CREDITS

Design and Writing: Joseph Goodman

Additional Design: Tavis Allison, Andy Frielink, Todd Kath, Doug Kovacs, Harley Stroh, Steven Thivierge, Dieter Zimmerman

Additional Writing: Michael Curtis, Harley Stroh, Dieter Zimmerman

Editing: Aeryn "Blackdirge" Rudel

Art Direction and Graphic Design: Joseph Goodman

Cover Art: Doug Kovacs

Endsheets: Doug Kovacs (front), Peter Mullen (back)

Interior Art: Jeff Dee, Jeff Easley, Jason Edwards, Tom Galambos, Friedrich Haas, Jim Holloway, Doug Kovacs, Diesel Laforce, William McAusland, Brad McDevitt, Jesse Mohn, Peter Mullen, Russ Nicholson, Erol Otus, Stefan Poag, Jim Roslof, Chad Sergesketter, Chuck Whelon, Mike Wilson

Special thanks to Doug and Harley for joining me on the expedition out of the underdark.

Roster
of
Heroes

DCC RPG was released as a beta version in June 2011. More than 20,000 gamers downloaded, played, and provided their feedback, which helped shape the final product. For two years prior to the public beta rules, hundreds of private playtesters assisted with their own input, at conventions, stores, and private sessions. We give our thanks to these brave playtesters, each of whom sacrificed several player characters to ensure this game is thoroughly entertaining: (DunDraCon 2010) Aldo Ghiozzi, Owen Hershey, Jon Leitheusser, Erol Otus, Richard Pocklington, Allan Sugarbaker; (Condor-Con 2010) Chris Czerniak, Kevin Cousineau, Matthew Davis, Kris K., Mac McEuen, Albert Park, Eric Silagi, Chris Webster; (GenghisCon 2010) Zoe Clark, Carl Collier, Diana Collier, Stormy Cone, Wendy Eberhardt, Jay Hafner, Jen Hymes-Balsley, Tonia Hymes-Balsley, Colette Kimes, Dean Kimes, Sam Lee, Sheila Smith, Harley Stroh, Jason Webster, James Wood, Valerie Wood; (GaryCon 2010) Tavis Allison, Matt Baker, Bill Barsh, David Bedell, Dex Briggs, Mark Clover, Marty Forbeck, Matt Forbeck, Alex Gygax, Mike Gygax, Scott Hirsch, Mike Johnston, Doug Kovacs, Greg Littlejohn, Don Manning, Pete Marron, Joel Mason, David Miller, James Mishler, James Nutter, Charley Phipps, Steve Polasky, Jeff Rients, John Seibel, Jim Skach, Keith Sloan, David Temporado, Adam Thornton; (North Texas RPG Convention 2010) Drew Balog, Steve "Balrog62" Balog, Martin Britt, Charles Cliff, James R. Cone, Scot H. P. Drew, Mark Greenberg, Kevin "Iron Phoenix" Highlander, Jimm Johnson, Joan McDonald, Ryan Simm, Jimmy Simpson, Rachel "Half-Dwarvish" Marsh; (Mount LeConte 2010) Alan Fishman, Mike Goodman, David Lepzelter, Seth Lepzelter; (Game Towne Game Fest 2010) David Aitken, Robert Jones, Eddy Ochoa, Ferris Ochoa, David Thurber; (SaurusCon) Alex Anderegg, Jon Obert, Matt Ruzicka, Will Stroh; (Anaheim Mini-Con) Joel Arellano, Louis Garcia, Rick Mobly, Gary Plover; (Tacticon 2010) Mike Crane, Bill Dawson, Pam Dawson, Jim Dotson, Christopher Dotson, Joshua Furtan, Rick W. R. Hill, Douglas S. Keester, Paul Lasnier, Thomas Lindgren, Lenny Logan, Troy Miller, Leif Olsen, Thomas Pasztor, Daren Pocus, Steven Slater, Bill Stilson, Scott Thorne, Linda Tschappat; (Fal-Con) Tavis Allison, Daniel Boggs, Jocelyn Stengel-Ahern, Brian Stith, Don and Joe; (Dicehouse Games / Dead Gamers' Society) John Armstrong, Andy Blanchard, Sam Carter, Greg Johnston, Timothy Johnston, Michael Cantin, Phil McCrum, Robert Reed, Joe Sosta; (Comic World) Mark Craddock, Matthew Gronner, Rob Hall, Gary Moreland, Dieter Zimmerman; (Erie Days of Gaming) Rob Conley, Greg Hofmann, Al Krombach, John Larrey, Jason Sholtis, Tim Shorts; (Anonycon) Tavis Allison, Emily Care Boss, Eric Gall; (Amazing Wonders) Kate Brown, James Flanagan, Jacob Folsom, Ben Parks, Gary Trumble, Dieter Zimmerman; Mike Adair, Kitty Faulhaber, Aaron Moreland, Bill Newsome, Tim Roberts, Jacob Woosley; (San Diego Playtest Group) Karina Benish, Kevin Cousineau, Jayson French, Becky Jones, Sam Carter, Steven Thivierge, Todd Thomas, Michelle Weisser; (New York Red Box Group) Eric Gall, George Strayton, Jed McClure, Paul Vermeren; (DunDraCon 2011) Cedric Alizado, Brian Chin, Jon Edwards, Duane Frederick, Guy Fullerton, Brad Neuberg, David Roth, Erol Otus, Derek Schubert, Rick Servande, Jon Wilson; (GenghisCon 2011) Andy Barnett, Andrew Becker, Dean Becker, Dave Brown, Rae Brown, Mike Crane, James Daton, Pam Dawson, Jeff Faller, Taylor Hellusch, Jon Hershberger, Bob Justus, Doug Keester, Tom Lindgren, Matt McConnell, Troy Miller, Dan Nelson, Kay Nelson, Leif Olsen, Thomas Pasztor, Daren Pocus, Keith Schooler, Bill Stillson, John Wolfenbarger, Kate Zaynard, Mark Zaynard; (Games Plus) Jeff Dean, Jeffrey Deb, Frank Flentge, Andy Frielink, Todd Kath, Tim Wadzinski; (GaryCon 2011) John Adams, David Bedell, Jen Deram, Jeremy Deram, Curt Duval, Kelsey Hines, David Koslowski, Jennifer Martin, Mark Martin, Travis Miller, Ryan Peel, Robert Phillips, Greg Potak, Jeff Rients, Jeff Runokivi, Adam Thornton, John Seibel, Mike Shorten, Jim Skach, Colin Skach, Haley Skach, Jeff Sparks, Erika Sparks; (Critical Hits) Matt Falduto, Robyn Meissler-Kubanek, Chris Mortika, Matt Sprengeler; (Gamex / Strategicon 2011) Chandler Bootchk, Isaac Bootchk, Benn Boyer, Andrew Linstrom, Brett Miller, Mike Olson, John Schroder; (Chicago group) Jeff Dean, Andy Frielink, Jeff Frohlich, Krissy Frohlich, Mike Lamczyk, Todd Kath, Sean Tragesser; Tim Wadzinski; (Doug's group) Art Braune, Daniel Kovacs, Doug Kovacs, Mike Milman, Rob Phillips, Vince Rock, Steve Vogel, and Senor Alec Tompson (who actually played the dog "Henson"); (Dicehead Games) Fred Dailey, Bill Guinan, Mel Grubb, Shane Grubb, Todd Hanson, Rick Hull, Brian LeGrand, David Parker, Logan Parker, Kim Swanson, Kyle Turner; (FCB Games) Patrick Anderson, Billie Abbitt, Patrick Campbell, Ray Franklin, Amy Jordan, Wayne Jordan, Amy Klinner, Brendan LaSalle, Cameron Martinez, Giles Othen, Lori Othen, Scott Sutherland, Billy Watford, Jim Williams, Bob Zimmerman; (Transylvanian Adventures) Mauricio Benitez, Alec Disharoon, Josh Durham, D. John Kennedy, Francois Levy, S. A. Mathis, Earl & Sydney, Stephen Zabel; (SoCal Mini-Con 2011) Joel Arellano, Reverend Dak, Simon Kesenei, Steve Ramirez, Daniel Waechter; (Tacticon 2011) Mike Crane, Erik Roach, Douglas S. Keester, C. Scott Kippe, Stephanie Latta, Tom Lindgren, Ron Ringenbach, Keith Schooler, Camdon Wright; (Finarvyn's Fellowship of Foragers) Alan Bean, Anna Breig, Dardrae Breig, Kaylina Breig, Marv Breig, Ryan Breig, Paul Luzbetak; (Brothers Grim) Michael Curtis, Mark Kellenberger, David Key, Mike Russo, Joe Scagluso, Jack Simonson; (Harley's youngsters) Chris Mullally, Connor Mullally, Zamira Mullally; (Con Nooga 2012) Paul Massingill, James LeRoy, Kyle Turner, Harrison Drew, Stephen Drew; (The Expendables) Dave Brown, Rae Brown, Patrick Carmichael, Michael Crane, Doug Keester, Kate Zaynard, Mark Zaynard; (Genghis Con 2012) Andy Barnett, Clint Black, Jason Dante, Shawn Davis, Jenni Hise, Zach Hodgens, Christoper Krieger, Tom Lindgren, Robert Potts, R. Kal "The Wolf King" Ringenbach, Mac Roger, Keith Schooler.

Joseph, Doug, and Harley
Return to the Source

GaryCon
Lake Geneva, WI

SoCal Mini-Con
Anaheim, CA

GaryCon
Lake Geneva, WI

DunDraCon
San Ramon, CA

Genghis Con
Denver, CO

DiceHead Games
Cleveland, TN

Game Towne
San Diego, CA

North Texas RPG Con
Bedford, TX

DCC RPG is dedicated to

Jim Roslof

1945-2011
TSR class of 1979

One of the great fantasy illustrators, who is already missed. His work for DCC RPG includes his last four illustrations, which appear on pages 76, 88, 110, and 205, as well as prior illustrations appearing on pages 13 and 375.

TABLE OF CONTENTS

bandon all presumptions, ye who enter here. Turn the pages of this tome only should you meet these qualifications:

hat you are a fantasy enthusiast of imaginative mind, familiar with the customs of role playing, understanding the history and significance of the Elder Gods Gygax and Arneson and their cohorts Bledsaw, Holmes, Kask, Kuntz, Mentzer, and Moldvay, and knowledgeable of the role of "judge" and the practice of "adventure."

hat you are in possession of the implements of role playing; namely, graph paper and an assortment of polyhedrons, including but not limited to d4, d6, d8, d10, d12, and d20; that you know the works of the great mage Zocchi and are prepared to exercise d3, d5, d7, d14, d16, d24, d30, or d% should they need to be deployed; and, although you may possess metal figurines and erasable mats for purposes of enjoyment, you understand their role as optional visualizers not prerequisites.

hat you understand and appreciate certain visual hieroglyphs derived from denizens of the higher planes whose deific identities among mortals are rendered, in the Common tongue: Otus, Easley, Roslof, Holloway, Caldwell, Trampier, and Dee.

hat you should be appreciative of a life of fantastic adventure and escapades, and acknowledge that a dungeon crawl facilitates the judging of a game focused thereon, but in no way excludes broader adventures in the wilderness, at court, on the outer planes, or on the sea, air, or other places.

hat you apprehend the fantasy pandect recorded in Appendix N with reverence and delight, acknowledging its defining place in creating this hobby.

hat you are prepared to pledge, with right hand upon your little brown books, that you shall uphold the honor of the hobby of role playing to all comers, whether young or old.

f these conditions are not met, then replace this book upon the shelf and flee with great celerity, for a bane befalls the heretical beholder of that which lies herein.

hould you meet these qualifications, be aware that you are indoctrinated into the order of Dungeon Crawl Classics and will find kind fellows of similar sentiment also within this order. You may proceed in good health.

INTRODUCTION

THE CORE MECHANIC

The core mechanic in the Dungeon Crawl Classics Role Playing Game is the d20 roll. You will frequently be asked to roll 1d20 and add or subtract modifiers. The goal is to roll high and beat a Difficulty Class, or DC. Sometimes the DC will have specific terms, such as an Armor Class, or AC, which is a combat variety of a DC. A higher DC is more difficult to beat, and a better-armored creature has a higher AC.

If you roll equal to or higher than the DC (or AC), you succeed. Otherwise, you fail.

A roll of 1 is an automatic miss and often results in a fumbling failure of some kind.

A roll of 20 is an automatic hit and often results in a critical success of some kind.

Occasionally a character may roll a die other than 1d20 when acting. 1d16, 1d24, and even 1d30 are used for weaker or stronger warriors and spellcasters.

HOW IS THIS GAME DIFFERENT FROM WHAT I HAVE PLAYED BEFORE?

If you are familiar with the d20 system (3.0 and 3.5):

- DCC RPG does not have prestige classes, attacks of opportunity, feats, or skill points.

- Classes and races are one and the same. You are a wizard or an elf.

If you are familiar with various iterations of AD&D:

- DCC RPG uses an ascending armor class system. A normal, unarmored peasant is AC 10, while a warrior in plate mail is AC 18.

- Attacks, saves, and skill checks all involve rolling 1d20, adding modifiers, and trying to beat a number.

- There are three saving throws: Fortitude, Reflex, and Willpower.

No matter what edition you've played before:

- Clerics turn creatures that are unholy to their religion. This may include un-dead and other creatures.

- All spells are cast with a spell check, where the caster rolls 1d20, adds certain modifiers, and tries to score high. The higher the roll the more effective the result. Each spell has a unique chart that adjudicates the spell's results.

- Wizards may or may not lose their spells after a casting. A low result means the wizard cannot cast the spell again that day. On a high result, he can cast the spell again.

- Cleric spellcasting works differently from wizard casting. Clerics never lose a spell when it's cast. However, when a cleric casts any spell and fails in his attempt, he may increase his "natural failure range." By the end of the day, a cleric may automatically fail on more rolls than just a natural 1.

- There is a critical hit matrix. Higher-level characters and martial characters generate critical hits more often and roll on more deadly result tables.

- You can burn off ability scores to enhance dice rolls. All characters can burn Luck, and wizards and elves can burn other abilities.

CHAPTER ONE

CHARACTERS

You're no hero.

You're an adventurer:
a reaver,
a cutpurse,
a heathen‑slayer,
a tight‑lipped warlock guarding long‑dead secrets.

You seek gold and glory,
winning it with sword and spell,
caked in the blood and filth of the weak, the dark, the demons, and the vanquished.

There are treasures to be won deep underneath,
and you shall have them...

ame play in the *Dungeon Crawl Classics Role Playing Game* starts at 0 level: untrained, uneducated peasants. Most of these characters die pitiful deaths in a dungeon. We highly suggest each player roll up multiple 0-level characters – at least three, possibly more. Don't get attached. Characters that survive their first dungeon then choose classes and become worth remembering.

Character creation in the DCC RPG follows these steps:

1. Roll ability scores. See page 18.

2. Determine 0-level occupation. See page 21.

3. Choose an alignment. See page 24.

4. Purchase equipment. See page 70.

5. Attempt to survive your first dungeon. If you survive and reach 10 XP, you advance to 1st level. At this point, you choose a class. See page 27.

6. Based on the class chosen, you may know some spells. See page 104.

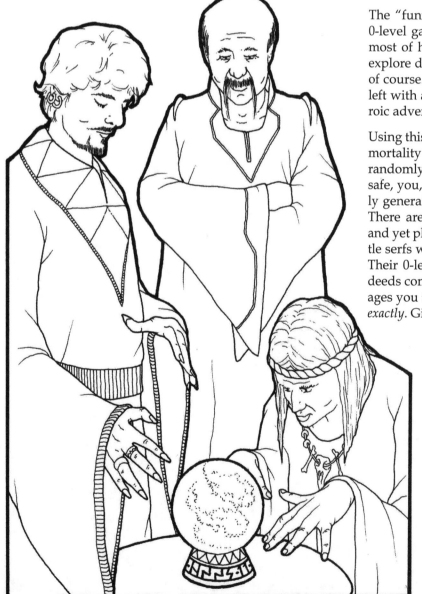

THE CHARACTER CREATION FUNNEL

Some role playing games codify "game balance" in an abundance of character options. The DCC RPG takes an anachronistic approach to this concept by pursuing an even playing field through *randomization* rather than *complexity*. The character creation steps that follow generate a play style unlike anything you have experienced in the last twenty-odd years – provided you follow the steps precisely. Omit any element, and you'll find that the process does not work. Here is why.

DCC RPG generates characters using what the author refers to as a "funnel." First, each *player* generates at least two, and possibly as many as four, 0-level characters. It is critical that the characters be generated using the process as described: completely random ability scores, random occupation, random Luck modifier, and random equipment. Each player ends up with an assortment of characters who could potentially serve as several different classes. When all characters are generated, have the players go around the table and introduce their 0-level peons to their peers.

The "funnel" takes place in 0-level play. During the first 0-level game, it is expected each player will lose some or most of his characters. When mere peasants and yeomen explore deadly dungeons, a high mortality rate is a matter of course. By the end of the first game, the players will be left with a motley crew of survivors, and this group of heroic adventurers becomes the 1st-level party.

Using this method of highly random character results, high mortality rates, and player choices as to which of their randomly-generated characters takes risks and which stays safe, you, the judge, will find you have a party of randomly-generated characters in which the players have agency. There are essentially no opportunities for min-max play, and yet players find themselves attached to their plucky little serfs who have done such amazing deeds at low levels. Their 0-level exploits will define them forever with great deeds completed at great risk. The author strongly encourages you to begin play using the method as described here *exactly*. Give it a chance; you may find you like it.

FUNKY DICE

This game utilizes polyhedrons of unusual shapes. Specifically, it utilizes the standard suite of dice, as well as what the author refers to as "Zocchi dice." As an experienced gamer, you undoubtedly own the following standard array of dice: d4, d6, d8, d10, d12, d20, and d%. DCC RPG also makes use of "Zocchi dice" in the following configurations: d3, d5, d7, d14, d16, d24, and d30. You may purchase these dice from your local game store (ask them to special order if they do not already stock them), and from www.gamestation.net, www.chessex.com, and www.koplowgames.com (as well as other select internet sites).

It is easy to substitute for the "funky dice" with a regular dice set. For a d3, roll 1d6 and divide by two; for a d5, roll 1d10 and divide by two. For a d7, roll 1d8 and re-roll on an 8. For d14 or d16, roll d20 and ignore rolls above the die-facing threshold. For d24, roll 1d12 and 1d6; if the 6-sider is odd, add 12 to the 1d12 roll. For d30, roll 1d10 with a 6-sided control die: add +0 on 1-2, +10 on 3-4, and +20 on 5-6.

THE DICE CHAIN

One of the most fun aspects of using funky dice in a rules set is getting to roll those dice! Many traditional RPGs utilize modifiers to dice rolls as a way to express improved success or failure in an action. For example, an attack with an off-hand weapon may incur a -4 penalty, or an attack against a motionless opponent may grant a +4 bonus.

DCC RPG utilizes this traditional modifier system but also employs a system of swapping out die types where the modifier is sufficiently large. Although d20 is the core die mechanic in the game, there are times when the player may be instructed to roll a d16 or a d24 instead, depending on whether the action has an improved or reduced chance of success.

Sometimes there will be multiple "dice swaps" impacting a die. For example, a spellcaster may be particularly good at one kind of magic, granting him an improved die, and he may also be operating under the influence of a magic item that grants him a further improved die. The system for moving "up and down" different die types is known as the dice chain.

The dice chain is represented as follows:

d3 – d4 – d5 – d6 – d7 – d8 – d10 – d12 – d14 – d16 – d20 – d24 – d30

Whenever the rules instruct the player to use an *improved die*, his dice choice moves one step to the right, culminating in a d30 (the largest die that can be used). When the rules instruct the player to use a *reduced die*, his dice choice moves one step to the left, culminating in a d3 (the smallest die that can be used). Multiple steps can switch the die type two or more steps, and combined improved and reduced results can offset each other. Modifiers to the roll (such as +1 or -2) are applied to the result on the new die type.

ABILITY SCORES

A character is defined in broad terms by six ability scores. For character creation, roll 3d6 for each ability score listed below in the order of Strength, Agility, Stamina, Personality, Intelligence, and Luck.

In DCC RPG character creation, you always roll 3d6, and you always roll and apply the scores in that same order. You do not roll more dice and drop the lowest die, you do not use a point-based buy system, and you do not assign ability scores in any order other than that defined above.

Why are we so explicit in the declaration of ability score process? Because you are an experienced gamer, and you know many other ways to determine ability scores. The open beta process revealed that ability score generation is the very first rule to be overridden by many players. This is your game and you should feel free to adapt it as you wish. We do encourage you to "buck tradition" and try at least one game using the precise method described here (3d6 straight down the line). It's a blast from the past, and something you probably haven't attempted in a decade or more. However, should you decide to house-rule otherwise, we expect this to be the place you begin.

Your character's score of 3-18 includes a modifier, as shown on table 1-1. This modifier applies to select rolls as described below.

Strength: Physical power for lifting, hurling, cutting, and dragging. Your Strength modifier affects melee attack and damage rolls. Note that a successful attack always does a minimum of 1 point of damage regardless of Strength. Characters with a Strength of 5 or less can carry a weapon *or* a shield but not both.

Agility: Balance, grace, and fine motion skills, whether in the hands or the feet. Your Agility modifier affects Armor Class, missile fire attack rolls, initiative rolls, and Reflex saving throws, as well as the ability to fight with a weapon in each hand.

Stamina: Endurance, resistance to pain, disease, and poison. Your Stamina modifier affects hit points (even at level 0) and Fortitude saving throws. Note that a character earns a minimum of 1 hit point per character level regardless of Stamina. Characters with a Stamina of 5 or less automatically take double damage from all poisons and diseases.

Personality: Charm, strength of will, persuasive talent. Personality affects Willpower saving throws for all characters. Personality is vitally important to clerics, as it affects the ability to draw upon divine power and determines the maximum spell level they can cast, as shown on table 1-1.

Intelligence: Ability to discern information, retain knowledge, and assess complex situations. For wizards, Intelligence affects spell count and maximum spell level, as noted on table 1-1. For all characters, Intelligence affects known languages, as described in Appendix L. Characters with an Intelligence of 7 or less can speak only Common, and those with an Intelligence of 5 or less cannot read or write.

Luck: "Right place, right time;" favor of the gods, good fortune, or hard-to-define talent. Players would be well advised to understand the goals of gods and demons that shape the world around them, for they are but pawns in a cosmic struggle, and their luck on this mortal plane can be influenced by the eternal conflict that rages around them. Luck affects several elements of the game, as follows:

Table 1-1: Ability Score Modifiers

Ability Score	Modifier	Wizard Spells Known	Max Spell Level**
3	-3	No spellcasting possible	No spellcasting possible
4	-2	-2 spells*	1
5	-2	-2 spells*	1
6	-1	-1 spell*	1
7	-1	-1 spell*	1
8	-1	No adjustment	2
9	None	No adjustment	2
10	None	No adjustment	3
11	None	No adjustment	3
12	None	No adjustment	4
13	+1	No adjustment	4
14	+1	+1 spell	4
15	+1	+1 spell	5
16	+2	+1 spell	5
17	+2	+2 spells	5
18	+3	+2 spells	5

Minimum of 1 spell.
** *Based on Intelligence for wizards and Personality for clerics.*

"With 8 INT you won't go far as a wizard, John, but as a warrior you can still earn a fine salary of 4d6 GP!"

- After rolling 3d6 to determine a player's Luck score, roll on table 1-2 to determine which roll is affected by the character's Luck modifier. This "lucky roll" is modified by the character's *starting* 0-level Luck modifier (for good or bad) in addition to all other normal modifiers. In some cases, the "lucky roll" is completely useless because the character chooses a class where it is not applicable.

- Note that the lucky roll modifier does *not* change over time as the character's Luck changes. For example, if a character's Luck modifier is +1 and his lucky roll is spell checks, he receives a +1 modifier to all spell checks henceforth. This modifier does not change if his Luck score changes.

- The character's Luck modifier affects other rolls in the game: critical hits, fumbles, corruption, and select other rolls, as described henceforth. In addition, Luck modifies a different element of play for each character class, as described in the class descriptions.

- Characters can burn off Luck to survive life-or-death situations. Any character can permanently burn Luck to give a one-time bonus to a roll. For example, you could burn 6 points of Luck to get a +6 modifier on a roll, but your Luck score is now 6 points lower.

- Characters can make Luck checks to attempt feats that succeed based on Luck alone. The judge will provide the specifics of any attempt, but the attempt is usually resolved by rolling equal to or less than the character's Luck score on 1d20.

- For all characters, Luck may be restored over the course of their adventures, and this restoration process is loosely linked to the character's alignment. Characters that act against their alignment may find themselves suddenly unlucky. Those who swear an oath to a patron of their newly desired alignment may find the change easier.

- Thieves and halflings have a particular affinity with luck. These classes renew their Luck score at a defined rate, as discussed in their class descriptions.

Table 1-2: Luck Score

d30	Birth Augur and Lucky Roll
1	Harsh winter: All attack rolls
2	The bull: Melee attack rolls
3	Fortunate date: Missile fire attack rolls
4	Raised by wolves: Unarmed attack rolls
5	Conceived on horseback: Mounted attack rolls
6	Born on the battlefield: Damage rolls
7	Path of the bear: Melee damage rolls
8	Hawkeye: Missile fire damage rolls
9	Pack hunter: Attack and damage rolls for 0-level starting weapon
10	Born under the loom: Skill checks (including thief skills)
11	Fox's cunning: Find/disable traps
12	Four-leafed clover: Find secret doors
13	Seventh son: Spell checks
14	The raging storm: Spell damage
15	Righteous heart: Turn unholy checks
16	Survived the plague: Magical healing*
17	Lucky sign: Saving throws
18	Guardian angel: Savings throws to escape traps
19	Survived a spider bite: Saving throws against poison
20	Struck by lightning: Reflex saving throws
21	Lived through famine: Fortitude saving throws
22	Resisted temptation: Willpower saving throws
23	Charmed house: Armor Class
24	Speed of the cobra: Initiative
25	Bountiful harvest: Hit points (applies at each level)
26	Warrior's arm: Critical hit tables**
27	Unholy house: Corruption rolls
28	The Broken Star: Fumbles**
29	Birdsong: Number of languages
30	Wild child: Speed (each +1/-1 = +5'/-5' speed)

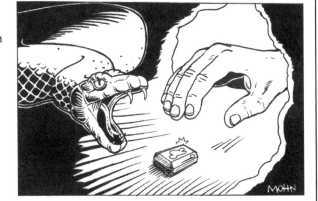

If a cleric, applies to all healing the cleric performs. If not a cleric, applies to all magical healing received from other sources.
** *Luck normally affects critical hits and fumbles. On this result, the modifier is doubled for purposes of crits or fumbles.*

SAVING THROWS

The DCC RPG uses three saving throws: Fortitude, Reflex, and Willpower. To make a saving throw, a character rolls 1d20, adds his modifier(s), and compares the result to a target number (DC). If the result is equal to or greater than the DC, the save is made. If not, dire effects may ensue.

Fortitude represents resistance to physical threats, such as poisons, gasses, acids, and stunning damage. A character's Stamina modifier influences his Fort save.

Reflex represents resistance to reaction-based threats, such as ducking a swinging axe trap, leaping aside as a doorway collapses, and twisting away from a dragon's flaming breath. A character's Agility modifier influences his Ref save.

Willpower represents resistance to mind-influencing threats, such as spells that charm or control, psychic effects that cause sleep or hypnosis, and mental domination. A character's Personality modifier influences his Will save.

All 0-level characters start with a base modifier of +0 to all saving throws, which is subsequently influenced by their ability modifiers. As characters gain class levels, their saving throws increase.

LANGUAGES

All characters know the Common tongue. For each point of Intelligence modifier, a character knows one additional language associated with the circumstances of his upbringing. These additional languages are established at 0-level. Dwarves, elves, and halflings with Int 8+ automatically know their racial languages as well.

Upon advancing to 1st level, a character may learn additional languages. Thieves learn a secret language called cant. Demi-humans learn one additional language. Wizards learn one additional language per point of Int modifier.

Additional languages commonly known include those of centaurs, giants, gnomes, goblins, and kobolds. Wizards may know magical languages and the animal tongues. More details on languages can be found in Appendix L.

0 LEVEL

All characters start at 0 level. Most will die in a dungeon, alone and unknown. The few who survive eventually choose a class in which to advance.

All 0-level characters start with the following:

- 1d4 hit points, modified by Stamina
- 5d12 copper pieces
- 0 XP
- One randomly determined piece of equipment (see table 3-4)
- One randomly determined occupation
- Based on the occupation:
    - Possession of one weapon and training in its use
    - Possession of some trade goods
- A +0 modifier to attack rolls and all saving throws; note that 0-level characters use a crit die of 1d4 on crit table I

As the character earns experience points, his XP total advances. When his XP total reaches 10, he may choose a class.

OCCUPATION

Your character once toiled away at mundane tasks, and his family and peers still do. Whether alongside his family or apprenticed to a master, a character's former occupation provides a set of skills. These skills may be useful to a character only as a fallback when he emerges crippled from the dungeon, but they are useful nonetheless. These skills also include training in a rudimentary weapon of some kind. Roll d% on table 1-3 to determine a character's background. Unless noted otherwise, a character is human.

Note that a character's occupation need not be determined randomly. If a player has a strong sense of the character's background, he should feel free to use it. Starting trained weapon and trade goods can be determined thematically with the judge's approval.

Demi-humans at level 0: Characters whose 0-level result includes a demi-human race must advance in class as that demi-human. For example, a dwarven miner levels up as a dwarf. 0-level demi-humans are able to utilize select racial traits as follows: dwarves have infravision and a base speed of 20'; elves are sensitive to iron and have heightened senses; and halflings have infravision and a base speed of 20'. Refer to the dwarf, elf, and halfling class descriptions for more information on these abilities. 0-level demi-humans speak Common plus their racial language, with additional languages gained as they level up. Just as all characters gain improved abilities and, sometimes, additional languages when they reach level 1, demi-human characters polish their natural talents through adventuring.

Table 1-3: Occupation

Roll	Occupation	Trained Weapon†	Trade Goods
01	Alchemist	Staff	Oil, 1 flask
02	Animal trainer	Club	Pony
03	Armorer	Hammer (as club)	Iron helmet
04	Astrologer	Dagger	Spyglass
05	Barber	Razor (as dagger)	Scissors
06	Beadle	Staff	Holy symbol
07	Beekeeper	Staff	Jar of honey
08	Blacksmith	Hammer (as club)	Steel tongs
09	Butcher	Cleaver (as axe)	Side of beef
10	Caravan guard	Short sword	Linen, 1 yard
11	Cheesemaker	Cudgel (as staff)	Stinky cheese
12	Cobbler	Awl (as dagger)	Shoehorn
13	Confidence artist	Dagger	Quality cloak
14	Cooper	Crowbar (as club)	Barrel
15	Costermonger	Knife (as dagger)	Fruit
16	Cutpurse	Dagger	Small chest
17	Ditch digger	Shovel (as staff)	Fine dirt, 1 lb.
18	Dwarven apothecarist	Cudgel (as staff)	Steel vial
19-20	Dwarven blacksmith	Hammer (as club)	Mithril, 1 oz.
21	Dwarven chest-maker	Chisel (as dagger)	Wood, 10 lbs.
22	Dwarven herder	Staff	Sow**
23-24	Dwarven miner	Pick (as club)	Lantern
25	Dwarven mushroom-farmer	Shovel	Sack
26	Dwarven rat-catcher	Club	Net
27-28	Dwarven stonemason	Hammer	Fine stone, 10 lbs.
29	Elven artisan	Staff	Clay, 1 lb.
30	Elven barrister	Quill (as dart)	Book
31	Elven chandler	Scissors (as dagger)	Candles, 20
32	Elven falconer	Dagger	Falcon
33-34	Elven forester	Staff	Herbs, 1 lb.
35	Elven glassblower	Hammer	Glass beads
36	Elven navigator	Bow	Spyglass
37-38	Elven sage	Dagger	Parchment and quill pen
39-47	Farmer*	Pitchfork (as spear)	Hen**
48	Fortune-teller	Dagger	Tarot deck
49	Gambler	Club	Dice
50	Gongfarmer	Trowel (as dagger)	Sack of night soil
51-52	Grave digger	Shovel (as staff)	Trowel
53-54	Guild beggar	Sling	Crutches
55	Halfling chicken butcher	Hand axe	Chicken meat, 5 lbs.
56-57	Halfling dyer	Staff	Fabric, 3 yards
58	Halfling glovemaker	Awl (as dagger)	Gloves, 4 pairs
59	Halfling gypsy	Sling	Hex doll
60	Halfling haberdasher	Scissors (as dagger)	Fine suits, 3 sets
61	Halfling mariner	Knife (as dagger)	Sailcloth, 2 yards
62	Halfling moneylender	Short sword	5 gp, 10 sp, 200 cp
63	Halfling trader	Short sword	20 sp
64	Halfling vagrant	Club	Begging bowl
65	Healer	Club	Holy water, 1 vial
66	Herbalist	Club	Herbs, 1 lb.
67	Herder	Staff	Herding dog**
68-69	Hunter	Shortbow	Deer pelt
70	Indentured servant	Staff	Locket
71	Jester	Dart	Silk clothes
72	Jeweler	Dagger	Gem worth 20 gp

Table 1-3: Occupation, continued

Roll	Occupation	Trained Weapon†	Trade Goods
73	Locksmith	Dagger	Fine tools
74	Mendicant	Club	Cheese dip
75	Mercenary	Longsword	Hide armor
76	Merchant	Dagger	4 gp, 14 sp, 27 cp
77	Miller/baker	Club	Flour, 1 lb.
78	Minstrel	Dagger	Ukulele
79	Noble	Longsword	Gold ring worth 10 gp
80	Orphan	Club	Rag doll
81	Ostler	Staff	Bridle
82	Outlaw	Short sword	Leather armor
83	Rope maker	Knife (as dagger)	Rope, 100'
84	Scribe	Dart	Parchment, 10 sheets
85	Shaman	Mace	Herbs, 1 lb.
86	Slave	Club	Strange-looking rock
87	Smuggler	Sling	Waterproof sack
88	Soldier	Spear	Shield
89-90	Squire	Longsword	Steel helmet
91	Tax collector	Longsword	100 cp
92-93	Trapper	Sling	Badger pelt
94	Urchin	Stick (as club)	Begging bowl
95	Wainwright	Club	Pushcart***
96	Weaver	Dagger	Fine suit of clothes
97	Wizard's apprentice	Dagger	Black grimoire
98-100	Woodcutter	Handaxe	Bundle of wood

† If a missile fire weapon (such as sling or dart), roll 1d6 to determine number of sling stones or darts.

* Roll 1d8 to determine farmer type: (1) potato, (2) wheat, (3) turnip, (4) corn, (5) rice, (6) parsnip, (7) radish, (8) rutabaga.

** Why did the chicken cross the hallway? To check for traps! In all seriousness, if the party includes more than one farmer or herder, randomly determine the second and subsequent farm animals for each duplicated profession with 1d6: (1) sheep, (2) goat, (3) cow, (4) duck, (5) goose, (6) mule.

*** Roll 1d6 to determine what's in the cart: (1) tomatoes, (2) nothing, (3) straw, (4) your dead, (5) dirt, (6) rocks.

WEAPON TRAINING

All 0-level characters are trained in the one weapon they possess from their former occupation. If a 0-level character handles multiple weapons over his career, he is considered trained in the *last* weapon he fought with. At 1st level, a character gains training in additional weapons, based on the class he chooses.

Generally, using a weapon without training imposes an attack penalty. However, this penalty is waived for 0-level characters. It is assumed that their naturally poor combat abilities reflect equal incompetence with the martial use of all weapons. (Not to mention that in playtests, applying the attack penalty increases the 0-level death rate to absurd proportions.)

TRADE GOODS

Novice adventurers typically hail from mundane backgrounds. The economics of a feudal setting involve more barter than coinage. The typical farmer or woodcutter may sustain his family for years of trade without ever setting eye on a metal coin. All 0-level characters start with trade goods of some kind, as indicated on table 1-3. These may be useful in the dungeon or may provide a starting point for trading up to a better status in life. In addition to their trade goods, each 0-level character starts with one randomly determined piece of adventuring equipment. Roll 1d24 on table 3-4 (page 73) for each character.

You will discover that 0-level characters individually possess almost no useful equipment. Begin play with a properly sized party (at least 15 PCs), and you will quickly learn what "wealth by attrition" means and how it applies to low-level play.

ALIGNMENT

In the beginning, there was the Void, where the Old Ones dreamed. In their dreams were Law and Chaos, inherent forces of unity and entropy. Through endless opposition these forces of unity and entropy elected champions who became gods, who in turn formed planes of existence that reflected their principles. On one such plane resides your trivial existence, tiny next to the vastness of Aéreth, even tinier next to the vastness of the cosmos. But you are connected back to the greater universe and the endless struggle by a fundamental choice: do you back the forces of Law or the forces of Chaos?

Alignment is a choice of values. In its simplest form it determines behavior. In higher forms it determines allegiance to a cosmic force. Characters choose an alignment at 0 level, and this choice determines their options for the rest of their lives.

Alignment functions on many levels, but there are two primary extremes: lawful and chaotic, with the balance of neutrality between. A character chooses one of these three alignments at 0 level.

Lawful characters believe fundamentally in unity and prioritize the values of mankind: order, authority, loyalty, and charity. They support organized institutions and "do what is right." They have a moral conscience that points them toward the appropriate action. Fundamentally, lawful characters choose the path of mankind over the path of supernatural dominance. At higher levels, lawful characters find themselves interacting with celestials, angels, demi-gods, and powerful Lords of Law. In mundane life, there are many shades of lawful behavior, and not all lawful characters agree on the same course of action at any time; though they invariably unite when mankind is threatened by outside forces.

Chaotic characters believe fundamentally in entropy and seek constantly to undermine or rule those around them. They are willing to disrupt the natural order of things – including established governments, guilds, and relationships – if they see a material benefit in doing so. They are open to agreements with supernatural powers, even if such agreements risk the primacy of man by allowing strange beings into the material plane. Fundamentally, chaotic characters choose the path of greatest personal power and success over any greater principle. At higher levels, chaotic characters find themselves aligned with demons and devils, sinister monsters, extraplanar creatures, and the supernatural Chaos Lords. In mundane life, chaotic behavior covers a wide spectrum of chicanery, subterfuge, aggression, and power politics, and chaotic characters are always looking for an advantage over their peers.

Neutral characters have not taken a stand between Law and Chaos. Neutrality is the balance of nature, the timelessness of eternity, and the nothingness of space. It can also reflect the neutrality of those who came before Law and Chaos: the Old Ones, the great Cthulhu, and the empty Void, and the emptiness of the time before gods. Neutrality between Law and Chaos can reflect a measured morality – balancing costs and benefits, without strong principles one way or the other. It can also reflect ambivalence or indifference. Fundamentally, neutral characters make choices based not on loyalty, values, or self-advantage, but by evaluating each and every opportunity that comes along. At higher levels, neutral characters find themselves aligned with elementals, extraplanar un-dead, and astral and ethereal beings.

The eternal struggle between Law and Chaos is real. Gods and demons battle on other planes for superiority, and the actions of man give those entities power. Make your choice carefully, for it will become increasingly important as you become more powerful.

LEVEL ADVANCEMENT

As a character completes adventures, he practices his skills and becomes more talented. Characters earn experience points (XP) that allow them to progress in level.

DCC RPG takes a different approach to experience points than the historical precedent and its modern interpretation. There is certainly a strong case for the historical approach which the author calls a "fiddly" system – a calculation-based method that accurately captures the abilities of a creature in a final XP-based number. There is also a case for an "encounter calculation" system – such as that used in 3E – that scales the XP awarded for each encounter based on the relative power of the characters and provides an ability to calculate the appropriate challenge rating of a set of opponents.

Another perspective is provided by Appendix N. The heroes of Appendix N did not always face enemies suitable to their power level nor did they proceed on a predictable path to greater competencies. Occasionally, they fled their enemies -- better to stay alive and fight another day. And as they advanced in power – for example, from wanderer to mercenary to king – they never quite knew exactly when the next opportunity for advancement would present itself.

The author has made one last consideration in his choice of XP system. As gamers grow older and must squeeze their sessions into complicated lives involving families, jobs, and other time commitments, the most enjoyable elements of the game must rise to the top. Bookkeeping related to XP tracking is not one of those elements.

Therefore, DCC RPG uses an extremely simple XP system. If this system is not to your liking, the author encourages you to adapt one of the many "fiddly" systems existing from prior and current editions. However, I urge you to give this system a try, as I suspect it will ease your game play experience considerably.

Basics of the XP System: The DCC RPG experience system works as follows:

- All character classes use the same advancement table.

- Each *encounter* is worth from 0 to 4 XP, and those XP are not earned merely by killing monsters, disarming traps, looting treasure, or completing a quest. Rather, successfully surviving encounters earns the characters XP in DCC RPG. A typical encounter is worth 2 XP, and the system scales from 0 to 4 depending on difficulty.

- All characters that participate in the encounter receive the same XP.

- The judge determines how much XP is awarded.

- Characters level up when they reach the XP threshold for the next level.

- The level thresholds become progressively higher. The number of "average adventures" required to advance to each subsequent level is higher than the preceding level.

The XP Table: The table below shows the experience points required for each level.

As an optional rule, consider allowing any 0-level characters that survive their first adventure to automatically advance to 1st-level and 10 XP. Zero-level adventures are a harrowing, deadly experience with particularly high fatality rates. As long as each player controls a portfolio of multiple 0-level PCs, such a play style can be fun. However, too many games with a 0-level character exchange novelty for enforced cowardice.

A 1st-level character retains his hit points from level 0, and gains new hit points according to his class. All characters of 1st-level or higher thus have their class hit dice *plus* 1d4 hit points from level 0.

Table 1-4: XP Level Thresholds

Zero-level characters start at 0 XP. The indicated level of XP is necessary to achieve each new level. For example, a 0-level character becomes a 1st-level warrior when he reaches 10 XP, a 2nd-level warrior when he reaches 50 XP, a 3rd-level warrior when he reaches 110 XP, and so on.

Level	XP Required
0	0
1	10
2	50
3	110
4	190
5	290
6	410
7	550
8	710
9	890
10	1090

CHOOSING A CLASS

What man calls free will is but the options remaining after destiny and the gods have made their plays. If your character survives to 1st level, you can choose a class. Your free will is constrained by the fatalism of the dice; pick a class that suits your randomly determined strengths and weaknesses. The demi-human classes of dwarf, elf, and halfling may only be selected by characters whose 0-level occupation was of that race.

The following terminology is introduced in the class descriptions:

Hit points: Each class uses a certain die to determine hit points. Note that all characters receive 1d4 hit points at 0 level, and their class hit points are *in addition to* the 1d4 hit points from 0 level. For example, a cleric has 1d8 hit points per level, so a 1st-level cleric actually rolls 1d4+1d8 to determine hit points. When that cleric achieves 2nd level, the player rolls another 1d8 hit points and adds it to the prior total.

Weapon training: Each class is trained in a certain list of weapons. Characters use their normal class action die when attacking with these weapons. When using other weapons, they roll a lower die (according to the dice chain).

Action dice: Action dice are used to make attacks, cast spells, and use skills. The most common use of an action die is to attack; most characters roll 1d20 for their attack rolls because they have a 1d20 action die. As characters advance in level, they may gain additional action dice. Typically, these start as additional dice of lower facings (i.e., a d14 instead of d20) to reflect that the character's secondary attacks are not as effective as his primary attacks. Character classes with spellcasting ability, or specialized skill uses, may be able to use action dice to cast additional spells or use additional skills rather than make attacks, as described in the class descriptions.

Title: Titles are included for characters of levels one through five. These titles reflect the most common terms for characters of that power level. In some cases, these titles are tied to formal orders; in other cases, they are generic terms. Formal orders (such as those noted in the thief and warrior descriptions) may have different titles. Characters of 6th level and above are extremely rare, so much so that no generic titles exist. Players are encouraged to develop their own titles for such levels using Appendix T for inspiration as needed.

BKM· 2011

CLERIC

There are rules that govern the multiverse, some deciphered by man and some opaque. The oldest rules are the Void, which no man or god understands, only Cthulhu and the Old Ones. Then the Old Ones established Law and Chaos, which created and divided the gods. From the gods came divine rules for the behaviors of mortal man, and if man lives by these rules, his gods reward him in this life or the next.

That is what your god tells you, and as his cleric, you will persuade, convert, or destroy those who speak otherwise. You adventure to find gold or holy relics, destroy abominations and enemies, and convert heathens to the truth. You'll be rewarded – even if you have to die to receive that reward.

An adventuring cleric is a militant servant of a god, often part of a larger order of brothers. He wields the weapons of his faith: physical, spiritual, and magical. Physically, he is a skilled fighter when using his god's chosen weapons. Spiritually, he is a vessel for the expression of his god's ideals, able to channel holy powers that harm his god's enemies. Magically, he is able to call upon his god to perform amazing feats.

Both clerics and wizards may gain powers from gods, but in different ways. A cleric worships a greater power and is rewarded for his service. A wizard unlocks the hidden mysteries of the universe in order to dominate powers both known and unknowable.

Hit points: A cleric gains 1d8 hit points at each level.

Choosing a god: At 1st level, a cleric selects a god to worship, and in doing so chooses one side of the eternal struggle. Clerics who worship demons and devils, monsters, fiends, Chaos Lords, and Set and the other dark gods of the naga are servants of Chaos. Clerics who worship lawful gods, nascent demi-gods, principles of good, immortals, celestials, guardians, and the prehistoric gods of the sphinxes are servants of Law. Clerics who stand at the balancing point, placing faith in the eternal struggle itself rather than the factions arrayed about it, are neutral in alignment. These "neutral" clerics may still be good, evil, or truly neutral, and as such are either druids, Cthulhu cultists, or guardians of balance.

All clerics pray to join their god in a never-ending afterlife. While still clothed in mortal form, clerics find a place among others with similar beliefs. The weak follow their order, the strong lead their order, and the mighty are living avatars of their gods. As a cleric progresses in level, he moves through these ranks.

A cleric's choice of god must match his alignment, and determines weapon groups, holy powers, and magical spells. Clerics may choose from the gods shown on page 32.

Weapon training: A cleric is trained in the weapons used by faithful followers of his god, as shown on page 32. Clerics may wear any armor and their spell checks are not hindered by its use.

Alignment: A cleric's alignment must match his god's.

Clerics of chaotic alignments belong to secret cults and strange sects. They travel the world to recruit new cultists and undermine their enemies.

Clerics of lawful alignments belong to organized religious groups. They may lead a rural congregation, adventure on great crusades to convert heathens, or defend holy relics as a militant arm of the church.

Neutral clerics tend toward philosophical affiliations. They may be druids who worship the oneness of nature or dark theosophists who research the dead gods that originally created the universe.

A cleric who changes alignment loses the support of his god. He loses access to all spells and powers from cleric levels earned under his old alignment.

Caster level: Caster level is a measurement of a cleric's power in channeling his god's energy. A cleric's caster level is usually his level as a cleric but may be modified under certain circumstances. Many clerics adventure in search of holy relics that bring them closer to their gods and thus increase caster level.

Magic: A cleric can call upon the favor of his god. This form of magic is known as idol magic. Its successful use allows a cleric to channel his god's power as a magical spell. A cleric has access to the spells of his god as noted on table 1-5.

To cast a spell, a cleric makes a spell check (see page 106). The spell check is made like any other check: roll 1d20 + Personality modifier + caster level. If the cleric succeeds, his god attends to his request – not always predictably, but with generally positive results.

If the cleric fails he risks disapproval. His god is preoccupied, annoyed, or facing its own battle – or questions the cleric's use of its power. Some of the most powerful gods are in turn the most fickle.

These rules apply to cleric magic:

- **Natural 1 means disapproval.** On a natural 1 during a spell check, a cleric discovers that he has somehow gained the disapproval of his deity. The spell check automatically fails, and the cleric must roll on the Disapproval Table (see page 122).

- **Each failed spell check increases the chance of disapproval.** After his first spell check fails in a day, a cleric's range of disapproval increases to a natural roll of 1 or 2. Thereafter, on any natural roll of 1 or 2, the spell automatically fails, and the cleric must roll on the Disapproval Table. After a second spell check fails, a cleric's range of disapproval increases to a natural roll of 1 through 3. And so on. The range continues increasing, and any natural roll within that range automatically fails. This means that a cleric could potentially reach a point where normally successful rolls automatically fail because they are in the disapproval range. For example, a cleric who fails 12 spell checks in a day would automatically fail any future spell check on a roll of 1 through 13, even though a roll of 13 would normally mean success on 1st-level spells. When the cleric regains spells on the following day, his disapproval range is reset to a natural 1. Probably. Clerics who test their gods may find they are not always forgiving.

- **Penalties can be offset by sacrifices.** Once a cleric's range of disapproval increases beyond a natural 1, he can reduce that range by offering sacrifices to his deity. See below for more information.

- **Sinful use of divine power.** A cleric may be capable of using his powers in ways that displease his deity. Doing so is a sin against his beliefs. Sinful activities include anything that is not in accordance with the character's or deity's alignment; anything that is not appropriate to the deity's core beliefs (e.g., being merciful to a foe while worshipping the god of war); healing a character of an opposed alignment or healing or aiding a character of an opposed belief or deity (even if of the same alignment); failing to support followers of the same beliefs when they are in need; calling on the deity's aid in a frivolous manner; and so on. When a cleric commits a sinful act, he may incur an additional increase in his disapproval range. This could amount to an increase of +1 for minor infractions all the way up to +10 for significant transgressions. These

additional penalties are always at the judge's discretion, and may manifest accompanied by thunder and lightning, plagues of locusts, water running uphill, and other signs of divine displeasure.

Sacrifices: A cleric may make sacrifices to his deity in order to regain favor. Sacrifices vary according to the nature of the deity, but, in general, any offering of material wealth counts. Other acts may count as well, at the discretion of the judge.

Sacrificing wealth means the items must be burned, melted down, donated to the needy, contributed to a temple, or otherwise relieved from the character's possession. They may be donated as part of a special rite or simply added to a temple's coffers. This is not a rapid combat action; it requires a minimum time of at least one turn and the cleric's full concentration.

For every 50 gp of sacrificed goods, a cleric "cancels" one point of normal disapproval range. For example, a disapproval range of 1 through 4 can be reduced to 1 though 3. A natural 1 still counts as automatic failure and disapproval.

A great deed, quest, or service to a deity may also count as a sacrifice, at the judge's discretion.

Turn unholy: A cleric wields his holy symbol to turn away abominations. At any time, a cleric may utilize a spell check to deter unholy creatures. An unholy creature is any being that the cleric's scriptures declare unholy. Typically this includes un-dead, demons, and devils. For more information on turning unholy, see page 96. As with all spell checks, the turn unholy spell check is made as follows: 1d20 + Personality modifier + caster level. Failure increases disapproval range, as noted above.

Lay on hands: Clerics heal the faithful. By making a spell check, a cleric may lay on hands to heal damage to any living creature. The cleric may not heal un-dead, animated objects (e.g., living statues), extraplanar creatures (e.g., demons, devils, elementals, etc.), or constructs (e.g., golems) in this manner. The cleric must physically touch the wounds of the faithful and concentrate for 1 action. The spell check is made as any other: roll 1d20 + Personality modifier + caster level. Failure increases disapproval range, as noted above.

The damage healed varies according to several factors.

- It is always a *number of dice*, with the type of dice determined by the hit die of the creature to be healed. For example, a warrior uses a d12 hit die, so a warrior would be healed with d12 dice.

- The number of dice healed *cannot exceed the target's hit dice or class level.* For example, a cleric healing a 1st-level character cannot heal with more than 1 die, even if he rolls well on his check.

- Finally, *before rolling his spell check*, the cleric may elect to heal a specific condition instead of hit points. Healed dice translate to conditions as noted below. In this case, the target's hit dice or class level do not act as a ceiling. If the cleric heals the indicated dice, the damaging condition is alleviated. "Overflow" hit dice do not become normal healing, and if the healed dice are too low, there is no effect.

  - Broken limbs: 1 die

  - Organ damage: 2 dice

  - Disease: 2 dice

  - Paralysis: 3 dice

  - Poison: 3 dice

  - Blindness or deafness: 4 dice

The cleric's alignment further influences the results, as follows:

- If cleric and subject are the same alignment, they count as "same" on the table below.

- If cleric and subject differ in alignment by one step (e.g., one is neutral and the other is lawful or chaotic), *or* have different but not antithetical gods, they count as "adjacent" on the table below. Such a healing action *may* constitute sin if not done in service of the faith.

- If cleric and subject are of opposed alignment (e.g., one

is lawful and one is chaotic), *or* have rival gods, they count as "opposed" on the table below. Such a healing *almost always* counts as a sin unless it is an extraordinary event in the service of the deity.

Then have the cleric make a spell check and reference the table below.

Spell check	Same	Adjacent	Opposed
1-11	Failure	Failure	Failure
12-13	2 dice	1 die	1 die
14-19	3 dice	2 dice	1 die
20-21	4 dice	3 dice	2 dice
22+	5 dice	4 dice	3 dice

Here is the same table presented slightly differently to match the format of the character sheet. The player should record the names of his party allies in the boxes for "same" (same alignment) or "adjacent" or "opposed" (based on alignment steps, as noted above). Then, the appropriate column shows the healing by check.

PC Names	Spell Check Minimum Result			
	12	14	20	22+
(same)	2	3	4	5
(adjacent)	1	2	3	4
(opposed)	1	1	2	3

Divine aid: As a devout worshipper, a cleric is entitled to beseech his deity for divine aid. Beneficent followers are already rewarded with spells and the ability to turn the unholy, so it must be recognized that requesting direct intervention is an extraordinary act. To request divine aid, the cleric makes a spell check at the same modifier that would apply were he casting a spell. This extraordinary act imparts a cumulative +10 penalty to future disapproval range. Based on the result of the spell check, the judge will describe the result. Simple requests (e.g., light a candle) are DC 10 and extraordinary requests (e.g., summon and control a living column of flame) are DC 18 or higher.

Luck: A cleric's Luck modifier applies to all spell checks to turn unholy creatures.

Action dice: A cleric can use his action dice for attack rolls or spell checks.

Table 1-5: Cleric

Level	Attack	Crit Die/ Table	Action Dice	Ref	Fort	Will	Spells Known by Level				
							1	2	3	4	5
1	+0	1d8/III	1d20	+0	+1	+1	4	–	–	–	–
2	+1	1d8/III	1d20	+0	+1	+1	5	–	–	–	–
3	+2	1d10/III	1d20	+1	+1	+2	5	3	–	–	–
4	+2	1d10/III	1d20	+1	+2	+2	6	4	–	–	–
5	+3	1d12/III	1d20	+1	+2	+3	6	5	2	–	–
6	+4	1d12/III	1d20+1d14	+2	+2	+4	7	5	3	–	–
7	+5	1d14/III	1d20+1d16	+2	+3	+4	7	6	4	1	–
8	+5	1d14/III	1d20+1d20	+2	+3	+5	8	6	5	2	–
9	+6	1d16/III	1d20+1d20	+3	+3	+5	8	7	5	3	1
10	+7	1d16/III	1d20+1d20	+3	+4	+6	9	7	6	4	2

Table 1-6: Cleric Titles

Level	Title by Alignment		
	Law	Chaos	Neutral
1	Acolyte	Zealot	Witness
2	Heathen-slayer	Convert	Pupil
3	Brother	Cultist	Chronicler
4	Curate	Apostle	Judge
5	Father	High priest	Druid

GODS OF THE ETERNAL STRUGGLE

The eternal struggle between Law and Chaos continues on a vast scale measured in the life and death of stars. In a man's brief time on earth, he chooses one antipode, and in doing so plays his tiny part in the eternal struggle. As such, a 1st-level cleric is either a cleric of Law, Chaos, or the balance. Within that scope, he chooses a god. The cleric displays the vestments of his god, preaches the god's good word, and carries the weapons considered holy by that god. The cleric's alignment further determines the creatures considered unholy for his turning ability.

Alignment	Gods	Weapons	Unholy Creatures
Law	Shul, god of the moon Klazath, god of war Ulesh, god of peace Choranus, the Seer Father, lord of creation Daenthar, the Mountain Lord, greater god of earth and industry Gorhan, the Helmed Vengeance, god of valor and chivalry Justicia, goddess of justice and mercy Aristemis, the Insightful One, demi-goddess of true seeing and strategy	Club, mace, sling, staff, warhammer	Un-dead, demons, devils, chaotic extraplanar creatures, monsters (e.g., basilisk or medusa), Chaos Primes, chaotic humanoids (e.g., orcs), chaotic dragons
Neutral	Amun Tor, god of mysteries and riddles Ildavir, goddess of nature Pelagia, goddess of the sea Cthulhu, priest of the Old Ones	Dagger, mace, sling, staff, sword (any)	Mundane animals, un-dead, demons, devils, monsters (e.g., basilisk or medusa), lycanthropes, perversions of nature (e.g., otyughs and slimes)
Chaos	Ahriman, god of death and disease Hidden Lord, god of secrets Azi Dahaka, demon prince of storms and waste Bobugbubilz, demon lord of evil amphibians Cadixtat, chaos titan Nimlurun, the unclean one, lord of filth and pollution Malotoch, the carrion crow god	Axe (any), bow (any), dagger, dart, flail	Angels, paladins, lawful dragons, Lords of Law, Lawful Primes, and Law-aligned humanoids (e.g., goblins)

THIEF

ou are a hulking, skulking thug waiting for your next victim, a dexterous wall-climber cozening treasures from ostensibly impenetrable vaults, a fleet-footed cutpurse outrunning shouting pursuers through a crowded market, or a brooding killer stalking a difficult target.

Thieves can be big or small, fast or slow, tall or thin, but they all have one thing in common: they survive not by sword or spell, but by stealth and cunning.

Hit points: A thief gains 1d6 hit points at each level.

Weapon training: A thief is trained in these weapons: blackjack, blowgun, crossbow, dagger, dart, garrote, longsword, short sword, sling, and staff. Thieves are careful in their choice of armor, as it affects the use of their skills.

Alignment: Although thieves have little regard for the laws of civilization, they are not necessarily chaotic.

Lawful thieves are ubiquitous, and they belong to institutions of organized crime: guilds of beggars who feign illness to fleece the generous, pirate gangs that hijack innocent travelers, or organized brigands who charge "protection fees" for certain routes. They are fences who dispose of stolen goods, enforcers who maintain the pecking order of the underworld, and petty burglars who work their way up to become mob bosses.

Chaotic thieves operate as independent agents. They are assassins and con artists, swindlers and sociopaths, or outright murderers and killers. They acknowledge no master aside from the glint of gold.

Neutral thieves are double agents: the kindly housekeeper who filches valuable baubles while the master sleeps, the "inside man" who leaves the vault unlocked one night, or the urban spy who sells secrets to his court's enemies.

Thieves' Cant: Thieves speak a secret language called the cant known only to members of their class. This is a spoken language with no written alphabet. Teaching the cant to a non-thief is punishable by death. Certain double-entendre phrases in Common have an alternate meaning in the cant and are used by thieves to identify their brethren covertly.

Thieving skills: A thief learns certain skills that aid his illicit pursuits. A thief can pick locks, find and disable traps, sneak silently, hide in shadows, climb sheer surfaces, forge documents, pick pockets, handle poison, and read languages.

The thief's alignment determines his interests, and those interests determine his rate of advancement in the various thieving skills. The thief receives a bonus to his skills based on level and alignment, as shown on table 1-9.

To use a thief skill, the player rolls d20 and adds his modifier. He must beat a DC assigned to the task at hand. An easy task is DC 5, while an extremely difficult task is DC 20 – for example, picking an extraordinarily well crafted lock, or picking the pocket of an alert guard. In some cases, the judge may make the roll for the character, and the result will not be known until some trigger event occurs (e.g., a forged document may not be truly tested until presented to the king's commissary).

A thief needs tools to pick locks, find and disable traps, climb sheer surfaces, forge documents, and handle poisons. A 1st-level thief must purchase a set of thieves' tools that allows him to use these skills.

Success when using a thief's skill means the following:

Backstab: The most successful thieves kill without their victims ever being aware of the threat. When attacking a target from behind or when the target is otherwise unaware, the thief receives the indicated attack bonus to his attack roll. In addition, if he hits, the thief automatically achieves a critical hit, rolling on the crit table as per his level (see page 37). Typically, backstabs are combined with checks to sneak silently or hide in shadows, such that a thief at-

tacks with surprise and is able to backstab. Certain weapons are particularly effective with backstab attempts and do additional damage, as noted in the equipment list. Backstab attempts can only be made against creatures with clear anatomical vulnerabilities.

Sneak silently: A thief never makes an opposed check to sneak silently; that is, the check is never made against the target's attempt to listen. The thief rolls against a hard DC, as noted below, and success means the thief did indeed sneak silently. With the exception of demi-gods and extraordinary magic, the thief's movement cannot be heard. This skill is often used to sneak up on unsuspecting guards and make a backstab attempt. The base DC for moving across stone surfaces is DC 10. Cushioned surfaces, such as grass or carpet are DC 5; moderately noisy surfaces, such as creaking wooden boards are DC 15; and extremely noisy surfaces, like crackling leaves, still water, or crunchy gravel are DC 20.

Hide in shadows: A successful hide in shadows check means the thief cannot be seen. As with sneaking silently, this check is never opposed, and is often used before a backstab attempt. The thief can attempt to hide in broad daylight should he be so bold! The base DC for sneaking down a hallway with moderate cover (chairs, bookcases, crevasses, nooks and crannies, alcoves, etc.) is DC 10. Hiding at night or in a shaded or dimly lit area is DC 5; hiding under a full moon is DC 10; hiding in daylight but in a dark shadow or behind a solid object is DC 15; and hiding in broad daylight with minimal obstruction is DC 20.

Pick pocket: The thief surreptitiously takes an object off a target's person. This skill also includes other feats of legerdemain such as card tricks, minor magic tricks, and so on. Stealing from an unaware target with a loose pocket and an unsecured coin pouch is DC 5; picking the pocket of a target that is actively watching and monitoring his or her belongings is DC 20; and the varying degrees of watchfulness in between define other check thresholds.

Climb sheer surfaces: As one would expect. DC 20 is a perfectly smooth surface with no visible handholds. A normal stone wall is DC 10.

Pick lock: A mundane lock is DC 10. An extremely well crafted lock is DC 20. Some locks of legendary manufacture and notable difficult are DC 25 or higher.

Find trap and *disable trap:* A large, bulky trap is DC 10. This would include traps like a pit in the floor, a spring-loaded axe, or a dropped portcullis. More subtle traps are DC 15, DC 20, or even higher. A natural 1 on a disable trap check triggers the trap.

Forge document: The DC varies with the complexity and originality of the source document, ranging from DC 5 to DC 20.

Disguise self: The degree of change determines the DC. The thief can transform himself to resemble someone of the same basic race and physical dimensions with a DC 5 check. Changing significant facial features requires a DC 10 check. Changing physical traits, like mannerisms and height, requires a DC 15 check. Fooling someone close to the target (such as a parent or spouse) requires a minimum DC 20 check.

Read languages: Interpreting simple meaning requires a DC 10 check. Interpreting anything more detailed is DC 15.

Handle poison: Any time a thief uses poison he must make a DC 10 safety check. On a failure, he accidentally poisons himself! This check is made each time poison is applied to a blade or other surface. Additionally, on a natural 1 on any attack roll with a poisoned blade, the thief automatically poisons himself, in addition to any fumble results.

Cast spell from scroll: Provided a spell is written on a scroll, a thief can attempt to read the scroll and cast the magical spell. The spell check DC is as standard, but the thief rolls the indicated type of die to attempt to beat that DC. The thief may not attempt spellburn.

Luck and Wits: Thieves survive on their luck and their wits, and the most successful thieves live a life of fortune on guts and intuition. A thief gains additional bonuses when expending Luck, as follows.

First, the thief rolls a luck die when he expends Luck. The luck die is indicated on Table 1-7: Thief. For each point of Luck expended, he rolls one die and applies that modifier to his roll. For example, a 2nd-level thief who burns 2 points of Luck adds +2d4 to a d20 roll.

Second, unlike other classes, the thief recovers lost Luck to a limited extent. The thief's Luck score is restored each night by a number of points equal to his level. This process cannot take his Luck score past its natural maximum. For example, a 1st-level thief with starting Luck score of 11 attempts to disable a trap and fails by 2 on his check. He burns 2 points of Luck to add 2d3 to his result, allowing him to succeed. His Luck is now 9. Because the thief is 1st level, his Luck score will be restored by 1 point on the following morning, bringing it back up to 10. Then, 1 additional point will be restored on the following morning, bringing it back to 11. The thief's Luck score cannot increase past 11.

Action dice: A thief uses his action dice for any normal activity, including attacks and skill checks.

Table 1-7: Thief

Level	Attack	Crit Die/Table	Action Dice	Luck Die	Ref	Fort	Will
1	+0	1d10/II	1d20	d3	+1	+1	+0
2	+1	1d12/II	1d20	d4	+1	+1	+0
3	+2	1d14/II	1d20	d5	+2	+1	+1
4	+2	1d16/II	1d20	d6	+2	+2	+1
5	+3	1d20/II	1d20	d7	+3	+2	+1
6	+4	1d24/II	1d20+1d14	d8	+4	+2	+2
7	+5	1d30/II	1d20+1d16	d10	+4	+3	+2
8	+5	1d30+2/II	1d20+1d20	d12	+5	+3	+2
9	+6	1d30+4/II	1d20+1d20	d14	+5	+3	+3
10	+7	1d30+6/II	1d20+1d20	d16	+6	+4	+3

Table 1-8: Thief Titles

Level	Title by Alignment		
	Lawful	Chaotic	Neutral
1	Bravo	Thug	Beggar
2	Apprentice	Murderer	Cutpurse
3	Rogue	Cutthroat	Burglar
4	Capo	Executioner	Robber
5	Boss	Assassin	Swindler

"Yes, well, you can't expect me to detect ALL the traps ALL the time..."

Table 1-9: Thief Skills by Level and Alignment

Skill	Bonus for LAWFUL Thieves (Path of the Boss)									
	1	**2**	**3**	**4**	**5**	**6**	**7**	**8**	**9**	**10**
Backstab	+1	+3	+5	+7	+8	+9	+10	+11	+12	+13
Sneak silently*	+1	+3	+5	+7	+8	+9	+10	+11	+12	+13
Hide in shadows*	+3	+5	+7	+8	+9	+11	+12	+13	+14	+15
Pick pocket*	+1	+3	+5	+7	+8	+9	+10	+11	+12	+13
Climb sheer surfaces*	+3	+5	+7	+8	+9	+11	+12	+13	+14	+15
Pick lock*	+1	+3	+5	+7	+8	+9	+10	+11	+12	+13
Find trap†	+3	+5	+7	+8	+9	+11	+12	+13	+14	+15
Disable trap*	+3	+5	+7	+8	+9	+11	+12	+13	+14	+15
Forge document*	+0	+0	+1	+2	+3	+4	+5	+6	+7	+8
Disguise self‡	+0	+1	+2	+3	+4	+5	+6	+7	+8	+9
Read languages†	+0	+0	+1	+2	+3	+4	+5	+6	+7	+8
Handle poison	+0	+1	+2	+3	+4	+5	+6	+7	+8	+9
Cast spell from scroll†	d10	d10	d12	d12	d14	d14	d16	d16	d20	d20

Skill	Bonus for CHAOTIC Thieves (Path of the Assassin)									
	1	**2**	**3**	**4**	**5**	**6**	**7**	**8**	**9**	**10**
Backstab	+3	+5	+7	+8	+9	+11	+12	+13	+14	+15
Sneak silently*	+3	+5	+7	+8	+9	+11	+12	+13	+14	+15
Hide in shadows*	+1	+3	+5	+7	+8	+9	+10	+11	+12	+13
Pick pocket*	+0	+1	+2	+3	+4	+5	+6	+7	+8	+9
Climb sheer surfaces*	+1	+3	+5	+7	+8	+9	+10	+11	+12	+13
Pick lock*	+1	+3	+5	+7	+8	+9	+10	+11	+12	+13
Find trap†	+1	+3	+5	+7	+8	+9	+10	+11	+12	+13
Disable trap*	+0	+1	+2	+3	+4	+5	+6	+7	+8	+9
Forge document*	+0	+0	+1	+2	+3	+4	+5	+6	+7	+8
Disguise self‡	+3	+5	+7	+8	+9	+11	+12	+13	+14	+15
Read languages†	+0	+0	+1	+2	+3	+4	+5	+6	+7	+8
Handle poison	+3	+5	+7	+8	+9	+11	+12	+13	+14	+15
Cast spell from scroll†	d10	d10	d12	d12	d14	d14	d16	d16	d20	d20

Skill	Bonus for NEUTRAL Thieves (Path of the Swindler)									
	1	**2**	**3**	**4**	**5**	**6**	**7**	**8**	**9**	**10**
Backstab	+0	+1	+2	+3	+4	+5	+6	+7	+8	+9
Sneak silently*	+3	+5	+7	+8	+9	+11	+12	+13	+14	+15
Hide in shadows*	+1	+3	+5	+7	+8	+9	+10	+11	+12	+13
Pick pocket*	+3	+5	+7	+8	+9	+11	+12	+13	+14	+15
Climb sheer surfaces*	+3	+5	+7	+8	+9	+11	+12	+13	+14	+15
Pick lock*	+1	+3	+5	+7	+8	+9	+10	+11	+12	+13
Find trap†	+1	+3	+5	+7	+8	+9	+10	+11	+12	+13
Disable trap*	+1	+3	+5	+7	+8	+9	+10	+11	+12	+13
Forge document*	+3	+5	+7	+8	+9	+11	+12	+13	+14	+15
Disguise self‡	+0	+0	+1	+2	+3	+4	+5	+6	+7	+8
Read languages†	+0	+1	+2	+3	+4	+5	+6	+7	+8	+9
Handle poison	+0	+0	+1	+2	+3	+4	+5	+6	+7	+8
Cast spell from scroll†	d12	d12	d14	d14	d16	d16	d20	d20	d20	d20

* The thief's Agility modifier, if any, also modifies checks for these skills.
† The thief's Intelligence modifier, if any, also modifies checks for these skills.
‡ The thief's Personality modifier, if any, also modifies checks for these skills.

A Man Among Men, A Thief Among Thieves

Career apogee for a thief is to be heralded for the most elegant of heists. To be a thief among thieves means stealing a famous treasure from a fabled tomb, a wizard's tower, or a king's treasury.

But while a warlord rules over the city he sacks, a mage commands the demon he masters, and a cleric proselytizes his flock, a great thief steals his prize and then slinks away, unseen and unknown, to enjoy his accomplishment alone.

In the rare circumstances where thieves do share their secrets, it is through business with trusted confederates: for example, by fencing a stolen jewel. The relationships that make these transactions possible – sometimes through trust, sometimes through leverage – are the social networks that form thieves' guilds and, in turn, gild a thief's reputation.

These are some examples of thieves' guilds. Your character may be part of such a guild.

The Mob: In the long-settled lands, chain-mailed bullies patrol a walled villa where a tiny, aged rogue holds court. Family ties form the background of his network. Nephews, uncles, and tenuous cousins are assigned territories to ply their illegal trades and advance or fall in the organization based on their business success. If your maternal uncle is a cousin to the boss, there may be an opening for you.

The Beggar King: The duchy's blind, lame, sick, and pestilent mendicants are easily robbed – unless they're protected by the Beggar King. This emaciated fiend collects a monthly tithe of one copper piece from every beggar under his service, and in return his bravos offer disinterested protection. Not every blindfolded beggar is really blind.

WANTED
DEAD OR ALIVE
REWARD!

NOTICE:
TO WHOM IT
MAY CONCERN
DAVID TRAMPIER
IS AN ARTIST
I ADMIRE
VERY MUCH
S.B.P.

The Warren: It has been decades since invaders last threatened the city's battlements, and outside the walls is now a warren of tents, shacks, shanties, and unkempt alleys known as the Warren. There are some legitimate businesses here, aye, as toothless women sell stunted turnips and day laborers lurch to work on uneven legs, but much of the Warren's population is sustained by brothels, taverns, slaving, opium dens, and other unsavory endeavors. Order (of a sort) is maintained by a pecking order of pilfery, with barkeeps, slavers, dealers, and petty thieves paying tribute up the ladder in a hierarchy of bosses and sub-bosses. A vault-like building down by the marsh is where the bosses meet. There are only rumors about who's at the top, but the system maintains order if not justice, and bucking the structure has been known to be dangerous.

The Twelve Spider-Assassins: A neighboring baron disputed the duke's claim to his throne. On his next stag hunt, the baron collapsed from his horse with no apparent wound. The dispute was dropped and the duke ascended. At the baron's public funeral, where the old women of the land lamented his early death, all remarked on the strange spider-shaped scar above his temple almost like a wound from a strangely-fanged arrow or dart. It must have been a coincidence that he scraped his head as he fell from his saddle. The twelve dark-cloaked men with hidden faces who made up the end of the funeral procession were remarked upon, as no one could identify them or their role. But, as of late, they have been seen in midnight audiences with the duke, who seems all the more harrowed now that he has a new throne.

WARRIOR

You are a mailed knight on a king's errand, a greedy brigand loyal to no man, a wild bear-skinned wanderer with an empty stomach, or a stout man-at-arms armored by a merchant's gold.

Of all the classes, warriors have the best attack bonus, the highest hit points, and the most potential for extra attack actions.

Hit points: A warrior gains 1d12 hit points at each level.

Weapon training: A warrior is trained in the use of these weapons: battleaxe, club, crossbow, dagger, dart, flail, handaxe, javelin, lance, longbow, longsword, mace, polearm, shortbow, short sword, sling, spear, staff, two-handed sword, and warhammer. Warriors wear whatever armor they can afford.

Alignment: Warriors can follow one of several paths based on their alignment, which in turn affects their title. Royal warriors, employed by nobility, are lawful. Lawless warriors, fighting merely for profit or carnage, are chaotic. Wild warriors, natives of the barren steppes or deadly forests, are neutral or chaotic. Hired warriors, loyal to a cause, a man, or simply the fattest purse, can be lawful, neutral, or chaotic.

Attack modifier: Unlike other classes, warriors do not receive a fixed attack modifier at each level. Instead, they receive a randomized modifier known as a *deed die*. At 1st level, this is a d3. The warrior rolls this d3 on each attack roll and applies it to both his attack roll *and* his damage roll. On one attack, the die may give him a +1 to his attack roll and damage roll. On the next attack, the die may give him +3! The deed die advances with the warrior's level, climbing to d7 by 5th level, and then higher up to d10+4 at 10th level. The warrior always makes a new roll with this die in each combat round. When the warrior has multiple attacks at higher levels, the same deed die applies to all attacks in the same combat round.

Mighty Deed of Arms: Warriors earn their gold with pure physical prowess. They swing across chapels on chandelier chains, bash through iron-banded oaken doors, and leap over chasms in pursuit of their foes. When locked in mortal melee, their mighty deeds of arms turn the course of battle: a brazen bull rush to push back the enemy lines, a swinging flail to entangle the beastman's sword arm, or a well-placed dagger through the enemy knight's visor.

Prior to any attack roll, a warrior can declare a Mighty Deed of Arms, or for short, a Deed. This Deed is a dramatic combat maneuver within the scope of the current combat. For example, a warrior may try to disarm an enemy with his next attack, or trip the opponent, or smash him backward to open access to a nearby corridor. The Deed does not increase damage but could have some other combat effect: pushing back an enemy, tripping or entangling him, temporarily blinding him, and so on.

The warrior's deed die determines the Deed's success. This is the same die used for the warrior's attack and damage modifier each round. If the deed die is a 3 or higher, *and the attack lands* (e.g., the total attack roll exceeds the target's AC), the Deed succeeds. If the deed die is a 2 or less, or the overall attack fails, the Deed fails as well.

Refer to the Combat section for additional information on Mighty Deeds of Arms (see page 88).

Critical hits: In combat, a warrior is most likely to score a critical hit and tends to get the most destructive effects when he does so. A warrior rolls the highest crit dice and rolls on tables with more devastating effects. In addition, a warrior scores critical hits more often. At 1st through 4th level, a warrior scores a crit on any natural roll of 19-20. The threat range increases to natural rolls of 18-20 at 5th level and 17-20 at 9th level. See the Combat section for more information on crits.

Initiative: A warrior adds his class level to his initiative rolls.

Luck: At first level, a warrior's Luck modifier applies to attack rolls with one specific kind of weapon. This kind of weapon must be chosen at first level and the modifier is fixed at its starting value – neither the weapon nor the modifier changes over the course of the warrior's career. The weapon type must be specific: longsword or short sword, not "swords."

Action dice: A warrior always uses his action dice for attacks. At 5th level, a warrior gains a second attack each round with his second action die.

Mighty Deeds in Action

The mechanic for Mighty Deeds of Arms was designed to encourage exciting stunts by ambitious warriors in the tradition of literary heroes. The goal was to create a rules system that encouraged situation-specific freedom without creating a lot of cumbersome rules. The author's original expectation was that this system would be used for disarms, parries, and other traditional combat maneuvers, but in actual playtesting the Mighty Deeds of Arms have been exciting and unpredictable. It's clear now that the system encourages creative actions, and the author believes it works best with creative warriors who devise interesting attacks. Here is a selection of actual Mighty Deeds of Arms performed by real players in real games, all of them declared on the spot in the midst of a grand adventure. Refer to the Combat section for more information on executing Mighty Deeds in play.

- When fighting opponents on a staircase, the character used a sword to stab an opponent and then lever him over the edge of the staircase. Later, the same character tried attacking the foe's legs to knock him over the edge.

- When facing a carven image with eyes that shot laser beams, the character used a mace to smash out the carved eyes (and thus disable the laser beams). In another game, a different player tried a similar attack to stab out the eyes of a basilisk and disarm its hypnotic gaze.

- When fighting a flying skull that was out of melee reach, a character leaped from the back of an ally into a flying lunge that brought him within reach of a melee swing at the skull.

- When hurling flasks of burning oil at a giant toad, the warrior aimed for the toad's open mouth to throw the oil down its gullet.

- When fighting enemies arrayed in a single-file line, a character hurled a javelin and tried to spear both of the front two enemies. The warrior impaled the first enemy, then speared the second, in effect pinning the second enemy to his ally's corpse.

- When fighting a chaos beast with a scorpion tail, a character attempted to chop off the tail.

Table 1-10: Warrior

Level	Attack (Deed Die)	Crit Die/Table	Threat Range	Action Dice	Ref	Fort	Will
1	+d3*	1d12/III	19-20	1d20	+1	+1	+0
2	+d4*	1d14/III	19-20	1d20	+1	+1	+0
3	+d5*	1d16/IV	19-20	1d20	+1	+2	+1
4	+d6*	1d20/IV	19-20	1d20	+2	+2	+1
5	+d7*	1d24/V	18-20	1d20+1d14	+2	+3	+1
6	+d8*	1d30/V	18-20	1d20+1d16	+2	+4	+2
7	+d10+1*	1d30/V	18-20	1d20+1d20	+3	+4	+2
8	+d10+2*	2d20/V	18-20	1d20+1d20	+3	+5	+2
9	+d10+3*	2d20/V	17-20	1d20+1d20	+3	+5	+3
10	+d10+4*	2d20/V	17-20	1d20+1d20+1d14	+4	+6	+3

A warrior's attack modifier is rolled anew, according to the appropriate die, with each attack. The result modifies both attack and damage rolls. At higher levels, the warrior adds both a die and a fixed value.

Table 1-11: Warrior Titles

Level	Lawful	Chaotic	Neutral
	Title by Alignment and Origin		
1	Squire	Bandit	Wildling
2	Champion	Brigand	Barbarian
3	Knight	Marauder	Berserker
4	Cavalier	Ravager	Headman/Headwoman
5	Paladin	Reaver	Chieftain

Militant Orders

Militant warriors of the feudal lands serve their lords by maintaining the rule of law, and, more specifically, the rule of their monarch's law. These warriors belong to knightly orders that serve their lord, their state, or their ideals. Your warrior may belong to such an order. Membership typically entails an oath to support the goals of the order and defend your fellow members, a pledge to provide service to the order's crusades when necessary (typically one or two full weeks out of every year or upon extraordinary circumstance such as war), and a tithe or dues of up to 10 gold pieces each year.

Membership in an order is reserved for noble warriors with steel weapons. Common footmen with their wooden spears and homespun clothes do not belong to knightly orders. Wildmen may be members of a totem-tribe where they fight in the style of bear, wolf, eagle, or other creature.

These are the best-known knightly orders.

Order of the Dragon

An association of high-born knights founded with intention to crush the pernicious deeds of the perfidious enemies of law and the followers of the evil dragons. The order is sponsored by the king, who serves as presiding officer, and all members display a dragon sigil on their shield.

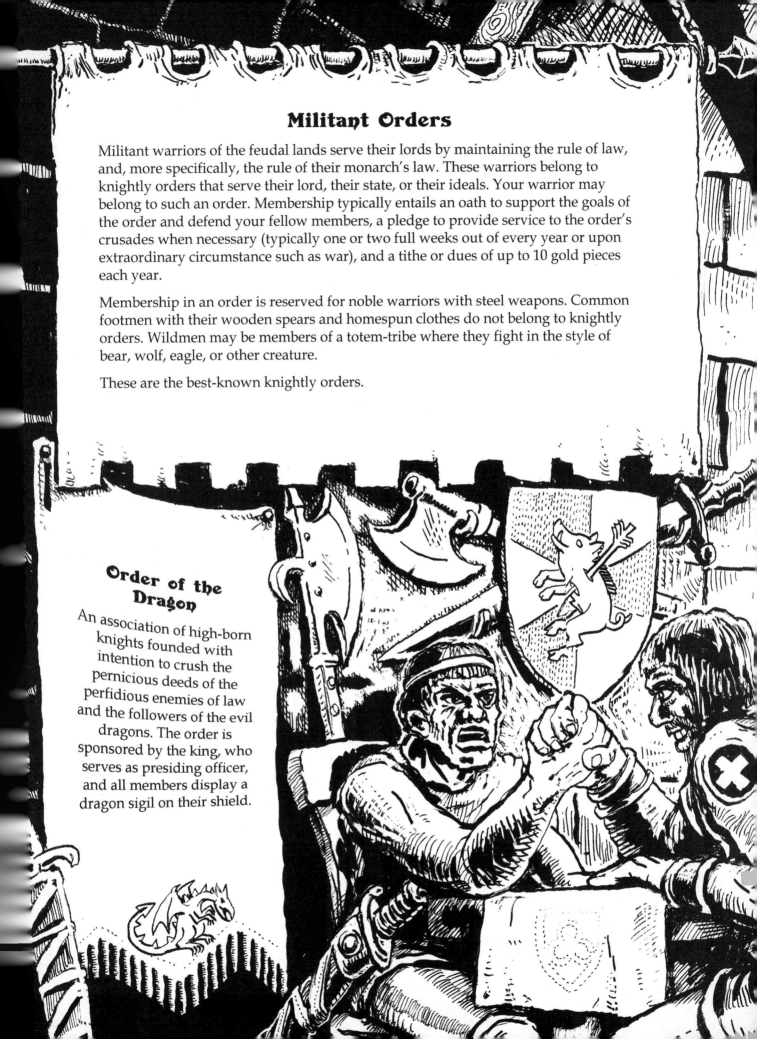

Order of Saint Stephen

An order founded by the grand duke to defend his lands in the tradition of valiant Saint Stephen, who died in single-handed combat against the giants. The order's emblem is a cross and they stand in staunch defense of all the grand duke's lands.

Fraternal Company of the Black Swan

A fraternal order of knights charged with cleansing a war-torn region of demi-human raiders. The company succeeded, and continued in peacetime as an ongoing society. All black swans must possess a war horse trained and equipped for mounted combat. Members display a black swan with red beak and feet on a white field.

Enterprise of the Green Shield with the White Lady

This chivalric order of twelve knights and their squires is led by the most senior knight. Each knight serves for five years and, inspired by knightly ideals, must defend women suffering any form of oppression, thievery, or dishonor. Their symbol is self-explanatory.

Order of the Golden Spur

This is an honorific society ruled by the highest-ranking cleric of the land. Knights who have distinguished themselves in the service of the church may be offered the chance to petition for membership in the Order of the Golden Spur. Petitioners must complete a great act of service to the church: for example, recovering a lost relic or defeating a chaos champion. If accepted as a member, the knight receives a medal and the right to wear a golden spur.

WIZARD

ou owe allegiance to no man, aye, but a demon or god may hold sway upon your soul. You are a tight-lipped warlock studying ancient tomes, a witch corrupted by black magic, a demonologist trading soul-slivers for secrets, or an enchanter muttering chants in lost tongues. You are one of many foul mortals clutching at power. Will you succeed? Low-level wizards are indeed very powerful, but high-level wizards fear for their souls.

Wizards control magic. At least, they attempt to. Mortal magic is unpredictable and wild but powerful. Unlike clerics whose faithful service is rewarded with divine powers, wizards wield magic through mastery and dominance of forces in which they are not always voluntary participants. Wizards are sometimes trained in combat, but are rarely a match for warriors or clerics in a clash of worldly weapons.

Hit points: A wizard gains 1d4 hit points at each level.

Weapon training: A wizard is trained in the use of the dagger, longbow, longsword, shortbow, short sword, and staff. Wizards rarely wear armor, as it hinders spellcasting.

Alignment: Wizards pursue magical arts according to their natural inclinations. Chaotic wizards study black magic. Neutral or lawful wizards seek control over elements. Wizards of all persuasions practice enchantment.

Caster level: Caster level is a measurement of a wizard's power in channeling a spell's energy. A wizard's caster level is usually his level as a wizard. For example, a 2nd-level wizard usually has a caster level of 2.

Magic: Magic is unknown, dangerous, and inhuman. Even the best wizards occasionally fail to properly harness a spell, with unpredictable results. Wizards thus inculcate their preferred magics, lest they err in casting a spell and corrupt themselves with misdirected magical energies. At 1st level a wizard determines 4 spells that he knows, representing years of study and practice. As his comprehension expands, a wizard may learn more spells of progressively higher levels. A wizard knows a number of spells as shown on table 1-12, modified by his Intelligence score.

Known spells are determined randomly (see Chapter 5: Magic). They may be of any level for which the wizard is eligible, as shown by the max spell level column. The wizard chooses the level before making his die roll. Higher-level spells are more powerful but harder to cast – and there are consequences for failure.

Wizards cast spells by making a spell check. A wizard's spell check is usually 1d20 + Intelligence modifier + caster level. In some cases, a wizard may roll a different die on the spell check (see Mercurial Magic).

Supernatural patrons: Wizards weave magic spells in consultation with powers from supernatural places and the outer planes. Demons and devils, angels, celestials, ghosts, outsiders, daevas, genies, elementals, Chaos Lords, spirits, elder gods, alien intelligences, and concepts foreign to mortal comprehension whisper secrets in exchange for favors best left unexplained. In everyday concourse, these secrets manifest as spells; in dire circumstances, the wizard can invoke one of his patrons directly and call for material assistance. This sort of request is called invoking a patron.

To invoke a patron, the wizard must spellburn at least 1 point of an ability score (see page 107) and cast the spell *invoke patron*. There may be additional requirements depending on the specific circumstances. Presuming the patron condescends to attend to the wizard, some negotiation may be required: a bauble exchanged, a secret name spoken, a sacrificial token burned, or maybe a quest performed. If the patron deigns to act, it sends an emissary to assist the wizard in the way the patron deems most appropriate.

Invoking a patron is powerful magic. Do not use it lightly.

Some common patrons include the following:

- Bobugbubilz, demon lord of amphibians
- Azi Dahaka, demon prince of storms and waste
- The King of Elfland, fey ruler of the lands beyond twilight
- Sezrekan the Elder, the wickedest of sorcerers
- The Three Fates, who control the fate of all men and gods to see that the world reaches its destiny
- Yddgrrl, the World Root
- Obitu-Que, Lord of the Five, pit fiend and balor
- Ithha, prince of elemental wind

Familiars: More than one wizard has found comfort in the company of a black cat, hissing snake, or clay homunculus. A wizard may utilize the spell *find familiar* to obtain such a partner.

Luck: A wizard's Luck modifier applies to rolls for corruption (see page 116) and mercurial magic (see page 111).

Languages: A wizard knows *two* additional languages for every point of Int modifier, as described in Appendix L.

Action dice: A wizard's first action die can be used for attacks or spell checks, but his second action die can only be used for spell checks. At 5th level, a wizard can cast two spells in a single round, the first with a d20 spell check and the second with a d14. Note that the results of mercurial magic may modify the action dice based on the dice chain.

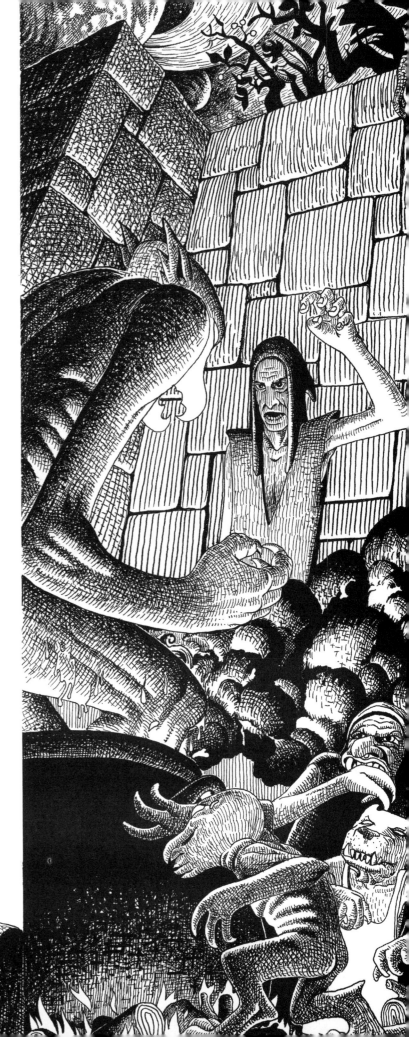

Table 1-12: Wizard

Level	Attack	Crit Die/Table	Action Dice	Known Spells	Max Spell Level	Ref	Fort	Will
1	+0	1d6/I	1d20	4	1	+1	+0	+1
2	+1	1d6/I	1d20	5	1	+1	+0	+1
3	+1	1d8/I	1d20	6	2	+1	+1	+2
4	+1	1d8/I	1d20	7	2	+2	+1	+2
5	+2	1d10/I	1d20+1d14	8	3	+2	+1	+3
6	+2	1d10/I	1d20+1d16	9	3	+2	+2	+4
7	+3	1d12/I	1d20+1d20	10	4	+3	+2	+4
8	+3	1d12/I	1d20+1d20	12	4	+3	+2	+5
9	+4	1d14/I	1d20+1d20	14	5	+3	+3	+5
10	+4	1d14/I	1d20+1d20+1d14	16	5	+4	+3	+6

Table 1-13: Wizard Titles

Level	Title by Alignment and Specialty		
	Chaotic	Lawful	Neutral
1	Cultist	Evoker	Astrologist
2	Shaman	Controller	Enchanter
3	Diabolist	Conjurer	Magician
4	Warlock / Witch	Summoner	Thaumaturgist
5	Necromancer	Elementalist	Sorcerer

DWARF

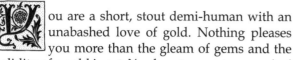

You are a short, stout demi-human with an unabashed love of gold. Nothing pleases you more than the gleam of gems and the solidity of a gold ingot. You love to count your coins! The sight of treasure sometimes makes you lose your head – just as does the swirling chaos of combat. You love to fight wildly, swinging a weapon with brutal effectiveness as you chop your way through your foes.

Dwarves live far beneath the ground and rarely set foot above it. Dark caves and deep cities were once your home, but now you live a wandering life: you are an exiled defender selling your martial might, a curious craftsman trading your talents, or a bitter renegade unwilling to settle for your lot in life. You are an object of suspicion to surface-worlders as well as other dwarves.

Dwarven societies are rigid, orderly, and prescribed, with clearly defined roles and responsibilities bound by byzantine rules of age and occupation. Any dwarf who rejects this lawful model of insular defensiveness to pursue a vocation of gregarious curiosity is, to his fellows, a loose cannon or even a traitor.

Hit points: A dwarf gains 1d10 hit points at each level.

Weapon training: Dwarves prefer to battle with a weapon and shield. A dwarf is trained in the use of these melee weapons: battleaxe, club, dagger, handaxe, longsword, mace, short sword, spear, two-handed sword, and warhammer. A dwarf is also trained in these missile fire weapons: crossbow, javelin, shortbow, and sling. Dwarves wear whatever armor they can afford.

Alignment: Dwarven life impresses lawful behavior forcefully. A dwarf who rejects this must have a good reason. Adventuring dwarves of a lawful alignment are syndics: agents of their native governments sent to spy, reconnoiter, procure goods, or build alliances. They are often possessed of many useful skills that represent their nations favorably, chosen for the traveling role based on fortitude and attitude.

Chaotic dwarves are exceedingly rare in their home countries. Death or exile is their natural fate; banishment due to rebellion and disobedience is the best they can hope for. Lacking the temperament to dedicate decades to learning a dwarven craft, they depend on martial skill and violence to endure their community's punishment for their tergiversation. Those who survive become adventurers.

Neutral dwarves adventure to learn of the world – a rare personality among this solipsistic race. A neutral dwarf is a master blacksmith, tanner, or miner seeking to expand his skills among the surface dwellers.

Attack modifier: Dwarves do not receive a fixed attack modifier at each level. Instead, they receive a deed die, just like a warrior. At 1st level, this is a d3. The dwarf rolls this d3 on each attack roll and applies it to both his attack roll *and* his damage roll. On one attack, the die may give him a +1 to his attack roll and damage roll. On the next attack, the die may give him +3! The deed die advances with the dwarf's level, climbing to d7 by 5th level, and then further to d10+4 by 10th level. The dwarf always makes a new roll with this die in each combat round. When the dwarf has multiple attacks at higher levels, the same deed die applies to all attacks in the same combat round.

Mighty Deed of Arms: Dwarves have a militant heritage that glorifies martial prowess. Like warriors, they can perform Mighty Deeds of Arms in combat. See the warrior entry for a complete description.

Sword and board: Dwarves excel at fighting with a shield in one hand and a weapon in the other. When fighting with a shield, a dwarf always gains a shield bash as a second attack. This shield bash uses a d14 to hit (instead of a d20). The dwarf adds his deed die to this number, as with all attacks, and can attempt Mighty Deeds of Arms involving the shield as well as his weapon. The shield bash does 1d3 damage. Some dwarves customize their shields with spikes or sharp edges to do more damage, while others enchant their shields with unique powers. Dwarves with multiple action dice (levels 5+) still receive only one shield bash each round.

Infravision: A dwarf can see in the dark up to 60'.

Slow: A dwarf has a base movement speed of 20', as opposed to 30' for humans.

Underground Skills: Long life beneath the ground trains dwarves to detect certain kinds of construction. When underground, dwarves receive a bonus to detect traps, slanting passages, shifting walls, and other new construction equal to their class level. Additionally, a dwarf can smell gold and gems. A dwarf can tell the direction of a strong concentration of gold

or gems within 100'. Smaller concentrations, down to a single coin, can still be smelled but require concentration and have scent ranges as low as 40' (for a single coin or gem).

Luck: At first level, a dwarf's Luck modifier applies to attack rolls with one *specific* kind of weapon (e.g., "longsword," not "swords"), just as a warrior's does. This kind of weapon must be chosen at 1st level, and the modifier remains fixed over time, even if the dwarf's Luck score changes.

Languages: At 1st level, a dwarf automatically knows Common, the dwarven racial language, plus one additional randomly determined language. A dwarf knows one additional language for every point of Int modifier, as described in Appendix L.

Action dice: A dwarf receives a second action die at 5th level. Dwarves always use their action dice for attacks. A dwarf's shield bash is always in addition to his base action dice.

Table 1-14: Dwarf

Level	Attack (Deed Die)	Crit Die/Table	Action Dice**	Ref	Fort	Will
1	+d3*	1d10/III	1d20	+1	+1	+1
2	+d4*	1d12/III	1d20	+1	+1	+1
3	+d5*	1d14/III	1d20	+1	+2	+1
4	+d6*	1d16/IV	1d20	+2	+2	+2
5	+d7*	1d20/IV	1d20+1d14	+2	+3	+2
6	+d8*	1d24/V	1d20+1d16	+2	+4	+2
7	+d10+1*	1d30/V	1d20+1d20	+3	+4	+3
8	+d10+2*	1d30/V	1d20+1d20	+3	+5	+3
9	+d10+3*	2d20/V	1d20+1d20	+3	+5	+3
10	+d10+4*	2d20/V	1d20+1d20+1d14	+4	+6	+4

* A dwarf's attack modifier is rolled anew, according to the appropriate die, with each attack. The result modifies both attack and damage rolls. At higher levels, the dwarf adds both a die and a fixed value.

** In addition to this basic action die, the dwarf receives a shield bash using a d14 action die.

Table 1-15: Dwarf Titles

Level	Title by Alignment		
	Lawful	Chaotic	Neutral
1	Agent	Rebel	Apprentice
2	Broker	Dissident	Novice
3	Delegate	Exile	Journeyer
4	Envoy	Iconoclast	Crafter
5	Syndic	Renegade	Thegn

ELF

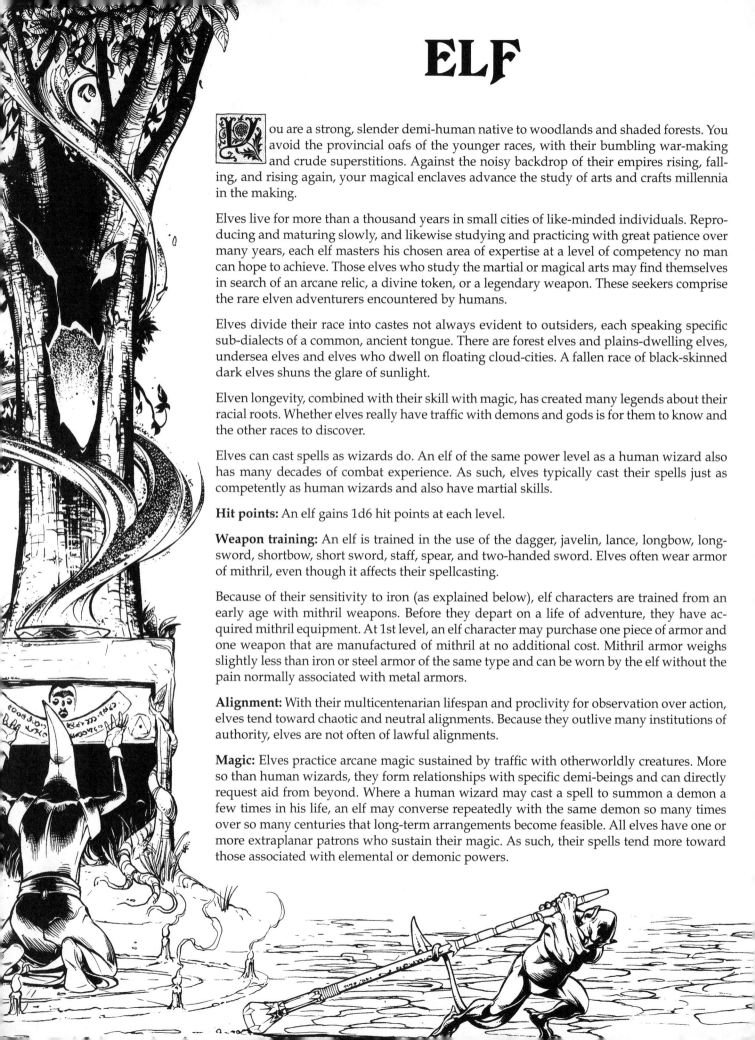

ou are a strong, slender demi-human native to woodlands and shaded forests. You avoid the provincial oafs of the younger races, with their bumbling war-making and crude superstitions. Against the noisy backdrop of their empires rising, falling, and rising again, your magical enclaves advance the study of arts and crafts millennia in the making.

Elves live for more than a thousand years in small cities of like-minded individuals. Reproducing and maturing slowly, and likewise studying and practicing with great patience over many years, each elf masters his chosen area of expertise at a level of competency no man can hope to achieve. Those elves who study the martial or magical arts may find themselves in search of an arcane relic, a divine token, or a legendary weapon. These seekers comprise the rare elven adventurers encountered by humans.

Elves divide their race into castes not always evident to outsiders, each speaking specific sub-dialects of a common, ancient tongue. There are forest elves and plains-dwelling elves, undersea elves and elves who dwell on floating cloud-cities. A fallen race of black-skinned dark elves shuns the glare of sunlight.

Elven longevity, combined with their skill with magic, has created many legends about their racial roots. Whether elves really have traffic with demons and gods is for them to know and the other races to discover.

Elves can cast spells as wizards do. An elf of the same power level as a human wizard also has many decades of combat experience. As such, elves typically cast their spells just as competently as human wizards and also have martial skills.

Hit points: An elf gains 1d6 hit points at each level.

Weapon training: An elf is trained in the use of the dagger, javelin, lance, longbow, longsword, shortbow, short sword, staff, spear, and two-handed sword. Elves often wear armor of mithril, even though it affects their spellcasting.

Because of their sensitivity to iron (as explained below), elf characters are trained from an early age with mithril weapons. Before they depart on a life of adventure, they have acquired mithril equipment. At 1st level, an elf character may purchase one piece of armor and one weapon that are manufactured of mithril at no additional cost. Mithril armor weighs slightly less than iron or steel armor of the same type and can be worn by the elf without the pain normally associated with metal armors.

Alignment: With their multicentenarian lifespan and proclivity for observation over action, elves tend toward chaotic and neutral alignments. Because they outlive many institutions of authority, elves are not often of lawful alignments.

Magic: Elves practice arcane magic sustained by traffic with otherworldly creatures. More so than human wizards, they form relationships with specific demi-beings and can directly request aid from beyond. Where a human wizard may cast a spell to summon a demon a few times in his life, an elf may converse repeatedly with the same demon so many times over so many centuries that long-term arrangements become feasible. All elves have one or more extraplanar patrons who sustain their magic. As such, their spells tend more toward those associated with elemental or demonic powers.

Elf spells are determined randomly like a wizard's, except for *invoke patron* and *patron bond*, as described below.

Caster level: Caster level is a measurement of an elf's power in channeling a spell's energy. An elf's caster level is his level as an elf. For example, a 2nd-level elf has a caster level of 2.

Supernatural patrons: Like wizards, elves can invoke supernatural patrons. An elf *automatically* receives the spells *patron bond* and *invoke patron* at 1st level in addition to his other spells.

Infravision: An elf can see in the dark up to 60'.

Immunities: Elves are immune to magical sleep and paralysis.

Vulnerabilities: Elves are extremely sensitive to the touch of iron. Direct contact over prolonged periods causes a burning sensation, and exposure at close distances makes them uncomfortable. An elf may not wear iron armor or bear the touch of iron weapons for extended periods. Prolonged contact with iron causes 1 hp of damage per day of direct contact.

Heightened Senses: Elves are astute and observant. All elf characters receive a +4 bonus to detect secret doors. Moreover, when simply passing within 10 feet of a secret door, elves are entitled to a check to detect it.

Luck: With their long lifespan, elves have ample opportunity to practice their magic craft. At first level, an elf may *choose* to apply his Luck modifier to spell checks on *one* spell of his choosing. That modifier does not change as the elf's Luck score changes.

Languages: At 1st-level, an elf automatically knows Common, the elven racial language, and one other language. An elf knows one additional language for every point of Int modifier. Additional languages are randomly determined as specified in Appendix L.

Action dice: An elf's action dice can be used for attacks *or* spell checks at any level. At 5th level, an elf can cast two spells in a single round, the first with a d20 spell check and the second with a d14; or he can make two attacks, the first with a d20 attack roll and the second with a d14; or he may combine an attack with a spell check. Note that the results of mercurial magic supersede the action dice, so an elf with a particularly high (or low) spell check die from mercurial magic uses that result instead (with his total actions still limited by his level).

Table 1-16: Elf

Level	Attack	Crit Die/ Table	Action Dice	Known Spells*	Max Spell Level	Ref	Fort	Will
1	+1	1d6/II	1d20	3	1	+1	+1	+1
2	+1	1d8/II	1d20	4	1	+1	+1	+1
3	+2	1d8/II	1d20	5	2	+1	+1	+2
4	+2	1d10/II	1d20	6	2	+2	+2	+2
5	+3	1d10/II	1d20+1d14	7	3	+2	+2	+3
6	+3	1d12/II	1d20+1d16	8	3	+2	+2	+4
7	+4	1d12/II	1d20+1d20	9	4	+3	+3	+4
8	+4	1d14/II	1d20+1d20	10	4	+3	+3	+5
9	+5	1d14/II	1d20+1d20	12	5	+3	+3	+5
10	+5	1d16/II	1d20+1d20+1d14	14	5	+4	+4	+6

* Plus *patron bond* and *invoke patron*.

Table 1-17: Elf Titles

Level	Title (all alignments)
1	Wanderer
2	Seer
3	Quester
4	Savant
5	Elder

HALFLING

You are a little man with a big appetite and a comfortable home, which you plan to return to as soon as this one little quest is completed. And once you're home, you plan to never leave again. The taller races might enjoy hunting for gold and glory, but all you ask for is a full stewpot, a cozy home, and pleasant interlocutors for teatime.

Halflings are un-ambitious country-dwellers who live in well-ordered peace and quiet. Their small stature and modest goals let them escape the notice of most major powers. They keep to themselves and make contact with others only when they are inadvertently drawn into the affairs of "the taller races," as they call elves, dwarves, and humans. Halflings prefer lives of farming, gardening, beer-brewing, and other simple crafts. The few that take up adventuring are usually traders or ne'er-do-wells who have somehow been thrust outside the ordered nature of their normal lives.

Hit points: A halfling gains 1d6 hit points at each level. They're small, but lucky.

Weapon training: Halflings prefer to battle with a weapon in each hand. A halfling is trained in the use of the club, crossbow, dagger, handaxe, javelin, shortbow, short sword, sling, and staff. Halflings usually wear armor – it's much safer, you know.

Alignment: Halflings value community, family, and kinship. They are usually lawful, or at the very extreme, neutral. Chaotic and evil halflings are extremely rare.

Two-weapon Fighting: Halflings are masters at two-weapon fighting, as follows:

- Normally, two-weapon fighting depends on the character's Agility to be effective (see pages 94-95). A halfling is always considered to have a minimum Agility of 16 when fighting with two weapons. This means he rolls at -1 die for his first attack and second, based on the dice chain (typically 1d16 for his first attack, and 1d16 for his second).

- A halfling can fight with two equal-sized one-handed weapons, such as two handaxes or two short swords.

- Unlike other characters, when fighting with two weapons, a halfling scores a crit *and* automatic hit on any roll of a natural 16.

- If the halfling has an Agility score higher than 16, he instead uses the normal two-weapon fighting rules for his Agility.

- When fighting with two weapons, the halfling fumbles only when *both* dice come up a 1.

Infravision: Halflings dwell in pleasant homes carved from the sod beneath hills. As such, halflings can see in the dark up to 30'.

Small size: Halflings are 2 to 4 feet tall, and the stoutest among them weighs no more than 70 pounds. This small size allows them to crawl into narrow passages and through tiny holes.

Slow: A halfling has a base movement speed of 20', as opposed to 30' for humans.

Stealth: Halflings are quite good at sneaking around. They receive a bonus to sneaking silently and hiding in shadows depending on their class level, as shown on table 1-18. This can be used in the same manner as a thief's abilities.

Good luck charm: Halflings are notoriously lucky. A halfling gains additional bonuses when expending Luck, as follows.

First, a halfling doubles the bonus of a Luck check. For every 1 point of Luck expended, a halfling gains a +2 to his roll.

Second, unlike other classes, a halfling recovers lost Luck to a limited extent. The halfling's Luck score is restored each night by a number of points equal to his level. This process cannot take his Luck score past its natural maximum. (The process works similar to how the thief ability is described, above.)

Third, a halfling's luck can rub off on those around him. The halfling can expend Luck to aid his allies. The ally in question must be nearby and visible to the halfling. The halfling can act out of initiative

order to burn Luck and apply it to the ally's rolls. The halfling loses the Luck, and the ally receives the benefit. The halfling's Luck modifier can apply to any roll made by an ally: attack rolls, damage rolls, saves, spell checks, thief skills, and so on.

Note that the good luck charm ability applies to only *one* halfling in the party. There is luck to having *a* halfling with an adventuring party, but there is not "more luck" to having more than one halfling. If multiple halflings accompany an adventuring party, only one of them counts as a good luck charm, and that cannot change through rearranging or separating the party. Luck is a fickle thing governed by gods and game masters, and players would do well not to attempt to manipulate the spirit of this rule.

Languages: At 1st-level, a halfling automatically knows Common, the halfling racial language, plus one additional randomly determined language. A halfling knows one additional language for every point of Int modifier, as described in Appendix L.

Action dice: A halfling's action dice can be used for attacks or skill checks.

Table 1-18: Halfling

Level	Attack	Crit Die/Table	Action Dice*	Ref	Fort	Will	Sneak & Hide
1	+1	1d8/III	1d20	+1	+1	+1	+3
2	+2	1d8/III	1d20	+1	+1	+1	+5
3	+2	1d10/III	1d20	+2	+1	+2	+7
4	+3	1d10/III	1d20	+2	+2	+2	+8
5	+4	1d12/III	1d20	+3	+2	+3	+9
6	+5	1d12/III	1d20+1d14	+4	+2	+4	+11
7	+5	1d14/III	1d20+1d16	+4	+3	+4	+12
8	+6	1d14/III	1d20+1d20	+5	+3	+5	+13
9	+7	1d16/III	1d20+1d20	+5	+3	+5	+14
10	+8	1d16/III	1d20+1d20	+6	+4	+6	+15

* Applies to attacks with one weapon. A halfling fighting with two weapons follows special rules, as outlined in the halfling class description.

Table 1-19: Halfling Titles

Level	Title (all alignments)
1	Wanderer
2	Explorer
3	Collector
4	Accumulator
5	Wise one

SMOKING WYRM

LOKERIMON THE LAWFUL

CHAPTER TWO
SKILLS

Outside of the skills required for combat, thievery, and magic, your character knows the skills dictated by the occupation he had before choosing a life of adventure.

Outside of the skills required for combat, thievery, and magic, your character knows the skills dictated by the occupation he had before choosing a life of adventure. When outside the dungeon – or even when inside the dungeon – there may be situations where a specific skill would be useful.

SKILLS BY OCCUPATION

A character's 0-level occupation determines the basic skills he can use. If the player can logically role-play the connection between his occupation and a skill in a way that the character's background supports the skill in question, then his character can make what is called a trained skill check. For example, a farmer would be able to identify seeds, a woodcutter could scale a wall, and a fisherman could swim an underground lake.

If your character's background does not support a skill use, your character is not familiar with the activity. In this case, he makes what is called an untrained skill check. For example, a former gravedigger could not identify strange seeds.

If there is ambiguity – for example, your character may have used the skill somewhat but not regularly – the character may make an untrained check with a +2 bonus. For example, a former miller may have some knowledge of the seeds his mill worked with.

Finally, if the skill is something that any adult could have a reasonable chance of attempting, then any character can make a trained skill check.

MAKING A SKILL CHECK

A skill check is made by rolling a die. If the skill is trained, the character rolls 1d20 for the check. Otherwise, he rolls 1d10. Then the appropriate modifiers are applied to the roll, and the total is compared to the difficulty challenge (DC) for the task at hand. If the roll beats the DC, the skill check succeeds. Otherwise, it fails.

Skill checks are modified by the appropriate ability score. This is described in more detail below. Generally speaking, a character's Strength, Agility, Stamina, Personality or Intelligence modifier apply to any skill check.

Example: A 2nd-level wizard was once a scribe. His friend, a 2nd-level warrior, was once a blacksmith. While adventuring, they discover a magical anvil. Any sword forged on the anvil gains special powers. The warrior can make a trained attempt to forge a sword, given his background in blacksmithing, and would thus roll 1d20 on a blacksmithing skill check. The wizard is untrained, and would roll 1d10 on his check. Later in the adventure, they find a strange tome with foreign writing. The wizard, with his background as a scribe, can try to translate the tome as a trained skill. The warrior would have to make the check untrained.

DIFFICULTY LEVELS

DC 5 tasks are child's play. Typically, these minor challenges aren't rolled unless there is a consequence for failure. Example: walking on a four-foot-wide castle wall requires no check, but walking a four-foot-wide bridge across a yawning chasm does, as there is a significant consequence to failure for this easy task.

DC 10 tasks are a man's deed. The weak and unskilled could not likely achieve these tasks. Example: kicking down a door, scaling a stone wall, or hearing the approach of a cautious footpad.

DC 15 tasks are feats of derring-do. It takes someone special to accomplish these tasks. Examples: leaping the gap between two city roofs, hurling a log at an oncoming bear, or grabbing a pouch lashed to the saddle of a galloping stallion.

DC 20 tasks are a hero's work. Only the most super-human characters attempt and succeed at these tasks.

OPPOSED SKILL CHECKS

Sometimes two characters attempt opposite actions. For example, a warrior may try to bash down a door while the orc on the other side holds it shut. In this case, roll the appropriate skill check for both parties – Strength for the warrior bashing the door and Strength for the orc holding it shut. The higher roll wins.

WHEN NOT TO MAKE A SKILL CHECK

Skill checks are designed for use when a system of abstract rules is necessary to adjudicate a situation. Only make a skill check when practical descriptions by the players will not suffice.

For example, imagine the characters are exploring a room whose walls are covered in clay tablets, one of which conceals a hidden door. Instead of asking the characters for a skill check, ask for their actions. If a player specifies that he is removing the clay tablets from the wall, his character discovers the hidden door. If the door is cleverly concealed behind a false wall, the players may have to further specify their characters tap the walls to listen for hollow sounds. No search check is necessary.

On the other hand, if the characters are in a dirt-walled cave attempting to sieve the floor until they find a dropped dagger, a search check may be perfectly appropriate to represent their chances of success.

SKILL CHECKS FOR COMMON ACTIVITIES

In general, skill checks are associated with either a field of knowledge (reflected in the 0-level occupation) or a specific ability score (such as Strength or Agility). Here is a list of common skill checks in a dungeon, and the ability scores associated with them.

Balancing: Agility

Breaking down doors, bending bars, and lifting gates: Strength

Climbing: Strength or Agility, as appropriate. A sheer wall uses Strength; a craggy cliff or tree uses Agility. Typically the player can choose to use one or the other ability, depending on how he wishes to approach the situation.

Listening: Luck

Searching and spotting: Intelligence

Sneaking: Agility

CHAPTER THREE
EQUIPMENT

Starting characters are peasants and serfs who
have never held a gold piece in their own hands.

he tables below show the costs of weapons, armor, and equipment. Starting characters are peasants and serfs who have never held a gold piece in their own hands. Their limited wealth is rarely maintained in coinage; usually it takes the form of hides, grains, implements, garments, meat, or other trade goods associated with their profession.

Starting gold: All 0-level characters start with 5d12 copper pieces (cp), a weapon from their 0-level occupations, and some form of trade goods. The plate mail and sword of a noble knight cost more gold than a 0-level character earns in a lifetime – the only hope of wealth is a life of adventure. Thus, a character's spending is likely to be light until he advances in level.

If you start a campaign at a level higher than 0, use the following dice rolls to determine a character's starting gold based on his class:

Class	Level 1	Level 2	Level 3
Warrior	5d12	5d12 +500	5d12 +1,500
Wizard	3d10	3d10 +(2d4x100)	3d10 +(5d4x100)
Cleric	4d20	4d20 +400	4d20 +1,300
Thief	3d10	3d10 +(1d6x100)	3d10 +(3d6x100)
Elf	2d12	3d12 +500	3d12 +2,000
Halfling	3d20	3d20 +250	3d20 +1,500
Dwarf	5d12	5d12 +700	5d12 +2,000

Coinage: The value of copper, silver, gold, electrum, and platinum is as follows:

10 cp =	1 sp			
100 cp =	10 sp =	1 gp		
1,000 cp =	100 sp =	10 gp =	1 ep	
10,000 cp =	1,000 sp =	100 gp =	10 ep =	1 pp

Check penalty: Plate mail is bulky, ill-fitting, and inflexible. Warriors who wear plate mail find the weight inhibits their ability to jump chasms, as do thieves when they try to scale walls. The check penalty applies to checks to climb, jump, balance, swim, move silently, and other such physical activities.

Wizards who wear plate mail find it hard to trace runes correctly, and the high iron content interferes with their spellcasting. The check penalty *also* applies to wizard and elf spell checks made while using this kind of armor. Cleric spell checks are not affected by armor check penalties in this manner.

Note that armor manufactured from mithril, adamantine, or other materials not containing iron may reduce the spell check penalty.

Encumbrance: A character who carries too much weight is slowed down. Use common sense. Players must explain how they are carrying their equipment: which hand holds which weapon, which sack or backpack contains which objects, and so on. A character carrying a substantial ratio of his body weight is slowed to half speed. A character cannot carry more equipment than half his body weight.

Fumble die: Heavy armor is clumsy and awkward. When a fumble occurs, characters wearing heavy armor tend to be affected more significantly. Armor determines the die used for fumbles, as noted on the table below (refer to the Combat chapter for more information on fumbles).

Table 3-1: Weapons

Weapon	Damage	Range	Cost in gp
Battleaxe*	1d10	–	7
Blackjack†	1d3/2d6***	–	3
Blowgun†	1d3/1d5	20/40/60	6
Club	1d4	–	3
Crossbow*	1d6	80/160/240	30
Dagger†‡	1d4/1d10	10/20/30**	3
Dart	1d4	20/40/60**	5 sp
Flail	1d6	–	6
Garrote†	1/3d4	–	2
Handaxe	1d6	10/20/30**	4
Javelin	1d6	30/60/90**	1
Lance#	1d12	–	25
Longbow*	1d6	70/140/210	40
Longsword	1d8	–	10
Mace	1d6	–	5
Polearm*	1d10	–	7
Shortbow*	1d6	50/100/150	25
Short sword	1d6	–	7
Sling	1d4	40/80/160**	2
Spear#	1d8	–	3
Staff	1d4	–	5 sp
Two-handed sword*	1d10	–	15
Warhammer	1d8	–	5

Two-handed weapon. Characters using two-handed weapons use a d16 on initiative checks.

** *Strength modifier applies to damage with this weapon at close range only.*

*** *Damage dealt is always subdual damage.*

† *These weapons are particularly effective when used with the element of surprise. A thief who succeeds in a backstab attempt with one of these weapons uses the second damage value listed. All other classes and all other thief attacks use the first value.*

‡ *Characters generally purchase normal straight-edged daggers, but cultists, cave-dwellers, evil priests, alien worshipers, and other menacing villains carry curvy or ceremonial daggers known as athame, kris, or tumi.*

These weapons inflict double damage on a mounted charge. A lance can only be used when mounted.

"How come your plate mail gives the same Armor Bonus as mine?"

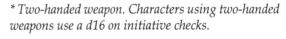

Table 3-2: Ammunition

Ammunition	Quantity	Cost in gp
Arrows	20	5
Arrow, silver-tipped	1	5
Quarrels	30	10
Sling stones	30	1

Table 3-3: Armor

Armor	AC Bonus	Check Penalty	Speed**	Fumble die	Cost in gp
(Unarmored)	+0	–	–	d4	Free
Padded	+1	–	–	d8	5
Leather	+2	-1	–	d8	20
Studded leather	+3	-2	–	d8	45
Hide	+3	-3	–	d12	30
Scale mail	+4	-4	-5'	d12	80
Chainmail	+5	-5	-5'	d12	150
Banded mail	+6	-6	-5'	d16	250
Half-plate	+7	-7	-10'	d16	550
Full plate	+8	-8	-10'	d16	1,200
Shield*	+1	-1	–	–	10

* Shields cannot be used with two-handed weapons.

** Human and elf base speed is 30'. Dwarf and halfling base speed is 20'.

Table 3-4: Equipment

Roll*	Item	Cost
1	Backpack	2 gp
2	Candle	1 cp
3	Chain, 10'	30 gp
4	Chalk, 1 piece	1 cp
5	Chest, empty	2 gp
6	Crowbar	2 gp
7	Flask, empty	3 cp
8	Flint & steel	15 cp
9	Grappling hook	1 gp
10	Hammer, small	5 sp
11	Holy symbol	25 gp
12	Holy water, 1 vial**	25 gp
13	Iron spikes, each	1 sp
14	Lantern	10 gp
15	Mirror, hand-sized	10 gp
16	Oil, 1 flask***	2 sp
17	Pole, 10-foot	15 cp
18	Rations, per day	5 cp
19	Rope, 50'	25 cp
20	Sack, large	12 cp
21	Sack, small	8 cp
22	Thieves' tools	25 gp
23	Torch, each	1 cp
24	Waterskin	5 sp

* Roll 1d24 to randomly determine equipment for 0-level characters. Characters who purchase their equipment at a later level ignore this column.

** A half-pint vial of holy water inflicts 1d4 damage to any un-dead creature, as well as to some demons and devils.

*** When ignited and thrown, oil causes 1d6 damage plus fire (DC 10 save vs. Reflex to put out or suffer additional 1d6 damage each round). One flask of oil burns for 6 hours in a lantern.

"Encumbrance? We always ignored that rule."

Table 3-5: Mounts and Related Gear

Item	Cost
Barding	x4*
Bridle and bit	2 gp
Donkey or mule	8 gp
Feed (per day)	5 cp
Horse, regular	75 gp
Horse, warhorse	200 gp
Pony	30 gp
Saddle, pack	15 gp
Saddle, riding	30 gp
Saddlebags	2 gp
Stabling (per day)	5 sp

* Relative to normal man-sized armor of this type.

Chapter Four
COMBAT

A bloody sword begets a wealthy adventurer.

bloody sword begets a wealthy adventurer. Combat is second nature to explorers, and all who would be mighty must master its arts.

The *Dungeon Crawl Classics Role Playing Game* assumes experience on the part of the judge. We assume you are competent in designing encounters, populating a dungeon, and finding challenges appropriate to your party's level of play. This chapter presents the basics of combat, but you are left to expand or discard the information here as you see fit.

Combat does not require a battle map or grid or miniatures. If you find these game aids helpful, by all means use them; however, the rules are written on the assumption that miniatures are optional.

OVERVIEW

Combat is very simple. The basic sequence is as follows:

- Before the first round, the judge checks for surprise.

- Based on the result of the surprise check, each player (not character) rolls for initiative. (At higher levels, initiative is instead rolled by character; see next page.)

- Characters and monsters act in initiative order.

- Attacks are resolved by rolling dice, adding modifiers, and comparing the result to the defender's Armor Class.

TIME KEEPING

Combat takes place in rounds. Each round is approximately 10 seconds. Dungeon exploration outside of combat takes place in turns. Each turn is approximately 10 minutes. The length of a complete combat should be rounded up to the next turn, with the additional time being spent on mending wounds, resting, repairing armor or weapons, and other such tasks.

BASICS OF THE ENCOUNTER

The encounter between characters and monsters forms the basic structure of the game. A well-crafted encounter includes deliberations by the judge regarding the monsters' reactions, their motivations, when they take actions, and whether they will negotiate or immediately enter combat. It is assumed the judge has considered these elements and properly adjudicated them in his adventures.

Be sure to account for the ability to see and hear the enemy, light sources, communication barriers such as different languages, and other such things.

MOVEMENT

Humans and elves move 30' per action. Dwarves and half-lings move 20' per action. If characters are encumbered with metal armor or a heavy load, they move more slowly. Outside of armor movement penalties shown on table 3-3, the judge determines what kind of encumbrance system to use.

MARCHING ORDER

Prior to entering combat, the players should determine the order in which their characters march.

In low-level play with hordes of 0-level and 1st-level characters, we recommend the "table center" method of determining marching order. Each player arranges his character sheets in order so the one closest to the table center is closest to the front of the marching order, and the one closest to the player is in the rear of the marching order. The assortment of character sheets closest to the "table center" then forms the front rank of the party.

INITIATIVE

Character death is frequent and merciless in the *Dungeon Crawl Classics Role Playing Game*, so the rules encourage each player to run more than one character at low levels. As such, we recommend two kinds of initiative.

In low-level play, especially with large masses of characters, use group initiative. Roll once for each player, applying the highest initiative modifier among his characters, then roll once for the monsters. When each player acts, he declares actions for all his characters.

In higher-level play, when each player has no more than two characters, use individual initiative by character. Roll once for each character and apply all appropriate modifiers.

But first, determine surprise. If the characters were not aware of their opponents (or vice versa), they are surprised. Being aware of an opponent means seeing them, making a check to hear them approach, or otherwise noticing them through magical or mundane means.

Surprised characters do not act in the first round of combat. After the first round they act normally on their initiative count.

An initiative check is conducted by rolling 1d20 and adding the appropriate modifier: Agility modifier, and, for warriors, class level. The highest initiative roll goes first, then next-highest, and so on. Ties are broken by highest Agility score, then by highest hit dice. A d16 is used instead of a d20 for characters wielding two-handed weapons. Initiative is rolled once at the start of an encounter, not each round.

ACTIONS

A character has one or more actions each round, expressed as action dice. Most characters have one action die, which is a d20. Higher-level characters may have two or more actions, expressed as action dice, such as d20+d16.

Each round, a character or monster may move its normal speed *and* do one thing for each of its action dice. The actions a character takes depend on his class.

- All characters can take another movement for their actions.
- A warrior can make an attack for each of his actions, rolling d20 for the first one and a different die for the second (generally d14 or d16).
- A wizard can attack *or* cast a spell with the first die and can *only* cast a spell with the second action die.
- An elf can attack *or* cast a spell with *any* action die.
- And so on, according to the class descriptions.

Spellcasting sometimes takes longer than one action. An action spent casting a spell either completes the spell, if it can be cast in one action, or contributes toward a total casting time if the spell requires more actions to cast.

In other words, a normal 0-level character with one action can move and attack once each round. A 6th-level warrior with action dice of d20+d16 can do any of the following combinations in one round: move only; move once, then attack once with a d20 roll; move, then attack once with a d20, then attack again with a d16; or simply stand and attack once with a d20 or a second time with a d16.

Other activities take time to complete as follows:

" SURPRISE!!! "

Activity	Time
Draw or sheathe a weapon	1 action*
Equip or drop a shield	1 action*
Open a door	1 action*
Light a torch or lantern	1 action
Uncork a potion or unfurl a scroll	1 action
Locate an item in a backpack	1 action
Stand up from a prone position	1 action
Mount or dismount a steed	1 action
Read a scroll or drink a potion	1 action

Can be included as part of a movement action.

TYPES OF COMBAT

When creatures fight within arm's reach (generally considered 5' for man-sized creatures), it is considered melee combat. Strength modifies melee attack and melee damage rolls.

When creatures fight beyond arm's reach, it is considered missile fire. Agility modifies missile fire attacks.

ARMOR CLASS

Armor Class is determined by armor, shield, Agility, and magical modifiers. An unarmored peasant is AC 10 – this is the baseline level. Armor Class *increases* with improved defensive capability, so wearing armor *increases* a character's Armor Class. For example, wearing leather armor takes a

character's AC from 10 to 12. Armor class *decreases* with reduced defensive capability, so a character with a negative Agility modifier has a lower AC. For example, a character with a -2 Agility modifier has his baseline Armor Class reduced from 10 to 8.

Agility modifies the defender's Armor Class for all kinds of combat. However, the defender must be able to maneuver in order to receive this modifier. If he is balancing on a pillar, climbing a wall, bound in rope, or otherwise constrained, the defender is not agile enough to receive the bonus from his Agility modifier.

THE ATTACK ROLL

The attacker rolls his action die (usually 1d20) and adds his attack bonus. He also adds any bonuses from spells, magic items, or class abilities (such as a thief's backstab ability). If the attack is made with a melee weapon, he adds his Strength bonus. If the attack is made with a missile weapon, he adds his Agility bonus.

This roll is compared to the defender's Armor Class. If the roll is equal to or higher than the defender's Armor Class, the defender is wounded.

Modifiers to attack rolls apply as shown on table 4-1.

A natural roll of 1 is a fumble. Fumbles automatically miss, and the attacker must roll the appropriate die on the fumble

Table 4-1: Attack Roll Modifiers

Condition	Attack Roll Modifier	
	Melee	Missile Fire
Missile fire range is…		
Short range	–	–
Medium range	–	-2
Long range	–	-1d
Attacker is…		
Invisible	+2	–
On higher ground	+1	–
Squeezing through a tight space	-1d	-1d
Entangled (in a net or otherwise)	-1d	-1d
Using an untrained weapon	-1d	-1d
Firing a missile weapon into melee*	–	-1
Defender is…		
Behind cover	-2	-2
Blinded	+2	+2
Entangled	+1d	+1d
Helpless (paralyzed, sleeping, bound)	+1d	+1d
Kneeling, sitting, or prone	+2	-2

And 50% chance of "friendly fire" if attack misses; see page 96.

table, with the result adjusted by the attacker's Luck modifier. Unarmored characters roll 1d4; others roll according to armor as indicated on table 3-3.

A natural roll of 20 is a critical hit. For some classes, other die rolls may also result in critical hits. See below for more details.

A higher-level character with multiple attacks may roll an action die other than 1d20. Similarly, a character attacking with two weapons may roll a die other than 1d20. A critical hit still requires a result of a natural 20 *or* the character's threat range, as detailed below – secondary dice results do not score critical hits as often.

ATTACK ROLL MODIFIERS

Attack roll modifiers come in two types. Some modifiers reduce the die type used to attack. These are noted as "-1d." The die types follow the dice chain. For example, a character attacking with a d20 die suffering a modifier of -1d would reduce his die type to d16. If a character has multiple active impacts on die type, follow the dice chain. For example, a character with a modifier of -1d using his second action die of d16 would attack with a d14.

FUMBLES

A natural roll of 1 is a fumble. Fumbles automatically miss, and the attacker must roll on the fumble table. Because "lower is better" on fumble table rolls, the roll is modified by *the reverse* of the character's Luck. For example, a +1 Luck modifier becomes -1 on the fumble table roll. The type of die rolled is determined by the attacker's armor, as follows.

Warriors and dwarves, and *only* warriors and dwarves, may burn 1 point of Luck to cancel a roll on table 4-2: Fumbles. The natural 1 still results in a miss but by burning a point of Luck they can avoid any further negative effects.

Heavy armor: If a character is wearing banded mail, half-plate, or full plate mail, he rolls 1d16 on the table, with the result adjusted by his Luck modifier.

Moderate armor: If a character is wearing hide armor, scale mail, or chainmail, he rolls 1d12 on the table, with the result adjusted by his Luck modifier.

Light armor: If a character is wearing padded, leather, or studded leather, or carrying only a shield, he rolls 1d8 on the table, with the result adjusted by his Luck modifier.

No armor: If a character is wearing no armor, including no shield, he rolls 1d4 on the table, with the result adjusted by his Luck modifier.

Table 4-2: Fumbles

Roll	Result
0 or less	You miss wildly but miraculously cause no other damage.
1	Your incompetent blow makes you the laughingstock of the party but otherwise causes no damage.
2	You trip but may recover with a DC 10 Ref save; otherwise, you must spend the next round prone.
3	Your weapon comes loose in your hand. You quickly grab it, but your grip is disrupted. You take a -2 penalty on your next attack roll.
4	Your weapon is damaged: a bowstring breaks, a sword hilt falls off, or a crossbow firing mechanism jams. The weapon can be repaired with 10 minutes of work but is useless for now.
5	You trip and fall, wasting this action. You are prone and must use an action to stand next round.
6	Your weapon becomes entangled in your armor. You must spend your next round untangling them. In addition, your armor bonus is reduced by 1 until you spend 10 minutes refitting the tangled buckles and straps.
7	You drop your weapon. You must retrieve it or draw a new one on your next action.
8	You accidentally smash your weapon against a solid, unyielding object (a rock, a wall, even the ground). Mundane weapons are ruined; magical weapons are not affected.
9	You stumble and leave yourself wide open to attack. The next enemy that attacks you receives a +2 bonus on its attack roll.
10	You should have maintained your armor! The joints of your armor seize up, freezing you in place. You cannot move or make an attack for 1d3 rounds. Unarmored characters are not affected.
11	Your wild swing leaves you off balance. You take a -4 penalty to your next attack roll.
12	You inadvertently swing at one randomly determined ally within range. Make an attack roll against that ally using the same attack die you just attempted to use.
13	You trip badly. You fall hard, suffering 1d3 damage in the process. You are prone and must use your next round to stand.
14	Like a turtle on its back, you slip and land upside down, flailing about and unable to right yourself. You must fight from a prone position for the next round before you can recover your balance and rise.
15	You somehow manage to wound yourself, taking normal damage.
16+	You accidentally strike yourself for normal damage plus an extra 1 point. In addition, you fall on your back and are unable to right yourself until you make a DC 16 Agility check.

Critical Hits

On a d20 roll, a natural roll of 20 is a critical hit. A natural 20 automatically hits and the attacker must roll his crit die on the appropriate critical hit table, with the result adjusted by his Luck modifier.

Crit dice and table are determined by class and level; refer to the character class tables. All 0-level characters roll 1d4 on crit table I.

Note that while higher-level warriors threaten critical hits on rolls other than 20, only a natural 20 is an automatic hit. Strikes that fail to hit do not incur critical hits. For example, a warrior with a threat range of 19-20 rolls a natural 19 against a foe with AC 21. If the warrior's deed die rolls a 1, the total attack is a result of 20, less than the AC, so this attack does not hit. It thus does not score a critical hit, even though it is within the threat range. If the deed die is a 2 or higher, the total attack roll is at least 21, so the attack hits and due to the natural 19 it counts as a critical hit.

When rolling dice greater than d20, a crit occurs based on the die's highest possible results. For example, when attacking with a d24, a crit occurs on a 24. A warrior with an improved threat range adjusts accordingly. For example, a threat range of 19-20 while rolling on a d24 becomes 23-24, with only the result of 24 being an automatic hit.

Given the wide range of foes encountered by the PCs, the judge should always adjust the description of the critical hit to suit the foe and the PC's weapon. If a result is completely inapplicable, use the next lower (less harmful) result on the table. Similarly, critical hits scored by monsters should be narrated in accordance to the monster's chosen attack.

Crit Table I: All 0-Level Characters and All Wizards

Roll	Result
0 or less	Force of blow shivers your weapon free of your grasp. Inflict +1d6 damage with this strike and you are disarmed.
1	Opportunistic strike. Inflict +1d3 damage with this strike.
2	Foe jabbed in the eye! Ugly bruising and inflict +1d4 damage with this strike.
3	Stunning crack to forehead. Inflict +1d3 damage with this strike, and the foe falls to the bottom of the initiative count next round.
4	Strike to foe's kneecap. Inflict +1d4 damage with this strike and the foe suffers a -10' penalty to speed until healed.
5	Solid strike to torso. Inflict +1d6 damage with this strike.
6	Lucky strike disarms foe. You gain a free attack if the enemy stoops to retrieve his weapon.
7	Smash foe's hand. Inflict +2d3 damage with this strike. You break two of the enemy's fingers.
8	Numbing strike! Cursing in agony, the foe is unable to attack next round.
9	Smash foe's nose. Inflict +2d4 damage with this strike and blood streams down the enemy's face.
10	Foe trips on his own feet and falls prone for the remainder of the round.
11	Piercing strike. Inflict +2d4 damage with this strike.
12	Strike to groin. The foe must make a DC 15 Fort save or spend the next two rounds retching.
13	Blow smashes foe's ankle; his movement speed is reduced by half.
14	Strike grazes temple; blood blinds the foe for 1d3 rounds.
15	Stab enemy's weapon hand. The weapon is lost and knocked 1d10+5 feet away.
16	Narrowly avoid foe's counterstrike! Inflict normal damage and make another attack roll. If the second attack hits, you inflict an additional +1d6 damage.
17	Blow to throat. Foe staggers around for 2 rounds and is unable to speak, cast spells, or attack.
18	Foe falls into your attack. He takes +2d6 damage from the strike and curses your luck.
19	Miracle strike. The foe must make a DC 20 Fort save or fall unconscious.
20+	Lucky blow dents foe's skull! Inflict +2d6 damage with this strike. If the foe has no helm, he suffers a permanent loss of 1d4 Int.

MULLEN

These footnotes apply to crit tables where indicated:

* Magical weapons never break due to critical fumbles. The target is disarmed instead, the weapon landing 1d10+5 feet away.

** A PC overcome by battle rage may temporarily expend points of his Personality or Intelligence score to enhance the damage on his critical hit. For every ability point he expends, he adds +1d12 to his damage roll.

Ability scores lost in this way return as the warrior heals. Each day thereafter where he does not succumb to battle rage, he recovers 1 point of the affected ability score. This rate is doubled if the character rests.

Crit Table II: All Thieves and Elves

Roll	Result
0 or less	Miss! Hesitation costs you the perfect strike!
1	Strike misses critical organs. Inflict a paltry +2d3 damage with this strike.
2	Slashes to head removes foe's ear. Inflict +1d6 damage with this strike and leave the enemy with a nasty scar.
3	Clean strike to back. Inflict +2d6 damage with this strike.
4	Blow to chest staggers foe. You can make an immediate free attack.
5	Blow pierces foe's kidneys. Inflict +3d3 damage with this strike, and the foe is stunned for 1 round.
6	Foe dazed by ferocious attack; his speed and actions are reduced by half.
7	Strike to chest grazes vital organ. Inflict +3d4 damage with this strike.
8	Strike cuts a line down foe's face. He is blinded by blood for 1d4 rounds.
9	Foe stumbles over his own limbs, falling prone. Make another attack.
10	Masterful strike! Inflict +2d6 damage with this strike.
11	Strike severs larynx. Foe is reduced to making wet fish noises.
12	Savage strike! Foe must succeed on a Fort save (DC 10 + PC level) or faint from the pain.
13	Foe disoriented by quick strikes. Foe suffers a -4 penalty to attack rolls for 1d4 rounds.
14	Strike to head. Foe must make a Fort save (DC 10 + PC level) or fall unconscious.
15	Blow drives foe to ground. Inflict +2d6 damage with this strike, and the enemy is knocked prone.
16	Lightning-fast shot to the face pops the foe's eye like a grape. Foe is permanently blinded in one eye and can take no actions for 1d3 rounds.
17	Strike pierces lung. Inflict +2d6 damage with this strike, and the foe can take only one action on his next turn.
18	Devastating strike to back of head. Inflict +1d8 damage with this strike, and the foe must make a Fort save (DC 10 + PC level) or fall unconscious.
19	Attack severs major artery. Inflict +1d10 damage with this strike, and the foe must make a Fort save (DC 10 + PC level) or fall unconscious from shock and massive blood loss.
20	Throat slashed! Inflict +2d6 damage with this strike, and the foe must make a Fort save (DC 13 + PC level) or die in 1d4 rounds.
21	Strike pierces spinal column. Inflict +3d6 damage with this strike, and the foe must make a Fort save (DC 15 + PC level) or suffer paralysis.
22	Chest skewered, spearing a variety of organs. Inflict +2d6 damage with this strike, and the foe must make a Fort save (DC 13 + PC level) or die in 1d4 rounds.
23	Strike through ear canal enters the brain. Ear wax instantly removed, and the foe must make a Fort save (DC 15 + PC level) or die instantly. Inflict an extra +2d6 damage on successful save.
24+	Strike through heart! Inflict +3d6 damage with this strike, and the foe must make a Fort save (DC 20 + PC level) or die instantly.

"I don't care about the delicate ecosystem, just kill the darn thing!"

Crit Table III: Clerics, Halflings, Level 1-2 Warriors, and Level 1-3 Dwarves

Roll	Result
0 or less	Battle rage makes friend and foe indistinguishable. Foe is hit for +1d12 damage, and the ally nearest him is also hit by a rebounding blow for 1d4 damage.**
1	Savage attack! Inflict +1d6 damage with this strike.
2	Attack sweeps foe off his feet. Next round, the enemy is prone.
3	Foe steps into attack. Inflict +1d8 damage with this strike.
4	Powerful strike hammers foe to his knees. Make another attack.
5	Smash foe's nose in an explosion of blood. Inflict +1d6 damage with this strike, and the foe loses his sense of smell for 1d4 hours.
6	Brutal strike to torso. Inflict +1d8 damage with this strike, and the foe suffers multiple broken ribs.
7	Strike to hand knocks weapon into the air. The weapon lands 1d20+5′ away.
8	Blow caroms off skull, deafening foe for 1d6 days. Inflict +1d6 damage with this strike.
9	Strike to leg splinters femur. Inflict +2d6 damage with this strike and foe loses 10′ of movement until healed.
10	Sunder foe's weapon! Shards of metal fill the air.*

Roll	Result
11	Strike hammers foe's belly causing massive internal bleeding. Unless he receives magical healing, the foe dies in 1d5 hours.
12	Blow to cranium staggers foe. The foe must make a Fort save (10 + PC level) or sink to floor, unconscious.
13	Strike breaks foe's jaw. Blood and shattered teeth ooze down the foe's face. Inflict +1d8 damage with this strike.
14	Attack hammers foe's torso. Inflict +2d8 damage with this strike.
15	Strike dislocates shoulder! Inflict +1d8 damage and shield arm hangs loosely by muscle and skin; no AC bonus from shield.
16	Attack reduces foe's attack hand to formless tissue; -4 penalty to future attacks.
17	Furious blows hammer target prone. Make another attack.
18	Blow hammers shards of bone into foe's forebrain; gray matter oozes out. Inflict +1d8 damage with this strike, and the foe suffers 1d4 points of Int and Per loss.
19	Devastating strike to the chest. Inflict +2d8 damage with this strike.
20	Chest strike stuns foe for 1d3 rounds. Inflict +1d8 damage with this strike.
21	Strike to leg shatters femur, knocking foe to the ground. Foe's movement drops by half. Inflict +2d8 damage with this strike and make another attack.
22	Weapon arm sundered by strike. The weapon is lost along with any chance of making an attack with this arm.
23	Blow craters skull. Inflict +2d8 damage with this strike, and the target permanently loses 1d4 Int and Per.
24	Masterful strike to throat. Inflict +2d8 damage with this strike and the foe staggers about gasping for air for 1d4 rounds.
25	Attack punches shattered ribs through lungs. Foe loses 50% of his remaining hit points and vomits copious amounts of blood.
26	Attack shatters foe's face, destroying both eyes. Inflict +2d8 damage with this strike, and the foe is permanently blinded.
27	Crushing blow hammers chest. Inflict +3d8 damage with this strike, and the foe must make a Fort save (DC 15 + PC level) or be knocked unconscious.
28+	Blow destroys spinal column. Inflict +3d8 damage with this strike, and the foe must make a Fort save (DC 15 + PC level) or suffer paralysis.

Crit Table IV: Level 3-4 Warriors, and Level 4-5 Dwarves

Roll	Result
0 or less	Battle rage makes friend and foe indistinguishable. Foe is hit for +2d8 damage, and the ally nearest him is also hit by a rebounding blow for 1d4 damage.**
1	Herculean blow. Inflict +2d12 damage with this strike.
2	Ferocious strike leaves foe's weapon hand dangling from the stump of a wrist. Inflict +1d12 damage with this strike.
3	Strike sweeps foe to the ground. Inflict +1d12 damage with this strike and make another attack on prone enemy.
4	Hammering blow drives nose cartilage into brain. Inflict +1d12 damage with this strike, and the foe suffers 1d6 Int loss.
5	Foe's weapon shattered.* If the foe has no weapon, inflict +2d12 damage with this strike.
6	Strike shatters foe's breastbone. The foe must make a Fort save (DC 15 + PC level) or fall unconscious as his internal organs collapse.
7	Foe driven back by furious assault. Inflict +2d12 damage with this strike, and the foe forgoes his next attack.
8	Concussive strike leaves foe dazed. Inflict +1d8 damage with this strike and make a second attack.
9	Blow to throat carries through to spinal column, reducing everything in between to pasty mush. Inflict +2d12 damage with this strike, and the foe loses speech for 1d4 weeks.
10	Blow craters temple. The foe must make a Fort save (DC 15 + PC level) or be blinded by pain and blood for 1d4 rounds.
11	Strike reduces face to a formless mass of flesh and bone fragments. Inflict +2d12 damage with this strike, and the foe has trouble making hard consonants.
12	You see red! Inflict +1d12 damage with this strike as you are overcome by battle rage!**
13	Hammering strike to torso crushes lesser organs into paste. Inflict +2d12 damage with this strike.
14	Blow to spinal column numbs lower limbs. The foe suffers a -4 penalty to AC as he learns to walk again.
15	Fearsome strike drives enemy to the blood-splattered floor. Foe cowers in fear, prone, for 1d4 rounds.
16	Blow shatters shield. Inflict +2d12 damage with this strike. If the foe has no shield, he is stunned by pain for 1d4 rounds.
17	Foe's kneecap explodes into red mist. Foe's movement drops to 0', and you make another attack.
18	Frontal lobotomy. Inflict +1d12 damage with this strike, and the foe must make a Fort save (DC 15 + PC level) or suffer amnesia. The foe is stunned for 1d4 rounds, regardless.
19	Strike to weapon arm. Foe takes triple damage from his own weapon as it is hammered into his face. Foe drops weapon in dumbfounded awe.
20	Blow crushes spinal cord. Inflict +3d12 damage with this strike, and the foe must make a Fort save (DC 15 + PC level) or suffer permanent paralysis.
21	Blow reduces internal organs to jelly. Death is inevitable in 1d8 rounds.
22	Target is disemboweled, spilling his entrails onto the ground. The foe dies of shock in 1d6 rounds.
23	Strike to chest explodes heart. Inflict +3d12 damage with this strike, and the foe must make a Fort save (DC 15 + PC level) or die instantly.
24+	Skull crushed like a melon. Inflict +3d12 damage with this strike, and the foe must make a Fort save (DC 20 + PC level) or die in 1d3 rounds.

Crit Table V: Level 5+ Warriors, and Level 6+ Dwarves

Roll	Result
0 or less	Battle rage makes friend and foe indistinguishable. Foe is hit for +3d8 damage, and the ally nearest him is also hit by a rebounding blow for 1d4 damage.
1	Foe's weapon shattered.* If the foe has no weapon, inflict +3d12 damage with this strike.
2	Furious assault hurls foe back 1d10'. Any adjacent foes accidentally strike the target for damage.
3	Blow to skull destroys ear. Inflict +1d12 damage with this strike, and the foe suffers permanent deafness.
4	Strike to gut! The foe must make a Fort save (DC 20 + PC level) or spend the next 2 rounds retching bile from a ruptured stomach.
5	Foe casts weapon away and wails for mercy. Inflict +1d12 damage with this strike and make another attack.
6	Strike scalps foe. Blood courses down his face, and the foe is effectively blinded until healed.
7	Foe entangled on your weapon, reducing his AC by -6 while caught. Make another attack.
8-12	You see red! Inflict +1d12 damage with this strike as you are overcome by battle rage!**
13-14	Strike to weapon arm. Foe takes quadruple damage from his own weapon as it is hammered into his face. Foe drops weapon in dumbfounded awe.
15	Blow sunders shield. Inflict +2d12 damage with this strike. If the foe has no shield, he must make a Fort save (DC 20 + PC level) or be knocked unconscious from the pain.
16	Strike to top of skull shortens spinal column, shortening foe by 6". Resulting nerve damage reduces foe's AC by -4.
17	Target is disemboweled, spilling his entrails onto the ground. Foe dies instantly of shock.
18	Blow destroys target's face. Foe is immediately rendered blind and deaf and is now capable of only wet, gurgling sounds.
19	Strike removes crown of target's skull. Foe dies from exposed brain matter in 3d3 rounds.
20	Blow severs shield arm. Inflict +2d12 damage with this strike. Foe's hopes of two-handed weapon mastery dashed.
21	Godly attack. Inflict +3d12 damage with this strike. If the target dies, move up to 10' and make another attack on any foe within 10'.
22	Blow severs leg. Inflict +2d12 damage with this strike, and the foe's movement drops to zero. Foe does nothing but wail in agony for 1d4 rounds.
23	Strike to skull stuns foe for 1d4+1 rounds and permanently reduces Int by 1d12. Make another attack on your inert foe.
24	Strike severs weapon arm. Inflict +2d12 damage with this strike, and the foe is disarmed, literally and figuratively.
25	Devastating strike to torso voids foe's bowels and crushes organs into paste. Foe loses 50% of current hit points and all dignity.
26	Strike crushes throat. Foe begins drowning in his own blood and expires in 1d4 rounds.
27	Crippling blow to spine. Inflict +4d12 damage with this strike, and the foe suffers permanent paralysis.
28+	Foe decapitated with a single strike. You are Death incarnate. Continue to make attacks against any foes within 10' until you miss.

MOUNTED COMBAT

The mounted knight is a classic archetype in medieval fantasy. While there is much room for lengthy, detailed rules on mounted combat, here is a quick and simple way to execute mounted combat rules in your game.

- A mounted character moves at the horse's speed but uses his own action dice.

- A trained warhorse can also make an attack using its own action die, even while mounted. A normal horse (not trained for combat) that attacks in combat forces its rider to make an Agility check to stay mounted (see below).

- One initiative check is rolled for both horse and mount, using the *worse* of the two creatures' initiative modifiers.

- A mounted character automatically receives a +1 AC bonus. When fighting an unmounted opponent, he counts as attacking from higher ground (+1 bonus to attack rolls). When charging with a lance or spear, a mounted character's damage dice are doubled. In addition, Mighty Deeds of Arms with a lance may send a defender flying from his saddle; see page 92.

- A rider's Agility score determines his ability to remain mounted on his horse. If his horse is spooked, he must make a DC 10 Agility check or be flung from the horse. A character trained in horseback riding rolls 1d20 on this check; untrained characters roll 1d10. (Training can be based on 0-level profession or subsequent training at the judge's discretion.) A character flung from a horse lands prone and must spend his next round standing up.

- A normal warhorse is only spooked when it first drops below half its hit points. All other horses are spooked any time they suffer a wound.

Combat statistics for a horse appear on page 418.

MIGHTY DEEDS OF ARMS

A warrior can declare a Mighty Deed of Arms, or a Deed for short, prior to any attack. If his deed die comes up as a 3 or better and the attack lands (e.g., the total attack roll exceeds the target's AC), the Deed succeeds. The higher the deed die, the more successful the Deed.

A warrior's Deeds should fit the situation at hand and reflect the might and daring of a great fighter. A terrific cleave of the axe that sunders an enemy's shield, a precise strike to the throat that silences the enemy leader, or a staggering uppercut that drops the gigantic gladiator are all examples of great Deeds. A warrior may even devise a "signature move" that he frequently attempts based on his particular proclivities. For example, he slashes a bloody red "Z" on an enemy's chest, or he lodges and leaves his bloody axe deep in the enemy's skull, inspiring terror among his opponents.

Certain magic weapons may grant a warrior particular prowess on certain kinds of Deeds, while some spells improve a warrior's ability to perform the same Deeds.

Performing a Deed: The following rules apply to Deeds:

1. The warrior must declare the Deed before his attack. If he rolls the dice before declaring what Deed he attempts, then no Deed takes place, even if he rolls well on his deed die.

2. The Deed must be within the reasonable ability of a warrior to perform, given the character's level and the enemy's size and power. Use the examples below and the judge's discretion to adjudicate. For example, a low-level warrior could not throw an arch-demon even with a great Deed roll, but a great Deed roll might let him throw a large orc that no normal man could budge.

3. The Deed succeeds at the most basic level if the attack hits and the deed die is a 3 or higher. The attack inflicts normal damage and the Deed takes place. The higher the deed die, the greater the Deed. The judge may still allow the enemy a saving throw or require an opposed check of some kind, depending on circumstances.

4. Finally, note that a Deed does not interfere with a crit and may stack with a crit if both occur with the same blow.

Examples of Deeds: Here are some example Deeds in action.

Example #1: A 1st-level warrior with a Strength of 16 (+2 bonus) has a d3 deed die. He is fighting a goat-headed demon that emerged from an extraplanar portal. The warrior declares his Deed will be to shove the demon back through the portal. He attacks, rolling 1d20 + 1d3 +2 (due to his Str). The result is a 16 on the d20, and a 3 on the 1d3, plus his +2 Str modifier, for a total attack roll of 21 (16+3+2). The demon's AC is 17, so the attack lands. Because the deed die came up a 3, the Deed also succeeds. The warrior does 1d8+3+2 damage with his longsword and shoves the demon back through the portal! (Note, depending on the size and strength of the opponent, the judge may still require an opposed Strength check for such a maneuver. In this case the demon is man-sized, and the judge rules that the push-back succeeds.)

Example #2: On his next combat round, the same warrior declares his Deed will be to shatter the demon's horns, a grievous insult to any horned denizen of the Nine Hells. He rolls 5 on his d20, 3 on his d3, plus his +2 Str modifier, for a total attack of 10 (5+3+2). This is below the demon's AC of 17. The attack misses, and even though the deed die came up a 3, the Deed fails.

Types of Deeds

There is no limit to the types of Deeds that a warrior can perform. Any situation-appropriate specialized attack should be encouraged. To help provide some general framework for understanding the concept behind Mighty Deeds of Arms, we have provided seven general categories below. *These are merely suggestions to give a sense of possibility and scale.* The guidelines that follow should help the judge decide which benefits to apply to a high deed die roll.

Creative players will certainly come up with new Deeds. Encourage and allow this.

Blinding Attacks

Blinding attacks usually involve making a called shot to an enemy's eyes. Examples include throwing sand in an enemy's face, stabbing a knife through a visor, or impaling a target's eyeball with an arrow. Blinding attacks obviously must take place where appropriate to the enemy; they are useless against oozes, for example. Against certain opponents, such as a cyclops, the judge may "bump up" results to the next-higher level, given the more serious effect of blinding blows against such creatures.

Deed Die	Blinding Result
3	Opponent's eyes are irritated and stinging, and he has difficulty seeing. On his next attack, the opponent suffers a -2 attack penalty.
4	Opponent is temporarily blinded. He suffers a -4 penalty to his next attack roll and may only move at half speed.
5	Opponent is completely blinded for 1d4 rounds. He flails about with wild attacks, suffering a -8 penalty to attack rolls, and can move only in a random direction at half speed.
6	Opponent is completely blinded, as above, for 2d6 rounds.
7+	Opponent is blinded for the next 24 hours. Additionally, he must make a Fort save against the warrior's attack roll. On a failure, he is permanently blinded.

Disarming Attacks

Disarming attacks include called shots to the hand, shattering an opponent's weapon, severing a spear shaft, entangling a sword arm, and using the flat of a blade to smack a weapon from an enemy's hand. Obviously, the opponent must have a weapon for this Deed to succeed; disarming an unarmed opponent would serve no purpose. Creatures with natural weapons – claws, fangs, horns, etc. – cannot be "disarmed" in the traditional sense but can have the use of their weapons limited. See the table below for examples.

Deed Die	Disarm Result
3	A humanoid creature with a weapon drops its weapon. There is a 50% chance the weapon is knocked out of reach. If the weapon is out of reach, the creature must move to retrieve it and cannot simultaneously attack on its next round (unless it chooses to fight unarmed or draw a new weapon). If the weapon is within reach, the creature can use its next action to recover the weapon and still attack. (Alternate results: stabbed hand throbs in pain, imposing a -1 attack penalty to future rolls; entangled sword arm is tied up, and as long as warrior devotes future combat rounds to maintain the entanglement, the enemy cannot attack.)
4	A humanoid creature with a weapon drops its weapon, which automatically lands out of reach (as above). There is a 50% chance a mundane weapon is sundered in the process. A sundered weapon is shattered or broken and cannot be used (except as an improvised weapon). Magic weapons are never sundered. (Alternate results: stabbed hand is crippled, imposing a -4 attack penalty to future rolls.)
5	A humanoid creature with a mundane weapon has it automatically sundered; a magical weapon is disarmed and lands out of reach. A monster with a natural attack method, such as claws or a bite, has its claws or teeth shattered, imposing a -4 penalty to damage rolls with the affected natural attack for the rest of the combat. Very large monsters, such as dragons, may not be affected or may receive a lesser penalty to damage rolls. (Alternate results: targeted hand is completely severed, requiring attacker to use off-hand for the balance of combat (reference two-weapon combat, below); sword arm is so thoroughly entangled that the warrior can release his weapon and make attacks with a new one while the target struggles to free itself in 1d4 rounds.)
6	Both humanoids and monsters have a weapon completely compromised. Manufactured weapons are either sundered or disarmed and land out of reach, while natural weapons are shattered. The attacking arm (or mouth or tentacle or whatever) is wounded and future attacks take at least a -4 penalty to damage rolls.
7+	As above, and the warrior can also affect creatures much larger and stronger than himself.

Pushbacks

Pushbacks include shield bashes, tackles, bull rushes, tables hurled into enemies, doors smashed into opponents on the other side, and so on. Generally speaking, any attempt to use brute strength to forcefully move an opponent is considered a pushback.

Deed Die	Pushback Result
3	A creature the same size as the warrior is pushed back a few feet – enough space to open access to a door or staircase the target was defending.
4	A creature the same size as the warrior is pushed back a distance equal to half the warrior's movement. A humanoid creature up to 50% larger than the warrior, such as a large orc or a small ogre, is pushed back a few feet. A stable, quadrupedal creature such as a horse or cow can also be pushed back a few feet.
5	The warrior can shove back a creature up to twice his size, such as a fully-grown ogre or a small giant, a distance equal to his full movement. Furthermore, he can pick up and hurl such a creature up to half his normal movement. This can allow the warrior to shove creatures off a nearby cliff, through a railing, out a chapel's stained-glass window, and so on.
6	The warrior can push back several oncoming opponents, such as a charging mass of goblins or a wall of marching men-at-arms. He can shove back a creature up to three times his size and can even budge creatures like small dragons and large basilisks.
7+	As above, and the warrior can affect creatures that would be seemingly impossible for someone his size to push back.

Trips and Throws

Trips and throws include any attempt to knock an enemy off its feet. Whether it's hooking an enemy's leg, stabbing a kneecap, knocking an opponent off-balance, hurling an enemy away, sweeping an enemy's legs, or some other maneuver, these Deeds allow the warrior to knock an enemy prone, limit his movement, and potentially keep him down.

Deed Die	Trips and Throws Result
3	The warrior can knock an enemy off-balance. The enemy gets a Ref save against the warrior's attack roll. Failure means the enemy is knocked prone and must spend its next attack action standing up. Remember that melee attacks against a prone opponent receive a +2 bonus.
4	Against a normal human-sized opponent, the warrior automatically knocks the target prone.

Creatures up to 50% larger than the warrior or those that are quadrupedal or otherwise sure-footed receive a Ref save to avoid being knocked prone.

5	A human-sized opponent is knocked down and thrown up to 10 feet away. Creatures up to twice the size of the warrior can be knocked down, but they receive a Ref save to avoid being knocked prone.
6	A creature up to twice the size of the warrior can be thrown up to 10 feet away automatically. Additionally, the warrior can use his next action to continue to pin down the opponent, forcing him to remain prone. Exceptionally strong opponents may be able to make an opposed Strength check to stand up.
7+	As above, and the warrior can trip or throw creatures that seem far too large to be affected.

Precision Shots

A precision shot is one that boggles the mind with its accuracy. These feats of precision include severing the hangman's noose with a well-placed arrow from twenty paces, lodging a sword in the dragon's mouth so it cannot use a breath weapon, and smashing the evil cleric's anti-holy symbol so he loses control over his un-dead minions. When declaring a precision shot, the warrior must declare exactly which target he is attempting to affect. For example, "I hurl my spear and try to shatter the hinge on the enemy's helmet visor" or "I swing my sword and try to sever the knight's stirrup."

This category also includes called shots that attempt to do additional damage. For example, aiming for an opponent's head, trying to sever a monster's neck, a belly shot against a lumbering chaos beast, and so on. Called shots may do additional damage based on the roll, as noted below.

Deed Die	Precision Shot Result
3	The warrior can hit a small object that is nearby – either at melee range or very close range via missile fire. For example, he can hit a holy symbol displayed by a cleric, a banner flown by a cavalier nearby, or an ogre's tusk. A called shot here may do up to 1d4 points of additional damage (judge's discretion).
4	The warrior can hit a target that is normally within the province of only the most skilled swordsmen or archers. For example, he can shoot an apple off someone's head or hit the bull's-eye at 100 yards. A called shot here may do up to 1d5 points of additional damage (judge's discretion).
5	The warrior can make a near-impossible shot that includes slicing a narrow rope with an arrow from 100 yards away, hurling a dagger

into a coin from across a moat, or stabbing a sword through the one vulnerable scale on the vast scaly hide of an ancient dragon. A called shot here may do up to 1d6 points of additional damage (judge's discretion).

6 The warrior can make precise shots, such as the ones above, while also blinded and deafened – he relies on his other senses to attempt such an incredible maneuver. A called shot here may do up to 1d7 points of additional damage (judge's discretion).

7+ The warrior can make precise shots that seem beyond the abilities of mortal man – provided he can contrive an explanation. For example, he can shoot an arrow through a doorway to hit the evil wizard in the throat in the room beyond, explaining that the arrow actually went through the narrowest crack between the door and its frame. He can hurl a stone more than half a mile to knock out the goblin kidnapper as he gallops away on horseback, explaining that a passing hawk carried the stone in its beak for several hundred yards, then let it continue on its original trajectory. A called shot here may do up to 1d8 points of additional damage (judge's discretion).

Rallying Maneuvers

The mighty hero, bounding to the front of combat, can restore order to broken ranks. A bellowing war cry, a heroic charge, a frothing bloodthirsty maniac exemplifying bloody prowess: the right rallying maneuver by a great warrior can make an army fight better than it ever has before.

Deed Die Rallying Maneuver Result

3 The warrior can let loose a war cry or perform some flashy maneuver that rallies his troops around him. Nearby hirelings and retainers that have failed a morale check get a second check and recover their wits if they succeed.

4 The warrior urges his allies to form up around him and leads the charge! He must be at the forefront of the battle, succeeding in his attacks and setting an example for his followers, who receive a +1 bonus to morale checks for the remainder of the round.

5 The warrior performs some dramatic combat maneuver that inspires courage. Allies and followers receive a +1 bonus to morale checks for the rest of the round. Additionally, if the warrior kills his opponent this round or causes a critical hit (or some other spectacular blow), all allies and followers receive a +1 attack bonus for the next round.

6 The warrior's incredible maneuver affects not only nearby allies and followers, but potential-

ly an entire army. The benefits are as above, but extend to as many as 100 followers, as long as they can see the hero.

7+   As above, and the benefits extend to as many followers as can see the hero – potentially an entire army of thousands of men!

Defensive Maneuvers

In certain circumstances, a warrior's greatest Deed may be allowing his comrades to live to fight another day. Shield walls, fighting withdrawals, and back-to-back combat maneuvers can sometimes allow the warrior to support his entire party.

Deed Die	Defensive Maneuver Result
3	The warrior fights defensively, improving his chances of surviving. He receives a +1 AC bonus for the next round.
4	The warrior organizes a defensive formation among his allies, such as a shield wall, that is well-suited to the opponent he fights. In addition to causing damage, he positions himself to "anchor" the defensive maneuver, granting a +1 AC bonus to himself and two allies who must be adjacent for the next round.
5	The warrior forms up his allies to best defend themselves. None of the participating allies can move or the defensive position is disrupted. As long as none of the allies move, the warrior and the allies receive a +1 AC bonus for the next round. Up to four allies can benefit.
6	As above, and the warrior organizes a particularly effective defensive position that grants a +2 AC bonus to himself and up to four allies, as long as no one moves. The warrior must continue using his Deed for this specific use to maintain the position. Subsequent Deed rolls do not need to roll 6 or higher, but the warrior cannot attempt another Deed without disrupting the defensive formation. If the warrior chooses to move and he scores a deed die roll of 6 or better, he can maintain a +1 AC bonus for himself and his four allies, provided they move in the same direction at the same speed and maintain their formation.
7+	As above, and the AC bonus is +3 if not moving or +2 if moving.

Signature Deeds

It is recommended that each warrior define his own "signature" Deed. You can think of this as a signature move for the character. If a player forgets to declare what his Deed will be, the assumption is that he attempted his signature move. The signature move can correspond to a defined Deed. For example, the Black Knight always attempts a disarm. Or it can be something highly specialized: a disarm if the result is 3, a blinding attack if the roll is 4, a trip if the roll is 5, etc.

You can use the back of your character sheet to write a deed table for recording your warrior's signature Deed.

Weapon-Specific Deeds

Select weapons bring with them certain abilities in the hands of an experienced warrior. For example, a battle axe is ideal for smashing an opponent's shield, while a war hammer can knock down an opponent. Another option for a player is to define a weapon-specific deed table, then make that his character's "default" action. You can use the deed die to provide an easy resolution in the form of a saving throw on the defender's part. Here are a few examples to provide ideas.

Battle Axe: Battle axes crush shields and rend armor. On any successful Mighty Deed of Arms, the defending party's armor is damaged so severely that the armor's AC bonus is reduced by the amount of the deed die *instead* of causing hit point damage. For example, the defender has full plate mail (AC bonus of +8). The attacker hits with a deed die of 3, so the defender's AC modifier from armor is reduced to +5. If the next attack hits with a deed die of 5, the defender's AC bonus drops to 0! If the defender has a shield, it is destroyed after the first point of reduced armor. After several battle axe hits, a defender's armor may be pulverized. Once the armor bonus is reduced to 0, the deed die translates to hit point damage as usual.

Flails: When aimed at an opponent's legs, a flail can entangle and trip an enemy. If a character with a flail does not declare any other Deed, he is automatically considered to be making a trip attack on any successful hit.

Lance: All of the Mighty Deeds of Arms discussed so far are for foot soldiers. It is perfectly acceptable to design a set of Deeds for a mounted knight. The lance is an excellent option for building a set of Deeds. A direct hit with a lance can shatter an opponent's shield and knock him to the ground. On any successful Mighty Deed of Arms, the defending party's shield is automatically shattered. In addition, the defender must make a Strength check against DC 10 + deed die. For example, if the attacker hit with a set of dice that included a deed die of 5, the defender would have to make a Strength check against DC 15. Failure on the Strength check indicates the defender is knocked prone. If he was mounted, he takes an additional 1d4 damage from the fall.

War hammer: War hammers swing with such momentum they can knock down an opponent. On any successful Mighty Deed of Arms, the defending party may be knocked off his feet. If a warrior with a war hammer does not declare any other Deed, he is automatically considered to attempt a pushback with any successful hit.

DAMAGE AND DEATH

If a defender is wounded, the attacker rolls for damage. Roll the appropriate die for the weapon.

If the attack was made with a melee weapon, add the attacker's Strength bonus. Add other bonuses due to spells, magic items, or class abilities.

Deduct this value from the defender's hit points.

A successful attack always inflicts a minimum of 1 point of damage, even if the attacker has a negative Strength modifier.

A character or monster dies when it reaches 0 hit points.

Bleeding out: There is a chance of saving a dead character by healing him very quickly (such as with a cleric's ability to lay on hands). A 0-level character that reaches 0 hit points is irrevocably killed, but a 1st-level character that reaches 0 hit points collapses and begins bleeding out. Such a character has 1 round in which he can be healed to prevent his death. If he is healed on the round he's reduced to 0 hit points or the next round, he is healed per the result of the lay on hands check (treat his hit points as starting at 0). If he is not healed before the second round, he may be permanently killed (see below).

For each level past the first, a character has one more round of bleeding before he is permanently killed. For example, a 3rd-level character can be saved if he is healed within 3 rounds.

A character that was bleeding out but was saved suffers permanent physical trauma from his near-fatal injuries. Anyone who is saved from bleeding out suffers a *permanent* loss of 1 point of Stamina. In addition, he gains a terrible scar from the wound that downed him.

Recovering the body: If the body of a dead ally can be recovered, there is a chance the ally may not be truly killed. He may have been knocked unconscious or simply stunned. If a character reaches a dead ally's body within one hour, the dead character may make a Luck check when his body is rolled over. On a successful check, the dead character was badly injured but is not permanently killed, and the ally is able to keep him alive. The "dead" character was simply knocked out, stunned, or otherwise incapacitated. Once an ally shakes the downed character awake, he recovers to 1 hit point. The character is groggy for the next hour (-4 penalty to all rolls) and sustains a permanent injury of some kind, reflected as a permanent -1 penalty to Strength, Agility, or Stamina (determine randomly).

HEALING

Wounds heal with rest. A healed character can never exceed his natural hit point maximum.

A character who actively adventures and gets a good night's rest heals 1 hit point. If the character gets a day of bed rest, he heals 2 hit points per night.

Critical hits heal when the associated damage heals. For example, imagine that a character takes a -10' penalty to speed due to a kneecap strike that also inflicted 4 extra points of damage. The wounded kneecap (and associated speed penalty) heals when the character has recovered 4 hit points. Note that some crits may create permanent injuries which can only be healed by magical or extraordinary means.

Ability score loss, except for Luck, heals at the same rate: 1 point with a good night's rest, and 2 points with a day of bed rest.

A character may heal both ability score loss and hit point loss on the same night's rest.

Luck, however, does not heal. Repeat: lost Luck does not heal. Except for the special abilities of halflings and thieves, a character who burns Luck does so permanently. Luck can be restored in the same way that a man normally gains good or bad luck – by appealing to the gods. Great acts of courage in defense of one's deity may earn a boon, just as acts in opposition to a devil may earn a curse. The judge can tell you more about Luck…

SAVING THROWS

Saving throws represent the character's ability to resist extraordinary trauma, whether it's poison, magical flame, or a dangerous trap. A character's class and ability scores determine his saving throw modifier for Fortitude, Reflex, and Willpower. To make a saving throw, roll 1d20 and apply the character's modifier. If the result is equal to or greater than the target DC, the saving throw succeeds. Otherwise, it fails.

MORALE

Not all monsters fight to the death – some flee or surrender. Monsters, retainers, and non-player characters (NPCs) make morale checks at certain times in battle. This determines if they stay to fight or retreat to live another day. Player characters never make morale checks; their behavior is up to the players.

A morale check is made at these times:

- With a group of monsters: when the first creature is slain and when half the creatures have been killed or incapacitated.

- With a single monster: when it has lost half its hit points.

- With a retainer: when he first encounters combat or danger (e.g., a trap) in each adventure and at the end of each adventure.

The morale check is made by rolling 1d20 and adding the creature's Will save. A result of 11 or higher is success – the creature can keep fighting. On a 10 or less, the check is failed – the creature attempts to flee the combat. Retainers also add their employer's Personality modifier. In some cases, the DC may be higher than 11, particularly when magical effects are involved.

The judge may apply a modifier of up to +4 or -4 to the check if the creature has sufficient motivation to fight or flee. For example, a mother defending her cubs would receive a +4 bonus as would a goblin shaman defending his sacred shrine. However, a goblin slave willing to see his ogre overlord slain might have a -4 modifier as would a mindless giant centipede that just wanted food, not a fight!

Some monsters are immune to morale checks. Automatons, animated statues, golems, and other mindless creations do not fear death and thus do not make morale checks. The same is true of unintelligent un-dead such as zombies and skeletons.

Table 4-3: Two-Weapon Attacks

Agility	Primary Hand Die	Off Hand Die	Critical Hits*
8 or less	-3 dice	-4 dice	Cannot score a critical hit fighting two-handed
9-11	-2 dice	-3 dice	Cannot score a critical hit fighting two-handed
12-15	-1 die	-2 dice	Cannot score a critical hit fighting two-handed
16-17	-1 die	-1 die	Primary hand scores a critical hit on a max die roll (16 on 1d16) that *also* beats target's AC (no automatic hit)
18+	Normal die	-1 die	Primary hand scores critical hits as normal

Warriors and others with improved crit threat ranges (i.e., those who can crit on 19-20 or better) lose that ability when fighting two-handed.

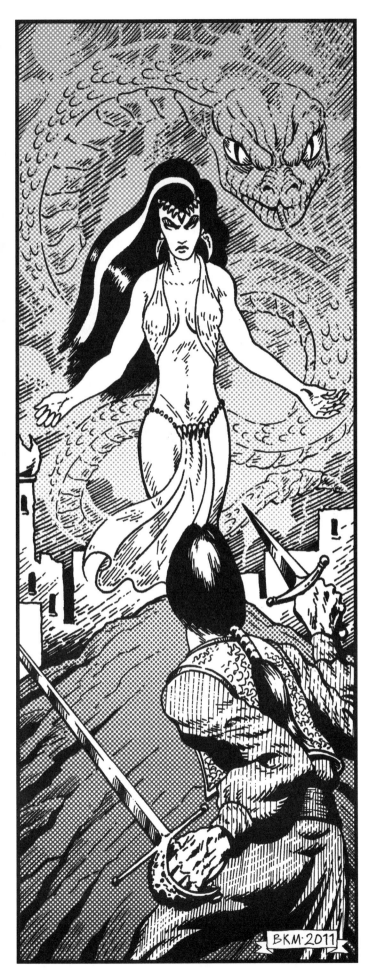

BURNING LUCK

As noted earlier, a character can permanently burn Luck to give a one-time bonus to a roll. For example, a character could burn 6 points to get a +6 modifier on a roll, but his Luck score is now 6 points lower. The following rules govern the burning of Luck:

- A character can only burn Luck to affect his own die rolls (except for halflings as noted in their class description). Luck cannot be burned to affect the die roll of other characters or monsters, even if they affect the character. (Note that the character's Luck modifier does apply to enemy crits against him, but this Luck *modifier* is different from burning off Luck.)

- Luck is typically used to affect a character's attack rolls, damage rolls, spell checks, thief checks, and saving throws, but it can also be used for other purposes.

- A character can declare his intent to burn Luck *before* or *after* his die roll. He then specifies how many points he will burn. But he can only burn Luck once per roll.

TWO-WEAPON FIGHTING

With sufficiently high Agility, a character can wield a lightweight secondary weapon (such as dagger, short sword, or knife) in his off hand while using a sword or other primary weapon in his natural hand. The character typically attacks using a smaller die, depending on the hand and the character's Agility, as shown on table 4-3. The table is based on the dice chain; i.e., "-1 die" means a normal d20 roll becomes a d16. This result stacks with secondary attacks, so a character with a d16 action die (for whatever reason) would revert to d14 if affected by "-1 die" on the table, based on the dice chain.

Two-weapon attacks are less likely to hit, but the character may make two attack rolls where he would normally make one. Because a character's off hand is usually not as strong or coordinated as his primary hand, his secondary attack rolls usually require a different deed die. Critical hits are determined as indicated on the table below.

Halflings are an exception to the two-weapon fighting rule, as described in the halfling class entry.

A character fighting two-handed cannot use a shield (obviously).

WITHDRAWAL

Once a character is engaged in melee, he cannot back away without opening himself up to attack. If a character or monster withdraws from an active melee – whether to retreat, move to a new position, or attempt some action – his opponents immediately receive a single free attack.

OTHER COMBAT RULES

Ability loss: Some attacks cause ability loss. A target reduced to 0 Personality or Intelligence is a babbling idiot incapable of feeding himself. A target reduced to 0 Strength or Agility is incapable of movement. A target reduced to 0 Stamina faints and remains unconscious. A target reduced to 0 Luck suffers such constant, bizarre mishaps that he is effectively unable to accomplish anything. Ability loss heals over time, as described on page 94.

Catching fire: A character who catches fire suffers 1d6 damage per round. He can put out the fire by spending an entire round doing "stop, drop, and roll," which grants him an opportunity to make a DC 10 Reflex save to put out the fire. Certain spells and monster attacks may produce hotter or more dangerous flames that cause more damage or are more difficult to put out.

Charge: A reckless character can use 1 action to declare a charge. In order to charge, he must move at least half his speed. A charging character gains +2 bonus to attack rolls but suffers a -2 penalty to AC until his next turn.

Dropping a torch: A torch dropped on the ground has a 50% chance of being extinguished.

Falling: Falling causes 1d6 damage per 10' fallen. For every damage die that comes up a 6, the victim breaks a bone. For each broken bone, the character permanently loses 1 point of Strength or Agility (player's choice). The affected limb, rib, or vertebrae never heals quite right and affects the character in some fashion from then on.

Firing into melee: Combat is a constant swirl of activity. A character who uses a bow, crossbow, dart, thrown dagger, or other missile fire weapon against an opponent engaged in melee may hit an ally. If the attack misses the intended target, there is a 50% chance it hits an ally engaged in the melee. Determine that ally randomly, then re-roll the attack roll against the ally's armor class.

Grappling: Each party makes opposed attack rolls, adding the higher of their Agility or Strength modifier. (Monsters add their hit dice instead.) An attacker twice the opponent's size adds +4 to the opposed roll; an attacker triple the opponent's size adds +8 to the opposed roll; an attacker quadruple the opponent's size adds +16 to the opposed roll; and so on. If the attacker wins the opposed roll, he has grappled and pinned his opponent. If the attacker loses the opposed roll, the grapple fails.

A pinned target cannot move or take any significant action until he frees himself from the pin. This is done by succeeding in another grapple check, as above.

Melee attacks against a grappled creature are treated similar to firing a missile into melee. Any failed melee attack against a grappled creature has a 50% chance of wounding the ally who is maintaining the pin.

Recovering armor: When someone is slain, the armor he wears ends up pierced, dented, and otherwise compro-

mised. Armor recovered from a fallen foe (or ally) has a 25% chance of being useless. It can be repaired by an armorer, typically for one-quarter to one-half the original cost of the armor.

Demi-humans are of an unusual physiognomy and cannot wear armor sized for a human. If not otherwise specified, there is a 75% chance that randomly discovered armor is human-sized.

Recovering missile fire weapons: Characters can recover missile weapons that miss their target. There is a 50% chance that recovered arrows, sling stones, javelins, and other weapons are destroyed; otherwise, they can be reused.

Subdual damage: You can use the flat of your sword to subdue an opponent you wish to capture alive. If a character is proficient in one of the following weapons, he can inflict subdual damage with it: swords, axes, clubs, spears, and staves. There is no attack penalty, but subdual damage is one die lower than normal for the weapon, according to the dice chain. An opponent brought to 0 hit points via subdual damage collapses unconscious.

Unarmed combat: Unarmed characters inflict subdual damage of 1d3 + Strength modifier.

TURNING UNHOLY

By wielding his holy symbol and uttering holy words, a cleric can turn away the enemies of his faith. A cleric can attempt to turn away un-dead, demons, and devils. Some clerics of particular faiths may be able to turn away other kinds of creatures, depending on what powers their deities award them.

A turn check is mechanically similar to a spell check, except that Luck matters. A d20 is rolled and added to the cleric's caster level. The cleric's Personality and Luck modifiers are also included. Compare the result of the turn check to table 4-4.

Turned monsters usually receive a Will save to resist being turned. The save is made against the cleric's turn check. At sufficiently high results, a cleric may turn groups of weaker creatures automatically; they do not receive a saving throw.

A failed turn check increases the cleric's range of natural disapproval, just as with a failed spell check.

If a cleric raises his holy symbol to turn a group of mixed creatures, the player should indicate a specific target. Apply the results of the turn check based on the HD of the target creature. "Overflow" HD affect lower-HD creatures at the indicated effect. For example, if a cleric were charged by a band of 1 HD skeletons led by a 4 HD vampire commander, the player could designate whether he targets the skeletons or the vampire. If he targets the skeletons and his check is 19, he turns 1d4+CL of these lesser un-dead but does not affect the vampire. If he targets the vampire and his next check is 24, he turns 1d3+CL 4 HD creatures. If he rolls 5, that means he could turn the vampire and 4 of the skeletons.

Table 4-4: Turn Unholy Result by HD

Check	Turn Range	Holy Smite	1 HD	2 HD	3-4 HD	5-6 HD	7-8 HD	9-10 HD	11-12 HD
1-11	–	–	NE	NE	NE	NE	NE	NE	NE
12-13	30'	–	T1	NE	NE	NE	NE	NE	NE
14-17	30'	–	T1d3+CL	NE	NE	NE	NE	NE	NE
18-19	30'	–	T1d4+CL	T1	NE	NE	NE	NE	NE
20-23	60'	–	T1d6+CL	T1d3+CL	T1	NE	NE	NE	NE
24-27	60'	Beam, 60', 1d3 dmg	T1d8+CL, D1d4 (no save)	T1d4+CL	T1d3+CL	T1	NE	NE	NE
28-29	60'	Cone, 30', 1d4 dmg	T2d6+CL, D1d4 (no save)	T1d6+CL	T1d4+CL	T1d3+CL	T1	NE	NE
30-31	120'	Cone, 60', 1d5 dmg	K1d8+CL (no save)	T1d8+CL, D1d4 (no save)	T1d6+CL	T1d4+CL	T1d3+CL	T1	NE
32+	240'	Cone, 120', 1d6 dmg	K2d6+CL (no save)	T2d6+CL, D1d4 (no save)	T1d8+CL, D1d4	T1d6+CL	T1d4+CL	T1d3+CL	T1

NE = No Effect.

T = Creatures up to this HD are turned in a quantity indicated. For example, "T1" means one creature is turned; "T1d4+CL" means a number of creatures of this HD are turned equal to 1d4 + caster level. Unless indicated, turned creatures receive a saving throw (Will vs. turn check DC). A turned creature moves away from the cleric at maximum speed or cowers if unable to retreat. A turned creature continues to flee for 3d10 minutes.

D = Creatures are turned, *and* they take the indicated damage on the first round of turning. For example, T1d4+CL, D1d4 means the cleric can turn a number of creatures of this HD equal to 1d4+CL, and those creatures *also* take 1d4 damage.

K = Creatures are automatically killed. The number of creatures killed is indicated after the K. For example, K1d8+CL means the cleric kills a number of creatures of that HD equal to 1d8 + caster level.

Holy Smite = At high levels, a cleric's turn attempt produces holy energy that smites unholy creatures in close proximity. This is in addition to the turning effect and can be directed in the same direction as the cleric's line-of-sight for the turning attempt. The effect and range varies, as described below, and all unholy creatures affected take the indicated damage *automatically* with no save. The damage occurs once per turn attempt; another turn check is required the following round to attempt again. Beam: a concentrated ray of light that the cleric can direct against one target within 60'. Cone: a cone 30' long and 30' wide at its end.

SPELL DUELS

A wizard seeks superiority over his fellows and attains that through demonstration of magical ability…at any cost. When two wizards meet, there is always conflict; and when wizards conflict, there are spell duels. A clap of thunder, the smell of brimstone, the staggering concussion of contested dominance, and, finally, the pile of ash where once a man stood – these are the marks of a spell duel.

Spell duel resolution: A spell duel is where one spellcaster casts a spell that is countered by a second caster, and the two proceed to throw spells until one dominates. These are the basic rules of spell duels. Full details are described below.

1. Both wizards and clerics can spell duel. A wizard can counter the spells of a cleric and vice versa. In rare circumstances, other classes can also spell duel (e.g., a thief reading from scrolls).

2. Spell duels are a special rule subsystem that breaks some standard combat mechanics, specifically parts of the initiative system. Casters involved in a spell duel may find themselves acting in response to each other prior to actions by other party members.

3. Only some spells can be used to counter each other. Generally speaking, there are two kinds of counterspells: "same spell" (i.e., *fireball* used to counter *fireball*) and "defensive" (i.e., *magic shield* used to counter *magic missile* or *fire resistance* used to counter *fireball*).

4. Spell duels proceed in initiative order. A wizard later in the initiative order may counterspell the spell cast by a wizard who went before him. A caster who is last in the order cannot have his spells countered.

5. Counterspell mechanics involve the comparison of the attacker's spell check to the defender's spell check and a resolution based on that comparison.

6. Successes build and failures compound in a spell duel. A wizard who wins a few counterspells will find himself building momentum.

7. Finally, untoward things can occur in a spell duel. It is, after all, a direct collision of unearthly energies.

Initiative: When one wizard or cleric casts a spell, a wizard or cleric *later in the initiative order* may immediately declare he is counter-spelling. If multiple casters attempt a counterspell, the outcome is resolved in initiative order.

The combat round immediately pauses for resolution of the spellcaster actions. When each spellcaster has completed his action, combat initiative resumes.

The spellcasters effectively "skip ahead" strictly for purposes of counterspelling, and then lose their normal initiative action.

However, the spellcasters *remain in their same initiative order.* On the next round they may choose to act normally, and thus initiative order must be maintained.

When a spellcaster chooses to counterspell, he may cast a counterspell *and that is all.* He may not take any other action that round. The counterspell action lets him skip ahead in order but limits his options.

The spellcaster who is last in initiative order has the advantage of being able to counterspell anyone before him and the disadvantage of only being able to respond to spells, not initiate the spell duel. The spellcaster who is first in initiative order has the advantage of setting the tone for the spell duel by choosing the initiating spell, but he cannot counterspell.

Spells that counter: Generally speaking, common sense dictates which spells can counter each other. Here is a general list:

Opposed Spells That Can Be Used to Counter Each Other

Fire resistance : Fireball, scorching ray

Magic shield : Magic missile, fireball, scorching ray, lightning bolt

Dispel magic : Any spell

Invoke patron : Invoke patron (depending on patrons)

Any attack spell : Counters same attack spell (for example, *fireball* counters *fireball*)

The Counterspell in Action: When a caster declares he is counterspelling, follow these steps:

1. First, at the very start of the spell duel, each player with a counterspelling caster sets a d20 in front of his character sheet. This is the momentum tracker. At the start of the duel, all casters set the d20 to 10.

2. Next, the attacker declares the spell he is casting and makes his spell check.

3. The defender (counterspeller) declares a counterspell and makes his spell check.

4. The winner is the high roller. Increment the winner's momentum tracker by 1. For example, if the attacker wins, move his d20 to 11. If the defender wins, his d20 is incremented by 1.

5. Cross-reference the two spell checks on table 4-5: Spell Duel Check Comparison.

6. Roll the indicated die and compare to table 4-6: Counterspell Power. If the attacker had the higher spell check, use the "Attacker High" column; otherwise, use the "Defender High" column. Modify the result by the *difference between the two momentum trackers.* For example, if the attacker's momentum tracker now shows 13 because he had 3 successes, and the defender's is still at 10, the Counterspell Power would be at +3 if the attacker won or at -3 if the defender won.

7. There is one exception: if the two spell checks are identical, table 4-5: Spell Duel Check Comparison will refer to Table 4-7: Phlogiston Disturbance. This is the most dangerous arena of magic, where different effects become commingled and extraordinary things may happen!

8. Resolve any spell effects at the resulting spell check.

9. Finally, proceed back to "normal" initiative. Other character classes receive their normal actions. When the counterspeller's count turns up, skip him and move onto the next character.

Special notes: Here are some clarifications on spell duels.

Spell check success: The attacker's spell check must succeed per the normal spell result table to have any effect (of course). The defender's spell check must also succeed (of course). This means that a level 1 spell check needs a minimum result of 12+ to counterspell; a level 2 spell needs a minimum result of 14+; and so on.

Who goes first? Generally speaking, the effects of counterspells happen simultaneously, unless noted otherwise. That means it is possible for two wizards to *both die* as they launch dueling fireballs. Sometimes the tables below will indicate that one wizard's spell takes effect first, which may affect the second spell. If order of resolution matters, the caster with the higher spell check always acts first.

Multiple counterspellers: Two spellcasters may attempt to counterspell a single caster. Resolve all spell check comparisons, then refer to the spell tables to determine what happens. Again, generally speaking, the effects of spells and counterspells happen simultaneously, unless noted otherwise on the tables.

Aiding a counterspell: Wizards may not "aid each other" in a spell duel. Each counterspell is determined separately, though results may stack against the caster. For example, if a wizard casts *fireball* and three defenders counterspell with returning *fireballs*, the impact of multiple mitigations of the attacker's *fireball* could mean his spell has no effect.

Patron invocation: A wizard who invokes his patron can be countered by a wizard invoking *the same* or *a different* patron. If a defender invokes the same patron as the attacker, and both spell checks succeed, *both spells are automatically cancelled* – ignore the results of tables 4-5 and 4-6. If the defender and attacker invoke different patrons, resolve the effect as normal.

Loss of spell: Certain spell duel results can reduce the check result of the attacker or defender. A wizard loses a spell for the day only if his *initial, unmodified* spell check is below the minimum threshold. If his initial check summons sufficient eldritch power to set the spell duel in motion, he does not count as losing the spell. The same goes for the defender's *initial, unmodified* spell check. For clerics, the same rule applies in regards to their accumulation of casting penalties.

Delaying actions: Wizards who are first in initiative order

Table 4-5: Spell Duel Check Comparison

Compare attacker's spell check (column headers) to defender's spell check (row headers). If a die type is indicated, roll that die on table 4-6: Counterspell Power. If the two spell checks are the same result, the table shows PD and you should refer to table 4-7: Phlogiston Disturbance.

Invoke patron has special results – see accompanying text.

		Attacker's Spell Check*															
		12	13	14	15	16	17	18	19	20	21	22	23	24	25	26	27	28+
Defend-er's Spell Check*	12	PD	d3	d4	d5	d5	d6	d6	d7	d7	d8	d8	d10	d10	d12	d12	d14	d16
	13	d3	PD	d3	d4	d5	d5	d6	d6	d7	d7	d8	d8	d10	d10	d12	d12	d14
	14	d4	d3	PD	d3	d4	d5	d5	d6	d6	d7	d7	d8	d8	d10	d10	d12	d12
	15	d5	d4	d3	PD	d3	d4	d5	d5	d6	d6	d7	d7	d8	d8	d10	d10	d12
	16	d5	d5	d4	d3	PD	d3	d4	d5	d5	d6	d6	d7	d7	d8	d8	d10	d10
	17	d6	d5	d5	d4	d3	PD	d3	d4	d5	d5	d6	d6	d7	d7	d8	d8	d10
	18	d6	d6	d5	d5	d4	d3	PD	d3	d4	d5	d5	d6	d6	d7	d7	d8	d8
	19	d7	d6	d6	d5	d5	d4	d3	PD	d3	d4	d5	d5	d6	d6	d7	d7	d8
	20	d7	d7	d6	d6	d5	d5	d4	d3	PD	d3	d4	d5	d5	d6	d6	d7	d7
	21	d8	d7	d7	d6	d6	d5	d5	d4	d3	PD	d3	d4	d5	d5	d6	d6	d7
	22	d8	d8	d7	d7	d6	d6	d5	d5	d4	d3	PD	d3	d4	d5	d5	d6	d6
	23	d10	d8	d8	d7	d7	d6	d6	d5	d5	d4	d3	PD	d3	d4	d5	d5	d6
	24	d10	d10	d8	d8	d7	d7	d6	d6	d5	d5	d4	d3	PD	d3	d4	d5	d5
	25	d12	d10	d10	d8	d8	d7	d7	d6	d6	d5	d5	d4	d3	PD	d3	d4	d5
	26	d12	d12	d10	d10	d8	d8	d7	d7	d6	d6	d5	d5	d4	d3	PD	d3	d4
	27	d14	d12	d12	d10	d10	d8	d8	d7	d7	d6	d6	d5	d5	d4	d3	PD	d3
	28+	d16	d14	d12	d12	d10	d10	d8	d8	d7	d7	d6	d6	d5	d5	d4	d3	PD

* Note that both spell checks must succeed at the normal spell check threshold as a prerequisite to comparison on this table. For example, a level 2 spells need a minimum result of 14 to be useful in a spell duel.

may wish to delay their initiative to be in a better position for counterspelling. This is acceptable. But if multiple wizards all decide to delay, the final "order of actions" is still resolved by initiative order, with the highest roll going first and the lowest roll going last.

A counterspell is all: A caster may use the counterspell mechanic *only* to cast a spell that specifically counters a previously cast spell. The counterspell "special initiative action" may not be used to "cast just any old spell."

The counterspell may kill creatures out of initiative order: A counterspell allows a wizard with a later initiative count to effectively "skip ahead," and thus the counterspell may have consequences for creatures that, technically, had a higher initiative count than the counterspeller. For example, a *fireball* countered with a *fireball* – where both spells go off – may kill warriors whose initiative count was before that of the wizard who counterspelled. So be it: counterspells are special.

Example of Spell Dueling: The combat consists of The Emerald Sorcerer, his two emerald soldiers, his nemesis Magnus the Gray, and Magnus' apprentice Athle the Astounding. Initiative rolls are as follows:

17 = The Emerald Sorcerer

15 = the two emerald soldiers

12 = Magnus the Gray

6 = Athle the Astounding

Round one. The Emerald Sorcerer casts *magic missile.* Magnus immediately declares a counterspell of *magic shield.* Athle the Astounding declines to counterspell. Even though the emerald soldiers are next in initiative order, the spell duel is resolved first.

Both players lay a d20 momentum tracker in front of them, showing a starting figure of 10.

The Emerald Sorcerer rolls 13 on his spell check, while Magnus rolls 16. Both checks succeed. The defender's roll is high. Therefore, Magnus the Gray's momentum tracker is incremented to 11.

Comparing the spell check results of 16 and 13 on Table 4-5: Spell Duel Check Comparison, we get a roll of d5. The difference in momentum trackers is 1 (11 on one die and 10 on the other), so the defender rolls d5+1 on Table 4-6: Counterspell Power.

Table 4-6: Counterspell Power

Roll	Defender High	Attacker High
1	Mitigate d4: roll d4 and subtract this from the attacker's spell check. Attacker's spell still carries through at this lower spell check; defender's spell is lost.	Push-through d4: roll d4 and subtract this from defender's spell check. Defender's spell takes effect at this lower result, and attacker's spell takes effect *simultaneously* at normal spell check result.
2	Mitigate d6: roll d6 and subtract this from the attacker's spell check. Attacker's spell still carries through at this lower spell check; defender's spell is lost.	Push-through d8: roll d8 and subtract this from defender's spell check. Defender's spell takes effect at this lower result, and attacker's spell takes effect *first* at normal spell check result.
3	Mitigate d8: roll d8 and subtract this from the attacker's spell check. Attacker's spell still carries through at this lower spell check; defender's spell is lost.	Overwhelm: attacker's spell takes effect and defender's spell is cancelled.
4	Mutual mitigation d10: roll d10 and subtract this from the attacker's spell check *and* the defender's spell check. *Both* spells take effect *simultaneously* at this lower spell check result.	Overwhelm: attacker's spell takes effect and defender's spell is cancelled.
5	Mutual cancellation: both attacker's and defender's spells are cancelled.	Overwhelm: attacker's spell takes effect and defender's spell is cancelled.
6	Push-through d6: roll d6 and subtract from defender's spell check. Defender's spell takes effect at this result, and attacker's spell is cancelled.	Overwhelm and reflect d8: roll d8 and subtract this from defender's spell check. Attacker's spell takes effect *simultaneously* at normal spell check result, and defender's spell check is reflected back on him at this lower spell check result.
7	Push-through d4: roll d4 and subtract from defender's spell check. Defender's spell takes effect at this result, and attacker's spell is cancelled.	Overwhelm and reflect d8: roll d8 and subtract this from defender's spell check. Attacker's spell takes effect *first* at normal spell check result, and defender's spell check is reflected back on him at this lower spell check result.
8	Overwhelm: attacker's spell is cancelled, and defender's spell takes effect at normal result.	Overwhelm and reflect d6: roll d6 and subtract this from defender's spell check. Attacker's spell takes effect *first* at normal spell check result, and defender's spell check is reflected back on him at this lower spell check result.
9	Reflect: defender's spell is cancelled, and attacker's spell reflects back on him at the spell check result rolled.	Overwhelm and reflect d4: roll d4 and subtract this from defender's spell check. Attacker's spell takes effect *first* at normal spell check result, and defender's spell check is reflected back on him at this lower spell check result.
10+	Reflect and overwhelm: defender's spell takes effect at normal result, and attacker's spell reflects back on him at the spell check result rolled.	Reflect and overwhelm: attacker's spell takes effect at normal spell check result, and defender's spell check is reflected back on him at normal spell check.

The result of 3 shows that Magnus's *magic shield* fails, but he reduces the *magic missile* check by d8. Magnus rolls 4 on the d8, so The Emerald Sorcerer's spell check of 13 becomes 9. That is below the minimum threshold of 12 for success, so *both* spells fail.

Even though both spells failed to take effect, both casters were able to summon sufficient energy to initiate their spells. Therefore, neither loses the ability to cast their spells.

Once the spell duel is resolved, the combat round proceeds:

- The emerald soldiers attack Magnus and the normal attack process is resolved.

- At Magnus' initiative count, he can take no action because he already counterspelled.

- Athle the Astounding did not counterspell, so he moves and casts *magic missile* against The Emerald Sorcerer. The Emerald Sorcerer could not counterspell anyway because he is first in initiative order, and because he already used his action. Athle rolls 15, succeeds in his check, and damages The Emerald Sorcerer with a spell check.

Round two. In the second round, The Emerald Sorcerer launches another *magic missile*. In this round, both Magnus the Gray and Athle the Astounding choose to counterspell. Magnus casts *magic shield* again, while Athle casts *magic missile*.

The Emerald Sorcerer rolls an 18 on his spell check. Magnus rolls 19, and Athle rolls 14.

A d20 momentum tracker set at 10 is now placed in front of Athle, since he has now entered the spell duel. The Emerald Sorcerer lost his comparison to Magnus, so Magnus' existing 11 is incremented to 12. The Emerald Sorcerer won his comparison to Athle, so his 10 is now incremented to 11.

Comparing The Emerald Sorcerer's 18 and Magnus' 19 spell checks to Table 4-5: Spell Duel Check Comparison, we get a roll of d3. The difference in momentum trackers is 1 (11 on The Emerald Sorcerer's die and 12 on Magnus'), so Magnus rolls d3+1 on the "defender high" column in Table 4-6: Counterspell Power.

Simultaneously, comparing the Emerald Sorcerer's 18 and Athle's 14 spell checks, we get a roll of d5. The difference in momentum trackers is 1 (11 on The Emerald Sorcerer's die and 10 on Athle's), so the Emerald Sorcerer rolls d5+1 on the "attacker high" column in Table 4-6: Counterspell Power.

And now our example ends, but you get the drift of it. At this point you can see how there can be multiple defending and attacking spells interacting with each other.

Table 4-7: Phlogiston Disturbance

Roll 1d10, regardless of spells involved.

Roll	Result
1	Pocket dimension. Both casters are instantaneously transferred to a pocket dimension that is spontaneously created by the interaction between their spells. They remain within the pocket dimension until one is killed, at which point the interaction of their spells ceases and the survivor is transferred back to the material plane one millisecond after his departure. Observers see only a brief flicker and the disappearance of the loser, whose body is lost forever. The pocket dimension appears as (roll 1d6) (1) a mountaintop surrounded by red clouds, (2) a bubble adrift in space, (3) a sweltering island in a sea of lava, (4) an upside-down forest where the trees grow down from the sky above, (5) a dust mote atop the point of a needle, (6) the left nostril of an intergalactic whale.
2	Alignment rift. Both casters are transferred to an alignment plane. If both are the same alignment, they go to that plane; if they are opposed, or if either is neutral, they transfer to the plane of neutrality. They return to the material plane after (roll 1d4) (1) one caster is killed (both bodies return), (2) 1d8 days, (3) 3d6 rounds for each caster, rolled separately, (4) The End of Days.
3	Time accelerates. Both casters see everything around them slow down; in reality, they are accelerating, and surrounding characters see them move at incredible speeds. Resolve an additional 2d4 rounds of combat between the casters only; no other characters may act in this time. At the end of this time, they slow back into the mainstream flow of time.
4	Time slows. The casters perceive the world around them as normal but observers see their reactions slow to a crawl. Roll 1d3 and resolve that many rounds of combat among other participants before the casters can react again.
5	Backward loop in time. The casters are tossed backward in time to relive the last few moments repeatedly. Roll 1d4 and repeat the last spell interaction that many times, re-rolling spell checks and incrementing momentum trackers but ignoring any subsequent Phlogiston Disturbance results (treat same-check results as "both spells cancelled"). For example, if the attacker cast *magic missile* and the defender cast *magic shield*, the two would repeat 1d4 repetitions of that same spell check result. No spell can be lost during this time – a below-minimum result indicates only a failure, and the spell cast repeats on the next loop. When this time loop is concluded, the two casters re-enter the normal initiative count.
6	Spells merge. In a freak of eldritch energy, the two spells merge to create something greater than both. This result requires judge mediation. Generally speaking, the resulting effect is centered directly between the two casters and is either: (a) twice as powerful as the normal spell (if two opposing spells had cancelled each other), or (b) some weird agglomeration of spell effects (if two different spells were used). For example, if two fireballs were cast, there may be a super-fireball that impacts between the two casters. Or, if fire resistance countered fireball, a flameless fireball could be set off, generating concussive noise and astounding force but no flames.
7	Supernatural influence. The casters create a rift in space and some supernatural influence filters through. Both spells fail and roll 1d4: (1) a randomly determined elemental energy suffuses the surrounding around, causing minor effects (for example, flames and heat fill the air to cause 1 damage to everyone within 50' or a massive rainstorm erupts centered on the casters); (2) negative energy drains through, granting +1d8 hit points to all un-dead and demons nearby; (3) shadow energy fills the air, limiting eyesight to half normal range; (4) ethereal mists swirl about, and 1d4 randomly determined ghosts enter the world.
8	Supernatural summoning. The combined spell results inadvertently pull a supernatural creature through the fabric of space and time. Randomly determine the nature of the supernatural creature: (roll 1d3) (1) elemental, (2) demon, (3) celestial. The creature has 1d4+1 HD. Determine the creature's reaction by rolling 1d5: (1) hostile to all, (2) hostile to one caster (randomly determined) and neutral to other, (3) friendly to one caster (randomly determined) and hostile to other, (4) neutral to all parties, (5) friendly to all parties.
9	Demonic invasion. 1d4 randomly determined demons are summoned at the exact midpoint between the two casters. Determine their reaction randomly as with result 8 above. The demons are of a type as determined here: (roll 1d4) (1) type I, (2) type II, (3) type III, (4) type IV.
10	Mutual corruption. Both spells fail, and both casters suffer 1d4+1 corruption results. Roll corruption as normal for the spells involved.

CHAPTER FIVE
MAGIC

Magic comes from gods and demons who are capricious and unconcerned with your character's flyspeck of a life. Those who would use magic are best served to always have a backup plan.

agic comes from gods and demons who are capricious and unconcerned with your character's flyspeck of a life. Those who would use magic are best served to always have a backup plan.

Summoning magical energies is arduous, expensive, and dangerous. No wizard does it lightly. As a result, there are no mundane magics, no spells used simply to light a corridor, for example. Use a torch, fool; it is much safer!

KINDS OF MAGIC

Wizards and clerics tap into different kinds of magic. Wizards specialize in the better-known fields of black magic, elemental magic, and enchantment. Clerics receive the direct assistance of their gods in a style of magic called idol magic, which may or may not be similar to the powers of wizards.

Black magic is learned from demons' lips. It includes witchcraft, shamanism, and totems, as well as necromancy, diabolism, mind control, and other concentrations of negative energy. Black practitioners hold power over mortals but are slaves to their demonic masters. Cthulhu cults practice black magic, as do zombie masters, witches, and voodoo shamans. Binding and summoning are considered black magic.

Elemental magic includes invocations relating to earth, air, fire, and water, including the energies and other forms associated with them (such as light, fog, flight, and other such things). Some elemental magics harness the purest form of an element, while others are based on pacts with mighty elemental lords.

Enchantment, also known as white magic, is the most mundane of the magics, as it is grounded in the overlap of the material plane of existence with other planes. White magicians manipulate the nature of things to conjure, divine, trick, and obfuscate. Astral projection, ethereal travel, and journeys to the lands of unnatural geometries are part of enchantment. Dwarves use runes to practice enchantment, and gypsies do it with entrails. The best alchemists often know a bit of minor enchantment. Astrologists practice a quotidian form of the extraplanar aspects of enchantment.

Idol magic, or divine magic, is any magic granted by worship of a god or other higher power. Most clerics practice idol magic. Falling out of favor with one's idol severs access to this kind of magic.

SPELL CHECKS

When your character casts a spell, you roll 1d20 and add your caster level. This is called a spell check. You also add your Personality modifier if you are a cleric or your Intelligence modifier if you are a wizard. Wizards also apply modifiers for wearing bulky armor (see Table 3-3), and there may be other modifiers specific to certain situations.

Compare the result to the casting table for that spell. In general, your spell succeeds if your spell check is equal to or higher than a base DC of 10 + (2x spell level). The higher

you roll, the more extraordinary the result, according to the casting table.

Make the spell check when the spell is first cast, even if the casting time is more than one round. High results may reduce casting time.

A novice wizard cannot cast magic beyond his comprehension, but he may attempt to cast a spell of any level he has learned. This means he may attempt to cast spells where he suffers a significant chance of failure, based on his spell check modifier. If he judges the attempt worthwhile, so be it; but there are consequences to failure.

Criticals and fumbles: A spell check result of a natural 20 is a critical success. The caster receives an *additional* bonus to his check equal to his caster level. Compare to the casting table for that specific spell for the result.

A spell check result of a natural 1 is always a failure. A result of 1 may also result in corruption or disapproval, as described below.

Concentration: Some spells require concentration. While concentrating, a wizard or cleric can take no action beyond walking at half speed. Combat damage, a fall, or other significant interruptions require the spellcaster to make a Will save against DC 11 or lose concentration.

Spell checks by other classes: Foolish warriors have been known to read magical scrolls in dangerous attempts to wield magic. A warrior, thief, or other character untrained in magic may attempt to cast a spell from magical instructions he encounters. A character from an untrained class rolls 1d10 for his spell check instead of 1d20. He does not add any modifier for an ability score or caster level. A trained thief may roll a higher die, as shown on Table 1-7: Thief.

Saving throws against spells: In general, a saving throw against a spell effect uses a DC equal to the spell check. For example, a *color spray* cast with a spell check result of 17 requires a Will save of 17 or higher to resist. If a spell does not specify a specific DC for a save, the save is made against the spell check result.

Reversing spells: Some spells can be reversed to perform the opposite function for which they were intended. For example, *mending* can be reversed to *tear* an object, or *enlarge* can be reversed to *shrink* an object. Although spell reversal sounds simple and straightforward as a concept, think about it in practical terms. It's not that easy. To use an analogy, can you un-cook a chicken pot pie by following the instructions in reverse? No. Magic cannot be simply reversed. To reflect the difficulty of reverse-spellcasting in practical terms, these simple rules apply:

- A wizard can learn a spell in one of its versions, normal or reversed. For example, he can learn *mending* as a spell slot, or he can learn *tear* as a spell slot. He casts either of these spells as normal.

- If the wizard attempts to cast the reverse of a spell in his repertoire, he makes the spell check at a reduced die type (based on the standard dice chain).

SPELLBURN

"Blood aids great sorcery," quoth the mummy, and he was right. A magic-user can harness more magical energies if he is willing to make mortal sacrifice: offer part of his soul to a demon, foster a demi-god's greedy growth by leeching his strength, or even burn the very life energy in his own cells. Before rolling any spell check, a wizard may declare that he will attempt spellburn. In attempting spellburn, the wizard temporarily expends points of his Strength, Agility, or Stamina score to enhance his spell check. For every ability point he expends, the wizard adds +1 to his spell check.

For example, a wizard in a life-or-death situation may need absolute certainty that his next spell functions. He calls to an archdemon with whom he has had past dealings. In offering the demon a share of his life-force, he trades 7 points of Strength to give himself a +7 bonus to his next spell check.

Ability scores lost in this way return as the wizard heals. Each day he does not attempt spellburn, he recovers 1 point of ability score.

Some spells and magical items require spellburn to function, as noted in their descriptions.

Automatic criticals: There is one additional option for spellburn. A wizard who sacrifices a full 20 points of ability scores in one fell swoop automatically treats his next spell check as a roll of natural 20.

Regaining spells via spellburn: A wizard may use spellburn to cast spells he has lost for the day (through previous casting, for example). If a wizard expends a lost spell's level in ability score points, he can cast the spell as if he still had it. For example, a wizard could burn 2 points of ability scores to cast a level 2 spell he had lost for the day. The wizard must expend additional spellburn to gain a bonus to the spell check. For example, a wizard could burn 4 points of ability scores to cast a level 2 spell at a +2 bonus to the spell check.

Failed spellburn: Any magic-user who rolls a natural 1 on a spell check while using spellburn suffers the loss of ability points and the associated corruption (see below), and also loses 1 point of ability score *permanently*.

Spellburn by clerics: Spellburn is a form of magic generally reserved for wizards. However, under highly unusual circumstances (mostly associated with great magic items or rare formulae), clerics can also utilize spellburn. Clerics can never utilize spellburn for normal spells; only under specialized circumstances the judge will specify. When a cleric does utilize spellburn, it invariably involves ritualized behavior associated with the rites of his deity.

Healing spellburn damage: In playtests, many wizards attempted to partner with clerics to reduce the impact of spellburn. A common action is to have a cleric handy to heal ability score damage as the wizard utilized spellburn. The author encourages the judge and players to remember the underlying role playing activities associated with these actions. Spellburn represents a mortal sacrifice to a supernatural entity for strictly selfish purposes. A cleric's ability to heal represents drawing on the power of a god to further that god's agenda in the mortal realms. *These are inherently contradictory activities.* A god that observes his follower repeatedly healing a devotee of another entity, whose self-inflicted wounds serve no greater agenda than a personal pursuit of power, will surely object to that cleric's action! Clerics who engage in this sort of behavior will soon find themselves out of favor with their divine allies.

Spellburn in practical terms: The wizard player should role-play the action that drives spellburn, as appropriate to the ability score sacrificed. Alternately, you can roll on table 5-1 to provide some illustration.

Table 5-1: Spellburn Actions

Roll (d24)	Result
1	The wizard sacrifices one pound of flesh per spell level, which he must carve from his own body with a knife that is holy to a powerful outsider.
2	The wizard must spill his own blood – one tablespoon per spell level.
3	The wizard swears an oath to a minor demi-god, who aids him in his time of need but curses him with weakness until the oath is fulfilled.
4	The wizard cuts off one of his fingertips.
5	The wizard must yank out his hair and burn it.
6	The wizard magically enervates his body in order to fuel the spell.
7	The wizard promises his soul to serve a powerful demon in the afterlife.
8	The wizard agrees to aid followers of a patron saint.
9	The wizard uses a hot iron to brand a supernatural symbol on his arm or torso.
10	The wizard must tattoo a mystical symbol on his cheek, forehead, or hand.
11	The wizard must pull out a fingernail and burn it with incense.
12	The wizard must speak aloud his own true name, weakening himself as a result.
13	The wizard develops a bleeding sore that will not heal until he pays back the aid of the power that assisted him.
14	The wizard must notch his ear in acknowledgment of each time he has been aided.
15	The wizard is required to ritually scarify his back, chest, or biceps with the symbol of a powerful supernatural creature.
16	The wizard sees maggots drip from his sleeves. When not wearing a shirt, nothing happens and his torso appears normal. However, when wearing a shirt, he constantly sees maggots falling from his sleeves.
17	The wizard starts to itch! He has strange, uncontrollable itches and scratches constantly.
18	The wizard develops an odd tic: he twitches his nose, tilts his head, or blinks one eye constantly.
19	The wizard begins muttering under his breath, repeating the name of the entity that has aided him. He can't stop.
20	The wizard must cut his cheeks and let the blood flow down his face.
21	The wizard must place his hand into an open flame.
22	The wizard must sacrifice one of his most favored possessions.
23	The wizard must walk on one leg for the remainder of the day.
24	Roll again twice.

REGAINING SPELLS

Spellcasting is draining. A spellcaster can exert himself a finite number of times in one day before he is exhausted and unable to cast another spell. Depending on the kind of magic, this can be a reflection of mental recall, godly favor, access to a demon's plane, soul-drain, magical ingredients, or other factors.

Each spell's casting table will indicate "lost" or "not lost" in each result entry. A result of "lost" means your character cannot cast that spell again in that day. "Not lost" means the character retains the use of that spell. Generally, only wizard spells are lost when a casting fails.

Clerics suffer a different difficulty. Each time a cleric fails to cast a spell, he suffers a cumulative increase to his natural disapproval range for the balance of the day. More information on this penalty can be found in the cleric class description.

In general, spells are regained within a day of being lost. The exact trigger depends on the magic in question. White magic is regained at the next sunrise; black magic upon the moon crossing the sky in full; demon magic after a full eight hours of rest; divine magic after resting and praying to the cleric's god; and so on, as agreed between player and judge based on the nature of the character's magic.

MERCURIAL MAGIC

The firstborn son of a witch hanged at trial wields black magic adroitly. An orphan raised by satyrs is a precocious student of druidry. Cosmic caprice determines skill in magic: birth order, family lineage, horoscope, and matters even more abstruse have as much influence on a wizard's spellcasting as his hard work and native intelligence.

As a result, the effect of a magical spell varies according to who casts it. A magical rite invoked by one mage may be more powerful – or even *different* – than the same ritual exercised by a peer. These variegations are not predictable, as the subtleties that produce them can never be fully catalogued.

The mercurial nature of magic is reflected in game terms. When a wizard learns a new spell, he rolls on table 5-2 to determine how that spell manifests *in his hands*. This percentile roll is adjusted by his Luck modifier x 10%; i.e., a +2 Luck modifier counts as +20% on the check.

The player rolls on table 5-2 for every spell he learns, and the effects are specific to that spell.

Table 5-2: Mercurial Magic

d%	Adjustment to spell effect
01	At great cost. Every time the wizard casts the spell, someone he knows dies (judge's choice).
02	Extremely difficult to cast. Instead of rolling as normal on a spell check, the wizard rolls a die type reduced by *two* steps on the dice chain (e.g., if he normally rolls 1d20, he now rolls 1d14).
03	Soul dedication. In order to cast the spell, the wizard must either dedicate the soul of the target to his patron or the soul of a creature with hit dice equal to that of the target. If the caster fails to claim the soul for his patron, the spell cannot be recast until the patron is appeased.
04	Health bane. Casting this spell always temporarily reduces the wizard's Stamina by 1d3 points. This ability loss is in addition to any spellburn and is deducted before spellburn occurs.
05	Difficult to cast. Instead of rolling as normal on a spell check, the wizard rolls a reduced die (based on the dice chain; i.e., d20 becomes d16).
06	Counter-magic bubble. In the round following the casting of this spell, all other spells (including the wizard's own) cast within 100' suffer a -4 penalty to spell checks.
07	Luck distortion. For 1d4 rounds following the spell, the wizard suffers a -2 penalty to all rolls.
08	Count of ten. Each time the wizard casts this spell, one of his fingers (or toes at the judge's discretion) melts away. For every two digits lost, he suffers a permanent -1 penalty to Agility. The digits can be replaced by magic, but if the wizard ever runs out of them, he cannot cast this spell.
09	Anima drain. The wizard suffers corruption every time he casts the spell, regardless of spell check, *unless* he spellburns.
10	Blood magic. The power of this spell is partially drawn from spilled blood, a sacrifice to the unknowable lords of Magic. A living creature with hit points equal to or greater than the spell's level must be offered up before the spell is cast; otherwise, the spell check suffers a -4 penalty or patron taint (judge's choice). The creature need not be sentient; chickens, goats, and other simple animals with the proper amount of hit points will suffice.
11	Planar rift. Casting the spell tears jagged hole in the warp and weft of the multiverse. There is a cumulative 1% chance that a horror from the outer dark steps through the rift. The fearsome creature has HD equal to the caster's level + 5. Roll 1d3: (1) the monster steals the spell from the PC's mind before vanishing forever; (2) the monster attacks the PC with the intent to slay the caster; (3) the monster seeks to strike a bargain with the caster, offering the PC forbidden knowledge (judge's choice) in exchange for the souls of the caster's party.
12	Magical reverb. For 1d4 rounds after the spell is cast, a backwash of eldritch energy passes over the wizard. Any spell checks the wizard makes during that time suffer a -4 penalty.
13	Slow cast. The spell requires twice the normal time to cast.
14	Sleep of ages. After casting this spell, the wizard must make a Fort save (DC 5 + the spell's level) or fall into a deep sleep for 1 day for each level of the spell. He cannot be awakened by any mundane or magical means during this time.
15	Material magic. The spell requires the caster to possess an uncommon substance or item to power its magic, beyond the normal components. This material component is determined by the judge and its rarity should be indicative of the spell's power. The object or item is consumed by a successful casting.
16	Primordial channel. Memories from before the time of Man flood the caster's mind as he takes on a primitive demeanor. Every time he casts this spell, the wizard devolves to sub-human tendencies for 1d4 rounds thereafter. During this time, he cannot speak intelligently, cannot cast other spells, cannot use complex devices, cannot read or write, etc.
17	Stolen knowledge. The formula for the spell was stolen from a powerful extraplanar being. Each time the spell is cast there is a 1% chance per spell level that the being emerges to take back its occult knowledge… the hard way. Roll 1d7: (1) Grand Sultan of the Efreet; (2) the great Cthulhu; (3) a Grand Prince of Hell; (4) an elephant-faced godling of the Outer Dark; (5) the spirit of a long dead archmage; (6) a mechanized brain from the distant future; (7) an elemental prince.

Table 5-2: Mercurial Magic, continued

18   Vermin attractor. The spell attracts a swarm of bothersome insects to the caster's location that arrive 1d4 rounds after the spell is completed. These insects mill about the caster, biting for 1 point of damage and causing the caster to suffer a -1 penalty to all saving throws, initiative rolls, and spell checks for 1d10 rounds or until he takes adequate measures to disperse or escape the swarm.

19   Siphon magic. Casting this spell has a 50% chance of causing the caster or another nearby person to forget a spell of equal level for the day as if they had failed a spell check. If it is determined that a spell caster loses a spell, there is a 3 in 4 chance it is the wizard himself and a 1 in 4 chance it affects the next closest spell caster. If the affected spell caster does not have a spell of the appropriate level, he takes damage equal 1d6 + the spell's level.

20   Rush of wind. A great rush of wind occurs every time the spell is cast, originating from the caster toward his target. Torches flicker and may go out (50% chance).

21   Corrosion touch. The casting of this spell causes a randomly determined item of steel or iron to corrode and pit in a 15' radius around the caster. The item corroded by the casting is always of dagger-size or larger and chosen at random. If the wizard voluntarily holds or touches a metal item of the appropriate size while casting, that object is destroyed and no other.

22   Sympathetic magic. The spell requires that the caster have a personal belonging or a physical piece of its target in order to function normally. The spell can be cast without this sympathetic connection, but the wizard suffers a -4 penalty to his spell check.

23   Cannibal magic. The caster suffers damage equal to 1d4+the spell's level each time he casts it, unless he is physically touching another individual willing to suffer the damage in his stead. Unwilling or unknowing individuals cannot be forced to suffer for the wizard.

24   Prismatic distortion. Nearby light is distorted. Roll 1d6: (1) area within 20' darkens to shadow; (2) all light sources (torches, lanterns, etc.) within 20' are extinguished magically; (3) incandescent flash upon completion of spell; (4) all colors are drained from within 20' of wizard for 1d4 rounds; (5) light takes on a green/orange/blue/yellow hue for 1d4 rounds; (6) shadows multiply from different directions, as if there were additional, invisible light sources, for 1d4 rounds after completion.

25   Terror-inducing. Casting the spell inspires terror in animals and creatures with an Intelligence score of 3 or less. All such creatures within 50' flee the caster as quickly as possible for 1d14 rounds. If restrained, the animals panic, insensate to all commands. The caster's familiar, if any, is immune.

26   Auditory feedback. Spell is always associated with unusual sounds. Roll 1d6: (1) crack of thunder, (2) loud buzzing, (3) faint whispers; (4) rush of water; (5) roaring of animals; (6) wailing of bereavement.

27   No range. The spell has no range, and can only be cast by touching the target. If the spell normally has a range of only touch, it can only be cast exactly 10 feet away from the target.

28   Odd growths. Strange growths appear in immediate area whenever spell is cast. Roll 1d6: (1) toadstools; (2) pools of slime; (3) flowers; (4) black fungus; (5) crystals; (6) fields of wheat.

29   Fear and loathing. The caster's forbidden knowledge inspires fearsome antipathy in intelligent beings. Friendly allies are immune, but all others are affected as follows: those of half the caster's HD or less must make a morale check or flee, those of greater HD focus all their attacks on the caster.

30   Memories of a dying god. Casting the spell accesses the memories of a dying god. The caster must succeed on a DC 13 Will save or be overcome by hallucinations of a bloody god-war that last 1d3 rounds. If the caster ever succeeds on the Will save with a natural 20, he triumphs over the god and is never troubled by the hallucinations again. Once dispelled, all future spell checks for this spell are made with 1d24.

31   Unwanted attention. Casting the spell draws the attention of a powerful supernatural being, who watches the wizard for 10 minutes. Roll 1d4: (1) a bloodshot eye opens on the wizard's forehead, seeing everything the wizard sees; (2) a small animal (crow, frog, cat, etc.) appears and follows the wizard around; (3) the wizard and his allies feel as if something huge and terrible is standing right behind them; (4) an agent of the supernatural being appears and interrogates the wizard on his use of the spell.

Table 5-2: Mercurial Magic, continued

32   Circumstantial magic. The wizard can only cast this spell under specific environmental or personal conditions. Roll 1d10 to determine the condition: (1) in the dark of night; (2) under the brightness of the sun; (3) while immersed in water; (4) while intoxicated; (5) after fasting for 24 hours; (6) underground; (7) during the cold of winter; (8) while naked; (9) from an elevated position; (10) when reduced to 50% or less of total hit points.

33   Hairy magic. The wizard's head hair (hair, beard, eyebrows, ear hair, etc.) grows 1" each time this spell is cast.

34   Thunderstruck. A clap of thunder and flash of heat lightning accompanies the casting of this spell, revealing the wizard's position to all within sight of him. This likely draws both attention and arrows.

35   Joe Average. Instead of a d20, the caster rolls 2d10 for spell checks on this spell. If his check die is another type, he rolls two "half-dice" instead (i.e., 2d7 instead of 1d14, 2d8 instead of 1d16, etc.).

36   Demonic voice. The words of the spell are in a demonic tongue unknown to mortals. A demon is compelled/allowed to speak the spell through the wizard's own throat. The strain of channeling the unnatural voice leaves the wizard unable to speak for 1d4 rounds after the spell has been cast.

37   Aura of decay. The spell drains the physical form of all material of a certain type within 20 feet of the caster, causing it to age quickly. Roll 1d6: (1) metal tarnishes and spots of rust appear on it; (2) wood dries out, becoming brittle and cracked; (3) stone becomes smooth and worn, with small cracks appearing in it; (4) fabrics and leathers fray and tear; (5) food and drink spoils; (6) flesh ages and all creatures within the effect age one year.

38   Whimsical patron. The spell draws upon the wizard's patron to succeed, but this entity's attentions are notoriously fickle. Whenever this spell is cast, roll 1d6 to determine what die is used whenever this spell is cast: (1-2) d16; (3-4) d20; (5) d24; (6) d30. This d6 roll supersedes the wizard's normal action die and the dice chain.

39   Blood sweat. Casting the spell causes blood to ooze from the wizard's pores. No damage is inflicted, but the wizard looks a gory mess. At the judge's discretion, this may also attract predators.

40   Ravenous. The wizard becomes ravenously hungry after casting the spell. Hungry people are often cranky, so the wizard suffers a -2 Personality until he is able to eat.

41-60   No change. The spell manifests as standard.

61   Loud enough for you? Due to the ineffable demands of magic, this spell must be shouted when cast, effectively negating any chance of the caster remaining undetected before the casting is completed.

62   Gender bender. Casting the spell causes the wizard to temporarily transform into the opposite gender. This sex change remains in effect for one hour per level of the spell. Recasting the spell shifts the caster back into his original sex, but a failure on the spell check causes the wizard to remain as the shifted gender until a full 24 hours have passed.

63   Diurnal/nocturnal magic. The spell's power is tied to either night or day. During the ascendant period, the wizard rolls 1d24 for spell checks; during the descendent hours he rolls 1d16. If the wizard's spell check does not use a 1d20, roll an appropriately higher and lower die according to the dice chain.

64   Wealful/woeful magic. Each time this spell is cast, there is a random 10%-60% chance that the wizard's Luck score is altered by its magic. If the wizard's Luck is affected, it is either raised 1d3 points (50% chance) or lowered 1d3 points (50% chance).

65   Casting circle. The spell's power can be amplified with the assistance of other wizards. For each wizard present and willing to assist the caster, the casting wizard gets a +1 modifier to his spell check. Assisting in spell casting does not require knowledge of the spell, but the assistant mages can perform no other action until the spell is cast.

66   Accidental alchemist. Each time the spell is cast, one random item within 20 feet of the caster is turned to lead and another is turned to gold. Both objects probably weigh more than they previously did, and the gold object is worth twice its normal cost or 1gp, whichever is more.

67   St. Gygakk's fire. Casting this spell results in the wizard being limned by flickering chartreuse fire for 1d4 rounds, granting opponents a +2 bonus to attacks against the caster. It also negates any concealment and invisibility enjoyed by the caster, but does provide a faint illumination to the area immediately surrounding the wizard.

Table 5-2: Mercurial Magic, continued

68   Mirror magic. This spell causes an eldritch echo that duplicates the wizard's appearance as if he had cast a *mirror image* spell with a spell check of 16-19. However, each duplicate image created saps the caster of a single point of Personality until the image is dispersed.

69   Skeletal caster. The wizard's skin and internal organs become transparent for 1d4 rounds after casting this spell, making him appear as a clothed skeleton. Although likely to be mistaken as an un-dead, the wizard also enjoys a +2 bonus to his AC against missile attacks.

70   Temporal echo. Each time the wizard casts this spell, he predicts the numerical result of his spell check roll. If he rolls this number exactly, the spell automatically re-casts itself each round for 1d3 rounds. The predicted result must be a successful spell check; predicting a failed result has no effect.

71   Worms of the earth. Pale white worms crawl forth from the earth whenever the wizard casts this spell, writhing in fiery agony (or unholy delight) before expiring on the open ground. Easily crushed underfoot, the worms disintegrate into greasy ash after 1d6 rounds.

72   Chain casting. Each successive casting of the spell grants a +1 bonus to wizard's spell check, up to a total bonus equal to the caster's Int or Luck modifier (whichever is higher). If the wizard casts another spell, he breaks the chain, resetting the modifier back to +0.

73   Karmic casting. Before making the spell check, the wizard can choose to add or subtract 1d5 from the roll. If the caster adds 1d5, the next time he casts the spell he must subtract 1d5, and vice versa. After two castings, the karma is reset, and the wizard again gets to choose what modifier to use, if any.

74   Tide of ash. All living vegetative matter within 10' per spell level is reduced to ash. Vegetative creatures caught within this radius take 1d14 points of damage per spell level. Dead vegetative matter is unaffected.

75   Spell by proxy. The wizard can choose another person or object to deliver this spell in his stead. He must first touch the proxy and then cast the spell, which does not take effect at that time. The proxy releases the spell a number of rounds later equal to 1d4+the spell's level. Non-intelligent proxies automatically release the spell at this time; intelligent proxies can release it at will at any point prior to the time indicated.

76   Silenced. At his discretion, the wizard is able to cast the spell silently. He need not speak, and any auditory effects of the spell can be suppressed.

77   Call of the Outer Dark. Strange chimes scream in the air and foreign stars waver above the wizard. All looking at the caster must make DC 10 Will saves or be entranced for 1d3 rounds. Attacking entranced characters instantly frees them from their enchantment.

78   Mentalism. The wizard can cast the spell using ESP alone. He need not move, speak, breathe, or use any material ingredients to invoke the effects.

79   Plague of rats. Thousands of rats, mice, moles and voles pour from the caster's sleeves, robes and pockets, scattering in every direction. Physical attacks against the caster are softened by 1d4 points of damage, the blow cushioned by the squealing tide of rodents.

80   Dimensional schism. By casting the spell, the wizard hurls himself into the warp of multiple realities. 1d7+1 duplicates of the caster appear, identical in nearly every respect, but each drawn from its own parallel universe. Attacks against the caster are randomly assigned across the doppelgangers. The doppelgangers remain for 1 round per spell level. There is a 1% chance per spell level that the original caster vanishes into one of the alternate realities, replaced by a nearly identical incarnation of opposite alignment and patron.

81   Terrible to behold. The wizard becomes fearsome when casting the spell. Roll 1d6: (1) he appears to grow in size; (2) he takes on a horrid expression; (3) he glows a fiery red; (4) his body is shadowed while his face is brightly lit; (5) the aspect of his patron towers above him; (6) the wind whirls around him.

82   Spell killer. Casting the spell steals energy from a dying world, and any use of the spell causes the death of untold thousands. Every night following a casting of the spell, the wizard is haunted by dream-communications from an ancient sorcerer-king desperate to save his people.

83   Blue star. A blue, seven-pointed star flares brightly on the wizard's forehead each time the spell is cast. The star casts a circle of glaring light 25' in diameter per spell level.

Table 5-2: Mercurial Magic, continued

84   Energy burst. When successfully casting this spell, the wizard is surrounded by a burst of energy. Roll 1d6: (1) wreathes of flame, which do not affect the wizard but ignite flammable objects within 5' and cause 1d6 damage to melee opponents; (2) crackles of electricity, which arc to the nearest enemy within 10' and cause 1d6 damage; (3) aura of frost, which causes 1d4 cold damage to everything within 10' and automatically snuff torches and lanterns in range; (4) cloud of ash, which the wizard can see through but obscures the sight of all others within 5'; (5-6) instead of determining effect at time of spell acquisition, roll 1d4 each time the spell is cast and compare to above results.

85   Psychic shield. In the round immediately following the casting of this spell, the wizard gains a +2 bonus to his AC and any Will saves, as he is encased in a protective barrier of psychic energy. It disperses the following round.

86   Mystic twin. Casting the spell causes a fully functioning twin face to appear in the caster's chest. The face remains for 1d3 rounds. During that time, this dual face has its own 1d20 action die under the control of the player, with which it can speak, cast spells as the caster, or spout cryptic wisdom.

87   Planar blink. After casting the spell, the caster unpredictably blinks in and out of this plane of existence, granting a +4 bonus to the wizard's AC at cost of a -4 penalty to all the wizard's attacks. The effect lasts for 1 round per spell level. There is a 1% chance per spell level that the wizard does not return from his involuntary jaunt across the cosmos.

88   Rain of frogs. Casting this spell sparks a tempest of amphibians that fall in a 30' diameter centered on the caster. All within that area must make a Ref and Fort save (DC 10+caster's Int modifier). Failing the Reflex save indicates the character slips on a frog and falls prone; failing the Fort save means the character has been hit by large batrachians for 1d3 points of damage.

89   Phase out. After casting this spell, the wizard shifts out of phase with the world, making him invisible and invulnerable to attack but preventing him from interacting with his environment. This state lasts for 1d6 rounds +1 round per level of the spell.

90   Weatherman. Casting the spell upsets local weather patterns. Roll 1d7: (1) drought: no rain or moisture falls on the land for 1d12 years; (2) bitter winter sweeps over the land for 1d3 years; (3) incessant rain douses the land for 1d20 weeks; (4) a freak lightning storm hammers the area for 1d100 hours; (5) hurricane-like wind scours the earth for 1d7 weeks; (6) a localized eclipse blots out the sun for 1d20 days; (7) no stars are seen in the sky for 1d100 years. The area of effect is up to the judge's determination.

91   Breath of life. Casting this spell imbues the caster and those around him with beneficial energies. All within 15' of the caster (both friend and foe) are healed 1d6 points of damage for every level of the spell (i.e., a level 3 spell heals 3d6 damage).

92   Gibbering allies. Chittering, mephitic, rat-sized demons scurry forth from the wizard's pockets and sleeves, scattering around him in a scratching fury. They attack enemies within 10' (atk +2, 1d4 dmg) and aid the spell as appropriate before dissipating in a cloud of ash after 1 minute.

93   Greater power. The caster is allowed to roll twice for any random element of the spell (duration, damage, number affected, etc.) and take whichever result he wishes.

94   Fine control. The wizard is adept at reigning in the magical energies of the spell and can choose any result on the spell chart equal to or lower than the one rolled.

95   Psychic focus. Casting this spell clears the caster's mind and prepares him to channel further energy. For 1d4 rounds after the spell is cast, the wizard receives a +4 bonus to *other* spell checks. This effect does not stack with itself.

96   Powerful caster. Instead of rolling as normal on a spell check, the wizard rolls a die improved by one step on the dice chain (e.g., d20 becomes d24).

97   Necrotic drain. The spell is powered by the energies of the living. The nearest creature (other than the caster) takes 1d6 hp of damage per spell level. For every 2 hp lost, the spell check result is increased by +1.

98   Natural-born talent. Instead of rolling as normal on a spell check, the wizard rolls a die type improved by *two* steps on the dice chain (e.g., if he normally rolls 1d20, he now rolls 1d30).

99   Roll again twice.

00   Roll again twice, but instead of rolling d%, roll 4d20 modified by the wizard's Luck adjustment (in increments of 10%).

CORRUPTION

Low-level wizards are powerful. High-level wizards fear for their souls. Continual use of magic results in...changes. Exposure to demons, radiation from other planes, elemental energies in toxic quantities, and the servants of Chaos all affect a wizard over the course of his career. Higher-level wizards seek pacts with demons and elementals to sustain their health so they may continue to advance.

Each and every time a wizard rolls a natural 1 on a spell check, he suffers the effect of the spell failure. Moreover, his spell may misfire and he may suffer corruption. The individual spell entries include specific results associated with a natural 1 on each spell check, as well as misfire and corruption results specific to the spell. Some results will further direct the player to roll on one of the corruption tables: minor, major, or greater. If this is required, the roll is 1d10 minus the spell's level plus the wizard's Luck modifier. In select circumstances, other modifiers may apply as well (e.g., a curse). Certain kinds of black magic may trigger corruption more often, as indicated and adjusted by the spell table.

Luck to avoid corruption: A wizard that suffers corruption may burn a point of Luck to avoid the corruption. The Luck can be burned *after* the player rolls to determine the specific corruption result. Note that Luck cannot be burned to avoid a spell misfire, only to avoid corruption. Patron taint is considered corruption for these purposes.

Table 5-3: Minor Corruption

D10	Result
1 or lower	Character develops horrid pustules on his face. These pustules do not heal and impose a -1 penalty to Personality.
2	Character's skin on one random portion of his body appears to melt. Like wax, it flows and reforms into odd puddles and shapes. This is an ongoing, constant motion that itches constantly and repulses others. Determine location randomly (1d6): (1) face; (2) arms; (3) legs; (4) torso; (5) hands; (6) feet.
3	One of the character's legs grows 1d6". Character now walks with an odd gait.
4	Eyes affected. Roll 1d4: (1) eyes glow with unearthly color; (2) eyes gain light sensitivity (-1 to all rolls in daylight); (3) character gains infravision (sees heat signatures at range of 100'); (4) eyes become large and unblinking, like a fish.
5	Character develops painful lesions on his chest and legs and open sores on his hands and feet that do not heal.
6	Ears mutate. Roll 1d5: (1) ears become pointed; (2) ears fall off (character still hears normally); (3) ears enlarge and look like an elephant's; (4) ears elongate and look like a donkey's (character also gains braying laugh); (5) ears shrivel and fold back.
7	Chills. Character shakes constantly and cannot remain quiet due to chattering teeth.
8	Character's facial appearance is permanently disfigured according to the magic that was summoned. If fire magic was used, his eyebrows are scorched and his skin glows red; if cold magic was used, his skin is pasty white and his lips are blue. If ambiguous magic was used, his appearance grows gaunt and he permanently loses 5 pounds.
9	Character's hair is suffused with dark energy. Roll 1d4: (1) hair turns bone white; (2) hair turns pitch black; (3) hair falls out completely; (4) hair sticks straight up.
10+	Character passes out. He is unconscious for 1d6 hours or until awakened by vigorous means.

Table 5-4: Major Corruption

D10	Result
1 or lower	Febrile. Character slowly weakens over 1d4 months, suffering a -1 penalty to Strength for each month.
2	A duplicate of the character's face grows on his back. It looks just like his normal face. The eyes, nose, and mouth can be operated independently.
3	Consumption. Character's body feeds on its own mass. Character loses 2d10 pounds in one month and suffers a -1 penalty to Stamina.
4	Corpulence. Character gains 6d12 pounds in one month. The weight gain imposes a -1 penalty to Agility, and the character's speed is reduced by 5'.
5	Character crackles with energy of a type associated with the spells he most commonly casts. The energy could manifest as flames, lightning, cold waves, etc.
6	Character's height changes by 1d20-10 inches. There is no change in weight; the character's body grows thin and tall or short and fat.
7	Demonic taint. Roll 1d3: (1) character's fingers elongate into claws, and he gains an attack for 1d6 damage; (2) character's feet transform into cloven hoofs; (3) character's legs become goat-like.
8	Character's skin changes to an unearthly shade. Roll 1d8: (1) albino; (2) pitch black; (3) clear; (4) shimmering quality; (5) deep blue; (6) malevolent yellow; (7) ashen and pallid; (8) texture and color of fishy scales; (9) thick bear-like fur; (10) reptilian scales.
9	Small horns grow on the character's forehead. This appears as a ridge-like, simian forehead for the first month; then buds for the second month; goat horns after the third month; and finally, bull horns after six months.
10+	Character's tongue forks and his nostrils narrow to slits. The character is able to smell with his tongue like a snake.

Table 5-5: Greater Corruption

D10	Result
1 or lower	A sliver of soul energy is claimed by a demon lord. Character experiences unearthly pain, suffering 3d6 damage, a *permanent* -2 penalty to all ability scores, and an additional -2 penalty to Luck.
2	Decay. Character's flesh falls off in zombie-like chunks. Character loses 1d4 hp per day. Only magical healing can stave off the decay.
3	Character's head becomes bestial in a painful overnight transformation. Roll 1d6: (1) snake; (2) goat; (3) bull; (4) rat; (5) insect; (6) fish.
4	Character's limbs are replaced by suckered tentacles. One limb is replaced at random each month for four months. At the end of four months, it is impossible to hide the character's inhuman nature.
5	Small tentacles grow around the character's mouth and ears. The tentacles are maggot-sized at first, but grow at rate of 1" per month to a mature length of 12".
6	Third eye. Roll 1d4 for location: (1) middle of forehead; (2) palm of hand; (3) chest; (4) back of head.
7	Fingers on one hand fuse while the thumb enlarges. After one week, the hand has transformed into a crab claw. Character gains a natural attack for 1d6 damage and can no longer grasp normal weapons and objects.
8	Character grows a tail over 1d7 days. Roll 1d6: (1) scorpion tail that can attack for 1d4 damage plus poison (DC 10 Fort save or target loses 1d4 Str permanently); (2) scaly snake tail; (3) forked demon tail (grants +1 Agility); (4) fleshy tail ending in a useable third hand; (5) fused cartilaginous links ending in spiked stump that can attack for 1d6 damage; (6) bushy horse's tail.
9	Bodily transformation. Roll 1d6: (1) character grows scales across his entire body; (2) character grows gills; (3) character sprouts feathers; (4) character develops webbed toes and feet.
10+	Character grows a beak in place of his mouth. Transformation starts as a puckering of the lips that slowly turns into a full-fledged bird or squid beak over the next 1d12 months. Character gains a bite attack for 1d3 damage.

Table 5-6: Generic Spell Misfire

Although every spell table includes results for a misfire, the judge may occasionally need generic effects. These can be useful when monsters use spell-like abilities, when the characters roll a natural 1 while using a magic item's powers, and other such situations. Here are some generic spell misfire tables for use when appropriate.

D8	Spell Misfire
1	Nearest ally is partially transformed into an animal (Will save to resist; DC = 10 + (2x spell level)). Roll 1d6 to determine body part: 1 = arms; 2 = legs; 3 = skin; 4 = head; 5-6 = body. Roll 1d8 for animal type: 1 = chicken; 2 = gorilla; 3 = cow; 4 = lizard; 5 = snake; 6 = horse; 7 = dragon; 8 = eagle. The duration of this effect is 1d7 days. On a roll of 7, re-roll as 1d7 weeks. On a second 7, re-roll as 1d7 months.
2	Different spell effect! The wizard inadvertently channels the wrong spell energies. Randomly determine a different spell of the same level. Have the wizard make a spell check roll for *that* spell. If the spell check is a failure, nothing happens. If it is a success, follow the results.
3	Rain! But it's not water. The wizard inadvertently causes a torrential downpour of (roll 1d6): 1 = flower petals; 2 = garden snails; 3 = cow dung; 4 = rotten vegetables; 5 = iron ingots; 6 = snakes (5% chance they are poisonous).
4	Explosion centered on nearest creature! That creature takes 1d3 damage per spell level.
5	Transformation! One randomly determined creature among the six closest is transformed into (roll 1d6): 1 = stone; 2 = crystal; 3 = earth; 4 = iron; 5 = water; 6 = fire. (Will save to resist, DC = 10 + (2x spell level)). There is a 10% chance the transformation is permanent; otherwise, the creature returns to normal in 1d7 days.
6	Inadvertent corruption! Roll d12+5 on the minor corruption table and apply the result to one randomly determined creature among the six closest (no Will save to resist).
7	Fireworks! Brilliant colored lights explode all around the caster, creating thundering booms. This effect deals no damage but draws attention to the caster.
8	Cloud of ash! Everyone within 20' of the caster is coated in fine ash.

DEITY DISAPPROVAL

A cleric must serve his immortal master well, lest he fall in disfavor. The cleric who risks the disapproval of his deity finds that he quickly loses access to the extraordinary benefits of being a cleric.

Each and every time a cleric rolls a natural 1 on a spell check, he must roll on table 5-7: Disapproval. In addition, any time a cleric rolls within his disapproval range (based on number of failed spell checks on this day), disapproval also occurs.

The roll is 1d4 for every point on the spell check. For example, if the cleric rolled a natural 1, he would roll 1d4. If he rolled a natural 4 and that counted as disapproval, he would roll 4d4. And so on. This roll is *reduced* by the cleric's Luck modifier.

Table 5-7: Disapproval

Roll	Disapproval
1	The cleric must atone for his sins. He must do nothing but utter chants and intonations for the next 10 minutes, starting as soon as he is able (i.e., if he is in combat, he can wait until the danger is over).
2	The cleric must pray for forgiveness immediately. He must spend at least one hour in prayer, beginning as soon as he is able (i.e., if he is in combat, he can wait until the danger is over). Failure to finish the full hour of prayers within the next 120 minutes is looked upon unfavorably; he incurs a -1 penalty to all spell checks until he completes the full hour.
3	The cleric must increase his god's power by recruiting a new follower. If he does not convert one new follower to his deity's worship by the next sunrise, he takes a -1 penalty to all checks on the following day. This penalty resets after 24 hours.
4	The cleric immediately incurs an additional -1 penalty to all spell checks that lasts until the next day.
5	The cleric must undergo the test of humility. For the remainder of the day, he must defer to all other characters and creatures as if they were his superiors. Failure (at the discretion of the judge) means he immediately loses all spellcasting ability (including healing and laying on hands) for the remainder of the day.
6	The cleric incurs an immediate -1 penalty to all attempts to lay on hands until he goes on a quest to heal the crippled. This quest is of his own design, but generally speaking must result in significant aid to the crippled, blind, lamed, sickly, etc. Once the quest is completed, the deity revokes the penalty. While the penalty remains, it applies to all attempts to lay on hands, even if the "normal" disapproval range has been reduced back to a natural 1.
7	The cleric must endure a test of faith. He gains an illness that costs him 1 point *each* of Strength, Agility, and Stamina. The ability score loss heals at the normal rate of 1 point per day. The cleric may not use magic to heal the loss. If the cleric endures the test to the satisfaction of the deity, he retains his magical abilities. If not (judge's discretion), his disapproval range immediately increases by another point.
8	The cleric immediately incurs a -4 penalty to spell checks on the specific spell that resulted in disapproval (including laying on hands and turning unholy, if those were the acts that produced disapproval). This lasts until the next day.
9	The cleric immediately incurs an additional -2 penalty to all spell checks that lasts until the next day.
10	The cleric loses access to one randomly determined level 1 spell. This spell cannot be cast until the next day.
11	The cleric is ordered by his deity to meditate on his faith and come to a better understanding of what he has done to earn disapproval. The cleric incurs an immediate and permanent -2 penalty to all spell checks. The only way to lift this penalty is for the cleric to meditate. For every full day of meditation, the cleric can make a DC 15 Will save. Success means the spell check penalties are removed.
12	The cleric is temporarily disowned by his deity. For the rest of the day, the character cannot accumulate XP and may not gain class levels as a cleric. After the time period expires, the character begins to accumulate XP again as normal but does not accrue "back pay" (so to speak) for XP missed while he was disowned.

Table 5-7: Disapproval, continued

13   The cleric loses access to two randomly determined level 1 spells. These spells cannot be cast until the next day.

14   The cleric's deity wishes to test whether the cleric is a man of the faith or a man of the flesh. Calculate the cleric's total net worth in gold pieces. The cleric immediately incurs a *permanent* -4 penalty to all spell checks. The *only* way to remove this penalty is for the cleric to sacrifice his material possessions. For every 10% of his net worth sacrificed to the deity, one point of penalty is removed. Or, in other words, sacrificing 40% of what he owns will return the cleric to a normal spell check penalty. A sacrifice can be destruction, consecration, donation, transformation into a temple or statue, etc.

15   The deity is not forgiving on this day. When the cleric rests for the night, he does not "reset" his disapproval range at the next morning – it carries over from this day to the next. The disapproval ranged resets as normal on the following day.

16   Cleric is temporarily barred from using his lay on hands ability. The deity will not grant healing powers for the next 1d4 days. After that time, the cleric regains the use of his healing abilities.

17   The cleric loses access to 1d4+1 spells, randomly determined from all the character knows. These spells cannot be cast for the next 24 hours.

18   Cleric is temporarily unable to turn unholy creatures. The cleric regains the ability after 1d4 days.

19   The cleric is stained with the mark of the unfaithful. This physical mark appears like a brand, tattoo, or birthmark, with the symbol determined by the cleric's faith. The symbol is automatically visible to all worshippers of the cleric's faith, even through clothing, but may be invisible to others. To all who see and comment on the mark, the cleric must explain his sin and describe what he is doing as penance. If he continues to sustain his faith for a week while retaining the mark, it disappears.

20+   The cleric's ability to lay on hands is restricted. The ability works only once per day per creature healed – no single character can be healed more than once per day. After 24 hours, the ability's use reverts to normal.

THE WIZARD GRIMOIRE

All wizards are jealous with their knowledge, as a wizard's safety is only ensured insofar as he can best his strongest rival. There are no schools of magic, only masters willing to take apprentices. Yet masters are miserly in their training, lest the prices of their devil-bargains be bargained higher by too many callers. There are secrets in the deep places, and he who knows the most gains an advantage.

As such, a wizard's spell book, or grimoire, is never particularly thick. Its contents are determined as much by the chance falling of cosmic dust as by anything else. Every spell is rare and powerful. Ingredients are scarce, rituals are lengthy, and mind, soul, and body can be threatened with each casting. Thus, grimoires are guarded fiercely.

A grimoire can have many forms. White wizards use spell books; shamans use strings of carved bones; necromancers record spells on scrolls of flayed flesh; Cthulhu cults have rune-inscribed stones; clerics use prayer beads; idolaters utilize sacred gongs; and star-sayers record constellations whose forms contains power.

An experienced wizard learns to recognize magic in all its form, so that he can better steal it.

Determining spells at a new level: A wizard knows spells as indicated on table 1-12: Wizard. At each level, the wizard learns new spells.

In the course of his travels, a wizard may come across recordings of spells. He may steal another wizard's grimoire. He may find etchings in a lost tomb. He may make acquaintance with a generous demon. He may consult with the corpse of a deceased rival. Should a wizard have a source of knowledge for a new spell, he may *choose* to learn that spell when he reaches a new level instead of rolling randomly.

If the wizard has not come across sources of such knowledge, then his spell choice is determined randomly. He chooses the level of spell he wishes to learn, as limited by the Max Spell Level for his wizard level, and randomly determines the spell. Duplicate results may be re-rolled. The random results reflect the chaos of fate: a spell is a result of finding a transcription, translating and understanding it, communing with whatever powers are necessary to cast it, acquiring the requisite ingredients, and, finally, succeeding in the associated rituals. At any given time a wizard may be working on unlocking a variety of spells, but the ones in which he succeeds are limited.

Learning a spell: Just because a wizard finds a description of how to cast a spell doesn't mean he can actually pull it off. Your character must make a check to learn the new spell to which he is exposed. Your judge will give you the criteria for this check.

Picking and rolling: Although the concept of randomly determined spells is entertaining and fits with the original concept of Vancian magic, the author has found that it can be disruptive in actual play. No one wants to play the wizard with four useless spells! If the random determination results in a level 1 wizard with useless spells, the author recommends allowing the player to drop up to half the randomly produced spells and choose replacements.

RITUALIZED MAGIC

The spells listed here are primarily oriented around an adventuring wizard. As such, they do not include the great rites and rituals of the era: those magical invocations which take weeks or months to complete and which can tap into recondite energies beyond the scope of Man. Know that there are more powerful rituals -- of a longer duration and more difficult casting time -- than those described here. These rituals typically mandate spellburn and sacrifices of various kinds, for which the caster can summon forth unearthly creatures from beyond space and time, whose powers are not limited by the physics we know. Such works of magic are reserved for future volumes.

With that caveat, it is also possible to cast ritualized versions of the spells presented here, which are more powerful than their more mundane brethren. Especially for wizards, a ritualized casting of a normal spell can generate exceptional results. Typically this ritualized version is actually a *different* incantation than the normal version of the spell, and as such is considered specialized knowledge that must be discovered or devised in its own manner. Ritualized magic for clerics can also involve some of the following conditions but is typically influenced by the highly specialized rites associated with the worship practices of the cleric's deity. The following conditions apply to ritualized magic, subject to the approval and interpretation of the judge.

Circle of mages: Having a spell invoked by multiple wizards at once can improve its power. One wizard amongst the circle is the primary caster and contributes his spell check and die type to the casting. Each wizard past the first adds half his spell check bonus (including spellburn) to the collective spell checks (tracking fractional benefits, so it takes two individual +1 contributors to grant a +1 bonus to the circle) to a maximum benefit of +10. When the spell check die is rolled, the casting mage can roll a number of times equal to the number of mages in the circle, keeping only the highest die roll and ignoring all lower results. For example, if there are five wizards in the casting circle, the caster can roll up to five times and keep the highest result. A casting circle has a *minimum* casting time of 1 turn per mage involved and is often closer to 1 hour per mage involved, and may be longer still depending on the nature of the spell. Additionally, if any corruption does occur, it is shared by *all* mages involved.

One additional benefit of a casting circle is the ability for multiple mages to contribute to any additional spells cast during the ritual. For example, the spells *wizard staff* and *breathe life* may require casting additional spells to imbue a staff or golem with a particular power. With multiple mages involved in a casting circle, the primary caster may have access to special properties beyond those in his own spell list.

Sacrifice: Sacrificing treasure or creatures can improve the result of a spell check. Treasure typically must have some relevance as an ingredient to the spell being cast (for example, a stash of gemstones may help a *color spray* casting). Depending on the nature of the spell, a benefit of up to +4

can be obtained via material sacrifice, in rapidly advancing increments: up to 500 gp = +1, 501-2,000 gp = +2, 2,001-5,000 gp = +3, and 5,001+ gp = +4. Sacrificing the enemies of the caster or his patron or creatures appropriate to the spell type (e.g., un-dead corpses for a *chill touch* spell) can grant a bonus of up to +1 for every 5 HD of creatures sacrificed, to a maximum benefit of +4. The judge's discretion and good taste is encouraged in limiting sacrifices of living creatures or humanoids within the game. Sacrifices always require a ritual in the manner of their offering, which typically takes an hour or more.

Location of power: Casting a spell at a place of power can improve its result. Sometimes this place of power is a ley line, a standing stone, a cemetery, or other place of natural magical significance; other times, it is a place specific to the spell, such as the elemental plane of fire for a *fireball* spell. Casting a ritualized version in a location of power typically increases the die type by one size (according to the dice chain) but adds at least 1 turn and possibly a full hour to the casting time.

Rare ingredients: Extraordinarily rare spell components may require a quest to obtain, but can aid in a casting with a bonus of up to +4. The ritual to prepare the ingredients takes time in the questing, time for pre-casting preparation, and time in the actual casting.

Automatic corruption: Offering one's own mortal shell for the consumption of supernatural powers can greatly aid a casting but is extremely painful. Any casting ritual where the caster offers to voluntarily accept corruption can add an extra +2 to +6 bonus to the spell check result, at the result of a mandatory corruption of minor (+2), major (+4), or greater (+6) variety.

Extra duration: Extended casting times, with relevant chanting, bell tolling, incense burning, and other contributions, can aid a spell check. Typically, every day spent in casting adds an additional +1 to the spell check. The wizard may be required to fast during this time to contribute to the duration. Any time spent casting does not count as normal rest, and the wizard catches only short, restless cat naps during this time; he is not well-rested and will not heal naturally or recover spells during this time.

KNOWN SPELLS OF THE CURRENT ERA

There are 716 wizard spells. No more, no less. This number is known because Leetore the Limicker, a great mage of the fourth aeon, successfully contacted a somnolent elder god that susurrated several secrets (in limerick form, of course) before drowsing off forever. It is the measure of success for every wizard to fill his spell book with as many of these 716 spells as can be found in his lifetime.

Thus, the spells that follow are by no means all the spells in the world. They are merely some that are known among the more quotidian wizards of Aéreth. As most wizards will never see more than a few of these spells recorded together, they are listed here as a convenience for play, nothing more. Should your character ever know more than this many spells, he will be a great mage.

Cleric spells are not so rigidly defined. Each god's domain offers both powers and limitations, such that the boundaries of a cleric's magic are a bit more flexible. And the gods themselves change over time, of course.

Spells are organized alphabetically. The tables below organize the spells by level, while each spell entry provides more detail.

Spell entries: Each spell includes the following elements:

Manifestation: When one spellcaster faces another, he does not necessarily know what spells are being thrown at him; all he can observe is the visual effect. This entry provides options for the visual manifestation of a spell. When a caster first learns a spell, he learns to create it with one of these manifestations. (The player can roll randomly or choose.) The same spell may have completely different manifestations in the hands of different casters.

Corruption: For wizard spells, a randomized list of potential corruption effects, which can potentially occur when the caster rolls a natural 1.

Misfire: For wizard spells, a randomized list of potential misfire effects, which can potentially occur when the caster rolls a natural 1.

Table 5-8: Wizard Spells (with page number)

	1st Level	2nd Level	3rd Level	4th Level	5th Level
1	Animal summoning 129	Arcane affinity 162	Binding* 270	Control fire 238	Hepsoj's fecund fungi 247
2	Cantrip 130	Detect evil* 259	Breathe life 202	Control ice 239	Lokerimon's un-erring hunter 249
3	Charm person 131	Detect invisible 165	Consult spirit 204	Lokerimon's orderly assistance 241	Magic bulwark 251
4	Chill touch 133	ESP 166	Demon summoning 206	Polymorph 243	Mind purge 252
5	Choking cloud 134	Fire resistance 169	Dispel magic 208	Transmute Earth 244	Replication 253
6	Color spray 135	Forget 170	Eldritch hound 211	Wizard sense 245	
7	Comprehend languages 136	Invisibility 172	Emirikol's entropic maelstrom 213		
8	Detect magic* 260	Invisible companion 173	Eternal champion 214		
9	Ekim's mystical mask 137	Knock 175	Fireball 216		
10	Enlarge 139	Levitate 176	Fly 217		
11	Feather fall 140	Locate object 178	Gust of wind 219		
12	Find familiar 141	Magic mouth 180	Haste 221		
13	Flaming hands 142	Mirror image 182	Lightning bolt 222		
14	Force manipulation 143	Monster summoning 184	Make potion 223		
15	Invoke patron** 144	Nythuul's porcupine coat 186	Paralysis* 264		
16	Magic missile 144	Phantasm 187	Planar step 225		
17	Magic shield 146	Ray of enfeeblement 190	Runic alphabet, fey 227		
18	Mending 147	Scare 191	Slow 228		
19	Patron bond** 148	Scorching ray 192	Sword magic 229		
20	Read magic 152	Shatter 193	Transference 232		
21	Ropework 153	Spider web 196	Turn to stone 233		
22	Runic alphabet, mortal 154	Strength 198	Water breathing 235		
23	Sleep 155	Wizard staff 199	Write magic 236		
24	Spider climb 156	(Patron spell)***	(Patron spell)***		
25	Ventriloquism 158				
26	Ward portal 160				
27	(Patron spell)***				

* As per cleric spell of same name. Because the wizard version of the spell is a different spell level, the wizard receives a -2 penalty to spell checks when casting it. For example, *binding* is a level 2 cleric spell but a level 3 wizard spell; therefore, when rolling on the spell table, the wizard applies a -2 penalty to spell checks. On a result of natural 1, the wizard suffers a 50% chance of major corruption *or* misfire, rolling on the generic tables as appropriate.

** If either *patron bond* or *invoke patron* is rolled, the wizard receives *both* of these spells, but they count as only one spell slot.

*** Ignore this result if the wizard does not have the spell *patron bond*. If the wizard has that spell, he also gains the appropriate patron spell. Consult your judge for more information.

Table 5-9: Cleric Spells (with page number)

	1st Level	2nd Level	3rd Level	4th Level	5th Level
1	Blessing 255	Banish 269	Animate dead 285	Affliction of the gods 295	Righteous fire 301
2	Darkness 258	Binding 270	Bolt from the blue 287	Cause earthquake 296	Weather control 302
3	Detect evil 259	Cure paralysis 272	Exorcise 288	Sanctify / desecrate 298	Whirling doom 303
4	Detect magic 260	Curse 273	Remove curse 289	Vermin blight 300	
5	Food of the gods 262	Divine symbol 275	Speak with the dead 290		
6	Holy sanctuary 263	Lotus stare 276	Spiritual weapon 291		
7	Paralysis 264	Neutralize poison or disease 277	True name 293		
8	Protection from evil 265	Restore vitality 278			
9	Resist cold or heat 266	Snake charm 280			
10	Second sight 267	Stinging stone 282			
11	Word of command 268	Wood wyrding 284			

Table 5-10: Patron Spells (with page number)

Patron spells are described in the judge's chapter. They are summarized here for easy reference.

Patron	*Invoke Patron* results	1st Level	2nd Level	3rd Level
Bobugbubilz	Page 322	Tadpole transformation 325	Glorious mire 326	Bottomfeeder bond 328
Azi Dahaka	Page 330	Snake trick 333	Kith of the hydra 334	Reap the whirlwind 335
Sezrekan	Page 336	Sequester 339	Shield maiden 340	Phylactery of the soul 341
The King of Elfland	Page 342	Forest walk 345	Warhorn of elfland 346	The dreaming 347
The Three Fates	Page 348	Blade of Atropos 351	Curse of Moirae 352	Warp & weft 353
Yddgrrl, the World Root	Page 354	N/A	N/A	N/A
Obitue-Que	Page 355	N/A	N/A	N/A
Ithha, Prince of Elemental Wind	Page 366	N/A	N/A	N/A

TABLE OF SPELL RESULTS
LEVEL 1 WIZARD SPELLS

Animal Summoning

Level: 1	Range: 20'	Duration: Varies	Casting time: 1 round	Save: None

General — The caster invokes animal spirits to summon forth a mundane animal. The caster must be familiar with the animal type and have some material remnant to expend in casting the spell (e.g., hair, fur, paw, tooth, skull, etc.).

Manifestation — Roll 1d4: (1) an egg shimmers into existence, then hatches into the animal summoned; (2) a flash of dark clouds and the animal appears; (3) the animal's skeleton appears first, then organs appear, then muscles knit them together, then skin grows, and the animal appears; (4) animal erupts from the ground fully formed.

Corruption — Roll 1d8: (1) wizard takes on minor facial trait of the animal he attempted to summon, such as whiskers, longer ears, cat eyes, etc.; (2) wizard emits an odor which humans find strange but animals find irresistible; (3-5) minor corruption; (6-7) major corruption; (8) greater corruption.

Misfire — Roll 1d4: (1) caster inadvertently summons a swarm of aggravating insects, such as bees, wasps, or locusts; (2) instead of summoning an animal, the caster inadvertently sends one away: The caster's familiar or the next-closest mundane animal vanishes for 1d4 rounds only to return dirty, wet, and angry; (3) caster summons only part of an animal, causing a pile of bloody rabbit ears, severed goat horns, dislocated wolf legs, or bloody viscera to appear; (4) caster correctly summons an animal but incorrectly places it inside a nearby building or terrain feature, or the floor/ground if there is no other nearby feature – the animal dies instantly and its body is difficult to recover now that it is fused with the object.

1 — Lost, failure, and worse! Roll 1d6 modified by Luck: (0 or less) corruption + misfire + patron taint, (1-2) corruption, (3) patron taint (or corruption if no patron), (4+) misfire.

2-11 — Lost. Failure.

12-13 — The caster summons one mundane animal of 1 HD or less. The animal remains for up to 1 hour, though it hungers, thirsts, and rests as normal. The animal obeys the caster's commands within normal bounds – suicidal commands or those contrary to its nature (e.g., ordering a rabbit to consume meat) have a 50% chance of releasing the animal from service, in which case it returns from whence it came. Due to the nature of the summoning, the caster cannot directly harm the creature summoned.

14-17 — The caster summons one mundane animal of up to 2 HD, or two animals of 1 HD or less. The animals remain for up to 1 hour, though they hunger, thirst, and rest as normal. The animals obey the caster's commands within normal bounds – suicidal commands or those contrary to its nature (e.g., ordering a rabbit to consume meat) have a 50% chance of releasing the animal from service, in which case it returns from whence it came. Due to the nature of the summoning, the caster cannot directly harm the creature summoned.

18-19 — The caster summons one mundane animal of up to 2 HD, or two animals of 1 HD or less. The animals remain for up to 2 hours, though they hunger, thirst, and rest as normal. The animals obey the caster's commands within normal bounds – suicidal commands or those contrary to its nature (e.g., ordering a rabbit to consume meat) have a 50% chance of releasing the animal from service, in which case it returns from whence it came. Due to the nature of the summoning, the caster cannot directly harm the creature summoned.

20-23 — The caster summons one mundane animal of up to 4 HD, two animals of 2 HD, or up to four animals of 1 HD or less. The animals remain for up to 2 hours, though they hunger, thirst, and rest as normal. The animals obey the caster's commands within normal bounds – suicidal commands or those contrary to its nature (e.g., ordering a rabbit to consume meat) have a 25% chance of releasing the animal from service, in which case it returns from whence it came. Due to the nature of the summoning, the caster cannot directly harm the creature summoned.

24-27	The caster summons one mundane animal of up to 8 HD, two animals of 4 HD, four animals of 2 HD, or up to eight animals of 1 HD or less. The animals remain for up to 2 hours, though they hunger, thirst, and rest as normal. The animals obey the caster's commands within normal bounds – suicidal commands or those contrary to their nature (e.g., ordering a rabbit to consume meat) have a 25% chance of releasing the animals from service, in which case they return to whence they came. Due to the nature of the summoning, the caster cannot directly harm the animals summoned.
28-29	The caster summons one mundane animal of up to 8 HD, two animals of 4 HD, four animals of 2 HD, or up to eight animals of 1 HD or less. The animals remain for up to a day, though they hunger, thirst, and rest as normal. The animals obey the caster's commands within normal bounds – suicidal commands or those contrary to their nature (e.g., ordering a rabbit to consume meat) have a 10% chance of releasing the animals from service, in which case they return to whence they came. Due to the nature of the summoning, the caster cannot directly harm the animals summoned.
30-31	The caster summons one mundane animal of up to 16 HD, two animals of up to 8 HD, four animals of up to 4 HD, or up to eight animals of 2 HD or less. The animals remain for up to a day, though they hunger, thirst, and rest as normal. The animals obey the caster's commands within normal bounds – suicidal commands or those contrary to their nature (e.g., ordering a rabbit to consume meat) have a 10% chance of releasing the animals from service, in which case they return to whence they came. Due to the nature of the summoning, the caster cannot directly harm the animals summoned.
32+	The caster summons a large group of mundane animals. This could be a herd of cattle, a pride of lions, a flock of geese, or a pack of wolves. All animals must be of the same type, and the total hit dice must be 100 HD or less. The herd remains for up to a week, though they hunger, thirst, and rest as normal. The animals obey the caster's commands and even undertake suicidal commands or those contrary to their nature (e.g., ordering a rabbit to consume meat). Due to the nature of the summoning, the caster cannot directly harm the animals summoned.

Cantrip

Level: 1	Range: Varies	Duration: Varies	Casting time: 1 action	Save: Will vs. spell check as applicable

General	As wizards learn their craft, they practice many minor incantations that produce simple visual or auditory effects. This spell can be used to apply magical energy to many minor tasks. With the inherent risks that come from spellcasting, few wizards are so bold as to frequently invoke *cantrips*, but their availability is sometimes valuable. The *cantrip* spell can be used to enact any effect the caster pronounces at casting, within the limits of the spell, as outlined on the spell check table below.

Manifestation	Varies
Corruption	N/A
Misfire	Roll 1d4: (1) caster accidentally summons a large bee that proceeds to chase him; (2) caster generates a patch of glue that attaches his boot to the floor until it is broken with a DC 15 Strength check; (3) caster's hair changes color (at judge's discretion); (4) caster's eyes change color (at judge's discretion).

1	Lost, failure, and misfire.
2-11	Lost. Failure.
12-13	The caster creates a simple visual effect at a distance of up to 20' per caster level. For example, a flash of light, dancing lights, a ray of moonlight, or a patch of darkness.
14-17	As above, *or* the caster can create a simple auditory effect at similar range. For example, a whispered sentence, enhancing his voice to a booming shout, a fake dog bark, or basic ventriloquism.
18-19	As above, *or* the caster can create a simple kinetic effect at similar range. For example, shove a mug off a table, tear the buttons off a dress, twist a knob, or cause a deck of cards to shuffle itself.
20+	As above, *or* the caster can generate a dangerous fluid or energy of some kind that does up to 1d3 damage. For example, a dollop of acid or a freezing chill.

Charm Person

Level: 1   Range: 120′   Duration: Varies   Casting time: 1 round   Save: Will vs. check

General	The caster charms an enemy to become a friend! Any mundane living humanoid can be affected normally. Druids can also use this spell on animals. Wizards can attempt this spell on monsters and un-dead with a -2 check penalty and attempt to affect outsiders and demons with a -4 check penalty.
Manifestation	Roll 1d6: (1) flash of light; (2) lulling harmony; (3) black cloud; (4) glittering pixie dust; (5) black beam; (6) moonbeam from above.
Corruption	Roll 1d6: (1-3) minor corruption; (4-5) major corruption; (6) greater corruption.
Misfire	Roll 1d4: (1) caster falls in love with intended target; (2) 1d4 randomly determined nearby creatures fall in love with each other; (3) caster inadvertently puts intended target to sleep (Will save to resist); (4) target is not charmed but instead repulsed and angered by caster.
1	Lost, failure, and worse! Roll 1d6 modified by Luck: (0 or less) corruption + misfire + patron taint; (1-2) corruption; (3) patron taint (or corruption if no patron); (4+) misfire.
2-11	Lost. Failure.
12-13	A single target must make a Will save or be dazed for 1d4 rounds. Dazed targets can move at half speed but can perform no other actions.
14-17	A single target must make a Will save or fall under the caster's complete control, as if it were his friend. However, the target will not perform actions that are suicidal or which a devoted friend would not otherwise perform. Unfortunately, the target's willpower must be forcibly subverted for the caster to exercise control, so it is but a shell of its former self, operating at a -2 penalty to all rolls, saves, checks, and ability scores while under the wizard's control. The target receives another save to break the charm according to its original Intelligence, as follows: Int 3-6 = one month; Int 7-9 = three weeks; Int 10-11 = two weeks; Int 12-15= one week; Int 16-17 = three days; Int 18+ = next day. While affected by the spell, the target is marked by a sign of the caster's control. Roll 1d4: (1) odd facial tic; (2) deep bags under eyes; (3) posture and facial expressions resemble caster; (4) hair stands straight up.
18-19	A single target must make a Will save or fall under the caster's complete control, as if it were his friend. However, the target will not perform actions that are suicidal or which a devoted friend would not otherwise perform. The target is able to operate at full normal functionality while charmed. The target receives another save to break the charm according to its original Intelligence, as follows: Int 3-6 = one month; Int 7-9 = three weeks; Int 10-11 = two weeks; Int 12-15= one week; Int 16-17 = three days; Int 18+ = next day. While affected by the spell, the target is marked by a sign of the caster's control, and its posture and facial expressions subtly change to resemble the caster's.
20-23	The wizard can target a number of creatures equal to his caster level. Each target must make a Will save or fall under the caster's complete control, as if it were his friend. However, the target will not perform actions that are suicidal or which a devoted friend would not otherwise perform. The target is able to operate at full normal functionality while charmed. The target receives another save to break the

charm according to its original Intelligence, as follows: Int 3-6 = one month; Int 7-9 = three weeks; Int 10-11 = two weeks; Int 12-15= one week; Int 16-17 = three days; Int 18+ = next day.

24-27	The caster can target a number of creatures equal to 1d6 + caster level. Each target must make a Will save or fall under the caster's complete control, as if it were his friend. However, the target will not perform actions that are suicidal or which a devoted friend would not otherwise perform. The target is able to operate at full normal functionality while charmed. The target receives another save to break the charm according to its original Intelligence, as follows: Int 3-6 = one month; Int 7-9 = three weeks; Int 10-11 = two weeks; Int 12-15= one week; Int 16-17 = three days; Int 18+ = next day.
28-29	The caster can target a number of creatures equal to 2d6 + caster level. Each target must make a Will save or fall under the caster's complete control, as if it were his friend. However, the target will not perform actions that are suicidal or which a devoted friend would not otherwise perform. The target is able to operate at full normal functionality while charmed. The target receives another save to break the charm according to its original Intelligence, as follows: Int 3-6 = one month; Int 7-9 = three weeks; Int 10-11 = two weeks; Int 12-15= one week; Int 16-17 = three days; Int 18+ = next day.
30-31	The caster can target a number of creatures equal to 3d6 + caster level. Targets of equal to or less HD than the caster do not receive a save. Those with greater HD than the caster must make a Will save or fall under the wizard's complete control, as if it were his friend. However, the target will not perform actions that are suicidal or which a devoted friend would not otherwise perform. The target is able to operate at full normal functionality while charmed. The target receives another save to break the charm according to its original Intelligence, as follows: Int 3-6 = one month; Int 7-9 = three weeks; Int 10-11 = two weeks; Int 12-15= one week; Int 16-17 = three days; Int 18+ = next day.
32+	The caster can influence the emotions of large groups of people, including crowds of public spectators or armies of angry warriors. The caster can attempt to charm up to 100 people at once, as long as they are within his line of sight – there is no effective range limit, and the targets need not be grouped together (e.g., if the wizard is using scrying means to observe multiple armies, he can target 20 people from each army). Targets of equal to or less HD than the caster do not receive a save. Those with greater HD than the caster receive a Will save. Failure indicates the targets fall under the caster's complete control and consider him their close friend. The targets receive another save to break the charm according to their original Intelligence, as follows: Int 3-6 = one month; Int 7-9 = three weeks; Int 10-11 = two weeks; Int 12-15= one week; Int 16-17 = three days; Int 18+ = next day.

Chill Touch

Level: 1	Range: Touch	Duration: Varies		Casting time: 1 action	Save: Will vs. check

General	This necromantic spell delivers the chill touch of the dead. The caster must spellburn at least 1 point when casting this spell.

Manifestation	Roll 1d4: (1) the wizard's hands glow blue; (2) the wizard's hands turn black; (3) the wizard emits a strong odor of corruption; (4) the wizard's hands appear skeletal.
Corruption	Roll 1d8: (1) skin on caster's face withers and dries out to give him a skull-like appearance; (2) skin on caster's hands falls away to give him skeletal hands; (3) caster permanently glows with a sickly blue aura; (4) un-dead are attracted to caster and flock to him like moths; (5-6) minor corruption; (7) major corruption; (8) greater corruption.
Misfire	Roll 1d3: (1) caster shocks himself with necromantic energy for 1d4 damage; (2) caster shocks one randomly determined nearby ally for 1d4 damage; (3) caster sends a blast of necromantic energy into the nearest corpse, animating it as an un-dead zombie with 1d6 hit points (if no nearby corpse, no effect).

1	Lost, failure, and worse! Roll 1d6 modified by Luck: (0 or less) corruption + misfire + patron taint; (1-2) corruption; (3) patron taint (or corruption if no patron); (4+) misfire.
2-11	Lost. Failure.
12-13	The caster's hands are charged with negative energy! On the next round, the next creature the caster attacks takes an additional 1d6 damage. Un-dead creatures take an additional +2 points of damage.
14-17	The caster's hands are charged with negative energy! On the next round, the caster receives a +2 to attack rolls, and the next creature the caster attacks takes an additional 1d6 damage. Un-dead creatures take an additional +2 points of damage.
18-19	The caster's hands are charged with negative energy! For the next turn, the caster receives a +2 to attack rolls, and every creature the caster attacks takes an additional 1d6 damage. Un-dead creatures take an additional +2 points of damage.
20-23	The caster's hands are charged with negative energy! For the next turn, the caster receives a +2 to attack rolls, and every creature the caster attacks takes an additional 2d6 damage. Un-dead creatures take an additional +2 points of damage.
24-27	The caster's hands are charged with negative energy! For the next turn, the caster receives a +4 to attack rolls, and every creature the caster attacks takes an additional 2d6 damage as well as 1d4 points of Strength loss. Un-dead creatures take an additional +4 points of damage.
28-29	The caster's hands are charged with negative energy! For the next *hour*, the caster receives a +4 to attack rolls, and every creature the caster attacks takes an additional 2d6 damage as well as 1d4 points of Strength loss. Un-dead creatures take an additional +4 points of damage.
30-31	The caster's hands are charged with negative energy! For the next *hour*, the caster receives a +6 to attack rolls, and every creature the caster attacks takes an additional 3d6 damage as well as 1d4 points of Strength loss. Un-dead creatures take an additional +6 points of damage.
32+	The caster's body glows a sickly blue light as he crackles with withering necromantic energy. Any creature within 10' of the caster takes 1d6 damage each round it stays within the field, and un-dead creatures take 1d6+2 damage. Until the next sunrise, the caster receives a +8 bonus to all attack rolls, and every creature the caster attacks takes an additional 3d6 damage (with un-dead suffering an extra +8).

Choking Cloud

Level: 1	Range: 50' or more	Duration: Varies	Casting time: 1 action	Save: None

General	The caster summons forth a cloud of caustic, acidic mist that chokes his target.

Manifestation	Roll 1d8: (1) black cloud; (2) translucent mist; (3) explosion of ash; (4) geyser that erupts from the ground below the target; (5) yellow-green cloud; (6) red mist; (7) thick, oily fog; (8) blue cloud.
Corruption	Roll 1d8: (1) caster's breath is now a toxic gas; whenever he exhales, anyone immediately adjacent must make a DC 12 Fort save or be ill for 1d4 hours (-1 to all rolls while sickened); (2) caster is surrounded at all times by a toxic cloud which automatically sickens everyone within 5' for 1d4 hours unless they make a DC 12 Fort save (-1 to all rolls while sickened); (3) caster's eyes change to translucent orbs which reveal a whirling cloud of gas; (4) certain kinds of creatures are able to detect the caster automatically if he is within half a mile and are attracted to him, notably incorporeal and ethereal creatures, as well as any monster from the elemental plane of air; (5-8) minor corruption.
Misfire	Roll 1d4: (1) cloud of toxic gas explodes at a point centered on the caster (1d4x10' radius, 1d4 damage to all within plus DC 12 Fort save or blinded for 1d4 rounds); (2) caster creates cloud successfully, but it is a *healing* cloud that heals 1d4 damage to all within 20' of intended target; (3) cloud of toxic gas inadvertently catches fire, sparked by some nearby torch or lantern, and explodes as it emerges from the caster's hand, causing 1d8 fire damage to the caster and everyone within 10' of him; (4) caster successfully creates cloud, but it is entirely useless, serving only to create a vague, misty cloud that has no other impact.

1	Lost, failure, and worse! Roll 1d6 modified by Luck: (0 or less) corruption + misfire + patron taint; (1) corruption; (2) patron taint (or corruption if no patron); (3+) misfire.
2-11	Lost. Failure.
12-13	One designated target is engulfed in a caustic, stinking cloud for 1d4 rounds, suffering a -1 penalty to all rolls (including attacks, damage, skills, and saves). The cloud follows the target; it cannot escape.
14-17	Up to 1d4 small individual clouds of toxic gas appear around selected multiple targets, all of which must be within range. Each cloud inflicts a -1 penalty to all rolls (including attacks, damage, skills, and saves) for 1d4 rounds. The clouds follow their targets; they cannot escape.
18-19	A single acidic, poisonous cloud appears with a radius of 20' centered on a target of the caster's choosing. For 1d4+2 rounds, targets in the cloud suffer a -2 penalty to all rolls (attacks, damage, skills, and saves) *and* take 1 point of damage each round. The caster can direct the cloud by concentrating; it moves up to 50' per round at his command.
20-23	A single acidic, poisonous cloud appears with a radius of 20' centered on a target of the caster's choosing. For 2d4+4 rounds, targets in the cloud suffer a -2 penalty to all rolls (attacks, damage, skills, and saves), take 2 points of damage each round, and must make a Fort save when first exposed or be poisoned (-1d4 Agility, duration 1 day). The caster can direct the cloud by concentrating; it moves up to 50' per round at his command.
24-27	A single acidic, poisonous cloud appears with a radius of 20' centered on a target of the caster's choosing within a 100' range. For 2d4+4 rounds, targets in the cloud suffer a -4 penalty to all rolls (attacks, damage, skills, and saves), take 4 points of damage each round, and must make a Fort save when first exposed or be poisoned (-2d4 Agility, duration 1 day). The caster can direct the cloud by concentrating; it moves up to 50' per round at his command.
28-29	A single acidic, poisonous cloud appears with a radius of 30' centered on a target of the caster's choosing within a 200' range. For 3d4+6 rounds, targets in the cloud suffer a -4 penalty to all rolls (attacks, damage, skills, and saves), take 8 points of damage each round, and must make a Fort save when first exposed or be poisoned (-3d4 Agility, duration 1d4 days). The caster can direct the cloud by concentrating; it moves up to 50' per round at his command.
30-31	The caster can create *two* acidic, poisonous clouds. Each appears with a radius of 30' centered on a target of the caster's choosing within a 200' range. For 3d4+6 rounds, targets in the clouds suffer a -4 penalty to all rolls (attacks, damage, skills, and saves), take 8 points of damage each round, and must make a Fort save when first exposed or be poisoned (-3d4 Agility, duration 1d4 days). The caster can direct the clouds at will, without concentrating; they move up to 50' per round at his command.
32+	The caster calls down three toxic clouds of unmatched lethality. For each cloud, he can choose a size ranging from a single target up to a 30' radius. The clouds can be targeted anywhere within 500'. The clouds come into existence instantly and remain for 1d4 turns. Each target within the clouds must make a Fort save or be killed immediately. Those that survive suffer a -6 penalty to all rolls (attacks, damage, skills, and saves) and take 10 points of damage each round from the toxic gases. The caster can direct the clouds at will, without concentrating; they move up to 50' per round at his command.

Color Spray

Level: 1	Range: 40'	Duration: Instantaneous	Casting time: 1 action	Save: Will vs. check

General	The caster summons forth a spray of brilliant colors that blind and dazzle the target.
Corruption	Roll 1d8, noting additional color change table at end of this one: (1) caster's skin permanently changes to a rainbow pattern; (2) caster's eyes each change to a new, different color; (3) caster's hair changes color; (4) caster's skin changes color; (5-7) minor corruption; (8) major corruption. Roll another 1d10 for color changes: (1) blue; (2) green; (3) yellow; (4) orange; (5) red; (6) purple; (7) silver; (8) gold; (9) white; (10) black.
Misfire	Roll 1d3: (1) colored energy blasts back on the caster, blinding him for 1d4 rounds; (2) *color spray* is delayed uncontrollably; judge secretly rolls a die type of his choice; spell is discharged that many rounds later on new re-rolled spell check result; (3) color sprays arc in different random directions rather than together in a cohesive rainbow; roll 1d12 for direction (clock face with 12:00 ahead of caster); 1d4+1 color hues blast out, each in a different direction, causing blindness (1d4 rounds, DC 12 Will save to resist) to first creature in that direction, whether friend or foe.
Manifestation	Roll 1d8: (1) spray of colored arrows; (2) rainbow from above; (3) flash of variegated hues; (4) spotlight of rotating colors from the sky; (5) cloud of many colors or a single color; (6) shadow of subdued, washed-out colors; (7) inversion of colors in the affected area; (8) rope-like coils of light that emanate from the caster's fingertips.

1	Lost, failure, and worse! Roll 1d6 modified by Luck: (0 or less) corruption + misfire + patron taint; (1) corruption; (2) patron taint (or corruption if no patron); (3+) misfire.
2-11	Lost. Failure.
12-13	One target within range must make a Will save or be blinded for 1d4 rounds. Sightless creatures are immune.
14-17	Up to two individual targets within range must make a Will save or be blinded for 1d4 rounds. Sightless creatures are immune.
18-19	Up to three targets within range can be targeted. Each target must make two Will saves or be affected. Targets that fail one save are blinded; targets that fail both saves are blinded *and* knocked unconscious. Duration is 2d4+1 rounds. Sightless creatures are immune.
20-23	Up to three targets within range can be targeted. Each target of 2 or less HD is automatically affected; targets of more than 2 HD must make two Will saves or be affected. Targets that fail one save are blinded; targets that fail both saves are blinded *and* knocked unconscious. Duration is 2d4+1 rounds. Sightless creatures are immune.
24-27	A blast of colored chaos affects all targets in a cone 40' long and from 10' to 30' wide (caster can decide). All targets, including allies, within the cone take 1d4 damage, are knocked unconscious for 3d4+1 rounds, and awake blinded for another 1d4+1 rounds. Creatures of 2 HD or less receive no save; others can attempt a Will save to resist. Sightless creatures are immune.
28-29	A blast of colored chaos affects all targets in a cone 40' long and from 10' to 30' wide (caster can decide). All targets, including allies, within the cone take 1d6 damage, are knocked unconscious for 3d4+3 rounds, and awake blinded for another 2d4+1 rounds. Creatures of 3 HD or less receive no save; others can attempt a Will save to resist. Sightless creatures are immune.
30-31	A blast of colored chaos affects all targets in a cone 100' long and from 10' to 40' wide (caster can decide). The caster may specify whether the cone affects all targets or only enemies. Affected creatures within the cone take 1d8 damage, are knocked unconscious for 3d4+3 rounds, and awake blinded for another 2d4+1 rounds. Creatures of 4 HD or less receive no save; others can attempt a Will save to resist. Sightless creatures are immune.
32+	An incredible surge of rainbow light blasts forth from the caster's fingertips. The spell creates an arcing pattern around the caster, forming a powerful rainbow shining down from the heavens toward the caster's fingers. The display of light is visible for several miles. All enemies within 200' of the caster's location are potentially affected: creatures of 5 HD or less are affected automatically; all others are affected on a failed save. Affected creatures take 2d6 damage, are knocked unconscious for 1d4+1 turns, and awake blinded for another turn. Moreover, *allies* who see the display are awed and inspired, and receive a +1 morale bonus to all rolls (attack, damage, saves, skills, etc.) for the next 1d4 rounds.

Comprehend Languages

Level: 1	Range: Self	Duration: Varies	Casting time: 1 turn	Save: None

General	The caster can understand non-magical words or images (such as treasure maps) that would otherwise be unintelligible.

Manifestation	Roll 1d4: (1) caster's eyes glow; (2) text glows; (3) letters of text flow into new, legible shapes; (4) none.
Corruption	Roll 1d8: (1) caster's eyes permanently glow a bright yellow; (2) skin is marred by faintly glowing tattoos of undecipherable enigmatic script; (3) afflicted speech: roll 1d12 any time caster speaks in any way, and on a 12 the words come out in a randomly determined language (each time, roll as wizard on Appendix L); (4) permanent interpretation: caster can permanently understand *all* spoken languages at juvenile level, including birdsong, insect buzzing, and subsonic speech like bat calls, such that constant drone of conversation around him makes it very difficult to concentrate (-1 to all concentration checks); (5) invisible heat rays from reading: whenever the caster reads any document, his eyes glow red and the document begins to heat up and eventually catches fire: paper in 2 rounds, papyrus in 3 rounds, cloth or vellum in 4 rounds; heat only manifests when reading and cannot cause damage to other creatures; (6) two dozen short tentacles sprout around each of the caster's eye sockets; (7) minor corruption; (8) major corruption.
Misfire	Roll 1d4: (1) caster speaks in tongues, indecipherable to all, for 1d4 hours; (2) nearest ally speaks in a randomly determined language (roll as wizard on Appendix L) for 1d4 hours; (3) *all* creatures within 30' radius (including caster) stricken with inability to speak for 1d6 minutes; (4) caster loses ability to read and write for 1d4 days.

1	Lost, failure, and worse! Roll 1d6 modified by Luck: (0 or less) corruption + misfire + patron taint; (1-2) corruption; (3) patron taint (or corruption if no patron); (4+) misfire.
2-11	Lost. Failure.
12-13	The caster can read writing in one terrestrial language for 1 turn. Terrestrial languages are those spoken by mortal, earthbound creatures, such as dwarves, giants, and goblins. Some sample of the language in question must be visible in front of you.
14-17	The caster can read *and* understand (but not speak or write) one terrestrial language for 1 turn. Terrestrial languages are those spoken by mortal, earthbound creatures, such as dwarves, giants, and goblins.
18-19	The caster can read, write, understand, and speak one terrestrial language for 1 turn. Terrestrial languages are those spoken by mortal, earthbound creatures, such as dwarves, giants, and goblins. The caster can speak the language in a very simple form, at the speech level of a young child. For example, he can communicate basic desires but nothing complex.
20-23	The caster can read, write, understand, and speak one language for 1 hour. The language can be terrestrial, supernatural or extraplanar in origin. For example, he could speak with a demon or an elemental. The caster can speak the language fluently.

24-27	The caster can fluently read, write, understand, and speak any one language for 1 hour per caster level *or* grant this ability to one creature he touches. If the target is unwilling, it can resist the casting with a Will save.
28-29	The caster can fluently read, write, understand, and speak any one language for 1 day per caster level, grant this ability to one creature he touches, *or* grant this ability to all creatures within 20', as long as they remain within that range. If any target is unwilling, it can resist the casting with a Will save.
30-31	The caster gains the *permanent* ability to fluently read, write, understand and speak any one language. He must have exposure to the language, in either written or spoken form, to gain the ability. The caster effectively learns at an extraordinary rate, such that limited exposure is enough to learn, but he must have at least 10 minutes of immersive exposure in the week following the casting of this spell.
32+	The caster gains the ability to read, write, understand, and speak all languages, regardless of origin or modernity, for a period of 1 day per caster level. He can speak to any creature, including unintelligent beasts (like eagles or ants) to the extent that they communicate.

Ekim's Mystical Mask

Level: 1   **Range:** Self   **Duration:** 1 round per CL   **Casting time:** 1 action   **Save:** See below

General	The caster conjures a mystical mask that covers his face and provides benefits against attacks, spells, and other conditions. On a successful casting, the wizard may choose to invoke an effect of lesser power than his spell check roll to produce a weaker but potentially more useful result.
Manifestation	Roll 1d4: (1) The caster plucks the mask out of thin air; (2) the flesh on the caster's face peels away to reveal the mask beneath; (3) the caster's head becomes momentarily blurred and the mask is in place once the distortion passes; (4) the caster's head appears to spin 180° revealing a masked face on the back of his head. In addition to these manifestations, each mask alters the caster's face in a different manner. These alterations are detailed on the spell check table below.
Corruption	Roll 1d4: (1) the caster's face takes on an emotionless, artificial mien; (2) the flesh on the caster's face turns dry and flakes away constantly; (3) the caster develops a phobia about revealing his true face and takes to wearing veils or hooded cloaks; (4) the caster's nose vanishes completely, leaving his face flat and mask-like.
Misfire	Roll 1d4: (1) caster is blinded by the mask for 1d3 rounds and suffers a -4 penalty to initiative rolls, attack rolls, saving throws, spell checks, and to avoid being surprised; (2) the caster's mouth vanishes for 1d3 rounds and no spells may be cast during that time; (3) for the next day, the caster's eyes become hypersensitive to light and he suffers a -2 penalty to all attacks, saves, spell checks, ability checks, and initiative rolls when in illumination brighter than candle light; (4) the caster's face vanishes completely, rendering him blind and mute; in addition, he must make a DC 10 Fort save each round or pass out from asphyxiation; his face returns to normal once the spell's duration has expired.

1	Lost, failure, and worse! Roll 1d6 modified by Luck: (0 or less) corruption + patron taint + misfire; (1-2) corruption; (3+) misfire.
2-11	Lost. Failure.
12-13	The mask grants infravision, allowing the caster to see in the dark up to 60' away. His eyes reflect light like a cat while this mask is in effect.
14-17	The mask helps protect the caster against gaze attacks such as that from a basilisk (q.v.). The caster enjoys a +4 bonus to saving throws of any type against gaze attacks for the duration of the spell. The caster's face takes on a mirror-like quality while this mask is in effect.
18-19	The mask helps defend the caster against baneful magical spells. All spells cast directly at the wizard suffer a -2 penalty to their spell checks. Area-of-effect spells or other magics that are not targeted directly at the mask wearer are unmodified. The caster's face takes on a faceted, quartz-like appearance while this mask is in effect.
20-23	The mask transforms the caster's face into a horrible visage. Each round he can attempt to *instill fear* in one creature. The target creature must make a Will save or flee from the caster's location for 1d4+CL rounds. The targeted creature must be able to see the caster clearly to be affected by the gaze. The caster

can attempt to affect one creature each round for the duration of the spell and can try to instill fear on the same creature more than once, requiring it to make a new saving throw with each attempt. The caster's face becomes monstrously demonic while this mask is in effect.

24-27   The mask protects the caster against physical attacks, granting him a +4 bonus to AC while the spell is in effect. In addition, the caster enjoys a +2 bonus to all saving throws for the duration of the spell. The caster's face appears encased in shining steel while this mask is in effect.

28-29   The mask reflects melee and ranged attacks back at unlucky assailants. Any attacker that successfully strikes the mask's wearer with a physical melee or missile attack must make a DC 10 Luck check or find their attack turned against them. The attacker's same attack roll (including any and all modifiers) is applied to its own AC and inflicts normal damage if the blow lands successfully. The caster's face appears to be that of his attacker(s) while the mask is in effect.

30-31   The mask transforms the caster's entire head into that of a snake. While in effect, the mask grants the caster both the illusion generating and hypnotic gaze powers of a serpent-man (see page 425). As an incidental benefit, it also allows the caster to pass himself off as a serpent-man under cursory inspection. The mask's effect on the caster's face is self-evident.

32+   With this powerful casting, the wizard's face is occluded by a mask that combines all the spell's possible effects into a single visage. The caster has infravision up to 60'; gains a +4 saving throw bonus against gaze attacks; harmful spells cast directly at the caster suffer a -2 penalty to spell checks; the caster can instill fear against any creature that fails a Will save, forcing it to flee for 1d4+CL rounds; the caster's AC is improved by +4, and all saves receive a +2 bonus (this stacks with the +4 bonus against gaze attacks); any attacker who successfully strikes the caster with a physical melee or missile attack must make a DC 10 Luck check or possibly be struck by its own attack (compare the initial attack roll against its own AC); and the caster's face is transformed into a serpent's head, granting him the illusionary and hypnotic capabilities of a serpent-man (see page 425). At this level of success, the mask makes no alterations to the caster's face other than the snake's head transformation (which can be obscured with the illusion generation ability granted by that alteration).

Enlarge

Level: 1   Range: Touch   Duration: 1 turn per caster level   Casting time: 1 round   Save: None

General	By touching a creature or object, or targeting himself, the caster causes the target to grow in size! In this manner, ropes can become longer, doors thicker, tables heavier, swords larger, and so on. Magical objects so increased retain their original magical potency; e.g., a *+1 sword* does not become a *+2 sword*, it simply becomes a larger magical sword. The caster can learn the reverse of this spell, *reduce*, which is used to make things smaller. Multiple castings of this spell do not stack, though *reduce* may be used to cancel *enlarge*.
Manifestation	Roll 1d4: (1) target visibly enlarges; (2) target disappears then re-appears at greater size; (3) hundreds of tiny workmen appear to chop apart the target's body and re-assemble it in greater volume; (4) target reverse-ages to the size and appearance of a baby, then amazingly grows back to adult appearance at larger than its former size.
Corruption	Roll 1d16: (1-6) one part of caster's body is permanently enlarged to (1d3+1)x normal size as follows: (1) eyes, (2) ears, (3) nose, (4) hands, (5) shins, (6) feet; (7-10) one part of caster's body is permanently reduced to half normal size as follows: (7) eyes, (8) nose, (9) arms (-1 Str), (10) legs (-5' speed); (11) hirsute: caster's body hair grows unstoppably for 1d4 days, covering body in gorilla-like fur; (12) caster permanently enlarges in size, increasing his height by 2d6", his weight by (1d6+1)x10 lbs., and his Str by +1, but his equipment does *not* enlarge; (13) caster's fingers each grow by 1d6", determined randomly by finger, making grasping difficult and inflicting a -1 Agility penalty; (14) minor corruption; (15) major corruption; (16) greater corruption.
Misfire	Roll 1d4: (1) nearest *enemy* is enlarged rather than ally by 50%, conferring a +2 bonus to Str (if no nearby enemy, ignore result); (2) all enemies within 50' are doubled in size, receiving a +3 bonus to Str; (3) target is *reduced* instead of enlarged, dropping in size by -25% and taking a -1 penalty to Str; (4) everything within 100', including living creatures, objects, plants, buildings, and other such things, is reduced to mouse-scale; i.e., humans drop to approximately 6" tall, buildings reduce in size to corresponding scale, weapons are the size of toothpicks, and so on; to those affected it appears the world beyond the range has just increased in size exponentially; affected creatures and objects remain affected even if they move beyond range and are restored to normal size in 1 day, but in the meantime they must survive as tiny creatures.

1	Lost, failure, and worse! Roll 1d6 modified by Luck: (0 or less) corruption + patron taint + misfire; (1-2) corruption; (3) patron taint (or corruption if no patron); (4+) misfire.
2-11	Lost. Failure.
12-13	The target increases in size and mass by 10%. It becomes visibly larger and potentially intimidating, but not enough to confer statistical bonuses. Depending on the situation, this may be enough to reach a ledge that was previously out of reach, or otherwise pass some barrier. Armor and equipment worn by the target are similar enlarged.
14-17	The target increases in size by 25%, conferring a +1 bonus to attacks, damage, and AC due to greater size and strength.
18-19	The target increases in size by 50%, conferring a +2 bonus to attacks, damage, and AC due to greater size and strength.
20-23	The target doubles in size. A normal man becomes ogre-sized with this result, receiving a +4 bonus to attacks, damage, and AC due to greater size and strength. In addition, the target receives +10 hp from the new size. These hit points are lost first when the target is wounded, and damage suffered while giant-sized transfers to his normal hit point pool only if he first loses all 10 bonus hit points.
24-27	The target triples in size. A normal man becomes giant-sized with this result, receiving a +6 bonus to attacks, damage, and AC due to greater size and strength. In addition, the target receives +20 hp from the new size. These hit points are lost first when the target is wounded, and damage suffered while giant-sized transfers to his normal hit point pool only if he first loses all 20 bonus hit points.
28-29	The caster is able to select up to three targets, which all triple in size. Each receives a +6 bonus to all at-

tack, damage, and AC due to larger size and strength. In addition, the targets receive +20 hp from the new size. These hit points are lost first when the targets are wounded, and damage suffered while giant-sized transfer to their normal hit point pools only if they first lose all 20 bonus hit points.

30-31	The caster is able to select up to three targets, which all triple in size. Each receives a +6 bonus to all attack, damage, and AC due to larger size and strength. In addition, the targets receive +20 hp from the new size. These hit points are lost first when the targets are wounded, and damage suffered while giant-sized transfer to their normal hit point pools only if they first lose all 20 bonus hit points. The duration is increased to one *day* per caster level, but can be individually ended by the decision of any target.
32+	The caster transforms himself or one target into a giant of truly godlike proportions. The target grows to a height of up to 100', at the caster's discretion. The target's statistics are similarly improved due to his new size, to a maximum benefit of +10 to attack, damage, and AC if he reaches the full 100' height. At that full height, he also receives a bonus of up to +100 hit points. These hit points are lost first when the target is wounded, and damage suffered while giant-sized transfers to his normal hit point pool only if he first loses all 100 bonus hit points. The duration of this extraordinary display of power depends on the size of the target: a target transformed to a 100' height stays at that size for only 1 turn, while sizes of progressively smaller 10' increments last 1 turn longer. For every 20' less in size, the benefit to attacks, damage, and AC drops by -1, and the bonus hit points drop by -10, but the duration is extended by 1 turn. For example, a height of 40' lasts 4 turns, and grants a bonus of +7 to attacks, damage, and AC, and +70 hit points.

Feather Fall

Level: 1	Range: 25'	Duration: 1 round per caster level or until landing	Casting time: instantaneous
	Save: Will to avoid		

General	The caster impedes his own or another person's rate of descent when falling. This allows the target to avoid injury or death or to glide upon the breeze. Note that this spell can be cast instantaneously, out of initiative order, if the caster or a target within range is falling.
Manifestation	Roll 1d4: (1) folds of aerodynamic flesh sprout from the target's arms and legs; (2) the target glows with a wispy, featherlike aura of canary yellow; (3) the target's body hair is replaced with downy feathers; (4) the target's body curls like a fallen leaf to rock upon the winds.
Corruption	Roll 1d5: (1) caster's hair stands on end as if permanently plummeting through the air; (2) the caster makes all descents (climbing down ropes, walking down stairs, sliding down poles, etc.) at half normal speed; (3) caster becomes subject to sporadic winds, which do not affect other characters, and must make a Strength check to stay upright (DC 5 for light winds, DC 10 for strong winds, and DC 15 against gusts); (4) caster's hair permanently replaced by feathers; (5) sound of whistling wind accompanies the caster wherever he goes.
Misfire	Roll 1d4: (1) caster's speed of descent is increased, resulting in an additional 1d6 damage upon impact; (2) caster abruptly rises 10' into the air before falling to the ground (taking 1d6 points of damage, or 2d6 if there is a hard surface 10' or less above the caster's head); (3) caster's clothing and other possessions turn ethereal for 1d6x10 minutes and cannot be worn or used; (4) caster is blown 10-30 feet in a random direction by a gust of ghostly wind.

1	Lost, failure, and worse! Roll 1d6 modified by Luck: (0 or less) corruption + patron taint + misfire; (1) corruption; (2) patron taint (or corruption if no patron); (3+) misfire.
2-11	Lost. Failure.
12-13	Caster reduces the speed at which he falls. With a successful Fortitude save (DC 10 +1 for each 10' fallen), he takes no damage. On a failed save, he suffers only half damage.
14-17	Caster falls at a graceful rate of 50' per round and takes no damage if he lands before the spell expires. Otherwise, he suffers half damage and is allowed a Fort save (DC 10 +1 for each 20' fallen) to avoid all damage.
18-19	Caster and three additional creatures within range fall at a rate of 50' round. They take no damage if they land before the spell expires. Otherwise, they suffer half damage and are allowed a Fort save (DC 10 +1 for each 20' fallen) to avoid all damage.

20-23	Caster and six additional creatures fall at a rate of 50' round. They take no damage if they land before the spell expires. Otherwise they suffer half damage and are allowed a Fort save (DC 10 +1 for each 20' fallen) to avoid all damage.
24-27	Caster gains the ability to glide on the air by leaping from a height 30' or more above the ground. The caster soars on the breeze, drifting back to earth at a vertical rate of 10' per round, arriving on the ground when he reaches the maximum distance he can glide. His movement rate is 60' per round while gliding, and if he fails to reach solid ground before the spell expires, he falls and suffers normal damage upon impact.
28-29	Caster and up to three additional creatures can glide on the winds. They soar on the breeze, drifting back to earth at a vertical rate of 10' per round, arriving on the ground when reaching the maximum distance they can glide. Their movement rate is 60' per round while gliding, and if they fail to reach solid ground before the spell expires, they fall and suffer normal damage upon impact.
30-31	Caster and up to six additional creatures can glide on the winds. They soar on the breeze, drifting back to earth at a vertical rate of 10' per round, arriving on the ground when reaching the maximum distance they can glide. Their movement rate is 60' per round while gliding, and if they fail to reach solid ground before the spell expires, they fall and suffer normal damage upon impact.
32+	Caster can fall any distance regardless of height or duration of fall without taking damage. Additionally, the caster is immune to any related hazards, such as thin atmosphere, intense cold, or even high temperatures generated by re-entry into an atmosphere from a vacuum.

Find Familiar

Level: 1	Range: Self	Duration: Lifetime	Casting time: 1 week	Save: None

General	This lengthy ritual prepares the caster to bond with a familiar. The familiar makes itself known during the ceremony 50% of the time; otherwise, the caster makes its acquaintance sometime in the weeks following the ritual. The spell check is made upon completion of the ritual, and a minimum spellburn of 10 points is required to cast this spell.
	The caster gains hit points equal to the familiar's and other powers as well, depending on the creature summoned. Once the caster has summoned a familiar (whether having met it or not), he cannot summon another until the current one dies and a full moon passes.
	If a familiar dies, the caster immediately keels over in intense pain, loses twice the familiar's hit points permanently, and suffers a -5 spell check penalty until the next full moon.
	The judge will provide more information (see page 316).

Manifestation	Varies
Corruption	Roll 1d6: (1-3) minor; (4-5) major; (6) greater.
Misfire	N/A

1	Lost, failure, patron taint, and corruption. Unlike normal spells, the spell is lost for an entire month, not simply one day.
2-11	Lost and failure. Unlike normal spells, the spell is lost for an entire month, not simply one day.
12-13	Per judge.
14-17	Per judge.
18-19	Per judge.
20-23	Per judge.
24-27	Per judge.
28-29	Per judge.
30-31	Per judge.
32+	Per judge.

Flaming Hands

| Level: 1 | Range: 15′ | Duration: Instantaneous | Casting time: 1 action | Save: None |

General	The caster produces gouts of fire from his bare hands to burn his enemies.
Manifestation	Roll 1d4: (1) caster's hands burst into flames; (2) fires spring from the wizard's fingertips; (3) caster's hands turn into roiling, smoking flame; (4) skin blackens and peels away to reveal skeletal hands dripping lava.
Corruption	Roll 1d4: (1) hands permanently blackened; (2) bare touch causes paper to ignite 25% of the time; (3) body hair burned away permanently; (4) caster suffers a permanent -2 penalty on spell checks to cold-based magics.
Misfire	Roll 1d4: (1) flame jets from random appendage, spoiling aim; randomly determine where and in what direction the flame gouts; jet causes 1d3 damage to everything within 15′ range in that direction; (2) caster's hands ignite causing him 1d3 damage (3); 1d4 random possessions of the caster catch fire and burn to char; (4) all fire within a 15′ radius of the caster is immediately snuffed out.

1	Lost, failure, and worse! Roll 1d6 modified by Luck: (0 or less) corruption + patron taint + misfire; (1-2) corruption; (3) patron taint (or corruption if no patron); (4+) misfire.
2-11	Lost. Failure.
12-13	A single blast of fire strikes one target within range for 1d3 points of damage.
14-17	Spell produces a blast of fire that burns a single target within range for 1d6 points of damage.
18-19	Spell produces a blast of fire that burns a single target within range for 1d6+CL points of damage.
20-23	Spell produces a blast of fire that burns up to three targets within range for 1d6+CL points of damage. All targets must be within 10′ of one another.
24-27	Spell produces a blast of fire that burns up to three targets within range for 2d6+CL points of damage. All targets must be within 10′ of one another.
28-29	Caster creates a single blast of fire 10′ wide and 30′ long that does damage equal to 3d6+CL to all caught in the blast.
30-31	Caster creates two blasts of fire 10′ wide and 30′ long. Each can be directed within a 180° arc of his position, doing damage equal to 3d6+CL to all caught in the blast.
32+	Caster can blast fire in a 360° arc outward from his body. Within that complete radius he can pick one "wedge" of 0-180° where fire does not blast (i.e., to protect allies in that position). All creatures within the affected arc, out to a range of 40′, are immolated, taking damage equal to 4d10+CL.

Force Manipulation

Level: 1	Range: 25'	Duration: Varies	Casting time: 1 action	Save: None

General	The caster conjures and shapes invisible force energy into useful objects or barriers of a solid nature. On a successful casting, the wizard may choose to invoke any effect of equal to or less than his spell check, allowing a range of options with every successful casting to produce a weaker but potentially more useful result.

Manifestation	Roll 1d4: (1) caster's hands shimmer and the air hums with power; (2) cloud of scintillating light motes takes the shape of the object created and then vanishes; (3) blocks of blue energy descend from above to form the object or barrier and then disappear; (4) caster traces the shape to be created in the air with a glowing finger tip.
Corruption	Roll 1d5: (1) caster loses his sense of touch as if his hands were permanently encased in an envelope of force; (2) small objects are knocked over around the caster by errant bolts of force energy (drinks spill, vases topple, potion bottles fall off tables) – this effect is seldom to the caster's benefit; (3) caster floats a half-inch above the ground at all time, but still puts pressure on the floor beneath him to set off traps, sink in water, and otherwise suffer the effects of poor terrain; (4) caster's face turns transparent on occasion to reveal the skull beneath; (5) once per day at the judge's discretion, a wall of force bars the caster's passage for 1d3 rounds.
Misfire	Roll 1d4: (1) caster is struck by force backlash, bludgeoned by invisible blows and must make a DC 13 Fort save or be knocked prone; (2) caster hoisted 3" aloft by force field and cannot move under his own power; must be pushed and pulled until effect wears off in 1 hour; (3) caster encases himself in force bubble and must make a DC 10 Reflex save each round or roll up to 30' in a random direction; bubble bursts in 1d6 rounds; (4) caster pelted by 1d4 force spheres doing 1 point of damage each.

1	Lost, failure, and worse! Roll 1d6 modified by Luck: (0 or less) corruption + patron taint + misfire; (1-2) corruption; (3) patron taint (or corruption if no patron); (4+) misfire.
2-11	Lost. Failure.
12-13	The caster creates an apple-sized sphere of force that can be hurled as a weapon. It can be hurled immediately or remain in the wizard's hand for up to one round per caster level. It inflicts 1d6 damage per caster level with a range of 25' per caster level.
14-17	The wizard forms a floating platform of force energy 3' above the ground. This disk-shaped, 3' diameter platform follows him at a distance of 5' but can be commanded to move up to 25' away from the wizard's position by thought alone. The platform can carry up to 100 lbs. per caster level and remains for 1d6+CL turns. If circumstances prevent the disk from remaining within range of the caster, the platform vanishes.
18-19	The caster calls into being a tower shield-sized wall of force at a point within 25'. It exists for 2d6 rounds and grants a +4 AC bonus to adjacent characters. The wall cannot move from where it was called into existence but remains in existence if the caster moves out of range.
20-23	As above, but the spell creates *two* shield walls. Each also provides protection against *magic missiles* 50% of the time.
24-27	The caster creates a wall of force 10' square per level in size. The wall cannot move but grants complete protection against all physical attacks, *magic missiles*, heat, cold, and lightning. The wall takes the damage inflicted by such attacks. The wall lasts until 1d6+CL turns have passed or it has absorbed 50 points of damage. The caster cannot attack or cast spells through the wall.
28-29	The caster creates a wall of force 10' square per level in size. He can form this wall into a spherical or hemispherical shape up to its maximum size in square feet. The wall cannot move, but grants complete protection against all physical attacks, *magic missiles*, heat, cold, and lightning. The wall takes the damage inflicted by such attacks. The wall lasts until 1d6+CL *hours* have passed or it has absorbed 100 points of damage. The caster cannot attack or cast spells through the wall.
30-31	The caster creates a wall of force 10' square per level in size. He can form this wall into any shape he can imagine, up to its maximum size in square feet. The wall cannot move, but grants complete protection against all physical attacks, *all spells*, and all dragon breath. The wall lasts until 2d6+CL *hours* have passed or it has absorbed 150 points of damage. The caster cannot attack or cast spells through the wall.
32+	The caster creates a wall of force 20' square per level in size. He can form this wall into any shape he can imagine, up to its maximum size in square feet. The wall can be moved up to 10' per round if the caster concentrates. It grants complete protection against all physical attacks, all spells, and all dragon breath. The wall lasts until 2d6+CL *days* have passed or it has absorbed 300 points of damage. The caster may cast spell through the wall at opponents while enjoying its protection.

Invoke Patron

Level: 1	Range: Self Duration: Varies Casting time: 1 round, and the spell may be cast only a limited number of times, according to results of *patron bond*. Save: None

General	In order to learn this spell, the caster must first cast *patron bond*. The particulars of this spell vary according to the terms of the patron. In casting this spell, the wizard invokes the name of a supernatural patron to request aid. This spell requires at least 1 point of spellburn. The patron responds by sending aid according to the nature of its followers; the judge will provide specifics. Note that continued casting of this spell may taint the wizard spiritually and physically.

Manifestation	Varies
Corruption	Roll 1d8: (1-4) minor; (5-7) major; (8) greater.
Misfire	N/A

1	Lost, failure, and worse! Roll 1d6 modified by Luck: (3 or less) corruption + patron taint; (4-5) corruption; (6+) patron taint.
2-11	Failure. Unlike other spells, *invoke patron* may not be lost for the day. Depending on the results of *patron bond*, the wizard may still be able to cast it.
12-13	Per judge.
14-17	Per judge.
18-19	Per judge.
20-23	Per judge.
24-27	Per judge.
28-29	Per judge.
30-31	Per judge.
32+	Per judge.

Magic Missile

Level: 1	Range: 150' or more Duration: Instantaneous Casting time: 1 action or 1 turn (see below) Save: None

General	The caster hurls a magical missile that automatically hits an enemy.

Manifestation	Roll 1d10: (1) meteor; (2) flaming arrow; (3) force arrow; (4) screaming, clawing eagle; (5) black beam; (6) ball lightning; (7) splash of acid; (8) ray of frost; (9) force dagger; (10) force axe.
Corruption	Roll 1d8: (1-4) caster's hands and forearms change color to match shades of most commonly cast magic missile: (1) electric yellow, (2) icy blue, (3) acid green, (4) vivid red; (5) pupils and irises vanish while eyes turn a chalky white; (6) fingertips turn translucent and nearly invisible, appearing ghost-like or as if they were composed of pure force energy; (7) from now on, every time he casts *magic missile*, the caster turns invisible for 1d6 rounds; (8) caster gains a permanent force stone that rapidly orbits his head, impacting with any creature that approaches within 3' to cause searing pain and 1 point of damage every round – which, unfortunately, includes allies attempting to heal or those who fight adjacent to the caster in melee.
Misfire	Roll 1d6: (1) explosion of missiles sprays in all directions – all creatures within 100' (allies and enemies) are hit by 1d4-1 missiles, each doing 1 point of damage; (2) missiles launch then ricochet back on caster, who is hit by 1d3-1 missiles for 1 point of damage each; (3) explosion of force energy centered on caster, causing 1d6 damage to caster and all within 10' (DC 10 Ref save for half); (4) delayed blast – no effect now, but at a random point sometime in the next 24 hours, determined whenever the caster rolls his next 1 on *any* dice roll (not just a d20), a single magic missile bolts forth to strike one randomly determined

character within 100' for 1d4 damage (strikes the caster if there are no other targets) – if no 1 is rolled in 24 hours, risk passes without damage; (5) caster becomes charged with force energy, such that the next creature or object he touches suffers a blast damage for 1d6+1 damage to target and 1 point of damage to caster; (6) force energy manifests in downward direction, burning a hole in the ground under caster – ground beneath him rapidly disintegrates to a depth of 1d20 feet, and he sinks with the falling depth of the ground to find himself at bottom of pit – there is no initial falling damage since he "rides" the drop in ground level but depth of pit may open to lower level of the dungeon (potentially causing damage), and he must now climb out.

1	Lost, failure, and worse! Roll 1d6 modified by Luck: (0 or less) corruption + patron taint + misfire; (1-2) corruption; (3) patron taint (or corruption if no patron); (4+) misfire.
2-11	Lost. Failure.
12-13	The caster throws a single missile that does 1 point of damage. He must have line of sight to the target. The missile never misses, though it may be blocked by certain magic (e.g., *magic shield*).
14-17	The caster throws a single missile that does damage equal to 1d4 + caster level. He must have line of sight to the target. The missile never misses, though it may be blocked by certain magic (e.g., *magic shield*).
18-19	The caster throws 1d4 missiles that deal damage equal to 1d4 + caster level. All missiles must be aimed at a single target to which the caster has line of sight. The missiles never miss, though they may be blocked by certain magic (e.g., *magic shield*).
20-23	The caster throws 1d4+2 missiles that do damage equal to 1d6 + caster level. Each missile can be aimed at a separate target to which the caster has line of sight. The missiles never miss, though they may be blocked by certain magic (e.g., *magic shield*).
24-27	The caster throws a single powerful missile that does damage equal to 4d12 + caster level. The missile must be aimed at a single target to which the caster has line of sight, at a maximum range of 1,000'. The missile never misses, though it may be blocked by certain magic (e.g., *magic shield*).
28-29	The caster throws 1d6+3 missiles that do damage equal to 1d8 + caster level. Each missile can be aimed at a single target at any range, as long as the caster has line of sight. The missiles never miss, though they may be blocked by certain magic (e.g., *magic shield*).
30-31	The caster throws 2d6+1 missiles that each do damage equal to 1d8 + caster level. Each missile can be aimed at a separate target. Range is line of sight, regardless of whether a direct path exists; e.g., the caster may launch a magic missile through a crystal ball or other scrying device. These missiles have limited ability to defy *magic shield* and other protections; compare this spell check against the spell check used to create the *magic shield*. If the *magic missile* check is higher, the *magic shield* has only a 50% chance of absorbing the missiles (roll individually for each missile). Any missiles that make it through do damage equal to 1d8 + caster level, as noted above.
32+	The caster throws 3d4+2 missiles that each do damage equal to 1d10 + caster level. He may direct these missiles individually as a single action, or he may direct them *all* at a *single target* that is not present or visible, provided he has specific knowledge of that target. In this case, the caster must have a physical memento of the target (hair, fingernail, vial of blood, etc.) and spend 1 turn concentrating to cast the spell, then continue concentrating as the missiles seek their target. The missiles seek out this target even if it is concealed or invisible, though they have a maximum range of 100 miles. The missiles turn, curve, retrace their route, and make every effort to reach the target, although they cannot cross planes. The missiles can travel up to 10 miles per second provided no obstacles are present, but speed is much lower if, for example, they must navigate underground caverns. Provided a direct route exists, the missiles strike the target unerringly.

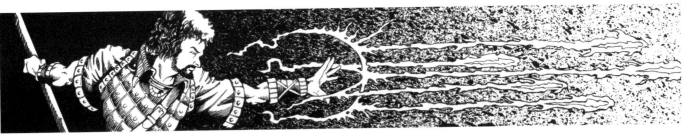

Magic Shield

Level: 1	Range: Touch	Duration: Varies		Casting time: 1 action	Save: None

General — The caster conjures up a magical shield that defends him from opponents.

Manifestation — Roll 1d6: (1) disc of shimmering blue force; (2) yellowish force-field; (3) giant hand that picks off attacks; (4) buckler that emits radiant light; (5) black, bottomless tear in the seam of reality; (6) whirlwind of air that buffets attackers.

Corruption — Roll 1d8: (1-4) minor; (5-7) major; (8) greater.

Misfire — Roll 1d4: (1) caster's shield appears as force burst aimed inward instead of spreading out, causing 1d4 damage as it explodes against him; (2) shield is accidentally summoned to benefit nearest enemy, granting that enemy a +4 bonus to AC for 1d3 turns; (3) caster accidentally summons shield horizontally below his feet, lifting him up 3" from the ground and causing him to "slide" on it for next 1d3+1 rounds; this increases his speed by +10' but imposes a -1 penalty to attacks, spell checks, damage, and AC as he slips and slides haphazardly; (4) caster completely encases himself in a shield that blocks all attacks, damage, spells, and physical contact between him and the rest of the world, such that he is completely encased in a transparent bubble which renders him invulnerable to attack but also unable to move or communicate outside the bubble for 1d4 rounds.

1	Lost, failure, and worse! Roll 1d6 modified by Luck: (0 or less) corruption + misfire; (1-2) corruption; (3+) misfire.
2-11	Lost. Failure.
12-13	The caster conjures a weak shield that provides a +2 bonus to AC for 1d6 rounds.
14-17	The caster conjures a shield that provides a +4 bonus to AC for 2d6 rounds.
18-19	The caster conjures shield that provides a +4 bonus to AC for 1d3 turns. When casting the spell, the caster can apply the shield to himself or one ally touched.
20-23	The caster conjures a shield that provides a +4 bonus to AC for 1d3 turns. When casting the spell, the caster can apply the shield to himself or one ally touched. In addition to the AC bonus, the shield also blocks *magic missiles* automatically (missiles usually have no effect; see *magic missile* spell description).
24-27	The caster conjures a shield that protects him or an ally touched. The shield lasts 1d4+1 turns and has three benefits: it provides a +4 bonus to AC; it blocks *magic missiles* automatically (see *magic missile* spell description); and it blocks most attacks from mundane projectiles, reducing damage from any arrow, sling stone, bolt, dart, or other ranged weapon by 10 points per attack for the duration of the spell.
28-29	The caster conjures *two* shields that protect him *and* one ally touched. Each shield lasts 1d4 hours and has *four* benefits: it provides a +4 bonus to AC; it blocks *magic missiles* automatically (see *magic missile* spell description); it blocks most attacks from mundane projectiles, reducing damage from any arrow, sling stone, bolt, dart, or other ranged weapon by 10 points per attack for the duration of the spell; and it provides a benefit in counterspelling equal to a +2 bonus to any subsequent spell check made as a counterspell.
30-31	The caster conjures a battalion of magical shields that protect him and his allies. The caster is automatically shielded, as are all allies within a 10' radius. Each shield lasts 1d4+1 hours and follows the allies even if they leave the caster's side. Each shield has *four* benefits: it provides a +6 bonus to AC; it blocks *magic missiles* automatically (see *magic missile* spell description); it blocks most attacks from mundane projectiles, reducing damage from any arrow, sling stone, bolt, dart, or other ranged weapon by 20 points per attack for the duration of the spell; and it provides a benefit in counterspelling equal to a +4 bonus to any subsequent spell check made as a counterspell.
32+	The caster calls forth a globe of shimmering magical energies that protects him and his allies. The caster is automatically encased in this magical shield, as are all allies within a 10' radius. The shimmering globes last until the next sunrise and follow the allies even if they leave the caster's side. Each globe has *five* benefits: it provides a +8 bonus to AC; it blocks *magic missiles* automatically (see *magic missile* spell description); it reduces damage on *all* attacks against its target by 2 points; it blocks most attacks from mundane projectiles, reducing damage from any arrow, sling stone, bolt, dart, or other ranged weapon by 20 points per attack for the duration of the spell; and it provides a benefit in counterspelling equal to a +4 bonus to any subsequent spell check made as a counterspell.

Mending

Level: 1　　Range: 5'　　Duration: Varies　　Casting time: 1 round　　Save: None

General	The caster can repair damaged objects, generally of a simple and mundane nature. The reverse spell, *tear*, can cause minor defects and offers a Fort save to the affected object.
Corruption	Always minor.
Misfire	Roll 1d6: (1) caster's clothes unravel and fall into a pile of threads at his feet; (2) all straps, laces, buckles, and fasteners within 20' of caster come undone, causing pants to fall off, shields to fall to the ground, sacks to spill their contents, boots to come unlaced, backpacks to slip from shoulders, etc.; (3) deep gouts of rust appear on all metal weapons within 10', imposing a permanent -1 penalty to damage; (4) a greenish patina tarnishes all precious metals on the caster's person, reducing their value (and making their metal content suspect) until they are polished; (5) the most complicated mechanical object within 20' (probably a crossbow but review character sheets to be sure) breaks in a manner that is very difficult to repair; (6) caster suffers a minor but aggravating wound, such as a stubbed toe or bad hangnail, which causes no damage but inflicts a -1 penalty to all rolls for 10 minutes.
Manifestation	Roll 1d4: (1) object glows; (2) object disappears then reappears mended; (3) swarm of tiny gnomes crawl out from under nooks and crannies to repair object with hammer and anvil, then they run away; (4) object melts and then reforms mended.

1	Lost, failure, and worse! Roll 1d6 modified by Luck: (0 or less) corruption + misfire; (1) corruption; (2+) misfire.
2-11	Lost. Failure.
12-13	The caster repairs a minor defect in a simple object of non-magical, non-living nature. The repair lasts for 24 hours. The defect to be repaired must be of a single material, be no more than 1 cubic foot in volume, and contain no moving parts or complex mechanisms. Once repaired, the object is as good as new. Examples: mend a torn shirt, repair a dent in a helmet, connect the two halves of a broken sword, or restring a broken bow.
14-17	The caster repairs a minor defect in a simple object of non-magical, non-living nature. The repair lasts for one week. The defect to be repaired must be of a single material, be no more than 1 cubic foot in volume, and contain no moving parts or complex mechanisms. Once repaired, the object is as good as new. Examples: mend a torn shirt, repair a dent in a helmet, connect the two halves of a broken sword, or restring a broken bow.
18-19	The caster *permanently* repairs a minor defect in a simple object of non-magical, non-living nature. The defect to be repaired must be of a single material, be no more than 1 cubic foot in volume, and contain no moving parts or complex mechanisms. Once repaired, the object is as good as new. Examples: mend a torn shirt, repair a dent in a helmet, connect the two halves of a broken sword, or restring a broken bow. There is a 50% chance that the repaired object is actually substituted for a similar whole object. For example, instead of mending a torn tunic, an intact but different tunic appears. Somewhere, someone's intact tunic was replaced by a torn one!
20-23	The caster permanently repairs one normal, complex object with moving parts and multiple elements. For example, he could repair a crossbow or a lock. The size of the object can be up to the caster's weight or volume. There is no chance of substitution.
24-27	The caster permanently repairs a *large,* complex object of mundane origin, with moving parts and multiple elements, at a range of up to 100'. For example, he could restore a crumbled statue to its original form or rebuild a collapsed wagon. The object can have a weight or volume up to four times the caster's own.
28-29	The caster permanently repairs a *very large,* complex object of mundane origin, even if it has moving parts and multiple elements, at a range of up to 100'. For example, he could reform the broken battlements of a tower with this spell. Larger objects take longer to mend, typically requiring concentration of one round per ton of weight.
30-31	The caster repairs very large objects of great complexity at a range of 100', even if they are magical in nature. Note that the specific object in question may require additional components beyond the scope

of the normal casting of this spell. For example, a chinked magic sword could be mended normally, but mending a broken wizard's staff may require the same elemental energies that were present when it was created.

32+   The caster repairs very large objects, even if they are complex or magical in nature, at a range of 100'. Optionally, the caster can cast this spell on a living creature to mend its wounds. Casting this spell on a living creature heals one debility per casting (e.g., blindness, deafness, a severed limb, etc.) or the equivalent of 2d6 hit points of damage.

Patron Bond

Level: 1   Range: Self or touch (see below)   Duration: Lifetime   Casting time: 1 week + quests as ordered   Save: None

General   The caster commits himself to the service of a supernatural lord, forming a pact to gain its support as his patron so long as he continues to please it with his service. This patron may be a demon, devil, ghost, spirit, elemental, angel, chaos lord, or other supernatural being who accepts the caster's service. The initial ceremony takes one week to complete. Once the pact is made, the caster may invoke the patron's support with the spell *invoke patron*, and it may or may not answer as it sees fit. In return for the patron's assistance, it may ask the caster to do certain things. The caster must act faithfully in its service at all times, lest it cast him off. The caster may perform more than one ceremony to serve multiple masters, but doing so may raise questions as to his true loyalties. This is dangerous magic; a supernatural patron is not the same as the deity that a cleric may worship. The caster should be forewarned that he is in communion with almighty spirits.

Alternately, once the caster has formed a bond with his patron, this spell may be cast to create a bond between another mortal and the caster's patron. The mortal need not be a spellcaster; in fact, the second mortal usually is not. In this case, both the caster and the recipient must spend a week on the ceremony, which requires a mighty oath to declare allegiance to the patron. Very powerful creatures are more likely to successfully bond with patrons (who look more favorably upon powerful followers). Typically, a casting of *patron bond* on behalf of another receives a bonus of +2 if the subject is of 5th-level (5 HD) or higher and +4 if the subject is of 9th-level (9 HD) or higher. At the end of the ceremony, the casting of the spell seals the bond. Recruiting additional followers for his patron brings the caster favor and may grant boons to the other followers; though, their patron will ask fealty of them in exchange.

Note that continued casting of this spell may taint the caster, both spiritually and physically.

Manifestation	Varies
Corruption	N/A – always patron taint
Misfire	N/A

	When Cast on Self	When Cast on Other
1	Lost and patron taint!	
2-11	Failure. Unlike normal spells, this spell is lost for an entire month, not simply one day.	
12-13	The caster makes contact with his patron and successfully negotiates the terms of the compact. He learns the spell *invoke patron* as it relates to his patron but may only cast it once per week. Each time the caster casts *invoke patron*, he is indebted to his patron, who will call in the debt at some point. The caster's patron marks him as its servant via an inconspicuous brand or symbol somewhere on the caster's body.	The caster forms a simple bond between the subject and his patron. The patron is aware of this subject, who is one among many. The subject may attempt a Luck check once per month, at a -4 penalty, to ask a *minor* favor from the patron, which manifests in a non-magical manner. (For example, if short of gold to pay for a ferry crossing, the subject may be lucky enough to find a fisherman willing to offer a free trip across the river.) Each time such a Luck check is attempted there is a 1% cumulative chance that the patron asks for something in return. The caster is viewed favorably for bringing more followers to his patron; for every 10 followers recruited and bonded, he receives a +1 bonus to future *patron bond* and *invoke patron* checks (max +5 bonus).
14-17	The caster makes contact with his patron and is considered a useful pawn. The caster receives a prominent mark of the patron on his hand or face. The caster learns the spell *invoke patron* as it relates to his patron and may cast it once per day. Each time he casts *invoke patron*, the caster is indebted to his patron, who will call in the debt at some point.	The caster forms a bond between his patron and the subject, who is attuned to the desires of the caster's patron. The subject receives a prominent mark of the patron on his hand or face, and may attempt a Luck check once per month, at a -2 penalty, to ask a *minor* favor from the patron, which manifests in a non-magical manner. Each time such a Luck check is attempted there is a 1% cumulative chance that the patron asks for something in return. The caster is viewed favorably for bringing more followers to his patron; for every 10 followers recruited and bonded, he receives a +1 bonus to future *patron bond* and *invoke patron* checks (max +5 bonus).
18-19	The caster makes contact with his patron and is granted a mark of favor. He receives a prominent mark of the patron on his face. The caster learns the spell *invoke patron* as it relates to his patron and may cast it once per day at a +1 bonus to the spell check. Each time he casts *invoke patron*, the caster is indebted to his patron, who will call in the debt at some point.	The caster forms a bond between his patron and the subject, who is important to the goals of the caster's patron. The subject receives a prominent mark of the patron on his hand or face, and may attempt a Luck check once per month to ask a *minor* favor from the patron, which manifests in a non-magical manner. Each time such a Luck check is attempted there is a 1% cumulative chance that the patron asks for something in return. The caster is viewed favorably for bringing more followers to his patron; for every 10 followers recruited and bonded, he receives a +1 bonus to future *patron bond* and *invoke patron* checks (max +5 bonus).
20-23	The caster arrives at an agreeable arrangement with his patron. He receives a prominent mark of the patron on his face. The caster learns the spell *invoke patron* as it relates to his patron and may cast it twice per day at a +1 bonus to the spell check. Each time he casts *invoke patron*, the caster is indebted to his patron, who will call in the debt at some point.	The caster forms a bond between his patron and the subject. For reasons unknown, the patron is inexplicably fond of this subject; the patron probably has some use for this subject in the future, which comes to light when the time is right. The patron bestows a minor boon on the caster in the form of a +2 bonus on the next casting of *invoke patron* or a patron spell. The subject receives a prominent mark of the patron on his hand or face, and may attempt a Luck check once per month, at a +1 bonus, to ask a *minor* favor from the patron, which manifests in a non-magical manner. Each time such a Luck check is attempted there is a 1% cumulative chance that the patron asks for something in return. The caster is viewed favorably for bringing more followers to his patron; for every 10 followers recruited and bonded, he receives a +1 bonus to future *patron bond* and *invoke patron* checks (max +5 bonus).

	Patron Bond (continued)	
	When Cast on Self	**When Cast on Other**
24-27	The caster is considered an important person in his patron's plans. He forms an agreement with his patron and is marked as one in the patron's service. The caster learns the spell invoke patron as it relates to his patron and may cast it twice per day at a +1 bonus to the spell check. The patron also gives the caster a gift (for which a counter-gift is to be expected, of course). The gift is a single patron spell, selected from the patron's spell list. The caster can cast this spell once per day in place of a casting of invoke patron. Each time he casts this patron spell or invoke patron, the caster is indebted to his patron, who will call in the debt at some point.	The caster forms a bond between his patron and the subject, who is very useful to the patron. The patron bestows a minor boon on the caster in the form of a +2 bonus on the next casting of invoke patron or a patron spell, and grants a minor boon to the subject in the form of a +1 bonus to his next action in the service of the patron. The subject receives a prominent mark of the patron on his hand or face, and may attempt a DC 16 Luck check once per month to ask a minor favor from the patron, which manifests in a non-magical manner. Each time such a Luck check is attempted there is a 1% cumulative chance that the patron asks for something in return. In addition, the patron sends followers to aid the subject's natural actions. The followers consist of 1d4+1 warriors, each of level 1d3. All bear the mark of the patron. The warriors serve with absolute loyalty (no morale checks are ever required) and ask for nothing in return save adherence to the principles of the patron. The caster is viewed favorably for bringing more followers to his patron; for every 10 followers recruited and bonded, he receive a +1 bonus to future patron bond and invoke patron checks (max +5 bonus).
28-29	The patron considers the caster indispensable to his long-term goals. The caster learns the spell *invoke patron* as it relates to his patron and may cast it up to three times per day at a +1 bonus to the spell check. The patron also gives the caster a gift (for which a counter-gift is to be expected, of course). The gift is a single patron spell, selected from the patron's spell list. The caster can cast this spell once per day in place of a casting of *invoke patron*. Each time he casts this patron spell or *invoke patron*, the caster is indebted to his patron, who will call in the debt at some point.	The caster forms a bond between his patron and the subject, who is extremely useful to the patron. The patron bestows a minor boon on the caster in the form of a +2 bonus on the next casting of *invoke patron* or a patron spell, and grants a minor boon to the subject in the form of a +1 bonus to his next action in the service of the patron. The subject receives a prominent mark of the patron on his hand or face, and may attempt a Luck check once per month, at a +2 bonus, to ask a *major* favor from the patron, which may manifest in a magical manner. For example, if attempting a ferry crossing without sufficient gold to pay the ferryman, the subject may suddenly find a giant eagle comes to fly him across the river. Each time such a Luck check is attempted there is a 2% cumulative chance that the patron asks for something in return. In addition, the patron sends followers to aid the subject's natural actions. The followers consist of 1d4+1 warriors, each of level 1d3. All bear the mark of the patron. The warriors serve with absolute loyalty (no morale checks are ever required) and ask for nothing in return save adherence to the principles of the patron. The caster is viewed favorably for bringing more followers to his patron; for every 10 followers recruited and bonded, he receives a +1 bonus to future *patron bond* and *invoke patron* checks (max +5 bonus).

	When Cast on Self	When Cast on Other
	Patron Bond (continued)	
	When Cast on Self	**When Cast on Other**
30-31	The caster's patron considers him indispensable to his long-term goals. The caster learns the spell *invoke patron* as it relates to his patron and may cast it up to three times per day at a +2 bonus to the spell check. The patron also gives the caster a gift (for which a counter-gift is to be expected, of course). The gift is a single patron spell, selected from the patron's spell list. The caster can cast this spell once per day in place of a casting of *invoke patron*. Each time he casts this patron spell or *invoke patron*, the caster is indebted to the patron, who will call in the debt at some point.	The caster forms a bond between his patron and the subject, who is indispensable to the patron. The patron bestows a major boon on the caster in the form of a *permanent* +1 bonus on all castings of *invoke patron* and patron spells, and grants a major boon to the subject in the form of a +1 bonus once per day to an action preformed in the service of the patron. The subject receives a prominent mark of the patron on his hand or face, and may attempt a Luck check once per month, at a +3 bonus, to ask a *major* favor from the patron, which may manifest in a magical manner. Each time such a Luck check is attempted there is a 2% cumulative chance that the patron asks for something in return. In addition, the patron sends followers to aid the subject's natural actions. The followers consist of 1d4+1 warriors, each of level 1d3. All bear the mark of the patron. The warriors serve with absolute loyalty (no morale checks are ever required) and ask for nothing in return save adherence to the principles of the patron. The caster is viewed favorably for bringing more followers to his patron; for every 10 followers recruited and bonded, he receives a +1 bonus to future *patron bond* and *invoke patron* checks (max +5 bonus).
32+	The patron considers the caster integral to his long-term goals. The caster learns the spell *invoke patron* as it relates to his patron and may cast it up to four times per day at a +2 bonus to the spell check. The patron also gives the caster a gift (for which a counter-gift is to be expected, of course). The gift is *two* patron spells, selected from the patron's spell list. The caster can cast either of these spells once per day in place of a casting of *invoke patron*. Each time he casts either of these patron spells or *invoke patron*, the caster is indebted to his patron, who will call in the debt at some point.	The caster forms a bond between his patron and the subject, who is indispensable to the patron. The patron bestows a major boon on the caster in the form of a *permanent* +1 bonus on all castings of *invoke patron* and patron spells, and grants a major boon to the subject in the form of a +1 bonus once per day to an action performed in the service of the patron. The subject receives a prominent mark of the patron on his hand or face, and may attempt a Luck check once per month, at a +4 bonus, to ask a *major* favor from the patron, which may manifest in a magical manner. Each time such a Luck check is attempted there is a 2% cumulative chance that the patron asks for something in return. In addition, the patron sends followers to aid the subject's natural actions. The followers consist of 1d4+1 warriors, each of level 1d3. All bear the mark of the patron. They warriors serve with absolute loyalty (no morale checks are ever required) and ask for nothing in return save adherence to the principles of the patron. The caster is viewed favorably for bringing more followers to his patron; for every 10 followers recruited and bonded, he receives a +1 bonus to future *patron bond* and *invoke patron* checks (max +5 bonus).

Read Magic

Level: 1	Range: 5′	Duration: Varies	Casting time: 1 round	Save: None

General	The caster can read magical text, such as magical scrolls, books, and tomes, as well as magical inscriptions on swords, arches, and the like. This allows comprehension but does not activate the spell. The caster can learn the reverse of this spell, called *obfuscate magic*, which renders magical text illegible (even with the aid of this spell).
Manifestation	Roll 1d4: (1) the caster's eyes glow; (2) text glows; (3) letters of text flow into new, legible shapes; (4) none.
Corruption	Roll 1d6: (1-2) minor; (3) caster's skin is inscribed with 1d6 glowing tattoos of mystic runes; (4) caster's eyes take on a yellow film whenever he looks upon the printed word; (5) caster's fingertips are permanently blotted in ink; (6) major.
Misfire	Roll 1d6: (1) caster's mind scrambles letters, preventing him from reading for 1d4 days; (2) caster scrambles visual perception for all allies within 20′, meaning none of them can read for 1d3 hours; (3) caster inadvertently enchants nearest text (probably a book on his person but could be further away), translating it into a magical text that can now only be read via *read magic*; (4) 1d6 printed pages within 100′ are magically distorted such that the letters un-ink, rearrange themselves, and then re-imprint, rendering the page completely unreadable unless the letters are manually resorted; (5) the nearest book is translated into another language entirely (reference Appendix L for ideas; roll d% as wizard); (6) for the next day, every word spoken by the wizard appears visually in front of him as a gust of dark smoke shaped like the appropriate letters, emanating from his mouth.

1	Lost, failure, and worse! Roll 1d6 modified by Luck: (1 or less) corruption; (2+) misfire.
2-11	Lost. Failure.
12-13	The caster can read magic text for 1 round, long enough to read a single sentence or phrase. He retains understanding of this phrase even after the duration ends. Reading a complete spell scroll typically takes 1 turn per spell level, so this is not enough time to read a complete spell.
14-17	The caster can read magic text for 1 turn, long enough to read a level 1 spell. He retains understanding of this phrase even after the duration ends.
18-19	The caster can read magic text for 2 turns, long enough to read a level 2 spell. He retains understanding of this phrase even after the duration ends. The caster can also read basic magic runes and glyphs, enough to decipher the general message of a *runic alphabet* spell or other rune-based inscription.
20-23	The caster can read magic text for 3 turns, long enough to read a level 3 spell. He retains understanding of this phrase even after the duration ends. The caster can also read basic magic runes and glyphs, enough to decipher the general message of a *runic alphabet* spell or other rune-based inscription.
24-27	The caster and one adjacent ally can read magic text for 1 hour. Both caster and ally can also read basic magic runes and glyphs, enough to decipher the general message of a *runic alphabet* spell or other rune-based inscription.
28-29	For a period of 1 day, the caster and all allies within 20′ can read all magic text, all runes and inscriptions, and 1d4 additional mundane written languages, starting with the first unfamiliar language encountered during the duration and ending after 1d4 have been encountered.
30-31	For a period of 1 week, the caster and all allies within 20′ can read all magic text, all runes and inscriptions, and 1d4+2 additional mundane written languages, starting with the first unfamiliar language encountered during the duration and ending after 1d4 have been encountered.
32+	For a period of 1 month, the caster can read *all writing* – whether mundane or magical, runic or alphabetic, inscribed or invisible. If there is text present within line of sight, the caster can read it.

Ropework

Level: 1	Range: 30' or more	Duration: Varies	Casting time: 1 round	Save: None

General

The caster summons a rope from nowhere and commands it to do his bidding. The rope can be used to entangle foes, climb walls, cross ravines, lift friends or enemies, shape itself into writing, or do other amazing things. Unlike other spells, casting *ropework* allows the caster to choose any result at or below the spell check.

Manifestation

Roll 1d4: (1) normal rope appears from thin air; (2) rope drops down from above; (3) rope explodes from the ground like a serpent, then changes to look like rope; (4) multi-colored threads sprout from the ground and coalesce into a rope.

Corruption

Roll 1d4: (1) caster's skin takes on ropy look and feel; (2) caster's arms elongate 1d4+4" and joints soften, giving the limbs a tentacle-like consistency; (3) caster grows a sixth finger on each hand; (4) caster grows a sixth toe on each foot.

Misfire

Roll 1d4: (1) for next 1d4 hours caster repels ropes as if by an invisible force field – ropes always "bounce away" when he approaches, and they slip out of his hand whenever he tries to grab one; (2) rope is summoned to immediately bind the caster securely (DC 15 Agi or Str check to escape, or rope must be cut); (3) caster plus 1d4 nearest allies are all drawn together by magically summoned rope which proceeds to bind them in a complex knot (DC 15 Agi or Str check to escape, or rope must be cut); (4) 1d4 animated ropes appear and begin attacking all nearby creatures! (AC 8, 5 hp each, atk whip +3 melee (dmg 1d3)).

1

Lost, failure, and worse! Roll 1d6 modified by Luck: (0 or less) corruption + patron taint + misfire; (1-2) corruption; (3+) misfire.

2-11

Lost. Failure.

12-13

The caster summons a rope of up to 100' in length from nowhere. The rope remains in existence for 1 turn.

14-17

The caster summons a rope as above. Using an existing rope or the summoned one, he can command the rope to rearrange itself into any shape. This can be a symbol (such as an arrow or square), writing (cursive or block), numbers, or anything else. The rope takes 1d4 rounds to arrange itself, depending on the complexity of the request.

18-19

The caster summons a rope as above. Using an existing rope or the summoned one, he can command the rope to entangle one target. The rope rapidly loops itself around the target, then constricts. The target receives a Reflex save against the spell check DC to escape; otherwise, it is constrained. A constrained target cannot move or take any action other than to talk. Once constrained, the target can attempt on future rounds to escape with a Strength or Agility check (to burst the rope or wiggle free) against the spell check DC.

20-23

The caster summons a rope as above. Using an existing rope or the summoned one, he can command the rope to rise into the air. The rope can rise straight up, at an angle, or hang in the air horizontally. It does not need to be anchored to anything and will support up to 400 pounds of weight without being anchored (anchoring it may allow it to support more weight). The rope can be climbed as normal. The rope remains in this position, magically floating in the air, for up to 1 turn, at which point it drops to the ground.

24-27

The caster summons a rope as above. Using an existing rope or the summoned one, he can command the rope to lift a target into the air. The rope loops itself lightly around the legs and waist of the target (requiring about 5 feet of its total length), then lifts the target to whatever height is indicates, as long as the base of the rope still touches the ground. The rope can lift a target that weighs up to 400 pounds. The target can be lifted straight up or at an angle, at a speed of 50' per round.

28-29

The caster summons a rope as above. Using an existing rope or the summoned one, he can command the rope to entangle a target (as result 18-19 above) or lift it up (as result 24-27 above), and then *also* have the rope drag target at a speed of up to 30' per round. The rope can be commanded to move up to 1 turn as long as one end of it is within 30' of you.

30-31

As any result above, and the spell's range is extended to 300'.

32+

As any result above, and the spell's duration is increased to 1 hour.

Runic Alphabet, Mortal

Level: 1   Range: One inscribed rune   Duration: Until triggered   Casting time: 1 turn

Save: Will save vs. spell check; -1 penalty if the target has an alignment opposed to the caster

General	Wizards learn alphabets of magic symbols, which, when traced, cause incredible things to happen. There are different alphabets: dwarven runes, elder sigils, the hieroglyphs of the sphinxes, and the signs of individual mages. With this spell, the caster can create the simplest runes, those comprehensible to mortals. The caster's alignment is imbued in the rune traced, and a being triggering the rune of an opposing alignment suffers more dire effects. The caster traces the sign using costly rare materials that must be purchased ahead of time for 50 gp per rune. The spell check is made, determining which energies are imbued into the rune; the caster can choose *one* rune at or below the result of the check, with the choice made when the rune is inscribed. The rune can be traced in any object: brooch, book, tombstone, archway, door, floor, tabletop, etc. Subtract -2 from the spell check to trace the rune in mid-air; -4 to trace the rune invisibly; or -8 to trace the rune permanently (does not vanish when triggered). The effect is triggered per the specific sign as described below: when touched, passed, gazed upon, etc. On a failed spell check, the sign fizzles and dissolves, and the materials use to make it are lost. On a success, the spell check becomes the DC for the opposing save. You can identify an unknown rune with a *read magic* spell or a successful *runic alphabet* spell check against the caster's check result.
Manifestation	Inscribed rune
Corruption	Roll 1d4: (1) caster has a non-magical runic shape permanently seared onto one cheek; (2) caster's forehead wrinkles such that it appears to house a third eye, which disappears upon close inspection; (3) minor; (4) major.
Misfire	Roll 1d4: (1) randomly determined rune (roll d10+10 on spell table) is inscribed on the caster's hand, then immediately detonated; (2) rune is traced but it will not activate under any circumstances, effectively providing a costly "tattoo" to the subject marked; (3) caster inadvertently sears a permanent symbol that resembles a silhouette of his face; (4) caster forgets how to read and write for 1d6 turns, during which time he cannot cast this spell or any other that is dependent on literacy.
1	Lost, failure, and worse! Roll 1d6 modified by Luck: (0 or less) corruption + patron taint + misfire; (1-2) corruption; (3) patron taint (or corruption if no patron); (4+) misfire.
2-11	Lost. Failure.
12-13	*Alarm.* A loud alarm sounds when the target object (up to man-sized) is disturbed (no save). Alternately, the alarm can notify the caster mentally and emit no audible noise. The notification has a range of 1 mile.
14-17	*Message.* The rune chants a predetermined message when triggered (no save). The message may be repeated up to three times.
18-19	*Block.* Creatures up to man-sized are unable to pass through or by the target door, window, portal, or inanimate object (Will save resists).
20-23	*Immobility.* Creatures attempting to move the target object (up to man-sized, including aggregated objects such as a pile of coins) cannot lift or move it (Will save resists).
24-27	*Veracity.* Creatures cannot lie or deceive within sight of this rune (Will save resists).
28-29	*Forgetfulness.* Creatures viewing the target object (up to the size of one man per caster level) forget that it exists the moment their attention is removed from it (Will save resists).
30-31	*Sleep.* Creatures viewing the triggering rune fall asleep (Will save resists). The sleep is normal and the target can be awakened through normal means.
32+	*Curse.* The rune delivers a minor curse to the creature that views it (Will save resists). The curse drains 1d3 points of Luck and may have one other irritating secondary effect. (See appendix C for more info.)

Sleep

Level: 1	Range: 60'	Duration: Varies	Casting time: 1 action	Save: Will vs. spell check DC

General	The caster lulls a target into a deep, sound sleep.
Manifestation	Roll 1d4: (1) ray of shimmering dust; (2) swan's wings which rise from the earth to enfold target; (3) soft white clouds that engulf target's head; (4) waves of blue light.
Corruption	Roll 1d6: (1) caster acquires persistent insomnia, which has no immediate obvious effect but manifests as an ongoing penalty to all rolls. as his sleep deprivation increases, starting with -1 and increasing to -2 after a week and -3 after a month; (2) caster emits a noxious odor that causes heads to turn within 20'; (3-4) minor; (5-6) major.
Misfire	Roll 1d4: (1) caster immediately falls into a natural sleep; (2) caster plus 1d4 closest allies immediately fall into a natural sleep; (3) caster collapses into a coma, from which he can only be awakened with medical attention or magical means; (4) caster jolts all creatures within 50' to total alertness, cancelling all sleep (magical or otherwise) as well as all dazes, hallucinations, and other distractions.

1	Lost, failure, and worse! Roll 1d6 modified by Luck: (0 or less) corruption + misfire; (1) corruption; (2+) misfire.
2-11	Lost. Failure.
12-13	One target within range must make its save or fall asleep for 1d6 turns. Target can be awakened through normal means. When casting the spell, the caster must specify an interrupt condition which automatically awakens the target. For example, being kissed by a prince, smelling the fragrance of a rose, or hearing a clock strike midnight. The caster must possess material components related to the interrupt condition.
14-17	Up to two targets within range must save or fall asleep for 1d6 turns. Targets can be awakened through normal means. When casting the spell, the caster must specify an interrupt condition which automatically awakens the target. For example, being kissed by a prince, smelling the fragrance of a rose, or hearing a clock strike midnight. The caster must possess material components related to the interrupt condition.
18-19	Up to three targets within range must save or fall asleep for 1d4 hours. Targets can be awakened through normal means. When casting the spell, the caster must specify an interrupt condition which automatically awakens the target. For example, being kissed by a prince, smelling the fragrance of a rose, or hearing a clock strike midnight. The caster must possess material components related to the interrupt condition.
20-23	Up to four targets must save or fall into a normal sleep for 1d6 hours, or one target can be placed in a supernatural sleep for 1d4 hours. While normal sleep can be interrupted by normal means, the supernatural sleep can be disrupted only via dispel magic or similar cancellation effects. However, both normal and supernatural sleep must have a specified interrupt condition which automatically awakens the target. For example, being kissed by a prince, smelling the fragrance of a rose, or hearing a clock strike midnight. The caster must possess material components related to the interrupt condition.
24-27	Up to eight targets must save or fall into a normal sleep for 1d7 days, or one target can be placed in a supernatural sleep for 1d3 days with no saving throw. While normal sleep can be interrupted by normal means, the

supernatural sleep can be disrupted only via dispel magic or similar cancellation effects. However, both normal and supernatural sleep must have a specified interrupt condition which automatically awakens the target. For example, being kissed by a prince, smelling the fragrance of a rose, or hearing a clock strike midnight. The caster must possess material components related to the interrupt condition.

28-29	With a range of 200', the caster can place a single target into a supernatural, ongoing, endless sleep with no saving throw; or normal ongoing sleep (with a save) to a group of up to 16 targets. While the normal sleep can interrupted by normal means, the supernatural sleep can be interrupted only by one specified interrupt condition (e.g., the kiss of a prince or the fragrance of a rose) or anti-magic effects such as dispel magic.
30-31	The caster puts great crowds of people to sleep. All unfriendly creatures within a 200' radius must make a saving throw or fall asleep. The sleep is natural and the targets can be awakened with normal means (rough shaking, water on the face, etc.). The creatures remain asleep for 1d7+1 days if not awakened.
32+	Natural slumber to all things: the caster causes the world around him to slow and sleep. All creatures within 500 yards fall asleep. Creatures of 4 or fewer HD receive no save. The affected creatures include birds, insects, and small animals as well as people. Both friendly and unfriendly creatures are affected. Plants are also affected; those that close their petals or retract flowers at night behave as if it is nighttime. The effect is supernatural in aspect and cannot be disturbed. The affected world continues to slumber until a specific interrupt condition occurs (e.g., the new moon rises, or 100 years have passed). Only powerful magic can end the effect sooner.

Spider Climb

Level: 1	Range: Self or touch (see below)	Duration: 1 turn per CL	Casting time: 1 action	Save: None

General	The caster gains the spider's ability to climb vertical surfaces.
Manifestation	Roll 1d4: (1) four extra spider-like limbs sprout from the caster's torso; (2) the caster's hands and feet ooze sticky goo; (3) the caster's fingers and toes glow with a strange orange light; (4) the caster grow six additional eyes.
Corruption	Roll 1d6: (1) caster grows four large spider-like limbs from his back; (2) caster can spin small webs like a spider and throw them up to 30' as a sticky goo (ranged attack roll, DC 12 Strength or Agility check for target to escape); (3) caster grows short, spindly hairs across the surface of his skin, much like a spider; (4) caster grows six extra eyes, clustered around his normal eyes, so they resemble a spider's; (5) caster's hands and feet excrete an oily, sticky substance that causes small objects to stick to them; (6) minor.
Misfire	Roll 1d5: (1) caster sticks himself to the floor and cannot move his feet until he makes a DC 16 Strength check; (2) caster makes his appendages magically slippery and has trouble standing straight for the next 1d6 rounds, falling over constantly unless he makes a DC 12 Agility check each round; (3) caster launches a glob of webby fibers at nearest ally, entangling his companion until the ally makes a DC 12 Strength or Agility check to escape; (4) caster summons a horde of poisonous spiders, which arrives one round later and swarm across all nearby creatures, inflicting scores of bites and forcing a DC 8 Fort save by all creatures within 50' with failure indicating a mild poison (1 hp damage plus -1 penalty to all rolls for 1 hour); (5) caster plus 1d4 nearby creatures are flipped upside down in mid-air, with their feet adhering to a point in the air about 8' above ground level, and although they are able to move about as normal in this upside-down station they remain upside down for 1d6 hours.
1	Lost, failure, and worse! Roll 1d6 modified by Luck: (0 or less) corruption + misfire; (1-2) corruption; (3+) misfire.
2-11	Lost. Failure.
12-13	The caster becomes much more skilled at climbing, gaining a +10 bonus to Climb checks as long as his hands and feet are bare. Items weighing less than 5 lbs. stick to the casters hands during this time, making spellcasting impossible for the duration.
14-17	The caster becomes extremely skilled at climbing, gaining a +20 bonus to Climb checks as long as his hands and feet are bare. Items weighing less than 5 lbs. stick to the caster's hands during this time, making spellcasting impossible for the duration.

18-19	The caster gains the actual climbing ability of a spider as long as his hands and feet are bare. He can hang upside down, climb completely vertical surfaces with no handholds, move across spider webs, and even scurry along upside down at obtuse angles. The caster moves at his normal speed and need never make Climb checks. He is immune to *spider web* spells. The caster's hands and feet must remain bare, and items weighing less than 5 lbs. stick to his hands during this time, making spellcasting impossible for the duration.

20-23	The caster gains the actual climbing ability of a spider, even when using gloves and shoes, and when carrying objects in his hands. He can hang upside down, climb completely vertical surfaces with no handholds, move across spider webs, and even scurry along upside down at obtuse angles. The caster moves at his normal speed, need never make Climb checks, and is immune to *spider web* spells.

24-27	The caster and one ally touched gain the actual climbing ability of a spider, even when using gloves and shoes, and when carrying objects in hand. The caster and his ally can hang upside down, climb completely vertical surfaces with no handholds, move across spider webs, and even scurry along upside down at obtuse angles. The caster and his affected ally move at their normal speeds, need never make Climb checks, and are immune to *spider web* spells.

28-29	The caster and all allies within 10' gain the actual climbing ability of a spider, even when using gloves and shoes, and when carrying objects in hand. The caster and affected allies can hang upside down, climb completely vertical surfaces with no handholds, move across spider webs, and even scurry along upside down at obtuse angles. Those affected move at their normal speeds, need never make Climb checks, and are immune to *spider web* spells.

30-31	For a duration of 1 hour per caster level, and the caster and all allies within 10' gain the actual climbing ability of a spider, even when using gloves and shoes, and when carrying objects in hand. The caster and his affected allies can hang upside down, climb completely vertical surfaces with no handholds, move across spider webs, and even scurry along upside down at obtuse angles. Those affected move at their normal speeds, need never make Climb checks, and are immune to *spider web* spells.

32+	For the next day, the caster and all allies within 20' gain all the abilities of a spider. First, those affected can climb as a natural ability, hang upside down, climb vertical surfaces and overhangs, and move on any surface regardless of handholds. Second, the recipients of this spell can launch sticky spider webs that can ensnare enemies. This counts as a ranged attack (at an additional +4 bonus) with a 50' range, and targets are unable to move or take any action until they make a DC 16 Strength or Agility check. Finally, the melee attacks of those benefiting from the spell carry a poison; any wound inflicted also imposes a DC 16 Fort save or the target takes an additional 1d6 damage and loses 1d4 points of Strength.

Ventriloquism

Level: 1   **Range:** 30' or more   **Duration:** 1 round or more   **Casting time:** 1 action   **Save:** Sometimes (Will; see below)

General	The caster projects the sound of his voice from another place, such as an adjacent room, an animal or statue, down a hallway, etc.
Manifestation	Varies with check (see below). Either no visual manifestation *or* roll 1d4: (1) "heat waves" in area of sound; (2) puffs of air and disturbance of dust, as if someone were speaking from that position; (3) sparkling air; (4) echo or reverberation.
Corruption	Roll 1d12: (1-6) caster can still speak normal languages but the sound of his voice permanently changes to resemble that of a (1) horse's neighing, (2) bee's buzzing, (3) goat's braying, (4) pig's oinking, (5) lion's roaring, (6) dog's barking; (7-12) caster's voice is permanently displaced to always emanate from (7) his feet, (8) his left hand, (9) his back (often making him hard to hear), (10) a point 20' above him, (11) the point of whatever weapon he carries, (12) the nearest person of the opposite gender.
Misfire	Roll 1d4: (1) caster creates an enormous booming noise centered on himself, drawing attention to his location; (2) caster scrambles all speech within 100' of himself for the next 1d4+1 hours, causing each person's voice to always issue from another nearby character, creating ongoing confusion about who is speaking; (3) caster changes his voice to that of a high-pitched squeal and throws the source towards his feet, such that all of his conversation for the next 1d4 hours sounds like they are coming from a mouse scurrying around his feet; (4) caster throws his voice onto another plane, to a place he has no knowledge of, so that every time he speaks, no noise issues forth, but a randomly determined demon is annoyed constantly in another place – caster is effectively mute for 1d4 hours and there is a 25% chance the annoyed demon tracks him down to shut him up.

1	Lost, failure, and worse! Roll 1d6 modified by Luck: (0 or less) corruption + misfire; (1-2) corruption; (3+) misfire.
2-11	Lost. Failure.
12-13	The caster projects one short phrase in his own voice to a place within 30' and line of sight. The position of origin is subject to the visual manifestation described above. Listeners that fail a Will save (rolled by judge) believe the noise to originate from the place designated; if they succeed on the save, they hear the voice from its true origin point of the caster's location.
14-17	The caster projects a short phrase to a place within 30' and line of sight. He can use his own voice, or he can simulate another voice or sound that he has previously heard. For example, the caster can make the goblin captain appear to shout "Retreat!" in the goblin's own voice. The position of origin is subject to the visual manifestation described above. Listeners that fail a Will save (rolled by judge) believe the noise to originate from the place designated; if they succeed on the save, they hear the voice from its true origin point of the caster's location.

18-19	The caster projects a short phrase to a place within 30' and line of sight. He can use his own voice, or he can simulate another voice or sound that he has previously heard. For example, the caster can make the goblin captain appear to shout "Retreat!" in the goblin's own voice. There is no visual manifestation, only the sound created. Listeners that fail a Will save (rolled by judge) believe the noise to originate from the place designated; if they succeed on the save, they hear the voice from its true origin point of the caster's location.
20-23	The caster projects a short phrase to a place within 30' and line of sight. He can use his own voice, or he can simulate another voice or sound that he has previously heard. For example, the caster can make the goblin captain appear to shout "Retreat!" in the goblin's own voice. There is no visual manifestation, and listeners receive no save; they automatically hear the noise from the point designated.
24-27	The caster projects sounds to a place within 60', even if it is beyond his line of sight. He can issue ongoing sounds for up to 1 turn as long as he concentrates. The caster can use his own voice, or he can simulate other voices or sounds he has previously heard. For example, he can simulate different voices in an ongoing conversation. There is no visual manifestation, and listeners receive no save; they automatically hear the noise from the point designated.
28-29	The caster projects sounds to a range of up to 300', even beyond his line of sight For every full turn the caster concentrates, he can create an ongoing effect that lasts 1 hour, for a maximum duration of 24 hours. For example, he could concentrate for 3 turns and then leave an ongoing sound effect that lasts for 3 hours. Once the caster stops concentrating, the ongoing effect is "prerecorded"; i.e., the ongoing spell simulates the sounds requested (running water, stamping hooves, ongoing conversation, crackling fire, etc.), but the caster cannot change those sounds. The sounds created can be any the caster imagines, though ensuring accuracy requires him to have some reference point or have heard the sound before. Listeners do not receive a save.
30-31	The caster projects sounds to a range of up to 1 mile, even beyond his line of sight. In addition, he can hear what is happening at the point where he throws his voice. For every full turn the caster concentrates, he can create an ongoing sound effect that lasts 1 day, for a maximum duration of 30 days. For example, he could concentrate for 3 turns and then leave an ongoing sound effect that lasts for 3 days (running water, stamping hooves, ongoing conversation, crackling fire, etc.). Once the caster stops concentrating, the ongoing effect continues, and he need only concentrate for one round to hear what is happening at the point of origin or change the running soundtrack should he so choose. The sounds created can be any the caster imagines, though ensuring accuracy requires him to have some reference point or have heard the sound before. Listeners do not receive a save.
32+	The caster can create nearly unlimited sound effects at will. He can create the sounds of massive thunderstorms, the crashing of waves on a cliff, the charge of a regiment of mounted knights, or the shouts of a thousand orcs. The sounds are true three-dimensional sounds; i.e., they surround the listeners and come from the appropriate directions not simply from a single origin point. The caster can extend these sound effects to a convincing range of 1 mile from the spell's target location, and that location can be anywhere that the caster has either personally visited (including other planes and dimensions) or currently has visibility to, even if that visibility is through scrying or a crystal ball. The caster can also hear all sounds from the target point as if he was standing there. Once he has cast the spell, the sound effect continues without concentration for up to 1 year or until the caster bids them cease. At any point, the caster can concentrate for one round to change the ongoing sound effect or hear what goes on at that place.

Ward Portal

Level: 1	Range: 10′	Duration: Varies	Casting time: 1 action	Save: None

General	The caster magically wards a portal against passage. Any door, trap door, gate, portcullis, grate, or other such portal can be affected.
Manifestation	Roll 1d6: (1) sigil engraved upon portal; (2) portal clouded by unnatural shadow; (3) portal turns to stone/iron/steel/rock; (4) magic circle encloses portal; (5) mass of chains and ropes binds portal; (6) no visible effect.
Corruption	Roll 1d6: (1-3) minor; (4-5) major; (6) greater.
Misfire	Roll 1d4: (1) for next 1d6 hours, any door the caster approaches automatically slams shut and locks; (2) all doors within 100′ slam shut and lock; (3) all doors within 100′ automatically unlock and open; (4) 1d4 illusory doors appear on wall beside nearest door.

1	Lost, failure, and worse! Roll 1d6 modified by Luck: (0 or less) corruption + patron taint + misfire; (1-2) corruption; (3+) misfire.
2-11	Lost. Failure.
12-13	Portal is stuck fast but can still be opened by mortal means with immense effort (DC 20 Strength check).
14-17	Portal is held in place for 2d6x10 minutes. It cannot be opened by mortal means, though a *knock* spell or powerful magical creature can open it.
18-19	Portal is held in place for 2d6 x 10 hours. It cannot be opened by mortal means, though a *knock* spell or powerful magical creature can open it.
20-23	Portal completely disappears, leaving in its place only a blank space of wall for 2d6 x10 hours. During this time, no passage is possible via normal means. Portal can be detected with a *detect invisibility* spell; if detected, it is treated as locked, and cannot be opened by mortal means except through a *knock* spell or similar powerful magic. When the portal re-appears, it remains locked for another 1d4 x10 hours.
24-27	Portal completely disappears, leaving in its place only a blank space of wall for 2d6 x10 *days*. During this time, no passage is possible via normal means. Portal can be detected with a *detect invisibility* spell; if detected, it is treated as locked, and cannot be opened by mortal means except through a *knock* spell or similar powerful magic. When the portal re-appears, it remains locked for another 2d6 x10 weeks. Additionally, any creature that opens the portal during the time of the ongoing effect (through magical means, of course) is subject to a curse: Will save or -2 Luck.
28-29	Portal completely disappears, leaving in its place only a blank space of wall for 4d6 x10 days. During this time, no passage is possible via normal means. Portal can be detected with a *detect invisibility* spell; if detected, it is treated as locked, and cannot be opened by mortal means except through a *knock* spell or similar powerful magic. When the portal re-appears, it remains locked for another 4d6 x10 weeks. Additionally, any creature that opens the portal during the time of the ongoing effect (through magical means, of course) is subject to a curse: Will save or -2 Luck.
30-31	Portal completely disappears, leaving in its place only a blank space of wall for 4d6 x10 days. The portal will reappear and unlock by the mental command of the caster. Otherwise, during this time, no passage is possible via normal means. Portal can be detected with a *detect invisibility* spell; if detected, it is treated as locked, and cannot be opened by mortal means except through a *knock* spell or similar powerful magic. When the portal re-appears, it remains locked for another 4d6 x10 weeks.
	Additionally, any creature that opens the portal during the time of the ongoing effect (through magical means, of course) is subject to a curse: Will save or -2 Luck.
	Finally, a guardian is summoned. Any creature that attempts to open the door is attacked by something that lashes out from the door with: (roll 1d4) (1) tentacles, (2) fangs, (3) claws, (4) barbed tail. The attacking appendage has the following statistics: Atk +6, 1d6 dmg, AC 16, 20 hp.

Portal completely disappears, leaving in its place only a blank space of wall. This is an ongoing permanent effect. The portal will reappear and unlock by the mental command of the caster, but until then, no passage is possible via normal means. Portal can be detected with a *detect invisibility* spell; if detected, it is treated as locked, and cannot be opened by mortal means except through a *knock* spell or similar powerful magic. Any creature that forces open the portal against the caster's intent is subject to a curse: Will save or -2 Luck.

Finally, a guardian is summoned. Any creature that attempts to open the door is attacked by something that lashes out from the door with: (roll 1d4) (1) tentacles, (2) fangs, (3) claws, (4) barbed tail. The attacking appendage has the following statistics: Atk +12, 2d6 dmg, AC 18, 40 hp.

LEVEL 2 WIZARD SPELLS

Arcane Affinity

Level: 2	Range: Varies	Duration: Varies	Casting time: Varies	Save: N/A

General   Some wizards choose to specialize in a particular kind of magic. They may be necromancers who study the lore of un-dead or pyromancers who control fire. They may be elementalists who can control free-willed elementals or summoners who bring material objects into existence from nowhere. These specialist mages go beyond the capabilities of normal magic-users by studying, pondering, and ultimately completely connecting to the school of arcane magic they choose. A necromancer may live with un-dead creatures to fully understand them. A pyromancer may dwell in a volcano. An elementalist may live on one of the four elemental planes, and a conjurer may study the atomic building blocks of matter.

This spell is the mechanism by which specialty magic happens. This spell forms an affinity between the caster and one kind of magic. This affinity comes after much time and labor is expended and has a cost: the spell slot is forever occupied by this very spell, and the caster is forever connected to the arcane element he chooses. However, this spell also has a benefit: it makes the caster more powerful in a specific school of magic.

Although this spell is listed in the caster's spellbook as the spell *arcane affinity*, it is really a different spell depending on each caster's goal. It truly represents the time and effort necessary to develop an affinity for a particular school of magic. The "casting time" is a set of rituals and actions necessary to form the affinity. This is a level 2 spell because a caster must understand the basic principles of magic before he can build an affinity. Traditional affinities and their "casting time" are as follows. Note the "casting time" can, in game terms, be considered to overlap with adventuring time or be a lull between adventures.

- **Illusionist:** A specialist in spells that alter perceptions or create false images and sounds. An illusionist must spend at least one year understanding how the human body processes sensory input and how it can be fooled.

- **Summoner:** A specialist in spells that summon animals, monsters, and other creatures to aid the caster, including elementals and demons. A summoner may further specialize in a particular kind of creatures summoned (e.g., elementals). Summoners may also specialize in summoning objects as well as creatures. A summoner must spend at least one year studying the creatures he wants to summon, both in captivity and in their natural surroundings.

- **Necromancer:** A specialist in the un-dead, their creation, their control, and their limits. A necromancer may ultimately pursue eternal life via his own transformation into an un-dead. A necromancer must spend at least one year in the presence of un-dead.

- **Transmuter:** A specialist in changing matter from one form to another, whether it be flesh to stone, iron to gold, or something in between. A transmuter must spend at least one year in a laboratory studying the properties of different materials.

- **Pyromancer:** A specialist in the study of fire. Pyromancers must spend at least one year in the presence of great flames, such as an active volcano or on the plane of fire. Pyromancers ultimately learn to create, control, and destroy flames at will. There are other specialists who study similar magical powers but control other elements; e.g., fulminators who study electricity, cryomancers who study cold, and aerialists who study air.

- **Demonologist:** A specialist in the summoning, control, exorcism, destruction, and lore of demons. This is a dangerous specialty, for demons are never willing to divulge the information necessary to control them. A demonologist must spend at least *three* years studying ancient tomes, consulting supernatural spirits, and traveling to distant planes to learn what he needs to control demons.

After a specialist has committed the necessary "casting time" to specialize in one field, a spell check is made. The spell check determines the benefit of specialization, as noted below. Many specialists utilize spellburn at this point to ensure a good result. Some specialists may attempt ritualized versions of this spell by casting it in a place of power, in concert with other mages, or with an appropriate sacrifice. The ritual rules at the beginning of this chapter, combined with the judge's discretion, determine the nature of the ritual.

The caster may choose to specialize in more than one field, provided he obeys the dictates given here and in the spell results. Because specialization typically results in improved spellcasting in certain spells and reduced spellcasting in others, a wizard with multiple specialties may find they begin to offset each other.

Manifestation	N/A
Corruption	Roll 1d4 according to specialty: **Illusionist:** (1) at every full moon, caster's face assumes the appearance of a randomly determined other humanoid; (2) all illusions created by the caster have an appearance of sadness or failure, and he is unable to create scenes of joy or happiness; (3) caster's form assumes an illusory appearance any time *any* die roll comes up on a natural 13 (roll % on the wizard table in Appendix L to randomly determine the nature of the illusion, treating the language as corresponding to its normal creature type; i.e., a result of "eagle" means the caster resembles an eagle); (4) each morning, roll 1d7, and on a 7, random illusions flicker into existence around the caster all day long, potentially ruining business deals and terrifying peasants around him; **Summoner/elementalist:** (1) caster inadvertently summons an aggravated mundane animal (or, if an elementalist, an elemental) any time *any* die roll comes up on a natural 13, such that the animal appears somewhere within 50' and immediately attacks the nearest creature out of confusion or rage; (2) the caster's appearance takes on traits of the last creature he summoned before casting this spell; (3) the caster always annoys his summoned creatures through some difficult-to-identify aspect of his spellcasting, so his summoned creatures are *always* hostile when they appear; (4) the caster himself is summoned to do the bidding of a greater power and disappears for 1d7 days; he reappears ragged and exhausted with 1d4 randomly determined diseases; **Necromancer:** (1) caster's head takes on the aspects of a skull: all fat disappears, skin pulls tight, nose pulls back to slits, hair falls out in tattered clumps, ears rot; (2) caster's eyes turn pitch-black; (3) caster stinks of the grave; (4) caster's flesh putrefies and melts, giving him a horrible appearance; **Transmuter:** (1) forevermore, any gold touched by the caster turns to iron; (2) whenever the player rolls a 13 on *any* dice roll, all metals within 20' change into another randomly determined metal, always of lesser value, such that treasure is always downgraded one notch (gold -> silver, silver -> copper, etc.) and weapons become less effective, giving them a -1 damage penalty as they become softer; (3) the caster's face is transmuted into a randomly determined metal, giving him a strange unearthly appearance; (4) the caster's left hand is changed into wood; **Pyromancer/fulminator/cryomancer/aerialist:** (1) caster's eyes change to resemble the appropriate substance (i.e., fire, electricity, ice, or air); (2) caster radiates aura of heat, static electricity, cold, or wind, as the case may be, which all creatures within 20' can't help but notice; (3) caster spontaneously summons painful burst of appropriate energy type (flame, electricity, cold, or sharp wind) on *any* die roll that comes up a natural 13, inflicting 1 point of damage to himself and one randomly determined creature within 20'; (4) caster's face permanently changes to appear as if he had excessive exposure to the appropriate element; **Demonologist:** (1) caster's face takes on demonic appearance, with pointed teeth, jagged eyebrows, and snake-like pupils; (2) caster's tongue is slit like a snake's; (3) caster gains cloven hooves in place of his feet; (4) caster's true name is learned by a demon, and each day there is a 1% chance the demon will use it to force him to perform some nefarious deed.

Misfire	N/A

1	The affinity fails *and* the caster automatically suffers corruption. The caster does not gain any particular insight or knowledge from his study and expenditure of arcane energy. The caster may not attempt another spell check without expending half again as much time in study (e.g., if he spent one year getting to this point, he must now spend another six months).
2-13	The affinity fails. The caster does not gain any particular insight or knowledge from his study and expenditure of arcane energy. The caster may not attempt another spell check without expending half again as much time in study (e.g., if he spent one year getting to this point, he must now spend another six months).
14-15	The caster establishes a nominal affinity with the school of magic he is studying. He may select *one* spell he already knows, which must be thematically associated with the school of magic. (For example, a pyromancer may select *fireball*.) Forevermore, the caster casts that spell with an improved die on his spell checks, based on the dice chain. However, the caster's great devotion means he was unable to practice other magics to the same extent as those in his chosen school. The caster must select one other spell he knows, which cannot be *arcane affinity*. Spell checks on the affected spell are automatically *reduced* by one die on the dice chain.
16-19	The caster establishes a strong affinity with the school of magic he studies. He may select *two* spells he already knows, which must be thematically associated with the school of magic. (For example, a pyromancer may select *fireball* and *fire resistance*.) Forevermore, the caster casts those spells with an improved die on his spell checks, based on the dice chain. However, the caster's great devotion means he was unable to practice other magics to the same extent as those in his chosen school. The caster must select one other spell he knows, which cannot be *arcane affinity*. Spell checks on the affected spell are automatically *reduced* by one die on the dice chain.
20-21	The caster establishes a powerful affinity with the school of magic he studies. He may learn one new spell from that school of magic that he did not know before. This spell is a bonus spell and does not count toward his normal spell slots. It is cast with a normal d20 spell check die. For example, a pyromancer who knows *fireball* and *fire resistance*, but not *scorching ray*, may select *scorching ray* as his spell. However, his knowledge of this spell comes at great cost. The caster permanently loses 1 hit point to reflect the physical duress required to expand his grasp of magic.
22-25	The caster gains a true understanding of the school of magic he studies. He may learn one new spell from that school of magic that he did not know before at the cost of 1 hit point, as result 20-21 above. Additionally, he may select *two* spells that he already knows and increase his spell check die at the cost of reducing the die on one other spell check result, as result 16-19 above.
26-29	The caster is a master of his specialty. He may select *three* spells thematically associated with the school of magic, which he forevermore casts at a higher spell check die (as result 16-19 above). If he so chooses, he may "hold" his selection of one, two, or all of these spells until he levels up. At any point in the future, when he gains a level, he may assign the higher spell check die to one spell he now knows. Once assigned, the spell check die cannot be changed, but the caster can "hold" his selection indefinitely. The caster must select *two* other spells he knows, neither of which can be *arcane affinity*, which are automatically *reduced* in spell check die by one progression (typically from 1d20 to 1d16). Finally, the caster permanently loses 1 hit point to reflect the physical strain of this process.
30+	The caster is a grand master of his specialty. He may select *three* spells to cast at a higher spell check die, as 26-29 above, but at a cost of only *one* other spell at a lower die. Additionally, he receives one free spell slot associated with his specialty at a cost of 1 hit point, as result 22-25 above.

"My henchmen have been so much more loyal since I turned them all into zombies."

Detect Invisible

Level: 2	Range: 60' or more	Duration: Varies	Casting time: 1 action	Save: Will vs. spell check DC (sometimes)

General — The caster activates an inner sight to see the true nature of things. In doing so, he is able to see invisible creatures and objects. If the target creature or object is protected by an invisibility shield (per the *invisibility* spell), the caster's spell check counts as the DC for the target's Will save.

Manifestation — Roll 1d3: (1) caster's eyes disappear, leaving only empty orbs; (2) caster's eyes turn black; (3) caster shrouded in a dim mist.

Corruption — Roll 1d6: (1-3) minor; (4-5) major; (6) greater.

Misfire — Roll 1d4: (1) caster inadvertently heightens the invisible effects of those around him, such that all invisible creatures automatically have the duration of their invisibility doubled; (2) caster causes his head to become invisible for 1d4 hours; (3) caster's shadow quadruples for 1d4 days, such that he always cast a total of 4 shadows in different directions, regardless of light sources, and they occasionally move independently, causing terror and panic among nearby peasants; (4) caster causes one randomly determined creature within 20' to become invisible for 1d4 rounds.

1 — Lost, failure, and worse! Roll 1d6 modified by Luck: (0 or less) corruption + patron taint + misfire; (1-2) corruption; (3) patron taint; (4+) misfire.

2-11 — Lost. Failure.

12-13 — Failure, but spell is not lost.

14-15 — For a brief moment, the caster can see all invisible inanimate objects within 60'. Unless protected by a powerful invisibility shield (per the *invisibility* spell), these objects flicker into sight then immediately disappear again, leaving the caster with an impression of their location. The caster cannot see invisible creatures.

16-19 — Until the end of the next round, the caster can see all invisible objects and creatures within 60'.

20-21 — For the next turn, the caster can see all invisible objects and creatures within 60'.

22-25 — For the next turn, the caster can see all invisible objects and creatures within 60'. Additionally, one ally touched is also able to see invisible things as the caster, as long as he maintains physical contact with the ally. The ally can change round-to-round if the caster touches a different person.

26-29 — For the next turn, the caster can see all invisible objects and creatures within 200'. Additionally, one ally touched is also able to see invisible things as the caster, as long as he maintains physical contact with the ally. The ally can change round-to-round if the caster touches a different person.

30-31 — For the next hour, the caster and all allies within 10' can see all invisible objects and creatures within 200'.

32-33 — For the next hour, the caster and all allies within 10' can see all invisible objects and creatures within 200'. Additionally, the caster can dispel invisibility. If the caster concentrates for one round on an invisible object or creature, it must make a Will save against his spell check DC. If the Will save fails, the target's invisibility is temporarily suppressed. The power is lost for one round per missed point of the check. For example, if the DC was 32 and the creature's Will save was 24, it would be visible for 8 rounds. This applies to creatures with native invisibility as well as spellcasters.

34+ — With a powerful burst of radiant light, the caster suppresses the invisible nature of all invisible creatures and things within his line of sight. All objects, and creatures of 3 or less HD, are automatically made visible for a period of one hour. Additionally, they must make a Will save or become *permanently* visible. Creatures of 4+ HD receive a Will save to resist the spell; failure means they also become visible for one hour. Visible creatures can be seen by *all* creatures. Note this effect includes friendly creatures who are invisible, as well as enemies. Finally, the caster (and only the caster) can see all secret doors, concealed compartments, hidden latches, and other such things. This ability lasts for the next hour.

ESP

Level: 2   Range: 100' or more   Duration: 1 round or more   Casting time: 1 round   Save: Will vs. spell check DC

General
The caster can detect the thoughts of other creatures. Lower check results allow the caster to read only surface-level thoughts. With higher check results the caster can concentrate and read deeper levels of thought with each round of continuous concentration, as follows. Detecting the answer to a specific question within the scope of the thoughts described below generally takes 1d4 rounds once the appropriate round of concentration is reached. For example, finding out where an evil necromancer hid his magic ring takes 1d4 rounds after the 4th round of concentration (recent memories), and understanding why the necromancer bears an irrational hatred toward the king takes 1d4 rounds after the 6th round of concentration (subconscious motivations).

Round 2: The caster understands any long-range goals and motivations associated with the creature's current thoughts and actions.

Round 3: The caster understands the creature's relationships with its friends and enemies.

Round 4: The caster can read the creature's recent memories. It still takes time to sort through all the thoughts – roughly one round for every day of memories.

Round 5: The caster can read the creature's historical memories – as far back as it can remember.

Round 6: The caster understands the creature's subconscious thoughts – motivations and underlying behaviors that it may not even be aware of.

Certain higher check results allow the caster to switch targets. Switching to a new target triggers a new Will save for the new target, and resets the "round counter" for purposes of reading deep thoughts. For example, if the caster concentrated for three rounds on one target, then switched to a second, then switched back to the first, it would be as if he was starting back at one round of concentration.

Manifestation
Roll 1d5: (1) nothing visible; (2) caster's head glows; (3) caster's eyes turn misty; (4) shimmering waves emanate from caster's skull; (5) flashes of light jump from caster periodically.

Corruption
Roll 1d8: (1) caster's skull expands grotesquely as his brain doubles in size; (2) caster's eyes turn permanently clouded; (3) caster's thoughts are visible (literally) as waves of shimmering light that radiate outward from his skull, expanding in frequency to torchlight-equivalent when he is deep in thought and fading to a slow pulse at night; (4) caster goes completely bald; (5-6) minor; (7-8) major.

Misfire
Roll 1d4: (1) caster accidentally broadcasts his thoughts to all creatures within 30', which suddenly know his mood and deepest opinions of them; (2) caster touches the darkest, most savage portion of the nearest animal mind, causing him to recoil in pain and suffer a -1 penalty to all rolls for 1d4 rounds as he recovers from the shock; (3) caster sends a burst of concentrated thoughts at 1d4 randomly determined creatures within 100', each of whom suffers 1 hp of damage as the psychic blast causes a mind-splitting headache; (4) one creature about whom the caster has a deeply guarded secret learns about that secret as he accidentally transmits thoughts instead of receiving them (e.g., a secret love, an ally he plans to double-cross, someone to whom he owes a debt he doesn't plan to pay, etc.).

1
Lost, failure, and worse! Roll 1d6 modified by Luck: (0 or less) corruption + patron taint + misfire; (1-2) corruption; (3) patron taint; (4+) misfire.

2-11
Lost. Failure.

12-13
Failure, but spell is not lost.

14-15
By concentrating for a full round, the caster can read the thoughts of one creature he can see within 100'. The creature receives a Will save and is aware of an attempt to read its thoughts (though it may not know the caster is the one attempting the action). If the caster is successful, he detects surface-level thoughts: the creature's emotional state, any actions it is intent upon, and so on. After the first round of concentration, the spell energy dissipates.

16-19
By concentrating for a full round, the caster can read the thoughts of one creature he can see within 100'. The creature receives a Will save, and is aware of an attempt to read its thoughts (though it may not know

the caster is the one attempting the action). If the caster is successful, he detects surface-level thoughts: the creature's emotional state, any actions it is intent upon, and so on. By continuing to concentrate, the caster can continue to read the surface thoughts of the target, as noted in the general spell description. If the caster stops concentrating, the spell ends.

20-21   By concentrating for a full round, the caster can read the thoughts of one creature he can see within 100'. The creature receives a Will save and is aware of an attempt to read its thoughts (though it may not know the caster is the one attempting the action). If the caster is successful, he detects surface-level thoughts: the creature's emotional state, any actions it is intent upon, and so on. By continuing to concentrate, the caster can continue to read the surface thoughts of the target, as noted in the general spell description. If the caster stops concentrating, the spell ends.

22-25   By concentrating for a full round, the caster can read the thoughts of one creature he can see within 100'. In addition, the caster can switch targets each new round, as long as he continues concentrating. Any target (whether the first or a later one) receives a Will save and is aware of an attempt to read its thoughts (though it may not know the caster is the one attempting the action). If the caster is successful, he detects surface-level thoughts: the creature's emotional state, any actions it is intent upon, and so on. By continuing to concentrate, the caster can continue to read the surface thoughts of the target, as noted in the general spell description. If the caster stops concentrating, the spell ends.

26-29   By concentrating for a full round, the caster can read the thoughts of one creature. If the caster has a physical memento associated with a specific target (a hair clipping, fingernail, favorite sword, drop of blood, etc.), he can detect its thoughts at a distance of up to one mile, without needing line of sight. Without a physical memento, the caster can attempt ESP on a target within line of sight at a distance of up to 1,000'. Viewing a target through a scrying device, such as a crystal ball, counts as line of sight. In addition, the caster can switch targets each new round, as long as he continue concentrating.

Any target (whether the first or a later one) receives a Will save and is aware of an attempt to read its thoughts (though it may not know the caster is the one attempting the action). If the caster is successful, he detects surface-level thoughts: the creature's emotional state, any actions it is intent upon, and so on. By continuing to concentrate, the caster can continue to read the surface thoughts of the target, as noted in the general spell description. If the caster stops concentrating, the spell ends.

30-31   By concentrating for a full round, the caster can read the thoughts of one creature. If the caster has a physical memento associated with a specific target (a hair clipping, fingernail, favorite sword, drop of blood, etc.), he can detect its thoughts at a distance of up to 100 miles, without needing line of sight. Without a physical memento, the caster can attempt ESP on a target within line of sight at a distance of up to 1 mile. Viewing a target through a scrying device, such as a crystal ball, counts as line of sight. In addition, the caster can switch targets each new round, as long as he continues concentrating.

Targets of 2 HD or less do not receive a save. Targets of 3+ HD receive a save but *are not aware of the attempt to read their minds*, even if they make the save. The judge should roll the save for these targets. If the caster is successful, he detects surface-level thoughts: the creature's emotional state, any actions it is intent upon, and so on. By continuing to concentrate the caster can continue to read the surface thoughts of the target, as noted in the general spell description. If the caster stops concentrating, the spell ends.

32-33   The caster can detect the thoughts of multiple creatures. For a period of one day, he gains awareness of the swirling morass of all thoughts within 100 miles of his position. Much like the background noise of a forest, the caster can "hear" all thoughts.

By concentrating, he can narrow the focus onto one creature. If the caster has line of sight, he can focus directly on that creature's thoughts; if the caster has a physical memento (a hair clipping or drop of blood), he can focus directly on that creature (even if not in his line of sight); and if the caster knows a creature personally and it is within range, he can focus on that creature. All other thoughts remain clouded and indistinct, much like a distant murmur.

When the caster has designated a specific creature, it receives no save if it is 2 HD or less and a Will save if 3 HD or more, but *it is not aware of the attempt to read its mind* even if it makes the save (the judge should roll). The judge should roll the save for these targets. If the caster is successful, he detects surface-level thoughts: the creature's emotional state, any actions it is intent upon, and so on. By continuing to concentrate the caster can continue to read the surface thoughts of the target, as noted in the general spell description. If the caster stops concentrating, the spell continues until the end of the day, and he need only focus on another target to resume reading minds.

34+ For a period of one month, the caster can detect the thoughts of multiple creatures. For a period of one day, he gains awareness of the swirling morass of all thoughts within 100 miles of his position. Much like the background noise of a forest, the caster can "hear" all thoughts.

By concentrating, the caster can narrow the focus onto one creature. If he has line of sight, he can focus directly on that creature's thoughts; if the caster has a physical memento (a hair clipping or drop of blood), he can focus directly on that creature (even if not in his line of sight); and if the caster knows a creature personally and it is within range, he can focus on that creature.

All other thoughts remain clouded and indistinct, much like a distant murmur, but the caster can choose to narrow the focus steadily. With a round of concentration, the caster can narrow the thoughts he hears to one category of creatures (for example, "all men" or "all warriors" or "all dwarves"). The caster can then continue to narrow the categories with subsequent rounds of concentration; each time he is aware of how many creatures remain part of the "murmur" and what general category of creature to which they belong. When there are only a dozen or so creatures left, the caster can sift through individuals, and choose to focus on one, even if it is unfamiliar to him.

When the caster has designated a specific creature, it receives no save if it is 3 HD or less and a Will save if 4 HD or more, but *it is not aware of the attempt to read its mind* even if it makes the save (the judge should roll). The judge should roll the save for these targets. If the caster is successful, he detects surface-level thoughts: the creature's emotional state, any actions it is intent upon, and so on. By continuing to concentrate, the caster can continue to read the surface thoughts of the target, as noted in the general spell description. If the caster stops concentrating, the spell continues until the end of the month duration, and he need only focus on another target to resume reading minds.

If the caster chooses, he can "anchor" his thoughts to those of a single target. This requires seven sequential rounds of concentration, and the target receives a second Will save after the seventh round. It is aware of this attempt and perceives that someone is trying to read its thoughts. If the target fails the save and the caster successfully anchors his thoughts, he remains aware of that target's ongoing thought processes at all times. The caster effectively maintains an ongoing link to read the target's mind. This link lasts until the end of the spell's duration. However, while anchored to one target in this manner, the spell blocks out other background thoughts and the caster cannot hear the "overall murmur" of other thoughts around him.

Fire Resistance

Level: 2   Range: Self or more   Duration: 1 turn or more   Casting time: 1 round   Save: N/A

General	The caster increases his resistance to heat and fire.
Manifestation	Roll 1d4: (1) caster's skin turns hard and black, like lava; (2) subject turns watery like an elemental; (3) shimmering white force globe envelops subject; (4) evanescent angels fan back flames.
Corruption	Roll 1d8: (1) caster's face takes on a burned, distorted look as if he had been caught in a terrible fire; (2) caster's eyebrows are scorched off; (3) caster's fingernails turn black; (4) caster's skin takes on a permanent sunburned hue; (5-6) minor; (7) major; (8) greater.
Misfire	Roll 1d4: (1) caster causes a fire to erupt on his person, as his clothing, scrolls, or other possessions suddenly catch fire, dealing 1d4 damage before sputtering out; (2) caster makes himself more vulnerable to fire; he receives a -2 save penalty against fire-based effects and suffers an additional point of damage from fire for the next 1d4 hours; (3) caster creates a wave of cold that passes instantaneously but not before deep-freezing all liquids on his person (including potions); (4) caster lights a fire at the feet of one randomly determined person within 50', inflicting 1d4 damage.
1	Lost, failure, and worse! Roll 1d6 modified by Luck: (0 or less) corruption + patron taint + misfire; (1-3) corruption; (4) patron taint; (5+) misfire.
2-11	Lost. Failure.
12-13	Failure, but spell is not lost.
14-15	The caster gains limited resistance to fire. For the next turn, he ignores 1 hp of fire damage each round.
16-19	For the next turn, the caster ignores up to 2 hp of fire damage each round. Additionally, the caster gains a +2 bonus to all saving throws to resist fire (include saves to resist fire- or heat-based spells).
20-21	For the next turn, the caster ignores up to 5 hp of fire damage each round. Additionally, the caster gains a +4 bonus to all saving throws to resist fire (include saves to resist fire- or heat-based spells). Finally, the caster and objects on his person cannot catch fire. Although intense heat and flames may still harm him and scorch his possessions, they will not ignite.
22-25	For the next turn, the caster ignores up to 10 hp of fire damage each round, and allies within 10' also resist up to 5 hp of fire damage each round. Additionally, the caster gains a +4 bonus to all saving throws to resist fire (include saves to resist fire- or heat-based spells). Finally, the caster and objects on his person cannot catch fire. Although intense heat and flames may still harm him and scorch his possessions, they will not ignite.
26-29	The caster creates a shield of fire resistance around himself for one turn. All heat or fire damage within 20' is suppressed: the caster and creatures within 10' ignore a *collective* 30 hp of fire damage each round. As the "heat sink" is absorbed, the caster selects where any overflow damage is directed. For example, if all allies within 20' take 17 hp of fire damage in a round, it is completely absorbed. However, if the next round produces 6 hits for a total of 34 points of fire damage, then 4 points of damage overflow. The caster selects which hits are completely resisted, partially resisted, and which bypass the shield to inflict those 4 points of overflow damage.
30-31	All fires within 30' of the caster are instantaneously extinguished. Additionally, all heat or fire damage within 30' is suppressed for one turn: the caster and creatures within 10' ignore a *collective* 40 hp of fire damage each round. As the "heat sink" is absorbed, the caster selects where any overflow damage is directed. For example, if all allies within 20' take 37 hp of fire damage in a round, it is completely absorbed. However, if the next round produces 9 hits for a total of 54 points of fire damage, then 4 points of damage overflow. The caster selects which hits are completely resisted, partially resisted, and which bypass the shield to inflict those 4 points of overflow damage.
32-33	The caster and all allies within 30' are completely immune to fire and heat for the next turn. The caster takes no damage from fire, lava, magma, fireballs, and so on. The caster cannot be set afire, nor will objects in contact with him ignite.
34+	The caster creates a shimmering bubble of cool, fresh air in which heat and fire cannot survive. The bubble appears like a calm blue cloud that surrounds the caster and extends to a radius of 30' in all directions. Fires that enter the bubble (either via the caster's movement or the fire being launched in his direction) are automatically extinguished. Air and water temperature within the bubble automatically drops to room temperature, regardless of outside influences. Fresh oxygen is constantly replenished in the bubble. The caster and all creatures within the bubble are effectively immune to fire and heat. The bubble lasts for one hour per caster level.

Forget

Level: 2   Range: Touch or more   Duration: 1 round or more   Casting time: 1 round   Save: Will vs. spell check

General	The caster makes a creature forget something.
Manifestation	Roll 1d3: (1) gray-toned fingertip; (2) flaming fingertip; (3) cone of mist.
Corruption	Roll 1d8: (1) caster's facial features "smooth out," becoming extremely generic and difficult to remember; (2) caster has difficulty remembering details, and each day tends to forget several minor details from the day previous, such that in adventures, whenever a detail of prior adventures need to be recalled, there is a 25% chance the character cannot remember it; (3-5) minor; (6-7) major; (8) greater.
Misfire	Roll 1d4: (1) among the spells the caster can still cast today, he forgets how to cast one randomly determined spell for the remainder of the day; (2) caster permanently forgets the last 24 hours of his life; (3) caster forgets his own name and for the next month has the hardest time remembering it, no matter how many times he is reminded; (4) caster accidentally installs his own childhood memories in the minds of all allies within 20', giving them a potentially confusing pastiche of memories and introducing many embarrassing childhood incidents into their awareness (e.g., bedwetting, spankings, first love, etc.).

1	Lost, failure, and worse! Roll 1d6 modified by Luck: (0 or less) corruption + patron taint + misfire; (1-3) corruption; (4) patron taint; (5+) misfire.
2-11	Lost. Failure.
12-13	Failure, but spell is not lost.
14-15	After spending a round casting this spell, the caster must attempt a touch attack on the next round. If he misses, the spell is wasted. If the caster touches a target, it receives a Will save; failure means it loses its memory of the last 1d6 rounds. To the creature, events in this time period never happened. Anything learned or memorized in this time period is also forgotten. This effect automatically disrupts concentration and typically disrupts any ongoing spells or magical rituals. The forgotten memories never return.
16-19	The caster can target one creature within 30'. The target receives a Will save to resist. Failure means it loses its memory of the last 1d6 turns. To the creature, events in this time period never happened. Anything learned or memorized in this time period is also forgotten. This effect automatically disrupts concentration and typically disrupts any ongoing spells or magical rituals. The forgotten memories never return.
20-21	The caster can target *an object* or one creature within 30'. If he targets an object (for example, a doorknob or a sling stone), the spell is triggered when that object next touches a living creature (*any* living creature – including the caster). The latent spell remains active for 1 day.
	Once the spell is triggered, either by direct targeting or via a touched object, the target receives a Will save to resist. Failure means it loses its memory of the last 1d6 hours. To the creature, events in this time period never happened. Anything learned or memorized in this time period is also forgotten. This effect automatically disrupts concentration and typically disrupts any ongoing spells or magical rituals. The forgotten memories never return.
22-25	The caster can target an object or one creature within 100'. If he targets an object (for example, a doorknob or a sling stone), the spell is triggered when that object next touches a living creature (*any* living creature – including the caster). The latent spell remains active for 1 week.
	Once the spell is triggered, either by direct targeting or via a touched object, the target receives a Will save to resist. Failure means it loses its memory of the last 1d7 days. To the creature, events in this time period never happened. Anything learned or memorized in this time period is also forgotten. This effect automatically disrupts concentration and typically disrupts any ongoing spells or magical rituals. The forgotten memories never return.
26-29	The caster can target an object or one creature within 100'. If the caster targets an object (for example, a doorknob or a sling stone), the spell is triggered when that object next touches a living creature (*any* living creature – including the caster). The latent spell remains active for 1 week.
	The spell can have one of two effects. If cast on an object, the spell trigger allows the target a Will save to resist. Failure means it loses its memory of the last 1d4+1 months. To the creature, events in this time

period never happened. Anything learned or memorized in this time period is also forgotten. This effect automatically disrupts concentration and typically disrupts any ongoing spells or magical rituals. The forgotten memories never return.

Alternately, instead of targeting a range of recent memories, the caster can target one specific memory he knows exists within a creature familiar to him. For example, if the target first met the caster two months ago, he can erase all traces of that encounter. If the target learned a new spell six months ago, the caster can make it forget that spell. This memory is lost permanently. When used in combat, this spell can cause an enemy caster to forget a spell he intends to use.

30-31   The caster can create a zone of forgetfulness that extends around him to a range of 40'. Any unfriendly creature entering this zone must make a Will save or potentially lose its recent memories. If the target fails, it immediately forgets why it is there or what it is trying to do. This can potentially cause hostile creatures to become neutral or even friendly. The zone of forgetfulness moves with the caster and lasts for one hour. While the effect is active, the caster can choose to expend all remaining spell energy to end the spell early by targeting one creature within 100' to wipe its memory blank. The affected creature experiences total amnesia, forgetting its name, its origin, and any and all class abilities. It may retain some skills (such as a warrior's attack bonus, based on years of muscle training) but mental talents (such as spellcasting) are lost.

32-33   The caster can create a zone of forgetfulness that extends around him to a range of 100'. Any unfriendly creature entering this zone must make a Will save or potentially lose its recent memories. If the target fails, it immediately forgets why it is there or what it is trying to do. This can potentially cause hostile creatures to become neutral or even friendly. The zone of forgetfulness moves with the caster and lasts for one hour. While the effect is active, the caster can choose to expend all remaining spell energy to end the spell early by targeting one creature within line of sight to wipe its memory blank. Line of sight can include scrying devices and crystal balls. The affected creature experiences total amnesia, forgetting its name, its origin, and any and all class abilities. It may retain some skills (such as a warrior's attack bonus, based on years of muscle training) but mental talents (such as spellcasting) are lost.

34+   The caster can influence the memories of vast groups of people and potentially even change them. By casting this spell, all creatures within 1 mile are caught within the caster's sphere of forgetfulness. Creatures of 1 HD or less are automatically affected, while those of 2+ HD receive a save that is adjudicated by the judge. Creatures that make their save do not have their memories altered, which may leave them feeling crazy when everyone around them remembers something different.

The caster can *change* the *common* memories of affected creatures in up to three important ways, with all minor details altered collectively to support the change. For example, the caster can change memories of what the king's face looks like, or whether last summer was hot, or the number of cows in Old Man Hanson's field.

Additionally, the caster can pick out a total of 10 HD of people within the affected area to affect more substantially. This can be ten characters of 1 HD, or one character of 10 HD, or any combination thereof. These affected creatures receive a second save, and on a failure they experience amnesia to a depth of time defined by the caster: a few weeks, several months, years, or their entire lives.

Invisibility

Level: 2   Range: Self or more   Duration: Varies   Casting time: 1 action   Save: Will vs. spell check DC (sometimes)

General	The caster makes himself invisible. This spell can also render allies invisible and can create an invisibility shield that prevents detection by other spells.
Manifestation	Subject turns invisible.
Corruption	Roll 1d16: (1-6) one portion of caster's body turns permanently invisible: (1) one hand, (2) one arm, (3) ears, (4) torso, (5) eyes, (6) one leg; (7) caster's head becomes permanently and irrevocably visible, such that when he is otherwise turned invisible, his head remains visible and appears like a floating orb with no body; (8-11) when caster turns invisible, his body polymorphs into another shape (visible to creatures that can see invisible): (8) bear, (9) ape-man, (10) wolf-man, (11) horse-man; (12-14) minor corruption; (15) major corruption; (16) greater corruption.
Misfire	Roll 1d4: (1) a wandering ghost that was formerly invisible is suddenly made visible within 15' of caster; (2) one randomly determined enemy within 20' is made invisible for 1 turn (no effect if no nearby enemies); (3) all enemies within 50' are made invisible for 1 turn; (4) for the next day, one randomly determined ally within 50' glows as if suffused in bright sunlight, becoming the target for any animal-minded creature that attacks.
1	Lost, failure, and worse! Roll 1d6 modified by Luck: (0 or less) corruption + patron taint + misfire; (1-3) corruption; (4) patron taint (or corruption if no patron); (5+) misfire.
2-11	Lost. Failure.
12-13	Failure, but spell is not lost.
14-15	The caster turns invisible. He must concentrate to remain invisible and cannot attack or move more than half speed. If the caster performs strenuous exertion, the invisibility dissipates. The spell lasts up to 1 turn or until dispelled.
16-19	The caster turns invisible and remains invisible for up to 1 turn. The spell remains as long as the caster does not attack another creature (either directly or by spellcasting). The caster does not need to concentrate to remain invisible.
20-21	The caster can turn himself invisible for 1 turn, as above, or one other man-sized creature or object he touches. If an object, it remains invisible for the full 1 turn. If a creature, it becomes visible the moment it attacks or at the expiration of the 1-turn duration.
22-25	The caster bestows invisibility on himself and all allies within 10'. Additionally, the caster can render select objects invisible if he concentrates. The zone of invisibility continues to emanate in a 10' radius around the caster as he moves. Allies that move in synch with the caster remain invisible. An attack by the caster or any ally in the zone of invisibility dismisses it. The zone lasts 1 turn.
26-29	The caster creates a zone of invisibility with a 20' radius for 1 turn, as above, or bestows invisibility only on himself for a duration of 1 hour.
30-31	The caster can create a limited invisibility shield. This magical effect counters efforts to see invisibility, and also allows the caster to take aggressive action within it. The invisibility shield renders the caster invisible for 1 turn. During this time, he can perform any action (including an attack) without becoming visible. Additionally, the invisibility shield provides the caster with a Will save against any effect that threatens to reveal him, such as *detect invisible*. The caster can also cast the invisibility shield on an object or an ally touched.
32-33	The caster creates an invisibility shield, as above, that extends in a 10' radius around him for 1 turn. It renders allies invisible, but does not make inanimate objects or enemies disappear. While within the shield, allies (and the caster) can make attacks or other actions without the shield disappearing. Furthermore, the caster and his allies receive a Will save against efforts to make them visible.
34+	As above, except the invisibility shield is a 20' radius and lasts for 1 hour. Furthermore, the caster can "throw" the shield up to 100' after a full round of concentration and then move it by up to 100' per round with continued concentration. For example, the caster could cast the invisibility shield over a distant bridge, so that any allies passing through that spot are invisible, and then move the shield downstream when cavalry charge across.

Invisible Companion

Level: 2	Range: Varies	Duration: Varies	Casting time: 1 turn	Save: N/A

General The caster summons forth an invisible creature to do his bidding. This invisible companion is under the caster's control and undertakes various tasks.

Manifestation N/A – invisible!

Corruption Roll 1d6: (1-3) minor; (4-5) major; (6) corruption.

Misfire Roll 1d4: (1) the caster accidentally turns his nearest ally invisible for 1d6 rounds; (2) the caster accidentally turns his nearest enemy invisible for 1d6 rounds; (3) the caster summons a visible companion which is deformed and horrible to look upon, such that until it is dismissed or 1d6 turns pass, the caster and all who look upon it must make DC 8 Fort saves or spend a round nauseated and vomiting; (4) the caster summons an invisible "companion" which is an obese, flatulent amphibian that will not leave until 1d6 hours have passed and makes constant noises and odors until then.

1 Lost, failure, and worse! Roll 1d6 modified by Luck: (0 or less) corruption + patron taint + misfire; (1-3) corruption; (4) patron taint (or corruption if no patron); (5+) misfire.

2-11 Lost. Failure.

12-13 Failure, but spell is not lost.

14-15 The caster summons an invisible companion who serves for up to 1 turn or until dismissed or killed and provided it is contained within a magic circle that the caster draws. After that turn, or when the circle is broken, the companion departs. The companion moves within the circle at 30', is considered to have ability scores of 12, can carry the same amount of gear as a strong man, and can perform any action a normal man could perform. It listens but never speaks. It has AC 16, 1d8 hp, and all attacks against it have a 50% chance of missing due to its invisibility. It can wield weapons at a +1 attack bonus. It is, of course, invisible, but does leave footprints or handprints depending on the activities directed by the caster.

16-19 The caster summons an invisible companion who serves for up to 1d6 turns or until dismissed or killed. No magic circle is required. It can venture up to 100' from the caster. The companion moves at 30', is considered to have ability scores of 12, can carry the same amount of gear as a strong man, and can perform any action a normal man could perform. It listens but never speaks. It has AC 16, 1d8 hp, and all attacks against it have a 50% chance of missing due to its invisibility. It can wield weapons at a +1 attack bonus. It is, of course, invisible, but does leave footprints or handprints depending on the activities directed by the caster.

20-21 The caster summons an invisible companion who serves for up to 2d6 hours or until dismissed or killed. No magic circle is required. It can venture up to 1 mile from the caster. The companion moves at 30', is considered to have ability scores of 16, can carry the same amount of gear as a strong man, and can perform any action a normal man could perform. It listens but never speaks. It has AC 18, 2d8 hp, and all attacks against it have a 50% chance of missing due to its invisibility. It can wield weapons at a +3 attack bonus. It is, of course, invisible, but does leave footprints or handprints depending on the activities directed by the caster.

22-25 The caster summons an invisible companion who serves for up to 1 day or until dismissed or killed. No magic circle is required. The companion moves at 60' and can fly. It leaves no footprints or handprints. It is considered to have ability scores of 16, can carry a man in its arms, and can perform any action a normal man could perform. It listens but never speaks. It has AC 20, 3d8 hp, and all attacks against it have a 50% chance of missing due to its invisibility. It can wield weapons at a +5 attack bonus.

26-29 The caster summons an invisible companion who serves for up to 1d6+1 days or until dismissed or killed. No magic circle is required. The companion moves at 120' and can fly. It is considered to have ability scores of 18 and can perform any action a normal man could perform. Its alien intelligence prevents it from carrying on mundane conversations, but it can communicate simple information verbally in the Common tongue. There is a 10% chance that it has some knowledge that is useful to the caster (whether from prior tasks or something from its native plane), provided he asks the right questions. It has AC 20, 5d8 hp, and all attacks against it have a 50% chance of missing due to its invisibility. It can wield weapons at a +6 attack bonus, and its attacks are considered magical.

30-31	The caster summons an invisible companion who serves for up to a month or until dismissed or killed. No magic circle is required. The companion moves at 120' and can fly. It is considered to have ability scores of 20 and can perform any action a normal man could perform. It can carry as much weight as a large mule. Its alien intelligence prevents it from carrying on mundane conversations, but it can communicate simple information verbally in the Common tongue. There is a 20% chance that it has some knowledge that is useful to the caster (whether from prior tasks or something from its native plane), provided he asks the right questions. It has AC 21, 7d8 hp, and all attacks against it have a 50% chance of missing due to its invisibility. It can wield weapons at a +7 attack bonus, and its attacks are considered magical.
32-33	The caster summons an invisible companion who serves for up to one year or until dismissed or killed. No magic circle is required. The companion moves at 120' and can fly. It is considered to have ability scores of 21 and can perform any action a normal man could perform. It can carry as much weight as a large mule. Its alien intelligence prevents it from carrying on mundane conversations, but it can communicate simple information verbally in the Common tongue. There is a 50% chance that it has some knowledge that is useful to the caster (whether from prior tasks or something from its native plane), provided he asks the right questions. It has AC 22, 9d8 hp, and all attacks against it have a 50% chance of missing due to its invisibility. It can wield weapons at a +8 attack bonus, and its attacks are considered magical.
34+	The caster reaches out into the infinite cosmos to call forth the invisible servant most useful to his purposes. This companion appears and pledges permanent service until it is dismissed, killed, or dies of old age (in 2d20+60 years). The companion moves at 150' and can fly. It is not man-shaped, and although its exact form is difficult to discern, it makes its capabilities known at the time most useful to the caster. As long as the companion is present, the caster can make a DC 10 Luck check once per week in a dire situation, and on a success it is revealed that the invisible companion has some heretofore unknown ability that is helpful in that situation (judge's discretion). For example, the companion may be able to pick locks, or create fresh water, or heal wounds. The companion is considered to have ability scores of 22 and can carry as much weight as a large draft horse. It can communicate simple information verbally in the Common tongue. There is a 75% chance that it has some knowledge that is useful to the caster (whether from prior tasks or something from its native plane), provided he asks the right questions. It has AC 23, 11d8 hp, and all attacks against it have a 50% chance of missing due to its invisibility. It can wield weapons at a +9 attack bonus, and its attacks are considered magical.

Knock

Level: 2	Range: 30' or more	Duration: Permanent	Casting time: 1 round	Save: N/A

General	The caster forces open a locked portal or object.
Manifestation	Roll 1d4: (1) resounding knocking sound; (2) loud smashing sound; (3) subtle sound of a lock clicking open; (4) flash of light.
Corruption	Roll 1d6: (1-3) minor; (4-5) major; (6) greater.
Misfire	Roll 1d3: (1) caster accidentally strengthens the lock on the targeted door, increasing DCs to unlock/break it by +4; (2) caster makes the targeted door invisible for 1d6 rounds; (3) caster causes all fasteners on his person to come undone, including shoelaces, belts, potion stoppers, scroll cases, and so on.

1	Lost, failure, and worse! Roll 1d6 modified by Luck: (0 or less) corruption + patron taint + misfire; (1-2) corruption; (3) patron taint (or corruption if no patron); (4+) misfire.
2-11	Lost. Failure.
12-13	Failure, but spell is not lost.
14-15	Targeting one locked chest, stuck door, bolted gate, tied rope, or other object or portal, the caster causes it to magically open. If locked by physical or mundane means, the targeted object automatically unlocks or unfastens – unless the object is of enormous size or supra-normal complexity. If locked by magical means, the spell has no effect.
16-19	Targeting one locked chest, stuck door, bolted gate, tied rope, or other object or portal, the caster causes it to magically open. If locked by magical means, the spell has no effect. If locked by physical or mundane means, the targeted object automatically unlocks or unfastens. Even objects of enormous size (e.g., the gates of a cloud giant's castle) or supra-normal complexity (e.g., the most complex clockwork lock ever devised by a level 20 gnomish locksmith) are opened, provided they are locked via a strictly physical nature.
20-21	Targeting one locked chest, stuck door, bolted gate, tied rope, or other object or portal, the caster causes it to magically open. If locked by physical or mundane means, the targeted object automatically unlocks or unfastens. Even objects of enormous size (e.g., the gates of a cloud giant's castle) or supra-normal complexity (e.g., the most complex clockwork lock ever devised by a level 20 gnomish locksmith) are opened, provided they are locked via a strictly physical nature. The caster may also be able to affect magically locked devices. If the result of this spell check is higher than the spell check result used to magically lock the object, it is opened. For example, a portal locked with *wizard lock* could potentially be opened if the *knock* check result exceeds the original *wizard lock* spell check.
22-25	The caster creates a zone of unlocking that potentially affects *all* locked objects within 30'. The caster gains instant awareness of all such objects within range (including secret doors, if they are locked) and may choose instantaneously which to unlock. This includes locked chests, stuck doors, bolted gates, tied ropes, and other objects or portals. Even objects of enormous size (e.g., the gates of a cloud giant's castle) or supra-normal complexity (e.g., the most complex clockwork lock ever devised by a level 20 gnomish locksmith) are opened. Objects locked via a physical nature are automatically unlocked, and objects locked by magic are unlocked if the result of this spell check is higher than the spell check result used to magically lock the object. For example, a portal locked with *wizard lock* could potentially be opened if the *knock* check result exceeds the original *wizard lock* spell check. The caster can use this spell to open extradimensional portals that have been locked or blocked.
26-29	The caster creates a zone of unlocking that potentially affects all locked objects within 60', *or* the caster can target all fasteners of any nature on a single target within 60'. If the latter, the spell affects belts, buttons, snaps, shoelaces, thongs closing sacks, cork stoppers in potions, and so on. A creature targeted with this effect receives no save, and typically finds itself suddenly naked and wet, as its clothes collapse around it, and ration and drinks begin to leak. If the former effect, the caster gains instant awareness of all blocked portals within range (including secret doors, if they are locked), and may choose instantaneously which to unlock. This includes locked chests, stuck doors, bolted gates, tied ropes, and other objects or portals. Even objects of enormous size (e.g., the gates of a cloud giant's castle) or supra-normal complexity (e.g.,

the most complex clockwork lock ever devised by a level 20 gnomish locksmith) are opened. Objects locked via a physical nature are automatically unlocked, and objects locked by magic are unlocked if the result of this spell check is higher than the spell check result used to magically lock the object. For example, a portal locked with *wizard lock* could potentially be opened if the *knock* check result exceeds the original *wizard lock* spell check. The caster can use this spell to open extradimensional portals that have been locked or blocked.

30-31	The caster instantly becomes aware of all portals, doors, and gates within 120′, including those that are invisible or extraplanar. All such portals are immediately unlocked unless subject to a magical effect created by a spell check higher than this one. Additionally, the caster can target one portal within range and permanently destroy it. Regardless of size, this door, gate, or window is instantly disintegrated, allowing permanent passage.
32-33	The caster instantly becomes aware of all portals, doors, and gates within 120′, including those that are invisible or extraplanar. All such portals are immediately unlocked unless subject to a magical effect created by a spell check higher than this one. Additionally, the caster can target up to three portals within range and permanently destroy them. Regardless of size, these doors, gates, or windows are instantly disintegrated, allowing permanent passage through them.
34+	In a staggering display of power, the caster causes all portals within 1 mile to blast open in a violent burst. This includes windows and shutters, cellar stairs and attic trapdoors, and oven doors and city gates, as well as normal doors and portals. Objects are affected regardless of size, complexity, or magic protection; even secret or invisible doors suddenly open, and passages concealed by tapestries are suddenly revealed as the tapestries fall or fray. There is a 25% chance that any given portal is also destroyed in the display of magic. Moreover, normal fasteners and stoppers are loosened or dislodged, such that wine corks fizz open, lids fall off dinner pots, shoelaces unlace, snaps loosen, belts unbuckle, and so on. The caster can vary the impact to range from "completely disassembled," where creatures' clothes fall off and their wineskins burst to dowse them, to "merely loosened" such that pants loosen and shoes are unlaced.

Levitate

Level: 2	Range: Self or further (see below)	Duration: Varies	Casting time: 1 action	Save: Will vs. spell check

General	The caster or a target chosen by the caster levitates into the air. This spell is useful for getting over walls or into canyons and handy for carrying heavy objects.

Manifestation	Roll 1d4: (1) target floats in air; (2) bluish disc of force appears beneath target to lift it into air; (3) a great winged bird descends from above to lift target; (4) pillar of phantasmal mist pushes creature into the air.
Corruption	Roll 1d6: (1) caster permanently float 1d6″ above the ground; (2) glass objects are permanently repelled whenever they come within 6″ of the caster, much like how magnets repel each other; (3) caster's hair stands permanently on end; (4-5) major; (6) minor.
Misfire	Roll 1d3: (1) caster is smashed 1d6+6″ down into the ground, sinking straight into mud or dirt, or blasting through stone for 1 point of damage; (2) caster rises 1d12″ in the air and hangs there, unable to get any traction for movement, for 1d4 rounds before dropping back to the ground; (3) caster shoots up violently into the air to a height of 1d4x10′, then falls to the ground, suffering 1d6 damage for every 10′ fallen; (4) all creatures within 20′ must make Will saves, and the creature with the lowest result shoots into the air, vanishing high in the sky, and is gone for 1d6+2 rounds before returning somewhere within a mile in a controlled descent from the sky (no damage).

1	Lost, failure, and worse! Roll 1d6 modified by Luck: (0 or less) corruption + patron taint + misfire; (1-2) corruption; (3) patron taint (or corruption if no patron); (4+) misfire.
2-11	Lost. Failure.
12-13	Failure, but spell is not lost.
14-15	For up to 1 turn, the caster can rise or descend through the air at a rate of 20 vertical feet or horizontal feet per round of concentration. In a single round, the caster can move horizontally *or* vertically, but not both – this is levitation not flight. Complex maneuvers are not possible, and the caster's AC is reduced by -2

while levitating. The caster may step off his vertical suspension at any point (for example, to step onto a castle wall). If the caster's concentration is broken while still in the air, he falls to the earth, suffering 1d6 damage for each 10' fallen.

16-19	The caster can affect levitate himself or a touched target of up to 300 pounds. If the target is unwilling, it receives a Will save. If the Will save fails, the target remains levitated as long as the caster concentrates. For up to 1 turn, the caster or the target rises or descends through the air at a rate of 20 vertical feet or horizontal feet per round of concentration. In a single round, the caster may move horizontally *or* vertically, but not both – this is levitation not flight. Complex maneuvers are not possible, and the caster's AC is reduced by -2 while levitating. The caster may step off his vertical suspension at any point (for example, to step onto a castle wall). If the caster's concentration is broken while still in the air, he falls to the earth, suffering 1d6 damage for each 10' fallen.
20-21	The caster designates a space of up to 10'x10'. For up to 1 turn, all creatures or objects in that space are levitated as if on an invisible rising platform. There is no weight limit. No save is possible, although an unwilling creature can run to the edge of the "platform" and jump off. The caster may move this platform of air at a rate of up to 20' vertically *or* 20' horizontally for every round of concentration.
22-25	The caster designates a space of up to 10'x10'. For up to 1 hour, all creatures or objects in that space are levitated as if on an invisible rising platform. There is no weight limit. No save is possible, although an unwilling creature can run to the edge of the "platform" and jump off. The caster may move this platform of air at a rate of up to 40' vertically *or* 40' horizontally for every round of concentration.
26-29	The caster designates a space of up to 20'x20'. For up to 1 hour, all creatures or objects in that space are levitated as if on an invisible rising platform. There is no weight limit. No save is possible, although an unwilling creature can run to the edge of the "platform" and jump off. The caster may move this platform of air at a rate of up to 40' vertically *or* 40' horizontally for every round of concentration.
30-31	The caster designates a space of up to 20'x20'. For up to 1 day, all creatures or objects in that space are levitated as if on an invisible rising platform. There is no weight limit. No save is possible, although an unwilling creature can run to the edge of the "platform" and jump off. The caster may move this platform of air at a rate of up to 60' vertically *or* 60' horizontally for every round of concentration.

32-33	The caster designates a space of up to 30'x30'. For up to 1 day, all creatures or objects in that space are levitated as one, as if on an invisible rising platform. There is no weight limit. No save is possible, although an unwilling creature can run to the edge of the "platform" and jump off. The caster may move this platform of air at a rate of up to 60' vertically *or* 60' horizontally for every round of concentration.
34+	The caster can levitate any object or creature he can see regardless of size or complexity. This could include an entire castle, a crowd of peasants, a massive boulder, or even a charging horde of barbarians. There is no weight limit, and the effect continues for up to 30 days or until dispelled. No save is possible, and an unwilling creature cannot escape. The caster may move the target in the air at a rate of up to 60' vertically *or* 60' horizontally for every round of concentration.

Locate Object

Level: 2   Range: Varies   Duration: 1 round or 1 hour   Casting time: 1 round   Save: N/A

General	This spell lets the caster locate an object. Weaker castings require a physical trace of the object, and it can only be located if it is on the same plane of existence. With more powerful castings, the caster can locate objects he has never beheld, even if they reside in a different plane or time.
Manifestation	N/A
Corruption	Roll 1d6: (1) for the rest of his life, the caster constantly misplaces things, such that any time he goes to retrieve an object, there is a 10% chance he's misplaced it; (2) the caster's eyes turn a deep purple color; (3) the caster becomes a magnet for the object-obfuscating magic of other sorcerers, such that every day there is a 10% chance that a new, randomly-determined object appears on his person, and a separate 5% chance that the angry owner of a formerly-appeared object arrives to reclaim it; (4-5) minor; (6) major.
Misfire	Roll 1d4: (1) one randomly determined object on the caster's person is transported 1d6x100 miles away, and the caster knows exactly where it is; (2) sometime in the next month the caster loses his favorite magic item and can't find it no matter where he looks; (3) the weapon of one randomly determined ally within 40' disappears, only to reappear 1d7 days later a little worse for wear; (4) the caster completely forgets all knowledge of the object he was going to locate.
1	Lost, failure, and worse! Roll 1d6 modified by Luck: (0 or less) corruption + patron taint + misfire; (1-2) corruption; (3) patron taint (or corruption if no patron); (4+) misfire.
2-11	Lost. Failure.
12-13	Failure, but spell is not lost.
14-15	The caster can attempt to locate a non-living, non-sentient thing, composed of metal, wood, cloth, or other mundane substances. The thing must be a specific object. For example, it cannot be "any lantern" but must be a certain lantern of which the caster knows. The caster must have a physical trace of the object for which he searches. For example, if he attempts to find a lost horde of pirate gold, he must have one gold piece from the horde; if he searches for a magic sword, he must have a suit of armor scored by the sword. Full concentration is required to cast the spell. If the object is within 100' of the caster and on the same plane of existence, he receives a sense of the direction in which it lays. This directional sense is three-dimensional, so an object on a lower level of a dungeon could produce a downward sense of direction.
16-19	The caster can attempt to locate a non-living, non-sentient thing, composed of metal, wood, cloth, or other mundane substances. The thing must be a specific object. For example, it cannot be "any lantern" but must be a certain lantern of which the caster knows. The caster must have a physical trace of the object for which he searches. For example, if he attempts to find a lost horde of pirate gold, he must have one gold piece from the horde; if he searches for a magic sword, he must have a suit of armor scored by the sword. Full concentration is required to cast the spell. If the object is within range of the caster and on the same plane of existence, he receives a sense of the direction in which it lays. This directional sense is three-dimensional, so an object on a lower level of a dungeon could produce a downward sense of direction. Range is increased with each round of full concentration, as follows: round 1 = 100', round 2 = 500', round 3 = half a mile, round 4= 1 mile, round 5 = 2 miles, round 6 = 5 miles, round 7 = 10 miles. The range does not go beyond 10 miles. The sense of location includes only direction, not distance, and exists only as of the moment in time when the spell was cast.
20-21	The caster can attempt to locate a non-living, non-sentient thing, composed of metal, wood, cloth, or other mundane substances. The thing must be a specific object. For example, it cannot be "any lantern" but must be a certain lantern of which the caster knows. The caster must have a physical trace of the object for which he searches. For example, if he attempts to find a lost horde of pirate gold, he must have one gold piece from the horde; if he searches for a magic sword, he must have a suit of armor scored by the sword. Full concentration is required to cast the spell. If the object is within range of the caster and on the same plane of existence, he receives a sense of the direction in which it lays. This directional sense is three-dimensional, so an object on a lower level of a dungeon could produce a downward sense of direction. Range is increased with each round of full concentration, as follows: round 1 = 100', round 2 = 500', round 3 = half a mile, round 4= 1 mile, round 5 = 2 miles, round 6 = 5 miles, round 7 = 10 miles. The range does not go beyond 10 miles. The sense of location includes direction and a very approximate sense of distance accurate to within 25%; this directional sense exists only as of the moment in time when the spell was cast.

22-25	The caster can attempt to locate a non-living, non-sentient thing, composed of metal, wood, cloth, or other mundane substances. The thing must be a specific object. For example, it cannot be "any lantern" but must be a certain lantern of which the caster knows. The caster does *not* need a physical trace of the object for which he searches, but he must have specific knowledge of the object. For example, he must have beheld it in the past, read accounts of it, or heard tell of it. Provided he can give an accurate description of the object, the spell will return the location of an object matching his description, if it is in range. Full concentration is required to cast the spell. If the object is within range of the caster and on the same plane of existence, he receives a sense of the direction in which it lays. This directional sense is three-dimensional, so an object on a lower level of a dungeon could produce a downward sense of direction. Range is increased with each round of full concentration, as follows: round 1 = 100', round 2 = 500', round 3 = half a mile, round 4= 1 mile, round 5 = 2 miles, round 6 = 5 miles, round 7 = 10 miles. The range does not go beyond 10 miles. The sense of location includes direction and a very approximate sense of distance accurate to within 25%. The spell's duration is a full hour. At any point during that duration, the caster can spend a full round concentrating and receive a new "ping" on the direction and distance of the object. A lapse in concentration during the duration does not cancel the spell; the caster must simply re-establish concentration.

26-29	The caster can attempt to locate a non-living, non-sentient thing, composed of metal, wood, cloth, or other mundane substances. The thing must be a specific object. For example, it cannot be "any lantern" but must be a certain lantern of which the caster knows. The caster does *not* need a physical trace of the object for which he searches, but he must have specific knowledge of the object. For example, he must have beheld it in the past, read accounts of it, or heard tell of it. Provided he can give an accurate description of the object, the spell will return the location of an object matching his description, if it is in range. Full concentration is required to cast the spell. If the object is within range of the caster and on the same plane of existence, he receives a sense of the direction in which it lays. This directional sense is three-dimensional, so an object on a lower level of a dungeon could produce a downward sense of direction. Range is increased with each round of full concentration, as follows: round 1 = 100', round 2 = 500', round 3 = half a mile, round 4= 1 mile, round 5 = 2 miles, round 6 = 5 miles, round 7 = 10 miles. The range does not go beyond 10 miles. The sense of location includes direction and a very approximate sense of distance accurate to within 25%. The spell's duration is a full hour. At any point during that duration, the caster can spend a full round concentrating and receive a new "ping" on the direction and distance of the object. A lapse in concentration during the duration does not cancel the spell; the caster must simply re-establish concentration.
30-31	The caster can attempt to locate a non-living, non-sentient thing. The thing need not be a specific object. The caster could choose to look for "any lantern" or a specific lantern he knows, or he could even look "for any water" or "for the nearest exit." The caster does *not* need a physical trace of the object for which he searches, nor does he need any specific knowledge of it. However, the more vague his description the greater the chance the spell will reveal an inaccurate read (at judge's discretion). Full concentration is required to cast the spell. If the object is within range of the caster and on the same plane of existence, he receives a sense of the direction in which it lays. This directional sense is three-dimensional, so an object on a lower level of a dungeon could produce a downward sense of direction. Range is increased with each round of full concentration, as follows: round 1 = half-mile, round 2 = 1 mile, round 3 = 5 miles, round 4= 10 miles, round 5 = 50 miles, round 6 = 250 miles, round 7 = 1,000 miles. The range does not go beyond 1,000 miles. The sense of location includes direction and a very approximate sense of distance accurate to within 25%. The spell's duration is a full hour. At any point during that duration, the caster can spend a full round concentrating and receive a new "ping" on the direction and distance of the object. A lapse in concentration during the duration does not cancel the spell; the caster must simply re-establish concentration.
32-33	The caster can attempt to locate a non-living, non-sentient thing, even if it is on another plane. The thing need not be a specific object. The caster could choose to look for "any lantern" or a specific lantern he knows, or he could even look "for any water" or "for the nearest exit." The caster does *not* need a physical trace of the object for which he searches nor does he need any specific knowledge of it. However, the more vague his description the greater the chance that the spell will reveal an inaccurate read (at judge's discretion). Full concentration is required to cast the spell. If the object is within range of the caster, he receives a sense of the direction in which it lays. This directional sense is three-dimensional, so an object on a lower level of a dungeon could produce a downward sense of direction. Range is increased with each round of full concentration, as follows: round 1 = half-mile, round 2 = 1 mile, round 3 = 5 miles, round 4= 10 miles, round 5 = 50 miles, round 6 = 250 miles, round 7 = 1,000 miles. After concentrating for seven rounds, on the eighth round the caster will know if the object is on a different plane. On the ninth round, he will have a sense of what plane that is. If he has visited that plane before, he will know specifically; if he has never visited, he will have a greater or lesser sense of which plane it is, depending on his knowl-

edge of the planes. Knowledge that the object is on another plane does not reveal direction or distance. If the item is on the same plane, the sense of location includes direction and a very approximate sense of distance accurate to within 25%. The spell's duration is a full day. At any point during that duration, the caster can spend a full round concentrating and receive a new "ping" on the direction and distance of the object. A lapse in concentration during the duration does not cancel the spell; the caster must simply re-establish concentration.

34+	The caster can attempt to locate any thing, whether living or non-sentient, specific or general, even if it is on another plane. The thing need not be a specific object. The caster could choose to look for "any lantern" or a specific lantern he knows, or he could even look "for any water" or "for the nearest exit." The caster does *not* need a physical trace of the object for which he searches nor does he need any specific knowledge of it. However, the more vague his description the greater the chance that the spell will reveal an inaccurate read (at judge's discretion). Full concentration is required to cast the spell. If the object is within range of the caster, he receives a sense of the direction in which it lays. This directional sense is three-dimensional, so an object on a lower level of a dungeon could produce a downward sense of direction. If the object is anywhere on the current plane of existence, the caster knows in the first round; if it is on a different plane, he knows the plane's identity on the second round; and on the third round, he knows the object's exact location on its plane of existence. The spell's duration is a full month. At any point during that duration, the caster can simply concentrate for one round to receive a new "ping" on the direction and distance of the object. A lapse in concentration during the duration does not cancel the spell; the caster must simply re-establish concentration.

Magic Mouth

Level: 2	Range: Varies	Duration: 1 hour or longer	Casting time: 1 turn	Save: N/A

General	This spell creates a magical mouth that speaks when certain triggers occur.

Manifestation	Caster's discretion.
Corruption	Roll 1d6: (1) the caster stutters terribly; (2) the caster mumbles constantly, even in his sleep; (3) the caster's teeth start to decay at an alarming rate and fall out at the rate of 1 every 1d7 days until magically healed; (4) the caster can't stop repeating the phrase his magic mouth was meant to impart; (5-6) minor.
Misfire	Roll 1d4: (1) a roughly human-sized magic mouth appears, but it does not speak and has absolutely terrible halitosis, which proceeds to stink up the entire area until it vanishes 1d7 days later; (2) a magic mouth appears for 1d6 hours but it mumbles and stutters such that it cannot be understood; (3) the caster inadvertently creates a 2' tall magic nose instead of a magic mouth, and the nose lasts for 1d8 hours during which time it oozes mucus in a rather disgusting display; (4) the magic mouth appears on top of the caster's *own* mouth and lasts for 1d6 rounds, during which time his speech is limited to the phrase he was planning to impart to the magic mouth.

1	Lost, failure, and worse! Roll 1d6 modified by Luck: (0 or less) corruption + patron taint + misfire; (1-3) corruption; (4) patron taint (or corruption if no patron); (5+) misfire.
2-11	Lost. Failure.
12-13	Failure, but spell is not lost.
14-15	The caster can create a magic mouth on an inanimate surface he touches. The magic mouth lasts 1 hour. It will speak a single phrase of up to 10 words whenever any creature approaches within 20'. The magic mouth's appearance is at the discretion of the caster (human, animal, etc.), as long as it is 2' wide or smaller. The mouth cannot attack or take any action other than speak.
16-19	The caster can create a magic mouth on an inanimate surface he touches. The magic mouth lasts 1 day. The caster can specify a trigger condition. For example, *any* creature approaching within a certain distance, a *specific* creature, a *certain kind* of creature, and so on. Assume the magic mouth can perceive its surroundings to a distance of 100' or as limited by line of sight. The magic mouth will speak a phrase of up to 20 words whenever the condition is triggered. The magic mouth's appearance is at the discretion of the caster (human, animal, etc.), as long as it is 2' wide or smaller. The mouth cannot attack or take any action other than to speak.

20-21   The caster can create a magic mouth on an inanimate surface he touches. The magic mouth lasts 1 day. The caster can specify a trigger condition. For example, *any* creature approaching within a certain distance, a *specific* creature, a *certain kind* of creature, and so on. Assume the magic mouth can perceive its surroundings to a distance of 100' or as limited by line of sight. The magic mouth will speak a phrase of up to 20 words whenever the condition is triggered. Once its phrase is spoken, the mouth has limited ability to converse on a single subject. Treat the mouth as Int 6; its knowledge is limited to a single subject that the caster can dictate in the 1-turn casting time. For example, the caster might describe the contents of a room or discuss the denizens of a dungeon. The magic mouth's appearance is at the discretion of the caster (human, animal, etc.), as long as it is 2' wide or smaller.

22-25   The caster can create a magic mouth on an inanimate surface within 100'. The magic mouth lasts 1 week. The caster can specify a trigger condition. For example, *any* creature approaching within a certain distance, a *specific* creature, a *certain kind* of creature, and so on. Assume the magic mouth can perceive its surroundings to a distance of 100' or as limited by line of sight. The magic mouth will speak a phrase of up to 20 words whenever the condition is triggered. Once its phrase is spoken, the mouth has limited ability to converse on a single subject. Treat the mouth as Int 6; its knowledge is limited to a single subject that the caster can dictate in the 1-turn casting time. For example, the caster might describe the contents of a room or discuss the denizens of a dungeon. The magic mouth's appearance is at the discretion of the caster (human, animal, etc.), as long as it is 4' wide or smaller.

26-29   The caster can create a magic mouth within 100'. It can be cast on a surface or in midair. The magic mouth lasts 1 month. The caster can specify a trigger condition. For example, *any* creature approaching within a certain distance, a *specific* creature, a *certain kind* of creature, and so on. Assume the magic mouth can perceive its surroundings to a distance of 100' or as limited by line of sight. The magic mouth will speak a phrase of up to 20 words whenever the condition is triggered. Once its phrase is spoken, the mouth has limited ability to converse on a single subject. Treat the mouth Int 6; its knowledge is limited to a single subject that the caster can dictate in the 1-turn casting time. For example, the caster might describe the contents of a room or discuss the denizens of a dungeon. The magic mouth's appearance is at the discretion of the caster (human, animal, etc.), as long as it is 4' wide or smaller.

30-31	The caster can create a magic mouth within 100'. It can be cast on a surface or in midair. The magic mouth lasts 1 year. The caster can specify a trigger condition. For example, *any* creature approaching within a certain distance, a *specific* creature, a *certain kind* of creature, and so on. Assume the magic mouth can perceive its surroundings to a distance of 100' or as limited by line of sight. The magic mouth will speak a phrase of up to 20 words whenever the condition is triggered. Once its phrase is spoken, the mouth has limited ability to converse on a single subject. Treat the mouth as Int 6; its knowledge is limited to a single subject that the caster can dictate in the 1-turn casting time. For example, the caster might describe the contents of a room or discuss the denizens of a dungeon. The magic mouth's appearance is at the discretion of the caster (human, animal, etc.), as long as it is 4' wide or smaller.
32-33	The caster can create a magic mouth within 100'. It can be cast on a surface or in midair and has a permanent duration. The caster can specify a trigger condition. For example, *any* creature approaching within a certain distance, a *specific* creature, a *certain kind* of creature, and so on. Assume the magic mouth can perceive its surroundings to a distance of 100' or as limited by line of sight. The magic mouth will speak a phrase of up to 20 words whenever the condition is triggered. Once its phrase is spoken, the mouth has limited ability to converse on a single subject. Treat the mouth as Int 6; its knowledge is limited to a single subject that the caster can dictate in the 1-turn casting time. For example, the caster might describe the contents of a room or discuss the denizens of a dungeon. The magic mouth's appearance is at the discretion of the caster (human, animal, etc.), as long as it is 4' wide or smaller.
34+	The caster can create a magic mouth within 100'. It can be cast on a surface or in midair and has a permanent duration. The caster can specify a trigger condition. For example, *any* creature approaching within a certain distance, a *specific* creature, a *certain kind* of creature, and so on. Assume the magic mouth can perceive its surroundings to a distance of 100' or as limited by line of sight. The magic mouth will speak a phrase of up to 20 words whenever the condition is triggered. Once its phrase is spoken, the mouth has limited ability to converse on a single subject. Treat the mouth as Int 12; its knowledge is limited to a single subject that the caster can dictate in the casting time. The caster can extend the casting time to up to 1 hour and impart additional knowledge to the mouth during this time. For example, the caster might describe the contents of a room or discuss the denizens of a dungeon. The magic mouth's appearance is at the discretion of the caster (human, animal, etc.), as long as it is 6' wide or smaller.

Mirror Image

Level: 2	Range: Self or touch	Duration: 1 round or longer	Casting time: 1 round	Save: Will vs. spell check DC

General	This spell creates illusionary doubles of the caster, which mimic his actions exactly. They appear in the space directly around him and distract opponents, who tend to strike the mirror images instead of the caster. More powerful castings can create duplicates of allies or objects. The total number of doubles the caster can create of himself, allies, or objects cannot exceed his Int score.

Manifestation	See below.
Corruption	Roll 1d6: (1-3) major; (4-6) minor.
Misfire	Roll 1d4: (1) the caster creates a "backward" mirror image of himself, such that the mirror image's left hand carries what the caster holds in his right hand, and so on, meaning the mirror image (which lasts for 1d6 rounds) is obviously different than the caster; (2) the caster creates 1d6 mirror images, but they're all different people, not "mirrors" at all, and frankly they have odd habits or strange tics that make them discomforting to be around for their 1d6+1 round duration; (3) the caster generates 1d4+1 extra *shadows* that dance around his feet, sometimes into the light rather than away from it, lasting the rest of the day; (4) the caster creates a mirror image of himself that is short and fat, like a funhouse mirror, lasting 1d6 rounds.

1	Lost, failure, and worse! Roll 1d6 modified by Luck: (0 or less) corruption + patron taint + misfire; (1-3) corruption; (4) patron taint (or corruption if no patron); (5+) misfire.
2-11	Lost. Failure.
12-13	Failure, but spell is not lost.
14-15	A single mirror image blinks into existence directly ad-

jacent to the caster. It looks exactly like him, and mimics his actions and speech. It must remain within 5' of the caster at all times. Any creature attempting to attack the caster automatically strikes the mirror image instead, which disappears instantly once hit. An opponent who concentrates for a full round can make a Will save to distinguish the caster's true self from the mirror image. Ranged attacks (e.g., dragon breath) may cause the mirror image to vanish and still wound the caster. The mirror image lasts for 1d4 rounds or until dispelled.

16-19	1d4+1 mirror images blink into existence next to the caster and must remain within 5' of him. They look exactly like him, and mimic his actions and speech. Any creature attempting to attack the caster automatically strikes a mirror image instead, which disappears instantly once hit. An opponent who concentrates for a full round can make a Will save to distinguish the caster's true self from the mirror images. Ranged attacks (e.g., dragon breath) may cause the mirror images to vanish and still wound the caster. The mirror images last for 1d6+1 rounds or until dispelled.
20-21	1d6+1 mirror images blink into existence next to the caster and must remain within 5' of him. They look exactly like him, and mimic his actions and speech. Any creature attempting to attack the caster automatically strikes a mirror image instead, which disappears instantly once hit. An opponent who concentrates for a full round can make a Will save to distinguish the caster's true self from the mirror images. Ranged attacks (e.g., dragon breath) may cause the mirror images to vanish and still wound the caster. The mirror images last for 1d4 turns or until dispelled.
22-25	The caster can create mirror images of himself or a creature he touches. 1d6+1 mirror images blink into existence next to the target and must remain within 5' of him. They look exactly like him, and mimic his actions and speech. Any creature attempting to attack the target automatically strikes a mirror image instead, which disappears instantly once hit. An opponent who concentrates for a full round may make a Will save to distinguish the target's true self from the mirror images. Ranged attacks (e.g., dragon breath) may cause the mirror images to vanish and still wound the target. The mirror images last for 1d4 turns or until dispelled.
26-29	The caster can create mirror images of himself or a creature he touches. 1d8+1 mirror images blink into existence next to the target and must remain within 5' of him. They look exactly like him, and mimic his actions and speech. Any creature attempting to attack the target automatically strikes a mirror image instead, which disappears instantly once hit. An opponent who concentrates for a full round may make a Will save to distinguish the target's true self from the mirror images. Ranged attacks (e.g., dragon breath) may cause the mirror images to vanish and still wound the target. The mirror images last for 1 hour or until dispelled.
30-31	The caster can create mirror images of any creature or object within 30', provided it is human-sized or smaller. Moreover, he can create different mirror images at once, such that he could create some duplicates of himself, some of his warrior ally, and some of his other thief ally. He can even mirror inanimate objects, meaning he could replicate a treasure chest or cause a door to have multiple iterations. The duplicates can still be dispelled with a strike, but using the spell in this manner may delay or confuse opponents or allow for a bluffing maneuver. Up to 1d10+2 mirror images can be created, and each must remain within 5' of the spell's target. Each mirror image looks exactly like the spell's target and mimics its actions and speech (if the original target is capable of such things). Any creature attempting to attack the target automatically strikes a mirror image instead, which disappears instantly once hit. An opponent who concentrates for a full round may make a Will save to distinguish the target's true self from the mirror images. Ranged attacks (e.g., dragon breath) may cause the mirror images to vanish and still wound the target. The mirror images last for 1 hour or until dispelled.
32-33	The caster can create mirror images of any creature or object within 30', provided it is human-sized or smaller. Moreover, he can create different mirror images at once, such that he could create some duplicates of himself, some of his warrior ally, and some of his other thief ally. He can even mirror inanimate objects, meaning he could replicate a treasure chest or cause a door to have multiple iterations. The duplicates can still be dispelled with a strike, but using the spell in this manner may delay or confuse opponents or allow for a bluffing maneuver. Up to 1d12+4 mirror images can be created, and each must remain within 5' of the spell's target. Each mirror image looks exactly like the spell's target, and mimic its actions and speech (if the original target is capable of such things). Any creature attempting to attack the target automatically strikes a mirror image instead, which disappears instantly once hit. An opponent who concentrates for a full round may make a Will save to distinguish the target's true self from the mirror images. Ranged attacks (e.g., dragon breath) may cause the mirror images to vanish and still wound the target. The mirror images last for 1 hour or until dispelled.

Additionally, if the caster replicates himself and then concentrates, he can send his doubles to perform illusionary assignments. The doubles can move up to 50' away from the caster and move or talk. They cannot physically interact with objects (e.g., open a door) or cause actual damage, but they can feign an attack and sow confusion.

34+   The caster can create mirror images of any creature or object within 30', provided it is human-sized or smaller. Moreover, he can create different mirror images at once, such that he could create some duplicates of himself, some of his warrior ally, and some of his other thief ally. He can even mirror inanimate objects, meaning he could replicate a treasure chest, or cause a door to have multiple iterations. The duplicates can still be dispelled with a strike, but using the spell in this manner may delay or confuse opponents, or allow for a bluffing maneuver. The caster can create a number of mirror images equal to his Int score, and each must remain within 5' of the spell's target. Each mirror image looks exactly like the spell's target, and mimics its actions and speech (if the original target is capable of such things). Any creature attempting to attack the target automatically strikes a mirror image instead, which disappears instantly once hit. An opponent who concentrates for a full round may make a Will save to distinguish the target's true self from the mirror images. Ranged attacks (e.g., dragon breath) may cause the mirror images to vanish and still wound the target. The mirror images last for 1 day or until dispelled.

Additionally, if the caster replicates himself and then concentrates, he can send his doubles to perform illusionary assignments. The doubles can move up to 50' away from the caster and move or talk. They cannot physically interact with objects (e.g., open a door) or cause actual damage, but they can feign an attack and sow confusion.

Monster Summoning

Level: 2	Range: 20'	Duration: Varies	Casting time: 1 turn or less	Save: None

General	The caster must spend half the casting time drawing pentacle, then the remaining casting time conjuring monster spirits. At end of the turn, the caster summons forth a monster. He must be familiar with the monster, and it must be native to this plane of existence. The master must have some material remnant of the monster to expend in the spell (e.g., hair, fur, paw, tooth, skull, etc.).
Manifestation	Roll 1d4: (1) egg shimmers into existence, then hatches into monster summoned; (2) flash of dark clouds and monster appears; (3) monster's skeleton appears first, then organs appear, then muscles knit them together, then skin grows, and animal appears; (4) monster erupts from ground fully formed.
Corruption	Roll 1d6: (1-3) minor; (4-6) major.
Misfire	Roll 1d4: (1) the caster summons forth 1d6 1 HD creatures that are not under his control and immediately attack him; (2) instead of summoning creatures, the caster sends himself to a place where the creatures live, arriving in a dark, dank cave where he must spend 1d4 rounds fighting an unknown monstrous opponent (judge's discretion at 1d4 HD) before returning wounded and bloody; (3) the caster sends his familiar away for 1d4 hours; (4) the nearest ally is transformed into an intelligent ape, dressed in the same clothes and equipment, for 1d4 rounds.
1	Lost, failure, and worse! Roll 1d6 modified by Luck: (0 or less) corruption + patron taint + misfire; (1-3) corruption; (4) patron taint (or corruption if no patron); (5+) misfire.
2-11	Lost. Failure.
12-13	Failure, but spell is not lost.
14-15	The caster summons one monster of 1 HD or less. The monster remains for up to 1 hour as long as it remains in the pentacle, though it hungers, thirsts, and rests as normal. It obeys the caster's commands within normal bounds; suicidal commands or those contrary to its nature have a 50% chance of releasing the monster from service. If the pentacle is broken or service is otherwise ended, the monster returns from whence it came. Due to the nature of the summoning, the caster cannot directly harm a creature he summons.
16-19	The caster summons two 1 HD monsters or one 2 HD monster. The monsters remain for up to 1 hour as long as they remain in the pentacle, though they hunger, thirst, and rest as normal. They obey the caster's commands within normal bounds; suicidal commands or those contrary to its nature have a 50% chance of releasing a monster from service. If the pentacle is broken or service is otherwise ended, the monsters return from whence they came. Due to the nature of the summoning, the caster cannot directly harm a creature he summons.

20-21	The caster summons two 1 HD monsters or one 2 HD monster. The monsters remain for up to 1 hour, though they hunger, thirst, and rest as normal. They obey the caster's commands within normal bounds; suicidal commands or those contrary to its nature have a 50% chance of releasing monster from service. If the pentacle is broken or service is otherwise ended, the monsters return from whence they came. Due to the nature of the summoning, the caster cannot directly harm a creature he summons.
22-25	The caster summons two monsters of 2 HD or less or one 4 HD monster. The monsters remain for up to 2 hours, though they hunger, thirst, and rest as normal. They obey the caster's commands within normal bounds; suicidal commands or those contrary to its nature have a 25% chance of releasing monster from service. If the pentacle is broken or service is otherwise ended, the monsters return from whence they came. Due to the nature of the summoning, the caster cannot directly harm a creature he summons.
26-29	With a reduced casting time of four rounds, the caster summons four 1 HD monsters, two 2 HD monsters, or one 4 HD monster. The monsters remain for up to 2 hours, though they hunger, thirst, and rest as normal. They obey the caster's commands within normal bounds; suicidal commands or those contrary to its nature have a 25% chance of releasing monster from service. If the pentacle is broken or service is otherwise ended, the monsters return from whence they came. Due to the nature of the summoning, the caster cannot directly harm a creature he summons.
30-31	With a reduced casting time of four rounds, the caster summons eight 1 HD monsters, four 2 HD monsters, two 4 HD monsters, or one 8 HD monster. The monsters remain for up to 4 hours, though they hunger, thirst, and rest as normal. They obey the caster's commands within normal bounds; suicidal commands or those contrary to its nature have a 10% chance of releasing monster from service. If the pentacle is broken or service is otherwise ended, the monsters return from whence they came. Due to the nature of the summoning, the caster cannot directly harm a creature he summons.
32-33	With a reduced casting time of only a single round, the caster summons eight 1 HD monsters, four 2 HD monsters, two 4 HD monsters, or one 8 HD monster. The monsters remain for up to 4 hours, though they hunger, thirst, and rest as normal. They obey the caster's commands within normal bounds; suicidal commands or those contrary to its nature have a 10% chance of releasing monster from service. If the pentacle is broken or service is otherwise ended, the monsters return from whence they came. Due to the nature of the summoning, the caster cannot directly harm a creature he summons.
34+	With a reduced casting time of only a single round, the caster summons sixteen 1 HD monsters, eight 2 HD monsters, four 4 HD monsters, two 8 HD monsters, or one 16 HD monster. The monsters remain for up to 24 hours, though they hunger, thirst, and rest as normal. They obey the caster's commands within normal bounds; suicidal commands or those contrary to its nature have a 1% chance of releasing monster from service. If the pentacle is broken or service is otherwise ended, the monsters return from whence they came. Due to the nature of the summoning, the caster cannot directly harm a creature he summons.

Nythuul's Porcupine Coat

Level: 2	Range: Self	Duration: 1 round per CL	Casting time: 1 action	Save: N/A

General	This spell cloaks the caster in a bristling layer of sharp quills. The quills act as armor, increases unarmed melee damage, and with more potent results, can be used as a ranged weapon.
Manifestation	The caster's skin is covered in long, sharp quills like that of a porcupine.
Corruption	Roll 1d4: (1) the caster's body hair becomes stiff and quill-like; (2) small quills speckle the caster's face and his nose assumes a hedge-hog-like quality; (3) the caster's skin constantly itches and may impose a -1 penalty to tasks that require finesse or concentration at the judge's discretion; (4) the caster develops a taste for worms and grubs, preferably freshly rooted from the earth.
Misfire	Roll 1d5: (1) the quills knit together, immobilizing the caster for 1d4 rounds until they fall out of his flesh; (2) the quills appear underneath the caster's flesh, causing 1 point of damage to him each round he moves more than 5' or engages in any spellcasting or physical attacks; (3) the quills are soft and oily, providing no protection and require a successful DC 8 Ref save each time the caster wishes to pick up an item or walk at more than half normal speed, with a failed save meaning the caster drops the item or slips and falls; (4) the caster's eyes turn small and beady, and his distance vision suffers (all attacks or spell checks against targets father than 10' away suffer a -2 penalty); (5) quills fire from the caster's body at random, requiring all within 15' of him to make a DC 10 Reflex save or suffer 1d4 damage.

1	Lost, failure, and worse! Roll 1d6 modified by Luck: (0 or less) corruption + patron taint + misfire; (1-2) corruption; (3) patron taint (or corruption if no patron); (4+) misfire.
2-13	Lost. Failure.
14-15	The caster's body erupts in stiff, sharp quills that provide a +1 bonus to his AC. These quills do not inhibit spellcasting and spell checks made by the caster are unmodified.
16-19	The caster's body erupts in stiff, sharp quills that provide a +1 bonus to his AC. These quills do not inhibit spellcasting, and spell checks made by the caster are unmodified. In addition, anyone that attacks the caster in melee combat must make a DC 10 Ref save immediately after his attack or suffer 1d3 points of damage from contact with the quills.
20-21	The caster's body erupts in stiff, sharp quills that provide a +2 bonus to his AC. These quills do not inhibit spellcasting, and spell checks made by the caster are unmodified. In addition, anyone that attacks the caster in melee combat must make a DC 15 Ref save immediately after his attack or suffer 1d4 points of damage from contact with the quills. The caster's quill-covered hands can also be used in melee combat. A successful attack with them inflicts 1d6 damage.
22-25	The caster's body erupts in stiff, sharp quills that provide a +2 bonus to his AC. These quills do not inhibit spellcasting, and spell checks made by the caster are unmodified. In addition, anyone that attacks the caster in melee combat must make a DC 20 Ref save immediately after his attack or suffer 1d4 points of damage from contact with the quills. The caster's quill-covered hands can also be used in melee combat. A successful attack with them inflicts 1d6 damage. Lastly, the caster can throw the quills as a missile attack. Each has a range of 20/40/60 and does 1d6 points of damage on a successful strike.
26-29	The caster's body erupts in stiff, sharp quills that provide a +3 bonus to his AC. These quills do not inhibit spellcasting, and spell checks made by the caster are unmodified. In addition, anyone that attacks the caster in melee combat must make a DC 20 Ref save immediately after his attack or suffer 1d4+CL points of damage from contact with the quills. The caster's quill-covered hands can also be used in melee combat and are considered magical weapons for the purpose of affecting targets protected from normal attacks. The quills impart a +2 bonus to attack rolls and inflict 1d8+2 damage on a successful hit. The quills can be thrown as a missile attack. Each has a range of 20/40/60 and does 1d6 points of damage on a successful strike.
30-31	The caster's body erupts in stiff, sharp quills that provide a +4 bonus to his AC. These quills do not inhibit spellcasting, and spell checks made by the caster are unmodified. In addition, anyone that attacks the caster in melee combat must make a DC 20 Ref save immediately after his attack or suffer 1d6+CL points of damage from contact with the quills. The caster's quill-covered hands can also be used in melee

combat and are considered magical weapons for the purpose of affecting targets protected from normal attacks. The quills impart a +4 bonus to attack rolls and inflict 1d8+4 damage on a successful hit. Lastly, up to three quills can be thrown as a missile attack against a single target each round. The quills have a range of 20/40/60, impart a +4 magical bonus to attack rolls, and do 1d8+4 points of damage on a successful strike. A separate attack roll is made for each thrown quill.

32-33	The caster's body erupts in stiff, sharp quills that provide a +5 bonus to his AC. These quills do not inhibit spellcasting, and spell checks made by the caster are unmodified. In addition, anyone that attacks the caster in melee combat must make a DC 20 Ref save immediately after his attack or suffer 1d8+CL points of damage from contact with the quills. The caster's quill-covered hands can also be used in melee combat and are considered magical weapons for the purpose of affecting targets protected from normal attacks. The quills impart a +5 bonus to attack rolls and inflict 1d8+5 damage on a successful hit. Lastly, up to *six* quills can be thrown as a missile attack against a single target each round. The quills have a range of 20/40/60, impart a +5 magical bonus to attack rolls, and do 1d8+5 points of damage on a successful strike. A separate attack roll is made for each thrown quill.
34+	The caster's body erupts in stiff, sharp quills that provide a +6 bonus to his AC. These quills do not inhibit spellcasting, and spell checks made by the caster are unmodified. In addition, anyone that attacks the caster in melee combat must make a DC 25 Ref save immediately after his attack or suffer 1d10+CL points of damage from contact with the quills. The caster's quill-covered hands can also be used in melee combat and are considered magical weapons for the purpose of affecting targets protected from normal attacks. The quills impart a +6 bonus to attack rolls and inflict 1d8+6 damage on a successful hit. Lastly, up to *six* quills can be thrown as a missile attack against a single target each round. The quills have a range of 20/40/60, impart a +6 magical bonus to attack rolls, and do 1d8+6 points of damage on a successful strike. A separate attack roll is made for each thrown quill.
	In addition, the caster gains the ability to simultaneously hurl all the quills from his body, filling a 30' radius area around him with flying, razor-sharp spikes. All targets within that area suffer (CL)d10 damage (i.e., a level 6 caster would inflict 6d10 damage) unless protected by solid cover, in which case they receive a DC 20 save for half damage but may still take damage from the razor-sharp spikes penetrating the cover. Those protected by a *magic shield* with a spell check of 24+ are also unaffected by this burst of quills. Once this effect occurs, the caster no longer gains the benefits of the *porcupine coat*.

Phantasm

Level: 2	Range: 100' or more	Duration: 1 round or longer, with concentration	Casting time: 1 round
	Save: Will vs. spell check DC		

General	With this spell, the caster creates a simple illusion. The illusion is strictly visual, with no aural, tactile, or olfactory components. With concentration, the caster can manipulate the illusion.
Manifestation	See below.
Corruption	Roll 1d6: (1) the caster's left hand is transformed into a phantasm, becoming insubstantial and unable to grasp objects, although it appears real; the caster can no longer use two-handed weapons or otherwise manipulate objects with his left hand; (2) the caster becomes a matter-magnet, automatically granting "real" solidity to any illusion he touches; (3-5) minor; (6) major.
Misfire	Roll 1d4: (1) the caster transforms one nearby ally into a phantasm, causing that ally's image to "loop" on the same motions taken over the last few rounds, until the ally re-appears in 1d6+1 rounds with no memory of what has happened; (2) the caster creates a completely unbelievable phantasm, such as a translucent man or a very poorly animated scarecrow, which proceeds to follow him around for the rest of the day; (3) the caster summons into existence an extremely believable illusion of a deadly beast (such as a lion) which appears nearby and lunges at him before vanishing at the moment of impact, forcing a DC 10 Fort save or inflicting a -1 shock penalty to all rolls for the next 1d6 rounds; (4) the caster cannot control his illusions and generates a series of fantastic images related to faeries, gnomes, and unicorns, which frolic about him for the next 1d4 hours, drawing attention to him in almost all circumstances.
1	Lost, failure, and worse! Roll 1d6 modified by Luck: (0 or less) corruption + patron taint + misfire; (1-3) corruption; (4) patron taint (or corruption if no patron); (5+) misfire.

2-11	Lost. Failure.
12-13	Failure, but spell is not lost.

14-15   With full concentration for one round, the caster can create an image up to man-sized. The image must be something of which the caster has visual reference (such as a table resting nearby, or an adjacent ally) or has seen recently and studied carefully for at least one hour. The image springs into existence at a point indicated by the caster within 100′ and line of sight. It cannot move. It remains in place up to a maximum of 2 turns, as long as the caster concentrates. A creature with reason to disbelieve the illusion can make a Will save to see through it. Any creature that touches the illusion automatically discovers it is not real.

16-19   With full concentration for one round, the caster can create an image up to man-sized. The image must be something of which the caster has visual reference (such as a table resting nearby, or an adjacent ally) or has seen recently and studied carefully for at least one hour. The image springs into existence at a point indicated by the caster within 100′ and line of sight. The caster can cause the phantasm to move up to 5′ per round with concentration, though it is not animated. For example, he could cause a phantasmal lantern to bob in the air as if carried by a man, but if he made a phantasmal man carrying a lantern, the entire phantasm would simply shift in place by 5′ rather than appear to actually walk. The phantasm remains in place up to a maximum of 2 turns, as long as the caster concentrates. A creature with reason to disbelieve the illusion can make a Will save to see through it. Any creature that touches the illusion automatically discovers it is not real.

20-21   With full concentration for one round, the caster can create an image up to man-sized. The image must be something of which the caster has visual reference (such as a table resting nearby, or an adjacent ally) or has seen recently and studied carefully for at least one hour. The image springs into existence at a point indicated by the caster within 100′ and line of sight. The caster can cause the phantasm to move up to 30′ per round with concentration, and the phantasm will animate as if it is actually moving, provided the caster has visual reference or has carefully studied examples. For example, he could cause a phantasmal soldier to appear to actually walk. The phantasm remains in place up to a maximum of 1 hour, as long as the caster concentrates, and must remain within 100′ of the caster even while moving. If it moves beyond this range, it vanishes. A creature with reason to disbelieve the illusion can make a Will save to see through it. Any creature that touches the illusion automatically discovers it is not real.

22-25   With full concentration for one round, the caster can create an image up to giant-sized, which he can cause to "loop" on a predetermined visual track. The image must be something of which the caster has visual reference (such as a table resting nearby, or an adjacent ally) or has seen recently and studied carefully for at least one hour. The image springs into existence at a point indicated by the caster within 1,000′ and line of sight. The caster can cause the phantasm to move up to 30′ per round with concentration, and the phantasm will animate as if it is actually moving, provided the caster has visual reference or has carefully studied examples. For example, he could cause a phantasmal soldier to appear to actually walk. To create a repeating visual loop, the caster must concentrate to establish the initial path of movement and motions. Thereafter, if his concentration lapses, the phantasm repeats that movement track until the spell expires or until the caster initiates concentration again to change the track. The phantasm remains in place up to a maximum of 1 hour, "looping" whenever the caster's concentration lapses. It must remain within 1,000′ of the caster, even while moving. If it moves beyond this range, it vanishes. A creature with reason to disbelieve the illusion can make a Will save to see through it. Any creature that touches the illusion automatically discovers it is not real.

26-29   With full concentration for one round, the caster can create an image of up to castle-sized, which he can cause to "loop" on a predetermined visual track. The image must be something of which the caster has visual reference (such as a table resting nearby, or an adjacent ally) or has seen recently and studied carefully for at least one hour. The image springs into existence at a point indicated by the caster within 1,000′ and line of sight, but once created it can move beyond this range. The caster can cause the phantasm to move up to 60′ per round with concentration, and the phantasm will animate as if it is actually moving, provided the caster has visual reference or has carefully studied examples. For example, he could cause a phantasmal soldier to appear to actually walk. To create a repeating visual loop, the caster must concentrate to establish the initial path of movement and motions. Thereafter, if his concentration lapses, the phantasm repeats that movement track until the spell expires or until the caster initiates concentration again to change the track. The phantasm remains in place up to a maximum of 1 day, "looping" whenever the caster's concentration lapses. It remains in existence even if the caster leaves the 1,000′ range, automatically "looping" when the caster is gone. A creature with reason to disbelieve the illusion can make a Will save to see through it. Any creature that touches the illusion automatically discovers it is not real.

30-31   With full concentration for one round, the caster can create an image up to castle-sized, which he can cause to "loop" on a predetermined visual track. The image must be something of which the caster has visual reference (such as a table resting nearby, or an adjacent ally) or has seen recently and studied carefully for at least one hour. The image can be complex, such as a castle with knights marching along its ramparts. The image springs into existence at a point indicated by the caster within 1,000' and line of sight, but once created it can move beyond this range. The caster can cause the phantasm to move up to 60' per round with concentration, and the phantasm will animate as if it is actually moving, provided the caster has visual reference or has carefully studied examples. For example, he could cause a phantasmal soldier to appear to actually walk. To create a repeating visual loop, the caster must concentrate to establish the initial path of movement and motions. Thereafter, if his concentration lapses, the phantasm repeats that movement track until the spell expires or until the caster initiates concentration again to change the track. The phantasm remains in place up to a maximum of 1 week, "looping" whenever the caster's concentration lapses. It remains in existence even if the caster leaves the 1,000' range, automatically "looping" when the caster is gone. A creature with reason to disbelieve the illusion can make a Will save to see through it. Any creature that touches the illusion automatically discovers it is not real.

32-33   With full concentration for one round, the caster can create an image up to castle-sized, which he can cause to "loop" on a predetermined visual track. The image must be something of which the caster has visual reference (such as a table resting nearby, or an adjacent ally) or has seen recently and studied carefully for at least one hour. The image can be complex, such as a castle with knights marching along its ramparts. The image springs into existence at a point indicated by the caster within 1,000' and line of sight, but once created it can move beyond this range. The caster can cause the phantasm to move up to 60' per round with concentration, and the phantasm will animate as if it is actually moving, provided the caster has visual reference or has carefully studied examples. For example, he could cause a phantasmal soldier to appear to actually walk. To create a repeating visual loop, the caster must concentrate to establish the initial path of movement and motions. Thereafter, if his concentration lapses, the phantasm repeats that movement track until the spell expires or until the caster initiates concentration again to change the track. The phantasm remains in place up to a maximum of 1 month, "looping" whenever the caster's concentration lapses. It remains in existence even if the caster leaves the 1,000' range, automatically "looping" when the caster is gone. A creature with reason to disbelieve the illusion can make a Will save to see through it. Any creature that touches the illusion automatically discovers it is not real.

34+   With full concentration for one round, the caster can create any image he can imagine, of any size or com-

plexity, and make it appear three-dimensional and real. The image can contain many complex motions. The caster need not have visual reference, and the strength of this spellcasting will "fill in the gaps" on images he imagines but has not seen, though sometimes such use of the spell creates inaccuracies in the details that may alert a viewer to the scene's illusionary nature. The image springs into existence at a point indicated by the caster anywhere within line of sight, but once created it can move beyond this range. The caster can cause the phantasm to move up to 100' per round, and the phantasm will animate as if it is actually moving. To create a repeating visual loop, the caster must concentrate to establish the initial path of movement and motions. Thereafter, if his concentration lapses, the phantasm repeats that movement track until the spell expires or until the caster initiates concentration again to change the track. The phantasm remains in place up to a maximum of 1 year, "looping" whenever the caster's concentration lapses. It remains in existence even if the caster leaves the scene of creation, automatically "looping" when the caster is gone. A creature with reason to disbelieve the illusion can make a Will save to see through it. Any creature that touches the illusion automatically discovers it is not real.

Ray of Enfeeblement

Level: 2	Range: 150′	Duration: Instantaneous	Casting time: 1 action	Save: Will vs. spell check

General
This necromantic spell requires at least 1 point of spellburn. The caster issues a dangerous strength-draining ray, which destroys the physical prowess of a target. Reducing a creature to 0 Strength transforms it into a jelly-like mass, unable to support its own weight or defend itself from attacks. If a target does not have a defined Strength score, assume 10 for normal humans and man-sized creatures. Lost ability scores heal back at the normal rate.

Manifestation
Roll 1d5: (1) black ray; (2) flaming ray; (3) wavering disruption of the air; (4) line of steam; (5) billowing jet of mist.

Corruption
Roll 1d10: (1) caster's muscles wither, causing him to permanently lose 1 point of Strength; (2) whenever the caster takes Strength damage in the future, he heals at an abnormally slow rate, requiring two days of healing to recover one lost Strength point; (3) the caster is no longer able to expend Strength points in spellburn; (4-7) minor; (8-9) major; (10) greater.

Misfire
Roll 1d4: (1) one randomly determined ally within range is stricken with a ray that causes him to temporarily lose 1d6 Strength points (no save); (2) all allies within range temporarily suffer a wave of weakness, causing them to drop weapons and shields, release their holds on ropes, and so on; (3) the nearest 1d4 enemies receive a ray of power, which grants them a +2 Strength bonus to attacks and damage for the next turn; (4) the caster shoots himself in the foot (literally) with a ray of enfeeblement, reducing the strength of his legs and cutting his movement rate in half for the next turn.

1
Lost, failure, and worse! Roll 1d6 modified by Luck: (0 or less) corruption + patron taint + misfire; (1-3) corruption; (4) patron taint (or corruption if no patron); (5+) misfire.

2-11
Lost. Failure.

12-13
Failure, but spell is not lost.

14-15
The caster can attack one target within range, which must make a Will save or temporarily lose 1d6 points of Strength.

16-19
The caster can attack one target within range, which must make a Will save or temporarily lose 1d8+1 points of Strength.

20-21
The caster can attack one target within range that temporarily loses 3d6+1 points of Strength. Creatures of 1 HD or less receive no save; others receive a Will save. Additionally, the caster *gains* 2 points of Strength for 1 turn (does not stack with multiple castings of this spell).

22-25
The caster can launch two rays. Each ray does 3d6+1 Strength damage. Creatures of 2 HD or less receive no save; others receive a Will save. Additionally, the caster *gains* 3 points of Strength for 1 turn.

26-29
The caster can launch three rays. Each ray does 4d6+1 Strength damage. Creatures of 2 HD or less receive no save; others receive a Will save. Additionally, the caster *gains* 4 points of Strength for 1 turn.

30-31
The caster can launch four rays. Each ray does 4d6+1 Strength damage. Creatures of 3 HD or less receive no save; others receive a Will save. Additionally, the caster *gains* 5 points of Strength for 1 turn.

32-33
The caster can launch five rays. Each ray does 4d6+1 Strength damage. Creatures of 3 HD or less receive no save; others receive a Will save. Additionally, the caster *gains* 6 points of Strength for 1 turn.

34+
The caster sends forth a burst of debilitating energy that weakens all enemies within a 150′ range! All enemies within range take 4d6+4 Strength damage. Creatures of 3 HD or less receive no save; others receive a Will save. Additionally, the caster *gains* 6 points of Strength for 1 turn.

Scare

Level: 2	Range: 30' or more	Duration: 1 round or longer	Casting time: 1 round

Save: Will save vs. spell check DC

General

This spell causes its victim to experience abject terror, potentially fleeing the scene or cowering in fright. The spell does not affect automatons, golems, mindless un-dead (such as zombies or skeletons), and other creatures that do not feel fear.

Manifestation

Roll 1d4: (1) caster's visage transforms into something horrible; (2) target's worst nightmare appears before its eyes for a brief instant; (3) nothing visual occurs but unreasoning fear grips target; (4) an image of a terrible monster momentarily flashes into existence then disappears.

Corruption

Roll 1d12: (1-6) the caster develops an irrational fear related to (1) chickens, (2) horses, (3) rocks, (4) clouds, (5) apples, (6) snakes, such that he must flee in fear if he fails a DC 10 Will save whenever he sees such a creature or object; (7) the caster is especially susceptible to fear, receiving a -2 penalty to saves to resist it from now on; (8) caster's face changes to resemble the monster that he fears most; (9-10) major; (11-12) greater.

Misfire

Roll 1d4: (1-2) nearest ally is absolutely terrified and must make DC 12 Will save or run in fear for 1d4+1 rounds; (3-4) caster's visage is momentarily transformed into something absolutely horrid, frightening his familiar, which runs away for 24 hours.

1

Lost, failure, and worse! Roll 1d6 modified by Luck: (0 or less) corruption + patron taint + misfire; (1-3) corruption; (4) patron taint (or corruption if no patron); (5+) misfire.

2-11

Lost. Failure.

12-13

Failure, but spell is not lost.

14-15

The caster can target one creature within 30' and line of sight. That creature receives a Will save to resist the effect. Failure indicates it experiences a moment of fright. It immediately flees the area at maximum speed. The scare lasts only one round; on the round following the failed save, the creature recovers its wits.

16-19

The caster can target one creature within 30' and line of sight. That creature receives a Will save to resist the effect. Failure indicates it experiences a moment of fright. It immediately flees the area at maximum speed. The scare lasts 1d4+1 rounds.

20-21

The caster can target two creatures within 60' and line of sight. Those creatures receive a Will save to resist the effect. Failure indicates they experience a moment of fright. They immediately flee the area at maximum speed. The scare lasts 1d6+1 rounds.

22-25

The caster can frighten three enemies within 60'. They receive a Will save to resist the effect. Failure indicates they experience a moment of fright. They immediately flee the area at maximum speed. The scare lasts 1d6+1 rounds.

26-29

The caster can frighten all enemies within 60'. Creatures of 1 HD or less are automatically frightened; others receive a Will save to resist the effect. Failure indicates they experience a moment of fright. They immediately flee the area at maximum speed. The scare lasts 1d6+1 rounds.

30-31

The caster can frighten all enemies within 60'. Creatures of 2 HD or less are automatically frightened; others receive a Will save to resist the effect. Failure indicates they experience a moment of fright. The fright is so painful they take 1d4 points of damage (potentially dropping dead from fear!), and then immediately flee the area at maximum speed. The scare lasts 2d6+1 rounds.

32-33

The caster can frighten all enemies within 90'. Creatures of 2 HD or less are automatically frightened; others receive a Will save to resist the effect. Failure indicates they experience a moment of fright. The fright is so painful they take 1d8 points of damage (potentially dropping dead from fear!), and then immediately flee the area at maximum speed. The scare lasts 3d6+1 rounds.

34+

The caster can frighten all enemies within 120'. Creatures of 3 HD or less are automatically frightened; others receive a Will save to resist the effect. Failure indicates they experience a moment of fright. The fright is so painful they take 2d8 points of damage (potentially dropping dead from fear!), and then immediately flee the area at maximum speed. The scare lasts 3d6+1 rounds.

Scorching Ray

| Level: 2 | Range: 80' | Duration: Instantaneous | Casting time: 1 action | Save: Ref partial (see below) |

General
The caster summons the flames of Hell to immolate his foes.

Manifestation
Roll 1d5: (1) arcing ray of fire; (2) laser beam; (3) flaming bullet; (4) sizzling gout of flame; (5) burning hands followed by spray of sparks. Color of fire varies – red, yellow, blue, or green.

Corruption
Roll 1d8: (1) all hair on the caster's head is permanently burned off (including eyebrows and facial hair); (2) the caster's hands and arms are blackened, as if they had been charred and burned; (3) the caster's skin is permanently sunburned, causing discomfort and pain when he wears armor or rough fabrics; (4) the caster's face is caught in a burst of flame, melting his flesh into a horribly grotesque appearance; (5) the caster develops an extreme sensitivity to heat, automatically taking an extra +1 damage on all dice related to fire damage from now on; (6) greater; (7) major; (8) minor.

Misfire
Roll 1d4: (1) caster explodes a ball of fire centered on himself, causing 1d6 damage and burning up all flammable objects on his person; (2) caster sends forth an errant ray of fire that causes 1d6 damage to one randomly determined ally within 30'; (3) caster lights the nearest ally on fire briefly for 1d4 damage; (4) caster inadvertently reverses the spell, summoning a wave of chilling cold that automatically extinguishes all flames within 100' of him.

1
Lost, failure, and worse! Roll 1d6 modified by Luck: (0 or less) corruption + patron taint + misfire; (1-2) corruption; (3) patron taint (or corruption if no patron); (4+) misfire.

2-11
Lost. Failure.

12-13
Failure, but spell is not lost.

14-15
One target takes 1d6 + caster level damage. Additionally, it must make a Reflex save vs. spell check or catch fire. Each round thereafter it suffers an additional 1d6 damage until it succeeds on a DC 15 Reflex save to extinguish the fire. Flammable objects on the target (e.g., scrolls or tomes) have a 75% chance of catching fire unless protected.

16-19
One target takes 1d8 + caster level damage. Additionally, it must make a DC 15 Reflex save or catch fire. Each round thereafter it suffers an additional 1d6 damage until it succeeds on a DC 15 Reflex save to extinguish the fire. Flammable objects on the target (e.g., scrolls or tomes) have a 75% chance of catching fire unless protected.

20-21
The caster can launch two rays, at the same target or at two targets. Each ray does 1d10 + caster level damage. Additionally, each target must make a DC 15 Reflex save or catch fire. Each round thereafter the target suffers an additional 1d6 damage until it succeeds on a DC 15 Reflex save to extinguish the fire. Flammable objects on the target (e.g., scrolls or tomes) have a 75% chance of catching fire unless protected.

22-25
The caster can launch three rays, at the same target or different targets. Each ray does 1d12 + caster level damage. Additionally, each target must make a DC 15 Reflex save or catch fire. Each round thereafter the target suffers an additional 1d6 damage until it succeeds on a DC 15 Reflex save to extinguish the fire. Flammable objects on the target (e.g., scrolls or tomes) have a 75% chance of catching fire unless protected.

26-29
The caster sends forth a fanning wave of flames. The attack is shaped like a cone, centered on the caster and expanding to a width of 40' at its farthest end 80' away. All targets within the cone take 1d12 + caster level damage. Additionally, each target must make a DC 15 Reflex save or catch fire. Each round thereafter the target suffers an additional 1d6 damage until it succeeds on a DC 15 Reflex save to extinguish the fire. Flammable objects on the target (e.g., scrolls or tomes) have a 75% chance of catching fire unless protected.

30-31
The caster detonates a blast of fire centered on himself. He suffers no damage, but all targets within 20' are automatically immolated for 1d12 points of damage. In addition, the blast sends out up to a dozen jets of flame, each 80' long and aimed at a single target. Each jet does 1d20 + caster level damage and automatically catches the target on fire for an additional 1d6 damage each round until the target makes a DC 15 Reflex save. Flammable objects on the target (e.g., scrolls or tomes) automatically catch fire. No target can be damaged by more than one jet of flame.

32-33	The caster detonates a blast of fire centered on himself. He suffers no damage, but all targets within 30' are automatically immolated for 1d20 points of damage. In addition, the blast sends out up to a dozen jets of flame, each 80' long and aimed at a single target. Each jet does 1d20 + caster level damage and automatically catches the target on fire for an additional 1d8 damage each round until the target makes a DC 15 Reflex save. Flammable objects on the target (e.g., scrolls or tomes) automatically catch fire. No target can be damaged by more than one jet of flame.
34+	The caster summons a jet of magma and flame from the earth's core, which explodes upward from his feet then blasts out at his enemies. He can direct a scorching ray of flame at any target he can see, to a range of 1,000'. The amount of damage done by each ray depends on how much the caster must dilute the pure magma of the earth's core. A single target takes 6d20+CL damage; 2-5 targets each take 4d20+CL damage; 6-10 targets each take 3d12+CL damage; 11-30 targets each take 1d20+CL damage; 31-50 targets each take 1d12+CL damage; 51-100 targets each take 1d8 damage; and 101 or more targets each take 1d6 damage. Every target must succeed on a DC 15 Reflex save or catch fire, suffering an additional 1d6 damage every round thereafter until they again succeed on a DC 15 Reflex save.

Shatter

Level: 2	Range: Touch or further	Duration: Instantaneous or longer	Casting time: 1 round	Save: N/A

General	The caster shatters a physical object. This spell causes damage to inanimate objects and is particularly effective at objects made of crystal or glass. It has the potential to not only damage the object immediately but also cause ongoing fractures that make it more susceptible to future damage.
Manifestation	Roll 1d4: (1) object simply shatters; (2) blast as if an explosion; (3) flash of light; (4) bolt of lightning from the sky strikes the object.
Corruption	Roll 1d6: (1-3) minor; (4-5) major; (6) greater.
Misfire	Roll 1d5: (1) one randomly determined object on the caster's person shatters; (2) randomly determine one ally within 20' (or caster if no nearby ally) and *all* mundane possessions of that ally have risk of shattering, as follows: magical objects have 10% chance, metal and stone objects have 25% chance, wooden and crystal/gemlike objects have 50% chance, cloth and all other soft objects have 75% chance of crumbling apart; (3) instead of shattering targeted object, spell infuses it with greater strength of construction, rendering it automatically resistant to the next *shatter* spell cast against it, but resistance wears off after one use; (4) *all* non-magical weapons in the hands of creatures (both allies and enemies) within 25' shatter (only affects those weapons held not those in backpacks or sheaths); (5) *all* armor within 25' (including shields and helms) comes apart and loses armor bonus (i.e., buckles unbuckle, straps fail, armor joints collapse, etc.).

1	Lost, failure, and worse! Roll 1d6 modified by Luck: (0 or less) corruption + patron taint + misfire; (1) corruption; (2) patron taint (or corruption if no patron); (3+) misfire.
2-11	Lost. Failure.
12-13	Failure, but spell is not lost.
14-15	By touching a mundane (non-magical) inanimate object made of wood, metal, crystal, glass, stone, or another similar substance, the caster creates a fracture at the point of contact. This automatically inflicts 1d4 points of damage to the object, bypassing any normal resistance to damage. Typically, a dagger has 1-4 hit points, a sword has 4-6 hit points, and larger objects have progressively more hit points, depending on their construction (glass is weakest, wood is stronger, stone is even stronger, metal is strongest). This effect is typically enough to break a doorknob or hinge, shatter a glass window, snap a dagger blade from its hilt, or crack a mirror, but not enough to burst down a door. Using this spell in combat is dangerous, as the caster is exposed to attack when he attempts to touch the target object; opponents receive a free strike if the caster tries to touch them with this spell, and the caster must also succeed in an attack roll to make contact.
16-19	By touching a mundane (non-magical) inanimate object made of wood, metal, crystal, glass, stone, or another similar substance, the caster creates a fracture at the point of contact. This automatically inflicts 3d4 points of damage to the object and an additional +2 points of damage if the object is glass or crystal or a gemstone, bypassing any normal resistance to damage. Typically, a dagger has 1-4 hit points, a sword

has 4-6 hit points, and larger objects have progressively more hit points, depending on their construction (glass is weakest, wood is stronger, stone is even stronger, metal is strongest). This spell result is usually enough to shatter a sword, shield, or helm, break a wagon wheel, explode a mirror, or shatter a valuable gem (but not a diamond). Using this spell in combat is dangerous, as the caster is exposed to attack when he attempts to touch the target object; opponents receive a free strike if the caster tries to touch them with this spell, and the caster must also succeed in an attack roll to make contact.

20-21   By touching a mundane (non-magical) inanimate object made of wood, metal, crystal, glass, stone, or another similar substance, the caster create a fracture at the point of contact. This automatically inflicts 3d6+CL damage to the object and an additional +4 points of damage if the object is glass or crystal or a gemstone, bypassing any normal resistance to damage. Typically, a dagger has 1-4 hit points, a sword has 4-6 hit points, and larger objects have progressively more hit points, depending on their construction (glass is weakest, wood is stronger, stone is even stronger, metal is strongest). This spell result is usually enough to break down a door, crack a suit of plate mail, burst an ironbound chest in half, break a wagon in half, or shatter a diamond. Using this spell in combat is dangerous, as the caster is exposed to attack when he attempts to touch the target object; opponents receive a free strike if the caster tries to touch them with this spell, and the caster must also succeed in an attack roll to make contact.

22-25   By touching an inanimate object made of wood, metal, crystal, glass, stone, or another similar substance, the caster creates a fracture at the point of contact. This automatically inflicts 4d6+CL damage to mundane objects or 1d6 points of damage to magical objects (such as magic weapons). It inflicts an additional +4 points of damage if the object is glass or crystal or a gemstone, bypassing any normal resistance to damage. Typically, a dagger has 1-4 hit points, a sword has 4-6 hit points, and larger objects have progressively more hit points, depending on their construction (glass is weakest, wood is stronger, stone is even stronger, metal is strongest). This spell result is usually enough to break down a door, crack a suit of plate mail, burst an ironbound chest in half, break a wagon in half, or shatter a diamond. Using this spell in combat is dangerous, as the caster is exposed to attack when he attempts to touch the target object; opponents receive a free strike if the caster tries to touch them with this spell, and the caster must also succeed in an attack roll to make contact.

26-29	By touching an inanimate object made of wood, metal, crystal, glass, stone, or another similar substance, the caster creates a fracture at the point of contact. Alternatively, the caster can imbue the power of this spell on a single object (such as an arrow or dagger point). The spell is triggered when the object strikes something within the next round; after 1 round, the power dissipates. This allows the caster to enchant an arrow that can then be used to shatter an enemy's armor (for example). The spell automatically inflicts 4d8+CL damage to mundane objects or 2d6 points of damage to magical objects (such as magic weapons). It inflicts an additional +4 points of damage if the object is glass or crystal or a gemstone, bypassing any normal resistance to damage. Typically, a dagger has 1-4 hit points, a sword has 4-6 hit points, and larger objects have progressively more hit points, depending on their construction (glass is weakest, wood is stronger, stone is even stronger, metal is strongest). This spell result is usually enough to break down a door, crack a suit of plate mail, burst an ironbound chest in half, break a wagon in half, or shatter a diamond. Using this spell in combat is dangerous, as the caster is exposed to attack when he attempts to touch the target object; opponents receive a free strike if the caster tries to touch them with this spell, and the caster must also succeed in an attack roll to make contact.
30-31	By touching an inanimate object made of wood, metal, crystal, glass, stone, or another similar substance, the caster creates a fracture at the point of contact. Alternatively, the caster can imbue the power of this spell on a single object (such as an arrow or dagger point). The spell is triggered when the object strikes something within the next turn. This allows the caster to enchant an arrow that can then be used to shatter an enemy's armor (for example). The spell automatically inflicts 4d8+CL damage to mundane objects or 2d6 points of damage to magical objects (such as magic weapons). It inflicts an additional +4 points of damage if the object is glass or crystal or a gemstone, bypassing any normal resistance to damage. Typically, a dagger has 1-4 hit points, a sword has 4-6 hit points, and larger objects have progressively more hit points, depending on their construction (glass is weakest, wood is stronger, stone is even stronger, metal is strongest). This spell result is usually enough to break down a door, crack a suit of plate mail, burst an ironbound chest in half, break a wagon in half, or shatter a diamond. Using this spell in combat is dangerous, as the caster is exposed to attack when he attempts to touch the target object; opponents receive a free strike if the caster tries to touch them with this spell, and the caster must also succeed in an attack roll to make contact.
32-33	Within a range of 60', the caster can target an inanimate object made of wood, metal, crystal, glass, stone, or another similar substance, to create a fracture at the point of contact. Alternatively, the caster can imbue the power of this spell on a single object (such as an arrow or dagger point). The spell is triggered when that object strikes something within the next turn. This allows the caster to enchant an arrow that can then be used to shatter an enemy's armor (for example). The spell automatically inflicts 4d8+CL damage to mundane objects or 3d6+CL damage to magical objects (such as magic weapons). It inflicts an additional +4 points of damage if the object is glass or crystal or a gemstone, bypassing any normal resistance to damage. Typically, a dagger has 1-4 hit points, a sword has 4-6 hit points, and larger objects have progressively more hit points, depending on their construction (glass is weakest, wood is stronger, stone is even stronger, metal is strongest). This spell result is usually enough to break down a door, crack a suit of plate mail, burst an ironbound chest in half, break a wagon in half, or shatter a diamond.
34+	Within a range of 1,000', the caster can target an inanimate object made of wood, metal, crystal, glass, stone, or another similar substance, to create a fracture at the point of contact. At this level of casting, the caster can also target golems, automatons, living statues, and other animated but non-sentient creatures, which count as magical objects for purposes of the spell. Alternatively, the caster can imbue the power of this spell on a single object (such as an arrow or dagger point). The spell power remains on the object permanently, and the spell is triggered when that object strikes something. This allows the caster to enchant an arrow that can then be used to shatter an enemy's armor (for example). The spell automatically inflicts 6d8+CL damage to mundane objects or 4d6+CL damage to magical objects (such as magic weapons). It inflicts an additional +6 points of damage if the object is glass or crystal or a gemstone, bypassing any normal resistance to damage. Typically, a dagger has 1-4 hit points, a sword has 4-6 hit points, and larger objects have progressively more hit points, depending on their construction (glass is weakest, wood is stronger, stone is even stronger, metal is strongest). This spell result is usually enough to break down a door, crack a suit of plate mail, burst an ironbound chest in half, break a wagon in half, or shatter a diamond.

Spider Web

Level: 2	Range: Varies	Duration: Varies	Casting time: 1 action	Save: Varies (see below)

General	The caster creates a sticky spider web with which to entangle his foes. Unless objects are trapped by the web, it is difficult to see, effectively invisible unless someone is searching for it. A creature that touches the web is held fast, able to escape only by a DC 20 Strength or Agility check. The web can be burned off (possibly wounding captured creatures) or hacked through with a very sharp blade by a creature not already caught (AC 16, 5 hp to free one creature). A dull blade or blunt object will simply become entangled; even a strike with an exceptionally sharp blade has a 25% chance of entangling the weapon. Melee attacks aimed at the creatures held by the web run a 10% risk per attack of entangling the attacker.
Manifestation	Some form of spider web, as determined by the caster (long and stringy, a clumped mass, elegant, torn, etc.).
Corruption	Roll 1d8: (1) cobwebs form permanently between the caster's fingers; (2) as the caster speaks, a dribble of webby mass forms at the corners of his mouth; (3) the caster's hair becomes sticky like a web, and small objects (leaves, twigs, dust, bird feathers, etc.) are constantly becoming stuck; (4) caster grows six extra eyes, like those of a spider, at the crown of his head; (5) caster's mouth forms fangs like those of a spider; (6) caster's skin emits an oily, friction-resistant residue, which makes him immune to tangling in spider webs (both magical or mundane) but also gives him a 10% chance of slipping off any rope, ledge, wall, or other climbing surface that relies on friction for success; (7) minor, (8) major.
Misfire	Roll 1d4: (1) globular mass of webbing plops from the caster's hand and explodes at his feet, entangling him and everything within 10' of him for 1d6 minutes (DC 20 Strength or Agility to escape); (2) the caster inadvertently summons not a spider web but instead the poisonous spider that lives in it, which immediately attacks him before scurrying away 1d4+1 rounds later (Atk bite +3 melee, dmg 1d3 + poison (DC 20 Fort or 2d4 Stamina), AC 8, HP 6); (3) the demon queen of the spider pits tires of her servants being misused by mortals and takes notice of the caster, who finds himself beset by arachnid opponents at all turns (judge's discretion) for the next 1d7+1 days – these spiders, both mundane and demonic, attack *exclusively* the caster and clearly seek to punish him; (4) the caster misfires a jet of spider web into the sky, which descends in clumpy strands; all creatures within 25' (including the caster) must make a DC 10 Ref save or be entangled in a small bit of web, which causes a -2 penalty to all actions for 1d4 rounds as the target untangles himself.

1	Lost, failure, and worse! Roll 1d6 modified by Luck: (0 or less) corruption + patron taint + misfire; (1-2) corruption; (3) patron taint (or corruption if no patron); (4+) misfire.
2-11	Lost. Failure.
12-13	Failure, but spell is not lost.
14-15	The caster weaves a spider web up to 10' in diameter. It can be placed in any static location (such as a door frame or hallway) touched. The web lasts for 1d6 hours before dissolving.
16-19	The caster weaves a spider web up to 20' in diameter. It can be placed in any static location (such as a door frame or hallway) touched. The web lasts for 1d6 hours before dissolving.
20-21	The caster weaves a spider web up to 30' in diameter. It can be placed in any static location (such as a door frame or hallway) touched. The web lasts for 1d6 days before dissolving.
22-25	The caster weaves a spider web up to 30' in diameter. The web lasts for 1d6 days before dissolving. The caster can place the web in a static location or fling the web a distance of up to 50'. If aimed at a living creature or small target, the caster must make a normal missile fire attack roll against the target, though he receive a +6 bonus to reflect the fact that the web need only touch the target not pierce its armor. A miss means the web lands 1d30' away in a random direction, still potentially capturing the target.
26-29	The caster weaves a spider web with a shape he can manipulate within a total mass of roughly 30' x 30' x 1'. For example, the caster could create a spidery rope 900' long or a rectangular web 10' x 90' that runs the length of a corridor floor. The web lasts for 2d6+CL days before dissolving. The caster can place the web in a static location or fling the web a distance of up to 200'. If aimed at a living creature or small target, the caster must make a normal missile fire attack roll against the target, though he receives a +6 bonus to reflect the fact that the web need only touch the target not pierce its armor. A miss means the web lands 1d30' away in a random direction, still potentially capturing the target.

30-31	The caster weaves up to *three* spider webs with shapes he can manipulate within a total mass of roughly 30' x 30' x 1'. For example, the caster could create a spidery rope 900' long, or a rectangular web 10' x 90' that runs the length of a corridor floor, or a single "personal" web 5'x5' designed to target one creature. Each web lasts for 2d6+CL days before dissolving. The caster can place a web in a static location or fling a web a distance of up to 200'. The caster can aim all three webs at living targets in the round of casting if he wishes. If aimed at a living creature or small target, the caster must make a normal missile fire attack roll against the target, though he receives a +8 bonus to reflect the fact that the web need only touch the target not pierce its armor. A miss means the web lands 1d30' away in a random direction, still potentially capturing the target.
32-33	The caster weaves up to *three* spider webs with shapes he can manipulate within a total mass of roughly 30' x 30' x 1'. For example, the caster could create a spidery rope 900' long, or a rectangular web 10' x 90' that runs the length of a corridor floor, or a single "personal" web 5'x5' designed to target one creature. Each web lasts for 1d6+CL months before dissolving. The caster can place a web in a static location or fling a web a distance of up to 200'. The caster can aim all three webs at living targets in the round of casting if he wishes. If aimed at a living creature or small target, the caster must make a normal missile fire attack roll against the target, though he receives a +8 bonus to reflect the fact that the web need only touch the target not pierce its armor. A miss means the web lands 1d30' away in a random direction, still potentially capturing the target.
34+	The caster can fill an enormous space with sticky cobwebs. The space can be up to a mile in diameter: the interior of a castle, the entire span of a battlefield, or the ceiling of a vast cavern. Alternately, the caster can choose to make the webbed space quite small and can restrict it to up to 10 human-shaped targets if he wishes. If the space covered is large, the caster can sculpt the mass of webbing to a general three-dimensional shape, but he does not have the control to individually exclude "holes" within the space (i.e., if he casts over a battlefield he can choose a rectangular shape, circular shape, oval shape, etc., but entangles all creatures inside the web). The webbing is particularly dense and can only be escaped with a DC 25 Strength or Agility check. It is also fire-resistant, with a 25% chance to resist new fires or extinguish existing fires each round. The webbing is permanent in duration until destroyed or magically dispelled.

Strength

Level: 2	Range: Varies	Duration: Varies	Casting time: 1 action	Save: N/A

General	With an arcane incantation, the caster grants physical strength to a willing target.
Manifestation	Roll 1d4: (1) biceps and muscles physically enlarge, potentially bursting clothing; (2) muscles glow with infernal light; (3) fierce aura surrounds target; (4) no change.
Corruption	Roll 1d8: (1) caster's muscles wither and age, permanently reducing his Strength by 1 point; (2) caster has great difficulty summoning any kind of supernatural strength, such that from now on all spellburn of Strength requires 2 points of spellburn for every +1 to a spell check; (3) caster permanently gains +1d4 points of Strength but at the cost of the same number of points of Intelligence; (4) caster's muscles bulge disproportionately and chaotically, giving him a lopsided, hunchbacked appearance; (5-6) minor; (7) major; (8) greater.
Misfire	Roll 1d4: (1) caster inadvertently weakens himself, losing 1d4+1 points of Strength temporarily; (2) caster saps the strength of those around him, reducing the Strength of everyone within 20' (allies and enemies alike) by 1d4+1 points; (3) caster channels his allies' strength of will to his enemies' strength, such that the highest allied Willpower save within 20' becomes the total Strength modifier of all enemies within the same range; i.e., a party of 10 adventurers whose greatest Will save is +4 would suddenly grant a +4 Strength modifier to all nearby enemies; (4) caster drops to the ground with the strength of an infant, completely unable to move (Str 0), and *all* of his Strength points flow to the nearest ally of his choice, whose Strength suddenly increases by the amount of the caster's decrease, with the lost Strength returning from target to caster at the end of 1d4 turns.

1	Lost, failure, and worse! Roll 1d6 modified by Luck: (0 or less) corruption + patron taint + misfire; (1-2) corruption; (3) patron taint (or corruption if no patron); (4+) misfire.
2-11	Lost. Failure.
12-13	Failure, but spell is not lost.
14-15	One target the caster touches (including himself) is enhanced to a prodigious Strength of 18 (+3 bonus), which lasts for 1d6+1 rounds.
16-19	One target the caster touches briefly gains superhuman strength. The target is treated as having a Strength modifier of +10 until the end of the next round. The superhuman Strength immediately fades after the end of that round.
20-21	One target the caster touches gains Strength 20 (+4 bonus), which lasts for 1d6 turns.
22-25	A single target touched receives Strength 20 (+4 bonus) or two targets each receive Strength 18 (+3 bonus). The bonus lasts for 1d6 turns.
26-29	All allies within 20' of the caster gain Strength 18 (+3 bonus) for next 1d6 turns.
30-31	All allies within 20' of the caster take their next activation as if they had a +10 Strength modifier. Additionally, they gain Strength 18 (+4 bonus) for the next 1d6 hours thereafter.
32-33	All allies with 100' of the caster receive Strength 20 (+4 bonus) for the next 1d4 days.
34+	If caster completes a week-long ritual casting with a minimum of 10 points of spellburn, and

both target and caster render appropriate sacrifices of great value, the target receives a one-time permanent bonus of +1 Strength. However, the target must make a Fortitude save or find his body unable to sustain the magical transformation. The save DC is equal to 15 + 2 for every point of Strength that has been magically added; i.e., the first save is DC 17, then if this spell is attempted again the save is DC 19, and so on. If the save is failed, the increased Strength fades after 1d6 weeks, and the caster finds that 1 point of his spellburn never truly heals (judge's discretion which ability is affected).

Wizard Staff

Level: 2	Range: Self	Duration: Permanent	Casting time: 1 week per caster level	Save: N/A

General	With this spell, the wizard crafts a staff and imbues it with magical energies linked to his soul. A wizard can create only one staff at a time and suffers great pains if it is destroyed. The material cost is 1,000 gp per caster level, plus any unusual materials (e.g., an adamantine staff requires sufficient adamantine), plus a minimum of 2 points of spellburn per caster level to properly bond the staff. One point of this spellburn never heals; it is permanent ability loss. Additionally, the caster must have the requisite spells that will be placed into the staff, and be able to utilize them without rest during the casting period. The casting period is ongoing with brief spurts of restless sleep, and the caster does not heal spellburn (or other wounds) during this time. The staff's efficacy is much greater at higher caster levels, and thus the time and material cost rises as the wizard progresses in power level. In the descriptions below, "original caster level" refers to the level at which the wizard crafted the staff – if he advances in level after creating the staff, abilities associated with original caster level do not increase.
Manifestation	One staff to be crafted by the caster, of any wood, metal, bone, or other material.
Corruption	Roll 1d8: (1-4) minor; (5-6) major; (7-8) greater.
Misfire	N/A

1	Lost, failure, corruption, and patron taint!
2-11	Lost. Failure.
12-13	Failure, but spell is not lost.
14-15	The caster succeeds in crafting a simple staff, which is linked to his soul. If the staff is ever destroyed, he immediately takes damage equal to 1d4 hit points per original caster level. The staff counts as a +1 magical weapon and inflicts damage equal to 1d4+1 + caster level (plus Str modifier). The staff also emits light in a 20' radius, which can be turned on or off and vary in intensity from candlelight to full daylight, at the caster's discretion.
16-19	The caster succeeds in crafting a simple staff, which is linked to his soul. If the staff is ever destroyed, he immediately takes damage equal to 1d4 hit points per original caster level. The staff counts as a +1 magical weapon and inflicts damage equal to 1d4+1 + caster level (plus Str modifier). The staff also emits light in a 20' radius, which can be turned on or off and vary in intensity from candlelight to full daylight, at the caster's discretion. During the casting time, the caster may attempt a single casting of one other spell he knows. If it succeeds, the staff's wielder receives a +1 bonus to spell checks when casting that spell or a +2 bonus if the original caster level is 4 or higher.
20-21	The caster succeeds in crafting a simple staff, which is linked to his soul. If the staff is ever destroyed, he immediately takes damage equal to 1d4 hit points per original caster level. The staff counts as a +1 magical weapon and inflicts damage equal to 1d4+1 + caster level (plus Str modifier). The staff also emits light in a 20' radius, which can be turned on or off and vary in intensity from candlelight to full daylight, at the caster's discretion. During the casting time, the caster may attempt a single casting of one other spell he knows. If it succeeds, the staff's wielder receives a +1 bonus to spell checks when casting that spell or a +2 bonus if the original caster level is 4 or higher. The staff also grants a +1 bonus to saving throws or a +2 bonus if the original caster level is 4 or higher.
22-25	The caster succeeds in crafting a simple staff, which is linked to his soul. If the staff is ever destroyed, he immediately takes damage equal to 1d4 hit points per original caster level. The staff counts as a +1 magical weapon and inflicts damage equal to 1d4+1 + caster level (plus Str modifier). The staff also emits light

in a 20′ radius, which can be turned on or off and vary in intensity from candlelight to full daylight, at the caster's discretion. During the casting time, the caster may attempt to cast two other spells he knows. If a casting succeeds, the staff's wielder receives a +1 bonus to spell checks when casting those spells or a +2 bonus if the original caster level is 4 or higher. The staff also grants a +1 bonus to saving throws or a +2 bonus if the original caster level is 4 or higher.

26-29	The caster succeeds in crafting a simple staff, which is linked to his soul. If the staff is ever destroyed, he immediately takes damage equal to 1d4 hit points per original caster level. The staff counts as a +1 magical weapon and inflicts damage equal to 1d4+1 + caster level (plus Str modifier). The staff also emits light in a 20′ radius, which can be turned on or off and vary in intensity from candlelight to full daylight, at the caster's discretion. During the casting time, the caster may attempt to cast two other spells he knows. If a casting succeeds, the staff's wielder receives a +1 bonus to spell checks when casting those spells or a +2 bonus if the original caster level is 4 or higher. The staff also grants a +1 bonus to saving throws *and* armor class or a +2 bonus if the original caster level is 4 or higher.
30-31	The caster succeeds in crafting a simple staff, which is linked to his soul. If the staff is ever destroyed, he immediately takes damage equal to 1d4 hit points per original caster level. The staff counts as a +1 magical weapon and inflicts damage equal to 1d4+1 + caster level (plus Str modifier). The staff also emits light in a 20′ radius, which can be turned on or off and vary in intensity from candlelight to full daylight, at the caster's discretion. During the casting time, the caster may attempt to cast three other spells he knows. If a casting succeeds, the staff's wielder receives a +1 bonus to spell checks when casting those spells or a +2 bonus if the original caster level is 4 or higher. The staff also grants a +1 bonus to saving throws *and* armor class or a +2 bonus if the original caster level is 4 or higher.
32-33	The caster succeeds in crafting a simple staff, which is linked to his soul. If the staff is ever destroyed, he immediately takes damage equal to 1d4 hit points per original caster level. The staff counts as a +1 magical weapon and inflicts damage equal to 1d4+1 + caster level (plus Str modifier). The staff also emits light in a 20′ radius, which can be turned on or off and vary in intensity from candlelight to full daylight, at the caster's discretion. During the casting time, the caster may attempt to cast three other spells he knows. If a casting succeeds, the staff's wielder receives a +1 bonus to spell checks when casting those spells or a +2 bonus if the original caster level is 4 or higher. The staff also grants a +1 bonus to saving throws *and* armor class or a +2 bonus if the original caster level is 4 or higher.

Additionally, the caster can imbue the staff with fixed charges associated with the three spells he casts. For the first spell, he makes a spell check. If it succeeds, he makes another spell check for the same spell, a number of times up to his caster level. For example, a level 4 caster could make up to 4 checks if each succeeds. Then he repeats this process for the second and third spells. For each check that succeeds, he imbues the staff with 1 charge of the relevant spell. For example, the level 4 caster could put up to 12 charges in the staff if every check succeeded (3 spells x 4 castings per spell = 12 charges). Thenceforth, the caster may burn those charges to cast the three spells stored in the staff, making a normal spell check to cast the spell, modified by the +1 or +2 bonus associated with that spell. Once expended, the charges are lost unless renewed. Renewal requires a modified casting of this spell, with a casting time of 1 week and no materials or spellburn required; if this modified version succeeds at DC 30 or better, the caster can repeat the process above to restore the castings, but cannot exceed the original number of charges.

For example: a level 4 caster attempts to burn the spells *sleep, spider web,* and *strength* into his staff. The minimum successful check result for *sleep* (a level 1 spell) is DC 12. His check results are 14, 16, 12, and 9. The first three checks succeed, so he imbues three charges into his staff. For *spider web* (a level 2 spell with minimum check result of DC 14), his first check is a 19 but his second check is a 12. He manages to imbue only one charge into the staff. Finally, he casts *strength* (minimum check result of DC 14) and rolls 20, 19, 17, and 18 – four successes! The final tally is a staff with 8 charges: 3x *sleep,* 1x *spider web,* and 4x *strength.* Because he was CL 4 when casting, each of these spells is cast with a +2 bonus.

34+	The caster succeeds in crafting a simple staff, which is linked to his soul. If the staff is ever destroyed, he immediately takes damage equal to 1d4 hit points per original caster level. The staff counts as a +1 magical weapon and inflicts damage equal to 1d4+1 + caster level (plus Str modifier). The staff also emits light in a 20′ radius, which can be turned on or off and vary in intensity from candlelight to full daylight, at the caster's discretion. During the casting time, the caster may attempt to cast three other spells he knows. If a casting succeeds, the staff's wielder receives a +1 bonus to spell checks when casting those spells or a +2 bonus if the original caster level is 4 or higher. The staff also grants a +1 bonus to saving throws *and* armor class or a +2 bonus if the original caster level is 4 or higher.

Additionally, the caster can imbue the staff with fixed charges associated with the three spells he casts. For the first spell, he makes a spell check. If it succeeds, he makes another spell check for the same spell, a number of times up to his caster level. For example, a level 4 caster could make up to 4 checks if each succeeds. Then he repeats this process for the second and third spells. For each check that succeeds, he imbues the staff with 1 charge of the relevant spell. For example, the level 4 caster could put up to 12 charges in the staff if every check succeeded (3 spells x 4 castings per spell = 12 charges). Thenceforth, the caster may burn those charges to cast the three spells stored in the staff, making a normal spell check to cast the spell, modified by the +1 or +2 bonus associated with that spell. Once expended, the charges are lost unless renewed. Renewal requires a modified casting of this spell, with a casting time of 1 week and no materials or spellburn required; if this modified version succeeds at DC 30 or better, the caster can repeat the process above to restore the castings, but cannot exceed the original number of charges.

For example: a level 4 caster attempts to burn the spells *sleep, spider web*, and *strength* into his staff. The minimum successful check result for *sleep* (a level 1 spell) is DC 12. His check results are 14, 16, 12, and 9. The first three checks succeed, so he imbues three charges into his staff. For *spider web* (a level 2 spell with minimum check result of DC 14), his first check is a 19 but his second check is a 12. He manages to imbue only one charge into the staff. Finally, he casts *strength* (minimum check result of DC 14) and rolls 20, 19, 17, and 18 – four successes! The final tally is a staff with 8 charges: 3x *sleep*, 1x *spider web*, and 4x *strength*. Because he was CL 4 when casting, each of these spells is cast with a +2 bonus.

Finally, the caster may grant the staff one unique ability. For example, the ability to wither an opponent's limbs or the power to transform into a serpent. These unique abilities require research, practice, and special materials. They should be determined with the aid of the judge.

LEVEL 3 WIZARD SPELLS

Breathe Life

| Level: 3 | Range: Touch | Duration: 1 turn or longer | Casting time: 1 turn | Save: N/A |

General

With an enchanted breath from his lungs, the caster brings life to an inanimate object. This spell can make statues move, turn clay figurines into obedient homunculi, cause spell books to defend themselves against interlopers, and transform dungeon doors into stalwart guardians. The spell requires a short ritual and a variety of special ingredients that vary according to the object to be animated. This spell does not work on the remains of living creatures and cannot be used as a substitute for *animate dead*.

The object moves according to its nature, typically at a speed of 20' or less: a book may move like an inchworm, a clay statuette may move according to the legs or wings with which it is endowed, a door might waddle about on its corners, and so on. In combination with other spells used in the casting ritual, the animated creature may speak (e.g., *magic mouth*), fly (e.g., *fly*), or have other properties (e.g., *invisibility*, *fire resistance*, etc.). The caster can include up to one additional spell effect per CL and must succeed in a casting of that spell with a minimum of 1 point of spellburn for it to take effect.

The animated creature does not always obey the whims of its creator. Except as noted below, the creator must make a DC 5 Personality check to elicit obedience to any specific command that places the object in danger or is opposed to its nature (i.e., sending a clay statue into a body of water or asking a book to leap above a fire).

The animated creature has statistics as noted below. Its AC varies according to material: paper is AC 4, cloth or straw is AC 6, leather or hide is AC 8, wood or clay is AC 10, stone is AC 12, and iron or steel is AC 14. Hit points are noted as below but are increased for particularly durable materials: wood or clay grants +1 per die, stone grants +2 per die, and iron or steel grants +3 per die. Unique or specialized materials may have other properties and benefits at the judge's discretion.

Manifestation

See below.

Corruption

Roll 1d6: (1) one of caster's fingers permanently transforms into material he intended to animate; i.e., if he was trying to animate a stone statue, his finger becomes living stone; (2) objects of the intended type (e.g., gemstones if the caster targeted a gem) become inexplicably animated around the caster, quivering or jumping or shaking; this effect extends to a 10' radius and affects objects of that type for the rest of the caster's life; (3-4) minor; (5) major; (6) greater.

Misfire

Roll 1d4: (1) targeted object does not come to life but instead takes 1d6 hit points of damage (which may be enough to destroy or shatter a small object); (2) the breath of life does come forth but it appears in the wrong object, such that one randomly determined small object within 20' (pebble, dagger, hat, boot, belt, pine cone, etc.) begins dancing about as it comes to life for 1d6 days; (3) re-roll spell check, ignoring failed results, until a success is rolled, so that target object *does* come to life but the hit points it is endowed with come from the caster, who immediately takes equivalent damage, which heals normally but may be sufficient to kill the caster if the object is large enough; (4) target object is not animated but *all* small objects weighing less than 5 pounds within 30' of the caster suddenly come to life for 1d10 turns, creating total pandemonium, as weapons, clothing, foodstuffs, and everything else dance around the party.

1

Lost, failure, and worse! Roll 1d6 modified by Luck: (0 or less) corruption + patron taint + misfire; (1-2) corruption; (3) patron taint (or corruption if no patron); (4+) misfire.

2-11

Lost. Failure.

12-15

Failure, but spell is not lost.

16-17

The caster breathes life into one small object. It must weigh 10 lbs. or less and be no larger than one cubic foot. For a period of 1d24 turns, the object is treated as a living creature with 1d4 hit points and the following ability scores: Int 2, Str 6, Agi 12. The animated creature's AC varies according to material.

18-21

The caster breathes life into one moderately sized object. It must weigh 100 lbs. or less and be no larger than man-sized. For a period of 1d24 turns, the object is treated as a living creature with 2d4 hit points and the following ability scores: Int 2, Str 10, Agi 10. The animated creature's AC varies according to material.

22-23	The caster breathes life into one large object. It must weigh 500 lbs. or less and be no larger than man-sized. For a period of 1d4 days, the object is treated as a living creature with 3d8 hit points and the following ability scores: Int 2, Str 16, Agi 10. The animated creature's AC varies according to material.
24-26	The caster breathes life into one large object. It must weigh 500 lbs. or less and be no larger than man-sized. For a period of 1d4 weeks, the object is treated as a living creature with 3d8 hit points and the following ability scores: Int 2, Str 16, Agi 10. The animated creature's AC varies according to material.
27-31	The caster breathes life into one large object. It must weigh 500 lbs. or less and be no larger than man-sized. For a period of 1d4 weeks, the object is treated as a living creature with 3d8 hit points and the following ability scores: Int 2, Str 16, Agi 10. The animated creature's AC varies according to material. Additionally, the caster has complete control over the creature. It never questions the caster's directives, even if asked to complete seemingly impossible or suicidal tasks.
32-33	The caster breathes life into one very large object that can be quite intelligent. It can weigh up to 2,000 lbs. and be up to three times man-sized. For a period of 1d4+1 weeks, the object is treated as a living creature with 6d8 hit points and the following ability scores: Int 8, Str 20, Agi 10. The animated creature's AC varies according to material. Additionally, the caster has complete control over the creature. It never questions the caster's directives, even if asked to complete seemingly impossible or suicidal tasks.
34-35	The caster breathes permanent life into an inanimate object. If the proper shell is built for the caster's creation, he can use this spell to create golems, living statues, homunculi, and other such things. The caster can construct a golem-like body, per the notes below, as a receptacle for the spell. Construction time is a minimum of 1 month. The target of the casting can weigh up to 10,000 lbs. and be up to four times man-sized. To attempt the creation of permanent life, the caster must cast a ritualized version of this spell requiring one week's time and a minimum of 10 points of spellburn; otherwise, a lesser casting of this spell is treated as result 32-33 above. The caster has complete control over the creature. It never questions the caster's directives, even if asked to complete seemingly impossible or suicidal tasks.

DCC RPG does not include complete statistics for golems and other such creatures, as the author prefers to leave the pursuit of such things up to the reader's creativity. As *general guidelines*, the creation of a *man-sized* golem-like shell for this spell can proceed with stats as follows. Larger or smaller golems can also be created, of course. The shells below do not include special properties; they are simply receptacles. See result 36+ below for more on special properties. A shell costs 10,000 gold pieces to create plus additional costs as noted below. Sufficient raw materials are obviously required.

Wood: Init -1; Atk fist +4 melee (dmg 1d6+3); AC 10; HD 6d8+6; MV 30'; Act 1d20; SP double damage from fire; SV Fort +2, Ref +3, Will +4; Int 8, Str 18, Agi 10. Construction costs: 10,000 gp + 1,000 gp.

Clay: Init -2; Atk fist +6 melee (dmg 1d8+3); AC 10; HD 6d8+6; MV 20'; Act 1d20; SP double damage from water-based attacks; SV Fort +3, Ref +2, Will +4; Int 8, Str 18, Agi 10. Construction costs: 10,000 gp + 5,000 gp.

Stone: Init -2; Atk fist +7 melee (dmg 1d8+4); AC 12; HD 8d8+16; MV 20'; Act 1d20; SV Fort +4, Ref +2, Will +4; Int 8, Str 20, Agi 8. Construction costs: 10,000 gp + 5,000 gp.

Iron: Init -2; Atk fist +8 melee (dmg 1d10+5); AC 14; HD 10d8+30; MV 20'; Act 1d20; SV Fort +6, Ref +3, Will +5; Int 8, Str 22, Agi 8. Construction costs: 10,000 gp + 10,000 gp.

Flesh: Init -1; Atk fist +5 melee (dmg 1d5+2); AC 12; HD 10d8; MV 30'; Act 1d20; SV Fort +8, Ref +4, Will +8; Int 12, Str 16, Agi 10. Construction costs: 10,000 gp + 15,000 gp.

Precious metal: Init -1; Atk fist +4 melee (dmg 1d4+2); AC 12; HD 8d8+16; MV 30'; Act 1d20; SP potentially unique properties according to metal used; SV Fort +6, Ref +3, Will +6; Int 12, Str 16, Agi 10. Construction costs: 10,000 gp + 50,000 gp.

Gemstone: Init -1; Atk fist +6 melee (dmg 3d6); AC 11; HD 8d8; MV 30'; Act 1d20; SP potentially unique properties according to metal used; SV Fort +8, Ref +4, Will +5; Int 10, Str 16, Agi 10. Construction costs: 10,000 gp + 100,000 gp.

36+	As result 34-35 *and* the caster can build a shell that is imbued with unique properties. For example, the caster could build a flesh golem that can absorb and heal itself from electrical shocks or an iron golem that can breathe poisonous gas. The caster can create one unique property per CL. The cost of creating the shell is increased by another 10,000 gp per unique property. For every unique property endowed, the casting time is increased by another week and another point of spellburn is required. In addition, the caster must successfully cast the necessary spells to imbue the special property.

Consult Spirit

| Level: 3 | Range: Self | Duration: 1 or more questions | Casting time: 1 hour | Save: N/A |

General

The caster consults with an extraplanar spirit in order to make inquiries or pass on information. The spirit may be the ghost of a deceased person, a demon residing on another plane, a nature spirit occupying a lake or tree, the caster's own supernatural patron, or even a god.

This spell is most effective if the caster consults with a spirit he already knows. If the caster consults with his patron (per the *patron bond* spell) or one of the patron's servants, add +1 to the spell check. If the caster consults with another specific spirit known to him from prior contact, legend, logical deduction (e.g., the caster sees a dead body and wishes to find its ghost), or research (e.g., the caster has visited his altar or read of his exploits), there is no modifier. If the caster has no knowledge of the spirit consulted, merely wishes to contact any spirit that will answer, or deliberately contacts a spirit of opposed alignment or interests, subtract -1 from the spell check.

If the spirit is known to the caster, roll d% to determine its attitude: (01-20) friendly, (21-80) neutral, (81-00) hostile. A friendly or neutral spirit answers honestly to the best of its ability and has a base 50% chance of knowing the answer to any given question appropriate to its area of knowledge, modified by the judge's discretion and the obscurity of the question. When questioning a hostile spirit, roll d%: it (01-50) provides misleading information; (51-80) refuses to answer; (81-95) attempts to probe the caster's mind (Will save vs. DC of 4d6 or take 1d4 temporary Int damage); or (96-100) uses this connection to attempt enter the material plane.

Note that establishing contact in this manner also enables the spirit to establish reverse contact on future occasions (by casting this same spell, if it is able, or other similar abilities). Furthermore, not all spirits are pleased at an interruption from a curious mortal. The ghost of a recently slain creature, for example, is probably quite angry at its death, and there may be consequences for awakening it.

Manifestation

Roll 1d3: (1) caster freezes and appears to do nothing for duration; (2) caster flickers in and out of existence as questioning occurs; (3) caster carries on one side of a conversation.

Corruption

Roll 1d6: (1) caster's face takes on the appearance of a randomly determined spirit (see page 319); (2) caster's consciousness is permanently linked to that of a randomly determined spirit, which has a 1% chance each day of taking possession of the caster's body for a duration of 1d4 rounds during that day; (3) caster's hair turns white and stands on end; (4) caster instantly ages 1d8+2 years; (5) caster's skin wrinkles as if he were 100 years old, but he does not actually age and has no other signs or consequences of aging; (6) caster's ears become sensitive to the noises of ghosts, and he can hear whenever spirits are near, even if no contact is made.

Misfire

Roll 1d3: (1) caster successfully contacts his *own* spirit, where it resides beyond life and death awaiting his mortal conclusion, which gives way to a bizarre sense of déjà vu and disorientation that causes a -1 penalty to all actions for 1 turn; (2) caster contacts a spirit that immediately takes over his body, causing him to fall under the judge's control for 1d6 rounds and act in a manner opposite of his normal tendencies and alignment; (3) caster forces his own spirit out of his body for 1d6 rounds, causing him to collapse into a catatonic state until his spirit returns.

1	Lost, failure, and worse! Roll 1d6 modified by Luck: (0 or less) corruption + patron taint + misfire; (1-2) corruption; (3) patron taint (or corruption if no patron); (4+) misfire.
2-11	Lost. Failure.
12-15	Failure, but spell is not lost.
16-17	The caster makes fleeting contact with the spirit, though contact is so brief he does not know to whom he speaks. The caster has just enough time to ask one simple question and hear an answer. The answer is of course from the spirit's perspective, which may not be objective or omniscient.
18-21	The caster establishes a simple rapport with the spirit and understands the nature of the entity to which he speaks. The caster has enough time to ask 2 simple questions.
22-23	The caster establishes a basic rapport with the spirit and understands the nature of the entity to which he speaks. The caster has enough time to ask 3 simple questions.
24-26	The caster establishes a basic rapport with the spirit and understands the nature of the entity to which he speaks. The caster has enough time to ask 4 simple questions.

27-31	The caster establishes a strong rapport with the spirit. He understands its nature and is able to communicate with it. The connection is strong enough for introductory conversation. The caster can ask up to 5 simple questions or carry on a short conversation (of 5 minutes or less) in order to hear a story, understand a magical ritual explained by the spirit, and so on.
32-33	In establishing a connection to the spirit, the caster immediately understands a great deal about it: its appearance, its motivations, its goals (either short-term or long-term), and its current state of mind (angry, pensive, calm, etc.). The caster can communicate with the spirit and can carry on a conversation of up to 1 hour in duration. This is enough time for a lengthy dialogue on any given subject. The caster can also get detailed information from the spirit on a subject in which it is an expert. Generally speaking, this is sufficient to confer a +1 bonus to activities based on the spirit's knowledge and expertise. For example, if the caster contacts the creator of a spell, then casts the spell, he would receive a +1 bonus to that spell check.
34-35	The caster establishes a powerful connection to the spirit. He immediately understands a great deal about it: its appearance, its motivations, its goals (either short-term or long-term), and its current state of mind (angry, pensive, calm, etc.). The caster can communicate with the spirit and can carry on a conversation of up to 1 hour in duration. In addition, the caster remains loosely connected to the spirit for the next 7 days. During this time, the caster can re-establish contact at any point with concentration of 1d10 turns, and this renewed concentration lasts for 1d5+1 turns before fading. This is generally enough time for a lengthy dialogue on any given subject. The caster can also get detailed information from the spirit on a subject in which it is an expert. Generally speaking, this is sufficient to confer a +1 bonus to activities based on the spirit's knowledge and expertise. For example, if the caster contacts the creator of a spell, then casts the spell, he would receive a +1 bonus to that spell check.
36+	The caster connects his mind to the spirit's and steps into the spirit's frame of reference. The caster's thoughts and the spirit's thoughts blur; he can access its memories and opinions; and it can do the same. For a period of 7 days, the caster is in constant contact with the spirit and occasionally loses track of his own self. While the spirit cannot control the caster's mortal form, its personality may occasionally break through in the caster's pattern of speech or body language. Great and powerful spirits may have profound knowledge beyond the caster's understanding (i.e., the memories of a god or the long-range intrigues of a demon prince), but to the extent that the caster's intelligence and mortal mind can understand the thoughts of the spirit in question, he can form an almost perfect link. The caster's questions are quickly and accurately answered by the spirit, and the caster can surrender his free will to allow the spirit's mind to guide his actions. Generally speaking, this is sufficient to confer a +4 bonus to activities based on the spirit's knowledge and expertise. For example, if the caster contacts the creator of a spell, then surrenders his free will to cast the spell, he would receive a +4 bonus to that spell check; or, if the caster contacts his patron and casts a patron spell, he would receive a +4 bonus to the spell check. However, each time the caster allows the spirit this level of control, there is a 1% chance it takes over the caster's body completely.

Demon Summoning

Level: 3	Range: 20'	Duration: Varies	Casting time: 1 turn	Save: Will vs. spell check

General This spell summons a demon to do the caster's bidding. Demons are intelligent, capricious, ambitious, and emotional, and do not always respond positively to summoning. The spell requires a darksome ritual and at least 1 point of spellburn. The effects of the spell vary according to the ritual performed. The caster can appeal to his patron if he has one; attempt to summon a specific demon if he knows its true name; or he can merely attempt to summon any demon. Use the appropriate column below depending on the intended result.

The demon summoned is not necessarily under the caster's control. Except as noted below, the demon always receives a Will save vs. the spell check result to resist control. If the demon succeeds in its save, it lashes out when summoned. There is a base 50% chance it attacks the caster, reduced by -20% if the caster summoned a demon in service to his patron, and another -20% if the caster knows the demon's true name. If the demon does not attack the caster, it attacks another nearby creature.

Manifestation Roll 1d4: (1) an egg shimmers into existence, then hatches into the demon summoned; (2) flash of dark clouds and demon appears; (3) demon's skeleton appears first, then organs appear, then muscles knit them together, then skin grows and the demon appears; (4) demon erupts from ground fully formed.

Corruption Roll 1d8: (1) caster's face takes on the appearance of the demon he attempted to summon; (2) caster's body takes on aspects of the demon he attempted to summon; (3) caster's face becomes pock-marked and he temporarily loses 1d4 points of Int as the demon struggles violently with the casting attempt; (4) caster wheezes and has trouble breathing in the presence of demons of the type he attempted to summon; (5) minor; (6) major; (7-8) greater.

Misfire N/A

	With Patron	Without Patron	True Name Known
1	Lost, failure, and worse! Roll 1d6 modified by Luck: (0 or less) corruption + patron taint; (1-4) corruption; (5+) patron taint (or corruption if no patron).		
2-11	Lost. Failure.		
12-15	Failure, but spell is not lost.		
16-17	The caster summons a type I demon in service to his patron that remains for 1d4+1 rounds.	The caster summons a randomly determined type I demon that remains for a single round.	The caster can summon a demon of type I, whose true name he knows. It is automatically under the caster's control for 1 round, then it receives a Will save to resist control. The demon remains on this plane for 1d4+1 rounds.
18-21	The caster summons a type I demon in service to his patron that remains for 1d4+1 turns.	The caster summons a randomly determined type I demon that remains for 1d4+1 rounds.	The caster can summon a demon of type I or II, whose true name he knows. It is automatically under the caster's control for 1 round, then it receives a Will save to resist control. The demon remains on this plane for 1d4+1 rounds.
22-23	The caster summons a type II demon in service to his patron that remains for 1d4+1 rounds.	The caster summons a randomly determined type I demon that remains for 1d4+1 turns.	The caster can summon a demon of type I, II, or III, whose true name he knows. It is automatically under the caster's control for 1 round, then it receives a Will save to resist control. The demon remains on this plane for 1d4+1 rounds.

Demon Summoning (continued)		
24-26	The caster summons a type III demon in service to his patron that remains for 1d4+1 rounds.	The caster summons a randomly determined type II demon that remains for 1d4+1 rounds.	The caster can summon a demon of type I, II, III, or IV, whose true name he knows. It is automatically under the caster's control for 1 round, then it receives a Will save to resist control. The demon remains on this plane for 1d4+1 rounds.
27-31	The caster summons a type IV demon in service to his patron that remains for 1d4+1 rounds.	The caster summons a randomly determined type III demon that remains for 1d4+1 rounds.	The caster can summon a demon of type I, II, III, IV, or V, whose true name he knows. It is automatically under the caster's control for 1 round, then it receives a Will save to resist control. The demon remains on this plane for 1d4+1 rounds.
32-33	The caster summons a type V demon in service to his patron that remains for 1d4+1 rounds.	The caster summons a randomly determined type IV demon that remains for 1d4+1 rounds.	The caster can summon a demon of type I, II, III, IV, V, or VI, whose true name he knows. It is automatically under the caster's control for 1 round, then it receives a Will save to resist control. The demon remains on this plane for 1d4+1 rounds.
34-35	The caster summons a type VI demon in service to his patron that remains for 1d4+1 rounds.	The caster summons a randomly determined type V demon that remains for 1d4+1 rounds.	The caster can summon a demon of type I, II, III, IV, V, or VI, whose true name he knows. It is automatically under the caster's control for 2 rounds, then it receives a Will save to resist control. The demon remains on this plane for 1d4+1 rounds.
36+	The caster summons a type VI demon in service to his patron that remains for 1d4+1 turns.	The caster summons a randomly determined type VI demon that remains for 1d4+1 rounds.	The caster can summon a demon of type I, II, III, IV, V, or VI, whose true name he knows. It is automatically under the caster's control for the entire time it is present. The demon remains on this plane for 1d4+1 turns.

"He had a pretty bad level drain last night."

Dispel Magic

Level: 3   Range: Touch or more   Duration: From instantaneous to permanent   Casting time: 1 round or longer
Save: Sometimes (Will vs. spell check DC)

General	With this spell, the caster disrupts arcane energies. This spell can break a pentagram, banish a summoned demon, neutralize a magical potion, or cancel another spell. At its most fundamental level, this spell is a test of wills: the caster attempts to master and break the magical energies already bound together by a rival magic-user. If the caster is stronger, he dispels the enemy magic. If his rival is stronger, the magic stays in place.

In most cases, concentration aids this spell immensely. A simple *dispel magic* can be cast in 1 round, and can achieve a maximum spell check result of 21, regardless of die roll, as noted below. For every round of concentration while casting the spell, the spell check can be incrementally higher, as noted on the table below. A higher casting time does not guarantee a better result, but spell check results are capped based on the casting time.

This spell may also be used to counterspell any opposed casting. When used in this manner it can achieve any level of effect regardless of casting time.

When casting this spell, the effect to be dispelled must have been created with a spell check of equal to or less than the caster's, and the opposing caster receives a Will save. For example, if the caster rolled 16 on the *dispel magic* spell check, he could cancel an enemy's *mirror image* that was created with a spell check of 15 or less. If the opposing spell check is not known, the judge should roll it on the spot. The caster does not necessarily know the strength of the magical spell or effect he is attempting to dispel.

In some cases, as noted below, the opposing caster may prevent a spell from being dispelled by making a Will save against the caster's spell check. For example, the owner of the *mirror image* spell could attempt to maintain its functioning by making a Will save of greater than or equal to the caster's spell check result.

Manifestation	Varies.
Corruption	Roll 1d6: (1) caster loses 10 pounds permanently; (2) caster absorbs traits of the spell he attempted to dispel, at the judge's discretion; for example, if he was trying to dispel *choking cloud*, then his breath becomes permanently noxious; (3) caster gains 20 pounds permanently; (4) minor; (5) major; (6) greater.
Misfire	Roll 1d4: (1) a randomly determined magic item on the caster's person (if any) is partially disenchanted, permanently losing one "plus" or special ability; (2) instead of targeting what the caster intended, the *dispel* effect targets one *randomly* determined spell effect within 50', which is automatically suppressed for 1d6 rounds; (3) the spell *enhances* magical effects instead of dispelling them, such that all spell checks made within 20' of the caster (including the caster's) receive a +1 bonus for the next 1d6 rounds; (4) the spell releases the energy of the last spell the caster dispelled and casts it at a spell check result of 1d10+14; for example, if the last spell dispelled was a *choking cloud*, then a new *choking cloud* suddenly appears; if the judge and player cannot remember the last spell dispelled, determine one randomly of level 1d4 on Table 5-8: Wizard Spells.

	Casting Time	Maximum Effect
1	1 round	Lost, failure, and worse! Roll 1d6 modified by Luck: (0 or less) corruption + patron taint + misfire; (1-2) corruption; (3) patron taint (or corruption if no patron); (4+) misfire.
2-11	1 round	Lost. Failure.
12-15	1 round	Failure, but spell is not lost.
16-17	1 round	The caster potentially cancels the *active effects* of a single spell with a non-permanent duration. The caster must touch the spell effect to dispel it. Depending on the specifics, this might mean he touches a summoned creature and causes it to return to its native place, disperses a *choking cloud*, causes an invisible creature to become visible, or awakens a person subjected to magical *sleep*. Spells with permanent durations or that create permanent bonds, such as *find familiar*, *patron bond*, or *wizard staff*, are not affected, nor are spells whose magical effects have now "passed," even though they generated a non-magical effect (for example, the caster could not "re-break" a broken sword that was repaired with a *mending* spell). The opposing caster may prevent his spell from being dispelled by making a Will save against the caster's spell check.

		Dispel Magic (continued)
18-21	1 round	The caster potentially cancels the *active effects* of a single spell with a non-permanent duration. The caster must be within 20′ of the spell effect to dispel it. Depending on the specifics, this might mean he touches a summoned creature and causes it to return to its native place, disperses a *choking cloud*, causes an invisible creature to become visible, or awakens a person subjected to magical *sleep*. Spells with permanent durations or that create permanent bonds, such as *find familiar, patron bond,* or *wizard staff,* are not affected, nor are spells whose magical effects have now "passed," even though they generated a non-magical effect (for example, the caster could not "re-break" a broken sword that was repaired with a *mending* spell). The opposing caster may prevent his spell from being dispelled by making a Will save against the caster's spell check.
22-23	2 rounds	The caster potentially cancels the *active effects* of *all spell effects within 20′* that have a non-permanent duration. This includes "friendly" spell effects. Spells with permanent durations or which create permanent bonds, such as *find familiar, patron bond,* or *wizard staff,* are not affected, nor are spells whose magical effects have now "passed," even though they generated a non-magical effect (for example, the caster could not "re-break" a broken sword that was repaired with a *mending* spell). Opposing casters do *not* receive a Will save against this casting to prevent the dispel. If the caster's spell check exceeds the spell check used to create opposed spells, the spells are automatically dispelled.
24-26	3 rounds	The caster potentially cancels certain spell effects within 20′. This includes "friendly" spell effects. All spell effects of a non-permanent nature are affected, as well as select magic items. Potions and magic scrolls within range are permanently neutralized. Magic staffs and weapons within the area of effect may have their magical effects (their "pluses" and other abilities) *temporarily* neutralized for 1d10 rounds, provided the spell check used to create them is less than the *dispel magic* spell check. Magic rods, wands, and unique magic items are *not* affected. Spells with permanent durations or which create permanent bonds, such as *find familiar* or *patron bond,* are not affected, nor are spells whose magical effects have now "passed," even though they generated a non-magical effect (for example, the caster could not "re-break" a broken sword that was repaired with a *mending* spell). Opposing casters do *not* receive a Will save against this casting to prevent the dispel. If the caster's spell check exceeds the spell check used to create opposed spells, the spells are automatically dispelled.
27-31	4 rounds	The caster potentially cancels certain spell effects within 20′. This includes "friendly" spell effects. All spell effects of a non-permanent nature are affected, as well as select magic items. Potions and magic scrolls within range are permanently neutralized. Magic staffs, rods, wands, weapons, and unique magic items within the area of effect may have their magical effects (their "pluses" and other abilities) *temporarily* neutralized for 1d10 rounds, provided the spell check used to create them is less than the *dispel magic* spell check. Spells with permanent durations or which create permanent bonds, such as *find familiar* or *patron bond,* are not affected, nor are spells whose magical effects have now "passed," even though they generated a non-magical effect (for example, the caster could not "re-break" a broken sword that was repaired with a *mending* spell). Opposing casters do *not* receive a Will save against this casting to prevent the dispel. If the caster's spell check exceeds the spell check used to create opposed spells, the spells are automatically dispelled.
32-33	5 rounds	The caster may choose to create a flash of dispelling magic, as result 27-31 above, or focus all spell energies on a single item, object, spell, or creature within 20′ to *permanently* disenchant it. If the latter, the spell check of the caster must exceed the spell check used to create the item, and a minimum spellburn of 1 point per "plus" of the item to be disenchanted is required. If successful, the item becomes a mundane example of its normal type. For example, with a successful check and 2 points of spellburn, a *+2 sword* becomes a regular longsword.

Dispel Magic (continued)		
34-35	1 turn	The caster creates a sphere of disenchantment that radiates 20' from his person at all times and travels with him. This sphere acts as an ongoing *dispel magic* spell that permanently dispels spells and magic items, as noted in result 27-31 above. Additionally, if the caster expends spellburn, the sphere can permanently disenchant items, objects, spells, and creatures of a permanent duration, up to a "plus" equal to the spellburn expended, as noted in 32-33 above. The sphere of disenchantment lasts for 24 hours. Note that the sphere affects the caster's own magic – he is effectively unable to cast magical spells while the sphere of disenchantment remains active unless he succeeds in a spell check greater than his original *dispel magic* check. He can dismiss the sphere at will.
36+	1 hour	The caster creates a sphere of disenchantment that radiates 20' from his person at all times and travels with him. The sphere can be placed on another object or person. The sphere then moves with that person or object. The subject need not be willing. This sphere acts as an ongoing *dispel magic* spell that permanently dispels spells and magic items, as noted in result 27-31 above. Additionally, if the caster expends spellburn, the sphere can permanently disenchant items, objects, spells, and creatures of a permanent duration, up to a "plus" equal to the spellburn expended, as noted in 32-33 above. The sphere of disenchantment lasts for 24 hours. Note that the sphere affects the caster's own magic – he is effectively unable to cast magical spells while the sphere of disenchantment remains active unless he succeeds in a spell check greater than his original *dispel magic* check. He can dismiss the sphere at will.

Eldritch Hound

Level: 3	Range: Varies	Duration: Varies	Casting time: 1 turn	Save: N/A

General

The caster summons forth an otherworldly hound to hunt for him. This eldritch hunter is a vile creature of the Abyss with no good intentions. This spell requires a minimum of 1 point of spellburn, and that spellburn *will not heal* until the eldritch hound returns from whence it came. It has no permanent form on the material plane and usually appears as a shadow or steaming mist. The caster must make known to the hound the object or person it seeks in clear and direct terms; ambiguity may result in the wrong target being sought. A physical sample, such as clothing, hair, or a vial of blood, is preferable; a painting, description, name (or true name) is of secondary value. The hound has an extraordinary sense of smell, as well as rudimentary ESP and second sight. Provided with sufficient foundational evidence and a trail to seek, it is usually very successful in finding its target. It will seek and return the specified person or object, dead or alive, to the place where it was first summoned. It has no preference between "dead" or "alive" and usually chooses the most expedient manner. Of course, if the object is on a distant continent or in a dangerous labyrinth, the eldritch hound may be in for a long and potentially unsuccessful journey. A caster who attempts to place terms on the hound – such as to retrieve an object alive or to make a retrieval only at a certain time or after a certain event, may or may not succeed, as noted in the spell check results below.

Unless noted otherwise, the hound flies at 100', has ability scores of 14, and can perform any action a normal man could perform. It listens but never speaks. It has AC 18, 4d12 hp, attacks at +8 (2d6 damage), and saves as the caster. It will not fight arbitrarily or even in the caster's defense – it will *only* fight to retrieve the specified person or object, and only then if combat is completely unavoidable. It is patient and would prefer to wait than fight. Provided with sufficient information, there is a base chance the hound succeeds in finding the trail of its target (as noted in the spell checks below), though it cannot shift between planes (unless noted otherwise below), and success in *locating the object* does not always mean success in *retrieving it within the indicated time*. The judge may modify this base chance as appropriate.

Manifestation

Roll 1d4: (1) an invisible presence that makes dogs and horses nervous; (2) a shadowy thing that never quite comes into focus; (3) a steamy mist that brings a dank humidity with it; (4) a shimmering heat wave that leaps from place to place.

Corruption

Roll 1d6: (1) caster's face takes on the appearance of a hound; (2) caster is a magnet to other eldritch hounds, and if one is ever set against him, its chances of success are increased by +25% (minimum 1% chance of failure); (3) whenever the caster attempts *any spell* going forward, a result of 1 always results in summoning an eldritch hound in addition to any other effects (corruption, misfire, patron taint, etc.), and the eldritch hound summoned makes one angry attack against the caster, then vanishes; (4) caster's skin grows a thin coat of hound-like fur; (5-6) greater.

Misfire

Roll 1d3: (1) the eldritch hound appears and immediately attacks the caster, fighting to the death; (2) the eldritch hound appears and misinterprets its mission, proceeding to track a randomly determined target friendly to the caster; (3) the eldritch hound summoned is weak and feeble and becomes associated with the caster's use of this spell in the future, such that when this spell is next cast, there is a 50% chance the feeble hound appears (AC 8, 5 hp, no attack); such a hound has a -50% chance in finding the trail of its target, and each time it appears, there is a new 50% chance it appears on the next casting, until such time as a casting finally succeeds without it appearing.

1

Lost, failure, and worse! Roll 1d6 modified by Luck: (0 or less) corruption + patron taint + misfire; (1-3) corruption; (4) patron taint (or corruption if no patron); (5+) misfire.

2-11

Lost. Failure.

12-15

Failure, but spell is not lost.

16-17

The caster summons an eldritch hound within a magic circle that he draws. Once the magic circle is rendered, the hound has 24 hours to pursue its target before it is drawn back from whence it came. Provided with sufficient information, there is a base 75% chance the hound succeeds in finding the trail of its target. The hound refuses any terms beyond "dead or alive."

18-21

The caster summons an eldritch hound within a magic circle that he draws. Once the magic circle is rendered, the hound has 1d6+1 days to pursue its target before it is drawn back from whence it came. Provided with sufficient information, there is a base 80% chance the hound succeeds in finding the trail of its target. The hound refuses any terms beyond "dead or alive."

22-23	The caster summons an eldritch hound within a magic circle that he draws. Once the magic circle is rendered, the hound has 1d7+7 days to pursue its target before it is drawn back from whence it came. Provided with sufficient information, there is a base 85% chance the hound succeeds in finding the trail of its target. The hound refuses any terms beyond "dead or alive."
24-26	The caster summons an eldritch hound within a magic circle that he draws. Once the magic circle is rendered, the hound has 1d7+7 days to pursue its target before it is drawn back from whence it came. Provided with sufficient information, there is a base 85% chance the hound succeeds in finding the trail of its target. The hound is able to switch planes in its pursuit and has a 25% chance of understanding and accepting up to 2 terms in its hunt (e.g., "return the creature alive" or "capture the target only after it has given birth"). The chance is rolled independently for each term.
27-31	The caster summons an eldritch hound that possesses vast knowledge of all things on the material plane. There is a 50% chance it has advance knowledge of the target, no matter how obscure, and may provide the caster with some previously unknown knowledge as it begins its search. The hound has 1d7+14 days to pursue its target before it is drawn back from whence it came. There is a base 90% chance the hound succeeds in finding the trail of its target. The hound is able to switch planes in its pursuit and has a 25% chance of understanding and accepting up to 2 terms in its hunt (e.g., "return the creature alive" or "capture the target only after it has given birth"). The chance is rolled independently for each term.
32-33	The caster summons an eldritch hound that possesses extraordinary knowledge of all things on the material plane. There is a 95% chance it has advance knowledge of the target, no matter how obscure, and may provide the caster with some previously unknown knowledge as it begins its search. The hound has 1d7+21 days to pursue its target before it is drawn back from whence it came. There is a base 95% chance the hound succeeds in finding the trail of its target. The hound is able to switch planes in its pursuit and has a 50% chance of understanding and accepting up to 2 terms in its hunt (e.g., "return the creature alive" or "capture the target only after it has given birth"). The chance is rolled independently for each term.
34-35	The caster summons an eldritch hound that possesses extraordinary knowledge of all things on the material plane. There is a 95% chance it has advance knowledge of the target, no matter how obscure, and may provide the caster with some previously unknown knowledge as it begins its search. The hound has 1d7+21 days to pursue its target before it is drawn back from whence it came. There is a base 95% chance the hound succeeds in finding the trail of its target. The hound is able to switch planes in its pursuit and has a 50% chance of understanding and accepting up to 3 terms in its hunt (e.g., "return the creature alive" or "capture the target only after it has given birth"). The chance is rolled independently for each term. The hound is extraordinary for its type: it flies at 200', has ability scores of 18, AC 20, 8d12 hp, attacks at +12 (3d6 damage), and uses the caster's saves with a +2 bonus to the roll.
36+	The caster summons an eldritch hound that possesses extraordinary knowledge of all things on the material plane. The hound has advance knowledge of the target, no matter how obscure, and may provide the caster with some previously unknown knowledge as it begins its search. The hound has 1d6+1 *months* to pursue its target before it is drawn back from whence it came. There is a base 99% chance the hound succeeds in finding the trail of its target. The hound is able to switch planes in its pursuit and automatically accepts up to 4 terms in its hunt (e.g., "return the creature alive" or "capture the target only after it has given birth"). The hound is extraordinary for its type: it flies at 400', has ability scores of 20, AC 22, 12d12 hp, attacks at +16 (4d6 damage), and uses the caster's saves with a +2 bonus to the roll.

Emirikol's Entropic Maelstrom

Level: 3	Range: 50' + 10' per CL	Duration: 1 round per CL	Casting Time: 1 action	Save: Fort save

General	This spell produces an entropic storm that fills a 40' square area. Those caught within this maelstrom are attacked by the elemental forces of Chaos, resulting in age, decay, or transformation. All creatures of Lawful alignment suffer a -1 to saving throws to resist the spell; Chaotic creatures enjoy a +1 bonus to their saves.
Manifestation	A bank of lightning-filled, purple-black fog appears, and the howling of the damned is heard within its misty confines.
Corruption	Roll 1d4: (1) caster's eyes are replaced by purplish-black orbs that crackle with silent lightning; (2) caster's body is mottled with veins of unseemly colors (bile yellow, dull tan, phlegm ochre, etc.); (3) caster is afflicted with premature aging (hair turns grey, wrinkles and liver spots appear, etc.); (4) garments of cloth and leather decay at an alarming rate when worn, forcing the caster to replace his wardrobe weekly.
Misfire	Roll 1d5: (1) caster must make a DC 10 Fort save or be temporarily aged 2d20 years for 24 hours; (2) all the caster's non-magical possessions suddenly rust or rot away; (3) entropic backlash knocks the caster back 15' feet and inflicts 1d4 damage; (4) a rain of fish or frogs falls in a 40' area around the caster, causing all to make a DC 8 Fort save or suffer 1d3 damage from bludgeoning; (5) caster and all other creatures within a 20' radius suddenly change places – the judge can reposition the affected targets by choice or at random.

1	Lost, failure, and worse! Roll 1d6 modified by Luck: (0 or less) corruption + patron taint + misfire; (1-2) corruption; (3) patron taint (or corruption if no patron); (4+) misfire.
2-11	Lost. Failure.
12-15	Failure, but spell is not lost.
16-17	The maelstrom affects non-living, non-magical metal and organic materials, causing them to decay and oxidize. Weapons, armor, and items made from iron, steel, wood, or leather must make a DC 10 Fort save or become brittle. These objects either impose a -2 penalty to attack and damage rolls or suffers a -2 reduction in AC, depending on the item. On a critical hit (by the weapon or against the armor), the item falls to pieces regardless of the critical hit roll result.
18-21	The maelstrom affects metal and organic materials, causing them to decay and oxidize. Even magical items and constructs of metal or organic materials are subject to this magical decay. Weapons, armor, and items made from iron, steel, wood, or leather must make a DC 15 Fort save or become brittle. These objects either impose a -2 penalty to attack and damage rolls or suffers a -2 reduction in AC, depending on the item. On a critical hit (by the weapon or against the armor), the item falls to pieces regardless of the critical hit roll result. Magical items must make a DC 10 Fort save to avoid the same fate and can add any "pluses" they possesses to the saving throw roll. Constructed, magical creatures must make a Fort save vs. spell check result or suffer 1d10+CL damage from the maelstrom's effects.
22-23	All living creatures within the spell's area of effect must make a Fort saving throw or be overwhelmed by weariness and ennui. They temporary lose 1d4 points of Strength and Stamina, and all attacks rolls, saving throws, spell checks, and ability checks are made at a -3 penalty for the duration of the spell.
24-26	All living creatures within the area of effect must make a Fort save or be affected by a random affliction. The judge should roll separately for each affected creature, as it is possible for different disabilities to affect the targets. Possible afflictions include: (roll 1d8) (1) blindness, (2) deafness, (3) paralyzation, (4) crippled (speed reduced to 5' round), (5) speak in tongues (no spell casting possible), (6) unconsciousness, (7) temporary insanity, and (8) temporary amnesia. The judge may substitute other afflictions as desired.
27-31	The maelstrom draws out and consumes magical energy within the area of effect, causing those who command spells to either feed the storm or suffer. Each round they are within the spell's area of effect, all spellcasters must make a Will save or be forced to release a portion of their magical energy in spell form. On a failed save, the caster's next action must be to cast a spell or suffer 1d6+CL damage. The caster can choose which spell he performs to feed the maelstrom and makes a spell check as normal. If the spell check is successful, the spell is devoured by the maelstrom and the caster takes no damage. On a failed

spell check, the caster loses the spell for the day (regardless of a spell check failure result indicating otherwise) and takes 1d6+CL damage. Non-spellcasters automatically take 1d3+CL points of damage for every round they are in the area of effect.

32-33	All living creatures within the area of effect are aged 2d10 years (or 2d10x10 years if an elf or other long-lived race). They permanently lose a point of Strength, Stamina, and Agility and may suffer other cosmetic changes (hair goes gray or is lost, wrinkles, liver spots, etc.) at the judge's discretion.
34-35	All living creatures within the area of effect must make a Fort save or be transformed by the maelstrom. The spell affects the targets' physical make-up, altering flesh and bone into other, less seemly substances. The judge should roll separately for each affected creature, as it is possible for different transformations to affect the targets. Possible transformations include (roll 1d8) (1) glass, (2) bile, (3) sand, (4) primordial ooze, (5) phlegm, (6) tin, (7) dead vermin, (8) cancerous tissue. The judge may substitute other substances as desired. Transformed creatures can be restored by powerful magics provided circumstances allow the majority of their altered form to be salvageable. For example, a creature transformed into bile while standing in a fast-moving stream has little chance of having all his material form collected and would be lost forever (barring divine intervention).
36+	All mortal creatures within the area of effect are torn apart by the uncaring, chaotic forces that reside in the heart of the cosmos. Their physical forms dissolve into primordial sludge, their possessions are destroyed on the atomic level, and their life forces are consumed by entropy. Any who witness this utter destruction are paralyzed by the futility of existence for 1d6 rounds and may develop nervous tics or have their hair turn white in fright. Those destroyed by the spell cannot be restored to life by any means, nor can their belongings be recovered or recreated. Entropy wins in the end.

Eternal Champion

Level: 3   **Range:** 1 mile   **Duration:** Until sunset   **Casting time:** One night's dreams   **Save:** N/A

General	By way of mystic draughts imbibed before sleep, the caster dream-speaks with the great warriors of ages past and future. One such warrior is summoned forth to fight for the caster's cause. When the caster wakes, the warrior steps forth from the next day's sunrise, and disappears at sunset with all his belongings. The warrior believes himself to be dreaming, but otherwise acts just as he would act in normal circumstances.
	The warrior summoned by this spell is inclined, by alignment and proclivities, to fight for the caster's cause and does so provided he is not offended or otherwise dissuaded. If slain, his body and all belongings vanish to mist. There is a 10% chance the warrior has ancient knowledge of immediate and practical use to the caster, provided the caster asks the right questions.
	The caster may only have one eternal champion at any time. Casting this spell while an eternal champion already exists from a prior casting will cause the second casting to fail.
	The summoned warrior has stats as noted in the spell check descriptions below.
Manifestation	See below.
Corruption	Roll 1d6: (1) caster is haunted by dream-like flashbacks to a primordial time, such that any time he rolls a natural 13 on *any* die roll (whether attack, spell check, saving throw, or anything else), he freezes up for 1d4 rounds and is unable to take any action during that time; (2) caster is marked by supernatural powers as a champion of a certain cause in the distant past, which is never revealed, but supernatural creatures now take on a markedly negative disposition toward the caster, and their chances of being hostile are generally increased by +25%; (3) the eternal champion the caster attempted to summon was posted as a permanent guard in the Courts of Chaos, and so displeased are the champion's superiors with the caster's failed summoning that he is marked with a sign of disfavor, visible only to chaos lords and their minions, who henceforth treat the caster with displeasure; (4) minor; (5) major; (6) greater.
Misfire	Roll 1d2: (1) caster marks an allied warrior as a candidate for the castings of *eternal warrior* by spellcasters of other times and places, such that this warrior has a 1% chance of randomly disappearing on any given day as he is summoned to fight for distant causes by others who cast this spell; (2) in casting this spell, the caster inadvertently reverses its parameters and sends himself to the time of the warrior instead of sum-

moning him for the caster's use, such that the caster disappears at the next sunrise and reappears at the next sunset, bloodied and weary as if he had fought the entire day (treat as 2d4 hp loss and 1d6 randomly determined spells expended); the caster has no memories of his time away.

1	Lost, failure, and worse! Roll 1d6 modified by Luck: (0 or less) corruption + patron taint + misfire; (1-3) corruption; (4) patron taint (or corruption if no patron); (5+) misfire.
2-11	Lost. Failure.
12-15	Failure, but spell is not lost.
16-17	A mighty fighter appears with stats as a level 3 warrior, normal ability scores, and mundane equipment.
18-21	As level 4 warrior with ability scores of 2d6+6 (judge rolls) and mundane equipment.
22-23	As level 5 warrior with all ability scores at 16 and a named *+1 sword*.
24-26	As level 5 warrior with all ability scores at 16, and the warrior is known to the annals of legend. He wields a legendary unique magic weapon of +2 enchantment. He inspires the caster's party's retainers and henchmen with an extra +1 morale bonus.
27-31	As level 5 warrior with all ability scores at 18, and the warrior is a well-known legend. He wields a legendary unique magic weapon of +3 enchantment. He inspires the caster's party's retainers and henchmen with an extra +1 morale bonus.
32-33	As level 6 warrior with all ability scores at 18. This warrior is one held in the greatest esteem; he is a living legend of deific proportions. Simply fighting at his side grants a +1 bonus to attacks and damage to the caster and all allies within 100'. The warrior wields a legendary unique magic weapon of +4 enchantment. He inspires the caster's party's retainers and henchmen with an extra +2 morale bonus.

34-35 As level 6 warrior with all ability scores at 20. This warrior is one held in the greatest esteem; he is a living legend of deific proportions. Simply fighting at his side grants a +1 bonus to attacks and damage to the caster and all allies within 100'. The warrior wields a legendary unique magic weapon of +4 enchantment. He inspires the caster's party's retainers and henchmen with an extra +2 morale bonus. In addition, the warrior brings with him three retainers who themselves have statistics as level 3 warriors with normal ability scores and mundane equipment.

36+ As level 7 warrior with all ability scores at 22. He is the greatest warrior ever known; in legends and stories, no warrior is his equal. Simply fighting at his side grants a +2 bonus to attacks and damage to the caster and all allies within 100'. The warrior wields a legendary unique magic weapon of +5 enchantment. He inspires the caster's party's retainers and henchmen with an extra +2 morale bonus. In addition, the warrior brings with him ten retainers who themselves have statistics as level 3 warriors with normal ability scores and mundane equipment.

Fireball

Level: 3	Range: 100' or more, exploding in a sphere of 20' radius or more
	Casting time: 1 round Save: Reflex vs. spell check Duration: Instantaneous

General

The caster points his finger at a target, speaks a magic word, and throws a jet of flame that explodes at the designated point. A *fireball* fills a sphere of 20' radius, affecting all creatures within the target point. All creatures take damage unless they succeed in a Reflex save against the spell check DC, in which case they take half damage. The *fireball* is a flash explosion and typically does not cause humans to catch fire, but there is a 50% chance that highly flammable objects (such as dry cloth or paper) within the blast area may catch fire.

Manifestation

Roll 1d4: (1) a flaming ball that catapults into the target and explodes in a fiery burst; (2) a stream of liquid flame that douses the target in a raining cloud of fire; (3) a singularity that appears at a point in space then explodes into a flowering burst of fire; (4) a collection of spinning, whirling, fiery seeds that bounce forth to the target point, where they explode in flames.

Corruption

Roll 1d8: (1) caster's hands and arms are blackened like charcoal; (2) caster's skin takes on a charcoal-like hue and texture; (3) all hair on the caster's body is burned off, and he is perpetually followed by a vague smell of burning hair; (4) a small, invisible portal to the elemental plane of fire opens right above the caster and remains open, dripping globules of fire or lava around him on a regular basis; this manifests as sparkling lights around him at all times, and there is a 1% chance each day that a spark will light something on fire at an inopportune time; (5) minor; (6-7) major; (8) greater.

Misfire

Roll 1d5: (1) a small *fireball* explodes on the caster, causing 1d6 damage to him; (2) a large *fireball* explodes centered on the caster, causing 3d6 damage to him and all creatures within 20'; (3) caster spontaneously combusts, taking 2d6 damage and causing all flammable objects on him (including clothes and scrolls) to instantaneously crumble to ash; (4) caster summons the wrong element, generating a spray of ice that showers everything within 20' of him, causing no damage but potentially dousing any existing flames; (5) caster's skin is badly sunburned across his entire body, and physical motion causes sharp pains (expressed as a -1 penalty to all physical actions) until the sunburn heals after one week.

1	Lost, failure, and worse! Roll 1d6 modified by Luck: (0 or less) corruption + patron taint + misfire; (1-3) corruption; (4) patron taint (or corruption if no patron); (5+) misfire.
2-11	Lost. Failure.
12-15	Failure, but spell is not lost.
16-17	The caster launches a *fireball* up to 100', doing 3d6 damage.
18-21	The caster launches a *fireball* up to 120', doing 4d6 damage.
22-23	The caster launches a *fireball* that jumps to different targets 1d4+1 times. The first target must be within 50', and that target takes 5d6 damage in an explosion of radius 20'. The fireball then skips to a second target that must be from 20' to 50' from the first target, and this second target takes 1d6 damage in a small explosion that only affects that single target. The second target must be *at least* 20' away from the first target; this is the minimum "skip" distance. If there is a third, fourth, or fifth target, it must be another 20' away from the previous target, and it takes 1d6 damage. The *fireball* must skip the indicated number of times. If the caster runs out of targets, he can skip the *fireball* against inanimate objects.
24-26	The caster launches a *fireball* up to 160', doing 6d6 damage. The fireball arcs up like a catapult to a maximum 40' above ground at its peak. As such, it can curve around or over intermediate obstructions.
27-31	The caster launches a spray of small *fireballs*. There are three sprays of 1d3+1 *fireballs* each. Each spray can target the initial target and up to two additional targets (up to three targets in total). The targets can be up to 200' away. Each mini-*fireball* does 1d6 damage and has no blast radius.
32-33	The caster launches a single *fireball* up to 200', doing 10d6 damage. The caster can choose an area of effect ranging from a single human-sized target up to the full sphere of 20' radius. The fireball arcs to a height of 40' at its peak and can avoid intermediate objects.
34-35	The caster calls down a *fireball* from the heavens, targeting a point up to 500' away and doing 14d6 damage. The caster can choose an area of effect ranging from a single human-sized target up to a sphere of 30' radius. Instead of projecting from his fingertip, the *fireball* falls from above like a meteor strike, exploding in a fiery burst. The caster must have line-of-sight to his target, but he can cast around obstructions in this manner. For example, he may be able to view the target through a periscope or via a crystal ball of some kind.
36+	The caster launches a *fireball* at a target up to 1 mile away, doing 20d6 damage. The caster can choose an area of effect ranging from a single human-sized target up to a sphere of 40' radius. The caster need not have line-of-sight to his target. He can choose a geographic point of which he has knowledge (such as a specific hill, tree, or room) or a target of which he has a physical trace (such as a lock of hair or fingernail). The *fireball* explodes at the designated point.

Fly

Level: 3	Range: Self or touch	Duration: 1 turn or more	Casting time: 1 round	Save: N/A

General — The caster grants flying ability to himself or another creature. The speed and duration vary according to the check result. The speed is halved when ascending and doubled when in a vertical dive. Heavily encumbered creatures fly at half the given speed. Maneuverability is generally good, equivalent to a large bird (such as an eagle or hawk). The duration is always rolled in secret by the judge, and the subject does not know when his flight will end until he falls to the ground.

Manifestation — Roll 1d4: (1) target manifests wings (angelic or demonic in appearance, depending on alignment); (2) target is surrounded by a thousand tiny birds that lift it into the air; (3) clouds manifest at the target's feet; (4) no visible manifestation.

Corruption — Roll 1d8: (1) caster grows fowl-like feathers around his ankles and feet; (2) the space between the caster's back and arms becomes webbed and feathered, almost like wings, but they are so spindly they do not grant any benefit; (3) caster becomes an object of attraction to birds, insects, and other flying objects, which frequently buzz about him, causing annoyance, making hiding difficult, and making him unpopular with civilized society; (4) caster gains 2d20+20 pounds, growing an enormous belly almost overnight and is suddenly more "earthbound" than he ever realized – the weight is impossible to lose no matter how hard the caster diets or exercises; (5) the caster becomes susceptible to attacks by elemental air, taking an additional +1 damage on all damage dice associated with air elementals, gusts of wind, cyclones, and other such effects; (6) major; (7-8) greater.

Misfire — Roll 1d4: (1) caster sinks 6″ into the ground, his feet cracking through dirt or stone, and cannot move until he spends a full round to extricate himself; (2) caster sends all his possessions into flight, but not himself, such that his clothes, weapons, spell books, and other things launch into the air for 1d4+1 rounds, moving 60′ per round in a randomly determined direction, leaving him naked and possession-less to chase them wherever they may fall; (3) caster sends all weapons within 30′ into the air, flying into a great flock then shooting off into the distance, moving at a speed of 60′ for 1d4+1 rounds; (4) caster and 1d4 randomly determined targets within 30′ grow enormously heavy and must move at half speed for the next turn.

1	Lost, failure, and worse! Roll 1d6 modified by Luck: (0 or less) corruption + patron taint + misfire; (1-3) corruption; (4) patron taint (or corruption if no patron); (5+) misfire.
2-11	Lost. Failure.
12-15	Failure, but spell is not lost.
16-17	The target flies at a speed of 30′. The flying ability lasts for 1 turn.
18-21	The target flies at a speed of 60′. The flying ability lasts for 1d6+1 turns.
22-23	The target flies at a speed of 90′. The flying ability lasts for 1d6+4 *hours*.
24-26	The caster can grant flight to up to two man-sized creatures (himself plus one other, or two others) or one creature twice the size of a man (such as an ogre). He must be touching the targets. The caster flies at 90′ while others fly at 60′. The spell's duration is 1d6+8 *hours*.
27-31	The caster can grant flight to up to four man-sized creatures (himself plus three others, or four others) or one creature up to four times the size of a man (such as a giant). The targets must be within 10′ of the caster. The caster flies at 90′ while other creatures fly at 30′. The spell's duration is one day. The flying creatures can each carry up to twice a normal man's load.
32-33	The caster draws a magic circle on the ground, and all creatures within that circle are granted flight. For each round spent drawing, the caster can render a circle up to 10′ in diameter. For example, if he spends 4 rounds drawing a magic circle, it will be 40′ in diameter. The magic circle can be a maximum of 100′ in diameter, and the spell is cast at the end of the round the caster finishes drawing it; e.g., if he spends 6 rounds drawing a 60′-diameter magic circle, the spell is cast on the end of the sixth round. All creatures within the circle, including the caster, are granted flight regardless of their size (e.g., even giants are granted flight if they are within the circle). The flight speed is 90′ for the caster and 60′ for all others. The duration is one day. The flying creatures can each carry up to twice a normal man's load.

| 34-35 | The caster raises his arms and grants flight to an entire army! All creatures within 300' of the caster, up to giant-sized, are granted flight. Their speed is 30' and they may fly for 1d4+1 turns. The caster himself can fly at 90' for one day, and any creatures he directly touches can fly at 60' for one day. (Typically, a maximum of 8 human-sized creatures can crowd around the caster and touch him during the casting.) All flying creatures can each carry up to twice a normal man's load. |

| 36+ | At this extraordinary level of casting, the caster can grant flight to geographical objects. Castles, mountains, towns, and lakes can be sent into the air. Additionally, when cast on a human target (including the caster), the spell can be rendered permanent. When targeting geographic objects or large groups of people, the caster can effectively grant flight in a manner that would normally be called "miraculous." The target can fly at a speed of 20' (for a mountain), 30' (for a giant), 60' (for a man-sized creature), and 90' (for the caster), for durations of up to a day. The caster can lift hundreds or even thousands of targets into the air at once or send them into the air in the city or castle they occupy. If aimed at a single target, a casting of this power level grants flight ability of great duration. The caster must expend a minimum of 1 point of spellburn. The duration starts at 1 week for 1 point of spellburn, and increases with every subsequent expenditure as follows: 2 = a month, 3 = six months, 4 = a year, 5 = five years, 6 = a decade, 7 = twenty years, 8 = forty years, 9 = sixty years, and 10 = permanent. |

Gust of Wind

Level: 3	Range: 10' or more	Duration: Instantaneous or longer	Casting time: 1 round	Save: N/A

General — The caster exhales and his breath becomes a mighty gust of wind. The wind is sufficient to extinguish small flames, like candles and torches, and may push back creatures flying or even walking in the caster's direction. The wind will fan large fires into larger conflagrations and send unattended objects skidding away.

Manifestation — Roll 1d4: (1) current of colored air that materializes into fast-moving gust; (2) storm of churning air behind caster, which whirls into gust of wind; (3) dozens of tiny cyclones that sweep outward from caster; (4) nothing more than a mundane gust of wind.

Corruption — Roll 1d5: (1) the caster attracts thunderstorms and lightning strikes like a living lightning rod, such that he takes an additional +1 damage from all lightning-based attacks and is perpetually the recipient of natural thunderstorms, eventually granting him a strange reputation amongst his peers; (2) the caster's sneezes become colossal in nature, sending forth gusts of wind that extinguish flames and send small objects flying; (3) when the caster talks, his breath is powerful enough to cause flames to waver 100' away and send small objects shooting away; (4) major; (5) greater.

Misfire — Roll 1d3: (1) a gust of errant wind sends the caster's belongings (weapon, backpack, spell book, etc.) flying 1d4x10' in a randomly determined direction; (2) the caster summons a torrential windstorm centered on himself, which presses him into the ground for 1d4 rounds and prevents him from moving or taking any action each round unless he can make a DC 20 Strength check; (3) all arrows within 100' are enchanted to ride the wind more effectively, and receive an additional +1 bonus to damage rolls for the next turn.

1 — Lost, failure, and worse! Roll 1d6 modified by Luck: (0 or less) corruption + patron taint + misfire; (1) corruption; (2) patron taint (or corruption if no patron); (3+) misfire.

2-11 — Lost. Failure.

12-15 — Failure, but spell is not lost.

16-17 — The gust of wind is a cone shape originating from the caster with a range of 10' and a final width of 10'. All creatures in the affected area must make a DC 14 Strength check or be forced back to the edge of the cone. Unattended objects of less than 10 pounds are also pushed back. If a target being pushed back impacts an obstruction before hitting the edge of the cone, it takes 1d6 damage.

18-21 — The gust of wind is a cone shape originating from the caster with a range of 20' and a final width of 20'. All creatures in the affected area must make a DC 16 Strength check or be forced back to the edge of the cone. Unattended objects of less than 20 pounds are also pushed back. If a target being pushed back impacts an obstruction before hitting the edge of the cone, it takes 1d6 damage.

22-23 — The gust of wind is a cone shape originating from the caster with a range of 40' and a final width of 20'. All creatures in the affected area must make a DC 18 Strength check or be forced back to the edge of the cone. Unattended objects of less than 30 pounds are also pushed back. Closed flames, such as those in a lantern, are extinguished 25% of the time. If a target being pushed back impacts an obstruction before hitting the edge of the cone, it takes 1d8 damage.

24-26 — The gust of wind is a cone shape originating from the caster with a range of 100' and a final width of 30'. All creatures in the affected area must make a DC 20 Strength check or be forced back to the edge of the cone. Unattended objects of less than 50 pounds are also pushed back. Closed flames, such as those in a lantern, are extinguished 50% of the time. If a target being pushed back impacts an obstruction before hitting the edge of the cone, it takes 1d10 damage.

27-31 — The gust of wind is a cone shape originating at any point designated by the caster within 200'. It has a range of 100' and a final width of 40'. The caster can use this cone to push objects *toward him* if he points the cone in such a direction. All creatures in the affected area must make a DC 22 Strength check or be forced back to the edge of the cone. Unattended objects of less than 75 pounds are also pushed back. If a target being pushed back impacts an obstruction before hitting the edge of the cone, it takes 1d12 damage and is pinned against the obstruction until it makes a DC 22 Strength check or the wind dies down. Closed flames, such as those in a lantern, are extinguished 50% of the time. Additionally, the gust of wind continues for up to 2 rounds for as long as the caster continues to concentrate. Creatures attempting to enter the area of the gust must make a DC 22 Strength check to do so, and missile weapons launched into the area of the wind take a -6 penalty to their attack roll.

32-33	The gust of wind originates at any point designated by the caster within 1,000′. The caster can control the vertical and horizontal shape of the wind gust and can send it snaking into the sky, around a corner, or down a pit. Creatures caught within the gust move along the designated vector. Those tossed into the air take normal falling damage when ejected (1d6 points per 10′ fallen). The gust has a range of 300′ and a final width of 100′. The caster can use this gust of wind to push objects *toward him* if he points the cone in such a direction. All creatures in the affected area must make a DC 28 Strength check or be forced back to the edge of the cone. Unattended objects of less than 200 pounds are also pushed back. If a target being pushed back impacts an obstruction before hitting the edge of the cone, it takes 1d14 damage and is pinned against the obstruction until it makes a DC 28 Strength check or the wind dies down. Closed flames, such as those in a lantern, are extinguished 90% of the time. Additionally, the gust of wind continues for up to 10 rounds for as long as the caster continues to concentrate. Creatures attempting to enter the area of the gust must make a DC 28 Strength check to do so, and missile weapons launched into the area of the wind take a -8 penalty to their attack roll.

34-35	The caster generates a massive gust of wind that emanates from him in an arc up to 360 degrees. If the caster wishes to protect allies (who are behind him, for example), he can limit the arc to less than the full 360 degrees; i.e., the wind could emanate in a 270-degree angle and the rear 90-degree arc could be protected. The gust of wind travels up to 400′ in all directions and can vector in a manner designated. For example, the caster could send the wind up into the sky or push targets down into the ground. Creatures that are at a vertical height when the wind diminishes take normal falling damage (1d6 per 10′ fallen). The caster can use this massive burst to send an entire army to the edges of the windstorm. All creatures in the affected area must make a DC 30 Strength check or be forced back to the edge of the effect. Unattended objects of less than 400 pounds are also pushed back. If a target being pushed back impacts an obstruction before hitting the edge of the cone, it takes 1d16 damage and is pinned against the obstruction until it makes a DC 30 Strength check or the wind dies down. All flames in the area are automatically extinguished. The gust of wind continues for up to 20 rounds for as long as the caster continues to concentrate. Creatures attempting to enter the area of the gust must make a DC 30 Strength check to do so, and missile weapons launched into the area of the wind take a -10 penalty to their attack roll.

36+	The caster calls forth a wind gust that is like a miniature thunderstorm, complete with dark gusts of rain, lightning, and thunder. The storm lasts for 1d4 turns (no concentration required) or until the caster ends the effect. The caster can protect a "bubble" centered around him and up to 40′ in diameter. All other creatures within 1,000′ in all directions are affected. All creatures are jostled by the winds for 1d6 damage per

round and steadily pushed by the winds to the outer edges of the storm at a rate of 100′ per round (DC 30 Strength check to resist). If a target being pushed back impacts an obstruction before hitting the edge of the cone, it takes 1d20 damage and is pinned against the obstruction until it makes a DC 30 Strength check or the wind dies down. In addition, creatures caught within the area of effect are struck by myriad flashes of ball lightning, taking 2d6-4 points of lightning damage each round (result of 0 or less indicates no lightning strikes this round). All caught within the gust are soaking wet; all flames are extinguished; and torches are difficult to re-light because of the moisture. Unattended objects of less than 500 pounds are also pushed back to the edge of the thunderstorm. It is impossible to launch missile fire weapons in the thunderstorm.

Haste

Level: 3	Range: Caster or 20' radius from caster	Duration: 1d4 rounds or more	Casting time: 2 rounds
	Save: N/A		

General

The caster gains quickness of motion. The caster's actions are amplified in speed such that he can move at twice the speed of a normal man – or faster! At higher levels, this spell also affects some creatures within a 20' radius of the caster. However, creatures affected by this spell age at an abnormal rate while under its influence. Additional actions gained are as follows:

Movement: *hastened* creatures double their movement speed. In some cases it may be tripled, as noted below.

Action dice: *hastened* creatures gain additional action dice. According to their class, these action dice may be used for attacks, spellcasting, turning, laying on hands, or skill checks. If the character currently has only one action die, the extra action die is the same as that one (usually a d20). If the character has multiple action dice (due to high class level or other factor), the extra action die is equal to the character's lowest action die. For example, if the character's action dice are 1d20+1d14, he gains an extra 1d14 as a third action die.

This spell can also be cast to cancel the spell *slow*.

Manifestation

Roll 1d3: (1) target appears blurred; (2) target is surrounded by a hazy aura much like a shimmering heat wave; (3) no manifestation when target stands still, but its movements are lightning-fast.

Corruption

Roll 1d8: (1) caster immediately ages 2d10+10 years; (2) caster ages himself, and everyone within 20' by 2d10+10 years; (3) caster acquires a series of tics and erratic motions that mark his every action, causing uncomfortable moments when in civilized society; (4) caster is perpetually nervous and on edge, flitting about in constant motion like a hummingbird, giving him a -1 penalty to any actions that require concentration; (5-6) major; (7-8) greater.

Misfire

Roll 1d4: (1) caster slows time for himself, causing him to miss his next action; (2) caster slows time for himself and 1d4 allies within 20', causing all of them to miss their next activation; (3) caster ages himself by 1d10+10 years; (4) caster grants *haste* to a nearby bug, which buzzes about viciously before flying off into the distance.

1	Lost, failure, and worse! Roll 1d6 modified by Luck: (0 or less) corruption + patron taint + misfire; (1-3) corruption; (4) patron taint (or corruption if no patron); (5+) misfire.
2-11	Lost. Failure.
12-15	Failure, but spell is not lost.
16-17	The caster gains double movement speed and one extra action die each round. The duration is 1d4+1 rounds.
18-21	The caster gains an immediate extra action die *this round* (after casting the spell), which can be used to attack or cast another spell. Thereafter, he gains double movement speed and one extra action die each round for 1d6+2 rounds.
22-23	The caster gains double movement speed and one extra action die. The caster gains an extra action die *this round* (after casting the spell), which can be used to attack or cast another spell. Additionally, one other designated creature within 20' is affected, beginning on its next activation. The duration is 2d4+1 rounds.
24-26	The caster experiences a moment of unnatural stillness. The world around him seems to slow to a near-immobility. He immediately gains 1d4 extra actions *this round* (after casting the spell), all at his normal action die (usually d20), which may be used to attack or cast spells. After this moment of pause, he gains double movement speed and one extra action die each round for 2d4+2 rounds.
27-31	The caster and up to three allies within range all gain double movement speed and one extra action die for a total of 2d4+2 rounds.
32-33	The caster gains triple movement speed and two extra action dice each round. Additionally, four other designated creatures within range gain double movement speed and one extra action die each round. The duration is 3d4 rounds.

34-35	The caster and four other designated creatures within range gain triple movement speed and two extra action dice each round. The duration is 3d4 rounds.
36+	The world around the caster slows. He and up to four designated creatures within range may take an additional 1d4+1 actions immediately. They proceed in initiative order as if they were in their own "time bubble" where they and only they can take actions; other creatures' initiative counts are simply skipped. Those affected by the spell can move, attack, cast spells, and perform other actions during this time, but these "extra rounds" of time count collectively as only one round for the purpose of spell durations or special effects. Once this time bubble evaporates, the caster and other affected creatures return to normal initiative order and regular combat order resumes. At that point, the caster gains *quadruple* movement speed and three extra action dice each round. Additionally, the other designated creatures within range gain *triple* movement speed and two extra action dice each round. The duration is 3d4 rounds.

Lightning Bolt

Level: 3	Range: See below	Duration: See below	Casting time: 1 round	Save: Reflex vs. spell check DC

General	With this spell, the caster summons forth a mighty discharge of electrical energy, sufficient to electrocute most creatures, splinter wooden objects, blast stone to bits, and melt metals.
Manifestation	See below.
Corruption	Roll 1d8: (1) caster is permanently charged with static electricity, causing him to take 1 point of shock damage every time he touches a metal object, and causing him to *inflict* 1 point of shock damage every time he touches a creature wearing metal armor; (2) caster's hair permanently stands on end, defying gravity in a most peculiar way; (3) caster is forever sensitive to electrical currents, allowing him to discover water underground as a dowser but also causing him to take +1 damage per die on all electrical attacks; (4) caster's brain is scrambled by electrical currents, causing his Intelligence and Personality scores to transpose; (5-6) major; (7-8) greater.
Misfire	Roll 1d3: (1) caster zaps himself for 2d4 damage; (2) caster zaps one randomly determined ally within 30' for 2d4 damage; (3) caster charges the point where he stands with electrical energy, such that any creature within 10' of that point on a following round who wears metal armor or carries metal weapons will take 2d6 damage as the electrical charge is released; the charge does not dissipate until released.

1	Lost, failure, and worse! Roll 1d6 modified by Luck: (0 or less) corruption + patron taint + misfire; (1-2) corruption; (3) patron taint (or corruption if no patron); (4+) misfire.
2-11	Lost. Failure.
12-15	Failure, but spell is not lost.
16-17	The caster releases a single lightning bolt aimed at one target. The target must be within 100', and it takes 3d6 damage.
18-21	The caster releases a single lightning bolt aimed at one target to which he has line of sight. The bolt has a range of 50' from the point of origination, which can be anywhere within 50' of the caster. The lightning bolt does 4d6 damage.
22-23	Static electricity! The caster designates a target within 100'. The target and all living targets within 30' of it (including allies and potentially the caster if he is in range) take 2d6 damage.
24-26	Chain lightning! The caster releases a single lightning bolt that jumps between up to four targets. The first target must be within 50' of the caster, and each subsequent target must be within 30' of the prior target. The lightning bolt cannot loop back to a prior target. The first target takes 4d6 damage, the second target takes 3d6 damage, the third target takes 2d6 damage, and the final target takes 1d6 damage.
27-31	Forked lightning! The caster releases five lightning bolts, one from each finger on one hand, but all targets must be within a 45 degree arc in front of the caster. A single target cannot be hit by more than one lightning bolt; if there are fewer than five eligible targets, then the last lightning bolts strike the ground and are lost. Maximum range of any single bolt is 150'. Each target takes 5d6 damage.

32-33	Ball lightning! The caster picks a point within 200'. A mighty charge of electricity explodes at that point. The target directly at the point of explosion takes 10d6 damage. All creatures within 20' take 6d6 damage.
34-35	Lightning storm! Dark clouds roll overhead as the caster directs blasts of electricity from the heavens. The caster may choose up to six targets within 500' and in line of sight. Lightning bolts arc down from the sky to strike these targets. Each target is hit by 1d7 bolts doing 1d12 damage each.
36+	The caster releases a single massive lightning bolt that forks to hit up to eight targets. The caster chooses a point of origination within 1,000'. The bolt has a range of 400' from the point of origination and does *total* damage of 24d6. The caster can divide that damage between up to eight targets as he sees fit. For example, the first target could take 17d6, then the next seven targets take 1d6 each.

Make Potion

Level: 3	Range: Self	Duration: Permanent brewing time (minimum one week)	Casting Time: 1d6+1 hours, plus material harvesting time and Save: None

General	The caster creates mystical brews that grant supernormal powers to those who consume them. The result of the spell check determines which kind of potion can be created, as indicated below; each casting allows the caster to *choose* one potion from the eligible results at his spell check *or less*. This portion of the spell requires 1d6+1 hours to cast. Once a potion is decided upon, the caster must spend money equal to half the potion's spell check number (rounded down) × 25 gp to procure the necessary equipment and base ingredients for the potion. In addition, each brew requires a special substance that must be harvested by the caster himself and then brewed, which takes roughly one week after the spell is cast. See below for suggested special ingredients and more details on potion effects. Unlike other spells, the judge, not the caster, makes the spell check roll to determine the caster's success.
Manifestation	Roll 1d4: (1) the liquid glows with scintillating colors; (2) small skull-shaped clouds rise from the brewing potion; (3) the brew churns and twists as if alive; (4) the liquid defies gravity, climbing the walls of its container and dripping up towards the ceiling.
Corruption	Roll 1d4: (1) caster's flesh takes on a permanent acrid smell; (2) caster's hand are mottled and stained by strange essences; (3) liquids writhe snake-like within any container handled by the caster; (4) liquids boil away in the caster's presence.
Misfire	Roll 1d4: (1) The potion explodes, resulting in 1d10 points of damage (Fort save against a DC equal to the intended potion's spell check number is allowed for half damage); (2) the potion seems fine, but in truth has no magical properties; (3) re-roll a normal result, and potion has the opposite intended effect as deemed appropriate by the judge; (4) re-roll a normal result, and potion functions as intended but for half the usual duration.

1	Misfire and corruption!
2-11	Lost. Failure.
12-15	Failure, but spell is not lost.
16-17	Love potion, poison.
18-21	Animal control, gaseous form, healing.
22-23	Shrinking, growth, levitation, water-breathing.
24-26	Polymorph, speed, heroism.
27-31	Invisibility, human control, fire resistance.
32-33	Un-dead control, extraordinary healing, flying.
34-35	Super-heroism, giant strength.
36+	Longevity, invulnerability.

Master Potion List			
Potion	Mini-mum DC	Special Ingredients	Effect
Animal control	18	A hair, scale, and feather from a gigantic specimen of mammal, reptile, and bird	For 2d6 rounds, all mundane animals within 30' obey the imbiber's commands, as follows: 1 or less HD = automatic; 2-4 HD = DC 16 Will save to resist; 5+ HD = DC 12 Will save to resist.
Extraordinary healing	32	The sweat of an angel or a piece of unicorn horn	Imbiber heals 3d6+3 hit points of damage immediately.
Fire resistance	27	A hell-hound's tooth	For 1d4 hours, imbiber resists first 10 points of fire or heat damage taken each round, and receives a +4 bonus to all saves to resist fire or heat-based effects.
Flying	32	A feather from a pegasus or a giant beetle's wing	Imbiber can fly at speed of 60' for 2d6+2 hours after drinking potion.
Gaseous form	18	Bottled essence of ghost	Imbiber transforms into gaseous form for 1d4 turns. While in this form he is immune to mundane physical attacks.
Giant strength	34	A giant's fingernail	Imbiber's Strength increases such that he has a +8 attack/damage bonus, which lasts 2d6 rounds.
Growth	22	A cyclops' eyebrow	Imbiber grows to double his normal size. His Strength increases by +6 and he gains 2d6 extra hit points. He returns to normal size in 2d6 rounds.
Healing	18	Spores from a giant mushroom	Imbiber heals 1d6+1 hit points of damage immediately.
Heroism	24	The spittle of a naga or the hair of a troll	For 1d6+1 turns, imbiber gains a +3 bonus to attacks, damage, saves, spell checks, and skill checks.
Human control	27	A serpent-man's eye or a harpy's tongue	For 2d6 rounds, all humanoids (including demi-humans, giants, and goblinoids) within 30' obey the imbiber's commands, as follows: 1 or less HD = automatic; 2-4 HD = DC 16 Will save to resist; 5+ HD = DC 12 Will save to resist.
Invisibility	27	The shadow of a shadow	Imbiber turns invisible for 1d4+1 hours. He returns to visibility if he attacks.
Invulnerability	36	A dragon's scale or a demon's claw	Imbiber gains resistance to *all* damage of 6 points; i.e., he resists the first 6 points of damage inflicted upon him every round. In addition, he gains an *additional* 6 points of resistance to fire, electricity, and acid damage; gains a +4 bonus to AC; and gains a +4 bonus to all saving throws. The duration is 1d6 turns.
Levitation	22	Webbing from a flying spider	Imbiber can levitate to a height of 10' for 1d4+1 turns. He can raise or lower himself at will. In addition, he can levitate one object of up to 400 pounds that he touches (such as a chest or another person).
Longevity	36	A piece of treant bark or lich's hair	Imbiber does not "grow young" – his physical form remains unchanged – but he effectively "does not count" the next 20 years of his life for purposes of aging. For example, if he were 60 years old when he drank this potion, he would remain at his same physical state for the next 20 years and only at age 80 would he begin to age again.
Love potion	16	A drop of honey from a killer bee hive	The imbiber falls in love with the first creature he sees after drinking this potion.

Master Potion List (continued)			
Poison	16	The poison glands of a giant scorpion or a titanic asp	Various potential effects per Appendix P, depending on materials used.
Polymorph	24	A piece of lycanthrope skin	The imbiber changes form into another man-sized creature (determined when the potion is crafted), which lasts for 1d4 days.
Shrinking	22	A drop of blood from a pixie	Imbiber shrinks to a height of 1', which lasts for 1d6 turns.
Speed	24	The venom of a giant wasp	Imbiber gains an extra action die (same as his lowest current action die) and double movement speed for 1 turn.
Super-heroism	34	A drop of dragon's blood	For 1d6+1 turns, imbiber gains a +6 bonus to attacks, damage, saves, spell checks, and skill checks.
Un-dead control	32	A pinch of mummy dust	For 2d6 turns, all un-dead within 30' obey the imbiber's commands, as follows: 1 or less HD = automatic; 2-4 HD = DC 16 Will save to resist; 5+ HD = DC 12 Will save to resist.
Water-breathing	22	A deep one's gill	Imbiber can breathe underwater for 2d6 turns.

Planar Step

Level: 3	Range: Potentially infinite (see below)	Duration: Permanent transfer of location
	Casting time: 1 round or more (see below)	Save: Unwilling targets receive Will save vs. spell check DC

General — With this spell, the caster steps to another place in the universe. At its lesser castings, this spell allows the caster to teleport to another place on the same world. At its higher castings, this spell takes the caster to other planes or even dimensions with a single step. The spell transports caster and all his belongings and potentially other creatures as well.

The higher the spell check, the further the caster travels and the more accurately he arrives. The success of this spell is determined in large part by the caster's familiarity with the location to which he intends to arrive. Each spell check result indicates the base chance of success depending on where the caster attempts to travel and his level of familiarity. This percentile chance is rolled when the caster decides where to travel. If the percentile indicates failure, the caster automatically suffers a misfire.

Manifestation — Roll 1d3: (1) targets simply vanish then reappear at target point; (2) targets explode in a cloud of smelly brimstone, then appear in a similar explosion at target point; (3) targets fade away, appearing to turn to mist then vanish into the air before reappearing in a similar manner.

Corruption — Roll 1d8: (1) caster's appearance ages nearly 100 years, although his body does not suffer any degeneration, but he appears wrinkled, haggard, and ancient; (2) caster is permanently unhinged from the material plane, such that whenever *any* die roll comes up as a natural 13, he flickers out of existence for 1d4 rounds, returning with no memory of where he has been and with a 10% chance of random wounds causing 1 point of damage; (3) caster is a dimensional magnet, attracting the attention of creatures that can leap through space and time, such that he inevitably draws the attacks of demons, elementals, and other extraplanar creatures when they are present (judge's discretion); (4-5) major; (6-8) greater.

Misfire — Roll 1d4: (1) caster and all nearby allies are transported 1d10 miles in a random direction, (2) caster and all nearby allies randomly swap positions and are physically rearranged; (3) caster's clothes and possessions are transported 1d20 miles in a random direction, but he remains in place, naked and without equipment; (4) the entire party's weapons are teleported to an unknown place.

1 — Lost, failure, and worse! Roll 1d6 modified by Luck: (0 or less) corruption + patron taint + misfire; (1-2) corruption; (3) patron taint (or corruption if no patron); (4+) misfire.

2-11 — Lost. Failure.

12-15 — Failure, but spell is not lost.

16-17	With a single step, the caster travels to a location up to 100 miles distant on this world, which he has personally seen before. The caster arrives with a margin of error equal to 1d10 miles, minus 1 mile per caster level; if the result is 0 or less, he arrives on target; otherwise he arrives at the indicated distance in a randomly determined with a 20% chance of arriving in a dangerous manner and taking 1d4 points of damage (partly embedded in the earth, above ground then experience a short fall, etc.).
18-21	With a single step, the caster travels to a location up to 200 miles distant on this world, which he must be familiar with, either via personal experience, detailed knowledge and study, or second-hand accounts. The caster arrives with a margin of error of 1d4 miles if he has personal experience with the location or 1d16 miles minus 1 mile per caster level if he doesn't. If the result is 0 or less, the caster arrives on target; otherwise he arrives at the indicated distance in a randomly determined direction with a 20% chance of arriving in a dangerous manner and taking 1d4 points of damage. The caster can take up to one other man-sized creature with him, who must be in physical contact. That creature receives a Will save to resist if unwilling.
22-23	With a single step, the caster travels to a location up to 500 miles distant on this world. The caster must be familiar with the location, either via personal experience, detailed knowledge and study, or second-hand accounts. The caster arrives with a margin of error of 1d3 miles if he has personal experience with the location or 1d14 miles minus 1 mile per caster level if he doesn't. If the result is 0 or less, the caster arrives on target; otherwise he arrives at the indicated distance in a randomly determined direction with a 20% chance of arriving in a dangerous manner and taking 1d4 points of damage. The caster can take up to four other man-sized creatures with him, who must be in physical contact. Creatures receive a Will save to resist if unwilling.
24-26	With a single step, the caster travels to a location up to 2,000 miles distant on this world or any adjacent moon or planet. The caster must be familiar with the location, either via personal experience, detailed knowledge and study, or second-hand accounts. The caster arrives with a margin of error of 1d3 miles if he has personal experience with the location or 1d12 miles minus 1 mile per caster level if he doesn't. If the result is 0 or less, the caster arrives on target; otherwise he arrives at the indicated distance in a randomly determined direction with a 20% chance of arriving in a dangerous manner and taking 1d4 points of damage. The caster can take up to four other man-sized creatures with him, who must be in physical contact. Creatures receive a Will save to resist if unwilling.
27-31	The caster draws a magic circle up to 40' in diameter, which requires one round of drawing time for every 10' of diameter. At the end of the last round of drawing, the spell is cast, and all creatures within the circle are transported to a distant location *anywhere* on this plane of existence *or* within 100 miles of the caster's equivalent point on another, *adjacent* plane of existence. Creatures receive a Will save to resist if unwilling. The caster must be familiar with the target location, either via personal experience, detailed knowledge and study, or second-hand accounts. If on the same plane, the caster arrives with a margin of error of 1d3 miles if he has personal experience with the location or 1d10 miles minus 1 mile per caster level if he doesn't. If on a different plane, the caster arrives with a margin of error of 1d10 miles if he has personal experience with the location or 1d20 miles minus 1 mile per caster level if he doesn't. If the result is 0 or less, the caster arrives on target; otherwise he arrives at the indicated distance in a randomly determined direction with a 20% chance of arriving in a dangerous manner and taking 1d4 points of damage.
32-33	With a wave of the hand, the caster transports himself plus a *selection* of creatures within 40' to another location. The caster can choose to transport *all* creatures within 40', up to a number equal to his caster level, or all *except* a number of exclusions equal to his caster level. The planar step transports the caster and the targets to a distant location *anywhere* on this plane of existence *or* within 1,000 miles of the caster's equivalent point on another plane of existence *that need not be adjacent*. Creatures receive a Will save to resist if unwilling. The caster does *not* need to be familiar with the target location; he can specify simply "a point on the elemental plane of fire." The caster arrives with a margin of error, which is a die roll less 1 mile per caster level if familiar with the location, or a die roll with no modifier if unfamiliar with the location. The die roll is 1d3 miles if on the same plane, 1d10 miles if on an adjacent plane, or 1d30 miles if on a non-adjacent plane. If the result is 0 or less, the caster arrives on target; otherwise he arrives at the indicated distance in a randomly determined direction with a 20% chance of arriving in a dangerous manner and taking 1d4 points of damage.
34-35	The caster transports boats, armies, fortresses, and even small cities between the planes. Unwilling targets always receive a Will save to resist. The caster can transport himself or a number of allies equal to his caster level with perfect accuracy to any point on this or an adjacent plane or within 1,000 miles of his equivalent point on a non-adjacent plane. Transporting greater targets has a margin of error equal to 2d30 miles less 1 mile per caster level. (The judge may adjust this per the guidelines on spell results

given above, depending on the size of the object being transported and the caster's familiarity with the target location.) Casting time is greatly increased due to the physical stress of moving large objects, and spellburn is required, as follows. The judge should use these general sizes as guidelines for the requirements of the specific objects at hand: boats require 5 points of spellburn and 1 turn of casting time; large groups of people or armies require 10 points of spellburn and 1 hour of casting time; fortresses, castles, and the like require 15 points of spellburn and 1 day of casting time; and small cities require 20 points of spellburn and 1 week of casting time.

36+	The caster transports boats, armies, fortresses, and even small cities as result 34-35 above, except he completes the spell with unerring accuracy and can even teleport objects to other *dimensions* beyond our conception of space and time, potentially visiting gods and alien intelligences. Alternately, the caster can create a permanent portal between the planes. The caster designates one object as the portal, typically a door, window, gate, archway, well, or cave mouth. The object need not require physical passage, though; the caster could also designate a pedestal, throne, obelisk, tile, or river, or even a boat or wagon that when utilized acts as the portal. A corresponding object on "the other side" is also designated, though the portals need not be two-way. The caster must spend one week at each location as the casting time for this spell and utilize exotic planar materials costing 50,000 gp per "direction" in addition to the cost of the objects (i.e., a one-way portal costs 50,000 gp, while a two-way portal costs 100,000 gp). A minimum of 10 points of spellburn is required. The objects become permanently linked up to any physical distance and across any number of planes or dimensions. Creatures passing through the portals are instantly transported back and forth with no save or other requirements.

Runic Alphabet, Fey

Level: 3	Range: One inscribed rune	Duration: Until triggered	Casting time: 1 turn
	Save: Will save vs. spell check; -1 penalty if of an alignment opposed to caster		

General	This spell grants the caster knowledge of the secret alphabet of the fey. The fey language is composed of eldritch sigils that house subtle but dangerous power. By casting this spell, the caster can trace a fey rune. The materials necessary to inscribe the rune cost 200 gp per rune. The spell check is made to determine which energies the caster can imbue in his rune; the caster can choose *one* rune at or below the result of the check, with the choice made when the rune is inscribed. The rune can be traced in any object: on a leaf or tree bark, on a cloak or ring, over a door, under a tabletop, and so on. Subtract -2 from the spell check to trace in mid-air; -4 to trace invisibly; or -8 to trace permanently (does not vanish when triggered). The effect is triggered per the specific sign as described below: when touched, passed, gazed upon, etc. On a failed spell check, the sign fizzles and dissolves and materials are lost. On a success, the spell check becomes the DC for the opposing save. The caster can identify an unknown rune with a successful spell check against the opposing caster's check result.
Manifestation	Inscribed rune.
Corruption	Roll 1d4: (1) caster has a non-magical runic shape permanently seared onto one cheek; (2) caster's forehead wrinkles such that it appears to house a third eye, which disappears upon close inspection; (3) minor; (4) major.
Misfire	Roll 1d4: (1) randomly determined rune (roll d16+10 on spell table) is inscribed on the caster's hand and immediately detonated; (2) rune is traced but it will not activate under any circumstances, effectively providing a costly and unsightly "tattoo" to the subject marked; (3) caster inadvertently sears a permanent symbol that resembles a silhouette of his face; (4) caster forgets how to read and write for 1d6 turns, during which time he cannot cast this spell or any other that is dependent on literacy for its effects.
1	Lost, failure, and worse! Roll 1d6 modified by Luck: (0 or less) corruption + patron taint + misfire; (1-2) corruption; (3) patron taint (or corruption if no patron); (4+) misfire.
2-11	Lost. Failure.
12-15	Failure, but spell is not lost.
16-17	*Pain.* The first creature to disturb the rune feels a sharp pang of intense pain. The target takes 2d6 damage immediately and sprouts a bloody wound, as if it had been stabbed. The rune dissolves once triggered.

18-21	*Burn.* The first creature to disturb the rune suffers a painful burning sensation. This causes 1d6+1 hit points of damage immediately, then 1d6 points one hour later, then 1d6-1 points an hour after that, then 1d6-2 and 1d6-3 points at the next two hour intervals. The rune dissolves once triggered.
22-23	*Rebuff.* A creature attempting to pass through the place protected by the rune feels a strong hand pushing it back. The target must make a Will save against the spell check. Failure indicates it is rebuffed and cannot pass and takes 1d4 points of damage. The target may continue to attempt to pass each round until it succeeds but continues to take damage on any failed save. The rune remains intact until it is passed.
24-26	*Explosive.* When triggered, the rune explodes in a fiery burst. All within 10' take 3d6 damage and flammable objects catch fire.
27-31	*Safety.* The object on which this rune is inscribed is protected. Creatures attempting to attack it must make a Will save. Failure indicates they lose the urge to attack, forget about the target, somehow miss wildly, or otherwise cannot succeed in an attack. Additionally, on a failed save the attacker immediately falls asleep for 1d4 rounds. Creatures that fail the save may attempt to attack on a subsequent round. The rune continues to protect its target until it is breached.
32-33	*Repulse.* Any attempt to pass through this rune triggers a powerful force that sends the target flying back 3d20 feet. The force of the repulsion is such that the creature takes 1d8 damage from the repulsion. This rune is often placed near ledges or pits so the repulsion sends the victim into a dangerous place.
34-35	*Lightning rod.* The first creature to disturb this rune observes the rune crackle and dissipate, but that is all. The target is now designated as a lightning rod. The next time the creature is in stormy weather of any kind, it automatically attracts 1d4 lightning bolts per minute, each doing 3d6 damage. If the creature is hit by a *lightning bolt* spell (or similar effect), it takes an additional 2d6 damage. The effect wears off after 7 days.
36+	*Rage.* The first creature to disturb this rune is enveloped in an overwhelming rage. It must make a Will save or attack the nearest living creature (ally or not). It fights to the death. The first death at its hands ends the effect.

Slow

Level: 3	Range: 20' + 10' per CL	Duration: Varies	Casting time: 1 round	Save: Sometimes (Will)

General	The caster impairs the ability of the targeted creature to move at its normal speed. This spell can also be cast to cancel *haste*.

Manifestation	Roll 1d3: (1) target appears elongated and stretched in several directions; (2) target is surrounded by a gray mist that partially obscures it; (3) target seems to droop toward the ground, moving with difficulty.
Corruption	Roll 1d8: (1) caster is returned to an age of 1d10+5 years, quite possibly reducing him to a child-like state; he retains all mental attributes but receives a -2 penalty to Strength, and +1 bonus to Stamina and Agility; he is treated as a child by all who encounter him; (2) caster makes himself and all within 20' younger by a factor of -2d10 years, possibly reducing already-young PCs to a child-like state; (3) caster's speech patterns slow significantly, such that it takes him twice as long as normal to communicate, and any time he casts a spell he must take twice the normal casting time *or* receive a -1 penalty to the spell check as he stutters and stumbles on his slurred, slow words; (4) the caster acquires a ponderous gait that permanently reduces his speed by -5'; (5-6) major; (7-8) greater.
Misfire	Roll 1d4: (1) caster slows time for himself, causing him to miss his next action; (2) caster slows times for himself and 1d4 allies within 20', causing all of them to miss their next action; (3) caster ages himself by 1d10+10 years; (4) caster grants *slow* to a nearby bug, which buzzes about somnolently before flying off into the distance.

1	Lost, failure, and worse! Roll 1d6 modified by Luck: (0 or less) corruption + patron taint + misfire; (1-3) corruption; (4) patron taint (or corruption if no patron); (5+) misfire.
2-11	Lost. Failure.
12-15	Failure, but spell is not lost.

16-17	One target within range immediately drops to the bottom of the initiative count (no save). If it has already acted this round, it does *not* receive another action at the end of the initiative count.
18-21	One target within range skips its next activation (no save).
22-23	One target within range is *slowed* to half its normal speed (Will save to resist). Its movement rate is halved, and it can take its normal actions only once every other round (with the first "skip" being its next activation). It automatically drops to the bottom of the initiative count. The effect lasts for 1d6+1 rounds.
24-26	The caster can target *two* creatures, each of which is *slowed* to half its normal speed (Will save to resist). The targets' movement rate is halved, and they can take their normal actions only once every other round (with the first "skip" being their next activation). They automatically drop to the bottom of the initiative count (in the same relative order of initiative). The effect lasts for 1d6+1 rounds.
27-31	The caster designates a target within range. That target and all other creatures (friendly or not) within 20' are potentially *slowed* (Will save to resist). Those that fail their save are slowed to half normal speed. Their movement rate is halved, and they can take their normal actions only once every other round (with the first "skip" being its next activation). They automatically drop to the bottom of the initiative count (in the same relative order of initiative). The effect lasts for 1d6+1 rounds.
32-33	The caster selects one target within range. If it fails a Will save, it is removed from the normal flow of time. Each round, roll d%. On a roll of 01-25, the creature can move and act as normal. A roll of 26-90 indicates it remains frozen in place and can take no actions. This effect continues until 91-00 is rolled, at which point the creature slips back into the normal flow of time and the effect ends.
34-35	The caster selects one target within range. That target and all creatures within 20' (friendly or not) are removed from the normal flow of time (no save). This is a one-time event; other creatures can subsequently move into the affected area without consequence. Each round, roll d%. On a roll of 01-25, all affected creatures can move and act as normal. A roll of 26-90 indicates those creatures remain frozen in place and can take no actions. This effect continues until 91-00 is rolled, at which point all affected creatures slip back into the normal flow of time and the effect ends.
36+	The caster creates a sphere of *slowness*. The caster designates a space within line of sight. All creatures within a 100' radius of that point are *slowed*. Additionally, any creature that enters that point is *slowed*. There is no visible indication of the field. Creatures receive a Will save to resist. Failure indicates they move at half speed and receive an activation only once every other round. The effect lasts as long as the targets remain within the sphere of *slowness* and extends for another 2d6 rounds thereafter when they leave. The sphere itself persists for 1d5 hours.

Sword Magic

Level: 3	Range: Self	Duration: Permanent	Casting Time: A month or more (see below)	Save: None

General

Magic weapons can be created by spellcasters using this spell. A spell check determines the *possible* abilities and properties of the weapon to be created. The specifics are determined by the material components, craftsmanship, and other elements incorporated by the caster. This spell is cast as an ongoing ritual through the weapon-forging process, and the caster may need a partner to forge the weapon if he is not a blacksmith himself. Spellburn utilized in the casting is lost for the duration of the casting and only heals when the spell is complete. All costs are expended before the spell check is made, and failure means all costs are lost; a weapon that is unsuccessfully enchanted can be re-forged to recover half the material costs involved. Generally speaking, follow this process to create a magic weapon:

Forge the weapon: The weapon must be forged while this spell is cast. A dagger, short sword, long sword, or two-handed sword is easily enchanted. Using this spell to enchant other kinds of weapons entails a -1 penalty to the spell check, increased to -2 if the caster is not proficient with the weapon in question. Construction of the physical weapon itself costs a minimum of 100x the cost of a normal weapon of that type in raw materials of the highest quality, plus any wages paid to the blacksmith(s).

The basic enchantment: The spell check determines the basic enchantment. The caster's level determines the maximum possible effectiveness of the weapon: CL5 = +1, CL6 = +2, CL7 = +3, CL8 = +4, CL10 = +5. Make the spell check and compare the result to Table 8-4 to determine the "plus" of the weapon. The cost of a plus, in addition to the weapon itself, is as follows, reflected in extraordinarily rare materials: +1 = 5,000 gp; +2 = 10,000 gp; +3 = 50,000 gp; +4 = 500,000 gp; +5 = 1,000,000 gp.

The weapon's intelligence: A magic weapon is always intelligent. The single spell check determines the basic enchantment, the weapon's intelligence, and all other aspects of the magic sword. Reference Table 8-4 to determine the dice rolled for the weapon's Intelligence and how it communicates. The weapon has a personality that is a blend of the caster's, the blacksmith involved, patrons invoked, and any other particulars of its creation (a dragon-bane weapon may be arrogant like a dragon).

Alignment: A magic weapon is usually, but not always, the same alignment as its creator. Reference Table 8-3 for the result of the spell check. Weapons of different alignments than their creators will not be easy to use.

Banes: A magic weapon can be constructed for the purpose of slaying a particular kind of foe. Reference Table 8-4 to determine the number of potential banes at any given spell check result and Table 8-5 for the effects of various banes. Each bane built into a weapon costs from 20,000 to 100,000 gp and requires voluminous material samples of the creature type in question (for example, a dozen dragon corpses or 100 orcs). The cost depends on the level of effect and is at the discretion of the judge (i.e., the most deadly result of instant death costs the most, while the simplest result of a bonus to hit is the cheapest). The caster must declare what kind of banes he is trying to instill in his weapon. Depending on the spell check, he may be successful in none, some, or all of those. If a limited number is granted, the judge randomly determines which are successful.

Special purpose: A magic weapon always has a special purpose, and it is not always under the control of the caster. The special purpose is determined by the most recondite of factors, ranging from astrological signs to natural terrain to the most subtle properties used in the crafting of the weapon. Table 8-4 indicates the dice rolled for a weapon's special purpose, based on the spell check; those dice are then rolled on table 8-6. The result is always random, *then* the caster can utilize spellburn to shift the table's results. For every point of spellburn, he can increase or decrease his roll by 1 point. This spellburn is determined *after* rolling for the special purpose. The level of spellburn employed determines the caster's knowledge of the process and how carefully he can actually influence the result of his crafting. Under certain circumstances, particularly if a caster has a powerful patron, the judge may *choose* a special purpose that is aligned with the caster's patron or some other greater power. There is no gp cost to a special purpose.

Powers: Sword powers come in three varieties: type I, type II, and type III (see tables 8-7, 8-8, and 8-9). The special check determines which powers a sword may have. The caster pays a cost to imbue a sword with powers: 10,000 gp for each type I power, 20,000 gp for each type II power, and 50,000 for each type III power. Depending on the result of the spell check, the weapon will have some number of those powers evident at the completion of the casting. It is quite possible that the caster will spend the money to imbue the powers but his spell check will not be sufficient to complete them, or his spell check results in a percentile chance which does not yield those powers.

Creation properties: Several of the entries above note specialized circumstances that can influence a sword's final traits. These creation properties are sometimes known factors, and other times are incidental events that affect the creation process inadvertently. Here are some potential creation properties, which can be used by the player to attempt to influence the final weapon created and by the judge to introduce unusual purposes or powers beyond the intent of the creator. *Creation properties:* crafter (not necessarily caster) is an elf, dwarf, giant, god, demon, last of a line, a wronged king, or seventh son; weapon is crafted on the plane of fire (or in a volcano or lava lake), on the plane of water (or under the sea, deep in a lake, or on a sailing ship), on the plane of earth (or far below in the underdeep, or within a mine), on the plane of air (or on a cloud, or atop a mountain above the clouds), on the plane of a demon prince or one of the Nine Hells, in the lair of a great dragon, in a graveyard or ossuary, a lich's crypt, a vampire's coffin, or a mummy's tomb, on a great battlefield, or in the fey lands; date of crafting is the birthday of a prince, the day a witch is hanged, or on the death of a god; moment of completion is at sunset, sunrise, high noon, during a full moon, during an eclipse; material components of sword include remnants of a pegasus, dragon, demon, un-dead, etc.; creator's Luck is at a certain level; iron or wood from which sword is forged is from a specific place; creator's spoken language includes a certain tongue; and so on.

Manifestation	Creation of a magic weapon.
Corruption	Roll 1d8: (1-3) minor; (4-6) major; (7-8) greater.
Misfire	N/A

1	Lost and corruption.
2-15	Lost. Failure.
16-17	Per above and table 8-4.
18-21	Per above and table 8-4.
22-23	Per above and table 8-4.
24-26	Per above and table 8-4.
27-31	Per above and table 8-4.
32-33	Per above and table 8-4.
34-35	Per above and table 8-4.
36+	Per above and table 8-4.

Transference

Level: 3   Range: 10' per level   Duration: Varies   Casting Time: 1 round   Save: Will to negate

General	The caster takes possession of another body, either temporarily or permanently.
Manifestation	Roll 1d4: (1) caster's body collapsed like an empty skin, leaving flaccid flesh behind; (2) target's features shift and bubble for a moment before returning to normal; (3) ectoplasm erupts from the caster's mouth and forces its way into the target's head; (4) ghostly doppelgangers of the caster and target wrestle briefly in the air between them before subsiding into the target's body.
Corruption	Roll 1d4: (1) caster ages 1 year; (2) caster's eyes take on a horrifically hypnotic cast, making others loath to meet his gaze; (3) caster occasionally speaks in tongues without being aware of it; (4) caster's reflection is that of another person.
Misfire	Roll 1d5: (1) all reflective surfaces within a 15' radius shatter (magic items allowed a DC 5 save to remain intact); (2) caster temporarily swaps souls with that of an inoffensive animal nearby (rat, louse, bird, etc); swap lasts 1d3 rounds; (3) spell targets the wrong victim; make a new spell check against a random target; (4) caster falls into a coma for 1d4 rounds; (5) psychic backlash allows all within 15' radius to read the caster's mind for 1d4 hours.

1	Lost, failure, and worse! Roll 1d6 modified by Luck: (0 or less) corruption + patron taint + misfire; (1-2) corruption; (3) patron taint (or corruption if no patron); (4+) misfire.
2-11	Lost. Failure.
12-15	Failure, but spell is not lost.
16-17	The caster insidiously inflicts his will upon his target, allowing him to control the target's action for a number of rounds equal to his CL. The victim is allowed a Will save each round to resist the caster's control for that round.
18-21	The caster can possess a sleeping victim and take control of the target's body for up to 8 hours. Roll 1d8 + the caster's Intelligence modifier to determine the number of hours this possession lasts, with a result of 8+ indicating the possession lasts a full 8-hour sleep cycle. The victim awakens exhausted with memories of horrible dreams symbolic of the actions his body performed in the night. The target gains none of the benefits granted by a full night's sleep.
22-23 and 24-26	The caster can take full possession of a target who fails a Will save. The caster's own body becomes inert during this time, falling into a comatose state. The target's soul is shunted into a tiny mental prison during this time, and it is forced to observe helplessly as its own body engages in any number of vile actions. During this period, the possessed body takes on minor physical changes that mirror the caster's own body (eyes change color, voice is altered slightly, poise is different, etc.). Friends of the possessed victim can make a DC 12 Int check to recognize something different about the target, but will not necessarily be aware that the target is under alien control.
	The duration of the control is one round per CL on result 22-23 and one turn per caster level on result 24-26. If the target is of higher level or has more hit dice than the caster, it is allowed a new Will save each round / turn to regain control of its body.
27-31 and 32-33	The caster can take full possession of a target who fails a Will save. The caster's own body becomes inert during this time, falling into a comatose state. The target's soul is shunted into a tiny mental prison during this time, and it forced to observe helplessly as its own body engage in any number of vile actions. If the target is of higher level than the spell caster, it is allowed a new Will save each hour to regain control of its body; otherwise the spell lasts a number of rounds equal to the caster's CL. During this period, the possessed body takes on minor physical changes that mirror the caster's own body (eyes change color, voice is altered slightly, poise is different, etc.). Friends of the possessed victim can make a DC 12 Int check to recognize something different about the target, but will not necessarily be aware that the target is under alien control.
	In addition, the caster can jump from body to body at will so long as his new chosen target fails a Will save each time a jump is attempted. A successful save indicates the caster cannot attempt to possess that body again during the duration of the spell. Each new body must be within spell range of the current

body in order to swap bodies. The owner of the body the caster vacates to possess a new form must make a DC 12 Fort save or be dazed for 1d4 rounds as it recovers from the possession.

The duration of the overall possession varies by spell check. On a result of 27-31 it is one hour per caster level and on a result of 32-33 it is 4 hours per caster level.

34-35	The caster can temporarily escape death by transferring his soul into a receptacle specially prepared to house it. This object can be most anything the spell caster desires (gemstone, statue, painting, book, etc.), but the special preparations needed to prepare the item cost 500 gold pieces for each decade the receptacle's power is intended to last. After the item is prepared, the caster can abandon his own body at any time thereafter and place his soul inside the object. His physical body dies and no spell can restore life to the corpse so long as the caster's spirit remains in the receptacle. The caster remains in the prepared object until he successfully takes possession of another body completely or the receptacle's prepared time period expires. To take possession of another, the caster must make a casting check of 22+ when a victim of lower level/hit dice *and* lesser Personality than his own comes within range of the receptacle. This can include animals, bugs, and so on. The target is allowed a Will save to avoid possession, and, if successful, can never again be targeted by the caster for possession. If no acceptable target comes within range of the receptacle or all targets make their saves before the receptacle's duration expires, the caster's soul is irretrievably lost when the last of the receptacle's power fails. If the target fails the Will save, its own spirit becomes housed in the receptacle and only powerful restorative magics or divine intervention (or other means devised by the judge) can ever evict the caster's spirit from the stolen form and restore the original soul to its proper body.
36+	The caster immediately obliterates the soul of his victim and takes permanent possession of its body. The caster's own physical form is destroyed in the casting, seemingly incinerated by spontaneous combustion. If the target makes the Will save, there is no effect.

Turn to Stone

Level: 3	Range: 30' plus 10' per caster level	Duration: Various	Casting Time: 1 round
	Save: Fortitude to avoid		

General	The caster turns other living beings to stone. A reverse version of this spell, *turn to flesh*, may be learned and can be used to cancel its effects. Note that casting this spell successfully against a creature of the water (such as a water elemental) automatically inflicts an extra 1d4 damage per caster level.
Manifestation	Roll 1d4: (1) caster's head turns medusa-like (horrible visage, snakes for hair, etc.); (2) caster's eyes become orbs of polished marble; (3) tendrils of stone rise from the ground to wrap around the target and burrow into its flesh; (4) the target sweats beads of quartz that accumulate to form a shell around it.
Corruption	Roll 1d4: (1) caster's hair become tiny, non-venomous serpents; (2) caster's hands become crude and rocklike; (3) the sound of grinding stone accompanies the caster when he walks; (4) the caster's voice becomes unnaturally gravelly like stone grinding together.
Misfire	Roll 1d5: (1) caster turns himself to stone for 1d6 rounds; (2) caster's body turns rocky and ungainly for 1d6 hours; (3) caster attracts loose stones and rubble to his position, inflicting anywhere from 1d3 to 1d30 points of damage at the judge's discretion depending on size and amount of available stones; (4) caster becomes stone deaf for 1d3 hours and suffers a -2 penalty to spell checks during that time; (5) caster inadvertently targets another creature; make a new spell check and apply the results to a random creature within range. If no other creature is within the area of the spell's power, the caster is afflicted by his own magic!

1	Lost, failure, and worse! Roll 1d6 modified by Luck: (0 or less) corruption + patron taint + misfire; (1-3) corruption; (4) patron taint (or corruption if no patron); (5+) misfire.
2-11	Lost. Failure.
12-15	Failure, but spell is not lost.
16-17	The caster turns the target's body partially mineral, making it heavy and causing it to sprout rock-like protrusions from the flesh. If the target fails a save, it suffers a -4 penalty to all attack rolls, Reflex saving throws, and initiative, as well as all skill checks involving mobility. This effect lasts 1 hour per caster level.

18-21	The target turns partially to stone if it fails the save. If the target's upper body is affected, it loses the ability to attack, speak, or cast spells, and must make a DC 10 Agility check to avoid falling prone. If the target's lower body is affected, it is immobilized until the spell expires or is removed. The portion affected by the spell is either targeted by the caster or, if not specified, randomly determined by the judge. This effect lasts 1 hour per caster level.
22-23	The target turns to stone if it fails the save. The target remains petrified for 1 day per caster level and cannot perform any action. The target remains aware of its surroundings as if buried beneath a thick layer of earth (sounds are muted and sight is hazy and narrow in scope) and is otherwise incapacitated but does not starve or suffocate.
24-26	Up to two targets within range can be affected, and turn to stone if they fail their saves. They remain petrified for 1 day per caster level and cannot perform any action. They remain aware of their surroundings as if buried beneath a thick layer of earth (sounds are muted and sight is hazy and narrow in scope) and are otherwise incapacitated but do not starve or suffocate.
27-31	Up to four targets within range can be affected, and turn to stone if they fail their saves. They remain petrified for 1 day per caster level and cannot perform any action. They remain aware of their surroundings as if buried beneath a thick layer of earth (sounds are muted and sight is hazy and narrow in scope) and are otherwise incapacitated but do not starve or suffocate.
32-33	The caster transforms one target into stone with no save allowed. In addition, the caster can cause the target to shatter with the flick of his wrist if the target fails a Fort save against this destructive gesture. If the save is successful, the target still remains petrified for a period of 1 week per caster level. During this time, the target remains aware of its surroundings as if buried beneath a thick layer of earth (sounds are muted and sight is hazy and narrow in scope) and is otherwise incapacitated but does not starve or suffocate.
34-35	The caster transforms all creatures within his sight to stone unless they make a successful Fort save. The caster cannot choose to affect certain creatures and spare others; the petrifying magic affects all within view. The effects last for 1 month per caster level. Victims remain aware of their surroundings as if buried beneath a thick layer of earth (sounds are muted and sight is hazy and narrow in scope) and are otherwise incapacitated but do not starve or suffocate.
36+	The caster turns a small geographic region to stone. All living creatures (animals, humanoids, monsters, trees, crops, etc.) are petrified unless they make a successful Fort save. The effect is permanent until negated by restorative magics, powerful artifacts, or divine influence. The area affected is equal to 100 yards per caster level. Victims remain aware of their surroundings as if buried beneath a thick layer of earth (sounds are muted and sight is hazy and narrow in scope) and are otherwise incapacitated but do not starve or suffocate.

"I told you not to turn on the light!"

Water Breathing

Level: 3	Range: Touch	Duration: 1 hour per caster level	Casting Time: 1 round	Save: Will to negate

General The caster grants himself and others the ability to breathe water and function beneath the waves.

Manifestation Roll 1d4: (1) target grows gill slits on the neck; (2) target's body becomes scaly and assumes a greenish-blue or silver hue; (3) target's eyes bulge fishlike in their sockets and its mouth puckers; (4) target's nose and mouth transform into thin slits.

Corruption Roll 1d4: (1) caster must immerse himself in water for 10 minutes each day or suffer great pain (manifested as -2 to all rolls); (2) caster's voice takes on a bubbling, distorted quality as if speaking underwater; (3) caster's flesh becomes permanently discolored and scaly; (4) caster's nose and ears vanish and are replaced with flaps of fishy flesh.

Misfire Roll 1d5: (1) caster gasps for breath and passes out for 1d10 minutes; (2) caster's skin becomes dry and cracked, and if not immersed in water for 1 hour immediately, he temporarily loses 1 point of Stamina; (3) caster and all within 10' of him are buffeted by a rain of fish that do 1d4 points of damage; (4) caster loses the ability to speak for 1d6 hours; (5) caster's skin becomes covered in slick mucus for 1d6 hours, reducing movement by 10 feet per round and inflicting a -2 penalty to attacks, spell checks, skill checks involving a firm grip, and initiative, but the slime does grant a +2 bonus to escape restraints.

1 Lost, failure, and worse! Roll 1d6 modified by Luck: (0 or less) corruption + patron taint + misfire; (1-2) corruption; (3) patron taint (or corruption if no patron); (4+) misfire.

2-11 Lost. Failure.

12-15 Failure, but spell is not lost.

16-17 Caster can breathe underwater for the duration of the spell. This does not protect his belongings or improve his movement rate underwater nor does it make him unable to breathe air.

18-21 Caster and up to three additional creatures can breathe underwater for the duration of the spell. This does not protect their belongings or improve their movement rate underwater nor does it make them unable to breathe air.

22-23 Caster and up to six additional creatures can breathe underwater for the duration of the spell. This does not protect their belongings or improve their movement rate underwater nor does it make them unable to breathe air.

24-26 Caster and up to ten additional creatures can breathe underwater for the duration of the spell. In addition, the caster (and only the caster) gains great swimming ability that lets him move at his normal rate beneath the waves, and all of his belongings are magically protected from the submersion. His allies' belongings are *not* similarly protected.

27-31 Caster and up to three additional creatures gain the ability to breath underwater, swim at normal speed while underwater, and have their belongings magically protected from the effects of submersion.

32-33 Caster and up to six additional creatures gain the ability to breath underwater, swim at normal speed while underwater, and have their belongings magically protected from the effects of submersion.

34-35 Caster and up to ten additional creatures gain the ability to breath underwater, swim at normal speed while underwater, and have their belongings magically protected from the effects of submersion.

36+ The caster becomes an aquatic creature for as long as he remains in the water. He can breathe water and air with equal ability, move normally underwater, suffer no damage from pressures found at extreme depths, and can speak with any intelligent aquatic creature. All of his possessions are protected from submersion. As a creature of the water, the caster gains a +2 bonus to *all* rolls made while in the water. Additionally, any creature that holds the caster's hand gains the same benefit as long as contact is maintained. The duration of this transformation is permanent or until the caster completely exits the water and steps foot on dry land once again.

Write Magic

Level: 3   Range: N/A   Duration: N/A   Casting Time: See below   Save: N/A

General	The caster transcribes magical writings onto a scroll, which can be read at a later time to create a spell-like effect. The result of the spell check determines the level of spell the caster can transcribe, the number of spells that can be written, and if the caster can create any unique properties as part of the casting. Most spellcasters sign their scrolls, and they may attach curses or wards to prevent others from reading them. The caster must provide the materials to transcribe the scroll, including paper, vellum, or other such materials; a writing utensil; and a specific kind of ink, at a base cost of 200 gp per spell per level inscribed on a scroll. For example, transcribing a level 1 spell costs 200 gp; transcribing three level 1 spells costs 600 gp; transcribing a level 1 spell and a level 3 spell costs 800 gp. The caster may also choose to inscribe on tusks, etch on stone tablets, or use other atypical surfaces, which doubles the cost. The time to transcribe the scroll is typically one full day per spell per level. Unlike other spells, the judge, not the caster, makes the spell check roll to determine the caster's success.
	The caster must inscribe a spell he already knows and must declare before making the spell check what spells he is attempting to inscribe on a scroll. All material costs and time are spent based on what the caster intends to create. The result of the spell check determines the caster's success, which can be total, partial, or nonexistent.
	A spell cast from a scroll typically requires the reader to make a spell check. However, with sufficiently high results, the caster can allow the spell to take effect at a defined result.

Manifestation	The caster creates a magic scroll.
Corruption	Roll 1d8: (1-4) minor, (5-6) major, (7-8) greater.
Misfire	Roll 1d4: (1) one of the spells the caster is attempting to inscribe is accidentally activated through the inscription process, causing the spell to take effect immediately; (2) the caster copies down the spell and in the process forgets it, such that he cannot cast it for the remainder of the day; (3) the caster has a terrible memory loss and forgets all spells for the rest of the day; (4) one of the spells the caster attempts to inscribe is gone from his memory for 1d4+1 days, and he simply cannot remember it under any circumstances.

1	Lost, failure, misfire *and* corruption!
2-11	Lost. Failure.
12-15	Failure, but spell is not lost.
16-17	The caster can transcribe one level 1 spell.
18-21	The caster can transcribe two level 1 spells.
22-23	The caster can transcribe one level 2 spell or three level 1 spells. Additionally, the caster can transcribe the scroll such that the reader other than himself or a designated subject may be subject to a curse or rune. The curse or rune must be generated via a separate spell, but that spell does not count toward the spells recorded on a scroll.
24-26	The caster can transcribe one level 3 spell or four spells of level 1 or 2. Additionally, the caster can transcribe the scroll such that a reader other than himself or a designated subject may be subject to a curse or rune. The curse or rune must be generated via a separate spell, but that spell does not count toward the spells recorded on a scroll.
27-31	The caster can transcribe one level 4 spell or five spells of levels 1, 2, or 3. Additionally, the caster can transcribe the scroll such that a reader other than himself or a designated subject may be subject to a curse or rune. The curse or rune must be generated via a separate spell, but that spell does not count toward the spells recorded on a scroll.
32-33	The caster can transcribe one level 5 spell or six spells of levels 1, 2, 3, or 4. Additionally, the caster can transcribe the scroll such that a reader other than himself or a designated subject may be subject to a curse or rune. The curse or rune must be generated via a separate spell, but that spell does not count toward the spells recorded on a scroll.

34-35	The caster can transcribe up to seven spells of any level. Additionally, the caster can transcribe the scroll such that a reader other than himself or a designated subject may be subject to a curse or rune. The curse or rune must be generated via a separate spell, but that spell does not count toward the spells recorded on a scroll. The caster can also transcribe the spells in a manner such that the spell check of the reader is influenced either positively or negatively. The caster can provide a modifier of -2, -1, +1, or +2 to the reader's spell check. This modifier can be conditionally based on the identity of the reader, the reader's alignment, or other conditions (for example, any chaotic reader of the scroll receives a -2 penalty to the check).
36+	The caster can transcribe up to eight spells of any level. Additionally, the caster can transcribe the scroll such that a reader other than himself or a designated subject may be subject to a curse or rune. The curse or rune must be generated via a separate spell, but that spell does not count toward the spells recorded on a scroll. The caster can also transcribe the spells in a manner such that the spell check is pre-determined. The caster must make a spell check for each spell he writes. When the scroll is read, the spells are cast at that spell check result automatically, with no need for an additional check by the reader.

Control Fire

| Level: 4 | Range: 15' | Duration: Varies | Casting Time: 1 action | Save: Fort partial (sometimes) |

General

The caster creates and manipulates fire to bar passage, immolate his opponents, and protect himself from damage. On a successful casting, the caster may choose to invoke any effect of equal to or less than his spell check, allowing a range of options with every successful casting to produce a weaker but potentially more useful result.

Manifestation

Roll 1d4: (1) caster's body ignites with harmless flame; (2) nearby flames leap from their sources to twist about the caster; (3) flame falls from the heavens to take the form of the caster's creations; (4) the caster vomits forth a gout of fire that fulfils the effect of the spell.

Corruption

Roll 1d6: (1) caster's hair turns to flickering flames that produce no heat; (2) caster leaves a trail of scorched footprints wherever he goes; (3) caster's clothes constantly smolder and must be replaced daily; (4) the odor of smoke permanently accompanies the caster; (5) caster's body becomes covered in burn scars; (6) caster must light a fire of campfire-size or greater each day and bask in its heat for at least 10 minutes or suffer a -1 penalty to all spell checks.

Misfire

Roll 1d4: (1) all creatures within 15' of the caster (including the caster) must make a Fort save equal to 5+CL or catch fire (1d6 damage each round until extinguished); (2) all fire sources within a 15' radius of the caster produces thick, obscuring smoke that fill a 10' cube around it each round for 1d4 rounds; (3) spell takes effect but in a random area or on a random creature within 30' of the caster (reroll spell check to determine effect and strength as if the caster were casting the spell again); (4) caster burns off all his own body hair.

1

Lost, failure, and worse! Roll 1d6 modified by Luck: (0 or less) corruption + patron taint + misfire; (1-2) corruption; (3) patron taint (or corruption if no patron); (4+) misfire.

2-11

Lost. Failure.

12-17

Failure, but spell is not lost.

18-19

The caster is wreathed in magical fire. Any creature attacking the caster in melee suffers damage equal to 1d6+CL. In addition, the caster suffers only half damage from cold-based attacks. This effect lasts 1 turn per caster level.

20-23

The spell caster produces spear-like manifestations of magical fire that he may hurl up to 25' feet + 5' per CL. The spears strike without fail (although *magic shield* and other similar effects deflect the spears as if they were *magic missiles*), inflicting damage equal to 1d8 points plus 2 additional points per caster level. The caster creates 1 spear per level of experience and may throw up to two per action die, beginning on his next action die. The spears remain in existence for one hour or until thrown.

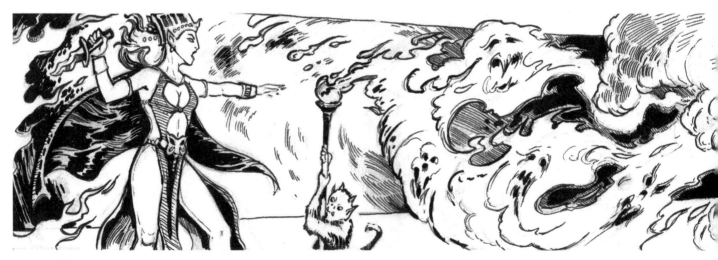

24-25	Caster creates a wall of fire up to 60' away. The wall is 20' high and 15' long per caster level or ring-shaped with a radius of 10' plus 5' per caster level. Creatures within 10' of the wall suffer damage equal to 1d6+CL. Creatures passing through the wall suffer damage equal to 4d6+CL. The wall stands for as long as the caster concentrates or 1 round per level if the caster chooses not to maintain the barrier.
26-28	The caster can create any single effect listed above, and all damage done is increased by 1 die (e.g., fire spears inflict 2d8 + 2 points per CL).
29-33	The caster can create any *two* of the effects listed above, and all damage done is increased by 1 die.
34-35	The caster can create *all three* of the effects noted above, and all damage is increased by 1 die.
36-37	The caster creates a conflagration that affects an area 50' in diameter. The range is any location within sight of the caster (including magical scrying). All creatures caught in the inferno suffer damage equal to 10d10 + 2 points per CL (Fort save for half damage). The fire ignites any naturally flammable substances and can be used to create a forest fire, burn down a town, etc. The magical flame remains in existence for 1 hour per caster level, though the mundane flames it creates will continue to burn as long as they have fuel.
38+	Caster creates a wildfire that ravages the landscape, destroys buildings, causes lakes to boil, and otherwise reduces the land to cinders. Fire is 100 square yards in size for each level the caster possesses and moves in a random direction for a distance equal to 1 mile per caster level. All creatures caught in the fire must make a Fort save or die. The magical flame remains in existence for 1 hour per caster level, though the mundane flames it creates will continue to burn as long as they have fuel.

Control Ice

Level: 4	Range: 20' per caster level	Duration: Varies	Casting Time: 1 action	Save: Fort partial (sometimes)

General	The caster creates ice walls or blasts of frigid cold to hinder or harm his enemies. On a successful casting, the caster may choose to invoke any effect of equal to or less than his spell check, allowing a range of options with every successful casting to produce a weaker but potentially more useful result.
Manifestation	Roll 1d4: (1) caster's eyes turn icy blue; (2) temperature drops in a 10' diameter around caster; (3) caster's skin and hair become covered in rime; (4) arctic winds appear from nowhere.
Corruption	Roll 1d6: (1) caster's touch freezes small volumes (cup-sized) of liquid; (2) caster's breath freezes normal plant life; (3) caster constantly shivers with cold; (4) caster's breath steams no matter what the surrounding temperature; (5) caster's eyes permanently become an unnatural icy-blue; (6) caster suffers a -2 penalty to spell checks, saves, and all other rolls related to fire-based magics.
Misfire	Roll 1d4: (1) caster encased in ice and immobilized; it takes 1d3 rounds to free the caster from his icy cocoon; (2) floor around caster becomes ice in a 15' radius, requiring all to make a DC 10 Reflex save or fall prone; (3) random ally of the caster is frozen in place as above; (4) all liquids on the caster (including magical ones) freeze suddenly and shatter their containers; liquids may thaw and be lost if steps are not taken to save them.

1	Lost, failure, and worse! Roll 1d6 modified by Luck: (0 or less) corruption + patron taint + misfire; (1-2) corruption; (3) patron taint (or corruption if no patron); (4+) misfire.
2-11	Lost. Failure.
12-17	Failure, but spell is not lost.
18-19	The caster blasts an area 40' in diameter with frigid sleet, doing 2d6+CL damage (Fort save for half) to creatures caught in its area of effect. Affected creatures are also blinded and their movement is reduced by half. Creatures attacking or moving within the area must make a Ref save or slip and fall prone. Sleet melts in 1d4+2 rounds.
20-23	The caster blasts an area 40' in diameter with frigid sleet, doing 3d10+CL damage (Fort save for half) to creatures caught in its area of effect. Affected creatures are also blinded and their movement is reduced by half. Creatures attacking or moving within the area must make a Ref save or slip and fall prone. Sleet melts in 1d6+2 rounds.
24-25	The caster conjures a vertical wall of solid ice to bar his enemies' passage and protect his allies. The wall is 1" thick per caster level and up to 10' square per caster level. Opponents can break through the wall with a Strength check vs. spell check DC but suffer 1d4+CL points of cold damage per round while doing so. The wall lasts for 1 turn per caster level. Magical fire destroys the wall in a single round.
26-28	The caster conjures a vertical wall of solid ice to bar his enemies' passage and protect his allies. Additionally, the wall emits painful waves of cold from the side opposite the caster. All within 30' of the wall suffer 1d4+CL damage each round. The wall is 1" thick per caster level and up to 10' square per caster level. Opponents can break through the wall with a Strength check vs. spell check DC but suffer 1d6+CL points of cold damage per round while doing so. The wall lasts for 1 turn per caster level. Magical fire destroys the wall in a single round.
29-33	The caster creates a cone of sub-zero cold that drains the heat from all creatures in its area of effect. The cone is 20' long per caster level and has a width of 10' per caster level at its terminus. Victims suffer 1d12 damage per caster level with no save.
34-35	The caster creates a cone of sub-zero cold that drains the heat from all creatures in its area of effect. The cone is 20' long per caster level and has a width of 20' per caster level at its terminus. Victims suffer 1d20+10 damage per caster level with no save (roll 1d20 per caster level, then add 10 x CL).
36-37	The caster creates a vicious ice storm that affects an area 100 yards in diameter. In addition to inflicting 6d10+CL points of damage on creatures within the area of effect, the storm destroys crops, causes roofs to collapse, freezes rivers, chokes roads with ice, and produces other destruction at the judge's discretion. The ice storm lasts for 1 hour per caster level, though the mundane ice that is created may take longer to melt.
38+	The caster creates a vicious ice storm that affects an area 1 mile in diameter for each level the caster possesses. In addition to inflicting 6d10+CL points of damage on creatures within the area of effect, the storm destroys crops, causes roofs to collapse, freezes rivers, chokes roads with ice, and produces other destruction at the judge's discretion. The ice storm lasts for 1 hour per caster level, though the mundane ice that is created may take longer to melt.

Lokerimon's Orderly Assistance

Level: 4   **Range:** Varies   **Duration:** Varies   **Casting Time:** 1 action   **Save:** Will vs. spell check DC

General	The caster creates a conduit between himself and other spellcasters, allowing him to assist their spellcasting and to offset the costs of spellburn. Provided the spell's duration allows, the caster can maintain the conduit and perform other actions with a DC 11 Will save. If the save fails, the conduit collapses, but the caster can perform his other action normally. For the purposes of this spell the caster initiating the spell is called the primary caster.
Manifestation	Roll 1d3: (1) a glimmering path of light connects the caster and his chosen target(s); (2) the eyes of the connected casters glow with the same eerie blue illuminations; (3) sparks of magical lightning flicker between the connected casters.
Corruption	Roll 1d4: (1) caster assumes alien personality traits borrowed from the connected casters; (2) caster must make a DC 10 Will check to avoid lending assistance to anyone who requests it from him; (3) caster suffers a permanent -1 to spell checks when alone; (4) physically touching another living person causes the caster great pain and inflicts 1 point of damage per round of contact if a DC 8 Fort save is failed.
Misfire	Roll 1d4: (1) all spellcasters within 20' suffer a -2 penalty to spell checks for 1d3 rounds; (2) caster temporarily loses a random point of Strength, Agility, or Stamina as spellburn ripples through his body (he gains no benefit from this spellburn); (3) caster's next successful casting causes an ally to lose a point of Strength, Agility, or Stamina as spontaneous spellburn wracks his body (the affected person is chosen by the judge and this spellburn provides no bonus to the cast spell); (4) caster makes two spell checks on his next spell and must apply the lower roll.
1	Lost, failure, and worse! Roll 1d6 modified by Luck: (0 or less) corruption + patron taint + misfire; (1-2) corruption; (3) patron taint (or corruption if no patron); (4+) misfire.
2-11	Lost. Failure.
12-17	Failure, but spell is not lost.
18-19	The caster opens a magical conduit to another spellcaster within 20' of his position. All spells cast by the connected caster gain a bonus to spell checks equal to the primary spellcaster's Intelligence modifier or +2 (whichever is higher). In addition, the primary caster can contribute a single point of spellburn to the connected caster if the connected caster casts a spell while connected. This connection lasts for a single round.
20-23	The caster opens a magical conduit to another spellcaster within 20' of his position. All spells cast by the connected caster gain a bonus to spell checks equal to the primary spellcaster's Intelligence modifier or +3 (whichever is higher). In addition, the primary caster can contribute up to two points of spellburn to the connected spellcaster if the connected caster casts a spell while connected. The conduit lasts for a number of round equal to the primary caster's CL or until he chooses to break the conduit.
24-25	The caster opens a magical conduit to up to two other spellcasters within 20' of his position. All spells cast by the connected casters gain a bonus to spell checks equal to the primary spellcaster's Intelligence modifier or +3 (whichever is higher). In addition, if the primary caster uses a point of spellburn immediately after casting this spell (after this result is determined), he does not benefit but can contribute that point of spellburn to each connected spellcaster's efforts. This connection lasts for one round.
26-28	The caster opens a magical conduit to any and all spellcasters of his choice within 40' of his position. All spells cast by the connected casters gain a bonus to spell checks equal to the primary spellcaster's Intelligence modifier or +3 (whichever is higher). In addition, if the primary caster uses a point of spellburn immediately after casting this spell (after this result is determined), he does not benefit but can contribute that point of spellburn to each connected spellcaster's efforts. This connection lasts for a number of rounds equal to the primary caster's CL or until he breaks the conduits. The primary caster can sever certain conduits while maintaining others if he wishes.
29-33	The caster opens a magical conduit to a single caster within 20' per CL. Spells cast by that connected caster gain a +4 bonus to spell checks. Each time the connected caster casts a spell, the primary caster can contribute points of spellburn up to his CL to assist the connected caster's spell checks. This connection lasts for a number of rounds equal to the primary caster's CL or until he breaks the conduit.

34-35	The caster opens a magical conduit to a single caster within 20' per CL. The next spell cast by that connected caster gains a bonus to the spell check equal to the primary caster's CL. Each time the connected caster casts a spell, the primary caster can contribute points of spellburn up to his CL to assist the connected caster's spell checks. In addition, each time the connected caster casts a spell, the primary caster can make a spell check using all his applicable modifiers. The connected caster can use his spell check or that of the primary caster's to determine the power of the spell. The primary caster need not know the spell to make a spell check; he is simply contributing magical power. If both spell checks fail and the spell is lost, the connected caster loses it not the primary caster. This connection lasts for a number of rounds equal to the primary caster's CL or until he breaks the conduit.
36-37	The caster opens a magical conduit to any and all casters of his choosing within 20' per CL. Spells cast by the connected casters gain a bonus to the spell check equal to the primary caster's CL. Each time the connected casters cast a spell, the primary caster can contribute points of spellburn up to his CL to assist the connected casters' spell checks. However, the primary caster cannot expend more points in spellburn than he has CL in a single round. Thus a 10th level caster could assist two other casters with 5 points of spellburn each, but could not assist a third because he has reached his maximum expenditure for the round. In addition, the primary caster can make a spell check with all applicable modifiers for any spell cast by the connected casters. The connected casters can use their own spell checks or that of the primary caster's to determine the power of the assisted spells. The primary caster need not know the spells he aids to make a spell check. If the spell checks fail and the spell is lost, the connected casters lose it not the primary caster. This connection lasts for a number of rounds equal to the primary caster's CL or until he breaks the conduits. The primary caster can sever certain conduits while maintaining others if he wishes.
38+	A sizzling web of magical energy forms around the caster connecting him with any other casters of his choice within 100'. This connection lasts for twice the primary caster's CL in rounds. During that time, the primary can either assist connected casters with a bonus to their spell checks equal to his CL or hinder them by reducing their spell checks by the same amount. In addition, the primary caster can choose to assist the connected casters with spellburn. All points contributed as spellburn are twice as effective (one point of spell burn adds +2 to the spell check). The primary caster can also dampen the spellburn efforts of hostile casters connected in the web, requiring them to spend twice as many spellburn points to receive a bonus (two points of spellburn add a +1 bonus). This connection lasts for a number of rounds equal to twice the primary caster's CL or until he breaks the conduits. The primary caster can sever certain conduits while maintaining others if he wishes.

Polymorph

| Level: 4 | Range: 30' | Duration: Varies | Casting Time: 1 round | Save: Will vs. Spell check DC |

General — The caster transforms himself or another into a different creature.

Manifestation — Roll 1d4: (1) target's body twists and boils like molten clay; (2) a puff of smoke obscures the target temporarily, revealing its changed form when the smoke disperses; (3) the target shines with blinding light that fades away, leaving it in its new shape; (4) the target's skin turns inside out, revealing its internal organs, before twisting back to take on a different shape.

Corruption — Roll 1d6: (1) one of the caster's appendages transforms into that of another creature; (2) caster's eyes become slitted like a serpent's; (3) caster gains a scaly tail; (4) caster's tongue becomes forked; (5) caster's hair is replaced by feathers; (6) caster's speech takes on an animalistic tone.

Misfire — Roll 1d4: (1) target is transformed into inoffensive animal or pest; (2) partial transformation leaves the target with a changed head but a normal body; (3) target's skin changes but that is all; (4) spell attracts 1d4 specimens of the intended transformation type to the caster's position unless completely inappropriate for type, climate, or terrain; creatures arrive in 1d100 minutes, angry and hungry.

1 — Lost, failure, and worse! Roll 1d6 modified by Luck: (0 or less) corruption + patron taint + misfire; (1-2) corruption; (3) patron taint (or corruption if no patron); (4+) misfire.

2-11 — Lost. Failure.

12-17 — Failure, but spell is not lost.

18-19 — The caster can transform himself into a creature with Hit Dice less than or equal to his own. He assumes the creature's form and manner of locomotion, as well as the ability to survive in the creature's normal habitat but gains no other powers. The transformation lasts 1 minute per caster level.

20-23 — The caster can transform himself *or another target* into a creature with Hit Dice less than or equal to his own. The target is allowed a Will save to negate the transformation if unwilling. The changed character assumes the creature's form and manner of locomotion, as well as the ability to survive in the creature's normal habitat but gains no other powers. The transformation lasts 1 minute per caster level.

24-25 — The caster can transform himself *or another target* into a creature with Hit Dice less than or equal to his own. The target is allowed a Will save to negate the transformation if unwilling. The changed character assumes the creature's form and manner of locomotion, as well as the ability to survive in the creature's normal habitat but gains no other powers. The transformation lasts 1 hour per caster level.

26-28 — The caster transforms himself into a creature with Hit Dice less than or equal to one and a half times his level. In addition, the caster can use one of the creature's racial powers or abilities. The change lasts 1 hour per level.

29-33 — The caster transforms himself *or another target* into a creature with Hit Dice less than or equal to one and a half times his level. The target is allowed a Will save to negate the transformation if unwilling. The target can use one of the creature's racial powers or abilities. The change lasts 1 hour per level.

34-35 — The caster changes himself completely into a new creature, gaining all of that creature's powers and abilities. This could include class abilities if appropriate. The creature cannot have more Hit Dice than twice the caster's level. The transformation lasts until the caster chooses to return to his normal form or 24 hours have passed.

36-37 — The caster changes himself *or another target* completely into a new creature, with all of that creature's powers and abilities. This could include class abilities if appropriate. The target is allowed a Will save to negate the transformation if unwilling. The creature cannot have more Hit Dice than twice the caster's level. The transformation lasts until the caster chooses to end the effect or 24 hours have passed.

38+ — The caster transforms himself or another target into a creature with HD up to the target's level and the caster's CL combined. The transformed creature possesses all the racial abilities and powers of the new form. The change is permanent and no saving throw is allowed.

Transmute Earth

Level: 4	Range: Touch or 30′	Duration: Varies	Casting Time: 1 round	Save: None

General The caster commands the earthly elements to do his bidding. On a successful casting, the caster may choose to invoke any effect of equal to or less than his spell check, allowing a range of options with every successful casting to produce a weaker but potentially more useful result.

Manifestation Roll 1d4: (1) caster's skin resembles rough-hewn rock; (2) caster's voice becomes gravelly; (3) earth rumbles at the caster's feet; (4) small, odd-colored crystals erupt from the ground around the caster.

Corruption Roll 1d6: (1) caster's skin turns slate-colored; (2) caster's hands become rock-like (+1 to damage in unarmed combats); (3) caster's body riddled with striations of quartz; (4) caster needs to eat 1 lb. of dirt each day; (5) caster must sleep on a bed of stone to gain a restful night's sleep; (6) caster cries tears of stone.

Misfire Roll 1d4: (1) minor tremor knocks all in a 30′ diameter to the ground unless a DC 10 Reflex save is made; (2) the ground beneath the caster turns to mud and he sinks up to his waist in the morass; (3) a hail of stones falls from the sky doing 1d3 damage to the caster and anyone else within 10′ of him; (4) the forces of Earth rebel against the caster: caster must make a DC 10 Fort save or turn to stone for 1d4 rounds. There is a 50% chance that the petrification is permanent, and the caster is transformed into a creature of living stone. Composed of rocky matter, living stone creatures have their movement rate reduced to 20′, have an Agility of 6, cannot swim (they sink automatically), and make a loud, grinding sound when moving. They do enjoy a +2 bonus to AC and gain a natural Strength of 18. Casting *transmute earth* again with a spell check of 34 or greater restores the caster to his fleshy form.

1 Lost, failure, and worse! Roll 1d6 modified by Luck: (0 or less) corruption + patron taint + misfire; (1-2) corruption; (3) patron taint (or corruption if no patron); (4+) misfire.

2-11 Lost. Failure.

12-17 Failure, but spell is not lost.

18-19 Caster turns natural rock up to 30′ away into mud. The area of effect is a 10′ cube of stone per caster level. The created mud has a maximum depth of half its length or width (whichever is greater). Creatures caught in the morass that cannot fly, levitate, or otherwise escape sink into the mud and drown if it is over their head. (Drowning creatures take 1d6 points of Stamina damage per round and die when Stamina reaches 0; lost Stamina is restored immediately if they are removed from the morass.) If the creature is taller than the depth of the mud, its movement is reduced by 50%. The mud hardens to stone in 1d6 days.

20-23 Caster creates a large opening in any stone, clay, mud, or iron barrier he touches. This breech is 5′ wide × 10′ high × 10′ deep and lasts for 1 hour + 1 turn per caster level. Multiple castings of this spell allow the caster to pass through thicker barriers.

24-25 Caster can mold stone he touches as if it were soft clay. The caster affects an area of stone equal to a half cubic foot per caster level. The level of detail is crude, but the object functions as intended (stone weapons inflict damage, stone trap doors open, stone manacles restrain prisoners, etc.).

26-28 Caster creates a wall of rock 3″ thick and 10′ square per caster level. There must be pre-existing stone for the wall to connect to in order to create this barrier. The wall can be vertical or horizontal and can be fashioned into a ramp or bridge as needed. The wall is permanent barring effects that destroy magic.

29-33 Caster conjures a wall of raw iron to bar passage and protect him and his allies. The wall is ¼″ thick per caster level and 10′ square per caster level. The wall must rest on a firm surface or it topples over, crushing anyone underneath it (1d10 damage per caster level). The wall is permanent unless affected by magic.

34-35 Caster can counteract petrification magics and attacks, restoring a touched victim and his belongings to their natural states.

36-37 Caster may transform himself into a more potent version of living stone. In this living stone form, he gains +4 to AC and a natural Strength of 18. His Agility cannot be higher than 9, his movement is reduced to 15′, and he cannot swim. He makes no additional noise when moving. The transformation lasts 1 round per caster level.

38-39	The caster gains *medusa eyes*. With a gaze, he can turn a target up to 30' away into stone (Fort save vs. spell check avoids). The transformation is permanent. The *medusa eyes* last for 1 round per caster level.
40+	The caster gains a fearful command of the earth. He can raise small mountains (500' per caster level in height), turn swaths of arable land into solid stone or liquid mud (1 mile diameter per caster level), and open gaping chasms (100' long and 50' deep per caster level). All of these effects destroy buildings, crops, alter the courses of rivers, collapse dams, and produce other destructive, landscape-altering effects at the judge's creation.

Wizard Sense

Level: 4	Range: 60' or more (see below)	Duration: 1 round per caster level	Casting Time: 1 round	Save: None

General	The caster extends his senses beyond the normal human range to observe distant events or glimpse the truth.

Manifestation	Roll 1d4: (1) caster's eyes turn dead white; (2) a third eye opens in the caster's forehead; (3) fleshy antennae extend from the top of the caster's head; (4) caster's eyes vanish completely from their sockets.
Corruption	Roll 1d6: (1) caster's eyes permanently vanish (sight is unaffected); (2) caster gains a permanent third eye; (3) caster's ears become bat-like; (4) caster's eyes never close, even in sleep; (5) caster sees meaningless visions from time to time that may interrupt his concentration (judge's discretion); (6) strange events from distant lands can be seen in the caster's eyes.
Misfire	Roll 1d4: (1) caster observes false events, believing them to be true; (2) caster struck blind and deaf for 1d4 hours; (3) caster broadcasts embarrassing or dangerous secrets to those under observation; (4) caster's eyes literally fall out of his head and roll away, blinding him until they are placed back in their sockets.

1	Lost, failure, and worse! Roll 1d6 modified by Luck: (0 or less) corruption + patron taint + misfire; (1-2) corruption; (3) patron taint (or corruption if no patron); (4+) misfire.
2-11	Lost. Failure.
12-17	Failure, but spell is not lost.
18-19	The caster can see magical auras, invisible creatures, and pierce illusions of all types to see creatures and objects in their true forms. This mystical sight also reveals secret doors and traps if they are present. The enhanced vision has a limit of 60'.
20-23	As above, but the caster also gains x-ray vision, allowing him to see through up to 30' of stone and 60' of wood or other less-dense material. Lead or gold foils x-ray vision.
24-25	The caster extends his hearing to detect sound and conversation at a distance. The caster must choose a location either well known to him (his own home, for instance) or within sight of his current position (beyond a closed door, a copse of trees, the roof of a nearby tower, etc.). The caster clearly hears any normal noises occurring within a 60' radius of that designated locale.
26-28	Similar to the above, but the caster extends his vision to observe whatever is in seeing distance from his designated location. Illumination is a factor, and the caster can only observe an area in a 10' radius from his chosen point if the space is dark. The caster's sight is considered normal for this effect and does not gain the additional spectrums of vision noted above.
29-33	The caster creates an invisible eye that he can send out to reconnoiter or spy for him. The eye moves at 30' per round and is incorporeal, so it can pass through solid matter. It "sees" up to 10' in darkness and up to 60' in brightly lit conditions. The eye can see magical auras, invisible creatures, and discern illusions. It sees traps if they are present. There is no limit on how far the eye may travel from the caster, but it vanishes when the spell expires regardless of position.
34-35	The caster can see and hear events occurring at a location up to 10 miles away for each level of experience he possesses. The location need not be familiar to him, but if it is not familiar, he must possess an object from the location he wishes to see (e.g., a leaf from a tree at that place, or a stone from a tower at that location, etc.). He is otherwise free to choose his target. Lead and gold shielding do not protect the site from

observation, but certain rare, mystic materials might at the judge's discretion. The caster has normal sight and hearing to a range of 60' from the chosen location and can also see invisible creatures, magic auras, traps, and the truth behind illusions.

36-37   The caster can see and hear events occurring at a location up to 100 miles away for each level of experience he possesses. The location need not be familiar to him, but if it is not familiar, he must possess an object from the location he wishes to see (e.g., a leaf from a tree at that place, or a stone from a tower at that location, etc.). He is otherwise free to choose his target. Lead and gold shielding do not protect the site from observation, but certain rare, mystic materials might at the judge's discretion. The caster has normal sight and hearing to a range of 60' from the chosen location and can also see invisible creatures, magic auras, traps, and the truth behind illusions.

38+   The caster witnesses events occurring on other planes of existence, with almost unlimited range. He can spy on the happenings in the Halls of Hell, in the palaces of the gods, in the realm of the dead, or into the cold depths of space to watch alien forms at play. The caster can see invisible or concealed creatures in these places. The judge has the final word on what is observed and where and whether those being watched detect the caster's prying eyes.

MULLEN

LEVEL 5 WIZARD SPELLS

Hepsoj's Fecund Fungi

Level: 5	Range: 100' plus 20' per CL	Duration: Varies	Casting Time: 1 action	Save: Varies

General	The caster draws upon and amplifies the ever-present spores of fungi and mold to produce spectacular effects, including choking clouds, ablative armor, restraining bonds, and spontaneous fungus generation. On a successful casting, the caster may choose to invoke an effect of lesser power than his spell check roll to produce a weaker but potentially more useful result.
Manifestation	Roll 1d4: (1) tiny tendrils of fungus sprout from the caster's fingers as he works his magic; (2) a cloud of scintillating spores wafts from the caster's mouth and nose before the magic takes shape; (3) small puffball fungi sprout out the caster's feet and spiral out towards the spell's target(s); (4) the caster's flesh becomes covered in fuzzy spores that then coalesce into the desired effect.
Corruption	Roll 1d4: (1) caster develops a chronic cough, hacking up mold spores; (2) small growths of leathery fungi develop on the caster's skin; (3) the perpetual odor of mold and mildew accompanies the caster; (4) the caster's head takes on a misshapen, mushroom-like form.
Misfire	Roll 1d5: (1) tiny mushroom homunculi appear at the caster's feet; they trip him and steal a small item from his possession before running off; (2) the air around the caster in a 10' radius is filled with thick spores making it difficult to see for 1d3 rounds (missile attacks and saving throws suffer a -2 penalty); (3) the caster's throat becomes choked with spongy fungi and he can do nothing but cough to clear it for 1d4 rounds; (4) painful fungal growths erupt from the caster's skin doing 1d6 damage; (5) the spell unwittingly summons either a primeval ooze or shrooman to the caster's location; the summoned creatures arrive in 1d5 rounds and are either hungry or unhappy at being called.
1	Lost, failure, and worse! Roll 1d6 modified by Luck: (0 or less) corruption + patron taint + misfire; (1-2) corruption; (3) patron taint (or corruption if no patron); (4+) misfire.
2-11	Lost. Failure.
12-17	Failure, but spell is not lost.
18-19	The caster causes the mildew and mold spores in the air to spontaneously multiply, creating a dense cloud of choking particles. The area of effect is 50' square and 10' in height. All air-breathing creatures within the cloud must make a Fort save or be incapacitated by wracking coughs and suffer 1d6+CL damage each round. Those that make their saves take no damage and may act freely, but the cough imposes a -3 penalty to all attacks, saves, spell checks, ability checks, and initiative rolls until the spell's duration expires. The cloud lasts for 1 round per CL.
20-23	The caster grows thick, leathery fungi over his body that prevents him from taking damage. This ablative armor protects the caster from a number of attacks equal to his CL. Each time the caster takes physical damage, he can make a Fort save with a DC equal to the amount of damage the attack caused. A successful save indicates damage, but the attack is deducted from the amount of defensive armor remaining. For example, a 10th level caster is protected against ten attacks. If he successfully makes his Fort save, he takes no damage and retains protection against nine more attacks. A failed Fort save indicates the caster takes normal damage, but doesn't reduce the amount of remaining armor. The fungus armor only defends against physical attacks of a magical or non-magical nature and provides no protection against psychic, illusionary, or other mental attacks. The armor remains until destroyed, dispelled, or for 1 hour per CL.
24-25	The caster summons thick, ropey strands of fungus that emerge from the ground and restrain and crush his enemies. These pale tendrils sprout in an area 60' square and attack all targets within that space. Each tendril attacks with a +4 bonus to hit. A successful strike indicates the target is entangled by the tendril and cannot move. In addition, the fungus constricts and targets suffer 1d8+4 damage each round until freed or the spell ends. A successful Ref saving throw by the entangled target indicates its arms are free and it can attempt to attack the tendrils with a weapon or cast a spell. These attempts suffer a -4 penalty. Tendrils have an AC of 15 and 25 hit points. A trapped target can also free itself with a DC 25 Strength check or an appropriate Mighty Deed of Arms at the judge's discretion.

26-28	The caster calls up thick stands of giant mushrooms to block passages, form protective walls, or create spongy ramps to reach higher ground. The amount of fungi generated can fill an area up to 150' square and 10' in height. It can be molded to take the shape of walls, pillars, cubes, ramps, and other solid shapes provided it has solid ground upon which to rest. Bridges, arches, and other curved forms are also allowed, but complete spheres are beyond the spell's ability. The caster can create openings in the fungi such as doorways, arrow slits, and vents at the time of the spell's casting, but later additions need be cut into the spongy material with edged weapons or tools. The fungi last for 30 minutes per CL and dissolves into a smelly, slimy mass once the spell ends. Hacking a man-sized hole through 10' of fungi requires 10 minutes of work; additional workers can reduce this time by 1 minute per assistant.
29-33	The caster calls into being a horde of shroomen (see page 426) to do his bidding. These laconic creatures emerge from the ground as puffballs that break open to reveal the fungoid humanoids within. The caster calls up 2 shroomen per CL. They remain under the caster's complete control until destroyed or released from service, upon which they depart slowly but peacefully. The shroomen have typical stats for their species.
34-35	The caster taps into the psychotropic nature of certain fungi to forge a mystic connection with the unseen realms. While under the effects of this hallucinogenic state, attempts to contact patrons, call for divine aid, summon demons, or use divination magic enjoy a +8 bonus to their spell checks if performed within the next hour. However, meddling with magic in this state can be detrimental to one's sanity. If the modified spell check fails, the caster must make a Will save or go permanently insane. Certain restorative magics may be able to restore the caster's sanity, but he never fully shakes the terrors he witnessed while under the psychotropic effects of this spell.
36-37	The caster causes the natural fungi that exist on and inside living creatures to rebel against their hosts, turning on them and destroying them from the inside out. The caster can affect a number of creatures within range equal to his CL. Each target must make a Fort save or suffer the effects of protoplasmic breakdown (see primeval slime, page 423). This destruction lasts for a number of rounds equal to the caster's CL but can be stopped with *neutralize poison or disease* with a spell check of 30+. Otherwise, the afflicted creatures suffer 1d4 Stamina loss each round until the spell runs its course. The spell lasts CL rounds.
38+	The caster contacts Mycetes-Thrax, the Great Sleeping Growth that lurks beneath the soil. This titanic entity is a single fungus that stretches for a hundred leagues under the earth and has grown sentient and wise with the eons. Mycetes-Thrax can serve as a patron if the caster knows the proper spells, and it rewards its servants with utterly alien but useful and fearsome powers (of the judge's choosing). Its wisdom is great and it knows much forgotten lore. The caster can ask a number of questions of Mycetes-Thrax equal to his CL, which it answers truthfully (if slowly). The judge will deem whether the Sleeping Growth knows the answers. Lastly, if the caster desires destruction, Mycetes-Thrax can ripple its great, slumbering corpus, causing destructive earthquakes, tsunamis, and avalanches in locations up to 300 miles away.

Lokerimon's Unerring Hunter

| Level: 5 | Range: Varies | Duration: Varies | Casting Time: 10 minutes | Save: None |

General

The caster conjures a magical hunter to kill or capture his quarry. This spell creates either a lesser or greater unerring hunter, whose statistics are as follows:

Unerring Hunter, Lesser: Init +3, Atk bite +6 melee (dmg 3d10+3) or paralyzing touch (Fort DC 12 or duration 1d5 days); AC 17; HD 8d8+3; MV 40'; Act 1d20; SP half-damage from normal weapons, camouflage, see invisible, SV Fort +5, Ref +3, Will +2; AL N.

Unerring Hunter, Greater: Init +5, Atk bite +8 melee (dmg 4d10+4) or paralyzing touch (Fort DC 15 or duration 2d4 days); AC 21; HD 10d8+8; MV 50'; Act 2d20; SP half-damage from normal weapons, camouflage, see invisible, SV Fort +7, Ref +5, Will +4; AL N.

Unerring hunters attack to either kill or capture, never both, and use their paralysis attack to incapacitate quarry to return to their master. Unerring hunters can carry a single man-sized or smaller creature without difficulty. They suffer normal damage from weapons of a +1 enchantment or greater and half-damage from normal weapons. They can occlude their forms with shadows to hide themselves and gain a +10 bonus to avoid detection. They can see invisible creatures. Hunters track their victims through magic; mundane means by the prey to hide its trail are never successful. Hunters cannot cross magical barriers but will wait patiently for wards to expire or for prey to leave the protected area. Slaying a hunter causes the spell to end and a new hunter cannot be sent against the target until 1 month has passed.

Manifestation

Roll 1d4: (1) the hunter coalesces from the shadows and then streaks off in search of its target; (2) caster vomits up a mass of bile and cancerous flesh that assumes the hunter's form; (3) the target dreams of a faceless entity pursuing him every night until the hunter finds him; (4) the target's possessions burst into flames and the hunter forms from the smoke it creates.

Corruption

Roll 1d4: (1) caster gains a mania about where his allies or enemies are at any given moment; (2) caster begins to eat like a hound, eschewing silverware to eat and drink with his mouth alone; (3) caster takes on a doglike appearance; (4) caster has horrible nightmares of being chased that might cause temporary Stamina loss at the judge's discretion.

Misfire

Roll 1d5: (1) a lesser unerring hunter appears and attacks the caster; (2) the caster offends the hunter race and cannot attempt to cast this spell again until either 1 year has passed or he undertakes steps to make amends (judge's discretion); (3) target becomes aware it is being sought and knows who is attempting find it; (4) target's possession is destroyed in the attempt and the caster must find a new item to replace it; (5) caster is targeted by a lesser unerring hunter that attempts to capture him and bring him to his intended target.

1

Lost, failure, and worse! Roll 1d6 modified by Luck: (0 or less) corruption + patron taint + misfire; (1-3) corruption; (4) patron taint (or corruption if no patron); (5+) misfire.

2-11

Lost. Failure.

12-17

Failure, but spell is not lost.

18-19

The caster conjures a lesser unerring hunter to locate, capture, or kill his enemies. It can take nearly any twisted form the caster desires so long as it is man-sized or smaller. The caster must have an object belonging to the target in order for the hunter to lock on to its victim. Without such an item, the spell fails. If given the wrong item (an object belonging to someone other than the intended quarry), the hunter carries out its mission on the owner of the item regardless of the caster's wishes.

The hunter can track down a single target up to 10 miles away and pursues its prey for up to 24 hours before fading out of existence.

20-23

The caster conjures a lesser unerring hunter to locate, capture, or kill his enemies. It can take nearly any twisted form the caster desires so long as it is man-sized or smaller. The caster must have an object belonging to the target in order for the hunter to lock on to its victim. Without such an item, the spell fails. If given the wrong item (an object belonging to someone other than the intended quarry), the hunter carries out its mission on the owner of the item regardless of the caster's wishes.

The lesser hunter can track its target up to 50 miles away or until 48 hours have passed.

24-25   The caster conjures a lesser unerring hunter to locate, capture, or kill his enemies. It can take nearly any twisted form the caster desires so long as it is man-sized or smaller.

The caster does *not* need an object belonging to the target, but without it there is a possibility that the hunter fails to "find the scent" of its intended prey. If the caster lacks an object but has seen the target personally, the hunter has a 90% chance of successfully tracking the victim. If the caster has seen an image of the intended target, the hunter has a 75% chance of finding its victim. If the caster has only a verbal description of the intended target, the hunter has just a 50% chance of locating its quarry. A hunter that fails to find the scent of its prey dissipates after an hour and the spell cannot be cast again until 24 hours have passed.

The unerring hunter can track its target up to 100 miles away or until 7 days have passed.

26-28   The caster conjures a lesser unerring hunter to locate, capture, or kill his enemies. It can take nearly any twisted form the caster desires so long as it is man-sized or smaller.

The caster does *not* need an object belonging to the target, but without it there is a possibility that the hunter fails to "find the scent" of its intended prey. If the caster lacks an object but has seen the target personally, the hunter has a 90% chance of successfully tracking the victim. If the caster has seen an image of the intended target, the hunter has a 75% chance of finding its victim. If the caster has only a verbal description of the intended target, the hunter has just a 50% chance of locating its quarry. A hunter that fails to find the scent of its prey dissipates after an hour and the spell cannot be cast again until 24 hours have passed.

The lesser unerring hunter can track its target up to 250 miles away or until two weeks have passed.

29-33   The caster conjures a greater unerring hunter to locate, capture, or kill his enemies. It can take nearly any twisted form the caster desires so long as it is man-sized or smaller. It tracks its target up to 500 miles away or until 1 month has passed. It always finds the trail of its target regardless of whether the caster has an object belonging to its victim or not.

34-35   The caster can either summon forth a lesser unerring hunter that pursues its target regardless of distance/time until it is either successful or destroyed, or the caster can set a greater unerring hunter against a foe that is up to 1,000 miles away or for up to 3 month's time. He does not need an object belonging to the target.

36-37   The caster can either summon up to three unerring hunters to pursue multiple targets or a single greater hunter that relentlessly tracks its target until successful or destroyed. Multiple lesser unerring hunters can be sent against a single target and all three must be destroyed to prevent the spell from being renewed against the target for one month's time. Regardless of whether multiple lesser hunters or a single greater hunter are summoned, there is no limit to time or distance on the hunt, and an object relating to the target is not required.

38+   The caster conjures up three greater unerring hunters to track down his target. These hunters can track their quarry across any distance and into other planes of existence if necessary. They hunt until successful or destroyed. An object belonging to the target is not required.

Magic Bulwark

Level: 5	Range: 10' radius centered on caster Duration: 10 minutes per CL Casting Time: 1 round Save: None

General The caster surrounds himself with a field that disrupts magic, provides him with a bonus to counterspell, and grants him immunity from low-power spells.

Manifestation Roll 1d4: (1) caster is encased in a field of coruscating light that flashes whenever targeted by magic; (2) a stream of small glowing orbs whirls around the caster, dissipating one by one when intercepting magical attacks; (3) shadowy mouths hang in the folds of the caster's garments, devouring spells cast against him; (4) a cloud of glowing smoke wreathes the caster's body.

Corruption Roll 1d4: (1) caster gains a new, violent red scar whenever he suffers damage from a magic attack; (2) caster becomes addicted to casting, temporarily losing 1 point of Stamina any day he does not perform a spell, and needing progressively more spells to avoid the Stamina loss in the form of 2 spells/day after 2 months, 3 spells/day after 3 months, 4 spells/day after 4 months, etc.; (3) caster permanently glows a soft blue color; (4) caster's eyes suffer magical trauma rendering him completely color-blind.

Misfire Roll 1d5: (1) the caster suffers a -2 penalty to any spell checks performed for the rest of the day; (2) magic is attracted to the caster and any spell cast at a target with 25' of him has a 50% chance of targeting him instead, but the effect fades after 1d4 hours; (3) caster cannot cast spells for the normal duration of *magic bulwark* and can only use magical items or counterspells during that time; (4) all spells cast within 15' of the caster (including his own) suffer a -2 penalty to spell checks; (5) caster loses one random spell for the day.

1 Lost, failure, and worse! Roll 1d6 modified by Luck: (0 or less) corruption + patron taint + misfire; (1-4) corruption; (5) patron taint (or corruption if no patron); (6+) misfire.

2-11 Lost. Failure.

12-17 Failure, but spell is not lost.

18-19 The magic field causes all spell checks made against the caster to suffer a -1 penalty. This adjustment requires no action on the part of the caster, and it does not apply to spell duel rolls or counterspell efforts. This protection remains in effect for the duration of the spell.

20-23 The magic field causes all spell checks made against the caster to suffer a -2 penalty. This adjustment requires no action on the part of the caster, and it does not apply to spell duel rolls or counterspell efforts. This protection remains in effect for the duration of the spell.

24-25 The magic field causes all spell checks made against the caster to suffer a -3 penalty. This adjustment requires no action on the part of the caster, and it does not apply to spell duel rolls or counterspell efforts. This protection remains in effect for the duration of the spell.

26-28 The magic field causes all spell checks made against the caster to suffer a -4 penalty. This adjustment requires no action on the part of the caster, and it does not apply to spell duel rolls or counterspell efforts. This protection remains in effect for the duration of the spell.

29-33 The magic field causes all spell checks made against the caster to suffer a -5 penalty. This adjustment requires no action on the part of the caster, and it does not apply to spell duel rolls or counterspell efforts. This protection remains in effect for the duration of the spell. In addition, the caster gains a +1 bonus to any attempt he makes to counterspell.

34-35 The magic field causes all spell checks made against the caster to suffer a -5 penalty. This adjustment requires no action on the part of the caster, and it does not apply to spell duel rolls or counterspell efforts. This protection remains in effect for the duration of the spell. In addition, the caster gains a +2 bonus to any attempt he makes to counterspell.

36-37 The magic field grants the caster immunity to all level 1 spells. It causes all other spell checks made against the caster to suffer a -5 penalty. This adjustment requires no action on the part of the caster, and it does not apply to spell duel rolls or counterspell efforts. This protection remains in effect for the duration of the spell. In addition, the caster gains a +3 bonus to any attempt he makes to counterspell.

38+ The magic field grants the caster immunity to all level 1 and 2 spells. It causes all spell checks made against the caster to suffer a -5 penalty. This adjustment requires no action on the part of the caster, and it does not apply to spell duel rolls or counterspell efforts. This protection remains in effect for the duration of the spell. In addition, the caster gains a +4 bonus to any attempt he makes to counterspell.

Mind Purge

Level: 5	Range: 20′ plus 10′ per level Duration: Varies Casting Time: 1 round Save: Will vs. Spell check DC

General   The caster blasts his victim's mind with magical amnesia, causing the target to temporarily or even permanently forget everything about itself.

Manifestation   Roll 1d4: (1) target spews smoke from nose, ears, and mouth; (2) a flash of crimson fire bursts from the target's eyes; (3) tendrils of evil-looking protoplasm erupt from the caster's hands to burrow into the target's head; (4) the caster inhales streams of sparkling energy from the target's mouth.

Corruption   Roll 1d4: (1) caster becomes absent-minded and must make a DC 7 Luck check each morning or misplace a randomly determined, useful object; (2) caster lacks name-recognition (he may be physically memorable, but nobody can ever place his name); (3) one person at random completely forgets the caster; (4) caster takes on habits or physical tics possessed by another (typically someone he has cast this or other mind control spells on in the past); habit/tic is determined randomly or chosen by the judge.

Misfire   Roll 1d5: (1) caster forgets who he is for 1d3 rounds (no spellcasting and stands befuddled trying to recall who he is and what he is doing); (2) all within 15′ radius must make a DC 10 Will save or forget 1 random memory; (3) universe forgets where the caster was and misplaces him (caster is randomly moved 1d10×10′ away from currently location and must re-roll initiative if in combat); (4) any allies (including caster) within a 15′ radius of the caster must make a DC 10 Will save or believe themselves to be another randomly determined ally for 1d3 rounds; (5) caster must make a spell check for his most powerful spell or forget it for the day.

1   Lost, failure, and worse! Roll 1d6 modified by Luck: (0 or less) corruption + patron taint + misfire; (1-2) corruption; (3) patron taint (or corruption if no patron); (4+) misfire.

2-11   Lost. Failure.

12-17   Failure, but spell is not lost.

18-19   The caster causes a spellcasting target to immediately make a spell check for every spell known. Any result of "lost" or "failure" on the spell check indicates the target loses the ability to cast that spell for the day. Corruption, misfires, or disapproval is never invoked as a result of these enforced spell checks.

20-23   The caster causes a spellcasting target to immediately make a spell check for every spell known. The target suffers a penalty to spell checks equal to the caster's Intelligence or Luck modifier (whichever is greater). Any result of "lost" or "failure" on the spell check indicates the target loses the ability to cast that spell for the day. Corruption, misfires, or disapproval is never invoked as a result of these enforced spell checks.

24-25   Target is afflicted with amnesia and completely forgets its identity. Victims of this spell lose their spellcasting abilities if they possess them. They remain in the amnesic state until a *remove curse* is cast upon them or until they make a successful Will save at the start of the next day (a new save is allowed each day).

26-28   The caster reduces the target's Personality and Intelligence to 3 if the victim fails a Will save. Targets that use spells suffer a -2 penalty to their saving throws. This effect is permanent until a *remove curse* or other powerful restorative magic is cast on the victim.

29-33   The caster can choose 1 target per level of experience and reduce the target's Personality and Intelligence to 3 if the victim fails a Will save. Targets who use spells suffer a -2 penalty to their saving throws. This effect is permanent until a *remove curse* or other powerful restorative magic is cast on the victim.

34-35   The caster purges knowledge of his target's identity from those around him, making the target a complete stranger to them for all intents and purposes. All friends, allies, and enemies (not including the spellcaster) within 100′ per CL must make a Will save or completely forget the victim's identity and any relationship they may have with it. The forgetfulness is permanent unless negated via *dispel magic, remove curse*, or similar great magic.

36-37   The caster purges knowledge of his target's identity from all who have ever met the target, making the target a complete stranger to them for all intents and purposes. All friends, allies, and enemies, including everyone the target has ever met regardless of distance from the target at the time the spell is cast, must make a Will save or completely forget the victim's identity and any relationship they may have with it. The forgetfulness is permanent unless negated via *dispel magic, remove curse*, or similar great magic.

38+   The caster removes the target's identity from the multiverse. Not only does the target lose all his mental facilities, but anyone who had ever heard of the target forgets it exists. Books mentioning the target's name become blank, songs written about the target are forgotten, and even stone carvings depicting the target become featureless. It is as if the target had never existed. Only the intervention of divine power can restore the target's identity to the cosmos.

Replication

| Level: 5 | Range: 100′ +10′ per CL or touch | Duration: Varies | Casting Time: Varies | Save: None |

General   The caster creates a magical double of himself to carry out actions, observe distant events, and possibly cheat death. On a successful casting, the caster may choose to invoke any effect of equal to or less than his spell check, allowing a range of options with every successful casting to produce a weaker but potentially more useful result.

Manifestation   Roll 1d4: (1) caster's skeleton glows orange-blue and steps from his body; (2) caster emits protoplasm from his body in the form of the duplicate; (3) the caster vomits up the duplicate form; (4) the caster peels his own skin from his body to create the duplicate.

Corruption   Roll 1d4: (1) caster's flesh becomes sentient and moves about his body uncontrollably; (2) caster's face becomes featureless and his body loses all distinctive marks; (3) caster is stalked by a homunculus, a twisted parody of himself standing 3′ tall and harboring ill will towards its creator; (4) caster's soul fragments from the casting and he loses a point of Personality permanently.

Misfire   Roll 1d5: (1) duplicate is created, but it is hostile towards the caster; (2) duplicate is flawed and cannot perform its normal tasks or possess typical abilities; (3) caster's body becomes semi-solid for 1d10 minutes (cannot move or perform any action other than speech until duration ends); (4) caster must make a DC 15 Will check or forget a random spell for the day; (5) caster becomes confused and believes himself to be an artificial creation. Nothing can convince him otherwise, and this mania can manifest itself as overconfidence (he's not real so what difference does his safety make?) to paranoia (his creator is after him and will destroy him) to constant fear (he could revert to base materials at any moment). This derangement lasts for 24 hours.

1   Lost, failure, and worse! Roll 1d6 modified by Luck: (0 or less) corruption + patron taint + misfire; (1-4) corruption; (5) patron taint (or corruption if no patron); (6+) misfire.

2-11   Lost. Failure.

12-17   Failure, but spell is not lost.

18-19   The caster creates a semi-solid illusion of himself that he can see, speak, and hear through. This projected duplicate can be placed anywhere within view of the caster up to 100′ +10′ per CL. If line of sight is ever broken, the image vanishes. This duplicate image reproduces the caster's movements and action, but these motions are illusionary and will only physically affect or injure a target who fails to make a Will save. The duration is one hour.

20-23   The caster creates a semi-solid illusion of himself that he can see, speak, and hear through. This projected duplicate can be placed anywhere within view of the caster up to 100′ +10′ per CL. If line of sight is ever broken, the image vanishes. The duration is four hours. This duplicate image reproduces the caster's movements and action. Physical motions are illusionary and will only physically affect or injure a target who fails to make a Will save, but the caster *can* cast spells through the duplicate image as if he were standing at its location. To do so, he must extend his concentration to the image's position, rendering him unaware of events occurring around his physical form for the duration of the spellcasting.

24-25   The caster creates an artificial duplicate of another creature out of base materials such as mud, clay, snow, ice, or dung. He must have a piece of the creature's body, such as hair, fingernail, or blood, to do so. The creation is physically identical to the original creature but possesses only half of the original's Hit Dice or levels (and a similarly reduced number of hit points, skills, and other abilities). The duplicate possesses none of the original's memories, and while it can learn, it can never increase in level or ability. It is permanent until reduced to zero hit points, at which point it collapses into a lump of the base material it was crafted from. The duplicate is under the caster's complete control, but commands must be given verbally or written, as no form of magical communication is granted by the spell. When the duplicate is killed, the original creature must make a DC 20 Fort save or take 1d4 damage. Only one such duplicate of a creature can exist at any time.

26-28	The caster can replicate himself in a physical form by creating a duplicate of himself from base materials such as mud, clay, snow, ice, or dung. The duplicate possesses half his hit points and levels and can never advance in power. The duplicate can cast spells at half its creator's level, but can never participate in a patron bond or summon a familiar as it is itself a servile creature. It has some degree of decision-making ability but is not sentient; it can handle open-ended directives but is completely under its creator's control and performs commands without hesitation. It lasts until reduced to zero hit points, at which point it collapses into a heap of the base material it was crafted from. When is the duplicate is killed, the caster must make a DC 20 Fort save or take 1d4 damage. Only one such duplicate of the caster can exist at any one time.
29-33	The caster creates a duplicate body to harbor the soul of a dead creature. Creating the clone requires 1 week's time, 1,000 gold pieces per level or Hit Die of the creature, and a portion of the dead creature's flesh. Once complete, if the soul of the intended creature is still free and not restrained by magical means or returned to life, it inhabits the duplicate form and effectively lives again. This cloned body possesses all the ability, levels, and knowledge the creature had at the time of its death. If the soul is bound, resurrected, or otherwise prevented from occupying its new form, the spell fails and the soul can never be cloned via *replication* again.
34-35	The caster creates a duplicate of his own body to harbor his soul in case of his sudden demise. The process involves 1 week's time, 1,000 gold pieces per caster level and a permanent sacrifice of the caster's hit points. At least one hit point must be given up by transfusing part of the caster's essence into the inert form. For each hit point transferred, there is a cumulative 20% chance that the caster's spirit will be drawn to this cloned body upon his death, allowing the caster to continue existence in a new form. The cloned caster retains all levels, abilities, and spells he possessed at the time of his death, but only has hit points equal to the amount poured into the duplicate body at the time the spell was cast. He can heal back to his full amount of health he possessed prior to casting *replication* (including the sacrificed points) with time or magical restoratives.
36-37	The caster can temporarily restore to life any creature of which he possesses a physical fragment. The creature must have died a physical death for this effect to work, but there is no time limit for the spell to be effective. Once cast, the creature immediately returns to life with all the levels, powers, spells, and other abilities it possessed in life. It is under the complete command of the caster. The replicated creature remains in this state until reduced to zero hit points or for 10 minutes per caster level, after which time it collapses back into fragments and cannot be revived with *replication* ever again.
38+	The caster can replicate up to 10 + CL dead creatures who return to life with all their levels, abilities, and powers they possessed in life. These duplicate creatures obey the caster unquestioningly and remain intact for 1 hour per CL. When reduced to zero hit points or when the spell expires, they collapse back into fragments and cannot be revived with *replication* ever again.

LEVEL 1 CLERIC SPELLS

Blessing

Level: 1   Range: Self or touch   Duration: 1 turn or more   Casting time: 1 action or more (see below)   Save: N/A

General   The cleric beseeches the blessing of his god. If bestowed, this blessing can be a great boon to the success of his endeavors. The spell can be cast on the cleric himself, on an object, or on one of the cleric's allies. The spell is most effective on allies with the same alignment. Casting this spell on a target with a different alignment incurs a -1 penalty to the spell check, and casting the spell on a target with an opposite alignment or in allegiance to an opposed deity incurs a -2 penalty.

The casting time reflects prayer and meditation as the cleric uses his holy symbol to conduct the blessing ritual. Blessings cast under auspicious circumstances receive a bonus of +1 to +4, according to the judge's discretion. Such circumstances include casting in the temple of the cleric's god, casting on a sacred holiday, or casting with the use of a holy relic. Likewise, casting under inauspicious circumstances, such as in an unholy enemy temple, receives a penalty ranging from -1 to -4.

Manifestation   Roll 1d4: (1) target glows; (2) target is limned in a brilliant aura; (3) target manifests an angelic crown; (4) the heavenly host sings softly when the blessing is present.

	When Cast on Self	When Cast on Ally	When Cast on Object
1-11	Failure.		
12-13	A god's favor grants success to the cleric's efforts. He receives a +1 bonus to all attack rolls for 1 turn.	The ally receives a +1 bonus to all attack rolls for 1 round.	Failure.
14-17	The cleric receives a +1 bonus to all attack rolls, damage rolls, saving throws, skill checks, and spell checks for 1 turn.	The ally receives a +1 bonus to all attack rolls for 1 turn.	The cleric can bless a vial of liquid to create holy water. The holy water does 1d4 damage when splashed upon unholy creatures. It remains holy for 1 day, as long as it is used in the service of the cleric's deity.
18-19	The cleric receives a +2 bonus to all attack rolls, damage rolls, saving throws, skill checks, and spell checks for 1 turn.	The ally receives a +1 bonus to all attack rolls, damage rolls, saving throws, skill checks, and spell checks for 1 turn.	The cleric can create holy water (as result 14-17 above) or bless a small amulet. The amulet is considered holy and magical for the duration of the spell, which is 1 day. The amulet grants its wearer a +1 bonus to the saving throws, as long as it is used in the service of the cleric's deity.
20-23	The cleric receives a bonus to all attack rolls, damage rolls, saving throws, skill checks, and spell checks. The bonus is equal to 1d3+CL (rolled at time of casting) and lasts for 1 turn. In addition, the cleric radiates a holy aura. Allies within 5' also receive the same blessing, as long as they remain within the aura.	The ally receives a +2 bonus to all attack rolls, damage rolls, saving throws, skill checks, and spell checks for 1 turn.	The cleric can create holy water (as result 14-17 above), a holy amulet (as result 18-19 above), or bless a weapon. A blessed weapon grants a +1 bonus to all attack and damage rolls *or* a +2 bonus to attack and damage rolls against unholy creatures. The weapon remains holy for 1 day and is considered magical.

Blessing (continued)		
24-27	The cleric receives a bonus to all attack rolls, damage rolls, saving throws, skill checks, and spell checks. The bonus is equal to 1d3+CL (rolled at time of casting) and lasts for 1 turn. In addition, the cleric radiates a holy aura. Allies within 10' receive the same blessing as long as they remain within the aura.	The ally receives a bonus to all attack rolls, damage rolls, saving throws, skill checks, and spell checks. The bonus is equal to 1d3+CL (rolled at time of casting) and lasts for 1 turn.	The cleric can create holy water, a holy amulet, or a holy weapon, as above with the following changes: holy water remains potent permanently, holy amulets grant a +2 bonus, and holy weapons grant a +2 or +3 bonus. However, the cleric asks much of his deity and loses the ability to cast this spell for the remainder of the day.
28-29	The cleric radiates an aura of exquisite holiness. All allies within 30' of the caster receive a blessing that grants a +4 bonus to all attack rolls, damage rolls, saving throws, skill checks, and spell checks. The bonus lasts for one hour.	The ally receives a bonus to all attack rolls, damage rolls, saving throws, skill checks, and spell checks. The bonus is equal to 1d3+CL (rolled at time of casting) and lasts for 1 turn. In addition, the ally radiates a holy aura. Allies within 5' of the ally receive the same blessing as long as they remain within the aura.	The cleric can create holy water, a holy amulet, or a holy weapon, as above with the following changes: holy water remains potent permanently, holy amulets grant a +2 bonus for one month, and holy weapons grant a +2 or +3 bonus for one month. The cleric asks much of his deity and loses the ability to cast this spell again for 1d7+1 days.
30-31	At this level of power, the blessing applies to the cleric and to an enterprise he serves in the name of his deity. This can be an army, a mission to liberate a princess, a castle, a sea voyage to new lands, or other such endeavors. The judge's discretion governs this power. All persons involved in the enterprise with the cleric receive a +1 bonus to all activities associated with the enterprise, as long as it remains in the service of the cleric's deity. In addition, the cleric can designate a number of individuals equal to his CL who receive an expanded bonus of +CL to all activities associated with the enterprise. The bonus lasts for 7 days. This is such a mighty drain of strength the cleric loses the ability to cast this spell for the same 7 days. If at any point the cleric falls out of favor with his deity, the blessing is revoked. The blessing is magical in nature and can be dispelled temporarily.	The ally receives a bonus to all attack rolls, damage rolls, saving throws, skill checks, and spell checks. The bonus is equal to 1d3+CL (rolled at time of casting) and lasts for 1 turn. In addition, the ally radiates a holy aura. Allies within 10' of the ally receive the same blessing as long as they remain within the aura.	The cleric can create holy water, a holy amulet, or a holy weapon, as above with the following changes: holy water remains potent permanently, holy amulets grant a +2 bonus for one year, and holy weapons grant a +2 or +3 bonus for one year. The cleric asks much of his deity and loses the ability to cast this spell again for 1d4 weeks.

Blessing (continued)

32+	At this level of power, the blessing applies to the cleric and to an enterprise he serves in the name of his deity. Moreover, the blessing bestowed to an ongoing enterprise is *permanent*, as long as it is favored by the cleric's deity, until either the completion of the enterprise or its dissolution. Note that there is a "reasonableness factor" in the deity's granting of this blessing. Attempting to abuse the definition of a "permanent enterprise" risk a deity's wrath. The enterprise can be a pilgrimage to a distant shrine, an army with a certain holy goal, a mission to liberate a princess, a sea voyage to encounter new lands, or other such endeavors. All persons involved in the enterprise with the cleric receive a +1 bonus to all activities associated with the enterprise, as long as it remains in the service of the cleric's deity. In addition, the cleric can designate a number of individuals equal to his CL who receive an expanded bonus of +CL to all activities associated with the enterprise. This is such a mighty drain of strength the cleric loses the ability to cast this spell for 1d20+10 days. If at any point the cleric falls out of favor with his deity, the blessing is revoked. The blessing is magical in nature and can be dispelled temporarily.	The ally receives a bonus to all attack rolls, damage rolls, saving throws, skill checks, and spell checks. The bonus is equal to 1d3+CL (rolled at time of casting) and lasts for 1 turn. In addition, the ally radiates a holy aura. Allies within 20' of the ally receive the same blessing as long as they remain within the aura.	The cleric can create holy water, a holy amulet, or a holy weapon, as above with the following changes: holy water remains potent permanently, holy amulets grant a +2 bonus permanently, and holy weapons grant a +2 *or* +3 bonus permanently. The duration is increased to permanent as long as the object remains in the service of the cleric's deity; if the object is used for an unholy purpose, its magic is revoked and forever lost. The cleric asks much of his deity and loses the ability to cast this spell again for 1d4 months.

Darkness

Level: 1   Range: 20' radius or more   Duration: 1 turn or more   Casting time: 1 action or more   Save: N/A

General   The cleric extinguishes the light of the sun, demonstrating the great power of his deity. From a distance, the darkness appears to be a space of deepest night; no light will penetrate it. Creatures within are blinded.

Manifestation   Roll 1d3: (1) shadowy cloud of darkness; (2) absolute blackness; (3) thick oily black mist.

1-11   Failure.

12-13   The space immediately surrounding the cleric, to a radius of 20', goes completely dark, as if all light had been extinguished. The darkness remains fixed to its location (it does not follow the cleric) and lasts for 1 turn.

14-17   The cleric can designate a point within 20' and create a 20'-radius sphere of darkness that remains fixed at that point for a duration of 1 turn.

18-19   The cleric can designate a point within 100' and create a 20'-radius sphere of darkness that remains fixed at that point for a duration of 1 turn.

20-23   The cleric can designate a point within 100' and create a 20'-radius sphere of darkness centered at that point. The darkness remains for a duration of 1 turn. By concentrating on future rounds, the cleric can move the sphere of darkness up to 40' per round, beyond the original 100' range if he so chooses.

24-27   The cleric can designate a point within 200' and create a sphere of darkness of up to 40' radius centered at that point. The darkness remains for a duration of 2 turns. By concentrating on future rounds, the cleric can move the sphere of darkness up to 80' per round, beyond the original 200' range if he so chooses.

28-29   The cleric can extinguish sources of light. He designates a point within 200', and a sphere of darkness up to 40' in radius appears at that point. The cleric can move this sphere at a speed of 80' per round. No concentration is required. The sphere lasts for 1 hour. In addition, all terrestrial sources of light within the sphere of darkness are extinguished. Torches go out, lanterns sputter and die, glowworms fade, and so on.

30-31   With a sweep of his arm, the cleric can cast an enormous space into darkness. The cleric can choose one of three effects: a cone extending 400' to a final width of 100'; a sphere up to 60' radius centered at any point within 300'; or a wide line, up to 1,000' long and 10' wide. Within the area of effect, total darkness reigns; no light source can penetrate. In addition, all terrestrial sources of light within the sphere of darkness are extinguished. Torches go out, lanterns sputter and die, glowworms fade, and so on. However, the cleric can see through the darkness. The dark space can be moved up to 100' per round without concentration. It lasts for up to 1 day or until dismissed.

32+   The cleric can blot out the sun, the moon, the stars, or other sources of light. This extraordinary display of divine power requires great concentration. If this result is achieved, the cleric may continue to concentrate. *All* light sources that illuminate a space 500' in all directions begin to fade. For every round the cleric concentrates, light sources fade by 1d20%. Torches still burn, but their flames seem to emit less light each round. The judge rolls each round the cleric continues to concentrate. When the total breaks 100%, all light sources have been completely extinguished, and the countryside around the cleric is completely darkened (at least to the eyes of all within 500' – the sun still seems to shine in other kingdoms). Once all light sources are extinguished, the radius of the effect begins to expand by another 1d20' per round of concentration. The maximum range is the cleric's CL x 1,000'. The effect continues as long as the cleric concentrates. When concentration is broken, the light reappears at the same rate it was extinguished; e.g., if it took 7 rounds to fade, it takes 7 rounds to reach full strength again.

Detect Evil

Level: 1   **Range:** 60' radius from cleric or more (see below)   **Duration:** 6 turns   **Casting time:** 1 action
Save: Will vs. spell check DC (sometimes)

General	The cleric holds up his holy symbol and detects emanations of evil within a ray that extends straight out 5' wide and 60' (or more) ahead of the symbol. The definition of "evil" is based on the cleric: generally it encompasses creatures of opposed alignment, those unholy to the cleric's deity, and those with clearly harmful intent. Depending on the strength of the spell, it may detect even more subtle dangers. This spell does not reveal creatures that are otherwise hidden but does inform the cleric that evil intentions radiate from a certain position. This spell may be reversed to detect good, which means creatures of allied alignment, common deity, or similar holy goals.
Manifestation	Roll 1d3: (1) evil creatures glow softly when viewed by the cleric; (2) a heavenly chorus trumpets strident tones of warning whenever the cleric views an evil creature; (3) evil creatures emit terrible, dark shadows in all directions, clouding their appearance with a deep shroud of darkness.
1-11	Failure.
12-13	Creatures of opposed alignment are potentially detected, as well as objects inherently dangerous in nature (such as traps and cursed weapons). Evil creatures receive a Will save vs. spell check DC to remain undetected by this spell.
14-17	Creatures of opposed alignment are automatically detected, as well as objects inherently dangerous in nature (such as traps and cursed weapons). Evil creatures do not receive a Will save to remain undetected.
18-19	To a range of 120' in all directions from the cleric, creatures of opposed alignment are automatically detected, as well as objects inherently dangerous in nature (such as traps and cursed weapons). Evil creatures do not receive a Will save to remain undetected.
20-23	The cleric is immediately aware of all evil creatures and objects within 180'. In addition, evil creatures and objects shine with a faint, unearthly glow that is obvious to the cleric's allies.
24-27	The cleric is immediately aware of all evil creatures and objects within 180'. In addition, evil creatures and objects shine with a faint, unearthly glow that is obvious to the cleric's allies. In addition, the cleric is also aware of creatures with intentions harmful to him, even if the creatures are not opposed in alignment. For example, a mindless but aggressive spider would be detected, as would a hungry bear thinking of eating the cleric.
28-29	The cleric is immediately aware of all evil creatures and objects within 180'. In addition, evil creatures and objects shine with a faint, unearthly glow that is obvious to the cleric's allies. In addition, the cleric is also aware of creatures with intentions harmful to him, even if the creatures are not opposed in alignment. For example, a mindless but aggressive spider would be detected, as would a hungry bear thinking of eating the cleric. The creatures detected by this spell are pained by the light of truth, suffering a -1 penalty to all attack rolls, damage rolls, skill checks, spell checks, and saving throws while in range.
30-31	The cleric is immediately aware of all evil creatures and objects within 240'. In addition, evil creatures and objects shine with a faint, unearthly glow that is obvious to the cleric's allies. In addition, the cleric is also aware of creatures with intentions harmful to him, even if the creatures are not opposed in alignment. For example, a mindless but aggressive spider would be detected, as would a hungry bear thinking of eating the cleric. The creatures detected by this spell are pained by the light of truth, suffering a -2 penalty to all attack rolls, damage rolls, skill checks, spell checks, and saving throws while in range.
32+	The cleric is immediately aware of all evil creatures and objects within 300'. In addition, evil creatures and objects shine with a faint, unearthly glow that is obvious to the cleric's allies. In addition, the cleric is also aware of creatures with intentions harmful to him, even if the creatures are not opposed in alignment. For example, a mindless but aggressive spider would be detected, as would a hungry bear thinking of eating the cleric. The creatures detected by this spell are pained by the light of truth, suffering a -4 penalty to all attack rolls, damage rolls, skill checks, spell checks, and saving throws while in range.

Detect Magic

Level: 1	Range: 30′ or more	Duration: 2 turns	Casting time: 2 actions	Save: Will vs. spell check DC (sometimes)

General	The cleric knows if there has been an enchantment laid upon a person, place or thing within range. The range is a cone, 30′ long and 30′ wide at its end, emanating from the cleric's holy symbol.
Manifestation	See below.

1-11	Failure.
12-13	The cleric is aware of magical enchantment on any object or creature within range. This includes weapons or armor worn by a creature, as well as spells. The cleric cannot distinguish which portions of the targets are magical. For example, a creature enchanted by a spell or carrying a magical weapon or item registers simply as "magical," so the true extent and nature of the magic is not always evident. The cleric does not receive any information on the nature of the magical enchantment, only its existence. Intelligent magic creatures and creations that wish to hide their magical nature can do so with a Will save. Objects behind 3′ of wood, 1″ of solid metal, or 1′ of stone are not detected.
14-17	The cleric is aware of magical enchantment on any object or creature within range. This includes weapons or armor worn by a creature, as well as spells. The cleric cannot distinguish which portions of the targets are magical. For example, a creature enchanted by a spell or carrying a magical weapon or item registers simply as "magical," so the true extent and nature of the magic is not always evident. The cleric does not receive any information on the nature of the magical enchantment, only its existence. Objects behind 3′ of wood, 1″ of solid metal, or 1′ of stone are not detected.
18-19	The cleric can determine exactly which objects or creatures are magically enchanted within range. He can tell if different weapons or items of equipment on a creature are enchanted and whether a creature that registers as "magical" overall does so because of its cloak (for example) or because of something inherent in its blood. Further, the cleric receives a rough gauge of the magic's strength, revealed as the approximate level of a spell, the general range of bonus (or plus) for weapons or armor, and so on. Objects behind 3′ of wood, 1″ of solid metal, or 1′ of stone are not detected.
20-23	The cleric can determine exactly which objects or creatures are magically enchanted within range. In addition, the spell reveals creatures of non-mortal origin (e.g., extraplanar creatures, demons, devils, celestials, un-dead, etc.). The cleric can distinguish between magical creatures and non-mortal creatures. He can tell if different weapons or items of equipment on a creature are enchanted and whether a creature that registers as "magical" overall does so because of its cloak (for example) or because of something inherent in its blood. Further, the cleric receives a rough gauge of the magic's strength, revealed as the approximately level of a spell, the general range of bonus (or plus) for weapons or armor, and so on. Objects behind 3′ of wood, 1″ of solid metal, or 1′ of stone are not detected.
24-27	The cleric can determine exactly which objects or creatures are magically enchanted within range. In addition, the spell reveals creatures of non-mortal origin (e.g., extraplanar creatures, demons, devils, celestials, un-dead, etc.). The cleric can distinguish between magical creatures and non-mortal creatures. He can tell if different weapons or items of equipment on a creature are enchanted and whether a creature that registers as "magical" overall does so because of its cloak (for example) or because of something inherent in its blood. Further, the cleric receives a very precise understanding of the magic's strength and nature: he knows an item is a +2 *sword* or that a door is guarded by a level 3 *ward portal* spell. Finally, the spell functions through any sort of impeding material (stone, wood, or iron, at any distance within range).
28-29	To an extended range of 120′, the cleric can determine exactly which objects or creatures are magically enchanted. In addition, the spell reveals creatures of non-mortal origin (e.g., extraplanar creatures, demons, devils, celestials, un-dead, etc.). The cleric can distinguish between magical creatures and non-mortal creatures. He can tell if different weapons or items of equipment on a creature are enchanted and whether a creature that registers as "magical" overall does so because of its cloak (for example) or because of something inherent in its blood. Further, the cleric receives a very precise understanding of the magic's strength and nature: he knows an item is a +2 *sword* or that a door is guarded by a level 3 *ward portal* spell. Finally, the spell functions through any sort of impeding material (stone, wood, or iron, at any distance within range).

30-31   To an extended range of 120' and for an extended duration of 4 turns, the cleric can determine exactly which objects or creatures are magically enchanted. In addition, the spell reveals creatures of non-mortal origin (e.g., extraplanar creatures, demons, devils, celestials, un-dead, etc.). The cleric can distinguish between magical creatures and non-mortal creatures. He can tell if different weapons or items of equipment on a creature are enchanted and whether a creature that registers as "magical" overall does so because of its cloak (for example) or because of something inherent in its blood. Further, the cleric receives a very precise understanding of the magic's strength and nature: he knows an item is a *+2 sword* or that a door is guarded by a level 3 *ward portal* spell. Finally, the spell functions through any sort of impeding material (stone, wood, or iron, at any distance within range).

32+   To an extended range of line-of-sight and for an extended duration of a full hour, the cleric can determine exactly which objects or creatures are magically enchanted. In addition, the spell reveals creatures of non-mortal origin (e.g., extraplanar creatures, demons, devils, celestials, un-dead, etc.). The cleric can distinguish between magical creatures and non-mortal creatures. He can tell if different weapons or items of equipment on a creature are enchanted and whether a creature that registers as "magical" overall does so because of its cloak (for example) or because of something inherent in its blood. Further, the cleric receives a very precise understanding of the magic's strength and nature: he knows an item is a *+2 sword* or that a door is guarded by a level 3 *ward portal* spell. Finally, the spell functions through any sort of impeding material (stone, wood, or iron, at any distance within range).

Food of the Gods

| Level: 1 | Range: 30' | Duration: 24 hours (see below) | Casting time: 1 turn | Save: N/A |

General   The cleric calls upon the power of his deity to feed the masses. This spell either makes inedible food edible or magically creates viands when no other food and drink is available. Magically-created food is a spongy, grey, and bland-tasting substance that spoils after 24 hours. Magically-created water is clean rainwater that remains drinkable for as long as it is properly stored.

Manifestation   Roll 1d4: (1) a glowing banquet table appears laden with food and then vanishes, leaving the meal behind; (2) food rains down from the heavens, collecting on flat surfaces or in upturned hands; (3) the cleric vomits up the magically-created food and water; (4) inedible substances such as wood, stone, and dirt are transformed into edible substances.

1-11   Failure.

12-13   The cleric can purify enough pre-existing spoiled food and tainted water to feed up to 1d6+CL people. This spell merely makes normally inedible food edible and has no effect on poison. This result does not create new food or water from thin air.

14-17   The cleric creates food and water from thin air, creating enough to feed 5+CL people.

18-19   The cleric creates food and water from thin air, creating enough to feed 10+CL people.

20-23   The cleric creates food and water from thin air, creating enough to feed 15+CL people.

24-27   The cleric creates food and water from thin air, creating enough to feed 20+CL people.

28-29   The cleric creates enough food and water from thin air to feed 30+CL people *or* produces a revitalizing heroic feast for 5 people. The food and drink of a heroic feast imparts all the benefits of a full night's sleep, restores a single point of temporary ability damage, and heals 1d4+CL points of damage.

30-31   The cleric creates enough food and water from thin air to feed 30+CL people *and* produces a revitalizing heroic feast for 10 people. The food and drink of a heroic feast imparts all the benefits of a full night's sleep, restores up to two points of temporary ability damage, and heals 1d6+CL points of damage.

32+   The earth opens up to provide a cornucopia of food and drink for the cleric's faithful followers. All food-producing locations within the cleric's line of sight burst forth to provide food and water. This includes natural sources, such as fields and fruit trees that are suddenly laden with grain and food; civilized sources, such as market baskets and cooking pots, which are suddenly filled with delicious substances; and even the animals of the wild, which march forth and rest at the feet of the cleric, offering themselves for slaughter. This divine spectacle produces enough nourishing food to provide a solid meal for up to 100 people. Moreover, the choicest meals produce a single revitalizing heroic feast for 15 people. The food and drink of a heroic feast imparts all the benefits of a full night's sleep, restores up to three points of temporary ability damage, and heals 1d10+CL points of damage.

Holy Sanctuary

Level: 1	Range: Self or more	Duration: 1 round or more	Casting time: 1 action	Save: Will save vs. spell check

General	The cleric invokes a place of sanctuary where he and his allies are safe from harm.

Manifestation	Roll 1d4: (1) glowing aura; (2) angelic halo; (3) beam of light from above; (4) "lightness of feet" that makes the cleric seem to float just above the ground.

1-11	Failure.
12-13	Enemies find it difficult to focus on attacking the cleric. They are distracted, and the cleric is more easily able to dodge their attacks. All attacks against the cleric for the next round suffer a -2 penalty.
14-17	Enemies are compelled to focus their attacks against other targets. As long as an attacker can reasonably attack some other target instead of the cleric, it must choose to do so. In order to resist this compulsion and attack the cleric, an enemy must make a Will save vs. spell check DC. If the cleric is the only reasonable target, the creature need not make a save to attack the cleric. This effect lasts for 1 turn. It is immediately dispelled if the cleric attacks or takes aggressive action in any way.
18-19	Enemies are compelled to focus their attacks against other targets. As long as an attacker can reasonably attack some other target instead of the cleric, it must choose to do so. In order to resist this compulsion and attack the cleric, an enemy must make a Will save vs. spell check DC. This Will save is required even if the cleric is the *only* reasonable target. This effect lasts for 1 turn. It is immediately dispelled if the cleric attacks or takes aggressive action in any way.
20-23	Enemies are compelled to focus their attacks against other targets. As long as an attacker can reasonably attack some other target instead of the cleric, it must choose to do so. Creatures of 3 HD or less cannot attack the cleric in any manner. Creatures of 4 HD or more may attempt a Will save to resist the compulsion and attack the cleric. This Will save is required even if the cleric is the *only* reasonable target. This effect lasts for 1 turn. It is immediately dispelled if the cleric attacks or takes aggressive action in any way.
24-27	The cleric can create a holy sanctuary that includes himself and up to two allies within 5'. The other protected allies must remain within 5' or the effect ends. Enemies are compelled to focus their attacks against other targets. As long as an attacker can reasonably attack some other target instead of the cleric and his protected allies, it must choose to do so. Creatures of 3 HD or less cannot attack in any manner; creatures of 4 HD or more may attempt a Will save to resist the compulsion. This effect lasts for 1 turn. It is immediately dispelled if the cleric *or any of his protected allies* attack or take aggressive action in any way.
28-29	The cleric may designate a place as a holy sanctuary. This must be a single building or self-contained location up to 5,000 square feet in area; e.g., a church, forest grove, or cave. This effect lasts for 1d7 days. Creatures within this place share the benefits of a *holy sanctuary* as follows, provided they are in the service of the cleric's deity: enemies of less than 6 HD cannot attack unless they use magical weapons, and enemies of 7+ HD or those using magical weapons must make a Will save vs. spell check DC to attack. The effect on any one individual is dispelled if that creature makes an aggressive action. Note that enemies can still *enter* the place and converse with its residents; they simply cannot attack or make other aggressive actions.
30-31	The cleric may designate a place as a holy sanctuary. This must be a single building or self-contained location up to 5,000 square feet in area; e.g., a church, forest grove, or cave. This effect lasts for 1d7+3 weeks. Creatures within this place share the benefits of a *holy sanctuary* as follows, provided they are in the service of the cleric's deity: enemies of less than 6 HD cannot attack unless they use magical weapons, and enemies of 7+ HD or those using magical weapons must make a Will save vs. spell check DC to attack. The effect on any one individual is dispelled if that creature makes an aggressive action. Note that enemies can still *enter* the place and converse with its residents; they simply cannot attack or make other aggressive actions.
32+	The cleric may designate a place as a holy sanctuary. This must be a single building or self-contained location up to 10,000 square feet in area; e.g., a church, forest grove, or cave. The place designated as a holy sanctuary becomes sanctified forever, as long as the cleric's deity retains respect for the cleric's work and actions. Creatures within this place share the benefits of a *holy sanctuary* as follows, provided they are in the service of the cleric's deity: enemies of less than 6 HD cannot attack unless they use magical weapons, and enemies of 7+ HD or those using magical weapons must make a Will save vs. spell check DC to attack. The effect on any one individual is dispelled if that creature makes an aggressive action. Note that enemies can still *enter* the place and converse with its residents; they simply cannot attack or make other aggressive actions.

Paralysis

Level: 1   Range: Touch or more   Duration: 1 round or more   Casting time: 1 action   Save: Will save vs. spell check

General	The light of the cleric's deity prevents his enemies from raising a hand to perform baleful deeds.
Manifestation	Roll 1d4: (1) crackle of electricity; (2) black ropy binds; (3) white pallor; (4) ethereal gray mist.
1-11	Failure.
12-13	The cleric's hands and melee weapons are charged with the energy of paralysis. The cleric must make a normal attack on his next round. If it succeeds, he causes normal damage and his enemy must make a Will save or be paralyzed. The paralyzed creature is unable to move or take any physical action for 1d6+CL rounds.
14-17	The cleric's hands and melee weapons are charged with the energy of paralysis. The charge remains for 1d4+CL rounds. Any attack by the cleric during this period delivers normal damage plus paralysis if the target fails a Will save. The paralyzed creature is unable to move or take any physical action for 1d6+CL rounds.
18-19	The cleric's melee weapons *and* missile fire weapons are charged with paralysis. The charge remains for 1d4+CL rounds. Any attack by the cleric during this period delivers normal damage plus paralysis if the target fails a Will save. The paralyzed creature is unable to move or take any physical action for 1d6+CL rounds.
20-23	The cleric designates one creature within 30' and paralyzes it with a word. If the creature is 2 HD or less, it is automatically paralyzed. If 3 HD or more, it receives a Will save to resist. Paralysis lasts for 1d8+CL rounds.

24-27   The cleric designates up to three targets within 100' and paralyzes all of them. Any creature of 4 HD or less is automatically paralyzed. Creatures of 5 HD or more receive a Will save. Paralysis lasts for 2d6+CL rounds.

28-29   The cleric imbues his touch with the power to paralyze an enemy. The cleric retains the latent paralysis touch for up to 24 hours. At any point during that time, he may discharge the paralysis with a spoken word. A melee attack may be necessary to touch a resisting target. The creature touched is automatically paralyzed if 6 HD or less. Creatures of 7+ HD receive a Will save. The paralysis lasts 4d6+CL hours.

30-31   Choose any one of the effects above, and the duration of the paralysis is doubled.

32+   Choose any one of the effects above, and the duration of the paralysis is permanent. The paralysis can only be cured via magical means, such as a cleric's ability to lay on hands or the spell *cure paralysis*.

Protection from Evil

Level: 1	Range: Self or more	Duration: 1 turn per CL	Casting time: 1 action	Save: Varies

General	The cleric calls upon his deity to protect him from harm. He is protected even if he is not aware of the danger. The definition of "evil" is based on the cleric: generally it encompasses creatures of opposed alignment, those unholy to the cleric's deity, and those with clear harmful intent. Depending on the strength of the spell, it may detect even more subtle dangers. This spell may be reversed to protect from good.
Manifestation	Roll 1d3: (1) translucent holy symbol; (2) soft, protective aura; (3) glowing halo.
1-11	Failure.
12-13	The cleric receives a +1 bonus to saving throws made against evil effects, evil creatures, un-dead, demons, and anything else unholy to his faith.
14-17	The cleric receives a +1 bonus to saving throws made against evil effects, evil creatures, un-dead, demons, and anything else unholy to his faith. In addition, all attempts to attack the cleric by evil or unholy creatures are made at a -1 penalty.
18-19	The cleric receives a +1 bonus to saving throws made against evil effects, evil creatures, un-dead, demons, and anything else unholy to his faith. In addition, all attempts to attack the cleric by evil or unholy creatures are made at a -1 penalty. Finally, all wounds suffered from evil or unholy sources have their damage reduced by 1 point per die (minimum damage 1 point per die).
20-23	In relation to evil effects, evil creatures, and anything else unholy to the cleric's faith, the cleric and all allies within a 10' radius receive a +1 bonus to saving throws against evil creatures, enemy attack rolls against them suffer a -1 penalty, and damage suffered from evil sources is reduced by 1 point per die (minimum damage 1 point per die).
24-27	In relation to evil effects, evil creatures, and anything else unholy to the cleric's faith, the cleric and all allies within a 20' radius receive a +2 bonus to saving throws against evil creatures, enemy attack rolls against them suffer a -2 penalty, and damage suffered from evil sources is reduced by 2 points per die (minimum damage 1 point per die).
28-29	In relation to evil effects, evil creatures, and anything else unholy to the cleric's faith, the cleric and all allies within a 30' radius receive a +3 bonus to saving throws against evil creatures, enemy attack rolls against them suffer a -3 penalty, and damage suffered from evil sources is reduced by 3 points per die (minimum damage 1 point per die).
30-31	Evil effects, evil creatures, and anything else unholy to the cleric's faith find it painful to come near the cleric. Any such creature that advances within 40' of the cleric takes 1d4+CL damage each round on the cleric's activation. This is automatic as a consequence of being near the cleric. Additionally, the cleric and all allies within a 40' radius receive a +4 bonus to saving throws against evil creatures, enemy attack rolls against them suffer a -4 penalty, and damage suffered from evil sources is reduced by 4 points per die (minimum damage 1 point per die).
32+	Evil effects, evil creatures, and anything else unholy to the cleric's faith find it painful to come near the cleric. Any such creature that advances within 40' of the cleric takes 2d6+CL damage each round on the cleric's activation. This is automatic as a consequence of being near the cleric. Additionally, the cleric and all allies within a 40' radius receive a +4 bonus to saving throws against evil creatures, enemy attack rolls against them suffer a -4 penalty, and damage suffered from evil sources is reduced by 4 points per die (minimum damage 1 point per die).

Resist Cold or Heat

Level: 1   **Range:** Self or more   **Duration:** 1 round or more   **Casting time:** 1 action   **Save:** N/A

General	The cleric repels the chilling effects of cold or heat, protecting himself and others. He can withstand such conditions without discomfort. When casting the spell, the cleric chooses which effect to resist (heat or cold). It is possible to cast the spell twice and create a resistance to both effects.
Manifestation	Roll 1d3: (1) reddish aura; (2) shimmering heat waves; (3) bluish skin tone.
1-11	Failure.
12-13	The cleric counteracts the harmful effects of cold or heat upon his body. He can ignore up to 5 points of cold or heat/fire damage in the next round. If more than 5 points are sustained, subtract 5 from the total dice result to determine the final damage suffered.
14-17	The cleric counteracts the harmful effects of cold or heat upon his body. He can ignore up to 5 points of cold or heat/fire damage for a number of rounds equal to 1d6+CL. If more than 5 points are sustained in a given round, subtract 5 from the total dice result to determine the final damage suffered.
18-19	The cleric counteracts the harmful effects of cold or heat upon his body. He can ignore up to 10 points of cold or heat/fire damage for a number of rounds equal to 1d8+CL. If more than 10 points are sustained in a given round, subtract 10 from the total dice result to determine the final damage suffered.
20-23	The cleric counteracts the harmful effects of cold or heat upon his body. He can ignore up to 10 points of cold or heat/fire damage for a number of rounds equal to 1d8+CL. If more than 10 points are sustained in a given round, subtract 10 from the total dice result to determine the final damage suffered. In addition, the cleric also receives a +4 bonus to all saving throws to resist cold- or heat-based effects.
24-27	The cleric can protect others as well as himself. The cleric produces a sphere of resistance that emanates 10' from his location. Everyone within this sphere can resist up to 10 points of cold or heat damage per round and receive a +2 bonus to all saving throws against cold- or heat-based effects. The cleric must concentrate to maintain the sphere, which can remain functioning for up to 1 turn.
28-29	The cleric can protect others as well as himself. The cleric produces a sphere of resistance that emanates 20' from his location. Everyone within this sphere can resist up to 20 points of cold or heat damage per round and receive a +4 bonus to all saving throws against cold- or heat-based effects. The cleric must concentrate to maintain the sphere, which can remain functioning for up to 1 turn.
30-31	The cleric can protect others as well as himself. The cleric produces a sphere of resistance that emanates 20' from his location. Everyone within this sphere can resist up to 20 points of cold or heat damage per round and receive a +4 bonus to all saving throws against cold- or heat-based effects. The sphere continues to function, without concentration, for a number of rounds equal to 1d10+CL. Each time it is about to expire, the cleric can concentrate for one round to extend the effect another 1d10+CL rounds, to a maximum duration of one hour.
32+	The cleric can protect others as well as himself. The cleric produces a sphere of resistance that emanates 50' from his location. Everyone within this sphere can resist up to 30 points of cold or heat damage per round and receive a +6 bonus to all saving throws against cold- or heat-based effects. The sphere continues to function, without concentration, for a number of *turns* equal to 1d6+CL. Each time it is about to expire, the cleric can concentrate for one round to extend the effect another 1d6+CL turns, to a maximum duration of one day.

Second Sight

Level: 1	Range: Self	Duration: 1 round or more	Casting time: 1 turn	Save: N/A

General	Using sortilege, haruspicy, or some other method appropriate to the cleric, he augurs the future. In doing so, the cleric gains insight about the consequences his actions will bring.

Manifestation	Roll 1d3: (1) a third eye appears in the cleric's forehead; (2) the cleric's eyes glow; (3) the cleric's eyes are fused shut but he can still see.

1-11	Failure.
12-13	For one round, the cleric glimpses the future. In doing so, he gains great insight into the most effective manner to complete any action. The cleric receive a +4 bonus to a single roll of his choosing on his next round, whether it's an attack roll, damage roll, skill check, spell check, or something else.
14-17	The cleric has a hint of possible outcomes. He must spend the following round concentrating on a choice that must be made in the next 30 minutes. For example, he may be deciding which direction to turn in a dungeon or whether to enter a room. The cleric gets a sense of whether the action will be to his benefit or harm. There is a 75% chance that the sense the cleric receives is accurate.
18-19	The cleric has a hint of possible outcomes. He must spend the following round concentrating on a choice that must be made in the next 30 minutes. For example, he may be deciding which direction to turn in a dungeon or whether to enter a room. The cleric gets a sense of whether the action will be to his benefit or harm. There is an 80% chance that the sense the cleric receives is accurate.
20-23	The cleric has a hint of possible outcomes. He must spend the following round concentrating on a choice that must be made in the next 30 minutes. For example, he may be deciding which direction to turn in a dungeon or whether to enter a room. The cleric gets a sense of whether the action will be to his benefit or harm. There is an 85% chance that the sense the cleric receives is accurate.
24-27	For the next *hour*, the cleric receives an ongoing sense of possible outcomes. At every significant decision or juncture, he receives a premonition regarding the decision he must make – a sense of foreboding or certitude depending on whether the action bodes well for him (or not). For any given action, there is an 85% chance that the sense is accurate. By concentrating, the cleric can receive a sense of whether a future action (one to be taken within in the next hour) will be a bane or boon.
28-29	For the next *hour*, the cleric receives an ongoing sense of possible outcomes. At every significant decision or juncture, he receives a premonition regarding the decision he must make – a sense of foreboding or certitude depending on whether the action bodes well for him (or not). For any given action, there is a 90% chance that the sense is accurate. By concentrating, the cleric can receive a sense of whether a future action (one to be taken within in the next hour) will be a bane or boon.
30-31	For the next *day*, the cleric receives an ongoing sense of possible outcomes. At every significant decision or juncture, he receives a premonition regarding the decision he must make – a sense of foreboding or certitude depending on whether the action bodes well for him (or not). For any given action, there is a 95% chance that the sense is accurate. By concentrating, the cleric can receive a sense of whether a future action (one to be taken within in the next day) will be a bane or boon. For example, a cleric could divine the results of a great battle to be fought on the morrow and gain a sense that although he will emerge unharmed from the battle, it will be harmful to his church.
32+	The cleric has read the tablets of time. For the next *month*, he receives an ongoing sense of possible outcomes. At every significant decision or juncture, he receives a premonition regarding the decision he must make – a sense of foreboding or certitude depending on whether the action bodes well for him (or not). For any given action, there is a 99% chance that the sense is accurate. By concentrating, the cleric can receive a sense of whether a future action (one to be taken within in the next day) will be a bane or boon. For example, a cleric could divine the results of a great battle to be fought on the morrow and gain a sense that although he will emerge unharmed from the battle, it will be harmful to his church. In addition, the cleric receive a +1 bonus to all rolls while the second sight is active, reflecting his general insight into the consequences of all actions.

Word of Command

Level: 1   Range: 30' or more   Duration: 1 round or more   Casting time: 1 round   Save: Will save vs. spell check

General	The cleric speaks a powerful word that carries with it the commanding will of his deity. Creatures hearing the word are bound to obey. The word must be a single word, which must describe an action. For example, "go," "attack," "retreat," "speak," "swim," "grovel," "silence," and so on. The word must be spoken in the direction of a single sentient target within range. That target receives a Will save to resist; if failed, it must obey the command for its next round. The command is interpreted by the creature's natural thought processes; e.g., issuing an "attack" command to an herbivore may have a different response than to a carnivore. The word of command cannot be longer in length than a single word and may be subject to misinterpretation. If the command is completely contrary to a creature's natural instinct, it receives a +4 bonus to its Will save to resist; for example, commanding a desert lizard to "swim" or any command of "suicide."
Manifestation	Roll 1d4: (1) word resounds in booming voice; (2) word echoes many times; (3) word seems to come from all around, including the air and ground; (4) word appears in the sky in fiery letters before dissipating.
1-11	Failure.
12-13	The cleric can speak a word at a target within 30'. If the creature fails its save, it must obey the command for one round.
14-17	The cleric can speak a word at a target within 30'. If the creature fails its save, it must obey the command for a number of rounds equal to 1d6+CL.
18-19	The cleric can speak a word at a target within 30'. He may combine the word of command with a gesture that clarifies its intent. For example, "attack" or "go" with a pointed finger. If the creature fails its save, it must obey the command for a number of rounds equal to 1d6+CL.
20-23	The cleric can speak a word at a target within 60'. He may combine the word of command with a gesture that clarifies its intent. For example, "attack" or "go" with a pointed finger. If the creature fails its save, it must obey the command for a number of *turns* equal to 1d6+CL.
24-27	The cleric can speak a word at multiple targets within 60' of his location. He can target up to six creatures, each of whom must be within range and within line of sight. The same command applies to all targets, and each target receives its own save. The cleric may combine the word of command with a gesture that clarifies its intent. For example, "attack" or "go" with a pointed finger. If a target fails its save, it must obey the command for a number of *turns* equal to 1d6+CL.
28-29	The cleric can speak a word at multiple targets within a range of up to 200'. He can target up to 1d6 targets per caster level, each of whom must be within range and within line of sight. The same command applies to all targets, and each target receives its own save. The cleric may combine the word of command with a gesture that clarifies its intent. For example, "attack" or "go" with a pointed finger. If a target fails its save, it must obey the command for a number of *days* equal to 1d7+CL. The target receives a new Will save each morning.
30-31	The cleric can speak a word at multiple targets within a range of up to a mile. He can target up to 50 targets per caster level (yes, 50), each of whom must be within range and within line of sight. The same command applies to all targets. Targets of 2HD or less are automatically affected; higher-level targets each receive their own save. The cleric may combine the word of command with a gesture that clarifies its intent. For example, "attack" or "go" with a pointed finger. The cleric's voice is magically amplified such that all targets can hear him. If a target fails its save, it must obey the command for a number of *days* equal to 1d7+CL. The target receives a new Will save each morning.
32+	The cleric can speak a word at all targets he can see. He can choose to *exclude* up to 10 targets per caster level, but otherwise all targets within line of sight are affected. The same command applies to all targets. Targets of 3HD or less are automatically affected; higher-level targets each receive their own save. The cleric may combine the word of command with a gesture that clarifies its intent. For example, "attack" or "go" with a pointed finger. The cleric's voice is magically amplified such that all targets can hear him. If a target fails its save, it must obey the command for a number of *days* equal to 1d7+CL. The target receives a new Will save each morning.

LEVEL 2 CLERIC SPELLS

Banish

| Level: 2 | Range: 30' or more | Duration: Varies | Casting time: 1 round | Save: Will vs. spell check DC |

General

The cleric banishes a creature from his presence and potentially forces it back from whence it came. This spell is usually employed to force a supernatural creature back to its native plane, though it can also be used to send mundane creatures back to their lairs.

The cleric specifies a single target. This can be a creature within line of sight or a creature that is not present, provided the cleric possesses a physical memento (lock of hair, fingernail, favored weapon, drop of blood, etc.). The cleric then casts the spell, and the target is affected as described below.

Manifestation

Roll 1d4: (1) silvery ethereal chains wrap themselves around the target and constrict it; (2) a dense mist settles on the target; (3) a clawed hand reaches down from the heavens to pluck the target back from whence it came; (4) the target simply blinks out of existence.

1-13

Failure.

14-15

For the next turn, the target must make a Will save to approach within 30' of the cleric. If failed, it cannot approach any closer than 30' nor can it hurl missile weapons, speak in the cleric's direction, or otherwise take action against him. If forced within 30', the target takes 1d4+CL divine damage each round, although this damage cannot kill the creature. If reduced to 0 hit points, the target collapses, unconscious, and heals normally when removed from the cleric's presence. If the spell is cast while the target is already within 30', it immediately takes damage and is forced back 30' per round until it is at the outer perimeter of the spell's area of effect.

16-19

For the next 1d6 turns, the target must make a Will save to approach within 60' of the cleric. If failed, it cannot approach any closer than 60' nor can it hurl missile weapons, speak in the cleric's direction, or otherwise take action against him. If forced within 60', it takes 1d8+CL arcane damage each round. This damage can kill the creature if it is reduced to 0 hit points. If the spell is cast while the target is already within 60', it immediately takes damage and is forced back 30' per round until it is at the outer perimeter of the spell's area of effect.

20-21

If the target is within 90' of the cleric, it must make a Will save or be forced back to its place of origin. Supernatural creatures, including demons, devils, elementals, and other denizens of foreign planes, are forced back to their native planes. Summoned creatures (as through an *animal summoning* or *monster summoning* spell) are sent back from whence they came. Mundane creatures are simply forced to the outer edge of the 90' range for the next 2d6+CL hours. Such targets cannot approach any closer than 90' nor can they hurl missile weapons, speak in the cleric's direction, or otherwise take action against him. If forced within 90', a mundane target takes 1d12+CL arcane damage each round. This damage can kill the creature if it is reduced to 0 hit points.

22-25

If the target is within 120' of the cleric, it must make a Will save or be forced back to its place of origin. Supernatural creatures, including demons, devils, elementals, and other denizens of foreign planes, are forced back to their native planes. Summoned creatures (as through an *animal summoning* or *monster summoning* spell) are sent back from whence they came. Mundane creatures are simply forced to the outer edge of the 120' range for the next 1d6+CL days. The creature receives a new save at the beginning of each new day. Such targets cannot approach any closer than 120' nor can they hurl missile weapons, speak in the cleric's direction, or otherwise take action against him. If forced within 120', a mundane target takes 1d12+CL arcane damage each round. This damage can kill the creature if it is reduced to 0 hit points.

26-29

Up to two targets within 120' must make a Will save or be forced back to their places of origin. Supernatural creatures, including demons, devils, elementals, and other denizens of foreign planes, are forced back to their native planes. Summoned creatures (as through an *animal summoning* or *monster summoning* spell) are sent back from whence they came. Mundane creatures are simply forced to the outer edge of the 120' range for the next 1d6+CL days. Such targets cannot approach any closer than 120' nor can they hurl missile weapons, speak in the cleric's direction, or otherwise take action against him. If forced within 120', a mundane target takes 1d12+CL arcane damage each round. This damage can kill the creature if it is reduced to 0 hit points.

30-31	Up to five targets within 120' must make a Will save or be forced back to their places of origin. Supernatural creatures, including demons, devils, elementals, and other denizens of foreign planes, are forced back to their native planes. Summoned creatures (as through an *animal summoning* or *monster summoning* spell) are sent back from whence they came. Mundane creatures are simply forced to the outer edge of the 120' range for the next 1d6+CL days. Such targets cannot approach any closer than 120' nor can they hurl missile weapons, speak in the cleric's direction, or otherwise take action against him. If forced within 120', a mundane target takes 1d12+CL arcane damage each round. This damage can kill the creature if it is reduced to 0 hit points.
32-33	Up to ten targets within 120' must make a Will save or be forced back to their places of origin. Supernatural creatures, including demons, devils, elementals, and other denizens of foreign planes, are forced back to their native planes. Summoned creatures (as through an *animal summoning* or *monster summoning* spell) are sent back from whence they came. Mundane creatures are simply forced to the outer edge of the 120' range for the next 1d6+CL days. Such targets cannot approach any closer than 120' nor can they hurl missile weapons, speak in the cleric's direction, or otherwise take action against him. If forced within 120', a mundane target takes 1d12+CL arcane damage each round. This damage can kill the creature if it is reduced to 0 hit points.
34+	The cleric can specify any number of targets within 120'. All targets must make a Will save or be forced back to their places of origin. Supernatural creatures, including demons, devils, elementals, and other denizens of foreign planes, are forced back to their native planes. Summoned creatures (as through an *animal summoning* or *monster summoning* spell) are sent back from whence they came. Mundane creatures are simply forced to the outer edge of the 120' range for the next 1d6+CL days. Such targets cannot approach any closer than 120' nor can they hurl missile weapons, speak in the cleric's direction, or otherwise take action against him. If forced within 120', a mundane target takes 1d12+CL arcane damage each round. This damage can kill the creature if it is reduced to 0 hit points.

Binding

Level: 2   Range: 30' or more   Duration: Varies   Casting time: 1 round   Save: Will vs. spell check DC

General	With this spell, the cleric binds a supernatural creature and forces it to obey his will. The spell is easiest if the creature has already been summoned for control via another spell. But the cleric may also cast this spell to control creatures encountered on their native planes.
	The cleric may target one creature already under the control of another spellcaster and summoned via another spell (for example, *animal summoning*, *monster summoning*, or *invisible companion*) or native to a non-material plane (for example, demons, devils, elementals, spirits, ghosts, etc.). The cleric binds that creature to obey his will instead of the will of its current master. A Will save is allowed to resist, but the Will save is made by *the other spellcaster* not the target creature, which is already dominated. If the check is successful, control of the bound creature transfers to the cleric casting *binding*. The cleric retains control for a time, after which control reverts back to the original caster (by which time the original summoning or controlling spell may have ended). This spell does not affect familiars or other creatures that voluntarily obey a spellcaster, only those under forcible control.
	Under certain circumstances, as noted below, the cleric may affect other targets as well.
	A creature under the cleric's control can be commanded to take any action normally within its power, similar to the *animal summoning* spell. The creature must be capable of hearing the cleric's commands and will execute them to the best of its ability. Suicidal or inherently contradictory commands grant the target another Will save to resist.

Manifestation	Roll 1d3: (1) glittery dust appears in a cloud surrounding the target; (2) a scintillating magical rope binds the target; (3) a sky-borne tether drops down and attaches to the target.

1-13	Failure.

14-15   The cleric may target a creature up to 2 HD. If the spell succeeds, the cleric controls that creature for 1d6 rounds.

16-19   The cleric may target a creature up to 4 HD. If the spell succeeds, the cleric controls that creature for 1d6+CL rounds.

20-21   The cleric may target a creature up to 6 HD. If the spell succeeds, the cleric controls that creature for 2d6+CL rounds.

22-25   The cleric may target a creature up to 6 HD. If the spell succeeds, the cleric controls that creature for 2d6+CL rounds. Alternately, the cleric may also choose to target one free-willed extraplanar creature of 4 HD or less currently on a non-native plane. It receives a Will save using its own modifier. The cleric controls the creature as if it were under the effects of an *animal summoning* spell of the same spell check. At the end of the duration, the creature reverts to its own free will.

26-29   The cleric may target a creature up to 8 HD. If the spell succeeds, the cleric controls that creature for 2d6+CL *turns*. Alternately, the cleric may also choose to target one free-willed extraplanar creature of 6 HD or less currently on a non-native plane. It receives a Will save using its own modifier. The cleric controls the creature as if it were under the effects of an *animal summoning* spell of the same spell check. At the end of the duration, the creature reverts to its own free will.

30-31   The cleric may target a creature up to 8 HD. If the spell succeeds, the cleric controls that creature for 2d6+CL *turns*. Alternately, the cleric may also choose to target one other creature of 8 HD or less, which can be any free-willed extraplanar creature currently on a non-native plane, any mundane animal, or any unintelligent monster. It receives a Will save using its own modifier. The cleric controls the creature as if it were under the effects of an *animal summoning* spell of the same spell check. At the end of the duration, the creature reverts to its own free will.

32-33   The cleric may target a creature up to 12 HD. If the spell succeeds, the cleric controls that creature for 2d6+CL *hours*. Alternately, the cleric may also choose any other target, whether intelligent or not, or extraplanar or not, of up to 10 HD or less. It receives a Will save using its own modifier. The cleric controls the creature as if it were under the effects of an *animal summoning* spell of the same spell check. At the end of the duration, the creature reverts to its own free will.

34+   The cleric may target any creature of any Hit Dice or power level and attempt to control that creature for 2d6+CL *days*. At the end of the duration, the creature reverts to its own free will.

Cure Paralysis

Level: 2   Range: Touch or more   Duration: One day or permanent (see below)   Casting time: 1 round   Save: N/A

General

The cleric frees a creature from paralysis. More powerful castings also cure petrifaction and other motion-limiting effects.

Manifestation

Roll 1d3: (1) target fades to invisibility then returns to normal state; (2) a host of fairy carpenters rise from the ground to hammer the target back into normal condition; (3) a glittering golden curtain falls before the target; when it is lifted the target is returned to normal state.

1-13

Failure.

14-15

One creature touched is immediately cured of paralysis. If the paralysis was due to mundane reasons (e.g., a severed spinal cord) or a magical effect of limited duration (e.g., a *paralysis* spell that is not permanent), the cure is permanent and ongoing. If the paralysis was due to a magical effect that is permanent, the paralysis is healed for one day but returns at the onset of the next day.

16-19

One creature touched is immediately and permanently cured of paralysis.

20-21

One creature touched is immediately and permanently cured of paralysis, as well as any other condition that limits motion. For example, a creature turned to stone is returned to its natural state. The spell also cures transformations to ice or other substances.

22-25

Up to two creatures touched are immediately and permanently cured of paralysis, as well as any other condition that limits motion. For example, a creature turned to stone is returned to its natural state. The spell also cures transformations to ice or other substances.

26-29

Up to two creatures within 30' of the cleric are immediately and permanently cured of paralysis, as well as any other condition that limits motion. For example, a creature turned to stone is returned to its natural state. The spell also cures transformations to ice or other substances.

30-31

All creatures within 30' of the cleric are immediately and permanently cured of paralysis, as well as any other condition that limits motion. For example, a creature turned to stone is returned to its natural state. The spell also cures transformations to ice or other substances.

32-33

All creatures within 60' of the cleric are immediately and permanently cured of paralysis, as well as any other condition that limits motion. For example, a creature turned to stone is returned to its natural state. The spell also cures transformations to ice or other substances.

34+

All creatures within 120' of the cleric are immediately and permanently cured of paralysis, as well as any other condition that limits motion. For example, a creature turned to stone is returned to its natural state. The spell also cures transformations to ice or other substances.

Curse

Level: 2	Range: Sight	Duration: Varies (see below)	Casting time: 1 round	Save: Will vs. spell check DC

General
The cleric utters a profound curse upon another creature, which always receives a Will save to resist. This spell must be used carefully, for it is considered a powerful act of intervention by one's deity. Uttering severe curses, such as those that affect entire families or communities or which extend across the generations, are considered a sin. Longer rituals entailing longer casting times may be appropriate for more sinister curses. See Appendix C for examples of simple curses with a background beyond game mechanics.

Manifestation
The cleric should articulate the manifestation as he casts the spell. The manifestation can include minor physical changes on the part of the target. For example, "Your hair will remain white for as long as this curse shall last," or "The mark of a sinner shall be visible on your breast for as long as this curse shall last."

1-13 Failure.

14-15 The cleric casts a simple curse on one target that inflicts a -1 Luck penalty for 24 hours.

16-19 The cleric casts a curse on one target that inflicts a -2 Luck penalty and a -1 penalty to one other statistic of the cleric's choice for up to a week. The statistic can be attack rolls, damage rolls, an ability score, saving throws, spell checks, Armor Class, speed (where -1 = -5'), hit points, and so on.

20-21 The cleric casts a curse on one target that inflicts a -2 Luck penalty and a -2 penalty to one other statistic of the cleric's choice for up to a week. The statistic can be attack rolls, damage rolls, an ability score, saving throws, spell checks, Armor Class, speed (where -1 = -5'), hit points, and so on. Alternately, the cleric may choose to invoke a specific physical or mental limitation for one week. For example, the target cannot speak, cannot walk, cannot sleep, cannot see, etc.

22-25 The cleric casts a curse on one target that inflicts a -2 Luck penalty, a -2 penalty to one other statistic, *and* a specific physical or mental limitation (e.g., cannot speak, sleep, see, walk, etc.). The statistic can be attack rolls, damage, an ability score, saving throws, spell checks, Armor Class, speed (where -1 = -5'), hit points, and so on. The duration is *ongoing* until some specific condition is met. The condition must have meaning to the cleric's deity or the target, and it must be within the target's power to achieve (even if very difficult). For example, "you cannot see until you kiss the medusa queen" or "you cannot sleep until you close your eyes beneath the tomb of the sleepless demon."

26-29 The cleric casts a curse on *a group of people*: a family, a community, a village, an adventuring group, etc. The cleric can affect up to 10 people at once as long as they are part of a single defined group. The curse inflicts a -2 Luck penalty, a -2 penalty to one other statistic, *and* a specific physical or mental limitation (e.g., cannot speak, sleep, see, walk, etc.). The statistic can be attack rolls, damage, an ability score, saving throws, spell checks, Armor Class, speed (where -1 = -5'), hit points, and so on. The duration is *ongoing* until some specific condition is met. The condition must have meaning to the cleric's deity or the target, and it must be within the target's power to achieve (even if very difficult). For example, "you cannot see until you kiss the medusa queen" or "you cannot sleep until you close your eyes beneath the tomb of the sleepless demon."

30-31 The cleric casts a curse on *a large group of people*: a family, a community, a village, an adventuring group, residents of a castle, etc. The cleric can affect up to 50 people at once as long as they are part of a single defined group. The curse inflicts a -2 Luck penalty, a -2 penalty to *two* other statistics, *and* a specific physical or mental limitation (e.g., cannot speak, sleep, see, walk, etc.). The statistics can be attack rolls, damage, an ability score, saving throws, spell checks, Armor Class, speed (where -1 = -5'), hit points, and so on. The duration is *ongoing* until some specific condition is met. The condition must have meaning to the cleric's deity or the target, and it must be within the target's power to achieve (even if very difficult). For example, "you cannot see until you kiss the medusa queen" or "you cannot sleep until you close your eyes beneath the tomb of the sleepless demon."

32-33 The cleric casts a curse on *a very large group of people*: a family, a community, a village, an adventuring group, residents of a castle, etc. The cleric can affect up to 100 people at once as long as they are part of a single defined group. The curse inflicts a -4 Luck penalty, a -2 penalty to *three* other statistics, *and* a specific physical or mental limitation (e.g., cannot speak, sleep, see, walk, etc.). The statistic can be attack rolls, damage, an ability score, saving throws, spell checks, Armor Class, speed (where -1 = -5'), hit points, and so on. The duration is *ongoing* until some specific condition is met. The condition must have meaning to the cleric's deity or the target, and it must be within the target's power to achieve (even if very difficult). For example, "you cannot see until you kiss the medusa queen" or "you cannot sleep until you close your eyes beneath the tomb of the sleepless demon."

34+ The cleric casts a curse on *an extremely large group of people*: a family, a community, a village, an adventuring group, residents of a castle, etc. The cleric can affect up to 1,000 people at once as long as they are part of a single defined group. *In addition*, the curse carries on to the heirs of those affected, and propagates through the generations until removed. The curse inflicts a -4 Luck penalty, a -2 penalty to *three* other statistics, *and* a specific physical or mental limitation (e.g., cannot speak, sleep, see, walk, etc.). The statistic can be attack rolls, damage, an ability score, saving throws, spell checks, Armor Class, speed (where -1 = -5'), hit points, and so on. The duration is *ongoing* until some specific condition is met. The condition must have meaning to the cleric's deity or the target, and it must be within the target's power to achieve (even if very difficult). For example, "you cannot see until you kiss the medusa queen" or "you cannot sleep until you close your eyes beneath the tomb of the sleepless demon."

Divine Symbol

Level: 2	Range: Self	Duration: 1d6 rounds or more	Casting time: 1 round	Save: N/A

General	The cleric channels the divine power of his deity into his holy symbol, which becomes a rallying point for the faithful, a weapon of righteousness, and a bane to the unholy.

Manifestation	The cleric holds his holy symbol aloft and utters words of prayer. He is suddenly illuminated in a bright light. Even as the light fades, the cleric's holy symbol burns with a brilliant radiance.

1-13	Failure.
14-15	For a duration of 1d6 rounds, the cleric can attack with his holy symbol as if it were a magical weapon of +1 enchantment. It deals 1d8+1 damage (modified by Str, as usual), with an *additional* +2 damage bonus against unholy creatures.
16-19	For a duration of 2d6+CL rounds, the cleric can attack with his holy symbol as if it were a magical weapon of +1 enchantment. It deals 1d10+1 damage (modified by Str, as usual), with an *additional* +2 damage bonus against unholy creatures.
20-21	For a duration of 2d6+CL rounds, the cleric can attack with his holy symbol as if it were a magical weapon of +2 enchantment. It deals 1d10+2 damage (modified by Str, as usual), with an *additional* +2 damage bonus against unholy creatures. *In addition*, as long as the cleric is visible to his allies and followers, they receive a +1 bonus to saving throws and morale checks.
22-25	For a duration of 3d6+CL rounds, the cleric can attack with his holy symbol as if it were a magical weapon of +2 enchantment. It deals 1d12+2 damage (modified by Str, as usual), with an *additional* +4 damage bonus against unholy creatures. *In addition*, as long as the cleric is visible to his allies and followers, they receive a +1 bonus to saving throws and morale checks.
26-29	For a duration of 3d6+CL rounds, the cleric can attack with his holy symbol as if it were a magical weapon of +2 enchantment. It deals 1d14+2 damage (modified by Str, as usual), with an *additional* +4 damage bonus against unholy creatures. *In addition*, as long as the cleric is visible to his allies and followers, they receive a +1 bonus to saving throws and morale checks. *Finally*, the cleric also receives a +4 bonus to all spell checks to turn unholy while using his holy symbol when under the influence of this spell.
30-31	For a duration of 3d6+CL rounds, the cleric can attack with his holy symbol as if it were a magical weapon of +3 enchantment. It deals 1d16+3 damage (modified by Str, as usual), with an *additional* +4 damage bonus against unholy creatures. *In addition*, as long as the cleric is visible to his allies and followers, they receive a +2 bonus to saving throws and morale checks. *Finally*, the cleric also receives a +4 bonus to all spell checks to turn unholy while using his holy symbol when under the influence of this spell.
32-33	For a duration of 1d6+CL *days*, the cleric can attack with his holy symbol as if it were a magical weapon of +4 enchantment. It deals 1d16+4 damage (modified by Str, as usual), with an *additional* +4 damage bonus against unholy creatures. *In addition*, as long as the cleric is visible to his allies and followers, they receive a +2 bonus to saving throws and morale checks. *Finally*, the cleric also receives a +6 bonus to all spell checks to turn unholy while using his holy symbol when under the influence of this spell.
34+	For a duration of 1d6+CL *days*, the cleric can attack with his holy symbol as if it were a magical weapon of +4 enchantment. It deals 1d20+5 damage (modified by Str, as usual), with an *additional* +4 damage bonus against unholy creatures. *In addition*, as long as the cleric is visible to his allies and followers, they receive a +2 bonus to saving throws and morale checks. *Finally*, the cleric also receives a +6 bonus to all spell checks to turn unholy while using his holy symbol when under the influence of this spell.

Lotus Stare

Level: 2	Range: Sight	Duration: 1 round or more	Casting time: 1 round	Save: Will vs. spell check DC

General	The cleric hypnotizes a target with the incomprehensible depths of the lotus stare.
Manifestation	The cleric's eyes swirl in a kaleidoscopic blur of light and dark. The eyes of affected targets swirl in the same manner.

1-13	Failure.
14-15	Making eye contact with one target, the cleric forces it to stare into the swirling hypnotics of his gaze. The target receives a Will save. If it fails, then as long as the cleric concentrates fully and maintains eye contact, the creature is held immobile and cannot take any action. If eye contact is broken – either voluntarily by the cleric or because the target is severely jostled, blindfolded, or otherwise removed from the cleric's sight – then the target regains its senses and can act as normal.
16-19	Making brief eye contact with one target, the cleric forces it to stare into the swirling hypnotics of his gaze. The target receives a Will save. If it fails, then the cleric can break contact and the target remains hypnotized for 1d6+CL rounds or until the hypnosis is broken. An attack or other physical trauma (including a vigorous shaking by an ally) will break the hypnosis. While the target is hypnotized, it acts on commands issued by the cleric, although it performs them as if a drugged zombie, moving at half-speed and taking a -2 penalty to all actions. The commands can be of any type, even those that are self-destructive. The target is considered to have animal-level intelligence while affected, so its ability to execute complex instructions (or cast spells, if it is a spellcaster) will be inhibited.
20-21	Making brief eye contact with one target, the cleric forces it to stare into the swirling hypnotics of his gaze. The target receives a Will save. If it fails, then the cleric can break contact and the target remains hypnotized for 2d6+CL rounds. The hypnosis cannot be broken by physical means (i.e., an attack or jostling). While the target is hypnotized, it acts on commands issued by the cleric, although it performs them as if a drugged zombie, moving at half-speed and taking a -2 penalty to all actions. The commands can be of any type, even those that are self-destructive. The target is considered to have animal-level intelligence while affected, so its ability to execute complex instructions (or cast spells, if it is a spellcaster) will be inhibited.
22-25	Making brief eye contact with one target, the cleric forces it to stare into the swirling hypnotics of his gaze. The target receives a Will save. If it fails, then the cleric can break contact and the target remains hypnotized for 1d4+CL *days*. The hypnosis cannot be broken by physical means (i.e., an attack or jostling). While the target is hypnotized, it acts on commands issued by the cleric, although it performs them as if a drugged zombie, moving at half-speed and taking a -2 penalty to all actions. The commands can be of any type, even those that are self-destructive for the target. The target is considered to have animal-level intelligence while affected, so its ability to execute complex instructions (or cast spells, if it is a spellcaster) will be inhibited. The target receives a fresh Will save each day to end the effect before the spell's duration expires.
26-29	Making brief eye contact with multiple targets, the cleric forces them to stare into the swirling hypnotics of his gaze. The cleric can affect up to 10 targets in a "gaze cone" up to 40' long and 40' wide at its endpoint. The targets receive a Will save. For any target that fails, the cleric can break contact and the target remains hypnotized for 1d8+CL *days*. The hypnosis cannot be broken by physical means (i.e., an attack or jostling). While the target is hypnotized, it acts on commands issued by the cleric, although it performs them as if a drugged zombie, moving at half-speed and taking a -2 penalty to all actions. The commands can be of any type, even those that are self-destructive. The target is considered to have animal-level intelligence while affected, so its ability to execute complex instructions (or cast spells, if it is a spellcaster) will be inhibited. The target receives a fresh Will save each day to end the effect before the spell's duration expires.
30-31	Making brief eye contact with multiple targets, the cleric forces them to stare into the swirling hypnotics of his gaze. The cleric can affect up to 10 targets in a "gaze cone" up to 40' long and 40' wide at its endpoint. The targets receive a Will save. For any target that fails, the cleric can break contact and the target remains hypnotized for 1d8+CL *weeks*. The hypnosis cannot be broken by physical means (i.e., an attack or jostling). While the target is hypnotized, it acts on commands issued by the cleric, although it performs them as if a drugged zombie, moving at half-speed and taking a -2 penalty to all actions. The commands can be of any type, even those that are self-destructive. The target is considered to have animal-level intelligence

while affected, so its ability to execute complex instructions (or cast spells, if it is a spellcaster) will be inhibited. The target receives a fresh Will save each day to end the effect before the spell's duration expires.

32-33	Making brief eye contact with multiple targets, the cleric forces them to stare into the swirling hypnotics of his gaze. The cleric can affect up to 20 targets in a "gaze cone" up to 80′ long and 80′ wide at its endpoint. The targets receive a Will save. For any target that fails, the cleric can break contact and the target remains hypnotized for 1d8+CL *weeks*. The hypnosis cannot be broken by physical means (i.e., an attack or jostling). While the target is hypnotized, it acts on commands issued by the cleric to the best of its normal, non-hypnotized ability. Targets move at normal speed and take no penalties to their actions while hypnotized. They retain their normal intelligence and can cast spells as normal (if applicable). However, they are still obviously hypnotized, for their eyes swirl with the strange patterns of the lotus. The target receives a fresh Will save each *week* to end the effect before the spell's duration expires.
34+	Making brief eye contact with multiple targets, the cleric forces them to stare into the swirling hypnotics of his gaze. The cleric can affect *all* targets in a "gaze cone" up to 80′ long and 80′ wide at its endpoint. Creatures of 2 HD or less are automatically affected; other targets receive a Will save. For affected targets, the cleric can break contact and the target remains hypnotized for 1d8+CL *weeks*. The hypnosis cannot be broken by physical means (i.e., an attack or jostling). While the target is hypnotized, it acts on commands issued by the cleric to the best of its normal, non-hypnotized ability. Targets move at normal speed and take no penalties to their actions while hypnotized. They retain their normal intelligence and can cast spells as normal (if applicable). However, they are still obviously hypnotized, for their eyes swirl with the strange patterns of the lotus. The target receives a fresh Will save each *week* to end the effect before the spell's duration expires.

Neutralize Poison or Disease

Level: 2	Range: Touch or further	Duration: Permanent	Casting time: 1 round	Save: N/A

General	This spell stabilizes further disruption from poison or disease and may reverse existing effects. The cleric may cast this spell on himself or someone he touches. While the effects of poisons are easily distinguished, some diseases may be fairly complex in nature and their "effects" may not be clear. The judge should adjudicate which are reasonably cured by this spell and which are not.
Manifestation	Roll 1d4: (1) the target is cured with no visible effect; (2) the target is cured and the mark of the cleric's deity appears as a birthmark or small scar in a place that was previously affected by the poison or disease; (3) the blinding rays of heavenly light shine forth on the target, making him feel an intense and almost painful heat, burning off the toxins that infest his body; (4) the target's skin peels instantaneously, as with a severe sunburn, and as the old skin sloughs off the new skin beneath appears younger and healthier as the toxins are removed.
1-13	Failure.
14-15	The cleric retards the subsequent effects of *one* poison or disease that is affecting the target and removes the remaining dosage or effect from the target's system. Any effects suffered already cannot be reversed. For example, an ally that has lost 3 points of Strength to an ongoing disease may stop future Strength loss, but the existing loss is not recovered.
16-19	The cleric retards the subsequent effects of *one* poison or disease that is affecting the target and removes the remaining dosage or effect from the target's system. In addition, any effects suffered already are reversed over the same time frame under which they were first suffered. However, a creature that has already been killed by the poison or disease is not brought back to life. For example, an ally that lost 3 points of Strength over the course of three weeks to an ongoing disease will recover those lost points over the next three weeks.
20-21	The target receives a +2 bonus to Fort saves to resist poison or disease for the next day. Additionally, the cleric retards the subsequent effects of *one* poison or disease that is affecting the target and removes the remaining dosage or effect from the target's system. In addition, any effects suffered already are reversed over the same time frame under which they were first suffered. However, a creature that has already been killed by the poison or disease is not brought back to life. For example, an ally that lost 3 points of Strength over the course of three weeks to an ongoing disease will recover those lost points over the next three weeks.

22-25	The target receives a +4 bonus to Fort saves to resist poison or disease for the next day. Additionally, the cleric retards the subsequent effects of *two* poisons or diseases that are affecting the target and removes the remaining dosage or effect from the target's system. In addition, any effects suffered already are reversed over the same time frame under which they were first suffered. However, a creature that has already been killed by the poison or disease is not brought back to life. For example, an ally that lost 3 points of Strength over the course of three weeks to an ongoing disease will recover those lost points over the next three weeks.
26-29	The cleric can lead a prayer in which up to 4 other creatures can participate. All creatures praying must link hands with each other and form a circle that terminates in the cleric's grasp. Those that pray with the cleric are completely cured of *all* poisons or diseases affecting them, and the poisons and diseases are removed from their systems. In addition, any effects suffered already are reversed over the same time frame under which they were first suffered. However, a creature that has already been killed by the poison or disease is not brought back to life. For example, an ally that lost 3 points of Strength over the course of three weeks to an ongoing disease will recover those lost points over the next three weeks. Finally, all allies participating in the prayer receive a +4 bonus to resist poisons and diseases for the next *week*.
30-31	The cleric can lead a prayer in which up to 12 other creatures can participate. All creatures praying must link hands with each other and form a circle that terminates in the cleric's grasp. All creatures that pray with the cleric are completely cured of *all* poisons or diseases affecting them, and the poisons and diseases are removed from their systems. In addition, any effects suffered already are reversed *over the course of the next 24 hours*. However, a creature that has already been killed by the poison or disease is not brought back to life. Finally, all allies participating in the prayer are completely immune to all terrestrial poisons and diseases for the next week and receive a +4 bonus to resist supernatural or magical poisons and diseases for the next *week*.
32-33	The cleric can lead a prayer in which up to 50 other creatures can participate. All creatures praying must link hands with each other and form a circle that terminates in the cleric's grasp. All creatures that pray with the cleric are completely cured of *all* poisons or diseases affecting them, and the poisons and diseases are removed from their systems. In addition, any effects suffered already are reversed *over the course of the next 24 hours*. However, a creature that has already been killed by the poison or disease is not brought back to life. Finally, all allies participating in the prayer are completely immune to *all* poisons and diseases for the next *month*.
34+	The cleric can lead a prayer in which up to 200 other creatures can participate. All creatures praying must be within the cleric's line of sight. All creatures that pray with the cleric are completely cured of *all* poisons or diseases affecting them, and the poisons and diseases are removed from their systems. In addition, any effects suffered already are reversed *immediately*. However, a creature that has already been killed by the poison or disease is not brought back to life. Finally, all allies participating in the prayer are completely immune to *all* poisons and diseases for the next *month*.

Restore Vitality

Level: 2	Range: Touch or further	Duration: Permanent	Casting time: 1 turn	Save: N/A

| General | The cleric restores lost vitality to a creature. Typically this restores lost ability scores or broken/severed limbs, though it can also heal. This spell cannot restore lost Luck. The spell can be cast on the cleric or an ally.

In playtests, some groups attempted to combine this spell with a wizard's spellburn to create a "one-two combo" – the wizard would burn points for spellburn, the cleric would immediately restore those points, then the wizard would burn those points again. Although legal within the letter of the rules, it is important that the judge recall that DCC RPG is a game where magic is *not* an act of chemistry; it is an invocation of the wills of supernatural creatures. Cleric magic is the act of divine creatures, and wizard magic is frequently the result of deals, agreements, and arrangements with demons, devils, ghosts, and supernatural patrons. Using *restore vitality* to offset spellburn will inevitably create trouble for the cleric, whose deity surely does not appreciate his power being used to heal wounds deliberately created to further the ends of *another* supernatural creature! |
|---|---|

Manifestation	Roll 1d3: (1) the target is cured with no visible effect; (2) the target is cured and the mark of the cleric's deity appears as birthmark or small scar in a place that was previously affected by the ability loss; (3) a shaft of heavenly light shines on the target, bathing him in light as his ability scores are restored.

1-13	Failure.
14-15	The cleric restores ability score drain that is non-permanent in nature. Whether caused by spellburn, monster attack, broken limbs, or other means, the spell restores 1 point of temporarily lost Strength, Stamina, Agility, Intelligence, or Personality. The ability score cannot be increased higher than the target's original maximum. Alternately, the cleric can heal 1 hit point of damage, up to the target's maximum.
16-19	The cleric restores ability score drain that is non-permanent in nature. Whether caused by spellburn, monster attack, broken limbs, or other means, the spell restores 2 points of temporarily lost Strength, Stamina, Agility, Intelligence, or Personality. The ability score cannot be increased higher than the target's original maximum. Alternately, the cleric can heal 4 hit points of damage, up to the target's maximum. The cleric cannot combine healing ability scores and hit points.
20-21	The cleric restores ability score drain, even if it is permanent in nature. Whether caused by spellburn, monster attack, broken limbs, or other means, the spell restores 1d4+CL points of lost Strength, Stamina, Agility, Intelligence, or Personality. If the restoration is associated with an injury, the injury is also healed. For example, if the lost Strength was from a broken limb or a severed hand, that limb is restored to functionality, provided the severed body parts were retained. The ability score cannot be increased higher than the target's original maximum. Alternately, the cleric can heal 2d4+CL hit points of damage, up to the target's maximum. The cleric cannot combine healing ability scores and hit points.
22-25	The cleric restores ability score drain, even if it is permanent in nature, *and* heals 2d6+CL lost hit points. Whether caused by spellburn, monster attack, broken limbs, or other means, the spell restores 1d6+CL points of lost Strength, Stamina, Agility, Intelligence, or Personality. If the restoration is associated with an injury, the injury is also healed. For example, if the lost Strength was from a broken limb or a severed hand, that limb is restored to functionality, provided the severed body parts were retained. The ability score cannot be increased higher than the target's original maximum.
26-29	The cleric restores ability score drain, even if it is permanent in nature, *and* heals 3d6+CL lost hit points. Whether caused by spellburn, monster attack, broken limbs, or other means, the spell restores 1d8+CL points of lost Strength, Stamina, Agility, Intelligence, or Personality. If the restoration is associated with an injury, the injury is also healed. For example, if the lost Strength was from a broken limb or a severed hand, that limb is restored to functionality, provided the severed body parts were retained. The ability score cannot be increased higher than the target's original maximum.
30-31	The cleric may designate up to four targets within 30' range. For all targets, the cleric restores ability score drain, even if it is permanent in nature, *and* heals 4d6+CL lost hit points. Whether caused by spellburn, monster attack, broken limbs, or other means, the spell restores 3d4+CL points of lost Strength, Stamina, Agility, Intelligence, or Personality. If the restoration is associated with an injury, the injury is also healed. For example, if the lost Strength was from a broken limb or a severed hand, that limb is restored to functionality, provided the severed body parts were retained. The ability score cannot be increased higher than the target's original maximum.
32-33	The cleric may designate up to 10 targets within 60' range. For all targets, the cleric restores *all* ability score drain, even if it is permanent in nature, *and* heals all creatures to their full hit point totals. Whether caused by spellburn, monster attack, broken limbs, or other means, the spell restores all points of lost Strength, Stamina, Agility, Intelligence, and Personality. If the restoration is associated with an injury, the injury is also healed. For example, if the lost Strength was from a broken limb or a severed hand, that limb is restored to functionality, provided the severed body parts were retained. The ability score cannot be increased higher than the target's original maximum.
34+	The cleric targets a single creature within 30'. It is restored to its full and perfect health: hit points are restored to maximum, ability scores are restored to their normal levels, and the creature is cured of all disease, illness, and infection, whether mundane or supernatural in origin. The creature is cured of any health problems not associated with its natural state, provided the body's functionality still exists. For example, if temporarily blinded, it has its sight restored; if deafened, it can now hear; if lamed, it can now walk. Lost limbs *do* re-grow, and defects caused by physical means (e.g. blindness caused by the plucking of eyeballs from the skull) *are* corrected, even if the missing body parts are not at hand. In addition, the creature permanently gains +1 hit point to its maximum total. This benefit may be received multiple times, but for each hit point permanently gifted to a single target *after* the first, the cleric permanently loses 1 hit point.

Snake Charm

Level: 2   **Range:** 30′ or more   **Duration:** Varies   **Casting time:** 1 round   **Save:** Will vs. spell check DC (sometimes)

General	The cleric can control snakes within his presence or potentially summon snakes to do his bidding. The snakes will threaten, guard, attack, or otherwise behave as commanded.
Manifestation	Roll 1d4: affected snakes (1) are surrounded in a shimmering blue aura, which also surrounds the cleric; (2) seem to have their faces change shape to resemble that of the cleric; (3) have their scales change into a colorful pattern reminiscent of the cleric's clothes or hair color/style; (4) turn pitch black.

1-13	Failure.
14-15	Nearby snakes acknowledge the cleric as their friend and ally. The range is 30′. Mundane snakes up to 2 HD are affected automatically. Mundane snakes of 3 HD or more, as well as supernatural snake-like creatures up to 4 HD (such as naga, medusae, snake-men, and so on) receive a Will save to resist. Snake-like creatures of 5 HD or more are not affected. Affected creatures will not attack the cleric under any circumstances. They do not actively assist the cleric, but will not impede his passing. When the cleric passes more than 30′ from any affected creature, it returns to its former attitude regarding him.
16-19	Nearby snakes submit to the cleric as their master. They obey the cleric's bidding and fight on his behalf. The range is 100′. The effect takes hold automatically on mundane snakes up to 3 HD. Larger mundane snakes and all other snake-like creatures receive a Will save to resist. Affected creatures will take simple actions on the cleric's behalf, such as "guard" or "attack." They continue to obey until the cleric is out of their sight or for 1 hour, whichever comes first.
20-21	Nearby snakes submit to the cleric as their master. They obey the cleric's bidding and fight on his behalf. The range is 100′. The effect takes hold automatically on mundane snakes up to 3 HD. Larger mundane snakes and all other snake-like creatures receive a Will save to resist. Affected creatures will take simple actions on the cleric's behalf, such as "guard" or "attack." They continue to obey until the cleric is out of their sight or for 1 day, whichever comes first.
22-25	The spell summons one friendly snake of up to 2 HD, and additionally causes nearby snakes to submit to the cleric as their master. They obey the cleric's bidding and fight on his behalf. The range is 100′. The effect takes hold automatically on mundane snakes up to 3 HD. Larger mundane snakes and all other snake-like creatures receive a Will save to resist. Affected creatures will take simple actions on the cleric's behalf, such as "guard" or "attack." They continue to obey until the cleric is out of their sight or for 1 day, whichever comes first. The summoned snake is AC 14, has 2d8 HD, and a bite at +4 attack for 1d6 damage that also inflicts a poison (DC 12 Fort or suffer one effect; choose from: 1d4 Strength loss, 1d4 Agility loss, 1d4 Stamina loss, blindness, sleep, or half-movement). The snake can be summoned to any point within the cleric's line of sight. The snake is permanently summoned; it is simply transported here from elsewhere on the planet.
26-29	The spell summons 1d4+1 friendly snakes of up to 2 HD, and additionally causes nearby snakes to submit to the cleric as their master. They obey the cleric's bidding and fight on his behalf. The range is 100′. The effect takes hold automatically on mundane snakes up to 3 HD. Larger mundane snakes and all other snake-like creatures receive a Will save to resist. Affected creatures will take simple actions on the cleric's behalf, such as "guard" or "attack." They continue to obey for one full day, even if the cleric leaves their sight. The summoned snakes are AC 14, have 2d8 HD, and a bite at +4 attack for 1d6 damage that also inflicts a poison (DC 12 Fort or suffer one effect; choose from: 1d4 Strength loss, 1d4 Agility loss, 1d4 Stamina loss, blindness, sleep, or half-movement). The snakes can be summoned to any point within the cleric's line of sight. The snakes are permanently summoned; they are simply transported here from elsewhere on the planet.
30-31	The spell summons 2d4+CL friendly snakes of up to 2 HD, or 1d4+1 large snakes of 5 HD, and additionally causes nearby snakes to submit to the cleric as their master. They will obey the cleric's bidding and fight on his behalf. The range is 100′. The effect takes hold automatically on mundane snakes up to 3 HD. Larger mundane snakes and all other snake-like creatures receive a Will save to resist. Affected creatures will take simple actions on the cleric's behalf, such as "guard" or "attack." They continue to obey for one full day, even if the cleric leaves their sight.

The summoned snakes are AC 14 and have 2d8 or 5d8 HD. Depending on their Hit Dice, they have a bite attack (2HD: +4 for 1d6 damage; 5HD: +8 for 3d6 damage). The bite also inflicts poison (DC 12 Fort or suffer one effect; choose from: 1d4 Strength loss, 1d4 Agility loss, 1d4 Stamina loss, blindness, sleep, or half-movement). The snakes can be summoned to any point within the cleric's line of sight. The snakes are permanently summoned; they are simply transported here from elsewhere on the planet.

32-33   The spell summons 2d4+CL friendly snakes of up to 2 HD, or 1d4+1 large snakes of 5 HD, and additionally causes nearby snakes to submit to the cleric as their master. They will obey the cleric's bidding and fight on his behalf. The range is 100'. The effect takes hold automatically on mundane snakes up to 3 HD. Larger mundane snakes and all other snake-like creatures receive a Will save to resist. Affected creatures will take simple actions on the cleric's behalf, such as "guard" or "attack." They continue to obey for one full *week*, even if the cleric leaves their sight.

The summoned snakes are AC 14 and have 2d8 or 5d8 HD. Depending on their Hit Dice, they have a bite attack (2HD: +4 for 1d6 damage; 5HD: +8 for 3d6 damage). The bite also inflicts poison (DC 12 Fort or suffer one effect; choose from: 1d4 Strength loss, 1d4 Agility loss, 1d4 Stamina loss, blindness, sleep, or half-movement). The snakes can be summoned to any point within the cleric's line of sight. The snakes are permanently summoned; they are simply transported here from elsewhere on the planet.

34+   The spell summons 2d4+CL friendly snakes of up to 2 HD, or 1d4+1 large snakes of 5 HD, and additionally causes nearby snakes to submit to the cleric as their master. They will obey the cleric's bidding and fight on his behalf. The range is 100'. The effect takes hold automatically on mundane snakes up to 3 HD. Larger mundane snakes and all other snake-like creatures receive a Will save to resist. Affected creatures will take simple actions on the cleric's behalf, such as "guard" or "attack." The duration is indefinite unless magically dispelled – the targets forever regard the cleric as a friend.

The summoned snakes are AC 14 and have 2d8 or 5d8 HD. Depending on their Hit Dice, they have a bite attack (2HD: +4 for 1d6 damage; 5HD: +8 for 3d6 damage). The bite also inflicts poison (DC 12 Fort or suffer one effect; choose from: 1d4 Strength loss, 1d4 Agility loss, 1d4 Stamina loss, blindness, sleep, or half-movement). The snakes can be summoned to any point within the cleric's line of sight. The snakes are permanently summoned; they are simply transported here from elsewhere on the planet.

Stinging Stone

Level: 2   Range: Objects touched   Duration: See below   Casting time: 1 turn   Save: Fort vs. spell check DC

General

The cleric transforms an object into a poisonous creature. For example, the cleric can change a sling stone into a spider, an arrow to an asp, or a staff into a serpent. The specifics are as follows:

- At low levels of effect (see below), the cleric can transform a small object into a poisonous spider. The object can be a coin, gem, sling stone, apple, beer mug, or other such small thing. The spell descriptions below assume a sling stone is used. For the spell's duration, the object retains its natural shape until it touches an enemy. So, for example, the cleric can hide a gemstone in a chest, which transforms into a spider when grasped; or launch an attack with his sling, and the stone transforms into a spider or scorpion when it strikes the enemy. Once the object touches an enemy (either through their grasp or via a successful hit as with a sling stone), it transforms into a spider, which remains for a certain amount of time. The spider receives one bite immediately on the round of attack and one additional bite each round until the spell ends. (A missed sling stone does not transform.) It reverts to its natural shape at the end of the spell. The poisonous spider is AC 14 (due to small size and agility) and has only 1 hp, but immediately scurries toward exposed flesh and strikes the enemy. On the first bite, the spider's attack automatically hits, causing damage 1 + poison. The target must make a Fort save against the spell check DC or suffer poison as per a (roll 1d3) (1) black widow; (2) tarantula; or (3) scorpion (see Appendix P). On future rounds the spider must make an attack roll at Atk +2 in order to inflict damage. Note that the spider continues to scurry about and bite for the duration of the spell. Strikes against it that miss have a 50% chance of hitting the spell's target for damage.

- At medium levels of effect (see below), the cleric can transform an arrow into an asp or adder. (He could also transform other similarly shaped objects into an asp or adder: a stick of wood, a lever, a metal rod, etc.) As above, the object retains its natural shape until it touches an enemy, at which point it transforms. The asp or adder receives one bite immediately on the round of attack and one additional bite each round until the spell ends. The first bite automatically hits, causing damage 2 + poison. The target must make a Fort save against the spell check DC or suffer the poison of an asp or adder (see Appendix P). On future rounds the snake must make an attack roll at Atk +4 in order to inflict damage. Note that the snake continues to slither about and bite for the duration of the spell. Strikes against it that miss have a 50% chance of hitting the spell's target for damage.

- At the highest levels of effect (see below), the cleric can transform a staff into a cobra or viper. (He could also transform other similarly shaped objects into a cobra: a tree branch, a pole arm, etc.) In this case, each time the cleric strikes with the staff, it transforms into a serpent, bites, and then transforms back into a staff. The serpent-staff is treated as a +4 magical weapon, so it attacks at the cleric's normal attack bonus with an additional +4 modifier. Any successful attack causes normal weapon damage, +4 for the magical modifier, and inflicts poison as per a cobra or viper strike (see Appendix P). The Fort save against the poison is the spell check result. If the cleric strikes with the staff and then releases it, the staff remains in serpent form and continues to attack with its bite for the duration of the spell; in this case, it attacks at Atk +6 and inflicts damage of 1d4+4 plus poison.

In all cases, the transformed spider or serpent is wild and uncontrolled. It will not obey commands from the cleric. An arrow that transforms into an asp, for example, cannot be commanded to return to the cleric after killing its target. It will simply slither off like any wild snake.

Manifestation   The object does not change in appearance but transforms at a touch.

1-13	Failure.
14-15	The cleric can transform a single small object, up to the size of a sling stone, into a poisonous spider. For a duration of 1d4+CL turns, the object retains its natural shape until it touches an enemy. Once it touches an enemy, it remains in spider form for 2 rounds.
16-19	The cleric can transform a single small object, up to the size of a sling stone, into a poisonous spider. For a duration of 1d4+CL days, the object retains its natural shape until it touches an enemy. Once it touches an enemy, it remains in spider form for 1d4+CL rounds.
20-21	The cleric can transform up to 5 small objects, up to the size of sling stones, into poisonous spiders. *Or* he can transform a single arrow into an asp or adder (see Appendix P). For a duration of 1d4+CL days, the

objects retain their natural shapes until they touch an enemy. Once an object touches an enemy, it remains in spider or snake form for 1d4+CL rounds.

22-25   The cleric can transform up to 10 small objects, up to the size of sling stones, into poisonous spiders. *Or* he can transform up to three arrows into an asps or adders (see Appendix P). For a duration of 1d4+CL days, the objects retain their natural shapes until they touch an enemy. Once an object touches an enemy, it remains in spider or snake form for 1d4+CL rounds.

26-29   The cleric can transform up to 25 sling stones into poisonous spiders, up to 10 arrows into asps or adders, or a single staff into a cobra or viper. For a duration of 1d4+CL days, the objects retain their natural shape until they touch an enemy. Once they touch an enemy, they remain in spider or snake form for 1d6+CL rounds.

30-31   The cleric can transform up to 25 sling stones into poisonous spiders, up to 10 arrows into asps or adders, or a single staff into a cobra or viper. For a duration of 1d4+CL *weeks*, the objects retain their natural shape until they touch an enemy. Once they touch an enemy, they remain in spider or snake form for 2d6+CL rounds.

32-33   The cleric can transform up to 50 sling stones into poisonous spiders, up to 20 arrows into asps or adders, or up to two staves into cobras or vipers. For a duration of 1d4+CL *weeks*, the objects retain their natural shape until they touch an enemy. Once they touch an enemy, they remain in spider or snake form for 3d6+CL rounds.

34+   The cleric can transform up to 100 sling stones into poisonous spiders, up to 40 arrows into asps or adders, or up to four staves into cobras or vipers. For a duration of 1d8+CL *weeks*, the objects retain their natural shape until they touch an enemy. Once they touch an enemy, they remain in spider or snake form for 3d6+CL rounds.

Alternately, the cleric can transform a single object *permanently*. Specify a single sling stone, arrow, or staff. It is permanently subject to transformation, as noted above. When it changes form into a spider or serpent, it stays in that form for the normal duration of 3d6+CL rounds, then reverts to its natural state until triggered again. If the "object" is killed while in serpent or spider form, it remains in its dead state and its magical properties are lost.

Wood Wyrding

| Level: 2 | Range: 30' + 5' per CL | Duration: Varies | Casting time: 1 round | Save: None |

General

The cleric destroys the functionality of wooden objects, rendering them useless or causing them to attack their owners.

Manifestation

Roll 1d4: (1) the target object(s) is limned with colored radiance appropriate to the cleric's deity; (2) the cleric's fingers temporarily become stick-like and leafed; (3) the smell of fresh-cut wood and fallen leaves fills the air around the cleric; (4) protoplasmic vines coil around the target object(s).

1-13

Failure.

14-15

The cleric causes a wooden object 5' square or smaller to bend and warp, destroying its functionality. Shutters spring open, arrows and spears become bent and useless, affected melee weapons impart a -4 penalty to attack rolls, chest lids pop open, etc.

16-19

The cleric causes a wooden object 10' square or smaller to bend and warp, destroying its functionality. Doors become jammed in their frames, small boats spring leaks, wagon wheels warp, etc. The cleric can affect multiple, smaller, wooden objects as long as they do not exceed the affected size in total.

20-21

The cleric causes a wooden object 20' square or smaller to bend and warp, destroying its functionality. Bridges break, roofs collapse, walls buckle, sailing ships spring leaks, etc. The cleric can affect multiple, smaller, wooden objects as long as they do not exceed the affected size in total.

22-25

The cleric causes a number of small wooden objects equal to his level to suddenly sprout long, sharp thorns that inflict 1d6+CL damage to any creature carrying, wearing, or otherwise touching the affected objects. Carried objects are automatically dropped. The affected objects cannot be larger than a spear or shield. Magical wooden objects are unaffected.

26-29

The cleric changes one wodden item per CL (of spear size or smaller) into a serpent that attacks other creatures as commanded by the cleric. Magical wooden objects are unaffected. Each serpent has the following stats: Init +1; Atk bite +2 melee (dmg 1d3+CL), AC 12, HD 1d8+CL; MV 30'; SV Fort +3, Ref +4, Will +2, AL N. In addition, there is a cumulative 5% per CL that the serpents are venomous (DC 12 Fort or 1d3 Stamina).

30-31

The cleric changes one wooden item per CL (of spear size or smaller) into an even larger serpent that attacks other creatures as commanded by the cleric. Magical wooden objects are unaffected. Each serpent has the following stats: Init +3; Atk bite +4 melee (dmg 1d6+CL), AC 14, HD 2d8+CL; MV 30'; SV Fort +4, Ref +6, Will +2, AL N. In addition, there is a cumulative 10% per CL that the serpents are venomous (DC 14 Fort or death).

32-33

The cleric has terrifying command over wooden objects. He may warp objects the size of tall trees, destroying wooden palisades, collapsing massive bridges, causing catapults and siege towers to fail spectacularly, etc. Moreover, using the same warped wood, he can transform any sufficiently shaped segment of the destroyed object (such as a fallen tree, log, or beam) into a titanic serpent with the stats of a giant boa constrictor (see Appendix P) that obeys his commands.

34+

With a startling invocation, the cleric invokes the power of his deity to destroy all wooden objects near him. To a range of 100' per CL, he causes all wood to instantaneously rot, leaving nothing but spongy powder behind. Even magical wood may be affected, with a chance of 5% per CL. This spell effectively disarms armed troops wielding spears, bows & arrows, or other wooden weapons; destroys wood-frame homes, possibly crushing those within; causes entire wooden palisades to vanish; sinks fleets of ships; and causes other spectacular effects.

LEVEL 3 CLERIC SPELLS

Animate Dead

Level: 3	Range: Touch	Duration: Varies	Casting time: 1 action	Save: N/A

General	The cleric calls upon the power of his deity to animate the rotted flesh and aged bones of slain creatures, creating mindless minions to serve his will and vex his enemies.
	The number of un-dead and type created is determined by the spell check and the number and type of dead creatures available; i.e., a cleric can create skeletons from bare bones but needs a complete corpse to create a zombie. He cannot create more of either type than he has "raw materials" available regardless of the spell check (e.g., creating five skeletons when only three sets of bones are present).
	The un-dead remain animated and under the cleric's control for an hour or more, depending on the spell check. When the spell duration ends, the un-dead collapse into the raw materials from which they were created.
	No cleric can control more than 4x his CL in Hit Dice of un-dead at any given time, but the cleric can "release" controlled un-dead to command other, possibly more powerful un-dead. Uncontrolled un-dead are likely to turn on their former master, however, so the cleric should be careful when releasing un-dead from his command.
	The player should reference the statistics of un-dead given later in this book for a sense of what can be created with this spell, but these should serve as guidelines not limitations. The typical humanoid corpse will produce a 1 HD skeleton or a 3 HD zombie. But there are more powerful skeletons to be created by using the bones of a giant. This work includes stats for the following un-dead, and of course a creative cleric may animate additional types of his own design: ghost (page 413), ghoul (page 416), mummy (page 422), shadow (page 425), skeleton (page 426), and zombie (page 431).

Manifestation	The air fills with the stench of corruption as the dead rise at the cleric's touch.

1-15	Failure.
16	The cleric creates a single skeleton of up to 1 HD, provided the necessary raw materials are present. The skeleton remains animated for a full day.
17	The cleric creates a single zombie or skeleton of up to 3 HD, provided the necessary raw materials are present. The un-dead remains animated for a full day.
18-21	The cleric creates a number of skeletons *or* zombies (one or the other) equal to his CL in Hit Dice. For example, a level 5 cleric could create five skeletons (5 HD) or a single zombie (3 HD). If multiple corpses are available, the cleric must choose which type of un-dead he is creating; he cannot animate both skeletons and zombies with a single casting of the spell. Excess Hit Dice have no effect if they exceed the number of available corpses. The un-dead remain animated for a full week.
22-23	The cleric creates a number of skeletons or zombies equal to 2x his CL in Hit Dice. For example, a level 5 cleric could create 10 skeletons (10 HD) or 3 zombies (9 HD). If multiple corpses are available, the cleric must choose which type of un-dead he is creating; he cannot animate both skeletons and zombies with a single casting of the spell. Excess Hit Dice have no effect if they exceed the number of available corpses. The un-dead remain animated for a full month.
24-26	The cleric creates a number of skeletons or zombies equal to 2x his CL in Hit Dice. For example, a level 5 cleric could create 10 skeletons (10 HD) or 3 zombies (9 HD). If multiples types are available, the cleric can produce a *mixture* of un-dead provided their combined Hit Dice do not exceed 2x his CL or the number of available corpses. In the example above, the level 5 cleric could create three zombies (3 HD x 3 = 9 HD) and one skeleton (1 HD), or two zombies (3 HD x 2 = 6 HD) and four skeletons (1 HD x 4 = 4 HD). Excess Hit Dice have no effect if they exceed the number of available corpses. The un-dead remain animated for a full month.
27-31	The cleric creates a number of more formidable skeletons and zombies equal to 3x his CL in Hit Dice. He can choose to animate the mortal remains of *larger creatures*, creating skeletons and zombies with above-average HD. For example, a 5th level cleric could animate the skeletal remains of a giant lizard (3 HD)

to create a 3 HD skeleton, or revivify a dead ogre (4 HD) to make a 4 HD zombie. He cannot animate a single creature with more Hit Dice in life than 2x his CL. If multiple corpses are available, the cleric can produce a mixture of un-dead provided their combined HD do not exceed his CL or the number of available corpses. These advanced un-dead retain none of their special abilities or movement means they possessed in life (no flight, breath weapons, etc.). The judge can rule that certain monster-types (demons, laboratory-born monstrosities, etc.) are exempt from reanimation. The un-dead remain animated for a full year.

32-33   The cleric creates a number of un-dead equal to 3x times his CL in Hit Dice. He may create any sort of unintelligent un-dead, provided the raw materials are available. This includes mummies, ghouls, ghosts, shadows, and other creatures, but excludes liches and vampires. He can also choose to animate the mortal remains of *larger creatures*, creating skeletons and zombies with above-average HD. For example, a 5th level cleric could animate the skeletal remains of a giant lizard (3 HD) to create a 3 HD skeleton, or revivify a dead ogre (4 HD) to make a 4 HD zombie. He cannot animate a single creature with more Hit Dice in life than 3x the cleric's CL. If multiple corpses are available, the cleric can produce a *mixture* of un-dead provided their combined Hit Dice do not exceed three times his CL or the number of available corpses. Excess Hit Dice have no effect if they exceed the number of available corpses. The un-dead remain animated for a full year.

34-35   The cleric creates a number of un-dead equal to 4x times his CL in Hit Dice. He may create any sort of unintelligent un-dead, provided the raw materials are available. This includes mummies, ghouls, ghosts, shadows, and other creatures, but excludes liches and vampires. He can also choose to animate the mortal remains of *larger creatures*, creating skeletons and zombies with above-average HD. For example, a 5th level cleric could animate the skeletal remains of a troll (8 HD) to create an 8 HD skeleton or revivify a dead dragon (15 HD) to make a 15 HD zombie. He cannot animate a single creature with more Hit Dice in life than 3x the cleric's CL. These advanced un-dead retain none of their special abilities or movement means they possessed in life (no flight, breath weapons, etc.). The judge can rule that certain monster-types (demons, laboratory-born monstrosities, etc.) are exempt from reanimation. If multiple corpse types are available, the cleric can produce a *mixture* of un-dead provided their combined Hit Dice do not exceed three times his CL or the number of available corpses. Excess Hit Dice have no effect if they exceed the number of available corpses. The un-dead remain animated *permanently* until killed or released from control.

36+   The cleric creates terrifying un-dead. He can animate any kind of un-dead, including intelligent un-dead such as liches and vampires, provided the raw materials are present and the correct rituals are performed. The created un-dead can be up to 4x his CL in Hit Dice. He can choose to animate the mortal remains of larger creatures, creating skeletons and zombies with above-average HD. If multiple corpse types are available, the cleric can produce a mixture of un-dead provided their combined Hit Dice do not exceed 4x his CL or the number of available corpses. In addition to their normal un-dead abilities and resistances, these animated dead can have strange traits. The character can pre-determine these traits with sufficient research, materials, and preparation, or the judge can roll to determine them randomly (e.g., refer to the table of special properties tables for skeletons on page 427). Animated dead of this type also retain special movement means at the judge's discretion. For example, a zombie dragon could still fly on rotting wings, but a skeletal one lacking wing membranes could not. The un-dead remain animated *permanently* until killed or released from control.

Bolt from the Blue

Level: 3	Range: 100′	Duration: 1 round	Casting time: 1 action	Save: See below

General	The cleric calls down divine vengeance upon those who stand in the way of his deity's agenda, causing physical and mental anguish, loss of ability scores, and other debilitating results.
Manifestation	A bolt of divine fire streaks down upon the enemies of the cleric's faith.

1-15	Failure.
16-17	A single bolt streaks down to strike one target of the cleric's choice within range. The bolt does 1d6 points of damage and the victim must make a successful Fort save or temporarily lose a single point from one of its abilities (determined by the judge or at random).
18-21	A single bolt streaks down to strike one target of the cleric's choice within the spell's range. The bolt does 1d8 points of damage and the target must make a successful Fort save the following round in order to perform any action.
22-23	The cleric can unleash a number of bolts equal to his CL, which must be aimed at a single target within the spell's range. Each bolt does 1d10 points of damage and requires the victim to make a successful Fort save. Failure indicates the target is paralyzed for 1d4 rounds and temporarily loses a single point from one of its ability scores (determined by the judge or at random). Paralysis and ability score loss from multiple failed saves do stack.
24-26	The cleric can unleash a number of bolts equal to his CL, which can be aimed at multiple targets within the spell's range. These bolts cause 1d12 damage, and cause each target to temporarily lose 1d2+1 points from a single ability score (determined by the judge or at random). In addition, each target must make a Will save or go insane for 1d4 rounds. The judge should check each round to determine the actions of the afflicted while the insanity lasts. Each round there is a 50% chance they do nothing other than tear at their hair, babble incoherently, and froth at the mouth; a 25% chance they attack a nearby creature at random; and a 25% chance they perform a normal action.
27-31	The cleric can unleash a number of bolts equal to *twice* his CL, which can be aimed at multiple targets within the spell's range. These bolts cause 1d14 damage and cause each target to temporarily lose 1d3 points from a single ability score (determined by the judge or at random). In addition, each target must make a Fort save or be crippled for 1d4 rounds. During this time, their movement rate is reduced to 5′ and they suffer a -4 penalty to all attacks, damage, saving throws, and spell checks.
32-33	The cleric can unleash a number of bolts equal to *twice* his CL, which can be aimed at multiple targets within the spell's range. These bolts cause 1d16 damage and cause each target to temporarily lose 1d4 points from a single ability score (determined by the judge or at random). In addition, each target must make a Will save or be *cursed* (as the cleric spell). Another spell check is made to determine the potency of the *curse* using all the same modifiers as the cleric's initial spell check for *bolt from the blue*, and the final result is compared to the *curse* spell table (see p. 273).
34-35	The cleric can unleash a number of bolts equal to *twice* his CL, which can be aimed at multiple targets within the spell's range. These bolts cause 1d20 damage and cause each target to temporarily lose 1d5+1 points from a single ability score (determined by the judge or at random). In addition, each target must make a Will save or permanently lose one point from that ability.
36+	The cleric can unleash a number of bolts equal to *twice* his CL, which can be aimed at multiple targets within the spell's range. These bolts cause 1d30 damage and cause each target to *permanently* lose 1d3 points from a single ability score (determined by the judge or at random). In addition, each target is branded with a symbol of the deity's displeasure. Such marked individuals are treated as enemies of the cleric's faith and attacked on sight by his followers. In addition, all spell checks against those targets by clerics of the offended deity enjoy a +10 bonus. Only miraculous magics by another powerful cleric or a sincere quest on behalf of the offended deity's church can remove this mark once it has been bestowed on a subject.

Exorcise

Level: 3   Range: 1 mile per CL (but see below)   Duration: Instantaneous   Casting time: 1 hour   Save: See below

General   The cleric calls upon divine forces to tear asunder the bonds linking mortals and their supernatural patrons, at the risk of drawing unwanted attention to himself. This spell requires much from the cleric and can only be performed once every seven days after a period of fasting, prayer, and mental preparation. Typically, an item belonging to the target, or a piece of the target's physical body (hair, blood, fingernail, etc.) is required to cast this spell. Attempting the spell without such an item imposes a -4 penalty to the spell check. Additionally, casting the spell without a physical link to the target reduces the range of the spell to 100' per CL.

When cast, the cleric makes a spell check as normal. If his spell check exceeds the spell check made when the original *patron bond* was cast, the bond is broken and the subject of the bond loses all benefits of that bond immediately. This can include losing patron spells he has previously learned. The subject cannot attempt to reform the *patron bond* until one month has past *or* some powerful magic has offset the exorcism. In addition, the subject may suffer side effects from the breaking of the bond (see below).

If the cleric's spell check is insufficient to break the *patron bond*, it is likely that the powers involved attempt to punish the cleric for his meddling. The cleric must make a Luck check to avoid drawing attention to himself and facing the wrath of the supernatural agents involved. If the Luck check fails, the cleric can expect to face the patron's minions, or at higher levels, the patron itself!

While the text of this spell refers to a *patron bond*, the spell could be used in a similar manner to break other, similar supernatural bonds, where they are encountered.

Manifestation   Ghostly representations of the cleric's deity or its agents appear and begin breaking the cosmic cords that bind the target to his supernatural patron.

1-15   Failure. The cleric must make a DC 5 Luck check to avoid attracting the patron's notice. If failed, the subject is alerted that someone is attempting to sever his *patron bond*.

16-17   The cleric exorcises a *patron bond* whose original spell check was less than the cleric's spell check roll. The subject of the bond is dazed for 1d6 rounds as the bond breaks, suffering a -2 penalty to all rolls during that time. If the cleric's spell check was insufficient to break the *bond*, he must make a DC 10 Luck check to avoid the patron's notice. If failed, a minor agent of the patron (judge's choice) seeks out the cleric with the intent to harm him. It arrives in 1d5 days after the failed casting.

18-21   The cleric exorcises a *patron bond* whose original spell check was less than the cleric's spell check roll. The subject of the bond is paralyzed for 1d6 rounds as the bond breaks. If the cleric's spell check was insufficient to break the *bond*, he must make a DC 12 Luck check to avoid the patron's notice. If failed, a minor agent of the patron (judge's choice) seeks out the cleric with the intent to harm him. It arrives in 1d4 days after the failed casting.

22-23   The cleric exorcises a *patron bond* whose original spell check was less than the cleric's spell check roll. The subject of the bond takes 1d6 + CL in damage as the bond severs. If the cleric's spell check was insufficient to break the *bond*, he must make a DC 14 Luck check to avoid the patron's notice. If failed, a moderately powerful agent of the patron (judge's choice) seeks out the cleric with the intent to harm him. It arrives in 1d3 days after the failed casting.

24-26   The cleric exorcises a *patron bond* whose original spell check was less than the cleric's spell check roll. The subject of the bond takes 1d8 + CL in damage and 1 point of temporary ability damage (chosen at random) as the bond severs. If the cleric's spell check was insufficient to break the *bond*, he must make a DC 16 Luck check to avoid the patron's notice. If failed, a moderately powerful agent of the patron (judge's choice) seeks out the cleric with the intent to harm him. It arrives in 1d2 days after the failed casting.

27-31   The cleric exorcises a *patron bond* whose original spell check was less than the cleric's spell check roll. As the bond severs, the subject of the bond takes 1d10 + CL in damage, 1 point of temporary ability damage (chosen at random), and loses the ability to cast one random spell for the day if a spellcaster. If the cleric's spell check was insufficient to break the *bond*, he must make a DC 18 Luck check to avoid the patron's notice. If failed, a moderately powerful agent of the patron (judge's choice) seeks out the cleric with the intent to harm him. It arrives in 1d2 days after the failed casting.

32-33	The cleric exorcises a *patron bond* whose original spell check was less than the cleric's spell check roll. As the bond severs, the subject of the bond takes 2d6 + CL in damage, 2 points of temporary ability damage (chosen at random), and must make a Will save or be struck senseless for 1d6 hours. If the cleric's spell check was insufficient to break the *bond*, he must make a DC 20 Luck check to avoid the patron's notice. If failed, a powerful agent of the patron (judge's choice) seeks out the cleric with the intent to harm him. It arrives the day the casting failed. If the Luck check is successful, the cleric still suffers cosmic backlash and becomes the subject of a minor *curse* of the judge's choosing.
34-35	The cleric exorcises a *patron bond* whose original spell check was less than the cleric's spell check roll. As the bond severs, the subject of the bond takes 3d6 + CL in damage, 3 points of temporary ability damage (chosen at random), and must make a Will save or lose all spells for 24 hours if a spellcaster. If the cleric's spell check was insufficient to break the *bond*, he must make a DC 22 Luck check to avoid the patron's notice. If failed, an extremely powerful agent of the patron (judge's choice) seeks out the cleric with the intent to harm him. It arrives within 1d12 hours of the failed casting. If the Luck check is successful, the cleric still suffers cosmic backlash and becomes the subject of a minor *curse* of the judge's choosing.
36+	The cleric exorcises a *patron bond* whose original spell check was less than the cleric's spell check roll. As the bond severs, the subject must make a DC 22 Fort save. If successful, he suffers 3d8+ CL damage, 4 points of temporary ability damage (chosen at random) and loses 1 permanent ability point. If the save is failed, he undergoes a horrific physical transformation, his body wracked by supernatural forces gone awry. The exact details of the transformation are left to the judge, but could include becoming a horrific monster, turned into mobile slime, transmutation into sentient, immobile stone, etc. If the cleric's spell check was insufficient to break the *bond*, he automatically attracts the attention of the subject's patron who immediately appears at the cleric's location with the intent of destroying him.

Remove Curse

Level: 3　　　Range: Touch　　Duration: Instantaneous　　Casting time: 1 round　　Save: See below

General	The cleric calls upon divine power to banish the baleful effects of a curse on a person or object. As referenced in the spell descriptions below, a minor curse is one that causes a loss of 2 or less ability score points; a moderate curse is one that impacts 3-4 ability score points or has a limiting effect of some kind (penalty to rolls, reduced speed, etc.); and a major curse is one that impacts 5+ ability score points or has a debilitating effect (blindness, deafness, immobility, etc.). When a save is called for, the affected individual or object either makes a second saving throw against the curse (save and DC are the same as the original curse), or, if no save was allowed against the original curse, the creature or object may make either a Fort or Will save (player's discretion) against a DC of 10 + the HD of creature that bestowed the curse. If the save is successful, the cursed creature or object is no longer affected by the curse. If the save fails, the curse remains in effect and 24 hours must pass before the cleric can again attempt to remove the curse.
Manifestation	Roll 1d4: (1) sparkling water flows from the cleric's hand to wash the target creature clean; (2) the target vomits up a black goop that quickly vanishes; (3) the cleric brushes the target with his hand, peeling away corrupt flesh to reveal unblemished skin beneath; (4) a divine fire burns away the curse.
1-15	Failure.
16-17	A single cursed individual or object is allowed to make a new saving throw to escape the effects of a minor curse.
18-21	A number of cursed individuals or objects equal to the cleric's CL are allowed to make a saving throw to escape the effects of a minor curse. If only a single cursed creature or object is targeted, they gain a bonus to their saving throw equal to the CL.
22-23	The cleric automatically removes a minor curse from a single individual or allows a saving throw to remove a moderate curse from a single cursed individual or object.
24-26	The cleric automatically removes a minor curse from a number of individuals or objects equal to his CL or allows a saving throw to remove a moderate curse from a number of cursed individuals or objects equal to his CL. If only a single cursed creature or object is targeted, it gains a bonus to the saving throw equal to the CL.

27-31	The cleric automatically removes a minor or moderate curse from a single individual or allows a saving throw to remove a major curse for a single cursed individual or object.
32-33	The cleric automatically removes a minor or moderate curse from a number of individuals or objects equal to his CL or allows a saving throw to remove a major curse for a number of cursed individuals or objects equal to his CL. If only a single cursed creature or object is targeted, they gain a bonus to their saving throw equal to the CL.
34-35	The cleric automatically removes any curse affecting a single creature or object, regardless of the curse's potency.
36+	The cleric automatically removes any curse affecting a number of creatures equal to his CL. In addition, if the creature or creatures that bestowed the curse(s) is currently alive, it automatically becomes the victim of its own curse regardless of its location or distance away from the cleric.

Speak With The Dead

Level: 3	Range: Self	Duration: Varies	Casting time: 1 hour	Save: N/A

General	The cleric speaks with a dead creature, and it answers his questions. The cleric must be in the presence of the dead creature's body and be able to speak in a language that the creature understands. It will answer the cleric's questions to the extent of its knowledge, which is the same it possessed in life. Note that creatures with stubborn or disobedient personalities may still exhibit the same personality traits in death.

Manifestation	Roll 1d4: (1) corpse miraculously "heals" such that it rises and talks conversationally with the cleric until returning to its rotting state at the end of the duration; (2) corpse glows in a soft light and its lips or jaws move to answer any questions; (3) the corpse's spirit appears as a ghostly apparition, floating above the corpse to answer any questions; (4) the corpse animates such that it writes answers to questions, such as by scratching the answers in the dirt or using its clotted blood to write on the walls.

1-15	Failure.
16-17	The cleric may ask one question of a creature dead up to one week and converse for up to one round. The creature's body must be largely intact; e.g., a fragment of a shattered skull is not sufficient to answer a question, but a cadaver is.

18-21	The cleric may ask two questions of a creature dead up to one month and converse for up to two rounds. The creature's body must be largely intact; e.g., a fragment of a shattered skull is not sufficient to answer a question, but a cadaver is.
22-23	The cleric may ask three questions of a creature dead up to one year and converse for up to two turns. The creature's body must be largely intact; e.g., a fragment of a shattered skull is not sufficient to answer a question, but a cadaver is.
24-26	The cleric may ask four questions of a creature dead up to 10 years and converse for up to two turns. The cleric need only have a fragment of the creature's body – for example, a skull or head – but the creature's ability to communicate is limited by its remaining anatomy. If the cleric possesses only a tooth or knucklebone, for example,

the deceased cannot speak, and he may need another spell to also establish a mode of communication. The cleric may communicate with the un-dead using this spell; they count as "dead" for purposes of the spell.

27-31	The cleric may ask five questions of a creature dead up to 100 years and converse for up to two turns. The cleric need only have a fragment of the creature's body – for example, a skull or bone chip – and the creature can communicate even with only a fragmented anatomy, as its spirit speaks through it. The cleric may communicate with the un-dead using this spell, as well as other creatures whose souls have departed due to supernatural means; they count as "dead" for purposes of the spell.
32-33	The cleric may ask six questions of a creature dead up to 1,000 years and converse for up to an hour. The cleric need only have a fragment of the creature's body – for example, a skull or bone chip – and the creature can communicate even with only a fragmented anatomy, as its spirit speaks through it. The cleric may communicate with the un-dead using this spell, as well as other creatures whose souls have departed due to supernatural means; they count as "dead" for purposes of the spell.
34-35	The cleric may ask any number of questions of a creature dead up to 10,000 years and converse for up to an hour. The cleric need only have a fragment of the creature's body – for example, a skull or bone chip – and the creature can communicate even with only a fragmented anatomy, as its spirit speaks through it. The cleric may communicate with the un-dead using this spell, as well as other creatures whose souls have departed due to supernatural means; they count as "dead" for purposes of the spell.
36+	The cleric may ask any number of questions of a creature dead up to 100,000 years and converse for up to a day. He can communicate mentally directly with the creature and need not have any physical specimen of its corpse, though the cleric does need specific knowledge of its identity and location of birth, death, or deeds.

Spiritual Weapon

Level: 3   Range: 60' + 20' per CL   Duration: 1 round per CL   Casting time: 1 action   Save: N/A

General	The cleric empowers his own personal weapon with his faith, allowing it to smite his enemies as if wielded by an unseen warrior. Attacks with this weapon use the cleric's normal melee attack modifier and his normal attack dice, although the melee attack roll is adjusted by the cleric's Strength *or* Personality modifier (whichever is higher). Greater spell checks increase attack and damage rolls, as well as add additional action dice. The weapon uses the cleric's crit die and table for determining the results of a critical hit. If cast upon a magical weapon, the cleric adds any "pluses" the weapon has to his spell check. The *spiritual weapon* itself cannot be targeted or damaged by physical attacks, but can be rendered harmless with a *dispel magic* or a similar magic-negating effect.
	Additionally, while the spiritual weapon is empowered, it also gains one or more special abilities. The cleric may choose one of the following, as noted in the spell descriptions:
	Unholy avenger: The weapon inflicts an additional +1 damage against unholy creatures.
	Holy shock: Creatures struck by the blade must make a DC 10 Fort save or be dazed (-1 to all rolls for next turn).
	Light of the lord: The weapon glows a brilliant yellow, providing illumination equivalent to torchlight.
	Sacred defender: The weapon parries attacks aimed at the cleric by the creature it is directed to fight, giving that creature a -2 penalty to all attacks against the cleric.
Manifestation	The cleric's weapon glows with a divine radiance and leaps into the air, moving about as if wielded by an invisible champion.
1-15	Failure.
16-17	The cleric can direct the weapon to attack a single target within range. The weapon has the cleric's normal chance to hit (modified by Strength or Personality) and inflicts normal damage (also modified by Strength or Personality). The weapon has one special ability, chosen by the character as noted above. The weapon continues attacking without any concentration on the cleric's part, but if the cleric wishes to attack a different target, he must first call the weapon back to his current position and direct it to the new target. This takes one action.

18-21	The cleric can direct the weapon to attack a single target within range. The weapon gains an additional +1 bonus to hit and inflicts an additional 1d3 damage (in addition to any other modifiers and damage dice). The weapon has one special ability, chosen by the character as noted above. The weapon continues attacking without any concentration on the cleric's part, but if the cleric wishes to attack a different target, he must first call the weapon back to his current position and direct it to the new target. This takes one action.
22-23	The cleric can direct the weapon to attack any target within range. The weapon gains an additional +2 bonus to hit and inflicts an additional 1d4 damage (in addition to any other modifiers and damage dice). The weapon has one special ability, chosen by the character as noted above. The weapon continues attacking without any concentration on the cleric's part, and he can direct it to a new target with only a thought. When the spell's duration ends, the weapon returns to the cleric's hand.
24-26	The cleric can direct the weapon to attack any target within range. The weapon gains an additional +3 bonus to hit and inflicts an additional 1d5 damage (in addition to any other modifiers and damage dice). The weapon has *two* special abilities, chosen by the character as noted above. The weapon continues attacking without any concentration on the cleric's part, and he can direct it to a new target with only a thought. When the spell's duration ends, the weapon returns to the cleric's hand.
27-31	The cleric can direct the weapon to attack any target within range. The weapon gains an additional action die for the purpose of making multiple attacks per round. The additional action die is the next lowest in the dice chain based on the cleric's current action dice. These attacks can be split between two targets so long as they are within 10' of one another. The weapon gains an additional +3 bonus to hit and inflicts an additional 1d5 damage (in addition to any other modifiers and damage dice). The weapon has *two* special abilities, chosen by the character as noted above. The weapon continues attacking without any concentration on the cleric's part, and he can direct it to a new target with only a thought. When the spell's duration ends, the weapon returns to the cleric's hand.
32-33	The cleric can direct the weapon to attack any target within range. He also gains an additional action die for the purpose of making multiple attacks per round. The additional action die is the next lowest in the dice chain based on the cleric's current action dice. These attacks can be split between two targets so long as they are within 10' of one another. The weapon gains an additional +4 bonus to hit and inflicts an additional 1d6 damage (in addition to any other modifiers and damage dice). The weapon has *three* special abilities, chosen by the character as noted above. The weapon continues attacking without any concentration on the cleric's part, and he can direct it to a new target with only a thought. When the spell's duration ends, the weapon returns to the cleric's hand.
34-35	The cleric can direct the weapon to attack any target within range. He also gains *two* additional action dice for the purpose of making multiple attacks per round. The additional action dice are the next lowest in the dice chain based on the cleric's current action dice. These attacks can be split between three targets so long as they are within 10' of one another. The weapon gains an additional +4 bonus to hit and inflicts an additional 1d6 damage (in addition to any other modifiers and damage dice). The weapon has *three* special abilities, chosen by the character as noted above. The weapon continues attacking without any concentration on the cleric's part, and he can direct it to a new target with only a thought. When the spell's duration ends, the weapon returns to the cleric's hand.
36+	The cleric can direct the weapon to attack any target within range. He also gains *two* additional action dice for the purpose of making multiple attacks per round, and both additional action dice are 1d24 dice. These attacks can be split between three targets so long as they are within 10' of one another. The weapon gains an additional +5 bonus to hit and inflicts an additional 1d8 damage (in addition to any other modifiers and damage dice). The weapon has all *four* special abilities. The weapon continues attacking without any concentration on the cleric's part, and he can direct it to a new target with only a thought. When the spell's duration ends, the weapon returns to the cleric's hand.

True Name

Level: 3   Range: 100' per CL or unlimited (see below)   Duration: Instantaneous   Casting time: 1 action
Save: Will vs. spell check DC

General	The cleric calls upon his deity to reveal the true name of an individual or creature, allowing him to more easily affect the named target with his magic. This spell works only on intelligent creatures and magical constructions that were named by their creator. Un-dead, slimes, animals, and similar creatures that do not possess names are immune to this spell. Other creatures may or may not be affected at the judge's discretion. A successful Will save indicates that the target's true name remains hidden from the cleric.
	In order to gain the knowledge of a creature's true name (or one of them; many creatures possess a number of secret names of varying power), the cleric must either be within range and have a clear view of the target or possess a personal item or physical component (blood, hair, fingernails, etc.) of the target. If the cleric has a portion of the target's physical body, this spell can be cast at any distance provided that the target is on the same plane of existence as the cleric.
	Once a creature's true name is known, the cleric permanently enjoys the benefits indicated by the spell check below. He can attempt to recast the spell to further deduce the target's secret name(s), but a failure on subsequent castings of the spell makes the target permanently immune to further attempts by the cleric – he has learned all he can about his target. Due to the complexities and magical nature of true names, the cleric cannot easily share a true name with another person. Attempts to write or speak the true name become garbled in the communication process and the would-be recipient of the name must make a spell check with a result equal to or greater than that of the cleric's spell check to comprehend the priest's attempt to share the true name. Failure means it is impossible for the recipient to understand the cleric and he cannot make another attempt to comprehend the true name unless the cleric recasts the spell.
	An individual whose true name has fallen into the possession of another can attempt to nullify that name and negate all bonuses granted to the possessor of the name. This usually requires the intervention of a patron or god, undertaking a quest, subjecting oneself to powerful memory- or identity-erasing magics, or other means determined by the judge.
Manifestation	Roll 1d4: (1) a divine servant of the cleric's deity appears and whispers the target's true name into his ear; (2) the true name appears in the air before the cleric, written in celestial fire and visible only to him; (3) the cleric is subject to a brief hallucination of the target's naming at birth; (4) a nearby animal croaks the target's true name in a harsh, unearthly voice.
1-15	Failure.
16-17	The cleric learns the simplest inkling of the target's lesser secret name. The target suffers a -1 penalty to all saving throws against spells cast by the cleric and/or others in possession of the target's true name.
18-21	The cleric learns the actual pronunciations of the target's lesser secret name. The target suffers a -2 penalty to all saving throws against spells cast by the cleric and/or others in possession of the target's true name.
22-23	The cleric learns of the target's greater secret name. The target suffers a -3 penalty to all saving throws against spells cast by the cleric and/or others in possession of the target's true name. In addition, all attempts to magically sway, dominate, or dismiss the target (*banish, binding, charm person, lotus stare, word of command*, etc.) gain a +2 bonus to the spell check.
24-26	The cleric learns of the target's greater secret name. The target suffers a -3 penalty to all saving throws against spells cast by the cleric and/or others in possession of the target's true name. In addition, all attempts to magically sway, dominate, or dismiss the target (*banish, binding, charm person, lotus stare, word of command*, etc.) gain a +3 bonus to the spell check.
27-31	The cleric learns the target's true secret name. The target suffers a -4 penalty to all saving throws against spells cast by the cleric and/or others in possession of the target's true name. Any attempt to magically sway, dominate, or dismiss the target (*banish, binding, charm person, lotus stare, word of command*, etc.) gain a +4 bonus to the spell check. In addition, all other spells checks made against the target enjoy a +1 bonus to the spell check.

32-33	The cleric learns the target's true secret name. The target suffers a -4 penalty to all saving throws against spells cast by the cleric and/or others in possession of the target's true name. Any attempt to magically sway, dominate, or dismiss the target (*banish, binding, charm person, lotus stare, word of command,* etc.) gain a +4 bonus to the spell check. In addition, all other spells checks made against the target enjoy a +2 bonus.
34-35	The cleric learns not only the target's true name but the true names of all its living blood relatives. Anyone within the target's family suffers a -5 penalty to all saving throws against spells cast by the cleric and/or others in possession of the target's true name. Any attempt to magically sway, dominate, or dismiss the target (*banish, binding, charm person, lotus stare, word of command,* etc.) gain a +5 bonus to the spell check. In addition, all other spells checks made against the target enjoy a +3 bonus.
36+	The cleric learns the true name of the target's dynasty, allowing him to better magically affect not only the target but any relatives living, dead, or yet to be born. Any creatures of the target's family line suffer a negative penalty equal to -5 or the cleric's CL +2 (whichever is greater) to all saving throws against spells cast by the cleric and/or others in possession of the target's true name. In addition, all spell checks (of any type) made against the target or his dynasty gain a positive bonus equal to +4 or the cleric's CL +2 (whichever is greater).

LEVEL 4 CLERIC SPELLS

Affliction of the Gods

Level: 4	Range: 50' + 10' per CL	Duration: Varies	Casting time: 1 action	Save: Fort vs. spell check DC

General
The cleric strikes down his enemies with afflictions, conditions, and wounds. Those who are opposed to the cleric's faith (considered unholy or of opposite alignment) suffer a -2 penalty to their Fort save. All others make their saving throws as normal. The spell affects all enemies in an area 10' square per CL. Allied creatures within the targeted area are not affected.

Manifestation
Roll 1d4: (1) the targets' skin roils and bubbles as the blight enters their bodies; (2) coils of divine light streak down from on high or burst from the ground, wrapping themselves around the targets; (3) rays of energy shine from the cleric's holy symbol and touch each affected target in turn; (4) ghostly figures coalesce around the targets, touching their faces with insubstantial hands.

1-17
Failure.

18-19
All enemies within the area of effect must make a Fort save or be deafened. Deaf creatures suffer a -4 penalty to initiative rolls and to avoid being surprised. Deaf spellcasters suffer a -2 penalty to all spell checks made while deaf. The affliction lasts for CL hours.

20-23
All targets within the area of effect must make a Fort save or be crippled. Crippled individuals have their movement rate reduced to 5' and suffer a -2 penalty to all attack and damage rolls, saving throws, and spell checks until the condition is removed. The affliction lasts for CL hours.

24-25
All targets within the area of effect must make a Fort save or be blinded. Blind creatures suffer a -4 penalty to initiative rolls, attack and damage rolls, saving throws, and spell checks, and are easy to surprise. In addition, a blind character firing a missile weapon is at -8 to hit and any missed shot has a 50% chance of striking a randomly determined ally. The affliction lasts for CL hours.

26-27
All targets within the area of effect must make a Fort save or temporarily lose 1d8 points of Strength per CL. The lost Strength returns at the normal rate once the spell has ended. Creatures whose Strength is reduced to zero fall unconscious until they've regained one or more Strength points. This weakness lasts for a full 24 hours.

28-33
All targets within the area of effect are afflicted with a hideous, flesh-eating bacteria. Each round, the affected must make a Fort save or take 1d6 points of *compounded* damage every round for CL rounds; i.e., 1d6 on the first round, 2d6 on the second round, 3d6 on the third round, and so on. Success on a Fort save avoids damage only on the current round; it does not stop the spell's effect on future rounds. The bacteria devour all organic materials worn or carried by the victims, destroying leather, cloth, wood, and similar materials in 1d4 rounds. A *neutralize disease* spell destroys the bacteria as does magical flame (*fireball, control fire,* etc.), but the target takes full damage from the fire.

34-35
All targets within the area of effect must make a Fort save or be stricken with a plague of divine origin. The disease immediately causes 1d10+CL damage to the targets and the loss of a point of Luck. The disease continues to ravage the targets' bodies after the spell ends and can easily prove fatal. Each subsequent day the target is diseased, it must make a DC 25 Fort save. Failure to do so means they remain ill and suffer the loss of another Luck point and an additional 1d6 damage. Each day after the first, the DC of the Fort save is reduced by 1 until the target makes his save, the disease runs its course, or the disease kills its subject. The disease lasts for 4 days plus 1 day per CL.

36-37
All targets within the area of effect must make a Fort save or spontaneously combust! They and all non-magical possessions burst into flames that do 1d10 points of damage each round they remain on fire. Extinguishing the magical flame requires a full round's action and the victim must make a DC 20 Ref check to put out the fire. The fires continue until extinguished or the victim dies.

38+
The gaze of the cleric's deity turns upon the heathens within the area of effect and completely decimates all who fail their Fort save. The targets melt into pools of bloody slime and runny flesh that quickly evaporates as if they had never been. Due to the deity's personal involvement in this effect, all spell checks by the cleric suffer a -10 penalty for a full week afterwards. His deity has helped him enough and is likely to ignore any further requests until a week's time has passed. This modifier can be removed at the judge's discretion if the cleric undertakes a great task in his deity's name.

Cause Earthquake

| Level: 4 | Range: Various | Duration: 1 round | Casting time: 1 action | Save: See below |

| General | The cleric creates an intense but centralized earth tremor, causing destruction in his immediate vicinity. The shockwave upsets creatures, knocks down structures, causes crevasses to open in the earth, and creates avalanches and landslides. |

| Manifestation | The earth begins to heave and toss when the cleric slaps the ground at his feet. |

| 1-17 | Failure. |

| 18-19 | The ground rumbles and heaves in a 40' radius area centered at a point up to 100' away from the cleric. All creatures standing in the area of effect must make a Ref save to remain standing. This is the only action allowable during the round; no attacks or spell casting is possible as the affected targets struggle to remain standing. Creatures in the area of effect suffer a -2 penalty to AC as they lose their defensive stance, and spellcasters concentrating on active spells must make a DC 11 Will save to maintain their castings. Flying and incorporeal creatures are obviously unaffected by the spell. |

| 20-23 | The ground quakes in a 60' radius area centered at a point up to 150' away from the cleric. All creatures standing in the area of effect must make a Ref save to remain standing; those who fail take 1d3 damage from a hard fall. Standing is the only action allowable during the round; no attacks or spellcasting is possible as the affected targets struggle to remain standing. Creatures in the area of effect suffer a -4 penalty to AC as they lose their defensive stance, and spellcasters concentrating on active spells must make a DC 13 Will save to maintain their castings. Flying and incorporeal creatures are obviously unaffected by the spell. Additional effects occur depending on the surrounding terrain:

Inside Caves, Tunnels, Buildings, or in Rocky Terrain: There is a 50% chance that the roof collapses, a wall falls down, or an avalanche begins, doing 6d8 points of damage to any creature in the area of effect as debris cascades down atop them. A Ref save reduces the damage by half. A failed save indicates the creature is buried and suffocating in the rubble. Such creatures must make a Stamina check (DC 10) each round or lose an additional 1d3 hit points until rescued or dead.

Open Ground: There is a 25% chance a fissure opens under the feet of each creature in the area (Ref save to avoid falling in). The fissure is 10' deep and creatures take 1d6 falling damage.

River, Marsh, or Lake: Fissures open beneath the surface, causing the waters to drain away and leave a morass of boggy muck behind. There is a 25% chance each creature in the area is trapped in the mud and must make a DC 10 Strength check to pull free. The following round, the remaining waters rush back into the area and possible drowning may occur. |

| 24-25 | The ground quakes violently in an 80' radius area centered at a point up to 200' away from the cleric. All creatures standing in the area of effect must make a Ref save to remain standing; those who fail take 1d6 damage from a hard fall. This is the only action allowable during the round; no attacks or spellcasting is possible as the affected targets struggle to remain standing. Creatures in the area of effect suffer a -4 penalty to AC as they lose their defensive stance, and spellcasters concentrating on active spells must make a DC 15 Will save to maintain their castings. Flying and incorporeal creatures are obviously unaffected by the spell. Additional effects occur depending on the surrounding terrain:

Inside Caves, Tunnels, Buildings, or in Rocky Terrain: There is a 75% chance that the roof collapses, a wall falls down, or an avalanche begins, doing 7d8 points of damage to any creature in the area of effect as debris cascades down atop them. A Ref save reduces the damage by half. A failed save indicates the creature is buried and suffocating in the rubble. Such creatures must make a Stamina check (DC 12) each round or lose an additional 1d4 hit points until rescued or dead.

Open Ground: There is a 50% chance a fissure opens under the feet of each creature in the area (Ref save to avoid falling in). The fissure is 1d4x10' deep and creatures take 1d6 falling damage for every 10' fallen.

River, Marsh, or Lake: Fissures open beneath the surface, causing the waters to drain away and leave a morass of boggy muck behind. There is a 50% chance each creature in the area is trapped in the mud and must make a DC 14 Strength check to pull free. The following round, the remaining waters rush back into the area and possible drowning may occur. |

26-27	The ground quakes tempestuously in a 100' radius area centered up to 400' away from the cleric. The quakes continue for 1d3+1 rounds, affecting all within as follows for each round: All creatures standing in the area of effect must make a Ref save to remain standing; those who fail take 1d8+1 damage from a hard fall. This is the only action allowable during the round; no attacks or spellcasting is possible as the affected targets struggle to remain standing. Creatures in the area of effect suffer a -4 penalty to AC as they lose their defensive stance, and spellcasters concentrating on active spells must make a DC 17 Will save to maintain their castings. Flying and incorporeal creatures are obviously unaffected by the spell. Additional effects occur depending on the surrounding terrain:

Inside Caves, Tunnels, Buildings, or in Rocky Terrain: There is a 90% chance that the roof collapses, a wall falls down, or an avalanche begins, doing 8d8 points of damage to any creature in the area of effect as debris cascades down atop them. A Ref save reduces the damage by half. A failed save indicates the creature is buried and suffocating in the rubble. Such creatures must make a Stamina check (DC 12) each round or lose an additional 1d5 hit points until rescued or dead.

Open Ground: There is a 75% chance a fissure opens under the feet of all creatures in the area (Ref save to avoid falling in). The fissure is 1d6x10' deep and creatures take 1d6 falling damage for every 10' fallen. In addition, there is a 25% chance that each fissure closes 1d4+3 rounds later. Any creatures caught in a closing fissure takes 10d10 damage as the earth grinds them to pulp. Creatures that survive begin suffocating and must make a Stamina check (DC 16) each round or lose an additional 1d6 hit points until rescued or dead.

River, Marsh, or Lake: Fissures open beneath the surface, causing the waters to drain away and leave a morass of boggy muck behind. There is a 75% chance each creature in the area is trapped in the mud and must make a DC 14 Strength check to pull free. The following round, the remaining waters rush back into the area and possible drowning may occur.

28-33	The ground quakes in a 125' radius area, centered up to 500' away from the cleric. The quakes continue for 1d4+1 rounds, affecting all within as follows for each round: All creatures standing in the area of effect must make a Ref save to remain standing; those who fail take 1d8+3 damage from a hard fall. This is the only action allowable during the round; no attacks or spellcasting is possible as the affected targets struggle to remain standing. Creatures in the area of effect suffer a -4 penalty to AC as they lose their defensive stance, and spellcasters concentrating on active spells must make a DC 19 Will save to maintain their castings. Incorporeal creatures are unaffected by the spell, but flying creatures may be caught in gusty updrafts; any creature flying within 50' of the ground must make a DC 20 Ref save or be tossed to the ground for 2d6 damage. Additional effects occur depending on the surrounding terrain:

Inside Caves, Tunnels, Buildings, or in Rocky Terrain: The roof collapses, a wall falls down, or an avalanche begins, doing 9d8 points of damage to any creature in the area of effect as debris cascades down atop them. A Ref save reduces the damage by half. A failed save indicates the creature is buried and suffocating in the rubble. Such creatures must make a Stamina check (DC 14) each round or lose an additional 1d6 hit points until rescued or dead.

Open Ground: A fissure opens under the feet of all creatures in the area (Ref save to avoid falling in). The fissure is 2d6x10' deep and creatures take 1d6 falling damage for every 10' fallen. In addition, there is a 50% chance that each fissure closes 1d4+1 rounds later. Any creatures caught in a closing fissure takes 10d10 damage as the earth grinds them to pulp. Even if they survive they begin suffocating, and must make a Stamina check (DC 16) each round or lose an additional 1d6 hit points until rescued or dead.

River, Marsh, or Lake: Fissures open beneath the surface, causing the waters to drain away and leave a morass of boggy muck behind. Each creature in the area is trapped in the mud and must make a DC 16 Strength check to pull free. The following round, the remaining waters rush back into the area and possible drowning may occur.

34-35	The ground quakes in a 150' radius area, centered up to 600' away from the cleric. The quakes continue for 1d5+2 rounds, affecting all within as follows for each round: All creatures standing in the area of effect must make a Ref save to remain standing; those who fail take 1d8+5 damage from a hard fall. This is the only action allowable during the round; no attacks or spell casting is possible as the affected targets struggle to remain standing. Creatures in the area of effect suffer a -4 penalty to AC as they lose their defensive stance, and spell-casters concentrating on active spells must make a DC 21 Will save to maintain their castings. Incorporeal creatures are unaffected by the spell, but flying creatures may be caught in gusty updrafts; any creature flying within 50' of the ground must make a DC 20 Ref save or be tossed to the ground for 2d6 damage. Additional effects occur depending on the surrounding terrain:

Inside Caves, Tunnels, Buildings, or in Rocky Terrain: The roof collapses, a wall falls down, or an avalanche begins, doing 10d8 points of damage to any creature in the area of effect as debris cascades down atop them. A Ref save reduces the damage by half. A failed save indicates the creature is buried and suffocating in the rubble. Such creatures must make a Stamina check (DC 16) each round or lose an additional 1d6 hit points until rescued or dead.

Open Ground: A fissure opens under the feet of all creatures in the area (Ref save to avoid falling in). The fissure is 3d6x10′ deep and creatures take 1d6 falling damage for every 10′ fallen. In addition, there is a 50% chance that each fissure closes 1d4+1 rounds later. Any creature caught in a closing fissure takes 10d10 damage as the earth grinds them to a pulp. Creatures that survive begin suffocating and must make a Stamina check (DC 16) each round or lose an additional 1d6 hit points until rescued or dead.

River, Marsh, or Lake: Fissures open beneath the surface, causing the waters to drain away and leave a morass of boggy muck behind. Each creature in the area is trapped in the mud and must make a DC 18 Strength check to pull free. The following round, the remaining waters rush back into the area and possible drowning may occur.

36-37	The cleric wreaks destruction upon an area a half-mile in radius, at a point centered up to 10 miles away. He need not have line of sight to the target location. Massive tremors topple entire fortresses; dams collapse; villages, farmlands, animals, and people are engulfed in chasms; roaring flames erupt from lava spouts; and other titanic examples of devastation occur. The judge may allow those in the area of effect a saving throw to avoid death, but the force of the quake and the damage caused by it is likely fatal to all. Even flying creatures are caught in the updrafts and stormy winds created by the event. The landscape remains permanently altered in the aftermath.
38+	The cleric wreaks destruction upon an area 3 miles in radius, centered at any point he can see, even beyond this plane. Scrying devices may allow him to cast this spell over great distances. Massive tremors topple entire fortresses; dams collapse; villages, farmlands, animals, and people are engulfed in chasms; roaring flames erupt from lava spouts; and other titanic examples of devastation occur. The judge may allow those in the area of effect a saving throw to avoid death, but the force of the quake and the damage caused by it is likely fatal to all. Even flying creatures are caught in the updrafts and stormy winds created by the event. The landscape remains permanently altered in the aftermath.

Sanctify/Desecrate

Level: 4	Range: 20′ square area per CL	Duration: Varies	Casting time: 1 turn	Save: See below

General

The cleric dedicates a physical space to his deity, granting it supernatural protection and attuning it to the will and agenda of his divine master. This sanctum becomes a refuge for the cleric and other worshippers of the deity. The spell can also be cast upon a space already sacrosanct to another deity. If the cleric's spell check is greater than that of the cleric who originally *sanctified* the space, the area becomes *desecrated* and no longer grants any benefits to those within. A space that has been *desecrated* must be cleansed of any lingering traces of its former divine connection (a month-long process) before it can be *sanctified* to a new deity. No cleansing is necessary to re-sanctify a space to its former divine protector.

The cleric, worshippers of the cleric's deity, and those of the same alignment of the cleric gain the full benefit of the sanctuary as determined by the spell check. Those of a different alignment who worship a deity not in direct opposition to the cleric's deity gain half the normal benefits of the sanctuary (rounded up), i.e. a cleric of a different, but not antagonistic, god would receive a +1 bonus to laying on hands if the cleric who cast the *sanctify/desecrate* spell scored a 20 on her spell check. Individuals who are unholy (according to the cleric's faith) or worship a deity opposed to the casting cleric's own suffer a negative penalty equal the bonus the sanctuary provides true believers and may be subject to physical damage as well.

Each sanctuary provides a bonus to spell checks, turning, laying on hands, and pleas for divine aid. In addition, the sanctuary provides a bonus to actions related to the deity to which it is dedicated. The judge must adjudicate these bonuses on a deity-by-deity basis, but they should always apply to actions favorable to the deity. For example, a sanctuary dedicated to Klazath, god of war, would modify all combat rolls made by the cleric and his followers while within the sacred space. The devotees of Amun Tor, god of mysteries and riddles, would gain the sanctuary's bonus to rolls made to decipher codes or uncover hidden clues; while those of Bobugbubilz, demon lord of evil amphibians, would discover that all batrachian servants or summoned creatures within the sanctuary add the bonus to their hit points, saving throws, and attack rolls.

Manifestation	Roll 1d4: (1) the affected area erupts in harmless, divine fire that leaves the sanctum magically cleansed; (2) the affected area glows with a divine radiance of a color appropriate to the cleric's deity; (3) a blast of celestial music spills from the cleric's mouth, causing the affected area to resonate with the music of the spheres; (4) tears of holy/unholy water flow from the cleric's eyes, anointing the affected area.

1-17	Failure.
18-19	The cleric creates a minor sanctuary. All spell checks, turning, laying on of hands, pleas for divine aid, and actions related to the sanctuary's deity receive a +1 bonus. The area remains a sanctuary for 3 hours.
20-23	The cleric creates a lesser sanctuary. All spell checks, turning, laying on of hands, pleas for divine aid, and actions related to the sanctuary's deity receive a +2 bonus. Unholy creatures (determined by the cleric's divine allegiance) with 1 HD or less must make a Fort save when entering the area or suffer 1d3 points of damage. The area remains a sanctuary for 6 hours.
24-25	The cleric creates a moderate sanctuary. All spell checks, turning, laying on of hands, pleas for divine aid, and actions related to the sanctuary's deity receive a +3 bonus. Unholy creatures (determined by the cleric's divine allegiance) with 2 HD or less must make a Fort save when entering the area or suffer 1d5 points of damage. Spells targeted at the cleric and allied individuals of the cleric's faith inside the sanctuary suffer a -1 penalty to spell checks. The area remains a sanctuary for 12 hours.
26-27	The cleric creates a greater sanctuary. All spell checks, turning, laying on of hands, pleas for divine aid, and actions related to the sanctuary's deity receive a +4 bonus. Unholy creatures (determined by the cleric's divine allegiance) with 3 HD or less must make a Fort save when entering the area or suffer 1d6 points of damage. Spells targeted at the cleric and allied individuals of the cleric's faith inside the sanctuary suffer a -2 penalty to spell checks. The area remains a sanctuary for 1 day.
28-33	The cleric creates a major sanctuary. All spell checks, turning, laying on of hands, pleas for divine aid, and actions related to the sanctuary's deity receive a +5 bonus. Unholy creatures (determined by the cleric's divine allegiance) with 4 HD or less must make a Fort save when entering the area or suffer 1d8 points of damage. Spells targeted at the cleric and allied individuals of the cleric's faith inside the sanctuary suffer a -4 penalty to spell checks. The area remains a sanctuary for 1 week.
34-35	The cleric creates a true sanctuary. All spell checks, turning, laying on of hands, pleas for divine aid, and actions related to the sanctuary's deity receive a +6 bonus. Unholy creatures (determined by the cleric's divine allegiance) with 5 HD or less must make a Fort save when entering the area or suffer 1d10 points of damage plus an additional 1 point of damage each round thereafter (Fort save to resist). Spells targeted at the cleric and allied individuals of the cleric's faith inside the sanctuary suffer a -4 penalty to spell checks. The area remains a sanctuary for 1 month.
36-37	The cleric creates a divine sanctuary. All spell checks, turning, laying on of hands, pleas for divine aid, and actions related to the sanctuary's deity receive a +7 bonus. Unholy creatures (determined by the cleric's divine allegiance) with 6 HD or less must make a Fort save when entering the area or suffer 1d20 points of damage plus an additional 2 points of damage each round thereafter (Fort save to resist). Spells targeted at the cleric and allied individuals of the cleric's faith inside the sanctuary suffer a -5 penalty to spell checks. The area permanently remains a sanctuary until *desecrated*.
38+	The cleric creates a place forever revered by those of his faith. The devout embark on pilgrimages to the sanctuary in order to glimpse it before they die. It becomes the site of miracles and the cleric's deity is known to make appearances there to speak to the faithful. To the enemies of the cleric's faith, the sanctuary becomes a symbol for all that is hated about the religion and crusades are organized to raze the site to the ground. All spell checks, turning, laying on of hands, pleas for divine aid, and actions related to the sanctuary's deity receive a +10 bonus. Unholy creatures (determined by the cleric's divine allegiance) with 8 HD or less must make a Fort save when entering the area or suffer 2d20 points of damage plus an additional 4 points of damage each round thereafter (Fort save to resist). Spells targeted at the cleric and allied individuals of the cleric's faith inside the sanctuary suffer a -10 penalty to spell checks. The area permanently remains a sanctuary until physically destroyed, *desecrated,* and the ground itself is salted or doused with cursed waters and oils.

Vermin Blight

Level: 4   Range: 200' + 10' per CL   Duration: 1 round per CL   Casting time: 1 action   Save: N/A

General	The cleric summons forth a swarm of insects to attack his foes. Refer to page 419 for statistics on the insect swarm.
Manifestation	Roll 1d4: (1) cleric emits a susurration of wings and the swarms appear; (2) insects pour from the cleric's open hands; (3) insects boil up from the ground at the targets' feet; (4) chrysalises sprout from the cleric's body and then open to release the swarm.
1-17	Failure.
18-19	The cleric summons a single insect swarm. The swarm attacks *any* creatures within its area but does not move from that spot, remaining there until the spell's duration expires. The swarm receives a +2 bonus to attacks and damage or +3 against unholy creatures.
20-23	The cleric summons two insect swarms that occupy any two areas adjacent to one another within the range of the spell. These swarms attack any hostile creatures within their areas, and will not attack friendly or allied creatures. They do not move from their locations, remaining there until the spell's duration expires. The swarms receive a +4 bonus to attacks and damage or +6 against unholy creatures.
24-25	The cleric summons three insect swarms that occupy any three areas of the cleric's choosing within the range of the spell. The swarms are not required to be adjacent to one another. These swarms attack any hostile or unfriendly creatures within their areas but do not move from those locations, remaining there until the spell's duration expires. The swarms receive a +6 bonus to attacks and damage or +9 against unholy creatures.
26-27	The cleric summons four insect swarms that he may direct as he wishes. The swarms creep and crawl after a target or targets of the cleric's choosing so long as they remain within the range of the spell. Directing a swarm does not require much concentration on the cleric's part, and he is free to engage in other actions while commanding the insect swarm. The insects will only attack the enemies of the cleric. The swarms receive a +8 bonus to attacks and damage or +12 against unholy creatures.
28-33	The cleric summons eight insect swarms that he may direct as he wishes. The swarms creep and crawl after a target or targets of the cleric's choosing so long as they remain within the range of the spell. Directing a swarm does not require much concentration on the cleric's part, and he is free to engage in other actions while commanding the insect swarm. The insects will only attack the enemies of the cleric. The swarms receive a +10 bonus to attacks and damage or +15 against unholy creatures.
34-35	The cleric summons a titanic swarm of insects that fills an area equal to 100' square per CL. All enemies within the area of effect are subject to attack. The swarm receives a +10 bonus to attacks and damage or +15 against unholy creatures. The insects also devour all organic substances in the area (whether used by friend or foe), including clothing, leather straps and sacks, saddles, etc.
36+	The sky turns black with a biblical plague of locusts. The cleric can send this plague against an entire region, affecting one square mile per CL. The locust plague endures for more than a week, devouring all living matter in the affected area. The insects ravage the land, devouring crops, stripping leaves and bark from trees, destroying animal herds, consuming stored grain, and otherwise laying waste to the surrounding area. *All* living creatures in the affected area suffer 1d4 points of damage per day from the biting and scratching of insects. The cleric's enemies automatically suffer 1d4+10 points of damage per *round*, and unholy creatures suffer 2d6+20 points of damage. The only way to protect against this damage is for a creature to enter an enclosed space (such as a stone tomb or underground vault) that locusts cannot penetrate.

LEVEL 5 CLERIC SPELLS

Righteous Fire

Level: 5	Range: 100′ + 10′ per CL	Duration: Instantaneous	Casting time: 1 action	Save: See below

General	The cleric invokes a conflagration of divine fire to burn his foes.

Manifestation	See below.

1-19	Failure.
20-21	The cleric designates one target, which is suddenly engulfed in holy flame. The creature takes 1d6+2 points of damage per CL (maximum 10d6+20). A Ref save reduces the damage suffered by half.
22-25	A column of fire roars down to fill a 20′ cubic area. The fire does 1d6+1 points of damage per CL (maximum 10d6+10). A Ref save reduces the damage suffered by half.
26-27	A column of fire roars down to fill a 20′ cubic area. The fire does 1d10+2 points of damage per CL (maximum 10d10+20). A Ref save reduces the damage taken by half. Any creature slain by the fire is completely incinerated, leaving no remains and likely no possibility of revivification.
28-29	The cleric calls down two columns of divine flame. They each fill a 20′ cubic area. The fires do 1d12+3 points of damage per CL (maximum 10d12+30). No save is possible. A creature caught in both columns only takes damage once. Any creature slain by the fire is completely incinerated, leaving no remains and likely no possibility of revivification.
30-35	The cleric calls down three columns of divine flame. They each fill a 20′ cubic area. The fires do 1d20+4 points of damage per CL (maximum 10d20+40). No save is possible. A creature caught in both columns only takes damage once. Any creature slain by the fire is completely incinerated, leaving no remains and likely no possibility of revivification.
36-37	The cleric designates a nearby cloud in the sky, which proceeds to rain burning fire and lava down upon the ground..This affects an area of up to half a square mile. (If indoors or underground, this spell is still effective.) All creatures caught by the conflagration suffer 1d20 points of damage per CL. In addition, all creatures must make a Ref save; those that fail catch fire and suffer an addition 1d6 points of damage each round until the flames are extinguished with a subsequent save. Any creature slain by the initial rain of fire is completely incinerated.
38+	Pointing to a nearby mountain, hill, or rock anywhere within line of sight, the cleric raises his arms and calls forth a volcano from the ground. Gouts of liquid fire burst forth from the ground as lava coalesces all around. All creatures within a mile of the volcano are instantly killed via immolation unless they are immune to fire, such as fire elementals, or have extraordinary magical protection. All creatures to a range of the next five miles take an initial damage of 6d6 from lava and fire, then an additional 2d6 damage per round (no save) from the rain of fire, soot, coals, and ash until they reach a safe distance of five miles away. The sky is blackened by volcanic ash, weather patterns are disrupted, crops are destroyed, cities are leveled, and the wrath of a deity is evident.

Weather Control

Level: 5   Range: 2 miles   Duration: 4d12+CL hours   Casting time: 1 turn plus 1 turn (see below)   Save: N/A

General   The cleric alters natural weather patterns to create conditions of his choosing, even to the extent of producing very unnatural effects for the season and region. This spell takes 1 turn to cast, after which another ten minutes is required for the change in the weather to appear. Winds always blow from a direction chosen by the cleric, and the weather change is usually (but not always) dependent on the season.

Manifestation   Roll 1d4: (1) flashes of lighting appear in the cleric's eyes; (2) the cleric's chest swells unnaturally before he exhales a gust of wind; (3) strange colored and shaped clouds form over the cleric's position; (4) the air grows completely still and animals quiet as the weather begins to change.

1-19   Failure.

20-21   The cleric alters the weather slightly to produce a more pleasant or inclement condition. A light fog appears on a clear day; a light rain clears up; a soft breeze stirs otherwise still air; a light snowfall begins, etc.

22-25   The cleric produces a noticeable change in the weather, creating small squalls or stilling the same. Fog rolls in; rain begins to fall; snow starts to accumulate; winds gain strength; etc. The cleric can create weather effects strong enough to alter a farming season's outcome.

26-27   The cleric creates strong alterations in local weather patterns to produce impressive meteorological effects. Heavy snowfall suddenly begins; rain falls in sheets; strong winds start to blow; dense fog blankets the land, etc. The cleric can create weather effects strong enough to affect the success of an army or navy in battle.

28-29   The cleric produces destructive weather or calms the same. A blizzard blankets the area; hailstones fall from the sky; gale-force winds tear at rooftops; thunderstorms throw lighting down; tornadoes begin to touch down; etc. These destructive conditions are powerful enough to cause environmental damage to creatures caught outside (typically 1 to 1d4 points per round of exposure). The weather change is dependent on the season and the cleric has no control over the direction the weather takes. He cannot steer tornadoes at specific buildings or cause lighting to strike a special target. He can still control the wind's direction, however.

30-35   The cleric produces weather that is highly destructive and blatantly unnatural. Snow falls in high summer; heat waves melt polar glaciers; sleet storms wreak havoc on the desert, etc. Destructive conditions are powerful enough to cause environmental damage to creatures caught outside (typically 1 to 1d4 points per round of exposure). The cleric can also produce anomalous weather events if he desires. These include snows of unusual hues, rains of fishes or frogs; clouds of specific shapes or pattern, etc.

36-37   The cleric's command of the weather is terrifying. Not only can he create weather that is obviously unnatural for the season and climate, but he can direct the weather as if it were an extension of his body. Lightning strikes at specific individuals (10d6 damage per strike), windstorms affect certain buildings while leaving others untouched; storm winds fill the sails of some ships while avoiding others; etc. The judge has final say on what the effect(s) of the directed weather is, but these effects are powerful enough to cause massive devastation.

38-39   The cleric creates a magical maelstrom of weather that is magnificent in its power. Up to three weather effects of his choosing occur simultaneously, provided they do not conflict with one another. The cleric can have gale force winds, freezing sleet, and lightning happen in the same storm; summon down tornadoes, bludgeoning hail, and blinding rain all at once; ravage coasts with water spouts, tsunamis, and impenetrable fog; or any other combination of his choosing. The cleric could not, however, have scorching heat and freezing snow happen together. The judge has the final word on what combinations are allowable and the effects they have.

40+   The cleric causes utter destruction or calm the same in the area of effect. Lightning-filled tornadoes lay waste to fortifications; tsunamis laden with icebergs tear apart coastlines; frigid sleet and glacier winds instantaneously freeze creatures and plant life; etc. The storm will go down in legend. The judge is the final arbitrator on the devastation caused, but it should be catastrophic beyond even the greatest "perfect storm."

Whirling Doom

| Level: 5 | Range: 50' per CL | Duration: 1 round per level | Casting time: 1 action | Save: See below |

General The cleric creates a motionless barrier of whirling blades to bar passage and eviscerate those who come into contact with it. Enemies can attempt to fire missiles through the curtain of steel, but all creatures on the opposite side of the barrier enjoy a +4 bonus to their AC and a +2 bonus to Ref saves made against attacks originating on the other side.

Manifestation A field of spinning, razor-sharp blades appear in the air.

1-19 Failure.

20-21 The curtain occupies a vertical wall 20' square. Those passing through the blades suffer 1d6 points of damage per CL. If the barrier is created in an area already occupied by living creatures, they receive a Ref save to leap out of the area of effect before the blades commence slashing. A successful save indicates half damage is taken.

22-25 The curtain occupies a vertical wall 40' square. Those passing through the blades suffer 1d8 points of damage per CL. If the barrier is created in an area already occupied by living creatures, they receive a Ref save to leap out of the area of effect before the blades commence slashing. A successful save indicates half damage is taken.

26-27 The curtain occupies a vertical wall 60' square or a ring-shaped wall 20' in diameter. Those passing through the blades suffer 1d10 points of damage per CL. If the barrier is created in an area already occupied by living creatures, they receive a Ref save to leap out of the area of effect before the blades commence slashing. A successful save indicates half damage is taken.

28-29 The curtain occupies a vertical wall 80' square or a ring-shaped wall 30' in diameter. Those passing through the blades suffer 1d12 points of damage per CL. If the barrier is created in an area already occupied by living creatures, they receive a Ref save to leap out of the area of effect before the blades commence slashing. A successful save indicates half damage is taken.

30-35 The cleric creates two separate barriers. Each is either a wall 40' square or a ring-shaped wall 20' in diameter. Those passing through the blades suffer 1d12 points of damage per CL. If the barrier is created in an area already occupied by living creatures, they receive a Ref save to leap out of the area of effect before the blades commence slashing. A successful save indicates half damage is taken.

36-37 The cleric creates two separate barriers. Each is either a wall 60' square or a ring-shaped wall 30' in diameter. Those passing through the blades suffer 1d20 points of damage per CL. If the barrier is created in an area already occupied by living creatures, they automatically take damage with no save.

Alternately, the cleric can create a barrier 10' square that moves at a rate of 20' per round in any direction of his choosing. Those caught in the barrier's path must make a Ref save of suffer 1d20 points of damage per CL. Those who make their save are unharmed. Moving the barrier requires complete concentration on the part of the cleric, but he can choose to perform other actions in a round if he leaves the whirling curtain of steel motionless for that time. He may then move the barrier on subsequent rounds until the spell's duration ends.

38+ The cleric creates a terrifying field of whirling death. This barrier fills an area equal to 20' square per CL and the blades can be angled to face any direction of the cleric's choosing (horizontal, vertical, angled, etc.). Those caught in the barrier's path must make a Ref save of suffer 2d20 points of damage per CL. No save is allowed. The barrier cannot be moved, but it takes up any and all available space within the area of effect, altering its shape to fit down long hallways, oddly shaped rooms, etc.

CHAPTER SIX
QUESTS & JOURNEYS

A hero answers his calling, be it the travails of his duchy or an ocean-traversing escapade.

hero answers his calling, be it the travails of his duchy or an ocean-traversing escapade. Journeying to distant lands and faraway places is a part of every adventure. So, too, is the quest for extraordinary capabilities. This short chapter discusses these subjects.

QUESTING FOR THE IMPOSSIBLE

Modern role playing games contain a surfeit of rules defining spells, rituals, feats, and other mechanics for all manner of supernatural accomplishments. Raising the dead, improving an ability score, gaining weapon skill, receiving a divine boon are acts of dice-rolling and nothing more. The DCC RPG argues against this approach, and instead makes one simple request of both player and judge: follow the examples set by mythology and fiction and resolve such acts with a quest!

Here is a list of extraordinary acts in which the characters may wish to indulge and a suggested quest to accomplish them. Each of these is, of course, an adventure in itself. The judge should most certainly allow for extraordinary accomplishments in the DCC RPG—provided the players earn them. This game is not about mechanical solutions to requests; it's about *adventure*!

Realize that there are powers beyond the ken of player characters. An NPC sorcerer can know a spell or ritual that solves a difficult problem for the characters—but that spell need not be learned by the characters. There is no reason to explain the rules of magic; recall that there aren't any true "rules" of magic. Magic is *magical*. Perhaps the PC wizard *cannot* learn that spell for obscure and abstruse reasons. Lead your characters on quests toward allies with powers beyond their own rather than toward mechanical solutions.

For characters who do wish for extraordinary abilities, here are quests that could discover such possibilities:

Blessing: Do a favor for a god, and the god will do you a favor, too.

Breathe underwater: Locate the merman king and give him a perfect pearl.

Find safe passage through a terrible place: Bargain with Lady Luck: a week of safe passage now for a week of dangers later…but she picks the week of dangers.

Heal a terrible poison or disease, or blindness or deafness: Recover the long-lost vessel of liquid that heals any malady, or act with good faith toward a wounded creature of kindness.

Raise the dead: Journey to the lands of the dead and recover the lost soul, possibly by dancing, gaming, or jousting with Death himself. (Note: a DCC module deals with this exact subject. Look for *DCC #74: Blades against Death* as an example of how to perform such a quest.)

Remove a curse: Aside from specific methods as noted in Appendix C, consider a trip to the cave of the Oldest Crone, patron of witches, where the black stone representing that curse must be destroyed.

Speak with the dead: Obtain the tongue of a still-living witch who gives it willingly, then place it in the mouth of the corpse.

Slay an immortal: Find the hall of souls, where a candle is lit for every living being, somewhere on a divine plane of existence, and snuff the candle that represents that immortal's soul.

Summon creatures from beyond: Find the creature's representation in the vast collection of statues kept by Gorgon, the medusa god, then carry that statue back to the mortal realms and turn it to flesh.

Tame a dragon mount: Simply steal a dragon's egg and raise it from birth. Or, to tame an adult dragon, find the eggshell from which it hatched, which most dragons secure in a secret location.

Total party kill: Don't end the game! Transport all the player characters to Hell—where they can give in to Death's demands or try to fight their way out!

Unparalleled power: To achieve unparalleled power, make a pact with a deity of enormous power and promise it that which it cannot otherwise obtain.

Weapon proficiency: Find a true master of the indicated weapon and adventure with him, earning a potential bonus of +1 to +3 on attacks with that weapon given sufficient time. Of course the master may have demands of his own, and will expect much of his apprentice.

Wield a legendary magic weapon: Recover the magic weapon from its last known location.

JOURNEYS IN A SMALL WORLD

This manuscript will repeatedly stress the limits of knowledge in a medieval world. You, good sir, who read this manuscript, have access to an extraordinary amount of information. There is the internet and cell phones, there is television and radio, there are printed books, and there are libraries and universities and experts in your world. In a medieval setting, none of this exists. Pens and paper are expensive, there are no printing presses, and it takes a scribe almost a year to manufacture a single book. Most people are illiterate; there is no mechanized transportation, no long-range communication, and no photography. Information is communicated at the speed of verbal conversation, without photograph or illustration, and that information moves only so fast as a traveler's feet or his horse and wagon. *The traveler is the primary source of information in this world.* With travel comes knowledge; without travel there is no information.

Most everyday peasants in a medieval setting never travel more than a few miles from their places of birth. Their lives

are circumscribed by local terrain boundaries: a river to the east, the hills to the north, the village one town over to the south. In a game that accurately attempts to capture the medieval adventuring experience—or, phrased differently, in a game that retains the spirit of Appendix N—you do not need a vast space for adventuring. An area of land only 100 miles square should provide years of adventure, for it is a space larger than most living men will ever explore.

TRAVEL IN A MEDIEVAL SETTING

Low-level heroes, bereft of wealth, travel on foot or as passengers in farmers' carts and caravans. As they advance in name and station, they may acquire donkeys, ponies, or even great steeds to carry them. Here are a couple important points to remember.

First, travel is dangerous. When a man goes beyond the reach of his lord's cavalry and sheriff, he is on his own. Even in "civilized" lands, brigands accost wayfarers. The knights of neighboring duchies may harass mercenaries. And of course there are monsters.

Second, travel is rarely direct. Especially at lower levels when characters are paying passengers on caravans, there is business to conduct other than the PCs'. The caravan makes stops wherever it can sell or acquire goods. There may be other passengers with destinations involving religious pilgrimages, visiting relatives, or special errands. There are places to avoid: dangerous aboriginal tribes, barons charging egregious taxes, and regions superstitiously labeled as "haunted."

Third, travel is not easy. A city may have a few cobblestone streets, and a great kingdom may have a paved King's Road. Otherwise, travelers mostly follow muddy roads, tracked lanes, footpaths, and dry stream beds. A day's travel may end several hours shy of nightfall, "wasting" good travel time simply because the next inn is too far to reach before dark.

OVERLAND SPEED

With those caveats in mind, here are approximate traveling speeds for different modes of transportation. These assume normal traveling conditions: good weather, passable roads, and no delays. The speeds may be reduced by half or more due to bad weather, difficult terrain, brigands (or other encounters), caravan stops, excessive encumbrance, and other such things. Speed may be increased by up to a third with a forced march (typically for military purposes), but a forced march may cause 1 hp of damage over the course of a day (DC 10 Fort save to avoid). Horses and other steeds may also be forced at the same risk, or a fresh steed can be alternated regularly to increase speed. Exceptional steeds may travel at greater speeds.

Transportation	Hourly Speed	Daily Distance*
Walking	3 mph	24 miles
Mule or donkey	3 mph	24 miles
Horse or pony	4 mph	32 miles
Warhorse	5 mph	40 miles
Farmer's cart**	2 mph	16 miles
Passenger wagon***	3 mph	24 miles
Merchant's caravan	3 mph	24 miles
Raft or barge	1/2 mph	5 miles
Rowboat	1.5 mph	15 miles
Sailing ship	2 mph	48 miles
Warship (sailed and rowed)	2.5 mph	60 miles
Longship (sailed and rowed)	3 mph	72 miles
Galley	4 mph	96 miles

Assumes 8 hours of traveling time for overland methods. Waterborne travel can continue longer for man-powered methods (e.g., barges and rowboats) and go overnight for sailing vessels, which is built into the daily distance.

** *Two-wheeled cart with mule designed for hauling vegetables.*

*** *Covered wagon designed for carrying paying passengers. Available only between major destinations (e.g., large cities or trading ports).*

SECURITY WHILE TRAVELING

Camping is dangerous. Creatures roam the night, as do brigands and savages. A party that does not keep watch will be set upon by predators. Parties that do keep watch should be constantly reminded of the benefits of doing so: glittering red eyes circle the fire's light, never coming into full view, while mysterious flapping noises and gusts of sudden wind signal flying beasts lurking at the edges of safety.

Travelers plan their routes based on safe locations to stay at night. Inns and farm houses that take in travelers can charge for their services, even if all they offer is a solid roof, a bed of lice-ridden hay, and boiled turnips for dinner. Those few noblemen wealthy enough to build secure castles find their protection in high demand. Travelers may be invited to stay in a castle, but the transaction is not always ensured. Do the travelers march under coats-of-arms unfriendly to the castle's allies? Are they willing to pay homage to the local lord? Is there an old grudge, never forgotten, between the lord's grandfather and a distant uncle of one of the characters? And will the heroes contribute a few gold pieces—or a debt of honor—toward the upkeep of the stone walls?

The castle is an important part of any medieval fantasy game, and it should remain always mysterious and be never taken for granted. Even if only a way station for the night, there should be stories: the walled-off tower where a princess once hanged herself; the collapsed east wing, never rebuilt after a strange fire took many lives; the bricked-over fireplace in the great hall, said to contain the bones of a jester that japed too sharply about the lord's homely wife; the shadowed staircase to the cellar, from which strange hoots erupt on moonless nights.

So, too, should the lord of each castle be a character in his own way. Give the lord personality and appearance. Let him pass on important news to carry to the next town or issue unusual demands. Give the lord peculiar hobbies and pastimes or odd pursuits and inquiries. Travel is a chance to see and meet new and interesting people in a world where most inhabitants rarely stray more than a few miles from their birthplace.

Let it be recalled that travelers are rare and brave in a medieval setting. They bring tidings both good and bad and are the primary medium of long-distance communication. As is stressed elsewhere in this manuscript, there are no mundane sources of rapid information exchange; the common man, without magic, relies on travelers for news. At each place the adventurers stop, they will be expected to share the news and will gain new information to carry forth. The judge is encouraged to supply them with rumors at each stop, ranging from the quotidian affairs of peasant gossip (who married whom, who is sick, who had a child, and so on) to the stories of politics, religion, and even magic (which monsters have been sighted, which armies are on the move, which priests have switched parishes). Information can be a form of payment for the traveler to his host.

THE GREAT WHEEL

Your characters live on the skin of the earth—what is known as the Known Realms or Middle-Earth. In the caves and dungeons underground is the underdeep, known also as the Under-Earth or underdark. In the spaces above and beyond mortal comprehension is the Overworld, a region of distant dimensions and other planes of existence. All of these places together comprise the Great Wheel, a simplistic representation of the many places and planes of existence.

Since the earliest days of fantasy role playing, there have been systems to organize the many planes. This work does not need to re-create the wheel, so to speak, and thus does not present yet another organization of the planes, aside from the general metaphor of the Great Wheel. The author encourages the judge to reference one of the many previously-published sources of planar structure to populate his game world. However, the author does offer these pieces of advice:

- In the interest of creating an experience grounded in the wonder that is Appendix N, the judge is encouraged to begin extraplanar encounters at low levels. This does not mean unconquerable opponents immune to every weapon possessed by the characters. It could mean a cave that has more space within than without and corresponds to a planar junction; or a strange crea-

ture that can be banished in a manner accomplished by the low-level characters, even if their steel weapons will not wound it; or a magical gate or doorway that leads to a dangerous, magical realm, which is only later discovered to be on a different plane. An extraplanar plane is simply a magical place, and let those magical places become part of the adventure early.

- Avoid an overly structured approach to the planes. Further, to the extent that there is structure, avoid giving the characters (and players) too much knowledge of that structure. Just as the geography of Earth was not truly understood for many centuries after the medieval era—with entire continents being misunderstood and misplaced on maps!—there is no reason to think that the geography of the planes is fully understood by mortals. Let there be confusing links between places, difficult transitions, and unclear passages. Understanding the structure of the planes should be a lifetime's accomplishment for the characters.

- The planes can include *time* as a destination—both the past and future. Time travel is a strong theme in the books of Appendix N. This doesn't mean the characters necessarily have to travel in time, but they may encounter time travelers from the future (see page 429) or perhaps be visited by great wizards from the past.

- The planes can include *other dimensions* as a destination. Bizarre four-dimensional places, weird conglomerations of angles, strange geographies—all these can be planes, as well as "places of shadow or fire." Again, reference Appendix N for inspiration.

- Finally, the solar system can be part of planar travel. To an unschooled peasant, travel to another region is extraordinary, much less travel to another planet. Let the moons, planets, asteroids, and suns be "extraplanar" in your world. Travel to other planets can even be magical in nature, just as travel to the plane of fire—the concept of "space travel" need not exist.

RETAINERS, HIRELINGS, AND FOLLOWERS

Adventurers of wealth and renown recruit hirelings and henchmen to explore with them. Danger and excitement do not motivate all men, and thus these retainers must be promised a fee or a share of treasures recovered. An adventuring party may hire on retainers using these rules.

Note, however, that not all retainers may wish to travel. Many want only to earn a few coppers to feed their families. Do not assume that adventurers can keep the same hired hands from one locale to another.

Recruiting: For every 100 residents of a town or village, 1 man—not necessarily able-bodied—is willing to risk his life as an adventurer's helper. Areas of famine or hardship, where there are no other opportunities, may produce more prospective retainers; bustling centers of trade, with many competing chances at wealth, may produce fewer.

Equipping: Retainers come equipped with simple hide or leather armor, caps, and an axe, club, or spear. Some 20% have their own longswords and possibly armor but expect extra payment for being so equipped. All other equipment must be supplied by the characters.

Payment: Simple military duty in mundane circumstances, such as a man-at-arms in an army, commands payment of food and lodging plus 1-4 copper pieces per week. If the retainers bring good equipment, they'll charge another 1-4 cp per week.

A retainer expected to face supernatural horrors, un-dead spirits, or ferocious monsters demands at least 1 silver piece per day and up to 1 gold piece per day if facing extraordinary challenges.

Retainers higher than level 0 are rare, but if recruited they will ask for double the above wages.

Upon seeing the treasures recovered, retainers may also ask for a share thereof.

Morale: As covered in the combat section, a retainer must check morale in his first encounter. It is quite possible that he will run away upon realizing what he's up against. Unlike with normal monsters, the retainer is affected by loyalty to his employer. A retainer's morale check is modified by his Will save and also by his employer's Personality modifier.

At the end of each adventure, a retainer must make another morale check. The judge applies a modifier from -4 to +4, reflecting the retainer's wounds, his treatment at the hands of the characters, his payment and share of treasure, and the party's general success. A retainer who fails this morale check is spooked by the life of an adventurer, and chooses to return to the toil of village life.

Statistics: Retainers are level 0 characters. They have average ability scores, 3 hit points, and +0 saving throws.

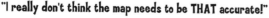

"I really don't think the map needs to be THAT accurate!"

CHAPTER SEVEN
JUDGE'S RULES

The judge is always right. Let the rules bend to you, not the other way around.

ADMONITIONS

 hight Joseph Goodman, author of this manuscript, and as ye suppose to be a judge, I admonish ye thus:

- The judge is always right. Let the rules bend to you not the other way around.

- Always roll your dice in public. "Let the dice fall where they may," as the saying goes. The players will learn fear, as they trust in the objectivity of your combat encounters.

- Let the characters die if the dice so dictate it. Nothing is as precious as a PC's life when it can be taken away — and nothing is so *unchallenging* as a game where the players know the judge will not kill their characters. The DCC RPG is designed for high character death rates — let this be true in your game as well. Achieving 5th level in the DCC RPG is a true accomplishment.

- Fear no rule. I know you will homebrew this game: I trust it will remain recognizable but different from as I conceived it. Such is as it should be.

THE KNOWN WORLD

he world is larger than your characters will ever know. As they explore, remember these facts of medieval life:

- Almost all common folk live and die within a few miles of their birthplace.

- Overland travel is dangerous and expensive. Most peasants can afford only to walk.

- Cultural variation is measured in towns and valleys not nations and continents.

- Most commoners are illiterate.

- Rare is the man who has traveled more than 20 miles from his home.

- There is no reliable form of long-range communication.

Make your world mysterious by making it *small* — very small. What lies past the next valley? None can be sure. When a five-mile journey becomes an adventure, you'll have succeeded in bringing life to your world.

WIZARD SPELLS

izard spells are not easily learned. While divine entities may place knowledge in the hearts of clerics, wizard spells result from dangerous interactions that do not follow predictable rules. Magic is not like physics. It is imprecise and the decimal point is hard to place, so to speak; as Harold Shea learned, summoning 1 dragon, 0.1 dragon, or 100 dragons is a matter of inculcation, not equations. A supernatural display can be accomplished in more than one way; one wizard may chant, another might practice a strange ritual, and a third may burn incense, all to produce the same result. Moreover, one wizard's method of magic may not work for another wizard due to some trick of bloodline, extraplanar allegiances, or simple cosmic fate. Magic is just that: *magic*.

The wizard's class progression table shows how many spells he knows. He does not simply learn new spells upon advancing a level, however. This rules convention of "spells known" plays out in game terms as follows.

GENERAL PRINCIPLES OF WIZARD SPELLS

In all conversations with a player about wizard spells, the judge should remember these principles.

1. Knowledge is scarce. There is no "encyclopedia of magic." The internet doesn't exist. Even the Gutenberg press does not exist! This is a medieval, feudal society without bookbinding technology. Knowledge is rare, and knowledge of spells and magic is even rarer. Obtaining that knowledge is as often as much a process of adventure than of reading. "Research" in the modern sense of going to a library with organized indices to retrieve certain books does not exist. Simply learning that a spell *exists* is a great accomplishment — much less learning how to cast it.

2. Wizards are jealous bastards. No offense, but it's true. When knowledge is scarce, he with the most knowledge holds an advantage over his peers — and wizards want that advantage. Identifying, obtaining, and learning a spell represents a significant investment; no wizard gives away that investment for free. A wizard must pay some price to loosen the lips of those who would share with him.

3. The means are mysterious. Even when a wizard learns that a spell exists and finds a source to teach him, the process of spellcasting may be beyond his grasp. Practice, practice, practice!

4. Obtaining magical knowledge should be part of the adventure. Finding new spells and magical knowledge should be a motivational goal for any wizard player.

5. Wizards seek understanding but are ever imperfect. While clerics *use* magic to further a cause, wizards seek to *understand* magic for its own sake. But they are

human, and their minds are finite. The fickle hand of fate—reflected in the randomness of the d20 die roll—shall always influence their efforts.

Learning new spells with level advancement: When a wizard advances to a new level, he knows a new spell. "Knowing" a spell works as follows.

1 If the wizard has heard stories of a new spell (through adventuring, another character, discovering a spell in a scroll or tome, or other game activities), he may identify that spell to learn. If not, his potential new spells are randomly determined (see below).

2 The wizard must dedicate some time to learning and practicing the spell. Assume at least one week per spell level, though it may vary.

3 The wizard may need to seek out a place where the knowledge is found, and may need to pay a price for that knowledge. See below for more on this.

4 When the wizard has studied the spell sufficiently, he makes a check against DC 10 + spell level. The check consists of 1d20 plus his caster level plus his Intelligence modifier. If he passes, he learns the spell. If he fails, he cannot attempt to learn that spell again until he has advanced another level.

DETERMINING NEW SPELLS

We encourage you to introduce knowledge of spells in-game through rumors, scrolls, demons, patrons, tomes, rare artifacts, conversation with peers, ancient lore, and myth and legends. Wizards who have not learned new spells through game experiences may randomly determine which new spells they are exposed to.

For every spell the wizard is eligible to learn, randomly identify 1-3 that he *can* learn. Presenting multiple options gives the wizard a "backup plan" if he fails to learn the first spell.

If the wizard fails to learn the first spell, give him the chance to learn another.

Finding knowledge: You can create adventures out of the search for knowledge. Since every wizard must learn many spells over the course of his career, it's best to reserve the adventures for important sources of multiple spells. Identifying a "fountain of knowledge" for that wizard can provide a great motivation for a long-term quest.

Here are some tables for randomly determining where spell knowledge can be found, what price must be paid for it, and which rare components are required to make it work. As the judge it's up to you to craft the story that turns these elements into an adventure.

Remember that spellcasting varies from wizard to wizard. A magician with a half-demon great-great-grandfather may cast fire-based spells more easily than a cultist who is purely mortal. Thus, the same spell cast by different wizards may have completely different requirements.

Table 7-1: Where is spell knowledge found?

1d16	Result
1	From the whispering lips of the corpse of Thaka-khan, a great wizard buried centuries ago under the desert sands
2	In the secret library of Alexandria, the only place in the world where more than 50 books can be found in the same room
3	With the witch-hags of Rahdomir, whose crazed chants bring insanity to all mortals who hear them
4	From the eldest sphinx
5	By gazing in the pool in the Hall of the Dragon Kings
6	In the Necronomicon, of which only seven copies exist, and the provenance of all seven copies is recorded on a scroll in the possession of a queer halfling now living in the forest
7	By clutching the magic sword Soulstealer, a black-runed, razor-edged warrior's blade that has not been seen for five hundred years
8	Carved in the ziggurats in the sunken city of Lemuria
9	By bargaining with demons on the plane of Asmodeus
10	In the purest drop of water in the morning dew
11	By translating the secret language of the dryads
12	In one's own soul, when viewed truly in a mirror of unparalleled purity
13	On the stone tablet of Hammurab
14	Inscribed on the back of a tombstone in the Necromancers' Graveyard
15	From consultation with the last cyclops
16	On the scroll of Shubteth, now frail with age

Table 7-2: What is the price of spell knowledge?

1d10	Result
1	One year of service
2	100,000 gold pieces
3	Defeating the greatest enemy of the person who shares the spell
4	A slice of the wizard's soul (causes ability score loss)
5	Marrying an ugly daughter
6	Sharing similar knowledge of spells unknown to the caster
7	Retrieving a unique object (the heart of a certain demon lord, the last ray of a dying sun, the rare blue flower of the Amazon, etc.)
8	Vow of silence
9	Building a great monument
10	Wearing hair in a topknot, in the custom of a rare sect of monks

Table 7-3: What components are required for the spell to function?

1d10	Result
1	Dragon's scale
2	Medusa's eye
3	Harpy's feather
4	Basilisk's gaze
5	Virgin's pure heart
6	The blood of an un-dead
7	A hyena's bark
8	A mother's love for her child
9	Utterance of a seventh son
10	The most brilliant diamond

SUMMONING A FAMILIAR

A wizard can summon a familiar with the spell *find familiar*. The resulting familiar is determined by his spell check and alignment. The higher the spell check, the more powerful the familiar and the greater effect it has on the wizard's magic.

Generate a familiar as follows:

1. Determine familiar type: guardian, focal, arcane, or demonic (see table 7-4).

2. Determine physical configuration (see table 7-5).

3. Determine personality (see table 7-6).

Step 1: Familiar type. Determine familiar type based on the spell check and caster's alignment. Familiars grant their caster abilities based on their type, as follows.

All familiars: All familiars have these traits:

- 1d4+2 hit points.

- AC 14 (due to small size and agility).

- Use the wizard's saving throws.

- Are unusually intelligent for their species, typically around an Int of 5 in human terms.

- The wizard and familiar can communicate telepathically, though this is limited by the familiar's senses and intelligence (e.g., a toad's 6-inch height limits its ability to see onto tabletops, and it cannot read).

- The familiar is absolutely loyal to its wizard master.

- The wizard gains bonus hit points equal to the familiar's.

- If the familiar has a natural ability, the wizard gains a +4 bonus when using that same ability. For example, a wizard with a cat familiar gains a +4 bonus to attempts to sneak silently.

Guardian familiars: Guardian familiars are combat-oriented. They focus on defending their wizard and are not afraid to enter combat. Guardian familiars have these traits:

- An additional 1d4+2 hit points (which the wizard also receives).

- An attack at +4 that does 1d6 points of damage (crit die 1d12, crit table III).

Table 7-4: Familiar Type

Spell check by Alignment	12-17	18-23	24-29	30+
Lawful	Guardian	Focal	Focal	Arcane
Neutral	Guardian	Arcane	Focal	Demonic
Chaotic	Guardian	Demonic	Arcane	Focal

- A +2 AC bonus (for a total AC of 16).

- A +1 to all saving throws.

- An incremental improvement to their attack equal to the wizard's attack bonus at each level. For example, when the wizard reaches level 2 and gains a +1 attack, the familiar's attack bonus goes from +4 to +5. When the wizard reaches level 5 and gains a +2 attack bonus, the familiar's bonus goes from +5 to +6.

Focal familiars: Focal familiars enable the wizard to concentrate magical energy at the familiar's location, casting a spell through the familiar. Focal familiars have these traits:

- In addition to communicating telepathically with the familiar, the wizard can actually *see* through the familiar's eyes.

- The wizard can cast spells with his familiar as the point of origin rather than himself. This ability lets the familiar deliver spells that normally require the caster to touch his target.

- Any spell that is cast through the familiar improves the wizard's spell check result by +1.

- An attack at +1 that does 1d3 points of damage.

Arcane familiar: Arcane familiars are magically imbued with a special power of some kind. They grant the wizard a spell or power that he may not have otherwise possessed. Arcane familiars have these traits:

- The familiar arrives knowing one randomly generated level 1 spell that the wizard does not already know. Alternately, the judge is encouraged to create an interesting spell-like power, potentially linked to the wizard's patron or Luck characteristics.

- The wizard may cast the familiar's spell at his normal spell check modifier, as if it were an additional spell in his repertoire. He may lose this spell for a day as normal, regain it the next day as normal, and so on.

- An attack at +1 that does 1d3 points of damage.

Demonic familiar: This is a familiar specifically sent from the nether regions, an outside plane, or in exchange for favors performed by a supernatural patron. The demonic familiar has an alien cast to its features. A demonic familiar has these traits:

- A sensitivity to corruption and negative energy. Any time the wizard rolls a 1 on a spell check which results in corruption, the familiar automatically absorbs half the effect of the corruption, rounding down in the wizard's favor. For example, if corruption resulted in loss of 1 point of Strength, the familiar would lose 1 Strength and the wizard would be unaffected. If the result were a loss of 2 Strength, both the familiar and the wizard would each lose 1 Strength.

- A claim to the wizard's soul. If the wizard dies while the familiar still lives, the wizard's soul is claimed by

the familiar. The wizard then cohabitates the familiar's body for all eternity (or until the familiar's physical form is slain). If the appropriate magic is performed, the wizard's soul may be transferred to another physical form.

- An immunity to many mortal diseases, poisons, and infections. As a result of this, the wizard gains a +4 bonus to Fortitude saving throws against any kind of infection, poison, disease, or other debilitating effect. Additionally, any effect that bypasses this improved protection is split between the wizard and familiar (rounding down in the wizard's favor). For example, if the wizard is afflicted by a spider bite that causes him to lose 2 Stamina, the familiar loses 1 Stamina and the wizard loses 1 Stamina. If the Stamina loss were only 1 point, only the familiar would be affected.

- An attack at +2 that does 1d4 points of damage.

Step 2: Physical configuration. Roll d14 on table 7-5, cross-referenced against the wizard's alignment, to determine the physical configuration of the familiar that arrives. Certain familiars have abilities particular to their form; their master receives a bonus when performing a similar action, as noted in parenthesis.

Step 3: Familiar personality. Roll 1d20 on table 7-6 to determine the familiar's personality.

Table 7-5: Familiar Physical Configuration (And Master's Benefit)

D14	Lawful	Neutral	Chaotic
1	Eagle (excellent vision)	Badger (melee attacks deal extra +1 damage)	Giant centipede (10' climb speed)
2	White cat (move very silently)	Wolverine (+2 hit points)	Black cat (move very silently)
3	Hawk (excellent vision)	Owl (can see at night as well as normal human can see in day, plus excellent hearing)	Bat (extraordinary hearing)
4	Brownie (excellent at hiding in forest)	Pixie (excellent at hiding in forest)	Cobra (poisoned bite; DC 16 Fort save or lose 1d6 Stamina)
5	Miniature armored knight with a visor that is never lifted (+1 AC)	Miniature minotaur (+1 Strength)	Tarantula (melee attacks deal poison: Fort DC 14 or temporary loss of 1 Agility)
6	Giant bee (melee attacks deal extra +1 stinging damage)	Giant cricket (loud, commanding voice)	Weasel (supernatural ability to squeeze into tight places)
7	Faithful hound (all followers, retainers, etc. receive +2 to morale checks)	Lizard (40' movement)	Spider monkey (20' climb speed)
8	Giant ant (+1 to all attempts at ESP, telepathy, scrying, etc.)	Turtle (+2 AC but movement reduced by -5')	Pseudo-dragon (breath weapon 1/day: cone, 20' long x 10' wide, 2d6 fire damage)
9	Extraplanar ant (+1 to all attempts at planar travel)	Toad (can breathe underwater for up to 20 minutes)	Miniature woman of extraordinary beauty (+2 Personality)
10	Miniature version of the wizard himself, but ancient in age (grants an extra life: the first time the caster dies of any cause, the familiar dies instead and wizard is restored to life with full hit points less consequences of familiar dying)	Tiny elemental (+1 to all checks/saves relating to that element; determine type randomly with 1d12: (1) earth, (2) air, (3) fire, (4) water, (5) ash, (6) lava, (7) ice, (8) mist, (9) dust, (10) steam, (11) mud, (12) something even more exotic (e.g., gold, silver, cyclone, dew, stone, etc.))	Python (melee attack causes constriction: automatic +1d4/+2d4/+3d4/etc. damage each round after first)
11	Giant wasp (melee attacks deal poison: Fort DC 12 or temporary loss of 1 Str)	Crow (uncanny ability to detect gems and shiny objects)	Tiny viper (extraordinary sense of smell)
12	Miniature robed wizard with a cowled face that is never revealed (+1 to spell checks on one randomly determined spell)	Horned slug (melee attack causes paralysis: Fort DC 12 or paralyzed for 1d4+CL rounds)	Tiny demon (i.e., imp or quasit; +2 Luck that, if used, restores naturally each night, similar to how a thief or halfling recovers Luck)
13	Miniature gorilla (+1 Strength)	Giant beetle (+1 AC)	Scorpion (+2 to Fort saves vs. poison)
14	Miniature version of the wizard himself, but young and spry (+1 Stamina)	Rat (120' infravision)	Skeletal rat (+1 damage against un-dead)

Table 7-6: Familiar Personality

D20	Personality
1	Grumpy
2	Angry
3	Eager and curious
4	Complains constantly about creaky joints
5	Normally mellow but becomes inexplicably animated when discussing (1d6) (1) opposite sex, (2) gnomes, (3) clouds, (4) flowers, (5) pancakes, (6) leather armor
6	Cranky
7	Narcissistic
8	Wide
9	Vapid (polishes nails constantly)
10	Garrulous (won't shut up)
11	Stingy
12	Jolly
13	Introspective
14	Convivial
15	Lazy
16	Aloof
17	Charitable
18	Sexy
19	Mellow
20	Sleepy

CONSULTING A SPIRIT

The spell *consult spirit* allows a wizard to reach out and make contact with an otherworldly spirit. Enterprising wizards can use this spell to reach the ghosts of slain creatures they encounter, perhaps to inquire as to how the creature died. Curious wizards may use this spell to ask open-ended questions of the spiritual powers around them, discovering valuable information or learning how certain magic works.

The judge is encouraged to use this spell as a means of moving along adventures or pushing wizards to new levels of knowledge. Should you need inspiration as to the type of spirit encountered, here is a simple table that can be used. Roll 1d10 randomly or choose:

Roll	Nature of spirit
1	Ghost of a deceased mortal creature. In life it was a (1d8) (1) wizard, (2) warrior, (3) thief, (4) cleric, (5) dwarf, (6) elf, (7) halfling, (8) goblinoid. It died (1d4) (1) naturally of old age, (2) in a terrible accident, (3) bravely in combat, (4) violently and seeks revenge.
2	Nature spirit that guards a nearby terrain feature (hill, lake, tree, mountain, grove, boulder, flower, etc.).
3	Low-ranking demon on one of the nine hells who knows very little but is willing to aid anyone who can promise him advancement.
4	Lordly djinni, satrap of his own mini-plane, who is (1d6) (1) annoyed at the intrusion, (2) curious about his interlocutor, (3) afraid of being discovered, (4) introverted and interested only in books, (5) grateful for the interruption in his boring life, (6) an aggressive conqueror intrigued by the prospect of a new land to invade.
5	An "average" elemental of no particular import, associated with the element of (1d12) (1) earth, (2) air, (3) fire, (4) water, (5) ash, (6) lava, (7) ice, (8) mist, (9) dust, (10) steam, (11) mud, (12) something even more exotic (e.g., gold, silver, cyclone, dew, stone, etc.).
6	An angel or celestial interested in (1d4) (1) protecting the weak, (2) punishing evil, (3) converting new believers, (4) destroying heathens.
7	A high-ranking demon, possibly (10% chance) a demon prince, who is most certainly annoyed, angry, or outright vengeful at the intrusion and adds the wizard to his list of enemies.
8	A chaos lord, possibly (10% chance) at the Courts of Chaos themselves, who is (1d4) (1) intrigued at the possibility of a mortal agent, (2) eager to sow chaos through misinformation, (3) afraid of rivals, (4) interested in raising a mortal army.
9	A nascent godling or demi-god (10% chance of a full-fledged god, 1% chance of an elder god) that is (1d4) (1) difficult to communicate with due to its long-term sense of time, (2) very focused on its own agenda and followers, (3) aggressively recruiting allies to oppose another god, (4) drowsy and not yet fully sentient.
10	An alien intelligence from beyond our universe so foreign that communication is difficult, with a frame of reference beyond mortal comprehension and a sense of place and time that is enigmatic.

USING MERCURIAL MAGIC TO DEFINE MAGIC SCHOOLS

Mercurial magic creates a unique version of each spell for every caster. As presented in the player chapter of this work, mercurial magic genuinely differentiates the casting of the same spell between two casters. The basic concept of mercurial magic can be further explored to create even more distinction between casters. Here are a few ideas presented to stimulate thought in the reader's own campaign.

Schools of Magic: When an illusionist casts a *magic missile*, does it derive from the same eldritch rites as the *magic missile* cast by a necromancer? Probably not. Consider creating your own custom mercurial magic tables that align with the schools of magic in your own campaign. Black magic and white magic; illusionists, elementalists, conjurers, diabolists, necromancers, and summoners; pyromancers and cryomancers; witches, warlocks, and wardens: each type of wizard can have its own mercurial magic table, thus further differentiating varieties of spellcasting.

Racial casting: Why should an elf's spell be the same as a wizard's? Furthermore, why should a dark elf's be the same as a high elf's? And further still, why would an orc shaman cast spells the same as either elf or human? Mercurial magic becomes another technique for distinguishing spellcasting by racial type.

Patron casting: Finally, consider creating customized mercurial magic tables for the supernatural patrons you design for your campaign. Once a wizard has cast *patron bond*, all further spells could be modified by the mercurial mark of that patron. In this way, the mercurial magic elements could resemble the taint of patrons as described above.

IULLEN

SUPERNATURAL PATRONS

Patron magic is powerful. It is the means by which wizards surmount the limits of mortal magic. At lower levels, an invoked patron provides material aid; at higher levels, it can substantially elevate the caster's level of magical ability.

Acquiring a Patron: While a cleric worships a deity out of shared belief, common alignment, similar ethics, and an affiliation for the deity's value, a wizard pursues a patron strictly in the pursuit of power—nothing more. A cleric may come to his deity after a life-long quest for meaning; a wizard discovers a terrible invocation that binds demon power to mortal control, and from thenceforth, demands service from said demon. Patron invocation is a function of a wizard gaining the upper hand on, or at least a good negotiation position with, a demon, ghost, spirit, elemental, or other supernatural being capable of supporting his spellcasting.

The bond between wizard and patron is established after the supplicant completes the appropriate ceremony using the *patron bond* spell. He then makes a single spell check. Failure means he must try the ceremony again; success means the patron accepts his new servant. Thenceforth, the wizard may invoke his patron with *invoke patron* at least once a day and possibly more often depending on the success of the *patron bond* spell.

Quid Pro Quo: The patron will ask things in return for his service. These may be sacrifices, quests, or objects. The judge should convey to the player what these requests may be. They may arrive as a whispered request at each invocation of the patron, come as dreams, or actually be spoken messages delivered by servants of the patron. A wizard who refuses to obey his patron—or is slow in acting—may find his patron less apt to aid him in the future.

A patron pact is not the same as worship. The patron's clerics smite his enemies, build temples in his name, and reinforce his creed with action; but a wizard patron simply negotiates for power, offering services for aid. It is a mercenary exchange, nothing more.

Patrons are not always gods. A patron can be any powerful supernatural creature. In fact they are usually demons, devils, and demi-gods, not full deities. To deign low enough to engage in compacts with mortals would not be flattering to a deity's ego.

Patron Spells: Invoking the aid of a patron is a highly unpredictable process. The whims of a demon are such that the aid sought is not always the aid that is given. When *invoke patron* is cast, the results can vary widely, as described below. But in some cases, a patron can also grant access to specific spells, according to its nature and whims.

The spell tables include an entry for a "patron spell" at each level. The examples below describe level 1, 2, and 3 patron spells for several patrons in detail. The judge should feel free to develop similar spells for other patrons.

Note that patron spells are, generally speaking, slightly more powerful than other spells of the same level. This comes at a cost. Just as with *invoke patron*, every casting of a patron spell represents an act performed on the wizard's behalf by the patron – who may demand recompense at some future date.

Spellburn: The player portion of this work includes a table for randomly determining the requests associated with spellburn. Role playing the spellburn interaction reinforces the connection between character and patron, and the judge is encouraged to always remind the players exactly what is happening when spellburn occurs: it is not just a mechanical game term but a transaction between a mortal and an immortal. Once patron magic is introduced into your game, the spellburn process can become even more engaging. As you create your own patrons, we encourage you to create customized spellburn tables for those patrons and perhaps even keep a handy list of what favors they currently have "available for lending," so to speak. That way, whenever a character spellburns, you can easily reinforce the patron bond and create adventure seeds as well. See below for examples of this in practice with several patrons.

Patron Taint: The spells cast by patron-based wizards eventually take on the aspect of the wizard's patron. A wizard of Azi Dahaka, for example, may find small clouds of dust kicked up when he casts *magic missile*, even though that spell is unrelated to his patron.

The first time a wizard casts *invoke patron, patron bond,* or any other patron-based spell, there is a 1% chance that his spellcasting becomes tainted by the patron. At each subsequent casting, that chance increases by 1%. The chance after the second casting is 2%, then 3%, then 4%, and so on. The 1% chance is based on *casting* a patron-based spell, whether the spell is successful or not.

The patron taint indicates that the wizard's ability to use magic is now so deeply integrated with the patron's aid that almost any spellcasting carries some engagement from the patron. This has visual implications, as noted below, and may also carry some benefit. But, again, the wizard is now even more indebted to the patron. The only way to remove a patron taint is to exorcise the relationship between patron and wizard once and for all.

If the dice indicate a patron taint is acquired, use the examples below to determine what it is. Each patron will have a number of indications of taint, and each die roll indicating taint gives the opportunity for one kind of taint to manifest. Eventually a spellcaster will acquire all the signs of taint, at which point there is no need to continue rolling.

Once a patron taint is obtained, the chance to gain a taint resets to 1% on each casting of a patron-based spell. It then increases to 2%, 3%, 4%, and so on until another taint is earned, at which point it resets again.

Full examples are given on the pages that follow for five patrons, and the judge is encouraged to develop detail for the other patrons given and for his own campaign.

Common Patrons: The following pages include detailed descriptions for some patrons well-known to those who seek power. They are:

- Bobugbubilz, demon lord of amphibians
- Sezrekan the Elder, the wickedest of sorcerers
- Azi Dahaka, demon lord of storms and waste
- The King of Elfland, ruler of the fey lands beyond the twilight
- The Three Fates, who control the fate of all men and gods to see that the world reaches its destiny

In addition, we have included simple entries for three more patrons. These patrons include only the results of an *invoke patron* spell check, without example spells or taint descriptions. Use these as examples and feel free to expand upon them for your own games!

- Yddgrrl, the World Root
- Obitu-Que, Lord of the Five
- Ithha, Prince of Elemental Wind

Creating Your Own Patrons: The judge is encouraged to devise his own supernatural patrons, both to fit his individual campaign and to fit the desires of the players. Some of the patrons in this work were designed to reflect the interests of DCC RPG playtesters. Designing a patron requires only five easy steps:

1. Theme. Each supernatural patron is a sentient being in its own right. It lives somewhere on the known planes, has interests and affinities, and pursues its own desires, whether these be material, spiritual, or emotional. Think through the nature of the patron you are creating, and how it would be reflected in spellcasting.

2. *Invoke patron* results. Design a table indicating how the patron responds to the spell *invoke patron*.

3. Patron taint. Design a randomized table indicating what kind of patron taint occurs.

4. Patron spells. Design one patron spell for each level.

5. Spellburn. Create a list or randomized table of "ready requests" that the patron would demand in return for spellburn.

You can use the examples on the following pages as templates.

BOBUGBUBILZ

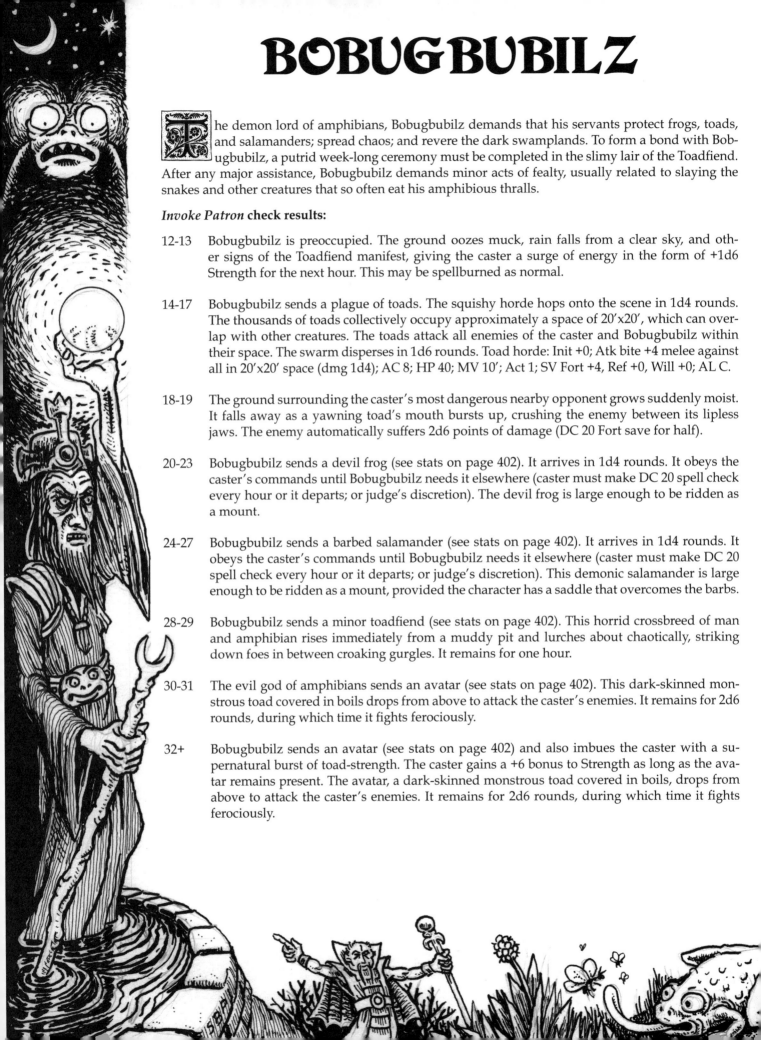

The demon lord of amphibians, Bobugbubilz demands that his servants protect frogs, toads, and salamanders; spread chaos; and revere the dark swamplands. To form a bond with Bobugbubilz, a putrid week-long ceremony must be completed in the slimy lair of the Toadfiend. After any major assistance, Bobugbubilz demands minor acts of fealty, usually related to slaying the snakes and other creatures that so often eat his amphibious thralls.

Invoke Patron check results:

12-13   Bobugbubilz is preoccupied. The ground oozes muck, rain falls from a clear sky, and other signs of the Toadfiend manifest, giving the caster a surge of energy in the form of +1d6 Strength for the next hour. This may be spellburned as normal.

14-17   Bobugbubilz sends a plague of toads. The squishy horde hops onto the scene in 1d4 rounds. The thousands of toads collectively occupy approximately a space of 20'x20', which can overlap with other creatures. The toads attack all enemies of the caster and Bobugbubilz within their space. The swarm disperses in 1d6 rounds. Toad horde: Init +0; Atk bite +4 melee against all in 20'x20' space (dmg 1d4); AC 8; HP 40; MV 10'; Act 1; SV Fort +4, Ref +0, Will +0; AL C.

18-19   The ground surrounding the caster's most dangerous nearby opponent grows suddenly moist. It falls away as a yawning toad's mouth bursts up, crushing the enemy between its lipless jaws. The enemy automatically suffers 2d6 points of damage (DC 20 Fort save for half).

20-23   Bobugbubilz sends a devil frog (see stats on page 402). It arrives in 1d4 rounds. It obeys the caster's commands until Bobugbubilz needs it elsewhere (caster must make DC 20 spell check every hour or it departs; or judge's discretion). The devil frog is large enough to be ridden as a mount.

24-27   Bobugbubilz sends a barbed salamander (see stats on page 402). It arrives in 1d4 rounds. It obeys the caster's commands until Bobugbubilz needs it elsewhere (caster must make DC 20 spell check every hour or it departs; or judge's discretion). This demonic salamander is large enough to be ridden as a mount, provided the character has a saddle that overcomes the barbs.

28-29   Bobugbubilz sends a minor toadfiend (see stats on page 402). This horrid crossbreed of man and amphibian rises immediately from a muddy pit and lurches about chaotically, striking down foes in between croaking gurgles. It remains for one hour.

30-31   The evil god of amphibians sends an avatar (see stats on page 402). This dark-skinned monstrous toad covered in boils drops from above to attack the caster's enemies. It remains for 2d6 rounds, during which time it fights ferociously.

32+   Bobugbubilz sends an avatar (see stats on page 402) and also imbues the caster with a supernatural burst of toad-strength. The caster gains a +6 bonus to Strength as long as the avatar remains present. The avatar, a dark-skinned monstrous toad covered in boils, drops from above to attack the caster's enemies. It remains for 2d6 rounds, during which time it fights ferociously.

PATRON TAINT: BOBUGBUBILZ

When patron taint is indicated for Bobugbubilz, roll 1d6 on the table below. When a caster has acquired all six taints at all levels of effect, there is no need to continue rolling any more.

Roll   **Result**

1   Buzzing, biting flies appear when the caster casts *any* spell. They distract and annoy but otherwise do no harm. If this result is rolled a second time, the effect is amplified such that a large black swarm of flies appears with each spell. The swarm is large enough to distract nearby creatures within 10', both friend and foe (DC 8 Will save or -1 to all rolls for one round), though the caster is immune. If this result is rolled a third time, the swarm of flies follows the caster constantly, day and night, whether he is casting spells or doing something else.

2   The caster is constantly wet with moisture, as if he were in a sauna or a humid swampland. His brow moistens, he sweats constantly, and by the end of every day his clothes are soaked through. This affects his ability to carry scrolls, paper books, and other such things. If this result is rolled a second time, the caster sweats so profusely that his clothes are soaked by noontime every day. If this result is rolled a third time, the caster actually exudes a constant trickle of moisture. He is constantly thirsty and must continually rehydrate his body, and he leaves puddles behind when he stops moving.

3   The caster's face gains a distinctly batrachian air. His eyes move apart, his brow thickens, and his lips extend and tighten. His voice deepens and takes on a croaking echo. If this result is rolled a second time, the caster's face transforms even further to resemble a frog, including the lengthening of his tongue and the appearance of eye ridges. At night he involuntarily and subconsciously makes croaking noises in his sleep. He can still pass for human, some of the time, although only by claiming he's deformed or otherwise strange. If this result is rolled a third time, the caster's head transforms completely into a frog's head. He can still speak, in a strange amphibious overtone, but there is absolutely no way he can pass for a normal human.

4   Every time the caster casts any spell, the area of effect is filled with a horrid swampland odor. Like a mix of rotting vegetation and fishy overtones, the smell is in no way pleasant. If this result is rolled again, a noxious smell accompanies the caster at all

times, and is sufficiently vile that passersby comment on it. If this result is rolled a third time, the caster stinks so badly he is not welcome in polite company (but is considered fragrant and delicious by the followers of Bobugbubilz).

5   Whenever the caster casts a spell, his legs extend and change their joint structure. They look deformed, and the caster must then move in short hops for a period of 1d4 rounds, at which point his legs return to normal. (If a spell effect interacts with this, the spell effect takes precedent.) If this result is rolled a second time, the transformation is more complete, such that the caster's legs truly resemble frog's legs for 1d4 turns. He does not gain any extraordinary leaping ability but must move in hops rather than steps, which looks strange. If this result is rolled a third time, the caster's legs permanently change into frog's legs. He gains the ability to leap his full movement speed in a single hop (e.g., if he moves 30' he can cover a full 30' with one hop, allowing him to jump across ravines and pits).

6   When the caster casts a spell, tiny toads appear around him. They drop from the air, crawl from the folds of his clothing, dig out of the ground beneath his feet, and sometimes materialize as part of the spell being cast. Then they scamper off into the underbrush. If this result is rolled a second time, the toads appear not just when the caster casts a spell but also 1d4 times randomly each day. It may be when the caster sits down to dinner, or tries to study a spellbook, or draws his dagger for combat: the toads just appear. If this result is rolled a third time, the toads become a permanent accompaniment to the caster. He is always followed by a retinue of croaking, burrowing, hopping frogs and toads of various sizes, ranging from newly natured tadpoles up to bullfrogs. No matter how many times he shoos them new ones arrive from unexpected sources. The caster has a very hard time fitting into polite society.

PATRON SPELLS: BOBUGBUBILZ

The demon lord of amphibians grants three unique spells, as follows:

Level 1: *Tadpole transformation*

Level 2: *Glorious mire*

Level 3: *Bottomfeeder bond*

SPELLBURN: BOBUGBUBILZ

Bobugbubilz does not reason like Man, and his requests do not always have an immediate end goal. When a caster utilizes spellburn, roll 1d4 on the table below when a request is made. These ideas should hopefully give you room to expand in your own campaign.

Roll   Spellburn Result

1   Bobugbubilz needs the blood of a dry-dweller (a creature that lives only on land). The caster's blood will do (expressed as Stamina, Strength, or Agility loss).

2   The demon lord of amphibians needs the feet of a man-creature. In this special situation, the character can spellburn up to 10 points of ability score loss, but need not take any physical action or damage. If he sacrifices the feet of a man-creature (any humanoid will do) to Bobugbubilz before the next sunrise, the character takes no spellburn. If he fails to find such a sacrifice, he takes the full 10 points, distributed across ability scores at the judge's discretion, at the next sunrise.

3   Bobugbubilz requires the sweet voice of the caster to make an invocation that his own amphibious servants cannot pronounce properly. Time slows to a crawl as the caster character is whisked away to a dizzying plane of close-quartered, moist, womb-like caverns, where is forced to read a text written in the words of his native language but with a recondite meaning utterly beyond his comprehension. Upon completing the invocation, he appears back on his native plane. No time seems to have passed, and he finds himself weakened by whatever extent he sacrificed ability score points for spellburn.

4   A slithering host of foul serpents wriggles forth from the ground at the caster's feet, where they promptly bite his ankles and begin sucking his blood. If the caster resists, the serpents flee and the spellburn fails. If he does not resist, the serpents suck blood until the spellburn is complete as normal, then they wriggle back into the earth. As they disappear below the ground, one turns its head back to offer thanks from Bobugbubilz…then it is gone.

Tadpole Transformation

Level: 1 (Bobugbubilz)	Range: Self	Duration: Varies	Casting time: 1 round	Save: None

General   A true servant of Bobugbubilz enjoys the calm of the deep swamp. The relaxing buzz of mosquitoes and biting flies, the cooling touch of muddy water, the irregular splashes of frogs and fishes, and the deep-throated calls of the swampland bullfrogs: these are the sounds and sights that bring happiness to Bobugbubilz and his thralls. This spell enables the caster to enjoy such sensations by changing his body to best accommodate them.

Manifestation   See below.

1   Lost, failure, and patron taint.

2-11   Lost. Failure.

12-13   The caster's legs double in girth, his ankle joints extend, and his legs double-back like a frog's. He can now hop distances equal to twice his normal walking speed. This means the caster can make a standing leap clear across chasms and pits or hop rapidly to move at twice his normal speed. The transformation lasts for 1d6 turns.

14-17   The caster grows a stiff, tadpole-like tail. He can now swim at a speed equal to double his normal walking speed. The transformation lasts for 1d6 turns.

18-19   The caster grows gills in the side of his neck. He can now breathe underwater for 1d6 turns.

20-23   The caster's mouth distorts into the wide, gulping maw of a frog, and his tongue lengthens. He gains a bite attack that deals 1d6 damage plus Strength modifier. Additionally, the caster can extend his sticky tongue with great accuracy. As a ranged attack, he can target any object within 40' with his tongue. Success indicates the caster latches onto the object and can reel it back with an effective Strength of 20 (for purposes of the sticky tongue only)—the target must make an opposed Strength check to resist. The effect lasts for 1d6 turns.

24-27   The caster undergoes a broad transformation that grants him frog legs, a stiff tadpole tail, gills, and a frog mouth, as the above four results. The effect lasts for 1d6 turns.

28-29   The caster gains all effects from results 24-27 above, and the duration is extended to 1d6 hours.

30-31   The caster is transformed into a walking avatar of Bobugbubilz. His girth and mass grows to roughly double normal. His arms and legs thicken, he grows a tadpole-like tail, and his frog-like mouth is imposing in size. He gains the hopping, swimming, breathing, biting, and tongue-lashing abilities outlined in results 12-23 for a period of 1d6 hours. In addition, due to his larger size and constitution, he gains 2d6 temporary hit points and is treated as having a Strength of 18 for all normal purposes (including melee combat).

32+   The caster is transformed into a walking avatar of Bobugbubilz. His girth and mass grows to roughly *triple* normal. His arms and legs thicken, he grows a tadpole-like tail, and his frog-like mouth is imposing in size. He gains the hopping, swimming, breathing, biting, and tongue-lashing abilities outlined in results 12-23 for a period of 1d6 days, which can be cut short at any point he wishes. In addition, due to his larger size and constitution, he gains 3d6 temporary hit points and is treated as having a Strength of 22 for all normal purposes (including melee combat).

Glorious Mire

Level: 2 (Bobugbubilz)   Range: Touch   Duration: Varies   Casting time: 1 round   Save: None

General   The demon lord of amphibians is most comfortable in the endless swamplands of his home plane. These pits of briny mud extend endlessly toward a low brown horizon, entangled in roots and sunk amidst stiff gray plants and furry mildewed ruins. With this spell, the caster transforms his immediate surroundings into the swampland that Bobugbubilz calls home. Stone floors soften and change to mud, trees destabilize and wobble on their newly liquid foundation, and castles sink into the mire. At low levels the caster can affect only a small volume of space, but at high levels, this spell can bring down castles.

Manifestation   See below.

1   Lost, failure, and patron taint.

2-11   Lost. Failure.

12-13   Failure, but spell is not lost.

14-15   The caster can transform a small space to swamp for 1d6 turns. He must touch the space to be affected. The space is equal to eight cubic feet or roughly the size of a human-sized door or a 2′ cube. Any mundane, non-living material can be affected (wood, stone, gold, dirt, etc.). The space changes into a semi-liquid muddy pool. If cast on a door, the door slides to the ground into a pool of gunk. If cast on a dungeon floor, the floor turns into a muddy pool a few inches deep. Living creatures are not affected, but their belongings (such as armor or a sword) can be. Magical items are not affected. At the end of the spell's duration, the space reforms to its original dimensions and nature.

16-19   The caster can transform a medium-sized space to swamp for 1d6 turns. He must touch the space to be affected. The caster can affect a space equal to 250 square feet or roughly the size of a large boulder 10′ x 5′ x 5′. Any mundane, non-living material can be affected (wood, stone, gold, dirt, etc.). The space changes into a semi-liquid muddy pool. If cast on a door, the door slides to the ground into a pool of gunk. If cast on a dungeon floor, the floor turns into a muddy pool a few inches deep. Living creatures are not transformed, but their belongings (such as armor or a sword) can be. Living creatures sitting or standing on the affected area sink into the mud as if they had been dropped into a swamp. If they are lightweight or can swim, there may be no impact, but heavily armored creatures may sink below the surface and drown. Magical items are not affected. At the end of the spell's duration, the space reforms to its original dimensions and nature.

20-21   The caster can transform a medium-sized space to swamp for 1d6 hours. He must touch the space to be affected. The caster can affect a space equal to 250 square feet or roughly the size of a large boulder 10′ x 5′ x 5′. Any mundane, non-living material can be affected (wood, stone, gold, dirt, etc.). The space changes into a semi-liquid muddy pool. If cast on a door, the door slides to the ground into a pool of gunk. If cast on a dungeon floor, the floor turns into a muddy pool a few inches deep. Living creatures are not transformed, but their belongings (such as armor or a sword) can be. Living creatures that were sitting or standing on the affected area sink into the mud as if they had been dropped into a swamp. If they are lightweight or can swim, there may be no impact, but heavily armored creatures may sink below the surface and drown. Magical items are not affected. At the end of the spell's duration, the space reforms to its original dimensions and nature.

22-25   The caster can transform a large field into swamp for 1d6 days. The caster touches the point of origin, then guides the dimensions of the space to be affected. He must have line of sight to the edges of the space. The caster can define a space up to 100′ wide on each side, which is transformed into a swampy pool of mud, muck, and shallow water up to a few feet deep at various points. The field becomes difficult terrain. Lightly armored creatures move at half speed, but heavily armored warriors, as well as heavy creatures such as cows, horses, or minotaurs, become mired and unable to move. Some creatures may actually drown in the shallow water if they cannot be freed. Houses, battlements, and other fixed structures may sink several inches or more into the swamp. Magical items are not affected. At the end of the spell's duration, the space reforms to its original consistency and nature, although objects that have sunk may now be partially underground.

Alternately, the caster can affect a large solid mass up to the size of a large house. Only mundane, non-living materials are affected (wood, stone, gold, dirt, etc.). The solid mass liquefies into a pile of mud and goo. The effect lasts for 1d6 days, at which point the object reforms to its original shape.

26-29	The caster can transform a large field into swamp *permanently*. The caster touches the point of origin, then guides the dimensions of the space to be affected. He must have line of sight to the edges of the space. The caster can define a space up to 100' wide on each side, which is transformed into a swampy pool of mud, muck, and shallow water up to a few feet deep at various points. The field becomes difficult terrain. Lightly armored creatures move at half speed, but heavily armored warriors, as well as heavy creatures such as cows, horses, or minotaurs, become mired and unable to move. Some creatures may actually drown in the shallow water if they cannot be freed. Houses, battlements, and other fixed structures may sink several inches or more into the swamp. Magical items are not affected. At the end of the spell's duration, the space reforms to its original consistency and nature, although objects that have sunk may now be partially underground. Alternately, the caster can affect a large solid mass up to the size of a large house, *permanently*. Only mundane, non-living materials are affected (wood, stone, gold, dirt, etc.). The solid mass liquefies into a pile of mud and goo.
30-31	The caster can *permanently* transform a vast expanse to swampy muck. The space is equal to up to 20,000 cubic feet or a field 200' x 100' to a depth of about a foot. This is also sufficient to affect a solid mass of almost 60' x 60' x 60' or a large castle. The caster can also use the ability to create a pit of mud; i.e., a space 10' wide at the very top and very deep. Heavy objects sink into the mud, armored humanoids may drown within it, and castles or houses can sink and be destroyed as their foundations shift. Magical items are not affected.
32-33	The caster can *permanently* transform a vast expanse to swampy muck *or* transform a single magic object permanently. If the caster transforms a vast expanse, the space is equal to up to 20,000 cubic feet or a field 200' x 100' to a depth of about a foot. This is also sufficient to affect a solid mass of almost 60' x 60' x 60' or a large castle. The caster can also use the ability to create a pit of mud; i.e., a space 10' wide at the very top and very deep. Heavy objects sink into the mud, armored humanoids may drown within it, and castles or houses can sink and be destroyed as their foundations shift. If the caster targets a magical item, he can target a single item up to human-sized (i.e., a sword, shield, staff, suit of armor, etc.), and that counts as the entire use of the spell. Magical objects receive a Fort saving throw to resist the effect. Otherwise, they are transformed to mud.
34+	The caster can *permanently* transform a vast expanse to swampy muck *or* transform a single magic object permanently *or* transform a single living creature to mud. If the caster transforms a vast expanse, the space is equal to up to 20,000 cubic feet or a field 200' x 100' to a depth of about a foot. This is also sufficient to affect a solid mass of almost 60' x 60' x 60', or a large castle. The caster can also use the ability to create a pit of mud; i.e., a space 10' wide at the very top and very deep. Heavy objects sink into the mud, armored humanoids may drown within it, and castles or houses can sink and be destroyed as their foundations shift. If the caster targets a magical item, he can target a single item up to human-sized (i.e., a sword, shield, staff, suit of armor, etc.) and that counts as the entire use of the spell. Magical objects receive a Fort saving throw to resist the effect. Otherwise, they are transformed to mud. If the caster targets a living creature, it must be touched to be affected. The living creature counts as the entire focus of the spell. Living creatures receive a Fort saving throw to resist the effect. Success indicates they are unaffected. Failure indicates they are transformed to mud and instantly slain.

Bottomfeeder Bond

Level: 3 (Bobugbubilz)   **Range:** 30' or more   **Duration:** 1 turn or more   **Casting time:** 2 rounds
Save: Will vs. spell check DC for intelligent creatures

General	Bobugbubilz holds court on a distant plane populated by endless horizons of swampland. In this place he is lord of all amphibians, as well as many other swamp dwellers, including crocodiles, catfish, venomous snakes, and biting flies. This spell reinforces the caster's bond to Bobugbubilz in the eyes of his mortal followers, and with such a bond the caster gains some degree of control over such creatures.
Manifestation	See below.
1	Lost, failure, and patron taint.
2-11	Lost. Failure.
12-15	Failure, but spell is not lost.
16-17	All mundane swampland creatures that come within 30' of the caster regard him with a neutral disposition. Swampland creatures include all amphibians, as well as crocodiles, fish, snakes and other reptiles, insects, and any other mundane creature that lives in a swamp. Intelligent swamp-dwellers, such as lizardmen, receive a Will save to resist the spell effect. If failed, they perceive the caster as non-threatening. The effect continues for 1 turn, or until the caster takes an action that threatens or harms the creatures.
18-21	As above, except even magical, un-dead, or extra-planar swampland creatures regard the caster as non-threatening. This includes lacedons (water-dwelling ghouls), swamp zombies, witch doctors, scrags (water-dwelling trolls), and primal variants of swamp-dwellers. Intelligent creatures receive a Will save to resist, as above.
22-23	As above, and the caster is regarded as non-threatening by *all* reptilian, amphibian, piscine, and insectoid creatures, as well as the specific swamp-dwelling varieties. Dragons are *not* considered reptilian for these purposes. Intelligent creatures receive a Will save to resist, as above.
24-26	As above, and the spell's range is extended to 100'.
27-31	As above, and the spell's duration is extended to 1 hour.
32-33	All reptilian, amphibian, piscine, and insectoid creatures within 100' regard the caster as not only neutral but potentially as a friend and ally. Unintelligent and mundane creatures of 4 HD or less are automatically affected, while intelligent, magical, and extraplanar creatures, or those of 5 or more HD receive a Will save to resist. Affected creatures hop, slither, and slide to the caster's side in an effort to nuzzle and offer their assistance. The effect lasts for 1d6+2 turns. While under this friendly influence, the creatures obey the caster's commands to the best of their ability (limited by their intelligence and physical capabilities, of course). Creatures sent into dangerous situations or those that oppose their nature receive another Will save at a +4 bonus to break the effect. Examples would include fish ordered out of the water, frogs ordered to fight a creature much larger than themselves, and so on.
34-35	As above, and the effect extends to 200' with a duration of 2d6+4 turns.
36+	As above, and the effect is ongoing for 1d6 days, to a range of 200'. Creatures affected remain under the spell's influence until its duration ends. By the time the spell ends, the caster is like the Pied Piper of swampland creatures, trailed by a train of crocodiles, snakes, fish, toads, frogs, and tadpoles, along with a veritable cloud of insects. When the effect disperses, this mass of creatures slithers off into the muck.

AZI DAHAKA

The demon prince of storms and waste, Azi Dahaka is anything but subtle. He is the blasting sand-storm, the deadly asp, and the desiccated corpse in scorching sun. He appears as an infernal hydra and expects his followers to bring ruin wherever they go. Eventually the world shall be a desert over which he will rule. His ceremony must be conducted in a desert at high noon where the caster has imbibed no liquid for one day and one night before. He demands much of his followers, causing them to be dehydrated and experience heat-induced visions where he gives them minor quests related to spreading chaos.

Invoke Patron check results:

12-13   Azi Dahaka sends a bolt of static lightning toward one of the caster's enemies, causing 2d6 damage (DC 15 Fort save for half). The caster can designate any target within 100'.

14-17   A cyclone erupts around the caster's enemies. The caster and his allies are unaffected, but all other creatures within a 30' radius of the caster suffer 1d8 points of abrasion damage per round. Additionally, each round, all enemies within the cyclone must make a Reflex save or be knocked prone by the storming winds. The cyclone continues for 1d4+CL rounds.

18-19   A sandstorm fills the air with blinding dust. However, the caster and his allies can still see normally. Enemies within a 60' radius are blinded as long as the caster continues to concentrate, for up to 1 minute.

20-23   A diminutive asp slithers forth from the caster's sleeve to coil around his hand. The asp will bite any enemy the caster touches until it vanishes in 1 minute. The caster must make a melee attack roll, but the asp grants a +4 bonus. The attack roll can involve a normal melee attack; i.e., the caster could stab with a dagger, and the asp would also make its bite attempt. Any enemy struck by the caster's melee attacks while the asp is present suffers from a terrible poison. The bite automatically does 1 point of damage the first round, then the poison sets in, automatically causing 2 points on the second round. On each subsequent round the target must make a DC20 Fort save or the damage doubles: potentially 4 points on the third round, then 8 points, then 16 points, and so on. The damage continues doubling until the target makes a Fort save.

24-27   Azi Dahaka sends a tangled mass of slithering snakes. The hissing swarm arrives in 1d3 rounds. The swarm occupies a space of 30' x 30' and attacks all enemies within that space. The individual snakes disperse after 1 minute. Snake swarm: Init +0; Atk bite +2 melee against all in 30' x 30' space (dmg 1d6 plus DC 20 Fort save or additional 1d6 points of poison damage); AC 12; HP 60; MV 30'; Act 1d20 (attack all enemies in space); SV Fort +2, Ref +2, Will +0; AL C.

28-29   Azi Dahaka sends a brawny three-headed snake to aid his follower. It arrives in 1d3 rounds. The 20' long creature obeys the caster's commands for 1 minute, then slithers away. Three-headed snake: Init +6; Atk bite +12 melee (dmg 2d8 plus DC 24 Fort save or additional 3d6 points of poison damage); AC 16; HP 24; MV 30'; Act 3d20; SV Fort +2, Ref +4, Will +0; AL C.

30-31   A spectral hydra shimmers into existence like a mirage above the sands. Its seven heads bite and breathe flame on the caster's enemies before vanishing on the following round. The caster may immediately direct seven attacks to any targets within 60' of himself. Each attack is either a bite (+10 attack, 4d6 damage) or a fiery breath weapon (+15 attack, 2d6 damage plus DC 20 Ref save or target catches fire, suffering additional 2d6 damage each round until the target makes a DC 20 Ref save).

32+   Azi Dahaka sends a spectral hydra, as above, which lasts for 1d4+CL rounds. The caster may direct 7 attacks on each round it remains. The caster must concentrate to direct these attacks.

PATRON TAINT: AZI DAHAKA

When patron taint is indicated for Azi Dahaka, roll 1d6 on the table below. When a caster has acquired all six taints at all levels of effect, there is no need to continue rolling any more.

Roll **Result**

1   Casting any spell produces a light coat of fine dust, which settles over everything within 20' of the caster; the dust seems to absorb moisture, leaving surfaces rough and dry. When the result is rolled a second time, the caster's desiccating cloud causes all natural plants within 25' of the caster to wither and die any time a spell is cast. If the result is rolled a third time, a cloud of dust and ash seems to follow the caster, his mere presence causes all natural plants within 10' to wither, shrivel and die.

2   The caster's spells draw destructive storms of unnatural wrath. There is a 10% chance after casting any spell that thunder booms somewhere in the distance. If the result is rolled a second time, any time the caster casts a spell, there is a 35% chance it is following by the immediate crash of localized thunder in 1d5 seconds. If the result is rolled a third time, there is a 50% chance that any spell causes a flash of lightning and the immediate crack of thunder. Those within 20' of the caster must succeed on a DC 10 Fort save of be deafened for 1d4 rounds.

3   The caster's presence brings ruin and decay to all things. Wooden and paper objects decay at his touch, crumbling into ash after a single week. If the result is rolled a second time, the caster's touch reduces cloth and leather to rags and then ash, after only ten days. If the result is rolled a third time, the caster's touch causes metal to rust and decay, crumbling into sand in a month's time. Magical objects resist the caster's casual touch, but still show wear where previously there was none, becoming pitted, mottled and worn.

4   Patches of the caster's torso skin peel away to reveal iridescent scales. If the result is rolled a second time, the skin on the caster's arms and legs is transformed into scales. If the result is rolled a third time, the caster's skin molts, revealing a body covered by scales.

5   The caster's wounds weep clear ooze—an offering to Azi Dahaka that leaves the caster parched and dry. Anytime the caster takes a wound, he loses 1 additional hp due to the seeping ooze. If the result is rolled a second time, the caster develops weeping sores on his body; if left untended and not bandaged, the sores cause the caster to lose 1d3 hp per day. If the result is rolled a third time, the caster's body is covered in scores of crusty wounds that threaten to tear open with any great exertion; any time the caster attempts to spellburn, he also loses 1 hp for every attribute point spent in the spellburn.

6   The caster takes on the aspect of Azi Dahaka, as a second pair of eyes buds somewhere on his shoulders or back. A ruin mutation, the eyes are blind, but blink disconcertingly every few moments. If the result is rolled a second time, two more sets of eyes bud somewhere on the caster's shoulders and back. If the result is rolled a third time, the budding faces fully emerge from the caster's body. The mouths moan strange dirges to Azi Dahaka in forgotten tongues, the nostrils flare wildly, and the blind eyes dart about unpredictably, as if tracking unseen beings.

PATRON SPELLS: AZI DAHAKA

The demon prince of storms and waste grants three unique spells, as follows:

Level 1: *Snake Trick*

Level 2: *Kith of the Hydra*

Level 3: *Reap the Whirlwind*

SPELLBURN: AZI DAHAKA

Azi Dahaka enjoys the wailing cries of his devotees and often encourages even non-followers to call out to him in their times of distress. When a caster utilizes spellburn, roll 1d4 on the table below or build off the ideas below to create an event specific to your home campaign.

Roll	Spellburn Result
1	A hot, searing wind centers on the caster, stripping him of bodily fluids, and leaving him parched, blistered and spent (expressed as Stamina, Strength, or Agility loss).
2	The demon prince demands more than the caster can offer. The caster can spellburn up to 10 points of ability score loss but must pay twice that, either in his own ability scores or in HD of creatures slain by the caster. For a sacrifice to qualify, the creature cannot have been summoned, and the caster *must* strike the killing blow with a ceremonial blade consecrated for the act.
3	Azi Dahaka craves a boon of the caster. Within 24 hours of the spellburn, the caster is struck by a burning fever. The caster loses the spellburned attributes while in the grip of the fever and sees a vision of his master's desire. If the caster successfully undertakes the quest (most often a side trek taking no more than 5 days), he is rewarded as Azi Dahaka sees fit.
4	The caster crumple to his knees and vomits forth a gout of wet, writhing serpents, leaving him exhausted from the exertion (expressed as Stamina, Strength, or Agility loss). The snakes slither away, vanishing into the ground.

Snake Trick

Level: 1 (Azi Dahaka)   Range: Varies   Duration: Varies   Casting time: 1 round   Save: Will vs. check if the item is held by an unwilling creature; magic items always receive a Will save

General
As a servant of Azi Dahaka, the caster is a friend to the common asp and lowly serpent. With a word, the caster transforms any non-living object into a writhing serpent. The serpent is not under the caster's control and does its best to defend itself, slithering away or striking, as appropriate. The target object must be roughly longer than it is wide. For example, a crown could be transformed into a snake but a wooden crate could not.

Manifestation
Roll 1d4: (1) caster's fingers become writhing snakes; (2) caster is shrouded in a black halo of snake-like forms; (3) the hissing of a thousand snakes fills the air; (4) caster's eyes flash with the steely gaze of the serpent.

1
Lost, failure, and patron taint.

2-11
Lost. Failure.

12-13
The caster transforms a non-magical object, up to the volume of a dagger, permanently into a snake of like size. The object must be within 15'. If in the hand of an enemy, the snake immediately strikes (Atk +1, dmg 1 plus poison (Fort DC 12 or 1 Str)) before slithering away.

14-17
The caster transforms a non-magical object, up to the volume of a longsword, permanently into a snake of like size. The object must be within 25'. If in the hand of an enemy, the snake immediately strikes (Atk +3, dmg 1d3 plus poison (Fort DC 15 or 1d4 Str)) before slithering away.

18-19
The caster transforms a non-magical object, up to the volume of a spear, permanently into a snake of like size. The object must be within 50'. If in the hand of an enemy, the snake immediately strikes (Atk +5, dmg 1d4+1 plus poison (Fort DC 18 or 1d6 Str)) before slithering away.

20-23
The caster transforms 1d3 non-magical objects, each up to the volume of a spear, permanently into snakes of like size. The objects must be within 100'. If in the hands of enemies, the snakes immediately strike (Atk +5, dmg 1d4+1 plus poison (Fort DC 18 or 1d6 Str)) before slithering away.

24-27
The caster transforms 1d12 non-magical non-living objects, or one magical object, each up to the volume of a spear, permanently into snakes of like size. The objects must be within sight. If in the hands of enemies, the snakes immediately strike (Atk +5, dmg 1d4+1 plus poison (Fort DC 18 or 1d6 Str)) before slithering away.

28-29
The caster transforms 1d24 non-magical objects, or one magical object, each up to the volume of a spear, permanently into snakes of like size. The objects must be within sight. If in the hands of enemies, the snakes immediately strike (Atk +5, dmg 1d4+1 plus poison (Fort DC 18 or 1d6 Str)) before slithering away.

30-31
The caster transforms 1d100 objects, or 1d4 magical objects, each up to the volume of a spear, permanently into snakes of like size. The objects must be within sight. If in the hands of enemies, the snakes immediately strike (Atk +5, dmg 1d4+1 plus poison (Fort DC 18 or 1d6 Str)) before slithering away.

32+
The caster transforms 3d100 objects, or 2d6 magical objects, each up to the volume of a spear, permanently into snakes of like size. The objects must be within sight. If in the hands of enemies, the snakes immediately strike (Atk +5, dmg 1d4+1 plus poison (Fort DC 18 or 1d6 Str)) before slithering away. Alternately, the caster can transform a single non-living man-made object of any size (a tower, a ship, a lighthouse, an inn) into a snake of like size. Generally this massive creature will have at least 10 HD and an attack at +20 for damage of 2d12, with a powerful poison (Fort DC 24 or 2d6 Str).

Kith of the Hydra

Level: 2 (Azi Dahaka)	Range: Self	Duration: Varies	Casting time: 1 hour	Save: None

General	Azi Dahaka is the sire and patron of all hydras. By embracing the secret of the hydra, the caster shirks death's coil, gaining the ability to return from the dead—but only at great sacrifice. Wounds knit, shattered bones mend, and even limbs grow back. However, ongoing damage (for instance, if the caster's body remains crushed beneath a boulder) does not cease. If the body is utterly and entirely destroyed, the spell fails. If a caster attempts to recast the spell while still under the influence of a previous casting, he is irrevocably transformed into a mindless hydra. This spell requires a minimum spellburn of 4 points.
Manifestation	Roll 1d4: (1) a single tendril of hair turns into a slender snake, rooted in the caster's scalp; (2) a snake takes form in the caster's throat, speaking his words with its forked tongue; (3) caster's eyes take on the serpentine cast of a snake; (4) caster molts like a snake, slowly shedding his skin.
1	Lost, failure, and patron taint.
2-11	Lost. Failure.
12-13	Failure, but spell is not lost.
14-15	If the caster dies within the next hour, his body is restored to full hit points upon the next new moon. Roll 1d3 upon rebirth: the caster suffers the permanent loss of (1) 1d5 Stamina, (2) 1d5 Strength or (3) 1d5 Agility.
16-19	If the caster is slain within the next six hours, his body is restored to full hit points with the coming dusk. Roll 1d3 upon rebirth: the caster suffers the permanent loss of (1) 1d4 Stamina, (2) 1d4 Strength or (3) 1d4 Agility.
20-21	If the caster dies in the next 24 hours, his body is restored to full hit points six hours following his death. Roll 1d3 upon rebirth: the caster suffers the permanent loss of (1) 1d3 Stamina, (2) 1d3 Strength or (3) 1d3 Agility.
22-25	If the caster is slain in the next week, his body is restored to full hit points one hour following his death. Roll 1d3 upon rebirth: the caster suffers the permanent loss of (1) 1d2 Stamina, (2) 1d2 Strength or (3) 1d2 Agility.
26-29	If the caster dies before the next full moon, his body is restored to full hit points the following round. Roll 1d3 upon rebirth: the caster suffers the permanent loss of (1) 1 point of Stamina, (2) 1 point of Strength or (3) 1 point of Agility.
30-31	If the caster is slain before the next solstice, his body is restored to full hit points the following round. The caster can return to life twice in this manner. Roll 1d3 upon each rebirth: the caster suffers the permanent loss of (1) 1 point of Stamina, (2) 1 point of Strength or (3) 1 point of Agility.
32-33	If the caster is slain in the next year, he is restored to full hit points the following round. The caster can return to life thrice in this manner. Roll 1d3 upon each rebirth: the caster suffers the permanent loss of (1) 1 point of Stamina, (2) 1 point of Strength or (3) 1 point of Agility.
34+	If the caster is slain in the next hundred years, he is restored to full hit points the following round. The caster can return to life a number of times equal to 1d7 + caster level. This roll *must* be made by the judge and *must not* shared with the player. Roll 1d3 upon each rebirth: the caster suffers the permanent loss of (1) 1 point of Stamina, (2) 1 point of Strength or (3) 1 point of Agility.

Reap the Whirlwind

Level: 3 (Azi Dahaka)   Range: Self   Duration: 1d5 rounds + CL   Casting time: 1 round   Save: None

General	Azi Dahaka is the patron of storms and waste. By transforming himself into a raging sandstorm, the caster embodies his patron's fiercest traits.
Manifestation	Roll 1d3: (1) caster and his equipment dissolve into whirling sand; (2) a howling wind erupts, reducing the caster to sand; (3) caster raises his head to the sky to as if to scream, and his insides pour out as sand.

1	Lost, failure, and patron taint.
2-11	Lost. Failure.
12-15	Failure, but spell is not lost.
16-17	The caster and all his equipment transform into a whirling vortex of sand. For the duration of the spell, he is immune to non-magical, physical attacks. While in sand form the caster cannot make physical attacks but can cast spells as appropriate to his new form.
18-21	The caster transforms into a whirling vortex of sand up to 25′ in height and 10′ in diameter. He can fly at twice his normal speed and is immune to non-magical, physical attacks. Any creature caught within the vortex must make a Fort save against the spell check or be scoured for 1d12+CL damage. Objects weighing less than 1 pound are lifted into the air and drawn into the whirlwind.
22-23	The caster transforms into a towering whirlwind up to 60′ in height and 30′ in diameter. He can fly at thrice his normal speed and is immune to non-magical, physical attacks. Creatures caught within the vortex are blinded and must make a Fort save against the spell check or be scoured for 1d16+CL damage. Objects weighing less than 25 pounds are lifted into the air and drawn into the whirlwind.
24-26	The caster transforms into a raging sandstorm up to 120′ in height and 60′ in diameter. He can fly at thrice his normal speed and is immune to non-magical, physical attacks. Creatures caught within the vortex are blinded and must make a Fort save against the spell check or be scoured for 1d24+CL damage. Objects weighing less than 50 pounds are lifted into the air and drawn into the whirlwind.
27-31	The caster transforms into a raging sandstorm up to 300′ in height and 150′ in diameter. He can fly at thrice his normal speed and is immune to non-magical, physical attacks. Creatures caught within the vortex are blinded and deafened and must make a Fort save against the spell check or be scoured for 2d12+CL damage. Objects weighing less than 100 pounds are lifted into the air and drawn into the whirlwind.
32-33	The caster transforms into a harrowing sandstorm up to 600′ in height and 300′ in diameter. He can fly at thrice his normal speed and is immune to non-magical, physical attacks. Creatures caught within the vortex are blinded and deafened and must make a Fort save against the spell check or be scoured for 3d12+CL damage. Man-sized objects or smaller must make a DC 15 Strength check or be torn from the ground. At the end of the spell's duration, they fall to the ground, suffering another 6d6 damage.
34-35	The caster transforms into a destructive sandstorm up to 1,000′ in height and 500′ in diameter. He can fly at thrice his normal speed and is immune to non-magical, physical attacks. Any creature caught within the vortex is blinded, deafened, knocked prone, and must make a Fort save against the spell check or be scoured for 4d12+CL damage. Horse-sized objects or smaller must make a DC 20 Strength check or be torn from the ground. At the end of the spell's duration, they fall to the ground, suffering another 6d6 damage. Wooden constructions are laid flat, and objects 4′ high or less are left buried in the sand.
36+	The caster transforms into a devastating sandstorm up to 2,000′ in height and 1000′ in diameter. He can fly at thrice his normal speed and is immune to non-magical, physical attacks. Any creature caught within the vortex is blinded, deafened, knocked prone, and must make a Fort save against the spell check or be scoured for 5d12+CL damage. Elephant-sized objects or smaller must make a DC 25 Strength check or be torn from the ground. At the end of the spell's duration, they fall to the ground, suffering another 6d6 damage. Stone constructions are hurled down, and objects in the caster's path are left buried beneath 10′ of sand.

SEZREKAN

Regarded as the wickedest of wizards ever to plague the Known World, Sezrekan the Elder was born to a peasant family and cursed with the knowledge of higher worlds. Straining to hear the music of the heavenly spheres, the aspiring wizard found only chaos and madness. Forsaking patron and liege alike, Sezrekan sought to free himself of the world and his mortal coil, regardless of the cost. Those who claim him as their patron are expected to follow in the Master's footsteps, sacrificing kith and kin in the single-minded pursuit of mastery of self and thereby the multiverse. The Old Master has little regard for those that cannot help themselves, offering his aid only to spellcasters of proven dedication and talent.

Invoke Patron **check results:**

12-13   Sezrekan cannot be troubled by such an insignificant petitioner. He grants the caster an additional 6d4 hit points. These may be burned in spellburn, with every 4 hp equaling a point of attribute. At the end of the hour, all the extra hit points are lost. Damage and spellburn are deducted first from the additional hit points. For example, a caster that is granted 16 hit points and takes 14 points of damage in the hour, would then lose only the 2 remaining hit points when the duration expires.

14-17   Sezrekan teleports the caster to a location 1d100 miles distant. The caster cannot choose the location, but is not in immediate danger upon his arrival.

18-19   Sezrekan permits the caster to recall a previously lost spell.

20-23   Sezrekan notes the caster's potential talent, granting +5 to the caster's next spell check.

24-27   Sezrekan teleports the caster and up to 8 allies to a location 5d100 miles distant. The caster cannot choose the location, but the party is not in immediate peril upon their arrival.

28-29   Sezrekan is impressed by the caster's might and deigns to grant a total of +10 to the caster's next two spell checks. The points can be allotted as the caster sees fit, but must be declared prior to the castings.

30-31   A phantasmal specter of Sezrekan appears, raining down hellfire on those that would dare challenge such a talented adept. Meteors and comets fall streaking from the sky, striking any foes within 50' for 3d8 damage (Ref save vs. spell check to avoid). The rain of fire continues for 1d3 rounds.

32+   Sezrekan recognizes the caster as a peer (albeit, a *lesser* peer) worthy of his aid in their shared efforts to cast off the shackles of an uncaring universe. He grants a total bonus of +30 to the caster's next five spell checks. The points can be allotted as the caster sees fit (up to +10 per spell check), but the allotment must be declared prior to the casting.

PATRON TAINT: SEZREKAN

Whereas other patrons scar their petitioners with foul taints, followers of the Old Master inflict injuries on themselves while in pursuit of the Sezrekan's mastery of magic. When patron taint is indicated, roll 1d6 on the table below. When a caster has acquired all six taints at all levels of effect, there is no need to continue rolling any more.

Roll	Result
1	Incited to madness and brimming with occult knowledge, the caster spends his next action carving a third eye into his forehead (inflicting 1d3 points of damage in the process). Upon return to civilization, the caster seeks out a tattooist who inks a third eye on the caster's forehead using exotic inks costing no less than 1d5 x 100 gp. If the result is rolled a second time, the caster insists on wearing a blindfold for the next 1d4 days, in the earnest hope of awakening his third eye. If the result is rolled a third time, the caster stabs a dagger into each of his real eyes, blinding himself. (There is a 3% chance, per level, that the self-mutilation brings the PC's third eye to life.)

2   Dazzled by his new insight into the terrifying nature of the multiverse, the caster is spurred into offering up sacrifices in thanks to the Old Master. The caster is driven to enact the ritual as soon as it is reasonably safe, though the caster's threat assessment may not agree with that of his peers. In a ritual lasting 1 turn, the caster offers up wealth totaling at least 1d5 x 100 gp in honor of Sezrekan. All the items are consumed in searing blue flames, and there is a 3% chance that Sezrekan honors the sacrifice with a +1 bonus to the caster's next spell check. If the result is rolled a second time, the caster must sacrifice a magic item; there is a 6% chance that Sezrekan honors the sacrifice with a +2 bonus to the caster's next spell check. If the result is rolled a third time, the caster must sacrifice a friendly ally to prove his single-minded devotion; there is a 9% chance that Sezrekan honors the sacrifice with a +3 bonus to the caster's next spell check.

3   In a passing moment of déjà vu, the caster realizes that Sezrekan demands his service. Subject to the judge's discretion, the caster must adventure to retrieve an occult item or lost relic for the Old Master, located within 1d4 days travel. The caster has a clear vision of the item, but only a rough sense of its location and wards. If the result is rolled a second time, the item is well warded and some 1d4 weeks distant. If the result is rolled a third time, the item is guarded by ancient wards, traps, and fiends, requiring 1d4 months of dangerous travel.

4   In a lucid dream of mighty Sezrekan, the caster realizes his own spells are terribly flawed and dependent on the aid of outsiders. Forsaking their influence, the caster gives up a known first level spell, vowing to never cast it again. (If, later, the caster discovers another spell of the same level, it can take the place of the original spell among the caster's known spells.) If the result is rolled a second time, the caster must surrender a second level spell. If the result is rolled a third time, the caster must surrender a third level spell. Should the caster refuse to give up any of the spells, he forsakes Sezrekan as his patron.

5   The daunting scope of the caster's knowledge induces a creeping madness that begins to seep into his everyday life. The caster must declare a common substance (iron, water, steel, cotton, gold, silver, silk, wood, leather, velum, meat, etc.) and declare it taboo. Henceforth, the caster makes every effort to avoid contact with the taboo substance. If the result is rolled a second time, the caster must

choose a second taboo; furthermore, contact with the forbidden substances causes searing burns that inflict 1 hp of damage per round of contact. If the result is rolled a third time, the caster must pick a third taboo, and contact inflicts 1d4 hp of damage per round of contact.

6   The caster is caught up in a dream world of hallucinations for the next 1d5 rounds, as a spectral image of Sezrekan strides through his vision. The caster can still interact with the real world, but if he chooses to ignore his surroundings and watch only the Old Master, he gleans hints and indications of Sezrekan's dweomercraft mastery. If the caster spends the next 1d4 days in solitary research, he is able to learn a new spell of his choosing. Failing to immediately retire to study causes the insights to be lost, like the fading memory of a dream. This result can be rolled up to three times.

PATRON SPELLS: SEZREKAN

Those daring to follow of the Path of the Mad Mage eventually learn three unique spells, as follows:

Level 1: *Sequester*

Level 2: *Shield Maiden*

Level 3: *Phylactery of the Soul*

SPELLBURN: SEZREKAN

Sezrekan does little to aid his followers. Those that are strong and willful distinguish themselves by their might, while the weak and pitiful are worthless tools to be discarded. And yet, the Old Master has been known to admire those that sacrifice their own bodies in pursuit of the impossible. When a caster utilizes spellburn, roll 1d4 and consult the table below or build off the suggestions to create an event specific to your home campaign.

Roll   Spellburn Result

1   The power of the spellburn opens the caster to the maddening horrors of the universe and leaves him weak (expressed as Stamina, Strength, or Agility loss) and disoriented. The caster must succeed on a DC 15 Will save or be unable to cast spells for 1d3 rounds. If the caster succeeds on the save, the caster gains a +1 bonus to all future attempts at the spell.

2   Admiring the caster's ambition, Sezrekan grants the caster the opportunity to burn an ally's attributes (Stamina, Strength or Agility) in place of his own. The target must be willing. For every point burned to augment the spell, the target loses 1d3 points of the same attribute. If any of the target's attributes fall to 0 or less, the target dies.

3   Sezrekan mocks the caster's feeble grasps at power. The caster receives but 1 point for every 2 points of attribute burned.

4   Horrific madness seizes the caster's mind, and the awful meaninglessness of the universe is driven deep into his mortal soul. The caster is granted a single DC 15 Will save; on a successful save the caster crumples to his knees, weakened by the spellburn, yet firmly grounded in the common reality. On a failed save—in lieu of the spellburn—the caster receives a +5 bonus to all spell checks for the next 1d6 rounds, yet perceives both friend and foe alike as all-devouring monsters from the outer dark, a truth far too real to contemplate.

Sequester

Level: 1 (Sezrekan)   Range: Varies   Duration: 1d24 hours per CL   Casting time: 1 turn   Save: Will or Skill check vs. spell check when appropriate (see below)

General	The Path of the Old One requires absolute attention and dedication. The caster secures an area against intrusion, permitting reflection and study so that he can plot his next move.
Manifestation	Roll 1d4: (1) a wash of arctic air chills the affected area, leaving a light sheen of ice; (2) the affected area glows faint green in dim light; (3) the sounds of latching locks, slamming doors, and eager workers speaking in alien tongues fills the air as the dweomer settles over the affected area; (4) the affected area takes on a forgotten air: dust settles in the corners, cobwebs hang from the ceiling, and the air grows staid and foul.
1	Lost, failure, and patron taint.
2-11	Lost. Failure.
12-13	The caster secures an area up to 100 square feet in size. Doors and windows are magically sealed, requiring a DC 15 Pick Locks check to open. The caster is instantly alerted to any being entering the warded area.
14-17	The caster secures an area up to 500 square feet in size. Doors and windows are magically sealed, requiring a DC 15 Pick Locks check or a password to open. The caster can declare up to 2 portals magically trapped (Find/Disable Traps DC 15; 1d10+CL fire damage). The caster is instantly alerted to any being entering the warded area.
18-19	The caster secures an area up to 1,000 square feet in size. Doors and windows are magically sealed, requiring a DC 18 Pick Locks check or a password to open. Lesser doors and windows are treated as stout wood for purposes of destruction (15 hp). The caster can declare up to 4 portals trapped (Find/Disable Traps DC 18; 1d12+CL fire damage). The caster is instantly alerted to any being entering the area.
20-23	The caster secures an area up to 3,000 square feet in size. Doors and windows are magically sealed, requiring a DC 20 Pick Locks check or a password to open. Lesser doors and windows are treated as iron bound for purposes of destruction (30 hp). The caster can declare up to 6 portals trapped (Find/ Disable Traps DC 18; 1d14+CL fire damage) and place a single pit trap up to 20' in depth (Find Traps DC 18). The caster is instantly alerted to any being entering the area.
24-27	The caster secures an area up to 6,000 square feet in size. Doors and windows are magically sealed, requiring a DC 20 Pick Locks check or a password to open. Lesser doors and windows are treated as iron for purposes of destruction (60 hp). The caster can declare up to 8 portals trapped (Find/ Disable Traps DC 20; 1d20+CL fire damage) and place 4 pit traps up to 40' in depth (Find Traps DC 20). The caster is instantly alerted to any being entering the area.
28-29	The caster secures an area up to 10,000 square feet in size. Doors and windows are magically sealed, requiring a DC 20 Pick Locks check or a password to open. Lesser doors and windows are treated as iron for purposes of destruction (60 hp). The caster can declare up to 8 portals trapped (Find/ Disable Traps DC 20; 1d24+CL fire damage) and place 4 pit traps up to 60' in depth (Find Traps DC 20). The caster and his allies within the sequestered area are immune to scrying. The caster and his allies are instantly alerted to any being entering the area.
30-31	The caster secures an area up to 10,000 square feet in size. Doors and windows are magically sealed, requiring a DC 20 Pick Locks check or a password to open. Lesser doors and windows are treated as iron for purposes of destruction (60 hp). The caster can declare up to 8 portals trapped (Find/ Disable Traps DC 20; 1d24+CL fire damage) and place 4 pit traps up to 60' in depth (Find Traps DC 20). The caster and his allies within the sequestered area are immune to scrying, summoning or teleportation. The caster and his allies are alerted to any being entering the area.
32+	The caster secures any single structure (a keep, tower, palace, dungeon, etc.) regardless of size. Doors and windows are magically sealed, requiring a DC 20 Pick Locks check or a password to open. Lesser doors and windows are treated as iron for purposes of destruction (60 hp). The caster can declare up to 8 portals trapped (Find/ Disable Traps DC 20; 1d24+CL fire damage), place 4 pit traps that teleport victims to an oubliette 100 miles distant (Find Traps DC 20), and a troop of 50 suits of animated armor (treat as skeletons that cannot be turned). The caster and his allies within the sequestered area are immune to scrying, summoning or teleportation. The caster and his allies are alerted to any being entering the area.

Shield Maiden

General

Stumbling across the ruins of a forgotten empire, Sezrekan the Elder discovered a dolmen holding the remains of 50 warrior-maidens. Bending their fierce spirits to his will, he struck a pact with the ghosts permitting him to summon each spirit once. A shield maiden is utterly loyal, interceding on physical attacks against her master, taking damage in his place on any successful attack within 4 points of the caster's target AC. Except as noted below, a maiden cannot attack and stand ready to defend her master in the same round. The death of any shield maiden causes the caster a loss of 1 point of Personality, and all arms and armor vanish upon a maiden's death. In the totality of a campaign, no more than 50 shield maidens can be summoned. Attempting to summon more than a single maiden at the same time causes both to turn on the caster, attacking for 1d6 rounds before vanishing into mist.

Manifestation

Roll 1d4: (1) a simple cloth doll grows to become a life sized shield maiden, replete with armor and wielding a spear; (2) a lock of blond hair is consumed in a burst of light, leaving a shield maiden standing in the dissipating smoke; (3) the caster draws a line across his palm with a dagger and a shield maiden emerges from the pooling blood; (4) the caster calls out to the sky and a shield maiden appears, stepping from between the rays of the dazzling sun.

1   Lost, failure, and patron taint.

2-11   Lost. Failure.

12-13   Failure, but spell is not lost.

14-15   A shield maiden appears with stats as a level 1 warrior, 10 hp, and mundane equipment. The maiden serves for 1 hour before vanishing into mist, freed from her indenture.

16-19   A shield-maiden appears with stats as a level 2 warrior, 15 hp, and mundane equipment. The maiden serves for 1 day before vanishing into mist, freed from her indenture.

20-21   A shield maiden appears with stats as a level 3 warrior, 20 hp, and mundane equipment. The maiden bears a kite shield, granting +1 to her master's AC against ranged attacks and +1 to saves against physical damage. The maiden serves for 1 week before vanishing into mist, freed from her indenture.

22-25   A shield maiden appears with stats as a level 4 warrior, normal ability scores, 25 hp, and armed with a *+1 spear*. The maiden bears a great shield, granting +2 to her master's AC, +3 vs. ranged attacks and +2 to saves against physical damage. The maiden serves for 1 month before vanishing into mist, freed from her indenture.

26-29   A shield maiden appears with stats as a level 4 warrior, one exceptional ability score, 25 hp, and armed with a *+2 spear*. The maiden bears a great shield, granting +2 to her master's AC, +3 vs. ranged attacks and +2 to saves against physical damage. Any time a physical attack succeeds against her master, the shield maiden can make an immediate counterattack against foe that struck her master. The maiden serves for 1 year before vanishing into mist, freed from her indenture.

30-31   A shield maiden appears with stats as a level 5 warrior, two exceptional ability scores, 30 hp, and armed with a *+2 spear*. The maiden bears a great shield, granting +2 to her master's AC, +3 vs. ranged attacks, and +2 to saves against physical damage. Any time a physical attack succeeds against her master, the shield maiden can make an immediate counterattack against foe that struck her master. The maiden serves for 1 year before vanishing into mist, freed from her indenture.

32-33   A shield maiden appears with stats as a level 6 warrior, three exceptional ability scores, 35 hp, armed with a *+2 spear*, astride a pegasus. The maiden bears a great shield, granting +2 to her master's AC, +3 vs. ranged attacks, and +2 to saves against physical damage. Any time a physical attack succeeds against her master, the shield maiden can make an immediate counterattack against foe that struck her master. The maiden serves for 10 years before vanishing into mist, freed from her indenture.

34+   A shield maiden appears with stats as a level 7 warrior, four exceptional ability scores, 50 hp, and armed with a *+2 spear*, astride a pegasus. The maiden bears a *+1 great shield*, granting +3 to her master's AC, +4 vs. ranged attacks, and +3 to saves against physical damage. Any time a physical attack succeeds against her master, the shield maiden can make an immediate counterattack against foe that struck her master. The maiden serves for the remainder of her master's life. Upon the caster's death, she vanishes into mist, freed from her indenture.

Phylactery of the Soul

Level: 3 (Sezrekan)   Range: Self   Duration: Variable   Casting time: 1 day   Save: See below

General   Following in the Old Master's path, the caster has succeeded in learning how to place his soul within an amulet or gem (worth no less than 1d8 x 100 gp) while still maintaining control of his mortal body. The caster has no awareness of the phylactery or its surroundings when inhabiting a body. If his mortal form is slain, his awareness returns to the phylactery and he has a variable period of time to inhabit a new body before his soul departs. Any new body must be living and physically touch the phylactery; the victim receives a Will save vs. spell check to resist being forced from its shell.

Manifestation   Roll 1d3: (1) caster's body takes on a pallid air and his eyes glaze over as his soul is sent into the phylactery; (2) a crack resounds in the heavens and the air smells of copper and burnt offerings; (3) the caster crumples to his knees, howling in spiritual agony as his soul is torn from his mortal shell.

1   Lost, failure, and patron taint.

2-11   Lost. Failure.

12-15   Failure, but spell is not lost.

16-17   The caster places his soul within the chosen phylactery. His body can travel no further than 10 miles from the phylactery; any further distance causes the body to die and the soul's awareness to return to its vessel. Without a body to sustain him, the caster has 1d6+CL hours to inhabit a new body before his soul dissipates into nothingness.

18-21   The caster places his soul within the chosen phylactery. His body can travel no further than 50 miles from the phylactery; any further distance causes the body to die and the soul's awareness to return to its vessel. Without a body to sustain him, the caster has 1d10+CL days to inhabit a new body before his soul dissipates into nothingness.

22-23   The caster places his soul within the chosen phylactery. His body can travel no further than 100 miles from the phylactery; any further distance causes the body to die and the soul's awareness to return to its vessel. Without a body to sustain him, the caster has 1d16+CL days to inhabit a new body before his soul dissipates into nothingness.

24-26   The caster places his soul within the chosen phylactery. His body can travel no further than 500 miles from the phylactery; any further distance causes the body to die and the soul's awareness to return to its vessel. Without a body to sustain him, the caster has 1d20+CL days to inhabit a new body before his soul dissipates into nothingness.

27-31   The caster places his soul within the chosen phylactery. His body can travel no further than 1,000 miles from the phylactery; any further distance causes the body to die and the soul's awareness to return to its vessel. Without a body to sustain him, the caster has 1d6+CL weeks to inhabit a new body before his soul dissipates into nothingness.

32-33   The caster places his soul within the chosen phylactery. His body can travel anywhere on this plane, but extraplanar travel (even for an instant) causes his body to die and the soul's awareness to return to its vessel. Without a body to sustain him, the caster has 1d10+CL weeks to inhabit a new body before his soul dissipates into nothingness.

34-35   The caster places his soul within the chosen phylactery. His body can travel anywhere in the multiverse without restrictions. If the caster's body is slain, he has 1d16 + CL weeks to inhabit a new body before his soul dissipates into nothingness.

36+   The caster places his soul within the chosen phylactery. His body can travel anywhere in the multiverse without danger. If the caster's body is slain, he has 1d100 + CL years to inhabit a new body before his soul dissipates into nothingness.

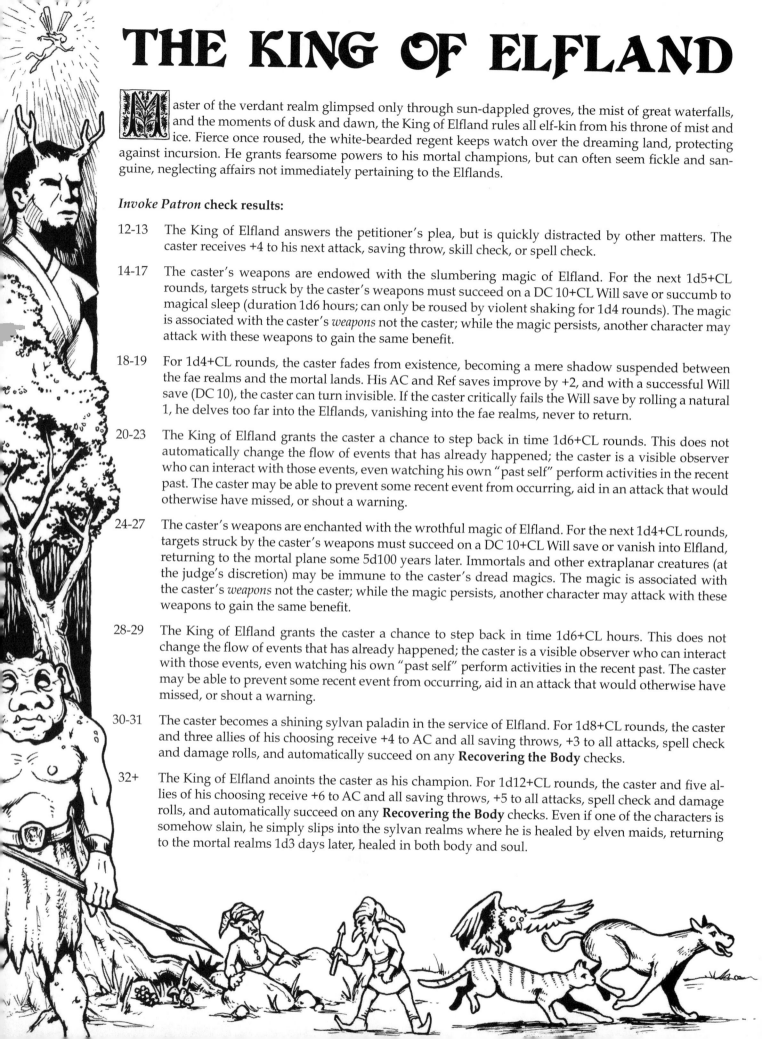

THE KING OF ELFLAND

Master of the verdant realm glimpsed only through sun-dappled groves, the mist of great waterfalls, and the moments of dusk and dawn, the King of Elfland rules all elf-kin from his throne of mist and ice. Fierce once roused, the white-bearded regent keeps watch over the dreaming land, protecting against incursion. He grants fearsome powers to his mortal champions, but can often seem fickle and sanguine, neglecting affairs not immediately pertaining to the Elflands.

Invoke Patron check results:

12-13	The King of Elfland answers the petitioner's plea, but is quickly distracted by other matters. The caster receives +4 to his next attack, saving throw, skill check, or spell check.
14-17	The caster's weapons are endowed with the slumbering magic of Elfland. For the next 1d5+CL rounds, targets struck by the caster's weapons must succeed on a DC 10+CL Will save or succumb to magical sleep (duration 1d6 hours; can only be roused by violent shaking for 1d4 rounds). The magic is associated with the caster's *weapons* not the caster; while the magic persists, another character may attack with these weapons to gain the same benefit.
18-19	For 1d4+CL rounds, the caster fades from existence, becoming a mere shadow suspended between the fae realms and the mortal lands. His AC and Ref saves improve by +2, and with a successful Will save (DC 10), the caster can turn invisible. If the caster critically fails the Will save by rolling a natural 1, he delves too far into the Elflands, vanishing into the fae realms, never to return.
20-23	The King of Elfland grants the caster a chance to step back in time 1d6+CL rounds. This does not automatically change the flow of events that has already happened; the caster is a visible observer who can interact with those events, even watching his own "past self" perform activities in the recent past. The caster may be able to prevent some recent event from occurring, aid in an attack that would otherwise have missed, or shout a warning.
24-27	The caster's weapons are enchanted with the wrothful magic of Elfland. For the next 1d4+CL rounds, targets struck by the caster's weapons must succeed on a DC 10+CL Will save or vanish into Elfland, returning to the mortal plane some 5d100 years later. Immortals and other extraplanar creatures (at the judge's discretion) may be immune to the caster's dread magics. The magic is associated with the caster's *weapons* not the caster; while the magic persists, another character may attack with these weapons to gain the same benefit.
28-29	The King of Elfland grants the caster a chance to step back in time 1d6+CL hours. This does not change the flow of events that has already happened; the caster is a visible observer who can interact with those events, even watching his own "past self" perform activities in the recent past. The caster may be able to prevent some recent event from occurring, aid in an attack that would otherwise have missed, or shout a warning.
30-31	The caster becomes a shining sylvan paladin in the service of Elfland. For 1d8+CL rounds, the caster and three allies of his choosing receive +4 to AC and all saving throws, +3 to all attacks, spell check and damage rolls, and automatically succeed on any **Recovering the Body** checks.
32+	The King of Elfland anoints the caster as his champion. For 1d12+CL rounds, the caster and five allies of his choosing receive +6 to AC and all saving throws, +5 to all attacks, spell check and damage rolls, and automatically succeed on any **Recovering the Body** checks. Even if one of the characters is somehow slain, he simply slips into the sylvan realms where he is healed by elven maids, returning to the mortal realms 1d3 days later, healed in both body and soul.

PATRON TAINT: THE KING OF ELFLAND

The King of Elfland is a vexing patron, indifferent and then demanding by turns. Those in his service must be dedicated to their liege and vengeful against his foes. Few can view the master of Elfland and not be influenced by his boundless lust for life.

When a patron taint is indicated, roll 1d6 on the table below. When a caster has acquired all six taints at all levels of effect, there is no need to continue rolling any more.

Roll	Result
1	The caster is seized by in explicable longing for the forests of Elfland and yearns to visit the mythic land. If the result is rolled a second time, the longing overcomes the caster; if the opportunity presents itself, he must make a pilgrimage to Elfland. If the result is rolled a third time, the caster can do naught but take steps that will return him to Elfland. If the caster succeeds in making a pilgrimage to the fabled land, he is free to depart after the briefest of visits (returning to the mortal world 3d100 years later).
2	The vibrant, verdant power of the Elflands seeps into the caster. The caster's skin takes on a green hue, especially at dusk and dawn. If the result is rolled a second time, the caster buds hints of velvet-covered antlers. If the result is rolled a third time, antlers sprout from the caster's forehead and his skin is covered in a soft coat of green-hued fur.
3	The caster adopts the sanguine indifference of his patron. He becomes aloof and easily distracted, reducing his Personality by -1. If the result is rolled a second time, the caster becomes withdrawn from mortal concerns—the promise of gold and glory have little draw; the caster's Personality is reduced by a further -1. If the result is rolled a third time, the caster fully withdraws from the world of mortal suffering, reducing his Personality by a further -1, and can only be motivated if the concern involves himself or the Elflands.

4   Animals are inexplicably drawn to the caster. Though they do not obey the caster's commands (and, indeed, ignore the caster's attempts to shoo them), domesticated animals of every sort long to be within the caster's presence. If the result is rolled a second time, the effect extends to small wild animals—birds, rats and the like—which accompany the PC wherever he goes. If the result is rolled a third time, the caster cannot go anywhere without being accosted by animals of all sort.

5   The caster sees sprites and the like out of the corner of his vision and just out of sight. If the result is rolled a second time, the caster comes to the very visceral realization that the entire world is alive with spirits and finds himself absent-mindedly consulting them when challenges arise. If the result is rolled a third time, his perception of the natural world of the spirit is far more real than the usual mortal realm, and the caster must make an effort (Will save, DC 15) in order to interact with mortals during anything other than life-threatening situations.

6   The caster is easily distracted and struggles to stay focused on the present: The judge may select a single spell that takes 1 round to cast; the caster must succeed on a DC 10 Will check or take an extra +1d3 rounds to cast the spell. If the result is rolled a second time, the judge should choose a second spell; the caster must succeed on a DC 15 Will check or take an extra +1d3 rounds to cast the spell. If the result is rolled a third time, the judge should choose a third spell; the caster must succeed on a DC 20 Will check or take an extra +1d3 rounds to cast the spell.

SPELLBURN: THE KING OF ELFLAND

The King of Elfland readily lends his strength to his champions, but few are those that can hold their master's attention for long. Those that do hope to win their patron's support must be cunning, clever and courageous. When a caster utilizes spellburn, roll 1d4 and consult the table below or build off the suggestions to create an event specific to your home campaign.

Roll   Spellburn Result

1   A fearsome, scintillating dragon appears over the caster's shoulder. As the spellburn takes effect, the dragon is drawn into the caster, the shock of the effect manifesting as stat point loss.

2   The caster is granted the spellburn bonus, but must succeed on a minor quest in the next 1d4 weeks; until the quest is completed, the caster cannot regain the burned stat points. The goal of the quest

is both trivial and difficult—typically to recover an item with a value only understood by the King of Elfland: a dwarven smith's favorite anvil; the tiara of a lady-in-waiting; the Black Knight's shield; the Emperor of the World's favorite diadem.

3   Calling on the sylvan realm causes a bit of the caster's shadow to leave for an errand in the Elflands; forcing one's own shadow away requires great mental force, manifesting as stat loss.

4   In order to succeed on the spellburn, the caster must come up with a pun, riddle or rhyme that delights the King of Elfland. If the King is amused, the PC need not spend any attribute points for the spellburn, but if the King is less than delighted, the caster must pay twice as many stat points for the burn.

PATRON SPELLS: THE KING OF ELFLAND

The King of Elfland grants three unique spells, as follows:

Level 1: *Forest Walk*

Level 2: *War Horn of Elfland*

Level 3: *The Dreaming*

Forest Walk

Level: 1 (The King of Elfland)   Range: Varies   Duration: Varies   Casting time: 1 action   Save: None

General	Conversant with the spirits and powers of Elfland, the caster employs the hidden byways and secret wynds of the fairy realm, teleporting from one tree to another. The caster must travel between trees of the same species, generally limiting his travel to similar biomes. For example, a caster cannot travel from a rain forest to a deciduous forest or from a northern conifer stand to a temperate broadleaf woodland. At the judge's discretion, appearing from within a tree typically confers surprise. The caster can specify a specific tree to emerge from of which he has knowledge, but he does not need knowledge of the place to which he travels: he can state, for example, "I wish to emerge from an oak tree in the orc realms 100 miles north of here."
Manifestation	Roll 1d3: (1) A door, set into the stump of a tree, is suddenly revealed; (2) caster slowly diminishes, fading into shadow, as he vanishes into the arbor; (3) caster sprouts leaves and bark skin and is quickly absorbed into the tree.
1	Lost, failure and patron taint.
2-11	Lost. Failure.
12-13	The caster steps through one tree and instantly emerges from another tree up 100 yards away.
14-17	The caster steps through one tree and instantly emerges from another tree within the same forest, up to one mile distant.
18-19	The caster steps through one tree and instantly emerges from another tree within the same forest, up to 100 miles distant.
20-23	The caster and up to 1d4 + CL allies step through a tree and are instantly transported to another tree within the same forest, up to 100 miles distant.
24-27	The caster and up to 1d8 + CL allies step through a tree and are instantly transported to another tree within the same forest, up to 100 miles distant.
28-29	The caster and up to 1d12 + CL allies step through a tree and are instantly transported to another tree within the same forest, up to 1,000 miles distant.
30-31	The caster and up to CL x 100 allies step through a tree and are instantly transported to another tree, anywhere on the same plane. This spell remains active long enough for all allies to step through the tree. This spell can be used to allow an army to march through a tree and arrive at a distance place. Allies can be mounted on horses or even in boats provided the tree is adjacent to a waterway.
32+	The caster and any number of allies can step through a tree to be instantly transported to another tree, on any plane. Of course, trees of the same species typically grow on similar planes of existence, so planar travel with this is limited, but a carefully cultivated specimen nurtured in advance of casting of this spell can be used as an "anchor point" on another plane. Servants of the King of Elfland use this spell to instantly travel between waystations on his realm of existence and many other planes.

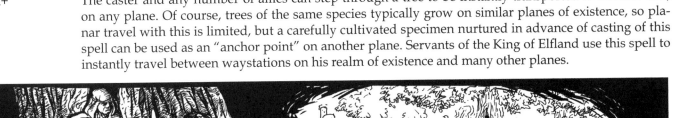

War Horn of Elfland

Level: 2 (The King of Elfland)	Range: Self	Duration: Varies	Casting time: 1 round	Save: None

General

The caster sounds a great war horn, calling the armies of Elfland to his side. Faithful unto death and fierce in battle, their tie to the mortal plane is but short and fleeting. The spell requires sounding a horn carved from a beast of 5 HD or greater. If the horn is set with precious jewels and metals (worth no less than 500 gp), the caster receives a +2 bonus to his spell checks (though a natural 1 still results in a patron taint). The horn must be held and sounded once every three rounds the spell is in effect. Sounding the horn requires an action, and if the horn fails to be sounded, the spell comes to an end. The warriors' bodies and kit vanish when slain or the spells ends. The stats for the various allies are as follows:

Trollish Spearmen: Init +0; Atk spear +1 melee (dmg 1d8); AC 15; HD 1d8; HP 1; MV 30'; Act 1d20; SV Fort +1, Ref +1, Will +0; AL C.

Brownie Slingers: Init +0; Atk sling +1 ranged (dmg 1d4) or short sword +1 melee (dmg 1d6-1); AC 14; HD 1d6; HP 1; MV 30'; Act 1d20; SV Fort +0, Ref +1, Will -1; AL C.

Hob Footmen: Init +0; Atk longsword +2 melee (dmg 1d8+2); AC 17; HD 2d8; HP 1; MV 30'; Act 1d20; SV Fort +1, Ref +1, Will +1; AL C.

Pixie Archers: Init +0; Atk Tiny sword +2 melee (dmg 1d4 plus *sleep*) or pixie bow +2 (dmg 1d4 plus *sleep*); AC 16; HD 2d6; HP 1; MV 40' flight; Act 1d20; SP pixie dust weapons (DC 15 Fort save on hit or *sleep* for 1d6 hours); SV Fort +1, Ref +2, Will +0; AL C.

Fomorians: Init +0; Atk Large morningstar +4 melee (dmg 1d12+4) or hurling stone +2 ranged (dmg 1d8+4); AC 16; HD 5d10; HP 1; MV 45'; Act 2d20; SV Fort +4, Ref +1, Will +0; AL C.

Manifestation

Roll 1d3: (1) hints of soldiers emerge from the shadows, coalescing into solid forms; (2) an emerald mist passes over the land leaving warriors in its wake; (3) a searing rainbow bridge arcs from over the horizon, bringing with it fierce warriors.

1

Lost, failure and patron taint.

2 -11

Lost. Failure.

12-13

Failure, but spell is not lost.

14-15

A group of 1d5 brownie slingers answer the call. Each is armed with a sling, a satchel of sling bullets, and a short sword, but vanishes after taking a single point of damage. The spell lasts for 1d6+CL rounds, as long as the horn is sounded once every three rounds, or until all the fae are dismissed.

16-19

A body of 1d5+CL trollish spearmen supported by 1d5 brownie slingers heed the call. The spearmen carry flashing long spears. Each ally vanishes after taking a single point of damage. The spell lasts for 1d8+CL rounds, as long as the horn is sounded once every three rounds, or until all the fae are dismissed.

20-21

A rough band of 1d12+CL trollish spearmen and 1d8+CL brownie slingers answer the call. All vanish after taking a single point of damage. The spell lasts for 1d10+CL rounds, as long as the horn is sounded once every three rounds, or until all the fae are dismissed.

22-25

A troop of 1d16+CL trollish spearmen, 1d8+CL brownie slingers, and 1d8 hob footmen answer the call. The spell lasts for 1d12 rounds, as long as the horn is sounded once every three rounds, or until all the fae are dismissed.

26-29

A marauding force of 1d20+CL trollish spearmen, 1d16+CL brownie slingers, 1d12+CL hob footmen, and 1d10 pixie archers answer the summons. The spell lasts for 1d16 rounds, as long as the horn is sounded once every three rounds, or until all the fae are dismissed.

30-31

A thundering company of 1d24+CL trollish spearmen, 1d20+CL brownie slingers, 1d16+CL hob footmen, 1d12+CL pixie archers, and 1d8 fomorians answer the summons. The spell lasts for 1d20 rounds, as long as the horn is sounded once every three rounds, or until all the fae are dismissed.

32-33

The caster's call for aid is answered by the full host of Elfland. The spell lasts for 1d24+CL rounds. Immediately re-roll the spell check to determine the type and number of fae that answer the call, re-rolling any spell failures or results of 32+. As long as the caster continues to sound the horn, re-roll the spell check again every third round, as new allies answer the call.

34+

The full host of Elfland comes to the caster's aid, stepping fully into the mortal realm. Immediately re-roll the spell check to determine the type and number of fae that answer the call, re-rolling any spell failures or results of 32+. As long as the caster continue to sound the horn, re-roll the spell check again every third round, as new allies answer the call. Each type of fae steps into the mortal realm with *full* hit points, not just 1 point, and are not dismissed until they reach 1 hit point. The spell ends when dismissed by the caster or by the King of Elfland himself.

The Dreaming

Level: 3 (The King of Elfland) Range: Self Duration: Varies Casting time: 1 round Save: None

General	The caster calls upon the ancient, slumbering magic of the Elflands. Time slows as the fey dreaming of twilight and dusk ooze into the mortal realms.
Manifestation	Roll 1d3: (1) glowing mist settles over the area; (2) scintillating dust and the peal of tinkling of bells fill the air; (3) a strange air settles over the caster, as if lit by the fading light of dusk.
1	Lost, failure and patron taint.
2-11	Lost. Failure.
12-15	Failure, but spell is not lost.
16-17	The dreaming magic of the faerie-realms spills into the world around the caster, slowing the passage of time. Versed in the ways of the Elflands, the caster may take an extra action each round and is granted a +1 bonus to his AC, Reflex saves, and attack rolls. The extra action is at the caster's lowest action die. The enchantment lasts for 1d4 rounds.
18-21	The caster's mastery of the Elflands is like an aura, protecting his allies from the fey and fell magics. The caster and all his allies within 50' may take an extra action each round (at each character's lowest action die) and are granted a +1 bonus to AC, Reflex saves, and attack rolls. The enchantment lasts for 1d4 rounds.
22-23	Time slows to a crawl. The caster and all his allies within 50' may take two extra actions each round (at each character's lowest action die) and are granted a +2 bonus to AC, Reflex saves, and attack rolls. The enchantment lasts for 1d3 rounds.
24-26	The caster and all his allies within 50' may take three extra actions each round (at each character's lowest action die) and are granted a +3 bonus to AC, Reflex saves, and attack rolls. The enchantment lasts for 1d3 rounds.
27-31	The caster and all his allies within 50' may take three extra actions each round (at each character's lowest action die) and are granted a +3 bonus to AC, Reflex saves, and attack rolls. The enchantment lasts for 1d3 rounds, and may be extended with spellburn. When the spell is about to expire, the caster may spellburn 1 point of attribute to extend the spell's effect by 1 round. He may continue to extend the spell's effect, round by round, in this manner. Using such spellburn requires an action on the caster's part (which can be one of several actions provided he extends the spell).
32-33	The passage of time stops for 1d3+CL rounds. The caster is the sole mortal immune to the effects of the enchantment, though gods and other immortals may also be immune. During this time, the caster may take normal activations, while other creatures are frozen in time. This can allow the caster to cast multiple spells, make multiple attacks, flee, or otherwise do whatever he wishes with no chance for others to react.
34-35	Time stops, resuming only when the caster or the King of Elfland dismiss the enchantment. The caster is the sole mortal immune to the effects of the enchantment, though gods and other immortals may also be immune. During this time, the caster may take normal activations, while other creatures are frozen in time. This can allow the caster to cast multiple spells, make multiple attacks, flee, or otherwise do whatever he wishes with no chance for others to react.
36+	Time stops, as result 34-35 above. Additionally, the caster may turn back time by *permanently* spellburning attribute points at the rate of 2 points for every 10 minutes.

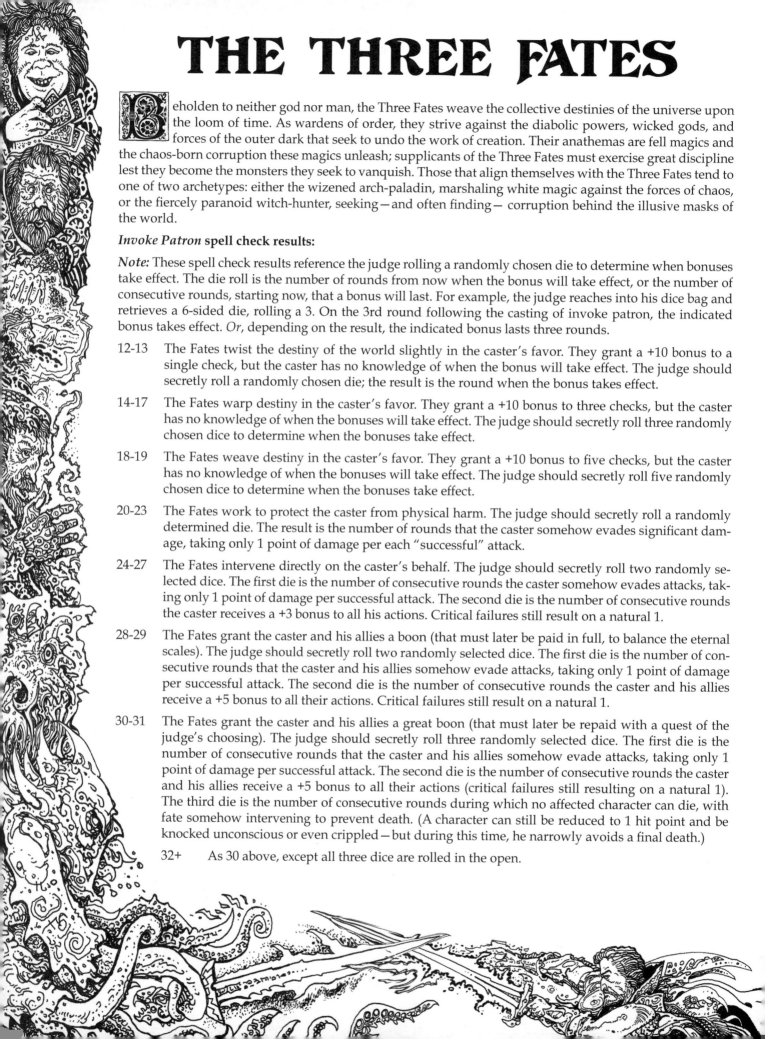

THE THREE FATES

Beholden to neither god nor man, the Three Fates weave the collective destinies of the universe upon the loom of time. As wardens of order, they strive against the diabolic powers, wicked gods, and forces of the outer dark that seek to undo the work of creation. Their anathemas are fell magics and the chaos-born corruption these magics unleash; supplicants of the Three Fates must exercise great discipline lest they become the monsters they seek to vanquish. Those that align themselves with the Three Fates tend to one of two archetypes: either the wizened arch-paladin, marshaling white magic against the forces of chaos, or the fiercely paranoid witch-hunter, seeking—and often finding— corruption behind the illusive masks of the world.

Invoke Patron **spell check results:**

Note: These spell check results reference the judge rolling a randomly chosen die to determine when bonuses take effect. The die roll is the number of rounds from now when the bonus will take effect, or the number of consecutive rounds, starting now, that a bonus will last. For example, the judge reaches into his dice bag and retrieves a 6-sided die, rolling a 3. On the 3rd round following the casting of invoke patron, the indicated bonus takes effect. *Or*, depending on the result, the indicated bonus lasts three rounds.

12-13　　The Fates twist the destiny of the world slightly in the caster's favor. They grant a +10 bonus to a single check, but the caster has no knowledge of when the bonus will take effect. The judge should secretly roll a randomly chosen die; the result is the round when the bonus takes effect.

14-17　　The Fates warp destiny in the caster's favor. They grant a +10 bonus to three checks, but the caster has no knowledge of when the bonuses will take effect. The judge should secretly roll three randomly chosen dice to determine when the bonuses take effect.

18-19　　The Fates weave destiny in the caster's favor. They grant a +10 bonus to five checks, but the caster has no knowledge of when the bonuses will take effect. The judge should secretly roll five randomly chosen dice to determine when the bonuses take effect.

20-23　　The Fates work to protect the caster from physical harm. The judge should secretly roll a randomly determined die. The result is the number of rounds that the caster somehow evades significant damage, taking only 1 point of damage per each "successful" attack.

24-27　　The Fates intervene directly on the caster's behalf. The judge should secretly roll two randomly selected dice. The first die is the number of consecutive rounds the caster somehow evades attacks, taking only 1 point of damage per successful attack. The second die is the number of consecutive rounds the caster receives a +3 bonus to all his actions. Critical failures still result on a natural 1.

28-29　　The Fates grant the caster and his allies a boon (that must later be paid in full, to balance the eternal scales). The judge should secretly roll two randomly selected dice. The first die is the number of consecutive rounds that the caster and his allies somehow evade attacks, taking only 1 point of damage per successful attack. The second die is the number of consecutive rounds the caster and his allies receive a +5 bonus to all their actions. Critical failures still result on a natural 1.

30-31　　The Fates grant the caster and his allies a great boon (that must later be repaid with a quest of the judge's choosing). The judge should secretly roll three randomly selected dice. The first die is the number of consecutive rounds that the caster and his allies somehow evade attacks, taking only 1 point of damage per successful attack. The second die is the number of consecutive rounds the caster and his allies receive a +5 bonus to all their actions (critical failures still resulting on a natural 1). The third die is the number of consecutive rounds during which no affected character can die, with fate somehow intervening to prevent death. (A character can still be reduced to 1 hit point and be knocked unconscious or even crippled—but during this time, he narrowly avoids a final death.)

32+　　As 30 above, except all three dice are rolled in the open.

PATRON TAINT: THE THREE FATES

Patron taint is a misnomer when referring to supplicants of the Three Fates. Rather, the caster believes that he has acquired a taint, real or imagined, from another, unclean source of magic (likely the residual chaos taint from a non-patron spell). As a result, the caster is driven to cleanse himself of the taint. Should the caster fail to excise the taint, he immediately loses all benefits of his patronage, including unique spells. When patron taint is indicated, roll 1d6 on the table below. When a caster has excised all six taints at all levels of effect, there is no need to continue rolling any more. Additionally, the caster is freed from all future corruption rolls.

Roll	Result
1	The caster perceives that his blood has been tainted with chaos magic. Before the next dawn, he must undertake a ritual bloodletting, reducing his Strength, Stamina and Agility by -1 for 1d3 days. If the result is a rolled a second time, the caster must go to even greater lengths, applying sanctified leeches to his veins within the next 24 hours. For the rite to achieve efficacy, the leeches must stay in place for one week, during which time the caster's Strength, Stamina and Agility are reduced by -3. If the result is rolled a third time, the caster submits his body to the Rite of Hooks and Needles, reducing his Strength, Stamina and Agility to 3 for the next month. Completing all three levels of effect cures the caster of 1d3 corruptions.
2	In horror, the caster perceives that his soul has been tainted in his battle against chaos magic. The caster redoubles his efforts to rid the world of corruption, undertaking a mission at the behest of his masters. Subject to the judge's discretion, the caster must adventure to destroy a fell relic of chaos located within 1d4 days of travel. The caster has a clear vision of the item, but only a rough sense of its location and wards. If the result is rolled a second time, the caster ventures to destroy a chaos-monster some 1d4 weeks distant. If the result is rolled a third time, the caster must venture to a capital city and slay a prominent citizen who has secretly sworn his soul to chaos. Completing all three quests cures the caster of 1d3 corruptions.
3	One of the caster's own limbs has become infected with chaos magic. The caster removes

his own finger (inflicting 1d2 points of damage), praying he acts quickly enough to stem the spread of corruption. If the result is rolled a second time, the caster recognizes that his eyes have been tainted from witnessing the horrors of chaos and takes out his own eye (inflicting 1d3 points of damage). If the result is rolled a third time, the caster believes that an entire limb has fallen prey to chaos. The caster subjects himself to a horrifying ritual, stripping key veins and muscles from his own limb, inflicting 4d8 damage upon himself in the process. If the caster survives the rite, he may attempt a DC 15 Fort save; on a failed check, the limb is lost to necrosis.

4   The caster perceives that his battle against chaos has released a shadow-self upon the plane. Subject to the judge's discretion, the caster must travel 1d4 days to discover and slay his mirror image. Both the caster and the shadow-self have a clear sense of the other's location, and are driven to slay one another. If the result is rolled a second time, the caster's doppelganger is some 1d4 weeks distant, 1d3 levels higher than the caster, and protected by the appropriate wards and minions. If the result is rolled a third time, the shadow-self is 1d3 months distant, 1d5 levels higher than the caster, and resides within a fell citadel defended by an army of fiends.

5   Having witnessed the horrors of chaos, the caster's own thoughts are irrevocably stained by chaos. The caster is driven to regain mastery of his own mind by submitting himself to meditation for the next 1d3 hours. If the result is rolled a second time, the caster must meditate until he succeeds on a DC 20 Will save, or 1 month has passed. The caster may attempt a Will save per day. If the result is rolled a third time, the caster must withdraw into meditation until he succeeds on a DC 25 Will save or one year has passed. The caster may attempt one Will save per day. Completing all three levels of effect grants the caster total mastery of his mind, mentally curing himself of 1d3 corruptions and receiving a +2 bonus to all future Will saves.

6   Believing himself to be the mortal hand of Fate, the CASTER loses all fear of death, accepting its role in the dance of worlds. If the caster dies, he is permitted a DC 15 Fort save; on a successful save, the caster miraculously survives, living on to serve the Three Fates. If the result is rolled a second time, the caster again grows to believe he has a role in the designs of the Fates, and a DC 20 Fort save permits him to escape death a second time. If the result is rolled a third time, a DC 25 Fort save permits the caster to escape death a third and final time.

PATRON SPELLS: THE THREE FATES

Agents of the Three Fates learn three unique spells, as follows:

Level 1: *Blade of Atropos*

Level 2: *Curse of Moirae*

Level 3: *Warp & Weft*

SPELLBURN: THE THREE FATES

While the universe can seem cold and uncaring, agents of the Fates understand that it is simply resolving toward a preordained destiny and that too much chaos threatens to tear the skein of creation. Thus spellburning in the name of the Three Fates most often manifests as an orderly rite, the caster petitioning the Fates for inner wisdom on the workings of the spheres. This, in turn, grants the caster's spells extra potency. When a caster utilizes spellburn, roll 1d4 and consult the table below or build off the suggestions to create an event specific to your home campaign.

Roll	Spellburn Result
1	Apprehending the majesty of his role in the ordered universe exhausts the caster (expressed as Stamina, Strength, or Agility loss). The caster must succeed on a DC 15 Will save or lose all benefits of the spellburn. If the caster succeeds on the save, his hard-won wisdom grants him a +1 bonus to all future attempts at the spell. (Such a bonus can only be gained once per spell.)
2	The caster draws upon the latent power of ley lines and telluric currents, utilizing the native forces to empower his spell. On a successful Int check (DC 15+spell level), the caster gains +3 to his spell check without expending any stats. (The caster is then free to spellburn stats to further augment the casting.)
3	The caster submits himself to the will of the Fates, who drain the caster of stat points according to their own, unknowable plan. Roll 1d4 to determine the stat drained in the spellburn: (1) Strength, (2) Agility, (3) Stamina, (4) the caster suffers no drain but still receives the spellburn bonus.
4	The caster cannot spellburn without resorting to a fell chaos rite. His oppressive guilt and the spell's grim requirements are expressed as Stamina, Strength, or Agility loss. Should the caster ever spellburn in the presence of other agents of the Fates, his life would surely be forfeit.

Blade of Atropos

Level: 1 (The Three Fates)   **Range:** Self   **Duration:** Varies   **Casting time:** 1 round   **Save:** Will save vs. 15+CL when appropriate (see below)

General	The Blade of Atropos is gifted to those willing to do the work of the Fates, bringing an end to chaos-creatures and those bearing the mark of arcane corruption. Casting the spell requires a non-magical sword; if the blade is decorated with jewels and precious metals (worth no less than 1,000 gp), the caster receives a +2 bonus to his spell check. If the blade leaves the caster's hand, the spell immediately ends. Strength modifiers (positive or negative) have no effect on the caster's to hit roll or damage rolls while wielding the blade.
Manifestation	Roll 1d4: (1) the caster's sword shines with righteous power, illuminating all within 60'; (2) the caster's blade crackles with magic, as electric-blue spider webs crawl up and down the sword; (3) the caster's blade shimmers in and out of existence, wreathed in tendrils of glowing green mist; (4) violet and purple light emanate from within the blade, shining through cracks that appear in the blade's surface.
1	Lost, failure, and patron taint.
2-11	Lost. Failure.
12-13	Attacks with the empowered blade are at a +1 to hit (+3 vs. chaos-creatures or corrupted casters) and inflict 1d12+CL in damage. The spell lasts for 1d3+CL rounds.
14-17	Attacks with the enchanted blade are at a +2 to hit (+4 vs. chaos-creatures or corrupted casters) and inflict 1d14+CL in damage. The spell lasts for 1d5+CL rounds.
18-19	Attacks with the enchanted blade are at a +3 to hit (+5 vs. chaos-creatures or corrupted casters) and inflict 1d16+CL in damage. The spell lasts for 1d6+CL rounds.
20-23	A second blade appears in the air, mirroring the first. The caster can direct the second blade to attack targets within 10' (at the caster's lowest action die), while he fights with the enchanted blade in his hand. No concentration is required to direct the second blade. Attacks with the blades are at a +3 to hit (+5 vs. chaos-creatures or corrupted casters) and inflict 1d16+CL in damage. The spell lasts for 1d8+CL rounds.
24-27	Two additional blades appear in the air, mirroring the first. The caster can direct the blades to attack targets within 50' (at the caster's lowest action die), while he fights with the enchanted blade in his hand. No concentration is required to direct the additional blades. Attacks with all three blades are at a+4 to hit (+6 vs. chaos-creatures or corrupted casters) and inflict 1d20+CL in damage. The spell lasts for 1d10+CL rounds.
28-29	Two additional blades appear in the air, mirroring the first. The caster can direct the blades to attack targets within sight and 100' (at the caster's lowest action die), while he fights with the enchanted blade in his hand. No concentration is required to direct the additional blades. Attacks with all three blades are at a +5 to hit (+7 vs. chaos-creatures or corrupted casters) and inflict 2d12+CL in damage, except against Chaos-creatures or corrupted casters, who must make Will saves or take damage equal to half their remaining hp (rounding up) or 2d12+CL, whichever is higher. The spell lasts for 1d12+CL rounds.
30-31	Two additional blades appear in the air, mirroring the first. The caster can direct the blades to attack targets within sight and 500' (at the caster's lowest action die), while he fights with the enchanted blade in his hand. No concentration is required to direct the additional blades. Attacks with all three blades are at a +6 to hit (+8 vs. chaos-creatures or corrupted casters) and inflict 2d14+CL in damage. Chaos-creatures or corrupted casters struck by the blades must make Will saves or be banished from this plane of existence. The spell lasts for 1d14+CL rounds.
32+	Two additional blades appear in the air, mirroring the first. The caster can direct the blades attack targets within sight (at the caster's lowest action die), while he fights with the enchanted blade in his hand. No concentration is required to direct the additional blades. Attacks with the blades are at a +7 to hit (+9 vs. chaos-creatures or corrupted casters) and inflict 2d16+CL in damage. Chaos-creatures or corrupted casters struck by the blades must make Will saves or be immediately and permanently struck dead. The spell lasts for 1d16+CL rounds.

Curse of Moirae

Level: 2 (The Three Fates)　　Range: Varies　　Duration: Varies　　Casting time: 1 round　　Save: Will vs. spell check when appropriate

General	The caster measures out the target's life as best a mortal can, increasing the likelihood of an untimely (though, ultimately, preordained) end. After casting the spell, the caster has 1d4+CL rounds to successfully make a touch attack against a target, triggering the curse. If the caster fails to bestow the curse on a target, the caster must succeed on a Fort save (DC 10+CL) or take 1d3 points of damage per CL.
Manifestation	Roll 1d4: (1) the caster's fingertips become smudged with soot that is transferred to the target with a successful attack; (2) a small black spider appears in the caster's palm that leaps to the target with a successful attack; (3) the caster's physical attacks manifest as a gout of black mist, exhaled onto the target; (4) the caster's lips blacken to the color of charcoal, and the curse is bestowed with a kiss (a successful attack).
1	Lost, failure, and patron taint.
2-11	Lost. Failure.
12-13	Failure, but spell is not lost.
14-15	The target suffers a -2 penalty to all saving throws, AC, and attacks against the caster and his allies for the next 1d4+CL rounds. The target takes an additional 1d4 damage each time it is struck for damage during the spell's duration.
16-19	The target suffers a -4 penalty to all saving throws, AC, and attacks against the caster and his allies for the next 1d6+CL rounds. The target takes an additional 1d6 damage each time it is struck for damage during the spell's duration.
20-21	The target suffers a -6 penalty to all saving throws, AC, and attacks against the caster and his allies for the next 1d8+CL rounds. The target takes an additional 1d8 damage each time it is struck for damage during the spell's duration.
22-25	The target suffers a -8 penalty to all saving throws, AC, and attacks against the caster and his allies for the next 1d10+CL rounds. The target takes an additional 1d10 damage each time it is struck for damage during the spell's duration.
26-29	The target suffers a -10 penalty to all saving throws, AC, and attacks against the caster and his allies for the next 1d12+CL rounds. The target takes an additional 1d12 damage each time it is struck for damage during the spell's duration.
30-31	The target suffers a -10 penalty to all saving throws, AC, and attacks against the caster and his allies for the next 1d12+CL rounds. The target takes an additional 1d14 damage each time it is struck for damage during the spell's duration.
32-33	The target suffers a -10 penalty to all saving throws, AC, and attacks against the caster and his allies for the next 1d12+CL rounds. The target takes an additional 1d16 damage each time it is struck for damage during the spell's duration. Finally, the target will die of natural causes (at the judge's discretion) at the end of 24 hours. This final curse is lifted if the target succeeds on a Fort save (DC 15+CL) or if the caster is slain before the spell reaches its grisly end.
34+	The target suffers a -10 penalty to all saving throws, AC, and attacks against the caster and his allies for the next 1d12+CL rounds. The target takes an additional 1d20 damage each time it is struck for damage during the spell's duration. Finally, the target will die of natural causes (at the judge's discretion) at the end of the next hour. This final curse is lifted if the target succeeds on a Fort save (DC 15+CL), but even slaying the caster does not bring the spell to an end.

Warp & Weft

Level: 3 (The Three Fates)   **Range:** 1d100' +10' per CL   **Duration:** 1d3+CL turns, except where noted
Casting time: 2 rounds   **Save:** Will save vs. spell check if unwilling

General	Servant to the Three Fates, the caster can bend, stretch—and in rare instances— weave the threads of destiny that rule the universe. Such power always comes with great risk, and even the caster's masters are loath to alter what has already been decided. Once cast, the spell effect can be declared at any time, regardless of initiative order. Each time the spell is unsuccessfully cast there is a cumulative 1% chance that the caster winks from existence, never to return. If the caster elects to turn the spell's effects on himself, he must first attempt a Will save vs. spell check or immediately cease to exist.
Manifestation	Roll 1d3: (1) caster freezes for the duration of the casting time, perceiving the strands and threads of fate that make up the universe; (2) large, pale, interdimensional spiders descend through rifts in reality, drawing threads of fate-silk behind them; (3) a dusky hue passes over the caster's vision and all living creatures within his sight appear as corpses, as he witnesses the inevitable end to all living things.
1	Lost, failure, and patron taint.
2-11	Lost. Failure.
12-15	Failure, but spell is not lost.
16-17	The caster can alter a single saving throw, ensuring that a failed save is successful or a successful save is failed.
18-21	The caster can alter 1d3 savings throws or attack rolls, making failed rolls successful or vice versa.
22-23	The caster can alter 1d5 savings throws, attack rolls, or damage rolls. He can make failed rolls successful or vice versa or ensure maximum or minimum damage on damage rolls.
24-26	The caster can alter 1d7 savings throws, attack rolls, spell checks, skill checks (including thief skills), or damage rolls. He can make failed checks successful or vice versa or ensure maximum or minimum results on damage rolls. Altered spells succeed at the lowest possible spell check result, or fail, but are not lost.
27-31	As result 24-26 above *or* the caster can cause 1d3 targets to suffer critical failures or successes to attack rolls or spell checks.
32-33	As result 24-26 above *or* the caster can cause 1d5 targets to suffer critical failures or successes to attack rolls or spell checks.
34-35	As result 24-26 above *and* the caster can cause 1d7 targets to suffer critical failures or successes to attack rolls or spell checks.
36+	The caster can alter 1d7 savings throws, attack rolls, spell checks, skill checks (including thief skills), or damage rolls, *and* cause 1d7 targets to suffer critical failures or successes to attack rolls or spell checks. *Alternatively*, for 1d5+CL rounds, the caster determines the failure or success of every die rolled within the spell's radius. This includes attacks, saving throws, spell checks, skill checks (including thief skills), and damage rolls. Damage rolls can be maximized or minimized. Altered spells succeed at the lowest possible check result, or fail, but are not lost. The caster's control of fate is not fine enough to determine critical failures or successes for attacks and spell checks (though such results can still be generated naturally). There is a 5% cumulative chance per round that the Fates reject the caster's intervention, ending the spell and inflicting 1d20 damage to all creatures within the spell radius.

YDDGRRL, THE WORLD ROOT

Y ddgrrl is the root from which all living plants grow. He is the guardian of the forest, worshipped by treants, sentient plants, and some druids. Yddgrrl's presence can be felt in the quiet dew-times and the deep calm of the green, when the meditating plant-life feels his nourishment. He controls the soil, the air, and the rain of the forest, and appears as a fast-growing root that breaks the surface of the forest floor to bring aid where needed. Yddgrrl asks little of his followers save that they meditate on the serenity of the green and defend the forests against all enemies, especially its greatest foes: fire and the axe. Yddgrrl dwells in a unique plane of existence at the intersection of the elemental planes of air, water, and earth, where he forever battles the forces of elemental fire.

Invoke Patron **check results:**

12-13 Yddgrrl protects the caster from the forest's enemies. Roots grow about his body and limbs with no negative impact to mobility. For 1d6+CL rounds, the roots protect the caster, who takes half damage from fire and bladed weapons.

14-17 Yddgrrl sends a torrential rain to protect the caster. A cloud materializes above the caster's head (even if underground) and the rainstorm erupts. The rain is centered on the caster and extends 1d4 x 10' from him in all directions. All natural fires are automatically extinguished. Magical fires are also extinguished unless they make a Will save against the spell check result (using the original caster's Will modifier). Fire-based magic used while the rainstorm is ongoing (e.g., *fireball*) is severely hampered and does only half damage. Visibility is restricted, inflicting a -2 attack penalty to all missile fire attacks. The rain storm continues for 1d6+CL rounds.

18-19 Yddgrrl strengthens the caster's skin to better resist the blade of the axe. The caster's skin thickens to resemble bark, and he gains a +4 AC bonus. The effect lasts for 1d4 turns.

20-23 Yddgrrl provides nourishment. The caster's legs sprout thin roots that seek out the ground. If the caster is standing on dirt or stone, he heals 1d8 hit points at the end of each round in which he does not move. This continues until he moves or returns to maximum hit points.

24-27   Yddgrrl sends the world-root to aid his follower. The tip of an enormous tree root bursts forth from the ground, swaying like a snake, and proceeds to attack a target of the caster's designation. It attacks with a +8 slam for 1d6+6 points of damage on the caster's initiative count. It can target any creature within 40' of the caster. The world-root remains for 1d6+CL rounds, and cannot be slain during this time; even if severed or killed, another root simply sprouts beside it. The caster does not need to concentrate in order to continue directing its actions.

28-29   A complex tangle of tree roots bursts from the earth to entangle an enemy of the caster's choosing. The enemy must be within 100'. He receives a Reflex save against the spell check DC to jump free; otherwise, he is trapped in place by the roots. The roots are permanent; the target can be freed only by chopping him free (must do 40 points of damage to the AC 12 roots).

30-31   A colossal tree-man bursts from the ground nearby and fights on behalf of the caster. He moves on the caster's initiative and the caster can perform other actions while directing him. The tree-man remains for 1d4+CL rounds. Tree-man: Atk slam +12 melee (dmg 2d6+6); AC 17; HD 6d8; MV 20'; Act 2d20; SP takes 2x damage from fire; SV Fort +8, Ref +1, Will +8; AL N.

32+   Yddgrrl sends *two* tree-men to fight for the caster, as result 30-31 above.

OBITU-QUE

The Lord of the Five is a pit fiend and balor general whose experimental mutations gave him five ruby-red eyes. His physical form was defeated by a line of noble barbarians but his dominating spirit survives in areas of blight and decay, where his ceremonies are performed. He demands that his subjects pursue his cryptic agenda of conquest. He is fast to respond to invocations, but the aid he sends may dominate the caster as much as aid him.

Invoke Patron **check results:**

12-13   Blight. All plants within 100' of the caster wither and die. All living creatures in range (excluding allies and the caster) grow suddenly weak, losing 1d4 Strength for the next hour.

14-17   Blight blade. The caster's weapon of choice (including staff or rod, as appropriate) grows black and dusky. Until the next sunrise, any creature struck by the blighted blade must make a DC 16 Fort save or be poisoned with a terrible blight that causes the permanent loss of 1d4 Strength.

18-19   Eldritch flames. The caster's body crackles with red flames, which give off no heat but are clearly visible. The flames grant a +6 bonus to attack rolls for the next turn, and whenever the caster attacks, they swirl above him and form the face of Obitu-Que, who sneers in profane delight.

20-23   Pit flames. The caster suffers 1 hp of damage as a bolt of black flame, jets from the ground through his body and arcs toward the nearest enemy. That enemy suffers 2d6 damage immediately and another 1d6 damage from burns on the following round.

24-27   Dominance. The demon's will surges into the caster's mind and from it to his nearest enemy. The caster loses 1d4 points of Personality for the next hour and feels irresistible compulsions to further Obitu-Que's agenda (at the judge's discretion). One designated enemy within 100' must make a DC 24 Will save or be dominated for 1d6 turns. While dominated, the caster controls the enemy's every action but must concentrate to do so. If the caster stops concentrating, the dominated enemy simply stands silent and immobile like a zombie.

28-29   As result 24-27, but the enemy must make a DC 28 Will save.

30-31   The five-eyed skull of Obitu-Que appears above the caster, sheathed in the ruby flames of Hell. It remains for five rounds, during which time the caster may cast no other spell. Each round, starting immediately (i.e., in the round of the spell-casting), the caster may direct one eye to dominate any enemy within 100'. The target must make a DC 30 Will save or be dominated. The domination lasts for 1d4 rounds past the end of the round following the disappearance of the skull. The caster controls the actions of all dominated creatures but must concentrate to do so. If the caster stops concentrating, the dominated enemies simply stand silent and immobile like zombies. When the effect ends, the caster temporarily loses 1d4 points of Personality and must follow the will of Obitu-Que for the next hour.

32+   As result 30-31, but the enemy must make a DC 32 Will save.

ITHHA, PRINCE OF ELEMENTAL WIND

thha, prince of elemental wind, serves as one example of the elemental pacts that can be made. Ithha is a demi-god who seeks to subjugate the earth elemental Grom and his minions. Ithha grants limited control over wind and the ability to summon air elementals.

Invoke Patron check results:

12-13   Earth-enemy. For the next turn, the caster and all allies within 10' gain a +2 bonus to attacks, damage, and spell checks against creatures of earth or stone.

14-17   Protective vortex. The caster is surrounded by a whirling vortex that flings aside all incoming missiles, and melee attackers must struggle to lift their blades against the wind. For the next turn, all missile fire attacks that "hit" the caster have an automatic 50% chance of missing, and the caster receives a +2 bonus to AC.

18-19   Sandstorm. A swirling, turbulent cone of air emanates from the caster's fingertip, pulling up sand and grit from the ground to produce a veritable sandstorm. The caster can target one enemy within 50', who takes 1d12 damage from abrasion. The sandstorm continues to whirl around that same target, following him if he moves and inflicting 1d10 damage on the next round, then 1d8, 1d6, and finally 1d4 on the fifth and final round. Each round, the target can make a DC 20 Fort save to avoid damage.

20-23   Suffocation. The caster targets one air-breathing enemy within 100' and points to him. All the air in the target's lungs is sucked out. The target begins suffocating, taking 1d6 Stamina damage immediately unless he succeeds on a DC 20 Fort save. If the save is failed, the target takes *another* 1d6 Stamina damage on the following round with another save to resist. Each time the target fails a save, the suffocation continues another round, lasting until he succeeds on a save or until he reaches 0 Stamina, at which point he dies.

24-27   Elemental transformation. The caster and all his equipment transform into gaseous form. He can fly at twice his normal speed and is immune to physical attack from mundane weapons, though he can be harmed by spells and magical attacks. The transformation lasts for 1 hour or until he wills it to end. While in gaseous form, the caster cannot attack physically but can cast spells that do not have limitations associated with his new form.

28-29   Summon invisible companion. The invisible companion performs the caster's bidding for 1 day. It can fly at a speed of 100' and can perform any task as a normal man, though it is invisible. It can attack enemies at +6 for 2d6 damage. If attacked, it has AC 16 and 60 hit points, although attackers can only fight it in melee (unless they cleverly reveal it somehow), and even then automatically miss 75% of the time.

30-31   Summon elemental. The caster calls forth a gust of sentient wind. It appears immediately and obeys commands for 2d6 rounds, then departs. It has the stats and abilities of an 8 HD air elemental (see page 411).

32+   Summon multiple elementals. The caster calls forth two gusts of sentient wind. They appear immediately and obey commands for 2d6 rounds, then depart. They have the stats and abilities of 12 HD air elementals (see page 411).

CLERIC SPELLS

Gods are not eternally patient. Clerical spell-casting is designed to reiterate this concept: the god may not be available when his servant needs him. In game terms, this is determined by a spell check; in story terms, the judge should strive to articulate why a spell check fails. If a cleric encounters a run of bad spell checks, perhaps introspection is in order. Has the cleric been faithful? Has he dedicated time to furthering his deity's agenda? Should he redouble his efforts?

Any time a cleric fumbles a spell check or fails more than three spell checks in a row— or, at the judge's discretion, when he has not acted as a faithful servant—the deity may issue a specific request. Table 7-7 offers 10 suggestions for the price of aid. In all cases, the judge can assess a penalty until the cleric obeys, with suggestions indicated below.

DIVINE AID

Clerics may request direct intervention from their deity. This is not an act to be taken lightly; however, pious followers may be granted frequent favors. The cleric wields his holy symbol, genuflects respectfully, and prays for assistance—often referencing his recent acts of devotion or promising future loyalties.

Calling for divine aid simply allows a cleric more flexibility in generating magical effects. There is a spell check DC associated with different kinds of divine aid. Simple requests are granted rather easily; more demanding requests, not as much. The judge must assign DCs on an ad hoc basis. As a rule of thumb, the ease of a request roughly mirrors casting a spell of the same level. Unlike spells, there is no sliding scale of effects; the request is either granted or not.

Any time a cleric requests divine aid, the deity requires a specific act in return, per Table 7-7.

Table 7-7: Deity Requests	
Roll	Request
1	The corpse of the cleric's next opponent animates momentarily and exhorts the cleric to slay twenty of his deity's enemies in as many days, lest he suffer great misfortune (in the form of a -4 Luck penalty) on the twenty-first day.
2	While meditating in his temple, the cleric hears a voice that encourages him to ransack the temple of the deity's rival, noting that his own prayers will henceforth go unheard until he prays in the ruins of the rival temple.
3	While trekking through an unsettled area, a passing deer or eagle pauses to speak to the cleric, instructing him to build a temple to his god and endow it with sufficient gold to operate for a year. Until this is complete, he loses contact with his god if he departs more than one mile from the region.
4	Over the course of a week, the cleric looks in his mirror each morning to see not his own face, but a different face on each of the seven different days. Somehow he knows that he must find these seven men and bring them to an appointed place and time for purposes unknown. During the seven days he suffers a cumulative -1 spell check penalty per day, to a maximum of -7 on the seventh day, which is relieved by -1 for each of the seven men located (eventually returning to a +/-0 modified to spell checks).
5	While traversing a busy city street, the cleric cannot help but notice that a particular object on the person of a stranger glows with a supernatural light. His companions do not see the light. He is compelled to steal this particular object from one person, then deliver it to another. Until the cleric does so, he can think of nothing else and suffers a -4 penalty to all other actions.
6	An ongoing religious crusade in a neighboring duchy requires assistance. The cleric is called to lead an army of minor followers on their raids, for which he will be rewarded with the trappings of leadership.
7	A holy relic dangerous to the deity has been discovered and must be destroyed. The cleric receives an urgent summons during his next prayers and is informed that should this relic be put to its intended use, the cleric will lose all access to spells as his god is shut off from the material plane.
8	The cleric must persuade a neutral party to take sides in a conflict. He learns this from a hobbling mendicant who admonishes detachment in the issue, declaring that his own penury shall befall the cleric should he fail.
9	The cleric must sacrifice something of personal value (suffering a -4 Luck penalty until he does). The deity requests the following sacrifice (roll 1d8, adjusting for alignment as appropriate): (1) 100 gold pieces, (2) treasured magic item, (3) holy symbol, (4) best weapon, (5) most villainous foe, (6) one of his fingers, (7) all his hair, (8) a favored mount.
10	The cleric must recruit a number of new followers (or lose access to half his spells until he does) (roll 1d4): (1) 100; (2) 7; (3) one per caster level, and another upon gaining each new level; (4) one, but he must be persuaded to abandon worship of an opposing god.

Table 7-8: Divine Aid Check DCs

DC 10: Very simple cantrips: light a candle, levitate a pebble, vanish a feather, sound a tweet.

DC 12: Minor mechanical effects (lift a latch), visual effects (lantern-like lights at a distance), or auditory effects (sound of footsteps); bless a course of action (+1 to +2 modifier to some roll for short duration); simple persuasions (induce suspicious or friendly tendencies in a single human).

DC 14: More complex physical or sensory effects (unlock a normal door or untie a rope; cause a mirror image to appear); stronger blessings (+4 to some action or affect more people); simple summoning (physical objects such as a weapon).

DC 16: Incredible physical acts (leap a gaping chasm, lift a boulder); impressive persuasion (amplify a voice to motivate an army); summon living aid (send divine warriors to aid a charge); smite an enemy (Will save or enemy suffers significant damage or ability score loss).

DC 18: Acts of clear divine intervention: affect the weather (draw down a lightning strike, dismiss storm clouds, summon a cyclone); superhuman feats of strength (topple a pyramid, smash a giant statue into a thousand pieces); incredible magical displays (control a swirling column of fire, split into a hundred mirror images).

DC 20: And so on. Higher-level acts are at the discretion of the judge.

MAGIC HERE AND MAGIC THERE

Spellcasters who are sensitive to the ebb and flow of natural energies can find the best places to effect their summonings. For example, fire energy is strong on certain elemental planes, while the brooding hollows of gray northern fens enhance the necromancer's efforts. You can further reinforce the *magical* nature of spell casting in your campaign by emphasizing environmental influences. There are two ways to do this.

In the simplest form, apply a bonus or penalty to spell checks. For example, all turning checks in a cursed graveyard receive a -2 penalty to spell checks while necromantic animations gain a +2 bonus. Ley lines may serve as conduits for magical energies over long distances and have chaotic effects when they cross. Standing stones or hideous primitive altars may produce similar modifiers to pagan magic.

A more exciting approach is to add secondary effects. Let the spell function as normal but with the addition of something special. For example, on the elemental plane of fire, all spells that affect an enemy with magical energy—such as *color spray* or *magic missile*—could be subject to the following side effects, according to the spell check. This is just one example; the reader is encouraged to create his own effects.

Check	Side effect
1-11	No side effect.
12-13	A cloud of ash explodes around the target, coating him in a fine gray mist.
14-17	Sparks trace a line from the caster's fingertips to his target, illuminating the arc in a flash of light. The sparks are insufficient to cause damage but easily ignited objects (such as paper or dry leaves) along the path, on the caster, or the target's person catches fire in a burst of flame.
18-19	A burst of red-hot cinders appears around the target. They cause an additional 1 point of burning damage as they scorch him.
20-23	A large pile of red-hot cinders appears around the target. They cause an additional 1d3 points of burning damage as they scorch him.
24-27	The target is enveloped in a corona of flame. The flash fire inflicts an additional 1d6 damage and ignites any flammable objects on his person.
28-29	The target is enveloped in a massive fireball. It inflicts an additional 2d6 damage and ignites any flammable objects on his person.
30-31	The spell manifests completely as a fire-based effect instead of its normal effect. It inflicts an additional 3d6 damage and the target catches fire, suffering an additional 1d6 damage each round until he makes a DC 10 Reflex save at the start of a round.
32+	The spell manifests completely as a fire-based effect instead of its normal effect. It inflicts an additional 4d6 damage and the target catches fire, suffering an additional 1d6 damage each round until he makes a DC 20 Reflex save at the start of a round.

HAAS'12

HEROES

eroes and monsters are both rare. When populating non-player characters in your world, use these guidelines for the frequency with which higher-level characters appear.

Level	Rank	Population Incidence
0	Commoner	95% of population
1	Expert in a field	2 in 100
2	Leader or master in a craft	1 in 100
3	Rare genius	1 in 1,000
4	Elder, learned genius	1 in 5,000
5	Once in a generation	1 in 10,000
6	Supra-mortal accomplishment	1 in 50,000
7	One per continent or century	1 in 250,000
8	Typically the greatest mind in a field	1 in 1,000,000
9	"The best there ever was"	1 in 10,000,000
10+	An immortal or demi-god—no longer mortal	2-3 per epoch

EXPERIENCE POINTS

hile brave adventurers explore strange dungeons, their compatriots toil in the fields, threshing wheat under a burning sun. When the adventurers emerge back into the sunlight who will be the higher level, them or their farmer friends? As just noted, only 1 in 100 men reach level 2—and only 1 in 10,000 reaches level 5. Whether farmer or fulgurator, level advancement is a slow, measured progress. Survival is its own reward; preeminence, a bonus.

In general, practicing one's profession earns experience points (XP), and accumulation of XP produces advancement in level. Adventurers practice their profession by challenging themselves in dangerous situations—usually, but not always, combat.

Scaling XP Awards: As introduced in the characters chapter, XP are a measure of level advancement. Your job as judge is to award XP to the players as they complete encounters. XP are always rewarded *by encounter* not creature or challenge. In general, most level-appropriate encounters should be worth 2 XP, with the scale going from 0 to 4 as follows:

XP	Description
0	Very easy encounter with little to no damage or resource loss for the adventurers. This is the kind of encounter that no longer challenges a group and clearly does not advance their skill level.
1	An encounter with damage and resource expenditure but relatively easy nonetheless. The typical "easy encounter" falls into this bracket.
2	A typical encounter. The characters incurred damage and were required to utilize resources to survive the encounter. No fatalities or significant losses.
3	A difficult encounter, even with good tactics. Significant damage and potentially permanent consequences, possibly even a fatality.
4	An extremely difficult encounter, one that the party barely survives. Multiple character fatalities, significant character damage, and potentially a retreat of some kind required.

XP for Non-Combat Activities: XP is always rewarded for combat. Non-combat encounters may also be worth experience points. Disarming or setting off traps provides guidance to characters of what to do (or not to do) in the future. Puzzles likewise build experience in navigating a dungeon. In broader terms, these criteria for earning XP can be interpreted as "bypassing hazards"; advancing past dangerous situations warrants the earning of XP. Thieves should receive XP for bypassing traps (typically 1-2 points, depending on the nature of the trap), and puzzles should likewise be worth XP to all who participated in solving them.

The judge may also choose to award XP for mundane, class-related activities. Just as there are level 2 wizards, there are also level 2 farmers and other non-character professions. These peasants advance through non-combat activities, and characters can, too. The rate of advancement for such activities is very slow—typically 1 XP for every period of activity. For a farmer, a period of activity might be one planting season; for a blacksmith, it could be a full year of work.

Characters can likewise be rewarded for non-combat activities as appropriate to their class, typically at the rate of 1-2 XP for every significant non-combat event. Here are some examples of appropriate non-combat events:

- Warrior: hiring a trainer to train in weapons, martial arts, archery, jousting, and other military activities; constructing a citadel or sailing vessel; hiring or recruiting men-at-arms to build a militia; equipping an expedition; paying tribute to a higher-ranking lord; and so on.

- Cleric: tithing to a temple on an ongoing basis; constructing a shrine, altar, or idol; donating to the needy; equipping a pilgrimage; translating or restoring sacred scrolls; recruiting followers; and so on.

- Wizard: forging magic items; researching or creating new magical spells; building a wizard's tower; building a golem or homunculus; acquiring rare or valuable spell components; and so on.

- Thief: paying for information; spending on drinks, food, and entertainment to establish contacts; acquiring blackmail material; constructing traps; building a secret vault; and so on.

- Elf: any activities associated with a warrior or wizard.

- Dwarf: any activities associated with a warrior.

- Halfling: any activities associated with a warrior or a thief.

Advancing in Level: When a character accrues enough XP to advance in level (per the XP table on page 26), he automatically acquires the benefits of that new level. No formalized training or other activity is necessary—though, as mentioned above, spending gold on training may accelerate the process.

LUCK

y now you know the universe is governed by rulers greater than the characters, and they are but pawns in this eternal struggle. Luck reflects that. In game terms it plays out as follows.

Modifiers: Luck modifies one die roll for each character, as determined by table 1-2. It also modifies rolls for fumbles and critical hits, as well as other class-specific rolls.

Luck checks: Characters can make Luck checks to survive impossible situations, at the judge's discretion. Luck can also be used for skill checks that could only be achieved through sheer luck alone.

Heroic effort: Any character can permanently burn Luck to give a one-time bonus to a roll. For example, you could burn 6 points to get a +6 modifier on a roll, but your Luck score is now 6 points lower.

Connection to alignment: Luck is a practical mechanism to ensure the characters act within their alignments. Characters who consistently act out of alignment should receive a permanent Luck penalty, which may become steadily worse if they continue to act out of character. Characters who consistently exemplify the virtues of their alignment may, over time, find themselves becoming luckier. In non-mechanical terms, this is a reflection of the characters being favored by gods and demons who share their alignments. A character who wishes to switch alignment may swear an oath to a new god in order to avoid the Luck penalties associated with an alignment change.

The stars align: Curses and calumny can bring changes to luck, as can blessings and benedictions. The judge is encouraged to create storylines that manipulate Luck as both a player incentive and as a plot mechanic. Certain classic fantasy characters were known to be doomed as part of their role in a greater drama complex beyond their understanding, while others were repeatedly luckier than they should have been. We offer these suggestions:

- Introduce villains that curse the characters, providing a negative modifier to their Luck. The curse can be countermanded via specific charms or amulets, nullified via curses or blessings to the opposite effect, or lifted via certain accomplishments. For example, a dying forest sprite curses its attacker to "a long and painful life" (reflected in a -4 penalty to Luck). To lift the curse, the unlucky fellow can find a charm, perform some service for the sprite's kin, or hope to be cursed to "a swift death"—the terms of which contradict and thus offset the curse of "a long and painful life."

- Introduce events that change the nature of Luck. For example, a particular constellation appears at the planar meridian for the first time in 1,000 generations, resulting in a new zodiac sign. *All* the characters' Luck modifiers are reset, such that either they all roll again individually on table 1-2, or the judge chooses one common result from table 1-2. Of course, a certain soothsayer avers that the changes can be averted by visiting a place distant in both space and time…

- Introduce supernatural patrons whose cosmic influence can change the course of history. Characters who challenge these beings do so at peril to their Luck. For example, a slumbering spirit of evil re-awakens, and in doing so revives an ancient lich to be its agent on earth. The characters challenge this lich but find themselves beset by bad luck in their battles against it. Only by identifying the underlying supernatural element of the adventure and specifically combating the evil spirit can they recover their natural luck.

Gaining and losing Luck: Regardless of greater plot themes, Luck is gained and lost over the course of adventures as shown on table 7-9.

Consequences of Low Luck: Some players treat Luck as a "battery" to burn at will. But the universe does not reward those who challenge the fates blindly! Characters with low Luck should suffer streaks of bad luck as they continue on their adventures. Here are suggestions for the judge on how to adjudicate this.

- Whenever the characters face opponents with little discretion in what they attack, such as oozes or wild beasts, have those creatures always target the character with the lowest Luck.

- When several characters are within range of a trap or spell that could affect only some of them, choose those with the lowest Luck.

- Once per hour of *real time* (i.e., every hour during your play session), have every character make a Luck check (roll 1d20 and attempt to roll under their Luck score). Those who fail suffer a random mishap sometime in the coming hour: they trip on a loose stone, they slip on the next staircase, the blade of their axe comes loose, the strap on their backpack comes off, etc.

Table 7-9: Luck Changes

Action	Modifier
Accomplishing certain objectives that are important to the Eternal Balance between law and chaos and favored by powers greater than man. In game terms, this represents the objectives of individual adventures, and Luck provides a way to reflect that characters are on the right (or wrong) path. In general, actions that strongly support a character's alignment provide a positive modifier to luck. Specific examples could include: righting a great wrong, aiding on an important quest, defeating an evil creature, etc.	+1 to +3, awarded at end of adventure
Offending a powerful demon, devil, or deity. This is not simply an action they would not support, but a meaningful affront worthy of the god's attention. For example: burning a deity's temple, assaulting a holy man, or slaying a loyal servant. Since many of these actions also have opposing gods that would support them, the Luck modifier may be offset if the character acts with supernatural backers. This is subtle and at the discretion of the judge.	-1, effective immediately upon completing offending act
Acting significantly outside of alignment. For example, a lawful character who flaunts an authority figure.	-1, effective immediately
Faithful obedience to a god, as reflected by a loyal cleric, or a binding oath that is fulfilled, or succeeding on a major quest, or building a major altar or temple.	+1, awarded at times of testing
Finding favor with a magical creature of great power, a supernatural creature, the gods of fate, or extraplanar denizens. The magical creatures that supposedly bring good luck often do!	+1, awarded at whim of the creature
Willfully disobeying the direct edict of a powerful supernatural patron, particularly for wizards associated with that patron, but also for other mortals who have entered into congress with powers greater than themselves.	-1, awarded at time of disobedience

CHAPTER EIGHT
MAGIC ITEMS

There is no such thing as a "generic" magic item. All magic items are unique.

here is no such thing as a "generic" magic item. All magic items are unique. In a fantastic medieval society, there are no blueprints, no factories, no assembly lines, and no centralized repositories of knowledge. Libraries are rare and fantastic. Wizards are jealous and power-hungry, unused to sharing. Clerics serve gods with selfish goals, locked in the power games of the eternal struggle. When it comes to creating magic items, there is no incentive to share knowledge, no place to communicate that knowledge, no forum for learning, and no one to learn from.

The possibility of possessing a magic item is sufficient motivation to embark on a great quest, murder a great rival, or begin a great war. Creating a magic item requires great sacrifice on the part of a spellcaster. Many wizards die having never created a magic item; the few who do are true masters of their craft. The rest pursue legends, whispers, secrets, and lies in their attempt to possess magic artifacts.

The rare wizard who imbues an object with magical power succeeds in unpredictable ways. When forging a magical dagger, a dwarven magician may use iron from deep in the earth, while a human wizard might melt down the legendary steel sword of a deceased hero. Each ends up with a magic dagger, but the specific mixture of materials, properties, and location that contributes to each dagger—not to mention the immense physical exertion required—means that each of the daggers will have different properties.

And few are the magic items created by mortal hands. Demons and deities have a part in many magical creations. As such these magic items may serve their creators (and true masters) just as much as their current owners. Rare is the magic item without a story or a greater purpose.

A SENSE OF SCALE

Here is a rough outline for the prerequisites of magic item creation, as a guide to their frequency of occurrence:

Magic staffs can be created by level 3 wizards (utilizing the 2nd-level spell *wizard staff*). Remember, only 1 in 1,000 people achieve level 3 in *any* class, and only a small number of those are wizards.

Magic scrolls can be created by level 5 clerics and wizards (utilizing the 3rd-level spell *write magic*). Recall from page 359 that only 1 in 10,000 people achieve level 5 in *any* class, much less as a wizard.

Potions can be created by level 5 wizards and clerics (utilizing the 3rd-level spell *make potion*).

Magic weapons can be created by wizards as low as level 5 (utilizing the 3rd-level spell *sword magic*). These are clumsy, obdurate things with modest bonuses to attack (equivalent to +1 or +2). Weapons that aid their wielder with zest need a higher-level wizard or the touch of a demon or demi-god.

Rods can be created by level 7 clerics (utilizing the 4th-level spell *magic rod*).

Wands can be created by level 7 wizards (utilizing the 4th-level spell *magic wand*).

Unique magic items are created by wizards and clerics of varying levels. The simplest objects, which only replicate a spell effect, typically require a creator of at least 7th level; more complex devices need creators of 10th level or deity status.

DISTRIBUTING MAGIC ITEMS

Most magic items have a greater purpose. This may be loyalty to a god, simple alignment, or a specific goal on Aéreth. Or the magic item could be intelligent with a complex set of objectives and the ego to override its wielder. Careful must the hand of a weapon be…

To ensure that magic items remain "special" in your campaign, we recommend that they never be given out as mere treasure. Magic items should always be deliberately distributed with great forethought. They should be the objects of quests or the possessions of great rivals.

Furthermore, each magic item should be individually created. The tables that follow list a wide variety of randomized properties suitable for association with magic items. With a few rolls of the dice, you can create any number of unique items.

When distributing magic items in your world, use these guidelines for the frequency with which they appear. An incidence of "1 in 1,000" means 1 person out of 1,000 has the skill to create such an item, and, concomitantly, 1 person out of 1,000 would possess such an item. Compare this table to the hero population distribution table on page 359 for a more comprehensive view.

Magic Item	Minimum Creator Level	Population Incidence
Staves	Level 3	1 in 1,000
Scrolls and potions; +1 weapons	Level 5	1 in 10,000
+2 weapons	Level 6	1 in 50,000
Rods and wands; +3 weapons	Level 7	1 in 250,000
+4 weapons	Level 8	1 in 1,000,000
+5 weapons	Level 10	Only 2-3 per epoch

IRE OF THE GODS

Magic items tear the veil that separates man from god; they break the rules. It is generally unwise to draw the attention of higher-order beings, lest their scrutiny find you wanting. A character who wields a magic item may suffer a penalty to his Luck score. This is a temporary penalty that remains in place as long as he wields the item. Generally speaking, the following actions draw a Luck penalty:

- Wielding a magic item of potentially sufficient power to challenge a demi-god. This is considered to be any rod or wand, any weapon of +2 enchantment or better, and any extremely powerful staff. Certain unique items may also qualify.

- Wielding any sort of magical artifact.

- Wielding any intelligent magic item or one that possesses (or traps) a soul.

- Wielding a lower-powered magic item that is not of the possessor's own personal creation.

The Luck penalty ranges from -1 to -4, depending on the nature of the item and the degree to which greater powers feel threatened. The final penalty is determined at the judge's discretion. Some magic items may have arcane powers that partially offset this Luck penalty, but that is rare.

OBJECTS FROM OTHER PLANES

To the extent that you wish to provide more frequent contact between player character and magic item, consider objects from the overworld. A sword forged on the elemental plane of fire has special properties on the prime material plane, even if it is but a common rapier at its place of origin. Acquisition of such weapons should of course require travel (or at least contact) with the appropriate plane.

CREATION SPELLS

Magic items are created using spells oriented toward that purpose. As noted above, those spells include *write magic, make potion, sword magic, wizard staff, magic rod,* and *magic wand.* Not all of those spells have defined spell tables in this work. That is deliberate. Magic item creation should remain something of a, well, *magical* process. We encourage the judge to come up with his own processes and spell tables for creating higher-level magic items.

SWORD MAGIC

The greatest legends, the deadliest fighters, the bravest champions, the holiest avengers, the heroes who transcend time: we know their names, we know their swords. The highest calling of a warrior is his sword, and the highest calling of a wizard is to create a magic sword.

Sword magic is the field of spells focused on the creation of magic swords. A sword is not merely enchanted, it is *forged* in places that trap spells within the folds of molten metal. Sword magic requires not only a wizard with magical proclivities, but one with strength and craftsmanship. Even then, the finest materials are a prerequisite, and the place of creation is key.

All magic swords share these properties:

- Each magic sword is unique. The same sword cannot be created twice; each combination of conditions ensures a new creation.
- Each magic sword is intelligent.
- Each magic sword has desires.
- Each magic sword has properties associated with the materials and conditions from which it was forged, the attributes of its creator, the place of its creation, and the cosmic circumstances at its point of completion. The greatest swords are crafted on a timetable associated with a specific astrological sign.

Creating A Magic Sword: A magic sword is created using the spell *sword magic*. The wizard makes several spell checks, depending on the circumstances, as noted in the spell description and on table 8-4.

Discovering A Magic Sword: The tables below can also be used to randomly determine the powers of a magic sword found during an adventure. Follow this process to randomly determine a magic sword:

- First, determine the type of sword by rolling d% on table 8-1.
- Next, roll on table 8-2 to determine the sword's alignment.
- Then roll d% on table 8-4. Read across the table to see how this result determines six aspects of the sword's abilities: plus, Int, banes, communication, special purpose, and powers.
- If the sword has banes, roll d% on table 8-5 *twice* for each bane.
- If the sword has a special purpose, roll the appropriate dice on table 8-6 for the special purposes.
- If the sword has a power, roll d% on table 8-7, 8-8, or 8-9 for each power.

Table 8-1: Type of Magic Sword

Roll	Sword Type
01-15	Dagger
16-30	Short sword
31-80	Long sword
81-00	Two-handed sword

Table 8-2: Magic Sword Alignment When Already Forged

d%	Alignment
01-40	Chaotic
41-60	Neutral
61-00	Lawful

Table 8-3: Magic Sword Alignment by Creator Spell Check and Alignment

Spell check	Lawful	Neutral	Chaotic
16-17	Chaotic	Neutral	Lawful
18-21	Neutral	Neutral	Neutral
22-23	Lawful	Neutral	Chaotic
24-26	Lawful	Lawful	Chaotic
27-31	Lawful	Chaotic	Chaotic
32+	Lawful	Neutral	Chaotic

Table 8-4: Magic Sword Characteristics

Spell check	d%	Plus**	Int*	Communication	Number of Banes	Dice Rolled for Special Purpose(s)	Powers
16-17	01-50	+1	1d6	None	None	1d12-6	50% chance of one type I power
18-21	51-75	+1	1d6+2	Simple urges	1	1d6	75% chance of one type I power
22-23	76-85	+1	3d4	Simple urges	1d3-1	1d6 then 1d6+6	One type I power, 50% chance of one type II power
24-26	86-90	+1	2d6	Empathy	1d4-1	1d12	1d3 type I powers, 75% chance of one type II power
27-31	91-94	+2	2d6+2	Empathy	1d4	1d8 then 1d14	1d4 powers of type I or II (50% chance of either for each power), 50% chance of one type III power
32-33	95-96	+2	3d6	Speech	1d3+1	1d14 three times	1d4+1 powers of type I or II (50% chance of either for each power), 75% chance of one type III power
34-35	97-98	75% +3, 25% +4	3d6+2	Telepathy	1d4+1	1d6 then 1d6+6	1d4+1 powers of type I or II (50% chance of either for each power), plus one type III power
36+	99-00	50% +3, 35% +4, 15% +5	3d6+4	Speech and telepathy	2d4	1d6 then 1d6+10	1d4+2 powers of type I or II (50% chance of either for each power), plus 1d3 type III powers

* Cannot be higher than creator's Intelligence.

** Capped by creator's caster level. Maximum bonus is as follows: CL5 = +1, CL6 = +2, CL7 = +3, CL8 = +4, CL10 = +5.

Table 8-5: Magic Sword Banes

For each bane (as determined by table 8-4), roll twice on this table: once to determine the type of bane and a second time to determine the effect when battling the bane.

d%	Type of Bane	Effect When Battling Bane
01-06	Goblinoids	Unreasoning hatred; sword urges wielder to attack bane at every opportunity (ego check)
07-10	Giants	Additional +1 attack bonus
11-15	Lycanthropes	Additional +1 damage bonus
16-24	Un-dead	Additional +1 bonus to attack *and* damage
25-34	Wizards	Berserker fury when facing bane; ego check or wielder gains +4 Strength and Stamina for 2d6 rounds, then is exhausted at -4 Strength and Stamina for 1d6 turns thereafter
35-41	Demons	Unerring throw; only against bane, sword can be thrown with a 60' range, and always returns to the attacker's hand; when thrown, it uses attacker's normal missile fire attack roll but includes his Strength modifier to damage
42-51	Dragons	Extended critical threat range; attacker scores criticals against bane at 1 more result on the die (e.g., if normally score criticals on 19-20, now score on 18-20)
52-54	Creatures of opposed alignment (lawful or chaotic)	Beacon of hope; allies within 100' engaged in battle against bane gain +2 bonus to all saving throws and morale checks
55-57	Vampires	Beacon of fury; sword attempts to persuade everyone that it can communicate with to attack the bane under any circumstances (ego check for wielder and potentially others)
58-59	Elves	Bleeding wounds; sword's wounds against bane continue to bleed, inflicting an additional 1 hp damage (cumulative) per round after hit until magically healed, so a bane target hit by three successive attacks from the sword takes 3 hp damage per round thereafter
60-62	Elementals (50% of all elementals, 50% chance of a specific type: (1) fire, (2) water, (3) earth, (4) air)	Neutralization; after a direct hit, sword prevents bane from using one of its natural powers (as determined by judge) for one full day; if bane does not have any specific natural powers (e.g., if bane is "men"), sword gives victim a cumulative -1 attack modifier for every direct hit (fades after 1 day)
63-64	Clerics	Ability score drain; sword inflicts normal damage *plus* 1d4 points of ability score drain per hit against bane; determine ability score with 1d5: (1) Strength, (2) Stamina, (3) Agility, (4) Personality, (5) Intelligence
65-66	Dwarves	Spotter; sword marks bane so it is more easily attacked; allies can fire into melee between wielder and bane at no penalty and no chance of hitting wielder, and allies attacking bane with missile fire within 100' of sword receive a +1 attack bonus
67	Halflings	Hardiness; when taking damage from the bane, wielder can make a Fort save (DC 1d20+10); success means the attack inflicts only half damage
68-69	Men	Shattering blow; on a critical hit, sword inflicts an additional 1d10 damage
70-72	Orcs	Banishment; with a successful hit, sword sends bane back to its native plane or lair (Will save to resist vs. DC 1d20+10)
73-75	Fey	Painful wound; sword inflicts an additional 1d4 damage to bane
76-77	Thieves	Festering wound; sword inflicts an additional 1d6 damage to bane, then *another* 1d4 damage on following round
78-80	Warriors	Summoning; when battling bane, sword can summon reinforcements, which are a creature type antithetical to the bane (per judge's discretion) of total HD equal to half of wielder; sword can summon 1/day with 50% chance of success for duration 1d4 turns

81-84	Serpents	Hunter; sword can detect bane creatures within 100', even if invisible or otherwise concealed, and can overcome magical defenses against detection as if with a +10 Will save or spell check
85-87	Naga	Defender; wielder gains a +2 AC bonus when defending against attacks from the bane
88-89	Sphinxes	Additional +2 attack bonus
90-91	Golems	Additional +2 damage bonus
92-93	Unicorns	Additional +2 bonus to attack *and* damage
94-95	Gods	Death dealer; when bane is struck, it must make a Fort save (DC = 1d20+10) or instantly die
96-00	Roll again; bane is a specific, unique named specimen of the indicated type	Roll again twice

Table 8-6: Sword Special Purpose

Roll dice as indicated by characteristics table, then cross-reference to sword's alignment.

Roll	Lawful	Neutral	Chaotic
0 or less	No special purpose	No special purpose	No special purpose
1	Enforce the law	Avoid conflict	Undermine authority
2	Protect the weak	Spill the blood of no man	Dominate all others
3	Punish evildoers	Bridge understanding between enemies	Reward the ambitious at all costs
4	Punish murderers	Live alone as a warrior-hermit	Punish interlopers and those who interfere
5	Punish thieves	Bring Balance to a specific place	Acquire wealth through theft
6	Jail the guilty	Take no sides	Free prisoners
7	Provide charity to the needy	Achieve perfect self-harmony	Spread the seven deadly sins
8	Defend against the incursion of Chaos	Become one with nature	Defend against the incursion of Law
9	Slay chaotic creatures*	Break all allegiances	Slay lawful creatures*
10	Slay chaotic dragons*	Purge the world of all paragons of Law and Chaos	Slay lawful dragons*
11	Slay chaotic demons*	Slay one lawful creature for every chaotic creature slain, and vice versa	Slay lawful outsiders*
12	Build monuments to great heroes	Bring peace between gods	Build a monument to Chaos from the rubble of civilization
13	Build the world's greatest city	Seek the Void	Destroy the world's kingdoms, one by one
14	Slay a specific Chaos Lord, demon or unique monster*	Deliver an esoteric item to an identified place at one point of time, performing one tiny step in a master plan beyond any man's understanding	Slay a specific hero of Law, such as an angel or celestial
15	Clear the world of all obstacles to the imposition of Law	Prepare the world for the return of the Old Ones	Clear the world for the invasion of Chaos
16	Roll again twice	Roll again twice	Roll again twice

* With this result, the indicated creatures are treated as banes.

Table 8-7: Sword Powers, Type I: Natural Powers

Roll	Power*
01-05	Read any non-magical map at will
06-10	Read 1d6 randomly determined languages
11-15	*Comprehend languages* 1/day
16-20	Speak thieves' cant
21-25	Detect secret doors within 1d6 x 10'
26-30	Detect gems within 1d4 x 10'
31-35	Detect gold within 1d8 x 10'
36-40	Detect evil within 1d4 x 10'
41-45	Detect good within 1d4 x 10'
46-50	Detect traps within 2d4 x 10'
51-55	*Detect magic* 1/day
56-60	*Detect magic* 2/day
61-65	*Detect invisible* 1/day
66-70	*Locate object* 2/day
71-75	Shed light with 20' radius at will
76-80	Obscure surroundings with 20' globe of darkness at will
81-85	Detect sloping passages within 1d10 x 10'
86-90	Detect water within 1d8 x 10'
91-95	Detect certain creature type within 1d10 x 100' (e.g., spiders, dragons, goblinoids, men, etc.)
96-00	Wielder gains infravision 120'

* If a spell, it is cast at a spell check of 1d10+20.

Table 8-8: Sword Powers, Type II: Combat

Roll	Power
01-05	*Crippler.* Always roll critical hits as warrior of one level higher than wielder.
06-10	*Flame brand.* Ignite in flame 3/day. Duration 6 rounds. Inflicts additional 1d6 damage and ignites targets on fire (Ref save to avoid; DC = 1d10+5).
11-15	*Flame tongue.* Launch jet of flame 1/day. Jet is cone, 40' long and 10' wide at end. All within take 2d6 damage and may catch on fire (Ref save to avoid; DC = 1d10+10).
16-20	*Frostburn.* Inflict additional 1d3 cold damage with every strike. Double damage to fire elementals.
21-24	*Cleave.* Each time an enemy is slain with this blade, the wielder automatically receive another attack (but cannot move). Note that certain bloodthirsty blades may attempt to force the wielder to attack an ally.
25-29	*Vampiric touch.* Any time the wielder inflicts 10 or more points of damage in a single strike, he heals 1 hit point.
30-32	*Life drainer.* The blade drains 1d4 XP with every blow, in addition to other damage.
33-37	*Regenerator.* When wielding this blade, the wielder's natural rate of healing is doubled. In addition, the wielder recovers twice as many hit points as usual whenever a cleric lays hands upon him.
38-39	*Energy mimic.* When attacked by any form of energy attack (e.g., fire, cold, force, electricity, etc.), the wielder may attempt to capture the energy within the sword. Make an attack roll. (This is not actually an attack, but reflects the sword's ability. Note that it does not prevent the wielder from taking damage; attempt saves as normal per the spell effect.) If the attack roll exceeds the spell check DC of the energy effect, the wielder captures that effect. He may unleash an identical effect as an attack action at some point within the next 24 hours. Once unleashed, the effect is lost. The sword only retains the most recent captured effect.
40-44	*Shock blade.* Inflict an additional 1d4 electrical damage with every strike, doubled to 2d4 if opponent wears metal armor, is in water, or is composed of metal (such as a golem or living statue).
45	*Vorpal blade.* On any critical hit, the wielder automatically decapitates enemy, causing instant death.
46-50	*Thunder blade.* In place of an attack, the wielder may strike the ground to create the resounding boom of thunder. All enemies within 40' take 1d8 points of sonic damage (no save).

51-55	*Eviscerator.* When rolling damage, the wielder rolls an additional damage die every time he rolls the highest result on a die. For example, if this weapon is a long sword and the wielder rolls an "8" on the 1d8 damage roll, he then rolls *another* 1d8 and adds that to the damage result. If that second 1d8 produces another "8", he rolls a third 1d8, and so on.
56-60	*Medusa's touch.* A creature struck by this blade must make a Fort save (DC = 1d10+10) or be turned to stone permanently.
61-70	*Great strength.* Wielder's Strength is increased by +4 while wielding blade.
71-75	*Holy brand.* Inflicts an additional +1d4 damage against unholy creatures.
76-81	*Precise strike.* Additional +1d4 bonus to attack rolls.
82-86	*Whirlwind strike.* Instead of making his normal attack, the wielder can make *two* attacks in a single round, but rolls 1d10 for each attack instead of 1d20. He applies his normal attack bonus. Critical hits are not possible when attacking in this manner.
87-91	*Armor-breaker.* On any critical hit, the opponent's armor is destroyed, in addition to other effects.
92-96	*Weapon-breaker.* On any critical hit, the opponent's weapon is destroyed, in addition to other effects. If the creature has natural weapons, they are maimed (e.g., claws are broken, teeth are shattered, etc.).
97-99	*Throwing blade.* Sword can be thrown up to 20' to make a ranged attack. It always returns to its owner's hand after a throw.
00	Roll again twice.

Table 8-9: Sword Powers, Type III: Magical

Roll	Power
01-07	*Spell healer.* Wielder heals spellburn at 3x the normal rate: with no rest, heals 3 points of ability score loss each night, and with rest, heals 6 points each night.
08-14	*Spellburn reservoir.* Each day, the wielder can burn up to 3 points of the *sword's* Intelligence on spellburn to affect his spellcasting as if he were spellburning his own abilities. The sword's lost ability scores heal in full each night.
15-20	*Spell magnifier.* The wielder casts all spells at +1 caster level.
21-25	*Shift planes.* The wielder can shift to an adjacent plane 1/day, arriving in the position corresponding to his current position. There is a 10% chance that the sword also allows him to take along up to 1d4+1 allies with each plane shift.
26-30	*Demon-binding.* With any successful strike against a demon or other extraplanar creature, the target must make a DC 20 Will save or be bound to its current exact location for 1d4 turns. It cannot take any steps or teleport out unless this effect is magically dispelled.
31-39	*Summon creature.* The sword is magically keyed to a specific creature type (e.g., wolf, lion, pegasus, etc.). The wielder can summon such a creature 1d3 times per day.
40-51	*Resistance.* The sword grants its wielder resistance to certain forms of attack. The wielder ignores the first 3 points of damage from that form of attack each round, and gains a +1 bonus to saving throws against that form of damage. The form of attack is (roll 1d6) (1) fire, (2) cold, (3) acid, (4) lightning, (5) poison, (6) drowning.
52-58	*Immune to non-magical attacks.* The sword makes its wielder resistant to non-magical attacks. The wielder resists the first 5 points of damage each round by attacks of a non-magical nature. Creatures of 5+ HD are considered "magical" for purposes of this effect.
59-65	*Resistance to critical hits.* The sword makes the wielder hard to inflict critical damage upon. The wielder receives an automatic Fort save whenever a critical occurs against him. The DC is equal to the natural die roll used to score the crit (usually 20 but not always). If he makes this save, the critical does not take effect.
66-75	*Flight.* The wielder can fly at a speed of 30'.
76-84	*Turn invisible.* Up to 1d3 times per day, the wielder can turn invisible for a duration of 1d4 turns. The invisibility vanishes immediately if the wielder attacks.
85-90	*Magic resistance.* All spells directed specifically at the wielder suffer a -2 spell check penalty.
91-94	*Supreme willpower.* The wielder receives a +2 bonus to Will saves.
95-97	*Un-dead touch.* The weapon scores critical hits as an un-dead creature, rolling 1d30 on crit table U whenever a crit is scored.
98-00	*Regeneration.* As long as he wields this weapon in his hand, the wielder regenerates 1 point of damage each round.

SCROLLS

A scroll records magical text of some kind. The physical form of the scroll may vary: rolled papers, flat parchments, and bound books are the most common, while primitive shamans may inscribe words of magic on carved bones, beaded thongs, and ivory tusks. We will assume henceforth that scrolls take the form of rolled papers. Scrolls are typically a recorded spell, where a familiar spell is written down. In some cases, a scroll may produce a unique magical effect of some kind, similar to a very specific spell.

Using a scroll: A scroll need only be read to be activated. The reader then makes the appropriate spell check to determine the results. Once a scroll is used, it loses its power. In most cases the words literally disappear from the parchment, leaving only blank paper. Some necromantic scrolls may turn to ash, while some divination scrolls may vanish in a puff of steam—the specifics vary.

A spell from a scroll can be recorded in one of two ways. The first manner allows the wizard or cleric to record the instructions for casting the spell, which he must cast using his typical spellcasting skills; i.e., a spell check must be made. The second manner allows the wizard or cleric to record a spell at a defined level of casting; i.e., equivalent to a *magic missile* with a spell check of 22. This process is much more difficult, but if executed, can allow a scroll to be read *by any character of any class* with no spell check required.

"Knowing" a spell vs. "reading" a spell: As described on page 315, a wizard must typically make a check to learn a new spell. This check determines whether the wizard can correctly memorize the poses, materials, invocations, and rituals required to draw power from the spell. Because a scroll contains precise instructions on the spell's casting, the wizard does *not* need to know a spell in this way to cast it from a scroll. If a wizard casts a spell from a scroll without "knowing" it, he cannot memorize the spell thereafter.

Copying scrolls into a spell book: Discovery of a magic scroll may be a wizard's first encounter with the spell copied thereon. If he studies the scroll and makes the appropriate check to learn the spell, he may then copy it into his spell book for future use. Copying a spell takes one day per level of the spell.

Non-spellcasters reading scrolls: Thieves have been known to read scrolls in desperate circumstances. Any character class may attempt to cast the spell on a scroll by making a spell check appropriate to their class (typically d10 but thieves may be higher).

Each scroll is unique: As stressed elsewhere, each scroll is unique. There is no such thing as a generic scroll. Use the tables below to determine unique characteristics of a given scroll.

Determining the results of a scroll: To randomly determine what is on a scroll, roll once on Table 8-10: Scroll Contents, once on Table 8-11: Scroll Casting Mechanism, and once on Table 8-12: Scroll Unique Traits.

Table 8-10: Scroll Contents

Roll	Scroll type
01-30	1 level 1 spell
31-45	1 level 2 spell
46-55	1 level 3 spell
56-60	1 level 4 spell
61-63	1 level 5 spell
64-73	1d4 level 1 spells
74-78	1d4 level 1 spells and 1 level 2 spell
79-85	1d4 level 2 spells
86-90	2 level 3 spells
91-93	1d4 level 1 spells, 1 level 2 spell, and 1 level 3 spell
94-95	1 level 2 spell and 1 level 4 spell
96-97	1 spell each of levels 1, 2, 3, 4, and 5
98-99	1 level 3 spell, 1 level 4 spell, and 2 level 5 spells
00	2 spells each of levels 1, 2, 3, 4, and 5

Table 8-11: Scroll Casting Mechanism

Roll	Result
1-75	Spell check must be made by reader, at his normal result.
76-85	Spell check must be made by reader, at a +2 bonus.
86-90	Spell check must be made by reader, at a -2 penalty.
91-95	Spell is automatically cast at minimal successful result (i.e., 12 for a level 1 spell, 14 for a level 2 spell, etc.)
96-00	Spell is automatically cast at a defined result (roll randomly or choose).

Table 8-12: Scroll Unique Traits

Roll	Result
1	Signed by creator, in his own name.
2	Signed by creator, in his own name, with the notation that, "This scroll is the property of the creator. All others who use it shall be subject to a curse." (Or something similar.)
3	Unsigned, but warded with a protective rune. Any spellcaster can tell that this rune is designed to prevent the scroll from being cast. Anyone attempting to read the scroll must make a DC 16 Will save or forget that the scroll exists.
4	Written in code. When properly deciphered the scroll can be read but not until then.
5	Written in a foreign tongue; for example, in orc, gnoll, or even celestial. Use Appendix L to randomly generate ideas, or create your own. Scroll can be cast only if translated.
6	Signed with the sigil of a wizards' conclave. Clearly this scroll was created for their use.
7	Signed by the signatures of three wizards, one of whom may have created it.
8	Sealed with wax, in which is stamped the sign of a powerful demon.
9	Stored in a scroll tube carved from exotic materials and etched with warnings against its use.
10	Spell on the scroll is a variant version that also unleashes a powerful watch-demon to hunt the caster when used.
11	Spell instructions are inter-mixed with the casting of a curse. Reader will not realize until about halfway through that the two spells are cast together. Reader can then choose to abandon casting both or finish casting both together. Curse automatically takes effect along with desired spell result.
12	Make up your own!

POTIONS

A selection of magic potions is presented in the description of the spell *make potion*. The judge should feel free to create additional ones as needed.

WANDS, RODS, RINGS, AND OTHER ITEMS

DCC RPG carries forth a legacy of magic item creation that stretches back to 1974. The author does not feel it necessary to include a list of magic items which, in all candor, will in many cases resemble the encyclopedic compilations of such items which have been published regularly in the preceding decades. These prior works are ample inspiration for magic items to be used within your DCC RPG adventures.

Here are a few notes on adapting magic items from other sources to your DCC RPG campaign.

Make it unique: A hallmark of fantasy literature, particularly that of Appendix N, is the feeling that magic items are rare, special, and worthy of epic quests. Would the quest for the Ring have been so important if there were dozens of such rings, freely available for purchase at local magic shops? The author encourages the judge to provide a back story and personality to *every magic item*. Each should have a lineage and history, and each should be special beyond the definition of its powers. More on that below.

Predictability of spell-use powers: The DCC RPG differs from traditional magic systems in randomization of results and unpredictable uses-per-day. While many other games define magic items in terms of "charges" related to a specific spell, DCC RPG does not employ that mechanism in its basic spellcasting rules. However, one way that magic items can be *special* in the realm of DCC RPG is to do exactly that: let them "break the rules" and define certain spellcasting results. For magic items — and *only* for magic items — the judge is encouraged to occasionally grant them highly predictable, charged results. For example, a *rod of magic missiles* might always produce the same result of three missiles that each do 1d6+4 damage, and such an effect can be generated once per day with unfailing regularity. That very predictability makes such an item special in world of unpredictable magic.

No production lines or schools of creation: The idea that there is a consistency in magic item creation (i.e., that there are rules for the creation of rods, wands, and scrolls) implies that there is a common approach to manufacturing these items, shared across many wizards. The DCC RPG rejects that notion. The author envisions wizards as power-hoarders who must spend decades accumulating the experience and knowledge to create even a single magic item.

In doing so, they expend tremendous amounts of energy (reflected in spellburn and other factors). The rarity of wizards in the world, the paucity of high-level characters in general, and the great stresses entailed in creating items means there are very few items being created in general, and even fewer situations where a wizard gains the chance to witness another wizard's creation process. It should be assumed that no two item creation processes are the same. This means one wizard's magic rod might follow a completely different process than another wizard's rod, and one rod may function in a very different manner than another. Let your imagination run wild, and do not feel constrained by a "taxonomy of magic items." There need not be hard definitions of what a rod does or what a ring does or what a wand does. Each can be special.

Random Generation of Item Provenance: It is strongly suggested that you create a "provenance" or "ownership history" of each item. Table 8-13 can get you started in determining the creator of a magic item. The author suggests you then also define the last three owners of a magic item, the inscriptions placed on a magic item (potentially by its creator as well as each owner since then), the languages of those inscriptions, the item's name, its packaging (i.e., is it contained in a rough iron chest or beautiful lacquered box?), its personality and motivations, and its craftsmanship (well-wrought or crude? artistic or shamanistic?). Note also the story behind the item's previous owners and those who wish to possess it: do they (or others) still seek it, or has it been forgotten? Finally, and last of all, you should determine the item's magic powers.

Table 8-13: Creator of a Magic Item

Roll	Result
1	Low-level wizard, dabbling in powers beyond his limits
2	Famous high-level wizard
3	Wandering cleric
4	Powerful cleric, head of a faith
5	Demon seeking escape from a prison
6	Devil trying to curry favor with a more powerful entity
7	A god, who planted the magic item knowing it will be used in the End Days for specific purposes
8	A nascent demi-god, whose dreaming semi-awareness on a distant plane formed the magic item from nothingness
9	A thief and magician working together, who intended to use the item on a great heist
10	A warlord ordered the item created so that he could conquer nations
11	A sorcerer who could not find love forged the item out of bitterness
12	An intelligent unicorn
13	A powerful elemental with magical abilities
14	A tribal shaman
15	A brooding witch
16	The seventh son of a seventh son

CHAPTER NINE
MONSTERS

This is a world where more is learned from the lips of man than the ink of pen, and accurate knowledge is a rare and valuable thing.

Thus, both judge and players know the creatures of their town and surrounding valleys, but what monsters lurk in the next mountain pass remains a thing of mystery.

he Dungeon Crawl Classics Role Playing Game dispenses with traditional monster assumptions. There are no "generic" monsters. The orcs that live in one region may differ from those in another region, and all monster statistics presented here are local variations. This is a world where more is learned from word of mouth than the written word, and accurate knowledge is a rare and valuable thing. Thus, both judge and players know the creatures of their town and surrounding valleys, but what monsters lurk in the next mountain pass remains a thing of mystery.

MAKING MONSTERS MYSTERIOUS

 key element of player experience in the Dungeon Crawl Classics Role Playing Game is a sense of wonderment. Your job as judge is to convey "the sense of the unknown" that was so easy to achieve when we were children who did not know all the rules. One way to achieve this is to make monsters mysterious. The less the players are able to predict about the specifics of an encounter, and the more they depend on role-played hearsay, legends, and lore, the more exciting their encounters will be—regardless of monster statistics.

There is a historical basis for this sense of the unknown. The availability of information in a medieval feudal society was severely restricted. In your game world, there is no internet. Pens and paper are expensive, there are no printing presses, and it takes a scribe almost a year to manufacture a single book. Most people are illiterate; there is no mechanized transportation, no long-range communication, and no photography.

The flow of information in a medieval fiefdom is no faster or more accurate than what can be communicated verbally, without illustration, over many slightly-varied repetitions, at the speed of a man walking, or at most on horseback. In other words: information is rare and usually inaccurate. Remember playing the telephone game when you were a child? Except for what your player character has personally experienced, every single scrap of information available to him is communicated in that manner.

This thought experiment defines the boundaries of a serf's knowledge of monsters. Common people—including player characters—know almost nothing about most monsters. When a monster is encountered, the peasants *flee* rather than fight, so they do not know what combat capabilities a monster possesses.

If you want your fantasy adventure game to be fantastic, you must remember this: monsters must be mysterious.

DESCRIPTIONS

Never describe a monster using a specific noun (e.g., "goblin" or "orc"). Always describe a monster using physical characteristics (e.g., "a four-foot-tall man-like creature with green skin and pointed ears"). Let players learn the capabilities and characteristics of monsters through experience. They can name these creatures as they see fit—but *they* should name them, not you.

Certain monster descriptors have specific meaning to adventurers (and fantasy role-players), but are very generic terms for peasants. For example, a village elder describes *every* monster as a "demon." He may know of a water-demon that inhabits a nearby lake, and man-demons that live in the forest, and a spider-demon that his second cousin heard was seen in the cliffs to the north. They're all "demons" to him.

LOCAL VARIATIONS

Just as the men of one nation may be smarter, hardier, or more dangerous than their neighbors, monsters may have local variations, as well. As your characters travel to new places, vary the monsters. Let them become faster, stronger, safer, and deadlier—let there be constant variation.

"THE" MONSTER VS. "A" MONSTER

Is there more than one minotaur in your game world? Is there more than one unicorn or more than one chimera? To a provincial farmer with a ten-mile-wide worldview, does it really matter? You can make monsters more special by referring to them as "the" monster (minotaur, unicorn, chimera, etc.) rather than "a" monster. Whether it is you as the judge describing the creature or an NPC speaking to the player characters, remind yourself that the in-game point-of-view is often from a perspective of limited knowledge. To any serf with a fearful view of monsters, "the" minotaur is *the only minotaur in the world.* Describe it as such, and its importance will grow in the mind of your players. They will be left wondering if there really is only one minotaur.

MONSTER NAMES

Intelligent monsters need not even be "the" orc, "the" giant, or "the" unicorn. Rather, they may have proper nouns, which they use to refer to themselves and which local peasants use as well. For certain classes of monsters, the world may have no generic term. There is no minotaur—there is only Mornoth the Bull-Head.

DESCRIPTIVE ENCOUNTERS

Although the monster statistics that follow present standardized varieties for many classic humanoids, we strongly encourage you to alter them in three ways.

1 Rarity is the very essence of fantasy. Which of these encounters sounds more interesting?

"The caravan was raided by twenty goblins."

"The caravan was raided by many dirty brigands in leather armor, led by a short red-skinned creature in a dark cloak."

The game statistics for each encounter could be identical, but the latter is more fantastic. Make humanoids rare. Have them lead parties of dangerous men or dwell in magical places.

2 Visualization brings fear. Use visual descriptions to alter encounters even when game statistics are the same. Which of these encounters sounds more interesting?

"The cave is occupied by six goblins throwing dice to pass the time."

"Several shapes step forward from the dark shadows of the cave, revealing scrawny, orange-skinned man-creatures with sharp fangs and glowing eyes."

3 Adventure is defined by the unknown. Although visual descriptors may accurately predict if an opponent is strong or smart or handsome, they should never fully reveal the monster's power level. Just as humans can have class levels, so too can humanoids. The meek kobolds could be led by a level 6 kobold wizard who looks just like his fellows. Let the players never be sure whether the humanoid they face is weak or mighty.

VARIETY IN HUMANOIDS

The stock inhabitants of low-level adventures are the classic humanoid archetypes of kobold, goblin, orc, gnoll, bugbear, and ogre. We highly recommend modifying these humanoids to instill wonder in your game. Some simple changes, such as skin color or appearance, can make a big difference in game play.

The author strongly recommends James Raggi's excellent sourcebook *Random Esoteric Creature Generator* for comprehensive inspiration in the realm of monster design. This book is available wherever Goodman Games products are sold. Expanding on Raggi's concept, we offer the following tables for investing mystery in the humanoids in your adventures. For any given "stock" humanoid, such as a goblin or orc, we recommend rolling once on each of the following tables to give it a degree of mystery in your game. Many of these variations *could* result in statistical changes, should you deem it necessary, or could simply be visual flavor.

Table 9-1: Humanoid Skin Color

D20

1. Chalky white
2. Albino
3. Pitch black
4. Dark gray
5. Light gray
6. Sky blue
7. Navy blue
8. Crimson red
9. Bright red
10. Yellow
11. Orange
12. Green
13. Brown
14. Purple
15. Translucent
16. Completely transparent
17. Human skin tone
18. Torso different than limbs; roll again twice, once for torso and once for limbs
19. Head different from body; roll again twice, once for head and once for body
20. As per typical specimen of that type

Table 9-2: Weaponry

d8

1. Unintelligent; can do little more than hurl stones
2. Net and spear
3. Fights with two weapons (long sword and dagger)
4. Bow and dagger
5. Sling and club
6. Sword and shield, with metal armor and heraldry, as a knighted order of humanoids
7. Javelins (6 each)
8. Two-handed battleaxes and swords

Table 9-3: Appearance

2d20

2. Dots or spots (as a giraffe)
3. No hair whatsoever
4. Hair in topknot
5. Thick, bushy beard
6. Bald head
7. Long mustache
8. Unusual facial hair: (1) handlebar mustache, (2) Fu Manchu mustache, (3) sideburns, (4) goatee
9. Glowing eyes
10. Three eyes
11. Blind: (1) white eyes, (2) eyes overgrown with skin, (3) ceremonial patches, (4) eye sockets empty with a 90% chance of "sight" through alternate source: (1) echolocation, (2) acute sense of smell, (3) heat sense, (4) ESP
12. Cyclops
13. Large, unblinking fish-like eyes
14. Glowing aura
15. No ears
16. Elephantine ears
17. Gills on neck and webbed appendages, with amphibious capability
18. Extra digit on hands and feet
19. Enormous claws on hands and feet
20. Extra joint in arms
21. Short and stocky
22. Corpulent
23. Well-muscled
24. Thick fur or long hair
25. Skinny
26. Fanged
27. Tusks
28. Horns: (1) as a bull, (2) as a ram, (3) as a goat, (4) as a demon
29. Unusual legs: (1) backward-bending, (2) only one leg (hops), (3) four legs, (4) very long
30. Long snout
31. Neanderthal physique (slouched, pronounced brow, knuckles drag on ground, etc.)
32. Monkey-like posture, face, and tail; able to climb walls
33. Gigantic—double normal size (8'-tall goblins!)
34. Unusual hair color: (1) blonde, (2) red, (3) brown, (4) green
35. Shy and furtive
36. Sickly: boils, feverish, weak
37. Stripes (as a zebra)
38. Skin covered in suckers (as an octopus)
39. Feathered
40. Cloven hooves

Table 9-4: Unusual Properties or Behaviors

d14

1. Wears strange animal skins not from this world
2. Refuses to fight back
3. Are always encountered herding a domesticated animal (goat, pig, chicken, sheep, etc.)
4. Rides bareback on giant steer, bears, frogs, lizards, snakes, deer, etc.
5. Forces slaves to fight for them
6. Would rather barter than fight
7. Fascinated with jewels, metal weapons, helmets, leatherworking, shoes, etc.
8. Prophesied a great hero to rescue them from bondage…who resembles a player character
9. Speaks a racial language other than their own (e.g., goblins that speak the kobold language)
10. Scared of the dark (or light)
11. Speak only in whispers
12. Never surrenders
13. Psychic
14. Chants in a strange rhythm as they work or fight

"For a half-orc, she really has a lot of charisma!"

VARIETY IN UN-DEAD

Pre-genre fantasy literature presents a number of "un-dead" creatures that do not resemble the stock monsters of modern role playing. Un-dead can mean "back from the grave," but it can also mean "without a soul," "eternal or undying," and "surviving only by force of will alone." Furthermore, the qualities of an un-dead creature are often linked to its nature and traits when it was alive. Not all skeletons are the same!

The author suggests consideration of this variety when populating your dungeons. Consider determining an un-dead creature's game statistics (Hit Dice, attack, etc.) independent of its physical form, based on its nature during life, and then applying the appropriate physical appearance and abilities to match the game's theme or mood. For example, a great sorcerer preserved in un-death by sheer force of will may have a decaying zombie-like body, while a soulless faerie king who lives eternally is surrounded by chilled air.

Furthermore, assign powers to un-dead based on their traits in life. Peasants become mundane skeletons. But the corpse of a wizard, brought back to life as a skeleton, could retain some ability to cast spells. A hulking zombie may in fact remember the great warrior skills it once possessed.

Remember: no monster is more frightening than the one that is unknown. Ten skeletons are frightening. Ten perfectly-preserved maidens, their voluptuous forms now encased in cold white skin and blank eyes are even more frightening.

Table 9-5: Physical Appearance of Un-dead

d20

1. Skeletal
2. Mummified
3. Emaciated, old, withered
4. Decayed and corpse-like; zombie
5. Partially preserved, partially decayed
6. Ashen-skinned and gray-eyed
7. Misty and translucent
8. Wrapped in chains
9. Retains appearance at moment of death (bloody wounds, terrified face, gasping for air, eternally drowning, etc.)
10. A trapped soul; ghost-like
11. A dark, polluted soul; a shadow form
12. Pieces and parts
13. Visible only in bright light or perfect darkness
14. Crazed and insane-looking
15. Perfectly preserved but ice-cold to the touch
16. Excoriated; muscular
17. Disemboweled
18. Appears normal but radiates an unholy air; dogs bark, horses jump, etc.
19. Vampiric – fangs, stark skin, etc.
20. Bestial

Table 9-6: Traits or Properties of Un-dead

d20

1. Energy-draining touch (ability score damage; Will save resists)
2. Level-draining touch (lose XP; Will save resists)
3. Searing gaze (1d6 damage with a look)
4. Touch of cold (1d4 damage; immune to fire spells)
5. Chill aura (all within 100' take 1d4 damage; immune to fire spells)
6. Blood drain (causes 1d4 damage + 1 Stamina point each round)
7. Flight
8. Transformation (rat, cat, bat, wolf, worm; or mist, dust, spirit; etc.)
9. Extraordinary strength (Str 22+)
10. Swift (2 actions per round)
11. Slow (1 action every 2 rounds)
12. Immune to non-magical weapons
13. Immune to non-silvered weapons
14. Resistant to spells (50% chance of any spell not affecting it)
15. Cannot be killed without special ritual (stake through heart, exorcism, destruction of phylactery, form burned in fire, etc.)
16. Paralysis with touch (Will save to resist)
17. Translucent/transparent/invisible
18. Issues a curse with every strike (see Appendix C)
19. Casts spells as wizard of level 1d4+1
20. Continues to worship a dark god in undeath; casts spells as cleric of level 1d4+1; can turn living as a cleric turns unholy

PRIMAL SERVANTS OF CHAOS AND LAW

Elsewhere in the cosmos beyond the ken of man, the armies of Law and Chaos do battle. On the material plane, where dwells man, agents of the cosmic powers infiltrate our daily affairs. Deployed to earth from the nether dimensions in the war of Law and Chaos, these progenitors spawn diluted descendants that lack the pure energy of the primes but still retain some spark of the beyond.

There is a 1% chance that any lawful or chaotic creature is an exemplar of the eternal struggle, and as such, demonstrates traits native to its original cosmic incarnation from beyond the material plane. These creatures are known as primes. For example, a prime basilisk would exhibit characteristics of the basilisk as it first arrived from the planes beyond.

Primes have 50% or more hit dice than usual, are bigger and stronger, are more intelligent, and generally have a number of magical abilities. They can often step between their original plane and the material plane. Chaos primes tend to be wildly mutated, while lawful primes are pure incarnations that seem ageless.

Be imaginative in your use of primes, and treat them as a chance to introduce even more fantastic encounters to your players.

ELDERS

Mortal creatures who originated on the material plane come from purebred specimens that dwell in remote valleys ringed by impassible peaks. Known as elders, these antecedents of all known monsters are wise, patient, and immortal. In rare cases, they may venture into mundane realms, where they review the progress of their descendents.

There is a 1% chance that any mortal creature is an elder specimen. Elders have a higher Intelligence and Personality and often evince the specialized wisdom of their race.

For example, an elder orc may be a great weapons-master who wields the mace with a skill not found in any living orc. Despite his frailty and age, the elder orc receives a +10 bonus to attack rolls with the weapon and fights with such strength and skill that orcs around the world seek to train with him. As another example, an elder manticore may have creaking joints and painful rheumatism, but when he takes flight he maneuvers with such grace that he can dodge arrows and missiles (treat as +10 AC when flying) and no living manticore can out-fly him.

Elders know great secrets of the past and are versed in the origins of their own kind. They know the origins of intraracial disputes and remember the very Beginning.

FALLIBLE FIENDS

Demons have personality quirks, too. There is a 5% chance that any given monster has an unusual trait. Here are 12 ideas:

Table 9-7: Unusual Traits

d12

1 Sneezes constantly

2 Smells like butter

3 Strange warts

4 Incredibly ugly – the ugliest example of that creature the heroes have ever seen

5 *Bad* halitosis

6 Alopecia (And yes, before you ask, there is such a thing as a self-conscious pit fiend with a comb-over…)

7 A bad flu – coughing, sneezing, runny nose

8 Flatulent

9 Loquacious

10 Toothless

11 Whistles incessantly

12 Two left feet

MONSTERS DON'T PLAY BY THE RULES

Why should they? Conan never knew what manner of foul beast he would face or whether his sword would overcome its sorcery. He feared no creature of flesh, but was justifiably terrified by the supernatural. Monsters and magic are not bound by the same laws that govern mortals. The creatures that follow demonstrate examples of this fact; and you should heed it in your own creature and encounter designs.

Spellcasters in particular, whether human or monstrous in nature, should have powers that are unavailable to the players. This does not mean fully defined spells of the same sort learned by the characters. This means a unique power of some kind that would provide a plot hook, leading the player characters to seek out the wizard character and attempt to enlist his services, either as a an ally, hireling, or hostage. On the next page is a table of inspiration, but note that these powers *should not be spells*. The NPC should be able to use these powers with predictability and accuracy in a way that player characters cannot. It is left up to you to flesh out these ideas, which can apply to any wizard, sorcerer, shaman, witch, warlock, acolyte, priest, cult leader, or other such figure.

DEATH THROES

Extraordinary creatures can remain extraordinary in death. Allow some creatures' last moments to carry on their mystery by randomly generating death throes on the table below. These are especially appropriate for wizards and priests, demons, extraplanar monsters, and strange spellcasters.

Table 9-8: Unique Powers

d12

1 Heal any wounds or a specific kind of injury (i.e., restore sight to the blind, let the lame walk again, bind the bloodiest of wounds, etc.)

2 See the future, either completely or a particular slice (i.e., see a character's doom, his future love, his descendents, his last breath, etc.), through some specific method (read palms, tea leaves, entrails, etc.), or simply via a third eye

3 Grant life to an unliving thing (i.e., allow the creation of Pinocchio-type creatures, animate a golem, etc.)

4 Restore life to a dead creature (either permanently or temporarily, and not always with completely desirable results; i.e., the wounds of the dead creature may not be healed in the process)

5 Speak with the dead, sometimes with conditions: only bodies occupied by the character's same soul, only ghosts that still walk the earth, only ancestors of the character, only if the body is present, only those dead that are now un-dead, only souls that have never been resurrected, etc.

6 Travel to distant realms, sometimes with specific conditions: only the realms of the dead, only the lands of the angels, only the elemental planes, etc.; but generally with flawless accuracy and at-will

7 Tame animals, monsters, un-dead, etc.

8 Cancel curses, restore good fortune, or end bad luck

9 Control the weather, in ways either small or large

10 Know the past of a person or item or animal by touching it or simply by description (i.e., reciting the complete history of a person's life story, or the provenance of an item including all owners since it was created, etc.)

11 Locate missing people

12 Summon monsters from beyond

Table 9-9: Death Throes

d12

1 Corpse dissolves into oily stain

2 Skin blackens

3 Skin withers and desiccates

4 Corpse dissolves into puddle of water

5 Skin turns deep red or yellow

6 Creature turns to ashen mold of its living shape; when touched, ash collapses into pile of dust

7 Flash of heat causing sunburn to nearby characters, then creatures dissolves into mist

8 Body vanishes with no trace

9 Puff of smoke then body is gone

10 Ghost of fallen creature rises, incorporeal and angry, then is painfully sucked into the ground, clearly destined for some subterranean hell

11 Earth opens to swallow body, then re-seals to conceal it

12 Shadowy simulacrum of creature rises into sky to disappear

BALANCING ENCOUNTERS

Modern role playing games include complex rules for encounter levels, challenge ratings, and other systems for balancing encounters. These rules do not capture the glory of classic fantasy! The DCC RPG has no such rules beyond the generalities of hit dice and dungeon levels. Let the characters learn when to charge, when to retreat, and when to bide their time until they are powerful enough to win. If they don't learn, let them suffer the consequences.

CRITICAL HITS BY MONSTERS

Monsters score critical hits, too. A natural 20 on an attack roll by a monster automatically scores a critical hit against a player character. Some monsters score crits on a wider threat range, as noted in the descriptions. The monster's Hit Dice determine its crit die, as shown below. The crit table may overlap with PC crit tables in the case of humanoids that use weapons, but in many cases there are special crit tables for certain monster types, as shown below.

A PC's Luck modifier always alters a monster's critical hit. A positive Luck modifier reduces the monster's roll, whereas a negative modifier grants a bonus to the monster's critical hit roll.

Note that extremely powerful monsters fighting weak PCs often cause instant death with a critical hit. (Gruesomely narrated by the judge for dramatic impact, of course!) Likewise, weak monsters fighting powerful PCs might not be able to score critical hits.

Table 9-10: Monster Critical Hit Matrix

Monster HD	Crit Table and Die by Monster Type					
	Humanoids w/ Weapons*	Dragons	Demons	Giants	Un-dead	All Other
Less than 1	III/d4	DR/d4	DN/d3	–	U/d4	M/d4
1	III/d6	DR/d6	DN/d4	–	U/d6	M/d6
2	III/d8	DR/d8	DN/d4	–	U/d6	M/d8
3	III/d8	DR/d10	DN/d4	–	U/d8	M/d8
4	III/d10	DR/d12	DN/d4	G/d4	U/d8	M/d10
5	III/d10	DR/d14	DN/d6	G/d4	U/d10	M/d10
6	IV/d12	DR/d16	DN/d6	G/d4	U/d10	M/d12
7	IV/d12	DR/d20	DN/d8	G/d4	U/d12	M/d12
8	IV/d14	DR/d20	DN/d8	G/d4	U/d12	M/d14
9	IV/d14	DR/d24	DN/d10	G/d4	U/d14	M/d14
10	IV/d16	DR/d24	DN/d10	G/d4	U/d14	M/d16
11	V/d16	DR/2d14	DN/d12	G/d4	U/d16	M/d16
12	V/d20	DR/2d14	DN/d12	G/d6	U/d16	M/d20
13	V/d20	DR/d30	DN/d14	G/d6	U/d20	M/d20
14	V/2d10	DR/d30	DN/d14	G/d7	U/d20	M/d20
15	V/2d10	DR/2d16	DN/d16	G/d7	U/d24	M/d20
16	V/2d12	DR/2d16	DN/d16	G/d8	U/d24	M/d24
17	V/2d12	DR/2d20	DN/d20	G/d8	U/d30	M/d24
18	V/2d14	DR/2d20	DN/d20	G/d10	U/d30	M/d24
19	V/2d14	DR/3d20	DN/d24	G/d10	U/d30	M/d30
20	V/3d10	DR/3d20	DN/d24	G/d12	U/d30	M/d30
21+	V/3d10	DR/4d20	DN/d30	G/d12	U/d30	M/d30

Includes orcs, kobolds, goblins, bugbears, lizardmen, etc.

Crit Table DR: Dragons

Roll	Result
1 or less	Dragon rakes target with its spiny hide. This attack inflicts +1d6 damage.
2	Dragon crushes PC's head between its jaws! The PC is stunned and falls to the bottom of the initiative count for remainder of battle.
3	Dragon smashes the PC's legs, knocking the PC prone. The character suffers -5' speed until healed.
4	Dragon targets the character's weapon. The character takes half damage, but must make an opposed Strength check against the dragon. Treat dragon as Strength equal to 10 + HD. If the check fails, dragon grabs weapon and hurls it 3d10x10' feet away.
5	Blow to shield arm! Normal damage and the shield is destroyed. If no shield, this attack inflicts +1d6 damage.
6	Scale, tooth, or claw lodged in the PC's chest! This attack inflicts +2d6 damage, plus an additional 1d6 damage next round.
7	Breath weapon splash! Spittle laced with dragon's breath weapon causes an additional 1d8 damage and any other side effects of breath weapon (poison, sleep, etc.) if appropriate.
8	Arm ripped from socket! Dragon hurls the arm away. This attack inflicts +1d12 damage, and the arm is forever useless unless recovered and magically healed.
9	Tail-sling! Dragon wraps its tail around the PC and slingshots him into the distance. The character is flung 3d6x10' away in a random direction. If a wall or other obstruction is in the way, the character slams into it. The PC takes normal damage from the blow plus an additional 1d4 damage per 30' (or portion thereof) he is thrown, plus an additional 1d6 if he hits a wall or obstruction.
10	Combination strike! Normal damage and the dragon follows up with a second attack of same type.
11	Claw through the throat! The PC can't speak until healed and spends the next round struggling to breathe (unable to act).
12	Dragon targets the PC's kneecap. PC's movement cut by half and this attack inflicts +1d10 damage.
13	Awe-inspiring blow! This attack inflicts +1d12 damage, and all nearby retainers and henchmen are forced to make a morale check. Additionally, PCs must make a Will save (vs. DC of 10 + dragon's HD) or take a -2 penalty to their remaining attacks this round.
14	Breath weapon combo attack! Dragon unleashes a tiny fraction of its power against the character. This does not count against its daily breath weapon use. The PC takes normal damage plus a breath weapon strike at half normal damage—in most cases this means half damage on a failed save and quarter damage on a save.
15	Dragon spears the PC with one of its leg spines, then moves away. The PC flails about trying to free himself from impalement. This attack inflicts +2d12 damage, and the PC can only free himself with a DC 16 Agility check. The PC can take no actions until freed, and moves with the dragon while impaled.
16	Dragon finishes its strike with a mighty head-butt! The character is sent flying 2d4x10' away from the dragon and takes an additional +3d6 damage from the head-butt and subsequent fall.
17	Dragon bends back the PC's leg in a way it was never meant to, snapping the leg in half. The character's movement is reduced by half, and he takes an extra 2d6 damage.
18	Dragon pins the character down with one claw before slashing with another. Dragon inflicts +1d6 damage and gets a bonus claw attack at +4 to hit.
19	Rag doll smash! Dragon locks onto the character's ankle, swings him up, and smashes him to the ground head-first. This attack inflicts +1d16 damage, and the PC must make a Fort save (DC 15 + HD) or fall unconscious.

Crit Table DR: Dragons (Continued)

Roll	Result
20	Dragon's spines pierce the character in 1d7 places. Long, sharp, lance-like dragon scales emerge from the character's back, piercing multiple important organs. The character takes double damage, and if he survives, he is automatically reduced to 1 Strength and 1 Agility as his organs fail one by one. However, the character is now stuck to the dragon (its head, claw, wing, or whatever part the dragon attacked with). The dragon must spend its next attack with that limb prying off the bleeding PC before it can use that attack mode again. Once the PC is pried off, he takes 1d8 damage per round from massive hemorrhaging. Only magical healing can arrest the bleeding and prevent death.
21	Dragon hooks the PC with its wing and does a lift-and-smash. The character takes an additional +2d8 damage and is automatically stunned for 1d4 rounds.
22	Dragon captures the PC with its tail and begins constricting like an anaconda. The PC automatically takes an extra 1d8 crushing damage. Additionally, the PC is held in place and begins suffocating. The character must make a Fort save each round thereafter (DC equals 10 + dragon's HD) or die of suffocation. The PC cannot escape (or move in any way) until he succeeds on an opposed Strength check (treat dragon as 10 + HD). The dragon cannot use its tail to attack while holding PC.
23	Dragon uses one claw to hold down the PC while it rips his limbs off with the other. The character loses 1d3+1 limbs, taking an extra 1d14 damage for each limb lost. The result is probably a paraplegic or quadriplegic PC. The dragon proceeds to swallow the limbs. Limbs can only be restored if they are recovered from the dragon's gullet and then magically reattached.
24	Dragon embeds its claw/tooth/spine in the PC and shreds the character's internal organs. The character takes an additional 1d16 damage and is pinned in place, unable to take any action. On the following round, the dragon finishes this attack by ripping out the character's guts. The character is disemboweled. The character automatically dies in 1d4 rounds as he bleeds out. The dragon proceeds to hurl the character's internal organs at another opponent, forcing a DC 20 morale check.
25	With staggering precision, the dragon plucks out both the character's eyes in a single strike. The character takes no additional damage but is permanently blinded. The dragon flings the eyeballs back at the PC, who, in his now-sightless state, fails to see them go rolling out of reach.
26	The dragon swallows the character whole in a single massive bite. The character takes normal damage and is now trapped in the dragon's gullet. The character automatically takes an additional 3d8 damage each round thereafter from suffocation, constriction, and stomach acids. If the character succeeds in a DC 22 Strength check he can force his hands to move against the crushing strength of the dragon's stomach, allowing an attack of some kind (e.g., drawing a dagger to try to cut his way out), but he cannot be freed until the dragon is killed and he is cut out.
27	The dragon's razor-sharp talons (or teeth or spines, as appropriate) slash the character in perfect synchronicity, rendering the character's body into equal thirds. Instant death!
28	Practicing a difficult draconic maneuver, the dragon executes a "reverse breath weapon," breathing out in a short burst then immediately inhaling. This focused attack does not count against the dragon's daily breath weapon use. The PC takes normal damage, *plus* a full breath weapon hit (with a normal save allowed). There is no area of effect, as the dragon immediately cuts off the breath weapon after a microsecond of attack.
29	The dragon pins the character down, cracks his rib cage open, reaches into his chest cavity, and rips out his heart. The character dies instantly. Brandishing the heart as a bludgeoning weapon, the dragon then makes one free claw attack against the nearest ally of the PC, splattering the character's heart on the ally.
30+	The dragon explodes the character's head into splinters with an incredible blow, causing instant death. Everyone who witnesses the attack must make a morale check vs. DC 25 or flee (for retainers) or remain stunned and motionless on their next round (for PCs). The dragon makes a free claw attack against the nearest PC, and may continue making additional claw attacks until it misses.

Crit Table DN: Devils and Demons

Roll	Result
1 or less	Piercing blow. The character takes an additional 1d8 damage.
2	Life burn. The character permanently loses an additional 2 hit points.
3	Head strike. The character takes an additional 1d10 damage.
4	Major life burn. The character permanently loses an additional 4 hit points.
5	Corruption. Character takes on corruption, similar to a wizard casting spells. Roll 1d10 on a corruption table. If the demon has 5 HD or less, use the minor corruption table; if 6-10 HD, use the major corruption table; if 11+ HD, use the greater corruption table.
6	Aging. The character ages 1d10 years instantly. If cumulative aging from this and other effects exceeds 20 years, the character suffers a -1 penalty to all physical ability scores.
7	Infernal weakening I. The PC loses 1d4 points of ability score for one week. Determine randomly: (roll 1d5) (1) Strength, (2) Agility, (3) Stamina, (4) Intelligence, (5) Personality.
8	Soul wound. The character loses 1 XP from the soul-burning touch of the demon.
9	Soul trade. The character's soul is swapped with that of a soul already owned by the demon. The demon takes possession of the character's soul while his body is now controlled by another life force. The character's physical stats remain unchanged, but re-roll the character's new Intelligence, Personality, and Luck with 3d6. The character loses all his normal memories and takes on the memories of the soul now in his body, including its most recent memories of infernal brimstone. He retains his class abilities and other training, but his new mental statistics may change the skill with which he uses his abilities. The character can recover his stolen soul only by journeying to the demon's home plane and recovering it. The judge is encouraged to come up with a new history for the soul now in his body.
10	Double corruption! The PC takes on corruption twice, similar to a wizard casting spells. Roll 1d10 twice on a corruption table. If the demon has 5 HD or less, use the minor corruption table; if 6-10 HD, use the major corruption table; if 11+ HD, use the greater corruption table.
11	Infernal weakening II. The PC loses 1 point of one ability score permanently. Determine randomly: (roll 1d5) (1) Strength, (2) Agility, (3) Stamina, (4) Intelligence, (5) Personality.
12	Luck burn. The touch of the demon brings bad luck upon the character! He loses 1 point of Luck. A halfling or thief can recover this loss through normal class means.
13	Severe soul wound. The character loses 3 XP from the demon's soul-searing touch.
14	Astral drift. The character's soul is sent adrift on the astral plane! The character drops to the ground, catatonic, and cannot be revived until his soul is located and returned to his body.
15	Confinement. The demon's strike breaks the magic bonds holding it on this plane and confines the character to the demon's current location. The character sees a burning circle of flame appear around him, sputtering black with dark energy. The circle is approximately 5 feet in diameter and traps the character within. It is considered powerful magic (treat as spell check 25 to dispel). The character cannot pass through it by any means until it is dispelled or the character is freed or "banished" back to his native free state. The demon, on the other hand, is now freed from any confinement or banishment to this plane and can return to its home plane at will.
16+	Banishment. The demon's strike banishes the character to the demon's home plane! The character vanishes from sight as he is instantly transported back to the demon's home. For all intents and purposes, the character is out of the game unless his allies immediately follow to save him.

Crit Table 6: Giants

Roll	Result
1 or less	Crushing blow. This attack inflicts +1d8 damage, and the character's spine is compressed. The PC permanently loses 1d6" of height.
2	Broken arm. This attack inflicts +1d10 damage and one arm is crippled. The character suffers *permanent* loss of 1 Strength (arm never heals back to original position properly), and the arm cannot be used until healed.
3	Broken leg. This attack inflicts +1d10 damage and one leg is crippled. The PC suffers *permanent* loss of 5' of speed (leg never heals properly) and moves at half speed until healed.
4	Crushed chest. This attack inflicts +1d12 damage and chest is caved in. Until completely healed, any sort of exertion (including combat, running, swimming, jumping, etc.) requires DC 6 Fort save. Failure indicates permanent loss of 1 Stamina (due to several organ damage; e.g., heart attack, lung failure, etc.).
5	Flattened. The PC is literally flattened into the ground by the sheer force of the blow, with multiple broken bones and several shattered ribs. The character takes an additional 1d12 damage *and* permanently loses 1 Stamina.
6	Ricochet blow. The giant's staggering attack sends the target hurling through the air up to 3d30' to collide with another victim (randomly determined). Both the original target and the secondary target take 1d10 damage from the collision (in addition to the giant's normal damage against the first target).
7	Colossal head strike. This attack inflicts +2d6 damage and the PC permanently loses 1 point of Intelligence. In addition, there is a 25% chance the character forgets the last 24 hours of his life.
8	Weapon smash. The giant's massive blow causes an additional 1d8 damage and splinters the character's weapons and equipment. The PC's weapons and equipment each have a 50% chance of being destroyed; roll for each item: armor is busted loose (straps broken and plates dented), shields are shattered, weapons splintered or cracked, etc. Magic items are destroyed only 10% of the time instead of 50%.
9	Sweeping blow. The giant's strike bowls over the character, and he takes an extra 1d8 damage and is knocked prone (must spend his next activation to stand). In addition, the giant can make another attack as long as it is directed against a *different* target, who must be within melee range and adjacent to the first target. If this second attack hits, the giant can attack *another* target, up to five in total, as it sweeps through its opponents.
10	Legs crushed into ground. The giant's blow hits the PC square on the head, driving him into the earth like a nail into a board. The character takes an additional 2d8 damage, and both his legs are broken as he is propelled 1d4 feet into the earth (reduced to 1d4 inches if surface is stone). The character suffers a permanent loss of 10' of speed and 1 Agility (legs never heal properly) and is temporarily reduced to a speed of 1' (yes, one foot per round) until his two broken legs are healed.
11	Roll again twice.
12	Roll again three times.

BKM·2·012

Crit Table V: Un-dead

Roll	Result
1 or less	Unnatural boils sprout spontaneously around the wound. These are extremely painful to the touch, and automatically inflict 1 point of damage in any round where the character exerts himself physically (such as running, jumping, and fighting). The boils can only be healed with magical healing.
2	The cold touch of un-death spreads across the wound. This attack inflicts +1d4 damage and the PC gets the chills, chattering his teeth noisily until magically healed.
3	The numbness of death spreads around the wounded area. This attack inflicts +1d4 damage and the PC slowly loses sensation. On the next round, he must make a Fort save against DC 2. Failure means he is paralyzed. This first save is easy, but he must make another save against DC 3 on the next round, then against DC 4, then DC 5, and so on. If he makes every save to DC 20, he shakes off the numbness and is unaffected. If a single save is failed, the PC is paralyzed—he is insensitive to any sensation and completely numb and unable to move. The paralysis can be cured by any magical healing.
4	The horrifying visage of life after death infects the PC's thoughts as the un-dead leers into his eyes with its attack. The PC must make a DC 15 Fort save or be shaken and unable to move or attack for the next 1d4 rounds.
5	The character is cursed from beyond the grave! Depending on his actions and the intelligence of the un-dead creature, the curse may have specific terms associated with the wishes of the un-dead (judge's discretion; see Appendix C). Alternately, the curse causes a -1 penalty to Luck and *all* dice rolls until lifted.
6	The wound blackens immediately and a horrid infection from beyond the grave begins to spread. The character must make a DC 10 Fort save or temporarily lose 1d4 Stamina. The infection continues to attack each day, forcing another DC 10 Fort save each morning (failure results in the loss of another 1d4 Stamina) until the infection is magically expunged. The character does not heal while infected.
7	Supernatural frost spreads out from the wound in a lacy web, causing an additional 1d8 damage and intense pain. The frost dissipates on the next round but until the next full moon, the PC takes an extra 1 point of damage from all cold-based attacks.
8	Necrotic energies leap from the un-dead in a sizzling flash, enervating the character. The PC loses 2d4 Stamina temporarily.
9	Faced with the very real prospect of unnatural un-death, the PC becomes unhinged. He immediately loses 1d4 Personality and goes temporarily insane, behaving erratically and strangely until the next new moon. The controlling player must make a percentile roll before any action, and on 01-10 the character makes an insane action (as determined by the judge) instead of what was intended. On 11-00 the intended action occurs.
10	The visage of rotting un-death brings the horror of the grave to the character's thoughts. He must make a DC 16 Fort save or be shaken with fear, unable to attack or do anything except quake in fear for 1d4 rounds.
11	Strange electrical sparks leap from the attacking un-dead, causing an additional 1d10 damage.
12	The attack is imbued with some unnatural remnant of un-dead slumber. The character must make a DC 16 Fort save or fall asleep, instantly and deeply. He will not awaken for 1d7 hours or until shaken violently.
13	The attack is infused with powerful necromantic energies which cause the character's skin to flake and rot! His flesh begins to fall off in large chunks, exposing the muscle and bone below. This is extremely painful and debilitating. The character loses an extra 1d8 hit points and 1 point of Personality immediately and again every morning thereafter as his flesh slowly rots. He dies when his Personality reaches 0. The rot can be arrested only by powerful magical healing.
14	The strike of un-death saps the PC's energy. The character temporarily loses 1d4 Str and must make a DC 12 Fort save or lose an *additional* 1d4 Str.
15	Strange spectral energies arc to the PC's body, making him temporarily incorporeal for 1d4 rounds. The PC cannot grasp physical objects. He cannot speak, make noise, attack, or be seen in bright light. He can fly at his normal movement rate and can pass through solid objects at half speed. He is considered un-dead while incorporeal. There is a 1% chance the transition is permanent.

Crit Table U: Un-dead (Continued)

Roll	Result
16	A disgusting grave rot immediately spreads around the wound, causing an additional 2d6 damage and forcing a DC 16 Fort save. Failure on the save causes an additional temporary loss of 1d4 Stamina. The rot gets progressively worse until magically cured, forcing another save each morning against the loss of another 1d4 Stamina.
17	The brief brush with death affects the PCs' memory. He loses all memory of the last 24 hours and must make a DC 16 Fort save or also lose memories of the past 1d7 days.
18	The blow smashes against the PC's temple and gives him a glimpse of his own death sometime in the future. This brush with death paralyzes the PC with fear for 1d6 rounds.
19	The wound immediately turns a deep yellow color and a dizzying madness infects the character. He temporarily loses 1d6 Intelligence and 1d6 Personality.
20	The wound takes the shape of an unholy mark. The character takes an additional 1d6 damage and is *marked*. Un-dead creatures are attracted to the PC from miles around. He cannot hide from un-dead, and they relentlessly hound him. The mark can only be removed by a blessing, holy cleansing, exorcism, or the like.
21	The character's soul is scarred by un-death. He permanently loses 1 point of Luck.
22	The wound erupts in a disgusting infestation of maggots. They cause an additional 2d6 damage plus an ongoing 1d6 damage per round until the wound is healed via magical means.
23	The un-dead's intensely concentrated aura of unholiness infects the PC with an unholy aura. Any magical *blessings* or similar effects are automatically cancelled, and the character takes 1d4 points of temporary Personality loss.
24	Grave rot! The wound bubbles and festers like a thing not from this earth. The rot causes an additional 1d12 damage and 1d6 Strength loss immediately, and the wound will not heal naturally. The damage and Strength loss can only be recovered via magical healing.
25	In a supernatural display, flesh melts away from the wound, revealing the bones beneath and causing an additional 1d6 damage and 1 point of Stamina loss. Each round thereafter, the radius of melted flesh expands, causing an additional 1d6 damage 1 point of Stamina loss. The melting flesh continues to expand until the PC dies. It can only be suspended via magical healing with a spell check of 20 or greater.
26	Death rattle! The stench of un-death chokes the character, who collapses in a fit of gagging that slowly begins to suffocate him. He must make a DC 20 Fort save or lose 1d4 points of Stamina. If he fails the Fort save, he must make *another* save on the next round. If that fails, he takes additional Stamina damage and must make *another* save. The pattern continues until he makes a save or dies.
27	The un-dead creature sucks life force from the character. The PC takes an additional 1d20 damage, and the un-dead creature *heals* that same amount (not to exceed its original total hit points).
28	The wizening. The character immediately ages 1d20 years. If the result is 15 or more, he *permanently* loses 1 point of Strength, Agility, and Stamina as his body weakens.
29	The end is always dust: the wounded area crumbles to dust, inflicting an extra 2d12 damage and permanently disfiguring the character. He loses the use of that arm, leg, hand, or whatever area was struck. On the following round, the area adjacent to the wound in turn crumbles to dust, inflicting an additional 1d6 damage. The radius of dust transformation continues to expand, inflicting an additional 1d6 damage each round until the character is dead. The transformation to dust can only be stopped by very powerful magic.
30+	Un-death seeks un-death: in a flash of thick black smoke, the un-dead creature expends some of the necromantic energies that sustain it to transform the PC into un-death. The un-dead attacker automatically loses 1d6 hit points and may be killed as a result. The PC collapses in a state of apparent death, only to arise 1d6 rounds later as an un-dead creature under the control of the judge. Roll 1d8 to determine the type of creature that arises: (1-4) zombie, (5-6) skeleton, (7) ghoul, (8) ghost.

Crit Table M: Monsters

Roll	Result
1 or less	Strike to chest, breaking ribs. This attack inflicts +1d6 damage.
2	Stunning blow! The PC falls to the bottom of the initiative count for the remainder of the battle.
3	Legs knocked out from beneath the character, knocking him prone.
4	PC disarmed. Weapon lands 1d12+5' away.
5	Blow to shield arm! If no shield, this attack inflicts +1d6 damage.
6	Weapon lodged in PC's chest! This attack inflicts +2d6 damage and an additional 1d6 damage next round.
7	Blow to jaw! The PC loses 1d8 hp and the same number of teeth.
8	Blow shatters PC's forearm. This attack inflicts +1d6 damage, and the arm is useless until healed.
9	Strike to helm! If no helmet, this attack inflicts +1d8 damage and forces a Fort save (DC 10 + HD). On a failed save, the PC falls unconscious.
10	Stunning blow! The world spins as the fell monster makes a second attack!
11	Strike to throat! The PC can't speak until healed and spends the next round struggling to breathe.
12	Blow smashes PC's kneecap. The character's movement is cut by half and this attack inflicts +1d10 damage.
13	Crushing blow! This attack inflicts +1d12 damage.
14	PC's weapon sundered in the violent assault.*
15	Strike to torso crushes internal organs. This attack inflicts +1d12 damage, and force the PC to make Fort save (DC 15 + HD) to remain conscious through the pain.
16	Devastating strike! This attack inflicts +1d16 damage.
17	PC's Achilles tendon is torn, snapping back into his thigh. The character's movement drops to 5' and the screaming can be heard for leagues.
18	Monster seizes PC by the neck. This attack inflicts +1d12 damage and the monster makes a second attack at +4 to hit.
19	Blow to cranium! This attack inflicts +1d16 damage and the PC must make a Fort save (DC 15 + HD) or fall unconscious.
20	Terrifying blow pierces several important organs. The PC spends the next 1d4 days dying a slow, painful death. Powerful magic (healing by a cleric of level 3 or higher) can arrest the dying.
21	Strike crushes skull, destroying the optic nerve and resulting in instant, permanent blindness.
22	PC's leg is shorn from his body. The character cannot move. This attack inflicts +2d12 damage.
23	Both the PC's arms are torn from his body. This attack inflicts +3d12 damage. Exceptionally cruel monsters may proceed to use PC's arms as weapons.
24	PC is disemboweled. Bloody guts spill to the ground. The PC spends the next 8 rounds dying as he futilely tries to feed the spooling intestines back into his body.
25	Attack craters PC's skull. This attack inflicts 1d8 Intelligence and Personality damage and puts the PC into an instant coma.
26	Strike crushes throat. The PC drowns in his own blood for 6 rounds.
27	Attack snaps the PC's spinal column like a twig. The attack causes permanent paralysis, and the PC watches the remainder of the battle from the floor.
28	Throat torn asunder. The panicked PC gargles wetly as blood gouts down his chest. He dies in 4 rounds.
29	Terrible blow to the chest explodes the PC's heart. Immediate and instantaneous death.
30+	Attack rends PC's head from his torso. Blood gouts from the collapsing body, and the monster moves on to the next foe, making attacks until it misses.

Magical weapons never break due to critical fumbles. The target is disarmed instead, the weapon landing 1d10+5 feet away.

TREASURE

The DCC RPG strives to avoid one aspect of the modern role playing experience that the author refers to as, "the economy of the adventurer." One goal of this work is to maintain verisimilitude in terms of the campaign world feeling like a feudal, medieval setting. In a medieval setting where most peasants survive on farming or trades, with an economy based primarily on barter, hard coinage is rare. This feudal environment is the essential starting point for most fantasy campaign settings.

However, the activities of wealthy adventurers quickly reveal a logical disconnect to this medieval world. If there is easy access to vast wealth simply by setting off on a life of adventure, how do peasants remain mere serfs? How does the overall environment remain an agrarian culture? When adventurers can delve into a tomb and return with hundreds or thousands of gold pieces—more wealth than a typical peasant will see in his entire lifetime, and more wealth than many low-level nobles will ever possess at one time—the local economy will necessarily tilt toward an overabundance of adventurers. Why farm or even live the leisurely life of a landed noble when a few dangerous journeys can produce extraordinary wealth beyond the compounded results of generations of land-holding?

Further, the essential paucity of hard coinage is called into question when adventurers have need of expensive goods and services. The very existence of "sages for hire" or a market for the sale and purchase of magic items raises severe questions about the flow of wealth through a medieval economy. When most peasants see a few gold pieces a year, if that, how does a sage charge 20, 50, or 100 gold pieces for a single consultation? If a magic item can be sold or bought for 5,000 gold pieces, where does the seller dispose of that kind of coinage? What local government is even minting such vast amounts of currency? What happens to the local economy when a seller of magic items suddenly has 5,000 gold pieces to spend? Remember that in a medieval economy, there are essentially no banks beyond a few government-chartered institutions in capital cities. It makes little sense to have a world where expensive adventurer-funded services coexist beside a supposedly feudal economy.

Finally, if monsters possess enormous quantities of gold and gems, where do they get it and what happens to the surrounding economy when a monster is robbed of such wealth? If defeating a terrible creature yields a take of 1,000 gold pieces in its lair, one must ask: where did the creature get 1,000 gold pieces? Or, phrased slightly differently, did 1,000 peasants lose a year's income to this creature? The very concept of "rich monster hauls" next to "feudal medieval economy" raises many questions. Monsters with even modest amounts of treasure must have accumulated that gold over centuries (in the case of dragons), or robbed vaults or individuals of legendary status in singular crimes that are well remembered (i.e., all remember the flying sorcerer-lizards who bankrupted the duke when they robbed all the gold in his family vault), or be located near places of incredible local wealth, such as noble courts or powerful cities (which calls into question how wild monsters can in turn be living near civilized lands). The only way that a monster could possibly possess such incredible wealth, while also existing in a feudal medieval environment, is if the wealth is in natural form (i.e., gold ingots from a mineral vein not yet found by man, or unworked gems from a rare crystal cave), or in a form not used by Man (i.e., the variegated shells of underground snails, which are treated as hard currency by drow and duergar, but essentially value-less above ground). All other large treasure hauls should logically be associated with a singular provenance (i.e., this treasure used to belong to the duke, or it follows from centuries of dragon-raids, or it comes from the lost city of Aa which fell into the sea 10,000 years ago, or it was recovered from the wreck of a galleon sunk to the sea-floor, or so on).

With this long preface, then, the author concludes the following.

First, treasures given out by the destruction of monsters or the completion of adventures should be reasonable in the context of a medieval economy, which is to say that in many cases treasure should not be particularly extraordinary.

Second, a core concept of the DCC RPG is *lack of predictability* in the nature of foes encountered, both in their combat abilities and the treasure that is rewarded. As has been stressed previously, the judge is held accountable for varying the nature of enemies and ensuring that no two encounters are similar. When it comes to treasure and other rewards, the players should never have a sense of entitlement associated with certain monsters always possessing large amounts of treasure. Equally important, they should occasionally be surprised by their good fortune in having slain, for example, the one goblin that happens to possess a flawless emerald.

Consequently, this work does not include detailed rules for assigning treasure to monsters or encounters. The existing volume of D&D work includes several such systems which are robust and well defined, and which can be easily adapted here. The author suggests you adapt an existing treasure system of your choice, but carefully and deliberately evaluate the randomized results. Always ask yourself: "Where did the monster acquire such wealth? And what happened to the local economy in the process?"

"Oooh! Dibs on the chainmail bikini!"

CYCLOPEDIA OF CREATURES MONSTROUS AND MUNDANE

With the caveat that every monster should be unique, judges will still need some basic creatures to use as opponents for the heroes when they play this game. Moreover, classic monsters provide a benchmark by which the judge can guide his own creations. Here is a short selection of monster statistics for classic creatures. Judges should have a frame of reference for each of these creatures from prior editions and other games, which should give them a sense of how the DCC RPG interprets them. Be sure to apply the above guidelines to make these monsters unique in your own game.

You may note that certain iconic monsters are not presented below. While there are statistics for demons, elementals, and giants, as well as a randomization system for dragons, there are no stats for devils, golems, fey, liches, lycanthropes, treants, or vampires, as well as select other classic monsters like the medusa, pegasus, sphinx, unicorn, wight, or wraith. What follows is enough for the judge to have a good sense of "benchmarks" for his own creations, as well as a number of examples of atypical creatures appropriate to a campaign inspired by the works on Appendix N. We encourage the individuality of each campaign by not presenting standardized versions of all monsters. Make your own stats for werewolves, liches, and devils!

Goodman Games publishes a variety of adventure modules designed specifically to be used with the DCC RPG rules. We encourage you to peruse these modules and note how few "typical" monsters are used within them. Almost all monsters within DCC RPG adventure modules are new – as should be in the case in your own adventures!

ANDROID

Android: Init -2; Atk sword +2 melee (1d8) or wand +4 missile fire (range 60', 1d4+2); AC 18; HD 3d8+12; MV 30'; Act 1d20; SP infravision 60', immune to mind-altering spells, heal 2 hp per round; SV Fort +5, Ref -2, Will +6; AL N.

Androids resemble man but have rubbery skin, black, soulless eyes, and strange metallic clothing. Created by a race from beyond the stars and preprogrammed by the time gods, they are still found wandering the depths of the underdeep or guarding long-buried space ships. A small number of androids are crafted to resemble normal men, and once every few centuries, a man of great longevity is discovered to be an android in disguise. Android innards are a mix of mechanical and organic. They are unaffected by mind-altering spells (such as hypnosis or fear). Their bodies self-repair at a rapid rate. They usually fight with razor-sharp swords or strange wands that burn on touch. (These are mechanical in nature, not magical, and typically fall into disrepair when in the hands of PCs, who do not know how to maintain them.)

ANT, GIANT

Ant, giant (worker): Init +0; Atk bite +2 melee (1d4+1); AC 16; HD 1d8+2; MV 50' or climb 50'; Act 1d20; SV Fort +5, Ref +1, Will -3; AL L.

Ant, giant (soldier): Init +2; Atk bite +6 melee (3d4+3); AC 18; HD 3d8+6; MV 50' or climb 50'; Act 1d20; SP 20% have poisoned stinger (+6 melee, dmg poison: DC 16 Fort save or 2d4 Stamina); SV Fort +7, Ref +3, Will -3; AL L.

Ant, giant (queen): Init -4; Atk bite +0 melee (1d3); AC 12; HD 5d8+10; MV 10' or climb 10'; Act 1d20; SV Fort +4, Ref -4, Will +8; AL L.

Giant ants are common in jungles, caves, and swamps, where these dog-sized predators terrorize other creatures. Their mindless determination and unflagging efforts to bring order to their surroundings frequently drive out other monsters.

When a young queen matures and is evicted from the anthill to colonize her own territory, she brings with her a retinue of 2d6 soldiers and 6d6 workers. These new colonies are often the ones that bring the most conflict, for they move into territory occupied by gnomes, kobolds, lizardmen, or other creatures that compete with the ants for food. If the colony establishes a foothold, it rapidly expands, and within a year may have hundreds of workers and approximately one-third as many soldiers. Such large colonies soon become the dominant life forms in their areas.

Up to 20% of giant ant soldiers are born with poisoned stingers. These creatures gain an additional stinger attack. The stinger can only be used once per hour, to allow time for the poison to regenerate.

Giant ants are common on the distant planes where icons of Law dwell. Extraplanar giant ants, as well as terrestrial primes, have skins of gold, silver, bronze, or copper, and are more mechanical than insectoid in nature. They make clicking and clacking noises as they build well-ordered structures around their nest.

APE-MAN

Jungle ape-man: Init +2; Atk bite +4 melee (1d4+3) or slam +6 melee (dmg 1d6+3) or thrown stone +3 missile fire (dmg 1d4); AC 13; HD 3d8; MV 20′ or climb 30′; Act 1d20; SP +10 to hide checks in jungle terrain; SV Fort +6, Ref +3, Will +1; AL L.

Four-armed ape-man: Init +3; Atk bite +6 melee (1d6+5) or slam +8 melee (dmg 1d8+5); AC 15; HD 6d8; MV 40′ or climb 20′; Act 4d20; SP rend for additional 1d8 damage if more than 2 slam attacks hit same target in one round; SV Fort +10, Ref +6, Will +2; AL C.

White ape-man: Init +1; Atk slam +5 melee (1d4+2) or thrown stone +3 missile fire (dmg 1d4); AC 12; HD 2d8; MV 20′ or climb 20′; Act 1d20; SP 5% have spells as level 2 cleric; SV Fort +5, Ref +3, Will +4; AL C.

Giant ape-man: Init +1; Atk bite +12 melee (2d6+10) or slam +14 melee (dmg 2d8+10); AC 17; HD 8d8+10; MV 40′ or climb 30′; Act 3d20; SP rend for additional 2d8 damage if more than 2 slam attacks hit same target in one round; SV Fort +14, Ref +8, Will +6; AL C.

The darksome wilds are ruled by ape-men: stolid, silent, enduring. Some live in the cyclopean ruins of cities built by their once-great progenitors; others peer from the sun-dappled shade of humid jungles, watching the modern races evolve. All share three traits: great strength, great stealth, and great intelligence. However, all are limited by a lack of ambition beyond animal survival. Varieties of ape-men include:

- Jungle ape-men: tribal gorilla-like hominids skilled at climbing and hiding.

- Four-armed ape-men: solitary and savage beasts that stand 10′ feet tall and can rend a man to pieces.

- White ape-men: highly intelligent anthropoids capable of great feats with the right leadership. Alien invaders and ambitious sorcerers have sought white apes to build their armies.

- Giant ape-men: rare, enormous gorilla-like creatures reaching 25′ in height that rival dinosaurs in their terrible ferocity.

BASILISK

Basilisk: Init -1; Atk bite +5 melee (1d10) or claw +3 melee (1d4) or gaze (special); AC 16; HD 5d8; MV 40'; Act 2d20; SP gaze (DC 14 Will); SV Fort +6, Ref +1, Will +1; AL C.

Basilisks are stout, six-legged lizards with tough hides and a paralyzing gaze. They came from another plane and now haunt mountains, hills, and dungeons in a relentless search for prey. A basilisk can use an action to lock eyes with a living creature; the target that looks a basilisk in the eye must make a DC 14 Will save or be paralyzed for 2d6 turns. Typically, a basilisk gazes to cause paralysis, then uses its second action to bite the target that same round. Ten percent of basilisks have eight legs and the ability to climb vertical surfaces at a speed of 40'. Five percent of basilisks have a gaze that instead turns their victim to stone permanently. The rarest type of basilisk is a variety that recently arrived from the Abyss. The abyssal basilisk possesses 8 HD and gains a +2 bonus to attack rolls. Prime basilisks may combine all special traits noted above and more.

BAT

Bat swarm, mundane: Init +4; Atk swarming bite +1 melee (1d3 plus disease); AC 10; HD 2d8; MV fly 40'; Act special; SP bite all targets within 20' x 20' space, half damage from non-area attacks, disease (see below); SV Fort +0, Ref +10, Will -2; AL L.

Bat swarm, vampiric: Init +6; Atk swarming bite +3 melee (1d4 plus disease and vampire drain); AC 12; HD 4d8; MV fly 40'; Act special; SP bite all targets within 20' x 20' space, half damage from non-area attacks, vampire bite (any target wounded by the swarm takes an additional 1 damage per round until entire swarm is killed), disease (see below); SV Fort +1, Ref +10, Will -2; AL L.

Bat, giant vampire: Init +6; Atk bite +4 melee (1d6 plus disease and vampire drain); AC 14; HD 2d8; MV fly 40'; Act 1d20; SP vampire bite (latches onto target and automatically inflicts an additional 1d4 damage per round until killed), disease (see below); SV Fort +4, Ref +4, Will -2; AL C.

Bat swarms are masses of hundreds of individual bats. They occupy spaces of roughly 20' to a side, though some may be larger or smaller. The swarm can bite all targets in that space. Because the swarm is composed of many individual elements, it takes half damage from normal weapons and any spell or effect that normally has an individual target. Slashing wildly with a sword or mace is unlikely to do much damage to a swarm of hundreds of bats! Attacks with area effects, such as *fireballs*, *choking clouds*, and the like, inflict normal damage.

Bats carry disease. A character bitten by a bat of any type receives a disease randomly determined from the table below.

D6	Fort Save	Effect on Failed Save
1	DC 8	Sickness and vomiting for 2 days; half movement and -4 to all rolls during that time.
2	DC 14	Terrible stomach pains; 1d4 damage and unable to heal normal damage for one week.
3	DC 16	Debilitating weakness. Temporarily lose 1d4 Strength and Stamina.
4	DC 10	System shock. Immediate death.
5	DC 20	Dizziness. Temporarily lose 1d4 Agility.
6	DC 12	Intense weakness. *Permanently* lose 1 Strength.

BEETLE, GIANT

Beetle, giant: Init -2; Atk mandibles +3 melee (1d4+2); AC 15; HD 2d8+2; MV 30' or climb 20'; Act 1d20; SP varies (see below); SV Fort +1, Ref +0, Will -3; AL N.

Giant beetles dwell beneath the earth in lands that time has forgotten. The click of their mandibles is a feared sound, for there is no reason behind their attacks beyond the urge to devour. There are many varieties of giant beetle, so the judge should roll 1d6 to determine the nature of the beetles in each encounter:

Roll Giant beetle type

1 Fire beetle. When the beetle bites, it exudes a glowing, acidic residue that causes an additional 1d4 damage. The glow is faint but does not fade for 1d3 days and cannot be washed off—characters bit by a fire beetle are a beacon to other curious creatures.

2 Stag beetle. The beetle's mandibles are enormous. Instead of the normal mandible attack, it attacks at +6 for 2d6+4 damage.

3 Spitting beetle. The beetle spits a sticky, caustic glob as it closes for melee. The spit attacks at +3, has a range of 60', and causes 1d6 points of acid damage on a hit.

4 Flying beetle. The beetle can fly at a speed of 30'.

5 Spiny beetle. The beetle's legs and carapace are coated in short, sharp spines. Anyone in melee with the beetle automatically takes 1 point of damage per round from the sharp spikes.

6 Armored beetle. The beetle's carapace is unusually dense, giving it an AC of 20.

BRAIN, ELDER

Brain, elder: Init +2, Atk mind blast +8 missile fire (3d4 Int damage, range 100'); AC 16; HD 10d12+30; MV 10'; Act 3d20; SP cerebral control, spells (5% chance as wizard of level 1d4+4), blindsense (perfect perception of all things, including invisible targets, within 500'); SV Fort +10, Ref +2, Will +12; AL N.

Elder brains are tough, leathery masses of tissue that were once the thinking portions of living creatures. Some come from the distant past, others from the unknowable future, and not all are the brains of Men. They are found in odd-shaped tanks, sometimes with mechanical components attached, buried in metal strongholds beneath the earth or floating with purpose through the astral realms. An elder brain's wizened outer hide conceals a functioning thought machine, and these living intellects still evince desires and emotions. They tend to be solitary and dislike disturbance. Some dominate nearby tribes of sub-humans, who are forced to serve their life-giving machines.

In combat, an elder brain launches mind blasts that wither the intellectual abilities of their targets. A single blast can reduce most commoners to dribbling idiots. An elder brain has three action dice each round and can thus launch multiple blasts. Intelligence lost to the mind blast heals normally *unless* the creature falls below 0 Intelligence, in which case the creature falls under the cerebral control of the elder brain. Its body becomes an extension of the elder brain's nervous system and is subject to complete control, indefinitely, until the elder brain is killed. An elder brain can control creatures totaling up to 1,000 points of Intelligence in this manner (i.e., a humanoid with starting Int of 9 counts as 9 points when reduced to Int 0 and taken over).

An elder brain can be an apt mastermind for an ongoing campaign—although the creature itself is not the most dangerous opponent, its centuries-long schemes can have storyline ramifications. Up to 5% of elder brains have psionic or magical powers that manifest in knowledge of spells, as noted in the stat block. Their great Hit Dice come from the complex, durable machinery that sustains and protects them.

BUGBEAR

Bugbear: Init +1; Atk mace +5 melee (1d6+5); AC 16; HD 4d8+4; MV 30'; Act 1d20; SP infravision 60'; SV Fort +4, Ref +0, Will +2; AL L.

Bugbears share a common ancestor with goblins, whom they dominate. A bugbear stands 8' tall but is somewhat pudgy and soft-looking. Its uninspiring appearance belies 500 pounds of mass, however, and the strength that goes with this mass is impressive. Bugbears are not overly intelligent but are smart enough to install themselves as the rulers of goblin tribes, who they abuse and misuse as their personal slaves. Typically, there will be one or two families of 3-4 bugbears for every band of goblins. Bugbears rule by brute strength from shabby throne rooms, sending their goblin slaves on raids against easy targets. If forced into direct combat, a bugbear fights with an enormous spiked mace and a mish-mash of scavenged armor. However, a threatened bugbear would rather retreat to find another easy life of ruling goblin slaves than stand and fight heroes!

CAVE CRICKET

Cave cricket: Init -1; Atk bite -2 melee (1d3); AC 13; HD 3d8; MV jump 80' or fly 30'; Act 1d20; SP buzz 1d4; SV Fort +2, Ref +0, Will -3; AL N.

Cave crickets are aggravating vermin found throughout the underdeep. They cluster in swarms of up to 20 creatures. Individually they are durable, but their weak bite is not to be feared. However, in numbers, their buzzing calls cause duress to humanoids. Instead of moving and attacking, a cave cricket can spend its entire round rasping its legs against each other. The low-pitched buzzing noise produced by this action is extremely painful to humanoids. For every cave cricket participating in the buzzing, roll 1d4. Sum the total and compare it to the Stamina of characters within 100' of the cave crickets. Any character with a Stamina less than the total automatically takes damage equal to the difference between the roll and his Stamina. For example, a group of six cave crickets would roll 6d4 when they buzz. If the result was a roll of 16, and the nearest character has a Stamina of 12, that character would take 4 points of damage. In great concentrations, cave crickets can be lethal.

CAVE OCTOPUS

Cave octopus: Init -2; Atk tentacle +2 melee (1) and beak +4 melee (1d8); AC 11; HD 2d6; MV walk 20' or swim 40'; Act 8d20; SP grasp 1d4, camouflage; SV Fort +2, Ref -2, Will +2; AL N.

Cave octopuses are clumsy eight-legged creatures that dwell in murky pools of water. They pull themselves ashore to pursue prey. In combat, they lash out with 8 tentacles, all of which can attack in a single round. The octopus will typically attack a single creature with all its tentacles, then hold down that creature and bite it.

For each tentacle that strikes the same character, the octopus receives 1d4 on an opposed Strength check to hold the character down. For example, if 6 tentacles hit a character in a single round, the character takes 6 points of damage, and the octopus rolls 6d4 on a Strength check against the character. If the octopus wins the Strength check, the character is grappled and cannot attack unless he spends the next round struggling and succeeds on an opposed Strength check.

A cave octopus can only use its beak once it has grappled a creature and won a Strength check.

Cave octopuses have a highly developed form of camouflage that lets them change color and pattern to match surfaces nearby. This grants them a +10 bonus to any attempt to hide.

CENTAUR

Centaur: Init +0; Atk hooves +1 melee (1d4+1) and sword +3 melee (1d8+1) or bow +3 missile fire (1d6+1) or other weapon; AC 14; HD 2d8; MV 50'; Act 2d20; SV Fort +2, Ref +1, Will +1; AL Varies.

Centaurs have the torso of a man set upon the body of a horse. They are proud and elusive. They are like men in that they have many peoples of varying customs and alignment. There are good centaurs dwelling in the pastures of the fey, evil centaurs in the dark woods, and others in between. Wild-born centaurs fight with clubs and their hooves; civilized centaurs fight with barding and steel weapons as well as their hooves. Many centaurs also use bows to launch arrows while charging.

CENTIPEDE, GIANT

Centipede, giant: Init +3; Atk bite +6 melee (1d6 plus poison); AC 14; HD 3d6; MV 60'; Act 1d20; SP detect thoughts 500', poison; SV Fort -1, Ref +2, Will -1; AL C.

Giant centipedes are predators that hunt by tracking psychic emanations. Mindless creatures (such as living statues or un-dead) are effectively invisible to giant centipedes, but creatures with thoughts find it impossible to lose the relentless predators. The centipedes dwell in pods of 3d6 creatures, and when hungry unravel their intertwined forms to converge on the creatures whose thoughts they detect.

CHIMERA

Chimera: Init +0; Atk lion bite +5 melee (2d4) or goat gore +4 melee (2d4) or snake bite +6 melee (1d10+2) or claws +4 melee (1d3) or breathe fire; AC 18; HD 5d8+8; MV 30' or fly 30'; Act 3d20; SP breathe fire 3/day; SV Fort +4, Ref +2, Will +2; AL C.

The chimera is a winged creature with the body and head of a lion, a second head of a goat, and a snake-headed tail. It is a flying predator that hunts the lowlands where the livestock it preys upon typically gather. Each round, it has three attacks, one from each head. The lion head bites, the goat head gores, and the snake-headed tail can breathe fire 3/day in a cone measuring 90' x 30', causing 3d8 damage (DC 15 Ref save for half). Ten percent of chimeras have a dragon's head at the shoulder instead of a snake-headed tail, and five percent have a bull's head (which also gores) in place of the goat head. Prime chimeras have all of the above, double HD, masses of tentacles at the joints, elongated claws granting another claw attack, and a *chimerical touch* ability (DC 18 Will save or target's touched body part mutates to lion, goat, snake, dragon, or bull).

COCKATRICE

Cockatrice: Init -1; Atk peck +2 melee (1d3 plus petrifaction; DC 13 Will); AC 13; HD 3d8; MV 20', fly 20'; Act 1d20; SV Fort +2, Ref +1, Will +1; AL C.

The cockatrice is a large bird-like creature with bat wings, a feathered snake's tail, and a rooster's head. It is a fantastical wild beast that hunts alone in warm regions. Its beak is not a powerful weapon, but anything touched by the creature must make a Will save or be turned to stone. Prime cockatrices are larger, have up to 6 HD, and have serrated beaks that deal 1d8 damage.

The bite of the giant centipede is poisonous. The poison varies according to the breed of the centipede. Determine randomly with 1d6:

d6	Fort Save	Effect on Failed Save
1	DC 10	Paralysis, duration 1d7 days
2	DC 12	Paralysis, permanent
3	DC 14	1d4 Strength loss (temporary)
4	DC 16	Immediate death.
5	DC 12	1d12 damage
6	DC 14	3d6 damage plus 1d4 Stamina loss (temporary)

CYCLOPS

Cyclops: Init +0; Atk huge club +8 melee (1d8+4); AC 16; HD 5d8+5; MV 40'; Act 1d20; SP *true sight*; SV Fort +6, Ref +1, Will +4; AL C.

Cyclopes are solitary one-eyed giants who traffic with ghosts. Their eyesight extends onto multiple planes of existence, including the astral and ethereal planes, as well as the invisible spectrums of the material plane. They can see invisible creatures and are never fooled by illusions. Cyclopes learn much from their conversations with spirits and astral travelers and can sometimes be persuaded to share secrets. Up to 25% of cyclopes know the spell *runic alphabet, mortal* (at +2d6 spell check). Prime cyclopes carry sacks of variegated eyeballs, which they exchange with the eye in their socket to expand their visual acuity into still broader expanses of space, time, and dimension.

DEEP ONE

Deep One: Init -2 Atk mace +2 melee (1d6+3) or other weapon; AC 13; HD 1d8+2; MV 20' or swim 40'; Act 1d20; SV Fort +3, Ref -1, Will +3; AL C.

The deep ones are tough, sluggish, goggle-eyed, amphibious fish-men who reek of brine. They live in dark cities under the sea and worship Cthulhu and his minions with human sacrifice and unspeakable rituals. All land-races fear deep ones, for when the deep ones come, it can only mean they seek slaves or sacrifices. Although they prefer humans, they are not above taking goblins, orcs, gnolls, or other humanoids.

Deep ones are always encountered in well-armed war parties supported by clerics of their enigmatic gods. There will be a minimum of 20 deep ones armored in sharkskin leather and shields and armed with barbed clubs and maces. War parties also carry nets and rope for retrieving victims alive. For every 10 warriors there is a level 1 cleric; for every 30 warriors there is a level 3 cleric; and for every 60 warriors there is a level 5 cleric. Up to 1d4 war-wizards accompany any sized force, each one possessing 1d3+1 levels of wizard spellcasting ability. The clerics worship enigmatic Cthulhu gods and wield spells designed to bind and subdue.

Deep ones mate as do fish, leaving eggs in undersea spawning grounds, but are also able to mate with surface-dwellers to produce horrid half-breeds. With sufficient generations some of these half-breeds resemble man save for subtle hints of ichthyoidal ancestry, such as gills, webbed feet, and wide unblinking eyes. Small communities of degenerate deep one hybrids exist on wind-swept ocean shores, shunned by their human cousins but willing to aid their deep one progenitors in their infrequent treks to the surface.

DEMON

A demon is a horrid creature native to the lower planes, Nine Hells, the 666 levels of the Abyss, the cold plains, the outer reaches, and select otherworldly places. Demons appear on the physical plane of existence when summoned, invoked, or bound, or occasionally, when visiting voluntarily. Demons find mortals repugnant and are disgusted by our blue skies and green vistas, and thus rarely visit corporeal realms except by compulsory means. On the other hand, they thrive on the energy in a human soul and are eager to take possession of souls that pass on to the afterlife. Demons that do find themselves stranded on the material plane may become more powerful by consuming the souls of those they meet.

The physics of extraplanar reality produce different forms of life, and thus demons have a variety of forms. Powerful demons may be unique in stature, and over a lifetime any given demon may change its form in subtle or dramatic fashion.

By mortal standards, demons are incredibly powerful and possess great magical powers. The impermanent nature of the outer planes manifests on the primary plane as an ability to alter physical reality, and thus many demons discover new powers when they visit our plane. Sorcerers pursue means to tap and control these powers, whether by forcibly binding demons to specific ends or by trading favors.

Demon planes are organized hierarchically. A demon typically owes fealty to a more powerful specimen and has some vassals of its own. Even the weakest demons bully lower life forms into submission. Powerful demons build strongholds and organize followers into armies, then war for control of their realms. A few ultra-powerful demon lords rule entire planes and serve as patrons for ambitious mortals.

Many mortals choose to serve demon lords in the pursuit of power. This is not a path to take lightly. While demons may bestow boons upon the faithful, they are likewise quick to punish those who fail, and capricious enough to revoke past gifts if so provoked. Wizards may declare fealty to a demon lord with the *patron bond* spell, while clerics can meditate and pray in the name of a demon lord.

A wizard can attempt to take control of a demon by casting the appropriate spell. The spell *binding* is the most basic method for this control, while *demon summoning* will summon a controlled demon for a limited duration. Demons that are slain on a non-native plane are not truly killed; they re-form on their native plane at a later time. Powerful demons may keep their life essence in a hidden vessel, which must be located and destroyed to truly kill them; otherwise, even if "slain," they simply re-form at the place of their life essence.

All demons are unique individuals, but they can be roughly classed as follows. Demons of each type share certain abilities and resistances, as indicated in their descriptions.

Demon	Communication	Abilities	Immunities	Projection	Crit Threat Range
Type I	Speech (Infernal, Common)	Infravision, *darkness* (+4 check)	Half damage from non-magical weapons and fire	Cannot travel planes of own volition	20
Type II	Speech, ESP (read minds but not converse)	Infravision, *darkness* (+8 check)	Immune to non-magical weapons or natural attacks from creatures of 3 HD or less; half-damage from fire, acid, cold, electricity, gas	Can teleport back to native plane at will, as long as not bound or otherwise summoned	19-20
Type III	Speech, telepathy	Infravision, *darkness* (+12 check)	Immune to weapons of less than +2 enchantment or natural attacks from creatures of 5 HD or less; half-damage from fire, acid, cold, electricity, gas	Can teleport back to native plane or any point on same plane, as long as not bound or otherwise summoned	18-20
Type IV	Speech, telepathy	Infravision, *darkness* (+16 check)	Immune to weapons of less than +3 enchantment or natural attacks from creatures of 7 HD or less; immune to fire, cold, electricity, gas; half-damage from acid	Can teleport back to native plane or any point on same plane, as long as not bound or otherwise summoned; can project astrally and ethereally	17-20
Type V and above	Speech, telepathy	Infravision, *darkness* (+20 check)	Immune to weapons of less than +4 enchantment or natural attacks from creatures of 9 HD or less; immune to fire, cold, electricity, gas, acid	Can teleport at will to any location, as long as not bound or otherwise summoned; can project astrally and ethereally	16-20

All demons roll on crit table DN and feature a threat range depending on their type, as noted below. While a natural 20 is always a hit, scoring a crit on another roll requires the demon to roll the natural result *and* beat the target's AC.

There are many demon lords and many thousands of demons. The table below lists some of the demons most applicable to a beginning DCC RPG campaign, organized by the demon lord to which they report. Stats are presented only for the demons of Bobugbubilz; the rest are yours to create. After all, most demons are unique!

Demons of Bobugbubilz

Devil frog (type I demon, Bobugbubilz): Init +1; Atk bite +6 melee (1d8+2); AC 13; HD 3d12; MV 20' or swim 10'; Act 1d20; SP demon traits; SV Fort +4, Ref +2, Will +0; AL C.

A devil frog is the size of a pony. It has unusually long legs and can stand upright for sustained periods. Its cavernous mouth is lined with sharp teeth. Devil frogs love the taste of fresh meat, particularly fish, and are not particularly intelligent.

Barbed salamander (type I demon, Bobugbubilz): Init +0; Atk bite +4 melee (1d8); AC 15; HD 4d12; MV 30' or swim 30'; Act 1d20; SP barbs, demon traits; SV Fort +4, Ref +4, Will +0; AL C.

The barbed salamander only nominally resembles its namesake. Its thick, stocky body and fleshy tail are covered with backward-pointing barbs. In melee it lashes about with the deadly barbs, automatically inflicting 1d3 damage each round to all adjacent opponents (DC 14 Ref save to avoid).

Minor Toadfiend (type II demon, Bobugbubilz): Init +4; Atk *+2 mace of chaos* +8 melee (1d6+4 plus 1d4 against lawful creatures) or claw +8 melee (1d8+2) or bite +10 melee (1d12); AC 18; HD 6d12; MV 30' or swim 30'; Act 2d20; SP disease, *detect good* (+6 spell check), demon traits; SV Fort +6, Ref +8, Will +6; AL C.

This horrid crossbreed of man and amphibian lurches about chaotically, striking down foes in between croaking gurgles. Toadfiends wield vicious spiked maces and radiate an aura of muck and disease. Any creature wounded by a toadfiend must make a DC 18 Fort save or contract a debilitating disease. The disease manifests 1d7 days later as terrible shakes and shivers, inflicting a -4 penalty to Strength and Agility until cured by magical means.

Toadfiend (type III demon, Bobugbubilz): Init +4; Atk *+2 mace of chaos* +10 melee (1d6+6 plus 1d4 against lawful creatures) or claw +10 melee (1d8+4) or bite +12 melee (1d12); AC 20; HD 8d12; MV 40' or swim 40'; Act 2d20; SP disease, *detect good* (+8 spell check), demon traits; SV Fort +8, Ref +10, Will +8; AL C.

This is a larger, more powerful version of the minor toadfiend. It has a similar ability to cause disease with its touch.

Toadfiend Avatar (type IV demon, Bobugbubilz): Init +6; Atk claw +12 melee (dmg 3d8+6) or bite +16 melee (1d12+4 plus swallow); AC 22; HD 10d12; MV 60' or swim 60'; Act 2d20; SP disease, swallow whole, spells (+8 spell check): *detect good, choking cloud, scare*, demon traits; SV Fort +12, Ref +10, Will +12; AL C.

This is an enormous, dark-skinned toad covered in boils and barbs. It is the size of a small house with dangerous talons on its webbed feet and a maw large enough to swallow a horse whole.

If the toadfiend avatar succeeds in a bite attack, it can make another bite attack that same round to attempt to swallow the target. If the second bite attack succeeds, the target does not take damage but is now trapped in the toadfiend avatar's stomach, where it takes damage each round thereafter equal to 1d8 acid and 1d8 constriction. A trapped creature can try to cut its way out with a small weapon (such as a dagger) by inflicting 15 points of damage against AC 22.

A toadfiend avatar can cast *detect good, choking cloud,* and

Rank	Bobugbubilz, Demon Lord of Amphibians	Azi Dahaka, Demon Prince of Storms and Waste	Obitu-Que, Lord of the Five	Nimlurun, The Unclean One, Lord of Filth and Pollution	Free-willed / varying allegiances
Type I	Devil frog, barbed salamander	Hell viper	First eye of Obitu-Que: fear	Filth-eater	Lemure
Type II	Minor toadfiend	Sun scorcher	Second eye of Obitu-Que: revulsion	Rat demon	Bone demon
Type III	Toadfiend	Sandman	Third eye of Obitu-Que: domination	Excretor	Barbed demon
Type IV	Toadfiend avatar	Infernal hydra	Fourth eye of Obitu-Que: destruction	Giant infester	Succubus / incubus
Type V	*Unknown*	Cyclone	Fifth eye of Obitu-Que: oblivion	Plague demon	Pit fiend
Type VI	*Unknown*	*Unknown*	The five-eyed skeletor	*Unknown*	Balor

scare at a +8 spell check. Any creature wounded by a toad-fiend avatar must make a DC 20 Fort save or contract a debilitating disease. The disease manifests 1d7 days later as terrible shakes and shivers, inflicting a -4 penalty to Strength and Agility until cured by magical means.

Unique Demons

There are an infinite number of planes and a nearly infinite variety of demons. To assist the judge in creating interesting encounters, the tables below contain a few inspirational results for generating unique demons. Use the table "Demon Statistics Range by Type" to get a sense of attack modifier and saving throw DCs depending on the Hit Dice range required. Roll 1d3 times for the demon's base type, combining the results to create an interesting visual type. Then add 1d4-1 traits, 1d2 basic attacks, and 1d4-1 special attacks.

Table 9-11: Demon Base Type (roll 1d3 times)

d30	Base type
1	Beetle or ant
2	Mantis
3	Bee or wasp
4	Elephant
5	Camel
6	Goat
7	Cow / ox
8	Horse
9	Armadillo
10	Rhinoceros
11	Bear
12	Skeletal
13	Zombie
14	Goblinoid
15	Humanoid
16	Snake
17	Lizard or crocodilian
18	Spider
19	Crab
20	Frog / toad
21	Ape
22	Mechanical
23	Clay, dust, or dirt
24	Metal (mundane or precious)
25	Gemstone
26	Elemental (fire or ice)
27	Vampiric or lich-like
28	Dog / wolf / coyote / hyena
29	Lion
30	Turtle

Table 9-12: Demon Traits (roll 1d4-1 times)

d30	Trait
1	Enormous
2	Tiny
3	Barbs / spines
4	Hairy / hairless
5	Scaled
6	Armored (i.e., armadillo)
7	Beautiful
8	Tusks
9	Horns
10	Wings
11	Tall
12	Obese
13	Smelly
14	Covered in rot or vermin
15	Cloud of flies
16	Telepathic
17	Telekinetic
18	Chameleon-like
19	Many eyes
20	No eyes
21	Antennae
22	Incredibly strong
23	Highly intelligent
24	Slavering
25	Amphibious
26	Fins
27	Sail-back (like *Dimetrodon*)
28	Teleportation
29	Elastic limbs
30	Plant-like

Table 9-13: Demon Basic Attacks (roll 1d2 times)

d8	Basic Attack
1	Claw
2	Bite
3	Tail
4	Sting
5	Constriction
6	Gore
7	Charge
8	Kick

Table 9-14: Demon Special Attacks (roll 1d4-1 times)

d12	Special Attack
1	Poison*
2	Curse**
3	Drain ability score
4	Drain XP
5	Sleep
6	Paralysis
7	Possession
8	Drain blood
9	Spells***
10	Suffocation
11	Swallow whole
12	Breath weapon

* See Appendix P.

** See Appendix C.

*** Of wizard type. 1d4 spells of random level; spell check modifier equal to HD.

Demon Statistics Range by Type

Type	HD	AC	Attack modifier	Target save DCs for special attacks
I	1-4	10-15	+2 to +6	10-14
II	4-8	13-18	+6 to +10	14-18
III	6-12	15-20	+8 to +12	18-20
IV	8-16	18-23	+10 to +16	20-22
V	10-20	20-25	+12 to +18	22-24
VI	15-30	22-28	+20 to +24	25-27

DIMENSIONAL SAILOR

Dimensional sailor: Init +2; Atk cutlass +5 melee (1d8+1); AC 15; HD 1d8+2; MV 30′; Act 1d20; SP astral flicker (50% chance of evading non-magical attacks), plane shift 2/day; SV Fort +1, Ref +1, Will +4; AL N.

Dimensional sailors are thin blue-skinned humanoids from another dimension. They ride skiffs that float in the air. Each skiff carries 5-8 dimensional sailors, one of whom is a captain with double hit points and an extra +2 to initiative, attack, and damage. Up to 50% of crews also have a wizard, who can cast 1d4 level 1 spells at a +3 spell check.

Dimensional sailors can plane shift 2/day. They are often encountered at moments of surprise, as their flying skiff simply sails out of thin air.

Each dimensional sailor is armed with a cutlass and buckler. They typically raid small communities and will occasionally take back prisoners. In combat, a dimensional sailor constantly flickers between material and astral form, giving them a translucent and evanescent appearance. Any attack against the dimensional sailor with a non-magical weapon has a 50% chance of striking when the dimensional sailor was in its astral state and thus missing. Magical strikes cause damage even when the sailor is in its astral state.

DRAGON

Dragons are powerful winged reptilian creatures, each unique and rare. They live thousands of years, and as each dragon matures it develops traits that its sires may never have evinced. Draconic intelligence can in some cases greatly exceed human limits, and elder dragons are quite learned. Many dragons have a proclivity for magic, and as such learn to cast spells at or above human levels.

Most dragons are covetous, prideful, and solitary. They make their lair in caves, castles, monuments, and aeries, where they accumulate prized possessions. Even young dragons have voracious appetites, and older specimens are multi-ton predators. A dragon is always the alpha predator in its region, emerging from its redoubt periodically to feed and fly.

Any dragon appearing in your game should be named. These creatures are so rare and special that mortals of a given region never refer to "a dragon" — it is always "the dragon," always with a specific name, typically the only dragon to reside within 100 miles of that place. When one dragon enters the territory of another, there is always conflict. Only in the case of mated pairs do they ever cohabitate.

Some dragons serve greater purposes. A dragon may be allied with Law or Chaos, the Elder Ones, select demons, demi-human lords, or rarely, mortal kingdoms. Their solitary nature makes dragons unsuitable as leaders, but there are cases where they have inspired cults and worshipful alliances of their own.

Basic Traits: In game terms, each dragon is unique. Use the tables below to randomly determine a dragon or select as you consider appropriate. Roll once on each table (I through VIII) to build the dragon. The guidelines below give some additional information.

Hit dice: Dragons use a d12 for their Hit Dice, with the number of Hit Dice determined on Table I.

Actions: A dragon automatically receives one d20 action die for every attack shown on table II. This action die can only be used for attacks. *In addition*, a dragon has one or more action dice for spells, as shown on table IV. Finally, a dragon *also* has a breath weapon, as determined on table III. Its age, as seen on table II, determines how many times it can use its breath weapon per day. Each use of a breath weapon requires one action die.

Attack modifier: A dragon's attack modifier equals its Hit Dice plus a die roll, as shown on table I. This roll is made once and applies to all of the dragon's attacks. It has one or more attacks as shown on table II.

Damage dice: A dragon will have one or more attacks, depending on its age, as shown on table II. The attacks do progressively more damage, as follows:

- Claw attacks do 1d8 damage
- Bite attacks do 1d12 damage
- Tail slaps do 1d20 damage
- Wing buffets do 2d12 damage
- A crush, where a dragon slams its entire body onto an opponent, does 3d12 damage

Critical hits: Dragons have their own crit tables, as noted earlier. A dragon scores critical hits on a natural 20. Most dragons roll multiple action dice each round and tend to score a fair number of critical hits.

Initiative: A dragon's initiative modifier is equal to its Hit Dice.

Movement: A dragon's speed is shown on table I. A dragon flies at twice its speed. Select dragons may also be able to swim, dig, or climb at their normal speed or faster.

Saving throws: A dragon's saves are all the same, each equal to its Hit Dice.

Table I: Dragon Size

D20	Dragon Size	Hit Dice	Die Used for Age	Speed	Attack Bonus
1	Pseudodragon (cat-sized)	1d3	1d4	30'	HD+1
2-5	Small (size range from horse to elephant)	1d6+2	1d6	40'	HD+1d3
6-15	Average (size of small house)	1d8+4	2d4	50'	HD+1d4
16-19	Large (up to the size of a small keep)	1d10+6	3d4	60'	HD+1d6
20	Godlike (size of a castle or larger)	3d6+10	1d8+4	80'	HD+1d8

Table II: Dragon Age

Roll*	Dragon Age	HP per HD	Daily Breaths	Die for Spells**	AC	Attacks
1	Very young (1-5 years)	1	1	d4-2	10+HD	1 claw
2	Young (6-15 years)	2	1	d6-2	11+HD	1 claw, bite
3	Sub-adult (16-25 years)	3	1	d8-1	12+HD	1 claw, bite
4	Young adult (26-50 years)	4	2	d8+1	13+HD	2 claws, bite
5	Adult (51-100 years)	5	2	d8+2	14+HD	2 claws, bite
6	Old (101-200 years)	6	2	d10+2	15+HD	2 claws, bite, tail slap
7	Very old (201-400 years)	7	3	d10+4	16+HD	2 claws, bite, tail slap
8	Ancient (401-600 years)	8	3	d12+4	17+HD	2 claws, bite, tail slap, wing buffet
9	Wyrm (601-1,000 years)	9	3	d14+4	18+HD	2 claws, bite, tail slap, wing buffet
10	Great wyrm (1,001-2,000 years)	10	4	d16+4	19+HD	3 claws, bite, tail slap, wing buffet, crush
11	Elder wyrm (2,000-5,000 years)	11	5	d10+10	20+HD	4 claws, bite, tail slap, wing buffet, crush
12	Immortal (5,001+ years)	12	6	d12+10	21+HD	4 claws, bite, tail slap, wing buffet, crush

* Use die as determined on table I.

** Roll this die on table IV.

Table III: Dragon Breath Weapon

D14	Breath	Save*	Damage	Shape
1-2	Fire	Ref	As dragon's hit points or half with save	Line, width 10', length 3d6 x 10'
3-4	Cold	Fort	As dragon's hit points or half with save	Cone, width 1d4x10', length 1d6 x 10'
5-6	Acid	Fort	As dragon's hit points or half with save	Cone, width 1d6x10', length 1d4 x 10'
7-8	Electricity	Ref	As dragon's hit points or half with save	1-4 line forks, width 5', total length 3d6 x 10'**
9-10	Poison gas	Fort	Death or no effect with save	Cloud, radius 1d3 x 10', aimed up to 90' away
11-12	Sleep gas	Fort	Fall asleep for 1d6 hours, no effect with save	Cloud, radius 1d4 x 10', aimed up to 60' away
13	Steam	Fort	As half dragon's hit points or quarter with save	Cloud, radius 1d4 x 10', aimed up to 60' away
14	Smoke	N/A	No damage but remains for 1d6 rounds***	Cloud, radius 1d3 x 10', aimed up to 90' away

* Save DC is equal to the dragon's Hit Dice plus 10. For example, a dragon of 8 HD would have a breath weapon with a save DC of 18.

** A dragon with an electrical breath weapon can target up to 4 creatures, with the electrical blast forking from target to target, as long as a line traced from the dragon to each target in turn does not exceed the total length of the breath weapon.

*** Smoke breath weapons obscure the target point. The dragon can use this to prevent archers from seeing it, to clog visibility down a tunnel, to conceal an escape, and so on.

Table IV: Dragon Spell Use*

Roll**	Spell Action Dice	Spell Check	Spells by Level Level 1	Level 2	Level 3
0 or less	No spells	N/A	0	0	0
1-2	1d20	+2	1	0	0
3-6	1d20	+4	2	1	0
7	1d24, 1d20, 1d16	+4	2	2	2
8	1d12	+6	6	0	0
9-10	1d30	+6	3	3	3
11-12	1d30, 1d20	+6	2	2	0
13-14	1d20	+8	3	2	1
15-18	1d20	+10	4	3	2
19+	1d20	+14	5	4	3

* A dragon casts spells as a wizard. Determine known spells randomly according to the levels specified.

** Use die as determined by age, as shown on table II.

Table V: Dragon Martial Powers

A dragon receives one martial power for every full 4 Hit Dice it possesses.

d%	Martial Power
01-05	Additional breath weapon. The dragon has a second, randomly determined breath weapon attack.
06-10	Amphibious. The dragon can breathe water and swim effortlessly.
11-15	Armored hide. The dragon's AC is increased by an additional +4.
16-20	Barbed tail. The dragon receives an additional attack equivalent to a tail slap, which also causes poison damage (determine type from Appendix P).
21-25	Burrow. The dragon can "swim" through sand and dirt at its normal speed.
26-30	Damage reduction. The dragon's tough hide reduces the damage of all blows against it by 1d4 points (roll at time of creation).
31-35	Dive bomb attack. When fighting from the air, the dragon's first round of claw and bite attacks receive an additional +4 attack bonus and +d8 damage.
36-40	Fast reflexes. The dragon's Ref save is increased by an additional +4.
41-45	Frightful presence. The dragon's visage and sheer mass are absolutely terrifying. All who look upon it must make a Will save (DC 10+HD) or flee in terror (duration 1d4 turns or until reach a safe distance).
46-50	Hurl rocks. The dragon can use its claws to pick up and throw small boulders. The attack requires one action die and is treated as missile fire at the same attack bonus with a range of 100' for average size dragons, 200' for large dragons, and 300' for godlike dragons. The hurled stone does 1d12 damage.
51-55	Hypnotic stare. The dragon can hypnotize targets with its gaze. The dragon can gaze into the eyes of one target per round by using one action die. A creature that meets the dragon's gaze must make a Will save (DC 10+HD) or stand stupefied as long as the dragon holds its gaze.
56-60	Immunity. The dragon is immune to (roll 1d12) (1) poison, (2) fire, (3) cold, (4) electricity, (5) arrows and bolts, (6) curses, (7) paralysis, (8) sleep, (9) gas, (10) suffocation, (11) force attacks (i.e., *magic missile*), (12) sonic attacks.
61-65	Infravision 100'
66-70	Magic resistance. All spells cast against dragon subject to 50% chance of failure before saves are rolled.
71-75	Petrifying gaze. The dragon can petrify targets with its gaze. The dragon can gaze into the eyes of one target per round by using one action die. A creature that meets the dragon's gaze must make a Will save (DC 10+HD) or be permanently changed to stone.
76-80	Retinue. The dragon is always accompanied by a retinue of loyal followers (warriors, cultists, allies, and slaves); 1d4+4 followers of 1d4+2 HD each, armed with swords and chain mail (or equivalent weapons).
81-85	Rusting hide. The dragon's hide causes rust in all normal metal objects. As a result, its treasure horde consists primarily of gems and magical items. Weapons used to attack the dragon crumble to rust upon touch (although magic weapons are immune).
86-90	Snatch attack. On a successful claw attack, the dragon snatches a target. The dragon can snatch up to one target per claw attack and cannot make the corresponding claw attack while a creature is snatched. A snatched creature takes 1d6 crushing damage each round. The dragon can fly with snatched creatures and can drop the grabbed target from any height, causing 1d6 damage per 10' fallen. Snatched creatures can attempt to escape with a Strength check (DC of 10 + dragon's HD).
91-95	Throw spines. The dragon's hide is filled with barbed spines that can be hurled as an attack. This takes the place of one claw attack, and the attack is made at the same attack and damage roll with a range of 100'. A dragon has enough ammunition to throw up to 4 spine attacks per day.
96-100	Weapon-resistant hide. The dragon's armor is so thick that it takes half damage from mundane weapons. Magical weapons do normal damage.

Table VI: Dragon Unique Powers

A dragon receives one unique power for every full 3 Hit Dice it possesses. Using a unique power requires one action die normally reserved for attacks *or* spells. The DC to resist all powers is equal to 10+HD.

d%	Unique Power
01-03	**Bless (1/day).** The dragon can grant a boon to one creature equivalent to a +1 bonus to all rolls for 24 hours. More powerful dragons may be able to bless more creatures or for longer periods; some use this ability to emulate godhood.
04-06	**Cause earthquake (1/day).** The dragon can create an earthquake centered on a point within 500'. Earth shakes for several seconds. All nearby creatures take 1d3 buffeting damage. Creatures within 50' of the epicenter are tossed into the earth for a fall of 1d8 x 10' (with falling damage of 1d6 per 10' fallen). Creatures further away must make a Reflex save or also be tossed into the earth. Concentration of enemies is disrupted, waterways may be diverted, buildings are shaken, creatures may fall from ramparts, etc.
07-09	**Change shape (1/day).** The dragon can transform into another creature, assuming all physical traits of that creature. Creature type: (roll 1d6) (1) man, (2) lion, (3) woman, (4) lizard, (5) stallion, (6) bee.
10-12	**Charm (1/hour).** The dragon can charm one living creature. Target considers the dragon its closest friend for 1d4 days or until attacked or betrayed by the dragon. Will save resists.
13-15	**Charm reptiles (1/hour).** All reptiles within 100' become friendly to the dragon (Will save to resist).
16-18	**Clear passage (at will).** The dragon can pass through vegetation without leaving any trace.
19-21	**Control fire (3/hour).** The dragon can take control of mundane flames, such as torches and lanterns, and cause them to dance, extinguish, or expand; can create line of flame up to 40' long per round. A character touched by line of flame (including one holding a torch or lantern) is engulfed in flames for 1d6 damage plus an additional 1d6 per round. Reflex save each round to extinguish.
22-24	**Corrupt water (at will).** The dragon can turn all water within 100' poisonous (Fort save or lose 1d4 hit points per sip).
25-27	**Curse (1/day).** The dragon can curse one creature with a -1 penalty to all rolls for 24 hours.
28-30	**Darkness (at will).** The dragon can cloak an area of 30' radius into absolute darkness. Target any spot within 100'.
31-33	**Detection (at will).** The dragon can detect object of one type within 100' at will. Level of precision depends on age and ranges from very specific (i.e., exact size and quantity of object) to vague (directional only). Object of detection: (roll 1d10) (1) gold, (2) silver, (3) precious metals, (4) gems, (5) iron, (6) steel, (7) plants, (8) living creatures, (9) men, (10) dwarves.
34-36	**Dust cloud (1/turn).** The dragon can summon a dust cloud that is 10' wide at base and up to 50' tall. Targets within suffocate (Fort save or 1d4 Stamina loss per round). Cloud remains while dragon concentrates; when concentration ends, cloud disperses in 1d4 rounds, retaining full strength until dispersed.
37-39	**Earth to mud (1/hour).** The dragon can transform an area of earth into sticky mud. The area transformed can be up to 50' x 50' in size. The mud, up to 3' deep, slows movement to half speed for all within.
40-42	**Earth to stone (1/day).** The dragon can transform an area of earth into solid stone. The area transformed, up to 100' x 20' x 5', is permanently changed into stone.
43-45	**Gust of wind (1/day).** The dragon can generate powerful hurricane-strength wind, blowing in a single direction originating from the dragon in cone shape up to 100' wide at termination. Creatures must make Strength check or be blown backward a distance equal to the dragon's HD x 10 in feet, taking 1d4 damage for every 10 feet blown.
46-48	**Heat metal (3/hour).** The dragon can heat one metal object to painful levels. This ability inflicts 1d8 damage per round to characters holding heated objects or 1d10 damage per round to characters wearing heated armor.
49-51	**Ice walking (at will).** The dragon can walk across icy surfaces as if they were normal ground.
52-54	**Light (at will).** The dragon can bring full light of daylight into an area of 30' radius. Target any spot within 100'.

Table VI: Dragon Unique Powers (continued)

55-57 Locate object (1/day). The dragon can locate an object known to itself. It receives an unerring sense of direction toward the object and the approximate distance. The range of this ability is: (roll 1d6) (1) up to 100' on this plane; (2) up to 1 mile on this plane; (3) up to 10 miles on this plane; (4) up to 100 miles on this plane; (5) any distance, as long as the object is on this plane; (6) any distance, including other planes.

58-60 Luck giver (1/day). The dragon can grant a permanent bonus of +1 Luck to one creature every 24 hours. The same creature cannot receive this bonus more than once per month.

61-63 Neutralize poison (1/day). The dragon can cancel the effects of any one poison by touching the affected creature.

64-66 Plant growth (1/hour). All plants within 100' grow to twice their current size in 1d4 rounds; targets within growth are entangled (half speed, -2 to attacks).

67-69 Reverse gravity (1/day). The dragon can reverse gravity in an area 100' surrounding itself. The dragon itself is not affected, but all other creatures "fall" upward, suffering falling damage of 1d6 per 10' fallen if they hit a ceiling. If they are under open skies, they rise to 100' in the air before stopping and bobbing in place. The dragon can continue this effect while concentrating or reverse it by taking any action. When reversed, affected creatures fall back to earth and suffer falling damage again.

70-72 Speak with animals (1/hour). The dragon can designate one animal and communicate effectively in that animal's native tongue for the remainder of the hour. The animal still cannot communicate beyond the limits of its intelligence and physical abilities.

73-75 Spider climb (at will). The dragon can climb any surface as if it were a spider.

76-78 Summon allies (1/turn). Allies arrive in 1d4 rounds. Roll 1d8 for ally type: (1) insect swarm, (2) 1d2 large snakes, (3) 1d3 large crocodiles, (4) 1d6+2 wolves, (5) 2d6 humanoids of allied type, (6) 1d4 lions, (7) 1d4 type I demons, (8) 1d10 zombies.

79-81 Telepathic (1/hour). The dragon can read the surface thoughts of one creature within line of sight.

82-84 Teleport (1/hour). The dragon can transport itself plus up to three other creatures instantaneously. Target location must be a place the dragon has seen before; 10% of dragons can teleport to another plane. Distance covered: (roll 1d4) (1) up to 100', (2) up to 1 mile, (3) up to 10 miles, (4) up to 100 miles.

85-87 Turn invisible (1/hour). The dragon can become invisible for up to 1 turn.

88-90 Ventriloquism (at will). The dragon can throw its voice to any point within 200'

91-93 Wall of fog (1/hour). The dragon can summon a wall of fog at will. The wall is up to 100' x 20' x 100'. Within the fog, targets suffer -4 to all attacks and move at half speed.

94-96 Water walk (at will). The dragon can walk across surface of water as if it were ground.

97-99 The dragon possesses – and uses – a powerful magical artifact of a design up to the judge.

00 Roll again twice.

Table VII: Dragon Appearance

d30	Appearance	d30	Appearance
1	Amethyst	16	Mercury
2	Black	17	Misty
3	Blue	18	Multi-chromatic
4	Brass	19	Platinum
5	Bronze	20	Purple
6	Brown	21	Red
7	Cloudy	22	Salamander-like
8	Copper	23	Sapphire
9	Crystal	24	Shadow
10	Emerald	25	Silver
11	Faerie-like	26	Steel
12	Fish-like	27	Topaz
13	Gold	28	Turtle-like
14	Green	29	White
15	Lion-like	30	Yellow

Table VIII: Dragon Alignment

d6	Result
1-2	Lawful
3-4	Neutral
5-6	Chaotic

ELEMENTAL

Distant in time and space are the elemental planes, which the Elder Ones conjured first as the raw stuff from which all material creation is derived, including the prime material plane, the very substance of man, and the daily objects with which he interacts. The elemental planes stand outside the cycle of growth and decay, roiling and reconstituting the same elements in an eternal, ongoing genesis, with their only change being the steady ebb and flow of elemental energies to the material plane. Elementals are the living, pseudo-intelligent manifestations of their planes, composed of the primal elements with no pollution from other materials. For the most part they are neutral in nature, acting as would animals in a forest. Their planes do harbor other kinds of life, including elemental princes who have taken sides in the eternal struggle between law and chaos, other natives (such as water weirds, salamanders, fire snakes, aerial servants, and hell hounds), and intelligent rulers (such as djinni), but the elementals themselves remain pure.

There are four elemental creatures: fire, earth, water, and air. In the spaces between these planes dwell the four pseudo-elementals: ash, lava, ice, and mist. Other minor elementals also exist at the rarest intersections of the planes: dust, steam, and mud.

Elementals are common on their native planes but extremely rare on the material plane. They are encountered when conjured or summoned by a wizard, in proximity to the few natural vortices that allow passage to the elemental planes, in places where the dimensional fabric has been torn, and in extreme concentrations of the elements that are pleasing to their senses (e.g., great oceanic depths, veins of rare minerals, colossal tornadoes, and volcanic pits). In a few cases they wander naturally when summoned by a wizard who died without breaking the spell—these elementals are trapped and cannot return, but are also without a master.

All elementals share these traits:

- As extraplanar creatures, they are impervious to normal attacks. They can only be wounded normally by magic weapons, spells, other extraplanar denizens, or creatures with naturally magical attacks (including paralysis, sleep, poison, acid, breath weapon, etc.). Creatures of at least 4 HD are powerful enough to wound an elemental for half damage, and creatures of at least 6 HD can cause normal damage.

- A summoned or conjured elemental must be controlled by a wizard in order for its actions to be directed. The controlling wizard must concentrate. If his concentration is broken, he may lose control of the elemental. Free-willed elementals attack in a rage, targeting the creatures that have dealt them damage

or controlled them. After 1d6 rounds they return to their original plane if they are able to do so.

- A wizard can attempt to take control of a free-willed elemental by casting the appropriate spell. When it comes to controlled elementals, a wizard can attempt to wrest control from another wizard by casting *dispel magic* against the controlling wizard's source of control, then casting the appropriate spell to control the elemental himself.

- Elementals that appear on the material plane have 8, 12, or 16 HD, depending on the mode of summoning. Elementals on their native planes are even more powerful and may possess 20 or more HD. Elementals of 12 or 16 HD receive one extra action die. Elementals of 20+ HD receive two extra action dice.

Elemental, Air: Init +8; Atk slam +8 melee (2d6) or hurled object +8 missile fire (1d6, range 100'); AC 16; HD 8d8, 12d8, or 16d8; MV 50' (flight); Act 1d20 (or more); SP cyclone, pick up opponent, elemental traits; SV Fort +6, Ref +10, Will +6; AL N.

Air elementals are living gusts of wind. When calm they are no more than gentle breezes, nearly invisible in the open air, but when angered they manifest as whirling vapor, swirling clouds, and glowering cyclones. Air elementals always fly and can carry man-sized creatures within their winds. They are known to pick up their opponents (opposed Str check, treating elemental as Str 22) and drop them from great heights (1d6 damage per 10' fallen). In combat they lash out with buffeting winds or pick up nearby objects and hurl them as high-speed projectiles. Once per hour, an air elemental can take a round to whip its winds into a full-fledged cyclone. On the second round, after the cyclone is formed, the elemental transforms into a reverse cone, 10' wide at the bottom and up to 50' tall, with a width equal to its height. The cyclone lasts only 1 round, but during that time, everything touched by the elemental's normal course of motion takes 8d6 buffeting damage.

A desert elemental is a lesser-known variety of air elemental that also inflicts heat damage. Every round spent in contact with a desert elemental—whether in cyclone form or when it picks up a target—inflicts 1d3 points of heat damage, as well as the effects indicated above.

Elemental, Fire: Init +6; Atk burning touch +12 melee (3d6) or flaming bolt +8 missile fire (2d6, range 40'); AC 18; HD 8d8, 12d8, or 16d8; MV 40'; Act 1d20 (or more); SP burning touch, vulnerable to cold and water, elemental traits; SV Fort +8, Ref +8, Will +8; AL N.

Fire elementals are living towers of flame, showers of sparks, or roaring bonfires. The air around them is unbearably hot, and they set fire to anything they touch, scorching or melting even the toughest metals. Any creature which touches a fire elemental—whether wounded in combat or initiating a melee attack—may catch fire. Targets on fire must make a DC 16 Ref save or take 1d6 damage each round until the fire is extinguished with another DC 16 Ref save (+4 if "stop, drop, and roll", +2 if aided by allies). Fire elementals are immune to heat and fire-based attacks. They cannot bear the touch of water and will not pursue prey under water, through streams, across lakes, or into waterfalls. They take double damage from cold and water attacks.

Elemental, Water: Init +6; Atk slam +10 melee (2d6); AC 16; HD 8d8, 12d8, or 16d8; MV 40' or swim 80'; Act 1d20 (or more); SP engulf and drown, vulnerable to fire and heat, elemental traits; SV Fort +8, Ref +8, Will +8; AL N.

Water elementals appear as living, ambulatory ocean waves. When calm they are soft and flowing; when angered, they are churning whitecaps. A water elemental attempts to move over its opponents, engulfing them within its space. It can still slam engulfed targets as it buffets them within its waves, and when a target is engulfed it may begin to drown. An engulfed target attacks at -4 and must make an opposed Str check (against Str 20) to push its way out. For each round it starts engulfed, the target must succeed in a DC 16 Stamina check. When the first check fails, the target is drowning. Once drowning, the creature loses 1d6 points of Stamina per round. Water elementals are immune to water-based attacks. They cannot bear heat and fire and take double damage from those attacks.

Elemental, Earth: Init +4; Atk slam +12 melee (4d6); AC 20; HD 8d8, 12d8, or 16d8; MV 30' or dig 30'; Act 1d20 (or more); SP elemental traits; SV Fort +10, Ref +4, Will +8; AL N.

Earth elementals are stolid, plodding masses of earth and stone. The largest ones resemble living hills. They attack with methodical, ponderous punches of their stone-hardened fists. They can dig through solid earth and stone at a rate of 30', and their stony hide is difficult penetrate.

The prairie elemental is a little-known subspecies of earth elemental. It appears as a flat, featureless expanse of terrain—the same volume as its terrene counterparts but flattened—and has the magical ability to elongate distances. Every step taken on the surface of a prairie elemental covers the distance of only one-third of a normal step. A character must pass a Will save against the elemental's HD to realize the slowing effect.

EXTRADIMENSIONAL ANALOGUE

Extradimensional analogue: All stats as character except for one (see below); XP as character.

Your world reflects an infinite number of times across the cosmos, and within the parallel universes there exists at least one analogue of each player character. This extradimensional analogue is a nearly-perfect replica of the character, and in fact may *be* the character at a different place in the space-time continuum. Planar travel and dangerous magic can bring a character in contact with his extradimensional analogue. In other circumstances, a character may find not his analogue but that of a villain, nemesis, or competitor—leading to cases of mistaken identity that are cosmic in resolution.

Because extradimensional analogues are *the same person as the matching character*—just displaced in space or time—they find that they live nearly-identical lives, with only the "set" changing around them. When two or more analogues are placed on the same plane of existence, their fates are merged. In combat, any damage done to one also affects the other. Healing magic, as well as natural healing, is likewise shared. Only rarefied forms of magic—or a planar separation of some kind—can result in damage to one without affecting the other.

To generate an extradimensional analogue, start with a character or creature's normal stat block. Then roll 1d6 and consult the table below or design your own based on this inspiration:

d6	Result
1	Elemental analogue composed of (roll 1d5): (1) fire, (2) water, (3) air, (4) earth, (5) pseudo-element—roll additional 1d5: (1) ash, (2) lava, (3) ice, (4) mist, (5) meta-element—roll additional 1d3: (1) dust, (2) steam, (3) mud. Adjust statistics to reflect abilities, strengths, and weaknesses of a comparable elemental.
2	Future analogue identical to character but aged 6d20 years—potentially far beyond normal human limits based on the nature of time in the alien plane. Mental attributes are much more advanced.
3	Heroic analogue identical to character but presented with world-shattering risks which, by conquering, elevated analogue to position of global leadership. Much higher level and possessed of amazing weapons and fanatically loyal retinue.
4	Primordial analogue from a world before literacy or technology. The analogue is physically superior but bestial in nature.
5	Transplanted analogue from planet-hopping race whose native star died one billion years ago. Identical personality and mental traits but placed into bizarre rugose body.
6	Insane analogue from world of broken minds. Illogical and self-destructive traits.

GARGOYLE

Gargoyle: Init +0; Atk claw +4 melee (1d4); AC 21; HD 2d8; MV 30' or fly 30'; Act 1d20; SP resistant to non-magical weapons, stand still; SV Fort +5, Ref +0, Will +0; AL C.

Gargoyles are winged stony creatures in the shape of man. They need no air, food, or water to survive but are evil in disposition and seek prey because they take pleasure in inflicting pain. When standing still they are completely motionless, and it cannot be discerned whether one is alive or an inanimate statue. A gargoyle's body is composed of organic stone and is practically immune to normal weapons. Weapons of +1 or better enchantment inflict normal damage, but all other non-magical weapons inflict only half damage and shatter against their stony hide 50% of the time.

An undersea variety of the gargoyle is known as a kopoacinth. Kopoacinths use their wings to swim, much like a manta ray. In all other respects they are like their surface-dwelling kin.

GHOST

Ghost: Init +2; Atk special (see below); AC 10; HD 2d12; MV fly 40'; Act 1d20; SP un-dead traits, immune to non-magical weapons, 1d4 special abilities; SV Fort +2, Ref +4, Will +6; AL C.

Ghosts are the spirits of the dead who cannot rest. They typically appear as shimmering, translucent apparitions close in appearance to their mortal selves. A ghost retains its final emotional state, which, in most cases, is the state of rage or terror that immediately preceded its mortal death. As such, they are typically hostile to the living.

Despite their hostility, each ghost has its own reasons for retaining life in un-death, and yearns to be put to rest. Satisfying the conditions that have forced it into un-death can provide eternal rest to a ghost. A ghost that is put to rest immediately dissolves into the ether, going on to its final reward. Characters that put a ghost to rest earn XP as if they had defeated it and also receive a bonus of +1 Luck as the natural balance of life and death is restored to a small degree. Determine a ghost's rest condition by rolling 1d6 or create one appropriate to your campaign:

d6	Rest Condition
1	The ghost was murdered violently and yearns to avenge its death. Killing its murderer brings it to rest.
2	The ghost was buried apart from its spouse and wishes to be reunited with him or her. Disinterring its remains and reburying them with the spouse will bring it to rest.
3	The ghost died searching for its child. Bringing it to the location of its child — whether dead or alive — will bring it to rest.
4	The ghost was killed on a religious pilgrimage to a sacred location. Transporting its physical remains to that location will bring it to rest.
5	The ghost died in search of a specific object. Bringing the object to the ghost will bring it to rest.
6	The ghost died on a mission for a superior. The nature of this mission could be military (e.g., to invade a nearby fort), religious (e.g., slay a vampire or convert a certain number of followers), civilian (e.g., carry a signed contract to a neighboring king), or something else. Completing this mission will bring the ghost to rest.

Ghosts are incorporeal and can pass through walls and other solid matter. They cannot be harmed by physical weapons unless the weapon is magically enchanted. They are un-dead, and thus can be turned by clerics. Ghosts are immune to critical hits, disease, and poison. As un-dead, they are immune to *sleep*, *charm*, and *paralysis* spells, as well as other mental effects and cold damage.

Each ghost has 1d4 special abilities. Roll on the following table to determine them.

d10	Special Ability
1	Horrid appearance. Simply glimpsing the ghost causes 1d4 damage and potential fear (DC 12 Will save to resist). A frightened creature runs away for one hour; if cornered, it can fight only at a -4 attack penalty.
2	Rattling chains. The ghost is accompanied by a constant noise of rattling chains, which can be heard up to 100 yards away.
3	Banshee scream. The ghost attacks with a bone-chilling scream. Every living creature within 100' automatically takes 1d4 sonic damage and is potentially deafened for 1d4 hours (DC 12 Fort save to resist). The ghost can issue this scream up to 3 times per hour. Dogs, horses, and other domesticated animals are automatically spooked by the scream.
4	Paralyzing touch. Any creature touched by the ghost may be paralyzed for 1d4 hours (DC 14 Fort save to resist). The ghost attacks at +6 melee.
5	Future sight. Any creature that gazes into the ghost's eyes receives a shocking glimpse of a possible future. A character attacking the ghost must make a DC 10 Reflex save or inadvertently gaze into the ghost's eyes to receive this glimpse. This glimpse is always a potential death of the most disturbing fashion. The judge is encouraged to describe the vision as one associated with a potential future encounter in the current adventure.

When the character reaches that encounter, he suffers a -2 penalty to all rolls due to fright and fear of death.

6 Bestow a boon. Ghosts of lawful inclinations before their death may bestow a boon on characters of similar alignment. This typically takes the form of a remarkable weapon made of solid ether. The weapon lasts for only a short time but will prove invaluable in conquering a future foe. (Treat as a magical weapon of +1 to +3 enchantment, typically a sword or dagger, given to one character in the party. The weapon is engraved with a symbol that somehow specifies its use and vanishes once used.)

7 Turn invisible. At will, the ghost can turn invisible. It can return to visibility on any following round.

8 Draining touch. Any creature touched by the ghost loses 1d4 points of physical abilities (Strength, Agility, or Stamina). The character chooses which points are lost. The ghost attacks at +6 melee.

9 Possession. The ghost can possess the material body of one mortal creature. The ghost must touch the target (+6 melee attack). The target receives a DC 12 Will save; on a failure, the ghost vanishes into its body and takes over. The possessed creature can attempt to reassert control of its body once per hour thereafter with another DC 12 Will save. If the possessed creature is killed, the ghost is expelled from its body. but the target is really dead.

10 Telekinesis. At will, the ghost can manipulate up to 4 objects within 100', each weighing no more than 50 pounds.

GHOUL

Ghoul: Init +1; Atk bite +3 melee (1d4 plus paralyzation) or claw +1 melee (1d3); AC 12; HD 2d6; MV 30'; Act 1d20; SP un-dead traits, paralyzation, infravision 100'; SV Fort +1, Ref +0, Will +0; AL C.

A ghoul is a corpse that will not die. Granted eternal locomotion by means of black magic or demoniac compulsion, these un-dead beasts roam in packs, hunting the night for living flesh. They appear as ragged dead men and attack with ferocious biting and clawing.

A man-type creature bitten by a ghoul must make a DC 14 Will save or be paralyzed, unable to move or take any physical action for 1d6 hours. Elves are not affected by this paralyzation. A creature killed by a ghoul is usually eaten. Those not eaten arise as ghouls on the next full moon unless the corpse is blessed.

Ghouls do not make any noise whatsoever. They are un-dead, and thus can be turned by clerics. They do not eat, drink, or breathe, and are immune to critical hits, disease, and poison. As un-dead, they are immune to *sleep, charm,* and *paralysis* spells, as well as other mental effects and cold damage.

Smaller ghouls of 1 HD or less are formed from the corpses of goblins or kobolds, and larger ghouls of up to 8 HD are formed from the corpses of ogres, giants, bugbears, and such. There exists a marine form of a ghoul called a lacedon.

GIANT

Giants are enormous humanoids of prodigious strength. They have little interest in the affairs of mortals, regarding humans and their ilk as mere gnats unworthy of notice. There are many varieties of giants, from realms both mundane and extraordinary, and within their similar breeds they typically organize themselves in family clans. These clans bicker, engaging in violent skirmishes based on centuries-old scores and long-forgotten slights.

As archetypal creatures, giants are surely familiar to the judge and thus the entries below do not present much description: you are capable of embellishing as needed. With that said, the author recommends that the judge treat each giant as a unique individual, just as each human is unique. The entries below present the basic statistics for a *standard* giant of each breed; beyond that, the judge is encouraged to personalize each and every giant encountered, using the table below, the previous discussion on making humanoids distinctive, or the judge's own invention:

d12 Giant personal trait

1 Unusual hair: mohawk, braids, ponytail, topknot, corn rows, balding (possibly with a clumsy comb-over), etc.

2 Broken or missing front teeth

3 Bad acne (on a gigantic scale)

4 Broken nose

5 Buck teeth

6 Only one eye; other eye is covered by homemade patch

7 Noticeably long, dirty fingernails and toenails

8 Missing several fingers on each hand

9 Missing an arm, severed at the elbow

10 Unusual facial hair; i.e., handlebar moustache, mutton chops, goatee, etc.

11 Highly visible tattoos (face, arms, hands, or legs)

12 Unusually fragrant odor

Giants attack with staggering blows, and as such, routinely cause incredible amounts of damage. In game terms, giants attack with a d24 die (as noted below), and they cause critical hits on any natural attack roll of 20-24 that also exceeds the target's AC. Giants have their own special crit table, as noted previously. This means most giants will routinely score critical hits about 1 out of every 5 attacks. They are fearsome opponents!

Giant, hill (12' tall, 1,200 lbs.): Init -2; Atk club +15 melee (2d8+8) or hurled stone +6 missile fire (1d8+6, range 100'); AC 16; HD 8d10; MV 30'; Act 1d24; SP infravision, crit on 20-24; SV Fort +10, Ref +5, Will +6; AL C.

Giant, stone (14' tall, 1,500 lbs.): Init +1; Atk club +18 melee (3d8+10) or hurled stone +10 missile fire (1d8+10, range 200'); AC 17; HD 12d10; MV 40'; Act 1d24; SP infravision, 50% chance of 1-2 cave bear companions, crit on 20-24; SV Fort +12, Ref +6, Will +8; AL N.

Giant, frost (16' tall, 2,700 lbs.): Init +3; Atk axe +21 melee (4d8+8) or hurled stone +12 missile fire (2d8+8, range 300'); AC 18; HD 14d10; MV 50'; Act 2d24; SP immune to cold, double damage from fire-based attacks, 75% chance of companions (2-4 wolves, 0-1 polar bears), crit on 20-24; SV Fort +14, Ref +7, Will +11; AL C.

Giant, fire (12' tall, 5,000 lbs.): Init +3; Atk sword +22 melee (4d10+10) or hurled stone +8 missile fire (1d8+10, range 200'); AC 17; HD 16d10; MV 30'; Act 2d24; SP immune to fire, double damage from cold-based attacks, 10% chance of magical flaming sword (+1d6 damage), 25% chance of 1-3 hellhound companions, crit on 20-24; SV Fort +15, Ref +5, Will +8; AL C.

Giant, cloud (20' tall, 7,000 lbs.): Init +1; Atk mace +24 melee (4d8+12) or hurled stone +12 missile fire (2d8+10, range 300'); AC 20; HD 17d10; MV 50'; Act 3d24; SP create fog (3/day; fog cloud up to 100' x 20' x 100'; reduces visibility to 5'), levitate (1/day; self plus 1,000 lbs.; duration 1 hour at speed of 50'), 50% chance of companions (3-18 giant hawks and 1-4 lions or 2-8 dire wolves), crit on 20-24; SV Fort +12, Ref +6, Will +8; AL C.

Giant, storm (22' tall, 10,000 lbs.): Init +3; Atk sword +26 melee (5d8+12); AC 21; HD 20d10; MV 50'; Act 4d24; SP immune to electrical damage, able to breathe underwater, spells (+12 spell check: lightning bolt, levitate, and gust of wind), crit on 20-24; SV Fort +16, Ref +8, Will +12; AL N.

GNOLL

Gnoll: Init +0; Atk bite +1 melee (1d3) or as weapon +1 melee; AC 13; HD 1d8; MV 30'; Act 1d20; SP invoke patron (Ithha) at 1d12 or better; SV Fort +1, Ref +0, Will +0; AL C.

Gnolls are violent hyena-headed cavemen who worship the wicked elemental deities. Wearing animal furs and wielding blunt clubs, they drag captives back to their deep caves for sacrificial rituals too horrible to describe. Their tribes are led by shamans who ordain the rituals according to some indescribable calendar they infer from the constellations. Using special spell suites proscribed by their wicked gods, the shamans send forth wild-eyed gnolls on brutal raids. They are no friends to the other goblinoids, as they do not discriminate between man, elf, dwarf, orc, goblin, hobgoblin, kobold, troll, or bugbear when they require blood.

Gnoll shamans are treated as level 4 clerics who know evil elemental spells and are quick to invoke the powers of Ithha and other hideous elemental princes. All gnolls can invoke patron (Ithha) with a spell check of 1d12; gnoll shamans invoke patron (Ithha) with 1d20 + caster level (usually 4th). For every 10 gnolls there is a beta male as a level 2 warrior; for every 40 goblins there is an alpha male as a level 4 warrior.

GOBLIN

Goblin: Init -1; Atk bite -1 melee (1d3) or as weapon -1 melee; AC 10 + armor; HD 1d6-1; MV 20'; Act 1d20; SP infravision 60'; SV Fort -2, Ref +1, Will -2; AL L.

Goblins are small, crooked-faced, bendy-backed, two-legged man-things with gray, tan, brown, or green skin and yellow or red beady eyes. They live in caves, under large rocks, and in the ruins of civilized lands, being incapable of architectural accomplishments. They are inveterate cowards and avoid conflict at all costs, prostrating and genuflecting with slavering, whimpering protestations of innocence. Typically, they would rather run than fight unless accompanied by their greater evolutionary cousins, the bugbears and hobgoblins, who rule some goblin tribes and motivate them to aggression with lashes and beatings. If a goblin tribes' bugbear or hobgoblin leader is killed, goblins in combat must make a DC 16 morale check or rout.

Goblins can see in the dark to 60' and attack with a -1 penalty in bright light. One quarter of goblins ride dire wolves or hunt with them. Goblins fight with slings, clubs, or dull swords and are armored in padded, leather, or hide.

GRIFFON

Griffon: Init +2; Atk bite +9 melee (2d6) and claw +5 melee (1d6); AC 17; HD 7d10; MV 30', fly 80'; Act 2d20; SV Fort +7, Ref +8, Will +4; AL N.

A griffon is a large magical beast resembling a winged lion with the head and feet of an eagle. Their wingspan often exceeds 20' and they can weigh upwards of 500 pounds. Griffons live in vast nests high in remote aeries. They love the taste of horse flesh.

HARPY

Harpy: Init +0; Atk claws +3 melee (1d4); AC 13; HD 5d8; MV 20', fly 70'; Act 1d20; SP captivating song (DC 13 Will); SV Fort +2, Ref +3, Will +6; AL C.

A harpy is an old woman with monstrous traits: scaly skin, bat-like wings, and a mass of tangled black hair. Harpies live on ocean cliffs and can use an action to sing. All creatures within 300' must make a DC 13 Will save or walk toward the harpy in a hypnotized state. The hypnotized creatures use the most direct path and may walk off cliffs to their death. Those who reach the harpy stand motionless as long as the song continues and can only be roused by magical means or after 24 hours have passed. Harpies build nests where they lay their eggs. Such nests are laced with precious metals and worth 500 gp or more if recovered.

HELL HOUND

Hell hound: Init +2; Atk bite +4 melee (1d6+2) or breath weapon; AC 12; HD 2d6; MV 40'; Act 1d20; SP immune to damage from fire or heat; SV Fort +1, Ref +2, Will +1; AL L.

Hell hounds are large, lean black-furred dogs with a smell of brimstone about them. Their skin is painfully hot to the touch. They are common on the elemental plane of fire and certain pits of the abyss, but are very rare on the material plane. Typically they are encountered when summoned by a wizard or employed in the service of an extraplanar master, although some packs of wild hellhounds now dwell in hot springs, volcanoes, scorching deserts, and other climes they find favorable. They are immune to damage from fire or heat. In combat they bite and can also unleash a breath weapon once per hour. The breath weapon is a cone 10' wide at its end and 30' long. All within the breath weapon must make a DC 12 Ref save or take 2d6 fire damage.

HOBGOBLIN

Hobgoblin: Init +2; Atk sword +2 melee (1d8+2) or whip +2 melee (1d6 plus DC 14 Ref save or be entangled); AC 14 (scale mail); HD 1d8+2; MV 30'; Act 1d20; SP infravision 60'; SV Fort +1, Ref +1, Will -1; AL L.

Hobgoblins are the evolutionary superiors to goblins. They superficially resemble goblins in skin tone and facial features but stand straight and tall as a man, are intelligent, utilize manufactured armor and arms, and demonstrate a proclivity for military organization. They battle in formation, designating sergeants and lieutenants to serve under a general, with each officer commanding a band of conscripted goblins. Were it not for hobgoblins, the goblin race would rarely be encountered by man, but hobgoblins have a racial affinity to ruling goblins (much as an older brother can command his younger siblings), and goblins are loath to disobey them. The relationship is a strange mixture of respect and fear. Where bugbears rule by force alone, hobgoblins do instill discipline and trust in their goblin charges.

Usually there is one hobgoblin corporal for every 10-20 goblins. There are three or four hobgoblin corporals to a sergeant, who has 2 HD and attacks with a +4 bonus to attack rolls. For every two or three sergeants, there is a lieutenant with 4 HD and a +6 bonus to attack rolls. Above the lieutenants is a general, with 6 HD and +8 bonus to attack rolls.

Hobgoblins hate elves above all else and attack them on sight. They treat bugbears as rivals for leadership of their goblin minions.

HOLLOW ONE

Hollow man: Init +0; Atk dagger +2 melee (1d4); AC 12; HD 2d8; MV 30′; Act 1d20; SP spells as level 4 wizard (spell check +6); SV Fort +1, Ref +2, Will +6; AL L.

Hollow spawn: Init +0; Atk tentacle +6 melee (1d6); AC 16; HD 2d8 (in addition to hollow man); MV 30′; Act 1d20; SV Fort +6, Ref +2, Will +1; AL L.

The hollow one is as a self-animated marionette: the strange tentacled mass at its nucleus is the puppeteer, directing the actions of the empty man-like shell around it. A hollow one first appears as a tall, gaunt humanoid wearing dark robes. It can cast spells as a level 4 wizard and is typically encountered in some ancient shrine. When the humanoid is slain, its skin splits at the seams and the slithering tentacled hollow spawn bursts forth, lashing about with its pseudopods. Only when the man-like shell operates in concert with its strange core can the combined creature cast spells; the spawn alone is nearly mindless. Hollow ones are typically encountered in small sects differentiated by their robe colors: red, green, black, and white. Each order practices a different type of magic. All prefer to be left alone to worship their terrible gods and study unnamable secrets.

HORSES, MUNDANE

Donkey/Mule: Init -1; Atk bite -1 melee (1d2); AC 11; HD 2d8; MV 30′; Act 1d20; SV Fort +4, Ref +2, Will +2; AL N.

Horse: Init +1; Atk hoof +2 melee (1d4+2); AC 14; HD 3d8; MV 60′; Act 1d20; SV Fort +4, Ref +3, Will +1; AL N.

Pony: Init +1; Atk hoof -2 melee (1d2); AC 11; HD 1d8+2; MV 40′; Act 1d20; SV Fort +2, Ref +3, Will -1; AL N.

Warhorse: Init +1; Atk hoof +5 melee (1d6+3); AC 14; HD 4d8; MV 60′; Act 1d20; SV Fort +6, Ref +4, Will +2; AL N.

These statistics are for mundane mounts without barding or armor.

HYDRA

Hydra: Init +4; Atk bite +6 melee (1d10+4); AC 16; HD 1d10 (7 hp) per head; MV 20′, swim 40′; Act 1d20 per head; SP 5-12 heads, crit on 19-20, regeneration of heads at 2x rate, heal 1 hp/round per remaining head; SV Fort +9, Ref +7, Will +5; AL C.

The hydra is a multi-headed reptile with four legs and a tail, typically residing in swamps, bogs, marshes, and oceanic environments. Each head can bite independently, and a hydra has from 5 to 12 heads (or, rarely, even more!). For each head, it receives 7 hit points (counting as a 1d10 Hit Die) and a bite attack with a 1d20 action die. Each head crits on a natural roll of 19-20; with so many heads and an extended threat range, hydras tend to score multiple crits.

Track a hydra's hit points in 7-hp increments. For example, if you had a 6-headed hydra, jot down its hit points like this:

Head 1: 7 hp

Head 2: 7 hp

Head 3: 7 hp

Head 4: 7 hp

Head 5: 7 hp

Head 6: 7 hp

For every 7 hit points of damage incurred by a single-weapon strike, one head is severed, and damage in excess of 7 hp on the last strike is lost. For example, a single sword blow inflicting 9 hit points of damage severs one head for 7 hp, and the remaining 2 hp "overflow" is lost. Area of effect attacks (such as a *fireball*) can damage more than one head at once, and do not lose overflow damage.

For every severed head, the hydra loses that head for two rounds…then on the third round following, two *new* heads grow from the old stump, and the hydra gains 14 hit points (two sets of 7 hp each). This regeneration can only be prevented by severing the heads with fire or acid.

Finally, all remaining hydra heads heal damage at the rate of 1 hp per round.

Up to 10% of hydras are pyrohydras, which can breathe fire. Every 1d4 rounds, all heads will let loose with a flaming jet, which attacks at +10, range 50', for 3d6 damage. Targets must make a DC 16 Reflex save or catch fire for another 1d6 damage per round until they pass a subsequent Reflex save. Pyrohydras are immune to fire and the stumps of their severed heads cannot be stopped from regenerating with fire, but cold will work.

Up to 5% of hydras are cryohydras, which can breathe frost. Every 1d4 rounds, all heads send out a jet of frost, attacking at +8, range 30', for 2d6 damage. Cryohydras take double damage from fire and are immune to cold.

Prime hydras can shoot jets of fire *or* cold, are immune to fire *and* cold damage, can have their head-stumps stopped only by acid damage, and typically have at least 20 heads.

INSECT SWARM

Insect swarm: Init +5; Atk swarming bite +1 melee (1 plus sting); AC 11; HD 4d8; MV fly 40'; Act special; SP bite all targets within 20' x 20' space, half damage from non-area attacks, sting (DC 5 Fort save or additional 1d4 damage); SV Fort +0, Ref +10, Will -2; AL N.

An insect swarm is a mass of flying wasps, ants, horseflies, bees, or other such noxious pests. The swarm occupies a 20' x 20' space and inflicts its bite damage on everyone within that space. Any creature bitten must make a Fort save or also suffer from a sting. Swarms take half damage from any attack that is not an area effect (i.e., swinging a sword is not nearly as effective as launching a *fireball* into the swarm).

IRON SHADOW

Iron shadow: Init -2; Atk slam +3 melee (1d6+2); AC 22; HD 2d8+4; MV 15'; Act 1d20; SP immune to critical hits; SV Fort +6, Ref +1, Will +0; AL L.

Cast from unknown molds in the perfect shape of man, iron shadows are ponderous 8-foot-tall living statues weighing thousands of pounds. They stand motionless until exposed to the light of the moon, at which point they lurch forward to patrol their station against intruders. The secret of their manufacture is now lost, though they are still found in ruins, guarding secrets long passed. Some iron shadows are also animated by torchlight and other light sources; the unwitting adventurer who brings one to life with his lantern need only extinguish his light source to survive.

KILLER BEE

Killer bee: Init +1; Atk sting +3 melee (1d4 + poison); AC 12; HD 2d8; MV fly 30'; Act 1d20; SP poison (DC 8 Fort save or death); SV Fort +2, Ref +3, Will +1; AL L.

The killer bee is a large dog-sized creature with a lethal sting. Killer bees usually appear in groups of 5-10 and are feared due to their poison. Although not particularly effective against an armored opponent, the sting of a killer bee frequently causes instant death against targets sensitive to the poison.

KOBOLD

Kobold: Init +1; Atk tiny sword -2 melee (1d4-1); AC 11; HD 1d4; MV 20'; Act 1d20; SP infravision 100'; SV Fort -2, Ref +0, Will -2; AL N.

Kobolds are rusty-skinned dog-headed demi-humans who despise fey. They hail from the deep pits underneath the lands of pixies, nixies, sprites, brownies, gnomes, and leprechauns. Some wizards believe kobolds are the reincarnations of damned fey. Kobolds associate elves with their fey enemies and seek to ambush and torture them.

A tall kobold stands barely four feet tall, with sharp teeth, pert horns, hideous red eyes, and clothing that tend toward warm hues. In their natural state, kobolds are squabbling, noisy creatures, and on the material plane they live in squalid swamps, oppressively dank jungles, and claustrophobic tunnels. However, they are sociable, at least with their own kind; kobolds are never found in numbers smaller than thirty, and they often live in overcrowded warrens with hundreds of occupants, including domesticated boars and weasels, as well as large incubation chambers for kobold eggs and young. For every thirty kobolds there is a leader and two guards with 6 hp each. For every hundred kobolds, there is a tribal leader with 9 hp and his retinue of five guards.

Kobolds have infravision to 100' but suffer a -1 penalty to attacks in bright light.

LEECH, COLOSSAL

Leech, colossal: Init -2; Atk bite +4 melee (1d6 plus blood drain); AC 14; HD 2d8; MV 10' or swim 30'; Act 1d20; SP blood drain (automatic 1d4 dmg per round after bite); SV Fort +4, Ref -2, Will -4; AL N.

Colossal leeches are bred by evil warriors to guard their fetid keeps and castles. The leeches live in moats, where they lurk below the water's brackish surface waiting for prey. When they sense vibrations, they converge on the source and thrash about violently, attempting to latch onto a target with a bite. Once they succeed in a bite, they automatically drain blood to cause an additional 1d4 damage each round until slain.

LIVING STATUE

Living statue: Init +6 (surprise); Atk weapon +3 melee (1d8); AC 14 (crystal), 16 (stone), 18 (iron); HD 2d8 (crystal), 3d8 (stone), 4d8 (iron); MV 30'; Act 1d20; SP surprises 50% of time; SV Fort +4, Ref -2, Will -2; AL N.

A living statue is an animated guardian programmed with simple instructions. It is completely motionless and causes surprise 50% of the time, even if the characters suspect its true nature. When causing surprise, the living statue receives a free attack then also uses its high initiative modifier to determine combat order. Living statues are only as intelligent as simple robots and can obey only the most basic instructions, typically related to guarding a location. The statue's material determines its combat statistics.

LIZARD, GIANT

Lizard, giant: Init -3; Atk bite +5 melee (3d4); AC 17; HD 3d8; MV 40' or climb 20'; Act 1d20; SP camouflage; SV Fort +2, Ref -2, Will -2; AL N.

The giant lizard is found in many varieties. Crocodiles guard the bogs, iguanas hang from trees, and geckos traverse cave walls. Regardless of type, all giant lizards are masters of camouflage—they receive a +10 bonus to all attempts at hiding.

LIZARDMAN

Lizardman: Init -2; Atk bite +3 melee (1d4 and roll) or club +2 melee (1d4); AC 14; HD 1d8; MV 30' or swim 30'; Act 1d20; SP roll, move silently; SV Fort +2, Ref -1, Will -1; AL N.

Lizardmen are the furtive, silent witnesses of the swamp. Hermitic by nature and living only in small family groups, they glide silently twixt the hollow reeds, slitted eyes watching eternal. When a fox is lamed, a fish trapped, or a man mired, the lizardman creeps forth to drag it into the shallow mud, gummy slavering jaws submerging its victim's last breath beneath the gurgling muck.

A lizardman moves silently in swamp or water (treat as +10 to all checks related to stealth). It attacks with a blunt-toothed bite. Any creature hit by the bite must succeed on an opposed Strength check. For purposes of this check, the lizard man's prognathous jaw and powerful bite grant it a +8 modifier. If the lizard man wins, it rolls the target under water. While trapped in this manner, the victim begins drowning. Each round the target takes 1d6 temporary Stamina damage. When Stamina is reduced to 0, the target dies. A lizardman occupied in this manner cannot attack other targets, and the ensnared victim can attack only at a -4 penalty.

Lizardmen hunting parties consist of 1d3+1 blood-related adults. There is a 25% chance they are accompanied by a tamed giant snake or giant crocodile (treat as giant lizard). Five percent of lizardmen are shamans (treat as 1st- or 2nd-level clerics).

MAN-BAT

MANTICORE

Man-Bat: Init +4; Atk bite +6 melee (1d6); AC 12; HD 2d8; MV 20', fly 40'; Act 1d20; SP carry off prey; SV Fort +1, Ref +4, Will +2; AL C.

Manticore: Init +5; Atk bite +6 melee (1d8) or claw +4 melee (1d3); AC 16; HD 6d8+6; MV 40', fly 50'; Act 3d20; SP tail spikes or barbed tail; SV Fort +5, Ref +4, Will +6; AL C.

Called chiropterans in their own language, but "man-bat" by all others, these demi-humans have two legs, rotund hairy bodies, and bat-like wings in place of arms. Their faces are a cross of human and bat, with large ears, flaring noses, and black, brown, or gray fur. They stand eight feet tall and have a 20' wingspan but weigh only a little more than a normal man. Chiropterans speak their own, subsonic tongue, and are incapable of normal speech. They feed indiscriminately and attack lone travelers opportunistically.

The manticore is a lazy predator that eschews battle in favor of opportunistic meals. It has the body of a lion, great bat-like wings, and the face of a bearded man. It craves the taste of man-flesh, and willingly attacks women and children, lone travelers, and the wounded survivors of battle—but is not often found seeking a meal from mail-armored swordsmen. It typically follows demi-human hunting parties, only to alight and steal their kills before they can react.

A man-bat utilizes sonar and thus is not affected by blindness or darkness. It typically attacks from the wing. A man-bat that scores a hit can attempt to carry off its prey by making an opposed Strength check at Str 16; if successful, the prey is captured in the man-bat's legs and lifted off the ground. Captured prey can still attack at a -2 penalty; a man-bat cannot make additional bite attacks while thus encumbered and moves at half speed in these circumstances. A dropped creature takes 1d6 damage for every 10' fallen.

Fifty percent of manticores have iron tail spikes embedded in their lion-tails. As a single action, the manticore can loose a volley of 6 tail spikes, which attack at +6 missile fire (range 100') for 1d6 damage each. A manticore can release four such volleys per day.

The other 50% of manticores have barbed scorpion-tails. In combat, they can use an action to lash out with a single tail strike per round at +8 melee (1d10 + poison). The poison requires a DC 16 Fort save or the target loses 1d6 Stamina with each strike.

Up to 10% of chiropterans have a vampiric bite that drains 1 XP with each bite (DC 14 Will save to resist). Prime chiropterans have double HD and two extra arm-wings (lifting at Str 22), as well as enormous gaping mouths with expanded vampiric abilities (drain levels, ability scores, magical ability, etc.).

MINOTAUR

Minotaur: Init +8; Atk gore +8 melee (1d8+4) or axe +8 melee (1d10+4); AC 15; HD 6d8+6; MV 30'; Act 2d20; SP bull charge, never surprised; SV Fort +6, Ref +8, Will +2 (see below); AL C.

Minotaurs are mighty bull-headed men created with divine purpose. They do not reproduce naturally and are rarely encountered in places not preordained by the gods. Little do the minotaurs understand their great purpose other than to rend, gore, and kill— functions they serve admirably.

A minotaur initiates combat with a powerful bull rush ending in its gore. This counts as a special charge: in addition to a +2 attack bonus and a -2 AC penalty, the minotaur gets an extra 1d8 damage (for total of 2d8+4), and the target must make an opposed Strength check (treat the minotaur as Str 24) or be hurled back 20'.

Minotaurs are never surprised and are utterly fearless. They are not smart but are cunning, like a hunting predator. Minotaurs are resistant to spells that affect their mental faculties (such as *charm, scare,* and so on), receiving an additional +6 bonus to Will saves against these spells.

MUMMY

Mummy: Init +0; Atk choke +5 melee (1d4 / 2d4 / 3d4 / etc.) or club +3 melee (1d6+2); AC 11; HD 8d12+8; MV 20'; Act 1d20; SP damage reduction 5, mummy rot, vulnerable to fire, un-dead traits; SV Fort +4, Ref +2, Will +10; AL C.

Draped in funereal wraps with misshapen lumps of preserved flesh shifting within, the mummy is a corpse preserved into un-death by strange oils, dangerous spices, and unknowable chants.

Mummies are ponderous and slow, cloaked only in ancient wraps, but their torsos are half-dust inside the crumbling linen. Strikes against them often find only empty spaces or rotted organs no longer of use; thus, they resist the first 5 points of damage caused by any strike.

A mummy typically wields a bludgeoning instrument of some kind and seeks to choke out the life of its target after closing the distance. A mummy that succeeds on a choke attack uses one or both hands to throttle its target. On the first round, this causes 1d4 points of suffocation damage. If the mummy succeeds in a second round of choking, the next attack causes 2d4 damage. If the third attack succeeds for a third round, the attack causes 3d4, then 4d4, and so on until either the mummy's attack fails or the target is suffocated.

Any creature that takes damage from a mummy may contract mummy rot (DC 12 Fort save). Mummy rot causes the victim's body to slowly shrivel and desiccate. Affected creatures take 1 Stamina damage each day and are constantly thirsty. The Stamina damage will not heal naturally until the rot is arrested by magic.

Mummy wraps are dried from years of subterranean exposure, so mummies take double damage from fire.

Mummies are un-dead, and thus can be turned by clerics. They do not eat, drink, or breathe, and are immune to critical hits, disease, and poison. As un-dead, they are immune to *sleep, charm,* and *paralysis* spells, as well as other mental effects and cold damage.

OGRE

Ogre: Init +2; Atk slam +5 melee (1d6+6) or great mace +5 melee (1d8+6); AC 16; HD 4d8+4; MV 20'; Act 1d20; SP bear hug; SV Fort +4, Ref +2, Will +1; AL C.

A gray-skinned ape with short legs, long arms, rotund torso, and the thick-featured face of a man, the ogre is a stupid bully easily conquered with guile. Living in fetid caves littered with bones, ogres scavenge and terrorize, but never plan further than their next meal. Their prodigious strength is put to use by the clever and the brave, who beguile them with promises of rich feasts and richer plunder. When not alone in their lairs, ogres serve as men-at-arms and mercenaries with the armies of giants, sorcerers, and desperate kings.

In single combat, an ogre grasps its enemy in a mighty bear hug to break his spine. If an ogre lands a slam successfully, its opponent must succeed at an opposed Strength check against the ogre's 22 Strength (+6). Failure means he has been trapped in a bear hug. Each round thereafter, the ogre automatically inflicts another 1d6+6 damage. The victim can attempt to escape each round with another Strength check on his action.

ORC

Orc: Init +1; Atk claw +1 melee (1d4) or as weapon +1 melee; AC 11 + armor; HD 1d8+1; MV 30'; Act 1d20; SV Fort +2, Ref +0, Will -1; AL C.

Orcs are brutish humanoids created in magical cauldrons by a long-dead wizard. They are a product of dark sorceries and sutured body parts. Once commanded by a great general, orcs now wander the wilderness in small bands, raiding and squabbling, never settling. They have piggish faces with tusked mouths and green or grey skin. Female orcs are as muscular as the males. Orcs are always prepared for war, wielding maces, bows, swords, axes, and shields, with armor of chain or plate. Every band has a boss with 4d8+4 HD and an attack bonus of +4. Bands with more than 30 orcs also have a witch doctor of 2d8 HD who knows 1d4 1st-level cleric spells and 1d3-1 2nd-level spells at a +3 spell check. Prime orcs are enormous and powerful, up to triple HD with an additional +4 bonus to attack and damage rolls from their earthy strength.

OWLBEAR

Owlbear: Init +1; Atk bite +6 melee (1d6+2) or claw +4 melee (1d4); AC 17; HD 3d8; MV 20' or climb 10'; Act 2d20; SP spell resistance; SV Fort +4, Ref +1, Will +8; AL C.

The transmogrifier and teratologist Xultich bred abominations in his laboratories. Loosed upon the grounds of his villa, some multiplied and thrived. The owlbear is one such success story. With the mighty-thewed body of a grizzly and the craggy beak, wings, and eyes of an owl, it is a ferocious predator. Owlbears cannot fly but do climb, and they prefer to attack from a position of height. Their sorcerous legacy grants them a natural defense against magic: they resist all magic, regardless of level or caster, with a 25% chance of success and gain a +8 on Will saves against spells that do affect them.

PRIMEVAL SLIME

Primeval slime: Init (always last); Atk pseudopod +4 melee (1d4); AC 10; HD 1d8 per 5' square; MV 5', climb 5'; Act 1d20 per 5' square; SP half damage from slicing and piercing weapons; SV Fort +6, Ref -8, Will -6; AL N.

Man evolved from croaking protoplasm, and his descendents still crawl amidst the murky swamps and tenebrous caves. Primeval slimes come in many varieties, none of them safe, all of them oozing slowly in search of organic matter suitable for dissolution.

Known to peasants as oozes, jellies, puddings, or slimes, these things are typically a few centimeters or inches thick and up to a quarter-mile in size. Most cover an area of 50 or 100 square feet but can ooze through openings as narrow as one centimeter. Some are lumpy masses many feet in depth or are cubic in shape. All can cling to vertical surfaces and hang upside-down.

For every 5' x 5' square, a slime has 1d8 hit points and can deploy one pseudopod in its defense. Slimes suffer half damage from slicing and piercing weapons (swords, daggers, arrows, axes, etc.), as their primordial mass quickly re-knits such wounds. They may be vulnerable to other attacks, as indicated below.

Roll 1d8 to determine a primeval slime's color: (1) yellow, (2) green, (3) red, (4) ochre, (5) black, (6) gray, (7) tan, (8) clear.

A slime has 1d4-1 special properties. Roll 1d10 to determine them randomly:

Roll	Ooze Special Property
1	Acidic touch. Pseudopods do an additional 1d6 damage. Additionally, any creature that steps on the slime takes 1d6 damage. The slime will attempt to move over adjacent targets and engulf them. Targets engulfed take 1d6 damage and cannot escape or take any action without making an opposed Strength check against the slime (treat the slime as Str 12 + 2 per 5' section).
2	Paralyzing touch. Pseudopod's or slime's touch requires target to make DC 14 Fort save. Failure causes paralysis for 1d6 hours.
3	Sticky. Any creature touched by the slime must make a DC 15 Str check to pull away. Stuck creatures attack at a -2 penalty to attack rolls and are dragged along by the slime until they pull free. The sticky skin of the slime is encrusted with 2d4 random objects picked up in its travels.
4	Protoplasmic breakdown. The slime digests its food by emitting acidic juices on contact. Any creature that contacts the slime (including by attack from a pseudopod) temporarily loses 1d4 Stamina from the digestive juices. A creature that reaches 0 Stamina is immediately killed.
5	Metal digestive. Any metal weapon touched by the slime or that strikes the slime is damaged. A weapon is rendered useless after one touch and metal armor loses one "plus" to Armor Class every round of contact. Magic items receive a save against DC 12 (add the weapon's "plus" to the d20 roll).
6	Rapid reproduction. For every 5 hit points of damage inflicted by the slime, its area grows by another 5'x5' and it gains 5 hit points.
7	Sensitive to light. The ooze is either drawn to light or takes 1 point of damage per round of exposure (50% chance of either).
8	Psionic. The ooze has a latent, primitive intelligence. It hurls mental blasts against nearby targets in an attempt to subdue them. Each round it gains a new action, which is a psychic blast. It can target any living creature within 100' with a psychic blast. A creature struck by the psychic blast must make a DC 14 Will save or take 1d6 points of damage as it reels back in intense mental pain, nose and ears bleeding from the pressure within its cranium.
9	Takes double damage from one source. Roll 1d6: (1) fire; (2) cold; (3) acid; (4) lightning; (5) force energy (e.g., *magic missile*); (6) necromancy (e.g., *chill touch*).
10	Immune to one kind of attack. Roll 1d6: (1) fire; (2) cold; (3) acid; (4) lightning; (5) force energy (e.g., *magic missile*); (6) necromancy (e.g., *chill touch*).

PTERODACTYL

Pterodactyl: Init +2; Atk bite +8 melee (1d10) or claw +2 melee (1d4); AC 15; HD 6d8; MV 10' or fly 50'; Act 1d20; SV Fort +6, Ref +5, Will +2; AL N.

These great flying lizard-creatures have a 25' wingspan and are often used as mounts by fiendish wizards.

RAT, GIANT

Rat swarm: Init +4; Atk swarming bite +1 melee (1 plus disease); AC 9; HD 4d8; MV 40' or climb 20'; Act special; SP bite all targets within 20' x 20' space, half damage from non-area attacks, disease (DC 5 Fort save or additional 1d3 damage); SV Fort +2, Ref +4, Will -2; AL N.

Rat, giant: Init +4; Atk bite +2 melee (1d4+1 plus disease); AC 13; HD 1d6+2; MV 30' or climb 20'; Act 1d20; SP disease (DC 7 Fort save or additional 1d6 damage); SV Fort +4, Ref +2, Will -1; AL N.

Rats are found in swarms by the hundreds or as giant specimens in packs of a dozen or more.

SCORPION, GIANT

Scorpion, giant: Init +3; Atk claw +12 melee (1d10+4) or sting +7 melee (1d6+2 plus poison); AC 18; HD 12d10+12; MV 50' or climb 30'; Act 3d20; SP poison (DC 15 Fort save or death in 1d4 rounds); SV Fort +9, Ref +4, Will -2; AL N.

The clicking, clacking, and snapping noises made by the armor-jointed, massive-clawed giant scorpion patrolling its native desert sands are feared by all creatures. This enormous predator, with a leg-span exceeding 40 feet, is king of its domain, surviving by both scavenging and aggressively pursuing anything that appears edible, whether man or beast.

SERPENT-MAN

Serpent-man: Init +1; Atk bite +3 melee (1d4 + poison DC 14 Fort) or as weapon +3 melee; AC 12 + armor; HD 1d10+2; MV 30'; Act 1d20; SP illusion 1/day, hypnosis; SV Fort +2, Ref +1, Will +2; AL L.

The serpent-men walk amongst us. Once vanquished millennia ago by the Elder Race, these secretive snake-headed men now lead cults of Set, god of serpents, within the cities of man. They use magic to take the form of humans, and in this guise rule their Shadow Kingdom—the secret government of serpent-man imposters who assassinate and then impersonate dukes, kings, and earls throughout the land. Their true form is revealed upon death, when their illusionary human features revert to a serpent's head. Until then, the only way to detect a serpent-man imposter without magic is to state a certain primordial phrase known to their ancient druidic enemies—a phrase which the jaws of a true man can pronounce, but which the bones of a serpent-man's mouth cannot form.

Serpent-men have human bodies with snake's heads. Once per day, a serpent-man can cast an illusion that causes its head to appear like that of a specific person. The illusion is complete—visual, tactile, auditory, olfactory—and is considered to have a spell check result of 30 for purposes of dispelling or disbelieving. The snake-man can reveal his true form if he so wishes.

A serpent-man can hypnotize lesser creatures. Any intelligent creature that looks into the serpent-man's eyes is susceptible. The hypnosis works even when the serpent-man is under illusion. The serpent-man casts the hypnosis at a +6 spell check; the victim must succeed on an opposed Will save or be under the control of the serpent-man. Hypnotized creatures appear as in a daze and will perform tasks as commanded. Any suicidal or dangerous task allows a new Will save to resist. The hypnosis fades after 1d4 hours.

Serpent-men fight with weapons and if revealed, with their bites, but they prefer skullduggery to combat. Serpent-man poison varies by individual; 25% cause blindness, 25% cause weakness (1d6 Str loss), and 50% cause painful spasms (1d6 damage).

Serpent-men are led by wizards of 3rd, 4th, or 5th level who specialize in illusions.

SERVITOR

Servitor: Init +4; Atk claw +6 melee (paralysis) or bite +1 melee (1d3); AC 16; HD 1d8+4; MV 40'; Act 2d20; SP paralysis (DC 16 Fort, duration 1d4 days), *cantrip* (spell check +4); SV Fort +3, Ref +6, Will +8; AL C.

Servitors are devilish creations of the Chaos Lords sent to serve their masters' ends. Servitors are never found alone but are always in small groups accompanying a necromancer, pagan, or warlock sent to adventure in service of Chaos. They appear as rotund little humanoids embellished with a myriad of sharp claws, barbs, spines, and teeth. They rarely weigh more than 20 pounds and are absolutely loyal to the creature their Chaos Lords assign them to, fighting to the death until reassigned. They can cast *cantrip* at will (never lost) with a +4 spell check and fight with a paralyzing claw, which they follow up on by gnawing on their paralyzed foes.

SHADOW

Shadow: Init +3 (able to always surprise); Atk debilitating touch +8 melee (1 Str); AC 17; HD 6d8; MV fly 40'; Act 1d20; SP stalk prey to guarantee surprise, incorporeal, immune to non-magical weapons, un-dead traits; SV Fort +5, Ref +10, Will +8; AL N.

In the hoary depths of the Nine Hells, vengeful lich lords send damnable vassals on mortal errands. Thus born is the shadow: a simple-minded un-dead that materializes in the crepuscular hours lit by neither sun nor moon. The shadow appears as a blotchy outline of a man or beast arcing from no light source. It moves across the ground or walls, as a normal shadow would, but without deference to any sun, star, moon, or torch—a shadow is literally unaffected by light. It attaches itself to its intended prey, merging with the creature's natural shadow, and sometime at dusk or dawn the adventurer becomes aware of a second shadow originating from their person—a trail of shade that misbehaves, that momentarily lags behind his actions, or manifests horns, or which walks when he stands and stands still when he walks. A time of terror then follows, until the tenebrous stalker finally lashes out at its prey.

A shadow typically stalks its target for many hours, merging with its natural shadow. Prior to the un-dead creature revealing itself, the target has a 5% chance per hour of noticing its natural shadow "misbehaving." This chance increases to 25% at dusk or dawn or at other times of less-than-natural light, including flickering torchlight and other environments where the shadow cannot easily conform to a clear outline.

If not detected stalking prey, the shadow chooses the moment of attack and always achieves surprise and a +4 bonus on its first attack. The shadow causes only one form of damage: a **permanent** Strength drain. A creature reduced to 0 Strength is slain by the shadow.

Shadows can be harmed only by spells, magic weapons of +1 or better enchantment, or creatures with naturally magical attacks (including paralysis, sleep, poison, acid, breath weapon; e.g., the basilisk's gaze would qualify). Creatures

of at least 4 HD are powerful enough to wound a shadow for normal damage.

Shadows are un-dead, and thus can be turned by clerics. They do not eat, drink, or breathe, and are immune to critical hits, disease, and poison. As un-dead, they are immune to *sleep*, *charm*, and *paralysis* spells, as well as other mental effects and cold damage.

Shadows are incorporeal. They can pass through walls, doors, and other material objects. They can fly and are not hindered by gravity or water. They can pass through humans and cannot be grappled.

SHROOMAN

Shrooman: Init -5; Atk slam +4 melee (4d4); AC 18; HD 2d8+6; MV 10'; Act 1/2d20; SP *fungal cloud*, half damage from bludgeoning weapons, infravision 100'; SV Fort +8, Ref -4, Will +4; AL N.

Shroomen are ponderous, laconic fungal creatures that live deep under the earth. They are encountered on the surface only in bogs or in monsoon conditions. They generally resemble living, walking mushrooms, but their forms vary widely, from wide and flat to tall and stout. All shroomen share these traits: a tough, rubbery hide; a saturnine disposition; a methodical, deliberate attitude; and a very slow mind.

They are intelligent and speak Undercommon as well as their own racial language, but their rate of speech is so ponderous that humans grow impatient. The shroomen breed many rare and potent mushrooms, but these are very expensive to obtain—not only for their cost in gold but because trade negotiations can drag on for months on a single transaction.

In combat, a shrooman takes one action every other round. Shroomen hides are so dense that they take only half damage from any bludgeoning weapon (club, mace, stave, etc.).

An agitated or threatened shrooman begins to emit spores that form a *fungal cloud* around it. Beginning on the second round of combat, any creature within 20' of the shrooman suffers a -2 penalty to attacks, damage, and saves due to the cloud. In addition, a target within the cloud must make a DC 14 Fort save or be poisoned, temporarily losing 1d4 points of Agility and taking 1d4 hit points of damage. A new save is required each round the creature remains within the cloud.

SKELETON

Skeleton: Init +0; Atk claw +0 melee (1d3) or by weapon +0 melee; AC 9; HD 1d6; MV 30'; Act 1d20; SP un-dead, half damage from piercing and slashing weapons; SV Fort +0, Ref +0, Will +0; AL C.

Brittle bones held together by eldritch energies, skeletons are un-dead creatures raised from the grave to do disservice to the living. They rattle and creak as they move across the graveyards and tombs where they can be found. If un-

der the command of a wizard or cleric, they understand and obey orders of a sentence or two in length. If found free-willed, they are always in places of death and attack the living on sight. Skeletons attack with claws or the pitted, rusted remains of whatever weapons they carried in life.

Skeletons take half damage from piercing and slashing weapons (such as swords, axes, spears, arrows, and pitchforks). They are un-dead, and thus can be turned by clerics. They do not eat, drink, or breathe, and are immune to critical hits, disease, and poison. As un-dead, they are immune to *sleep, charm,* and *paralysis* spells, as well as other mental effects and cold damage.

The skeletons of larger or small creatures—from goblins to giants—may have less than 1 HD or up to 12 HD. Skeletons can be animated by many means, and some have special traits. Determine special traits randomly with d%:

d%	Skeleton Trait
01-60	No special trait.
61-65	The skeleton was cursed before it reanimated. On any successful attack, there is a 25% chance that it also invokes a minor curse (see Appendix C).
66-70	Carrier of grave rot. Any creature damaged by the skeleton must make a DC 12 Fort save or contract grave rot. Grave rot can take one of many forms (roll 1d4): (1) loss of 1 hp per day, and no natural healing; (2) temporary loss of 1d4 Strength; (3) temporary loss of 1d4 Stamina; (4) loss of touch sensation, resulting in a -2 penalty to all attack rolls. Grave rot can be healed only through magical means.
71-75	Animated by harnessed lightning. Electricity courses through the skeleton's body, giving off brief sparks periodically. A lightning-charged skeleton inflicts an additional 1d4 points of shock damage on each hit.
76-80	Reanimated with gemstones in its eye socket. Roll 1d5 to determine gemstone: (1) pearl eyes affect a viewer as a *sleep* spell; (2) obsidian eyes radiate darkness (as the spell); (3) emerald eyes issue forth a *ray of enfeeblement*; (4) ruby eyes launch flaming bolts (as if a *magic missile*); (5) diamond eyes accelerate the skeleton's speed such that it has an extra action each round. All spell effects are as if a +4 spell check.
81-85	The bones are animated independently of the skeleton itself. When this skeleton is killed, it collapses into shards of bone that continue to attack. The shards have 1d6 hp and attack with a slash at +0 melee (1d3). Great piles of these animated bone shards can move at a speed of 5' and engulf creatures, inflicting an automatic 1d3 damage each round, and can hold the target in place (opposed Str check vs. Str 16). Piles of bone shards have 1d6 hp per 5' x 5' square.
86-90	This skeleton is formed from a higher-level warriors or the more recently dead. It has an additional 1d3 HD, attacks with a +3 bonus to attack rolls and carries intact plate mail armor, shield, and sword. These creatures are much more deadly and sometimes lead their more decayed brethren.
91-95	Chilling touch. Any creature touched by the skeleton takes an additional 1d3 points of cold damage.
96-100	Necromantic touch. Any creature touched by the skeleton loses 1d2 points of Strength.

SLUG, UNDERDARK

Slug, underdark: Init -6; Atk acidic touch +3 melee (1d4 plus slime); AC 18; HD 3d6; MV 10'; Act 1d20; SP slime; SV Fort +5, Ref -6, Will -2; AL C.

Underdark slugs are oozing stalk-eyed tubes of disgust. They patrol the corridors of the underdark, leaving trails of dangerous slime in their wake. The slugs move at a ponderously slow rate, and are easily to avoid; the real danger lies in their slime trails, which crisscross many regions and can be very dangerous.

Roll 1d6 on the table below to determine the nature of the slug's slime. An underdark slug's touch causes 1d4 damage plus one additional type of slime damage. Additionally, pools and trails of slug slime are found throughout the open spaces of the underdark. The slime remains potent for days after the slug's departure, and characters who accidentally walk through the nearly-invisible slime trails may suffer effects as noted below.

Roll	Slime effect
1	Sticky. The character is fixed in place and cannot move until he succeeds on a DC 20 Str check.
2	Acidic. The character takes 1d4 damage immediately, plus 1d4 again on the next round.
3	Hallucinogenic. The character sees strange visions. He is mentally incapacitated for 1d4 rounds, unable to attack or focus on any other activity.
4	Poisonous. The character succumbs to a neurological poison. He must succeed on a DC 14 Fort save or fall to the ground twitching for 1d6 hours.
5	Glowing. The slime glows brightly upon contact. The glow draws attention to the character and cannot be eliminated without being doused in a rare chemical.
6	Smelly. The character smells wretched. The chance of attracting wandering monsters is doubled.

SNAKE, GIANT

Boa constrictor, giant: Init +4; Atk bite +10 melee (1d6 + constrict); AC 18; HD 5d8; MV 30'; Act 1d20; SP constriction 1d6; SV Fort +6, Ref +3, Will +2; AL N.

Cobra, giant: Init +8; Atk bite +6 melee (2d4 + poison DC 20 Fort or death); AC 14; HD 3d8; MV 40'; SP 25% spitting; Act 1d20; SV Fort +3, Ref +8, Will +2; AL N.

Viper, giant: Init +6; Atk bite +8 melee (3d6 + poison DC 12 Fort or 1d4 Stamina); AC 16; HD 4d8; MV 30'; SP 15% spitting; Act 1d20; SV Fort +6, Ref +4, Will +2; AL N.

Giant snakes are not always natural; many are summoned or created by wizards. They can be as long as 50' and weigh a thousand pounds or more.

Constrictors that score a bite attack immediately wrap their coils around the victim. Each round thereafter, the constrictor attempts another bite (always against the grappled target) and also constricts the same target for an automatic 1d6 points of damage.

A small number of cobras and vipers can spit poison once per hour. The spittle is a spray 30' long and 20' wide at its terminus. All within are affected by the snake's poison.

Up to 5% of all giant snakes have two heads. Half of these are two-headed at the neck. The rest, known as amphisbaena, have their second head at the end of their tail and move by grasping one neck in the other head and rolling like a hoop. The second head grants an additional action which is always another bite attack.

Some very rare giant snakes possess gaze attacks like a medusa's.

Magical giant snakes are found in wizards' lairs. Necromancers have skeletal snakes; summoners have vermilion serpents from other planes; and enchanters sheathe their snake-pets in emerald armor.

SUBHUMAN

Subhuman: Init -1; Atk club +3 melee (1d4+2); AC 13; HD 1d8+2; MV 30'; Act 1d20; SV Fort +2, Ref +1, Will -2; AL C.

Cavemen, degenerates, mutants, goat-headed beast-men, swamp-dwellers, cult-worshippers, lost tribesmen, and jungle natives all fall under the category of subhuman. Subhumans are of a low intelligence and are always led by a higher-order humanoid: a sorcerer, priest, cult leader, demon, or king of pure bloodline. In combat they swarm mindlessly, beating viciously with their clubs. Outside of combat they grunt and leer, communicating monosyllabically only about subjects of the flesh.

TIME TRAVELER

Time traveler: Init +3; Atk laser sword +8 melee (2d6) or blaster +8 missile fire (3d6, range 400'); AC 21; HD 4d10; MV 30' or fly 30'; Act 1d20; SV Fort +3, Ref +3, Will +10; AL N.

Time travelers are men from 1,000,000 years in the future. They wear white togas and speak in two voices, one their own and one an electronic intonation that comes from a blinking, boxy apparatus they carry. They wear no visible armor but blows against them are disrupted by a shimmering force field, and they have wrist and ankle bracelets that can do amazing things, like launch fiery beams, levitate, and manifest a lightning-like sword. Time travelers appear only rarely, typically in places where significant events are taking place. They observe from a distance and rarely interfere but are sometimes forced to defend themselves.

TROGLODYTE

Troglodyte: Init +2; Atk bite +2 melee (1d6) or spear +5 melee (1d8+4); AC 15 (chain mail); HD 1d8+4; MV 30' or climb 10'; Act 2d20; SP infravision 100'; SV Fort +2, Ref +2, Will +3; AL L.

Degenerate reptilians of the deep, troglodytes are subhumanoid conquerors whose nomadic raiding parties are greatly feared. Hunchbacked and cruel, they lurch forward on crooked legs with hissing sounds and flickering forked tongues. Despite crooked spines and odd musculature, they are immensely powerful, and many a careless warrior has died transfixed by a troglodyte spear.

Troglodyte raiding parties consist of 10-30 warriors led by a chief. The chief has 4 HD and an additional +4 to attack and damage rolls. Every chief has 4-6 henchmen with 2 HD and an additional +2 to attack and damage rolls. Magic-wielders are rare amongst troglodytes.

TROLL

Troll: Init +6; Atk bite +10 melee (2d8+6) or claw +8 melee (dmg 2d6); AC 19; HD 8d8+6; MV 40'; Act 3d20; SP stench, regeneration, immune to critical hits, immune to mind-affecting spells, vulnerable to fire; SV Fort +10, Ref +5, Will +8 (see below); AL C.

Few living man have seen a troll, for to behold one is to die. The troll is a relentless pursuer, a calm hunter, a non-sentient beast that ravishes all it encounters. Like a mindless slime or an unthinking insect, it simply *hunts*, striving evermore to satiate an endless hunger, devouring man, metal, flesh, and vegetable—not to mention offal, tree trunks, and, on occasion, rocks and bones. Standing twice the height of a man with rangy limbs, it has a rubbery flesh, a long green nose, and no internal organs. Its beady black eyes stare from a winding cavernous lair whose stench wafts on the breeze for miles around.

When not encountered in its lair, a troll typically attacks from ambush. Each round it can bite then claw twice. A troll stinks so badly that men within 20' must make a DC 12 Fort save each round or succumb to a fit of retching (-2 to all rolls while retching). The troll is immune to mind-affecting spells, such as hypnosis or *charm*, due to its lack of sentience. It has no internal organs, brain, skeleton, or concentrations of nerves, and is thus immune to critical hits, as well as poison and disease. Finally, it heals at a prodigious rate, regenerating 1d8 points of damage at the *end* of each round, including the round it is killed. It can only be truly put down by taking its hit points negative such that its final regenerative burst does not raise its total above 0. A troll's severed head or limbs will even crawl back and re-attach. The troll's only vulnerability is to fire, from which it does not regenerate.

Prime trolls are horrible to behold, standing twice or thrice the normal height with corresponding hit points and attacks. Some have four limbs and the ability to swallow a man whole.

There exist water-dwelling trolls, known as scrags. A scrag has gills, fins, and webbed digits. Scrags can breathe underwater indefinitely and swim at their normal movement rate. They are vulnerable to fire like normal trolls.

TROLL LORD

Troll lords are hilarious raconteurs indigenous to southern climes. They have a staggering capacity for alcohol consumption, a fondness for large swords and other weapons, an inherent aversion to discipline and order, and yet a strong martial tendency and knowledge of military tactics. They possess sagely knowledge of many subjects, which is typically dispensed only while imbibing brewed confections. One in four troll lords are supernaturally barred from entry to 1d6 randomly determined planes by the Lords of Law, and every 1d7 days a troll lord awakens in a new location with no memory of how it arrived. Troll lords grow whiskers at an alarming rate, and invariably appear unshaven no matter how frequently they bathe. All troll lords carry clubs and sacks of randomly determined goods. They always maintain their treasure in one-copper-piece increments, never consolidating into larger denominations, for reasons known only to the males of the species. When encountered in the wilderness, there is a 1 in 6 chance that a troll lord will be en route to a conclave of other trolls, in which case it will be predisposed to games of chance and strategy, by which clever characters can escape its clutches. In combat, a troll lord mutters constantly to itself about "those darn distributors," whatever that means.

The Ghiozzar is an unusual mutation of the common troll lord. Unlike its hirsute companions, it is always beautiful and clean-shaven. Ghiozzars are native to the western climes, though they travel frequently, often by sea. They utilize a rare magic device known as a "timeshare" to dwell in multiple caves at once. A ghiozzar is inherently loquacious, and wizards of the species cannot cast the spell *silence*. Ghiozzars are inventive and often have new business opportunities to present, though these are invariably centered on either games or beauty pageants, both of which they love to partake in.

VOMBIS LEECH

Vombis leech: Init -1; Atk bite +0 melee (0); AC 10; HD 1d6+1; MV 15'; Act 1d20; SP *cranium bore*; SV Fort +1, Ref -2, Will Immune; AL N.

Vombis leeches are vicious predators resembling leathery, eyeless cowls. The leeches cling to the undersides of cavern ceilings and moldering tombs, dropping on their unsuspecting prey (+4 to hit if undetected), enveloping the victim's head.

On the round following a successful attack, the leech affixes itself to its target skull with hundreds of tiny, spiral-mawed suckers in a *cranium bore*. The maws dissolve hair, bone and flesh, inflicting 1d8 damage each round the leech remains in place. After 4 successive rounds, the leech begins to feed upon the victim's brain, irrevocably slaying the target and transforming it into a vombis zombie.

The leech's unknowable intelligence renders it immune to attacks with Will effects.

VOMBIS ZOMBIE

Vombis zombie: Init +1; Atk unarmed strike +1 melee (1d6+2); AC 13; HD 2d8+1; MV 40'; Act 1d20; SV Fort +0, Ref +1, Will Immune; AL N.

Vombis zombies are corpses animated by vombis leeches. Though not zombies in the un-dead sense, the mindless corpses are driven to inhuman strength and speed by the affixed cowl-like leeches.

Destroying a zombie does not slay the affixed leech, which can go on to attack, slay, and animate another target. The leech's unknowable intelligence renders the zombie immune to attacks with Will effects.

WOLF

Wolf, common: Init +3; Atk bite +2 melee (1d4); AC 12; HD 1d6; MV 40'; Act 1d20; SV Fort +3, Ref +2, Will +1; AL L.

Wolf, dire: Init +5; Atk bite +6 melee (1d6+2); AC 14; HD 2d6; MV 40'; Act 1d20; SV Fort +4, Ref +4, Will +3; AL L.

Dire wolves are large creatures that often lead packs of regular wolves.

ZOMBIE

Zombie: Init -4; Atk bite +3 melee (1d4); AC 9; HD 3d6; MV 20'; Act 1d20; SP un-dead; SV Fort +4, Ref -4, Will +2; AL C.

Zombies are the walking dead. These horrid remainders of life departed lurch drunkenly forth at the command of a necromancer. If encountered without a master, they stand dumb and mute, awakening to chase any living creature that wanders too close. Zombies are slow and easy to wound but very difficult to kill, being mere hunks of flesh that can sustain injury, dismemberment, and even decapitation before finally being dissembled sufficiently to render them immobile.

Zombies are un-dead, and thus can be turned by clerics. They do not eat, drink, or breathe. As un-dead, they are immune to *sleep*, *charm*, and *paralysis* spells, as well as other mental effects and cold damage.

MEN AND MAGICIANS

The fantasy world is populated primarily by men of medieval ranks: serfs and peasants; journeymen and master craftsmen; men-at-arms and knights; and dukes, earls, kings, and other nobles. Among these many mundane inhabitants are some with special abilities. Here are sample men you can use to populate your world.

As noted previously, "monsters break the rules"—and that applies to men as well. When sending your players to face a magician or warrior, you need not spend the time to create a complicated leveled-up player character according to the class rules. Make it fast and make it interesting!

ACOLYTE

Acolyte: Init -1; Atk mace +1 melee (1d4) or charm (see below) or harmful spell (see below); AC 11; HD 1d8; MV 30'; Act 1d20; SP *charm* 1/day, harmful spell 2/day; SV Fort +1, Ref +0, Will +2; AL varies.

Acolytes are novice clergy in a church. They are encountered in groups of 2-8, generally leading a flock of followers and often accompanied by a friar. Acolytes can use a simple *charm* once per day that turns any humanoid friendly to their cause for 1d4 hours (DC 11 Will save to resist). They can also cast minor harmful spells, which typically manifest as sparks of flame, cold rays, or electrical shocks. Each acolyte can cast two harmful spells per day, each of which causes 1d6+1 damage at a range of 50' (DC 11 Will save for half damage).

ASSASSIN

Assassin: Init +4; Atk poisoned dagger +9 melee (1d12 then 1d4, plus poison) or poisoned dart +12 missile fire (1d8 then 1d3, plus poison); AC 14; HD 3d6; MV 30'; Act 2d20; SP poison (Fort DC 18 or death, dmg 1d12+1d4 Str on successful save), thief skills 75% (disguise, move silently, climb, pick locks, hide in shadows); SV Fort +3, Ref +8, Will +4; AL C.

Assassins are rare masters of the subtle strike who infiltrate, attack, then vanish into the night. An assassin's poisoned dagger or dart does additional damage on its first strike, as noted in the stat block above, to reflect the careful aim and deadly accuracy of the assassin's premeditated attack. All assassin strikes are treated with poison, which is typically fatal, though Appendix P can be referenced for additional options. An assassin can disguise himself, move silently, climb walls, infiltrate locked areas, and hide in shadows successfully 75% of the time.

BANDIT

Bandit: Init +2; Atk scimitar +2 melee (1d8+1) or javelin +3 missile fire (1d6); AC 15; HD 1d8; MV 20'; Act 1d20; SV Fort +2, Ref +2, Will +0; AL C.

Bandit hero: Init +4; Atk scimitar +4 melee (1d8+2) or javelin +5 missile fire (1d6); AC 16; HD 2d8; MV 20'; Act 1d20; SV Fort +3, Ref +3, Will +1; AL C.

Bandit captain: Init +5; Atk scimitar +6 melee (dmg 1d8+3) or javelin +7 missile fire (1d6); AC 17; HD 3d8; MV 20'; Act 1d20; SV Fort +4, Ref +4, Will +2; AL C.

Bandits are untrustworthy men who steal, pillage, ambush, and rob. They are usually encountered in large bands. For every 10 bandits there will be one bandit hero, and for every 20 bandits there will be one bandit captain.

BERSERKER

Berserker: Init +2; Atk axe +3 melee (1d8+2); AC 14; HD 2d12; MV 30'; Act 1d20; SP battle madness; SV Fort +3, Ref +2, Will +0; AL varies.

Berserkers are savage warriors. When in combat, they fly into a battle madness that makes them even more dangerous. A berserker fights normally until wounded. When first wounded, he undergoes the battle madness. He gains +5 hit points and a +2 to all attacks, damage, and saving throws while in combat. After 1 turn this madness fades. He then loses the extra hit points, and drops dead if this brings his total below zero.

FORTUNE TELLER

Fortune teller: Init -1; Atk club -1 melee (1d4-1); AC 9; HD 1d4; MV 30'; Act 1d20; SP tell fortune; SV Fort -2, Ref -1, Will +4; AL varies.

A fortune teller uses divination to reveal a character's future. Any character who spends 10 minutes with a fortune teller can learn something about his future. Roll 1d20 and compare it to the character's Luck score. On a result less than or equal to the character's Luck, the fortune teller provides information that is genuinely useful, conveying a +1 bonus to some upcoming check related to that fortune (at judge's discretion). On a roll of a natural 1, the fortune teller glimpses the character's doom, becoming shaken and distraught as a result, and hinting at terrible things to come.

FRIAR

Friar: Init +0; Atk cudgel +3 melee (1d4+1) or sling +3 missile fire (1d4) or harmful spell (see below); AC 13; HD 3d8; MV 30'; Act 1d20; SP heal 2/day, harmful spell 3/day, turn 3/day; SV Fort +2, Ref +1, Will +4; AL varies.

Friars are religious leaders. A friar is often accompanied by acolytes and followers but may also be found on a solitary pilgrimage. Twice a day, a friar can heal 1d4 hit points from any follower simply by laying on hands. Each friar can cast three harmful spells per day, similar to an acolyte, each of which causes 1d8+2 damage at a range of 100' (DC 13 Will save for half damage). Finally, a friar can use his religious symbol to turn away his foes. This can be done three times per day, and the foes must make a DC 13 Will save or be held at bay, unable to approach within 20' of the friar. Such foes can still make ranged attacks.

KING

King: Init +0; Atk longsword +4 melee (1d8) or bow +4 missile fire (1d6); AC 11; HD 2d8; MV 30'; Act 1d20; SP rally; SV Fort +1, Ref +2, Will +4; AL varies.

A king inspires his allies and followers. When in the presence of their king, all loyal followers receive a +1 bonus to all saving throws against fear or charms and may re-roll one failed morale check per day.

KNIGHT

Knight: Init +1; Atk longsword +3 melee (1d8) or bow +3 missile fire (1d6); AC 16; HD 2d8; MV 20'; Act 1d20; SV Fort +2, Ref +1, Will +1; AL varies.

A doughty knight has earned his title by completing valorous deeds.

MAGICIAN

Magician: Init +0; Atk dagger -1 melee (1d4-1) or harmful spell (see below); AC 10; HD 3d4; MV 30'; Act 1d20; SP prestidigitation, harmful spell 3/day; SV Fort +1, Ref +1, Will +4; AL varies.

Magicians use their powers to create distractions and illusions. They are skilled with fireworks and startling displays

NOBLE

Noble: Init +2; Atk longsword +4 melee (1d8) or bow +4 missile fire (1d6); AC 18; HD 2d8; MV 20'; Act 1d20; SV Fort +1, Ref +2, Will +2; AL varies.

Nobles are skilled in swordplay and invariably well-armored and well-equipped.

PEASANT

Peasant: Init -2; Atk club -1 melee (1d4-1); AC 9; HD 1d4; MV 30'; Act 1d20; SV Fort -1, Ref -2, Will -1; AL varies.

The category of peasants also includes tradesmen and craftsmen, pilgrims, farmers, villagers, and any other common man encountered out and about.

SAGE

Sage: Init -2; Atk punch -2 melee (1); AC 9; HD 1d4; MV 30'; Act 1d20; SP knowledge; SV Fort -2, Ref -2, Will +2; AL varies.

A sage is learned in general studies and well-educated in 1d4+1 subjects. There is a base 50% chance that a sage knows the answer to any general question. Within the scope of his subjects of expertise, this chance increases to 75%. Very easy questions are 10-20% more likely to be known, while difficult questions are 10-20% less likely to be known. A sage typically charges a minimum fee of 5-20 silver pieces for a consultation, and increases this amount to 10-30 gold pieces if the answer requires some degree of research or study. Determine the sage's subjects of expertise by rolling 1d20: (1) history, (2) geography, (3) religion, (4) politics, (5) economics, (6) literature, (7) philosophy, (8) art, (9) music, (10) anthropology, (11) archaeology, (12) psychology, (13) chemistry, (14) physics, (15) logic, (16) mathematics, (17) agriculture, (18) architecture, (19) engineering, (20) law.

WITCH

Witch: Init -2; Atk claw -2 melee (1d4-1) or curse (DC 16 Will save; see below) or spell; AC 9; HD 3d6; MV 20'; Act 1d20; SP familiar, curse, spellcasting (+8 spell check); SV Fort +4, Ref +0, Will +8; AL C.

Witches are servants of Satan that live deep in swamps, wastelands, and deserts, where they putter about doing odd magic. They dwell alone but gather on full moons in covens of 12 plus a demonic master. They are evil creatures best destroyed when encountered.

A witch can issue a curse as an attack action. The victim receives a DC 16 Will save to resist the curse. See Appendix C for suggestions. A witch always knows 1d10 spells, randomly determined as follows (re-roll duplicates): (1) *charm person*, (2) *chill touch*, (3) *detect good*, (4) *forget*, (5) *demon summoning*, (6) *sleep*, (7) *ray of enfeeblement*, (8) *darkness*, (9) *paralysis*, (10) *second sight*. Additionally, all witches can make magic items as if they had the appropriate spells (*mix potion, sword magic*, etc.).

A witch always has a familiar, usually a bat, rat, cat, or toad, that has 1d4 hp, AC 14, and a +2 attack that does 1d3 damage. If the witch is killed while the familiar still lives, the witch's soul flees to the familiar's body, which runs away to restore its power to fight another day.

of colorful magic. In combat they can use prestidigitation to cause enemies' weapons to disappear; as an action, the wizard can target any weapon within 30', and the target must make a DC 12 Will save or see his weapon vanish! This is actually an illusion that fades after 1d6+1 rounds, but the victim believes it absolutely. In addition, up to three times a day a magician can throw a harmful spell that causes 2d4 damage to any target within 30' (no save).

MAN-AT-ARMS

Man-at-arms: Init +0; Atk axe +1 melee (1d6); AC 14; HD 1d8; MV 25'; Act 1d20; SV Fort +1, Ref +1, Will +0; AL L.

The stout, loyal man-at-arms is the background of any local militia.

APPENDICES

Additional information for the thorough judge.

APPENDIX C: CURSES

n-dead, witches, demons, and other vile creatures can inflict curses with a solemn word, as described in the monster descriptions. A curse can be cured by slaying the original invoker, fulfilling some specific terms of the curse, nullifying the curse with a more powerful blessing, or in some cases, by acquiring a different, competing curse which counters the terms of the first one. For example, a creative thief cursed to "a quick and painful death" may seek out another curse that condemns him to "a life of eternal suffering"—thus nullifying the deadly time frame of the first curse!

Curses provide entertaining fodder for adventure stories. They open up angles of exploration centered on the possible methods of resolution. They have a strong foundation in the literature of Appendix N and classical fantasy mythology, and the inclusion of a Luck attribute in this game provides a game mechanism for resolving curses.

In game terms, a curse typically applies an immediate penalty to the bearer's Luck score, as well as one or more specific other penalties. The curse must be invoked via a profound statement, and can be cured by fulfilling its terms. Those terms may sometimes be evident in the nature of the curse, but in most cases some degree of lore and knowledge is required to understand and remedy the curse.

Here are some examples of curses. If you need to generate them randomly, use these guidelines:

Issuer's Strength	Curse
Minor (4 HD or less)	Curse of blindness
	Curse of goblin sight
Moderate (5-8 HD)	Curse of lost love
Major (9+ HD)	Curse of locusts

CURSE OF GOBLIN SIGHT

This curse is typically carried by witches and un-dead of the underdark, such as ghouls and vampires. It is invoked by touching the target's eye and reciting this phrase:

While the sun is in the sky,
You'll wish the eagle's eye.
But what you'll see is goblin night
'Til caveland biers restore your sight.

The curse carries a -2 Luck penalty and makes the victim's eyes and body extremely sensitive to sunlight (much like a goblin). The victim suffers a -2 penalty to all rolls in daylight (attack rolls, damage rolls, skill checks, saving throws, etc.) and a -1 penalty in lesser lights up to torchlight. Only in torchlight or dimmer environments does the victim feel comfortable. Note that the victim cannot see in the dark.

The curse can be remedied by locating the burial place of the un-dead creature that issued the curse ("caveland biers") and performing holy rites to bless the creature's corpse and bury it according to proper rituals.

As the judge, you can substitute the word "biers" in line four of the curse for other terms to create something more specific to your game. For example, "'Til caveland gems restore your sight" could refer to some legendary jewels of your game world.

CURSE OF LOST LOVE

This curse is common to un-dead who were once pirates, sailors, and sea captains, and who left behind mourning wives on their home shores. The wives passed away never knowing what became of their husbands, who now roam the ocean's waves as death-less remnants of their former selves. The curse is delivered by a raking blow to the heart while the issuer recites these lines:

At seaside's edge she waits for me,
To return from distant sea.
But these bones are soaked with ocean's bottom brine,
While her heart remains forever mine.
The pain of longing now you will sing:
Forever you'll desire what no ship can bring.

The curse carries a -2 Luck penalty and fills the victim with a sense of endless longing. The sense of longing is hard to place. It's not clear to the cursed victim exactly what or who he longs for, but the things he once valued—companionship, gold, principles, power—no longer seem as important. In game terms, this manifests as a -2 penalty to all Will saves, as the victim sees no reason to go on living.

The curse can be remedied by recovering the bones of the un-dead that issued it, and re-uniting them with the body (living or long since passed) of its longing wife.

CURSE OF LOCUSTS

This powerful curse comes from the lips of Satanic creatures that are hateful to all mortal life. It is typically recited by demons, the evilest witches, and intelligent un-dead who desire an innocent babe for their foul doings. The curse is usually issued to an entire community of farmers at once. Adventurers may receive this curse accidentally because they are in the community at the time of delivery or via an evil creature that wishes them to become blight-carriers. The curse is delivered by sprinkling grave dirt on the target and reciting these lines:

The blackening hordes descend down,
To blot the green of your farming town.
They'll destroy to dirt your greening fields,
'Til your first borne to the Lord you do yield.

The curse carries a -4 Luck penalty and a -2 penalty to Fort saves. In addition, the target permanently loses 1 hit point per Hit Die, and is afflicted with the black thumb: his touch is anathema to plants and agriculture. Farms under his care invariably perform poorly; gardens die, crops wither, livestock sicken, and the weather does not cooperate. Communities affected with this curse become dust bowls.

The curse can be remedied by sacrificing the first child born after its issuance. The child must be delivered to the curse's issuer on a full moon. Usually this is the first child born in a community, though if an adventurer is stricken it could be that person's first child.

This is a very powerful curse and requires a great deal of exertion to cast. It is not taken lightly.

CURSE OF BLINDNESS

This is a fairly common curse delivered by witches and minor, sightless un-dead. More powerful than the curse of goblin sight, it sentences the victim to total blindness for a short duration—typically until the next full moon, until the next witch's coven meets, for a year and a day, or for some time period associated with the act that provoked the curse. A sightless skeleton or zombie, rendered blind by the witch's curse then slain before cured, might pass on the curse by pronouncing these words to an adventurer:

Sixteen words I spoke to her,
Declaring her "witch" I did aver.
"For sixteen moons, no sun you'll see,"
She cackled as dark passed over me.

The curse carries a -1 Luck penalty and inflicts total blindness. It can be remedied by waiting the indicated time or by slaying the witch that invoked it.

APPENDIX L: LANGUAGES

All characters begin the game knowing the Common tongue. More intelligent characters know additional languages. For every point of Int modifier, a character learns one more language. Finally, some characters may also learn more languages when they advance to level 1 in a class, as noted below:

Wizard: automatically know *two* additional languages for every point of Int modifier, meaning that when they advance from level 0 to level 1, they roll an additional language for every point of Int modifier in addition to the languages they knew at level 0.

Thief: automatically learn thieves' cant at level 1.

Elf, dwarf, and halfling: at level 1, demi-humans learn one *additional* language beyond Common, their racial language, and the languages earned by Int modifiers.

Warrior, cleric: do not earn any additional languages when advancing from level 0 to level 1. However, they may learn languages due to magic or improved ability scores, so their class entries are also included below.

Known languages are randomly determined by rolling d% on the table on the opposite page.

Language	% Chance to Know Language, by Class							
	0-Level Human†	Warrior	Cleric	Thief	Wizard	Halfling	Elf	Dwarf
Alignment tongue*	01-20	01-20	01-20	01-15	01-10	01-25	01-20	01-20
Chaos**	–	–	–	16-20	11-13	–	21-25	–
Law**	–	–	–	21-25	14-16	–	26-30	–
Neutrality**	–	–	–	26-30	17-19	–	31-35	–
Dwarf	21-30	21-30	21-25	31-32	20-21	26-35	36-40	–
Elf	31-35	31-35	26-30	33-34	22-23	36-40	–	21-25
Halfling	36-40	36-38	31-35	35-44	24-25	–	41-45	26-35
Gnome	41-45	–	36-40	45-49	26-27	41-50	–	36-40
Bugbear	46-47	39-43	41-45	50-54	28-29	51-55	–	41-45
Goblin	48-57	44-53	46-55	55-64	30-35	56-70	46-48	46-55
Gnoll	58-60	54-58	56-60	65-69	36-39	–	49-50	56-60
Harpy	–	59-63	–	70-71	40-41	–	51-52	–
Hobgoblin	61-65	64-70	61-65	72-74	42-45	71-80	53-54	61-65
Kobold	66-75	71-78	66-75	75-78	46-49	81-90	55-57	66-75
Lizard man	76-80	79-81	76-78	79	50-53	–	58	–
Minotaur	81	82-83	–	–	54-55	–	59	76
Ogre	82-83	84-88	79-80	–	56-57	–	60	77-81
Orc	84-93	89-95	81-82	–	58-62	–	61-63	82-86
Serpent-man	–	96	83	80-81	63-65	–	64	–
Troglodyte	94-99	97-98	84-88	82-83	66-68	–	65	87-91
Angelic (a.k.a. Celestial)	–	–	89-92	–	69-72	–	66-70	–
Centaur	–	–	93	–	73	–	71-75	–
Demonic (a.k.a. Infernal/Abyssal)	–	–	94-97	84	74-79	–	76-80	–
Doppelganger	–	–	–	85	80	–	–	–
Dragon	–	–	98	86-87	81-84	–	81-85	92-93
Pixie	–	–	99	88-89	85-86	91-93	86-90	–
Giant	100	99-100	100	90-91	87-88	–	–	94-97
Griffon	–	–	–	–	89	–	–	–
Naga	–	–	–	–	90	–	91-92	–
Bear	–	–	–	–	91-92	–	–	98
Eagle	–	–	–	–	93-94	–	93-94	–
Ferret	–	–	–	–	–	94-98	–	–
Horse	–	–	–	–	95-96	–	95-96	–
Wolf	–	–	–	–	97-98	–	–	–
Spider	–	–	–	–	99	–	–	–
Undercommon	–	–	–	92-100	100	99-100	97-100	99-100

† Use the elf, dwarf, or halfling column for 0-level demi-humans.

* Chaos, Law, or Neutrality depending on character's alignment.

** Re-roll if this duplicates a result of the character's alignment tongue.

APPENDIX N: INSPIRATIONAL READING

n the 1979 publication of the AD&D DMG, the last entry before the glossary is Appendix N, in which Gary Gygax lists the fantasy and sci-fi novels that inspired his work on the game. This oft-ignored bibliography has received renewed attention in recent years. It is in fact one of the foundations on which fantasy role playing was built. Reading the books referenced by Gygax, one understands three important facts.

First, that D&D was not spawned from the imagination wholly formed, but was in fact an incremental iteration of literary mechanism, one more step in a march begun by Burroughs, Lovecraft, Vance, and Howard many decades prior—a very important step, true, but nonetheless an evolution.

Second, that many (many!) of the conventions of D&D are not in fact unique but share a clear and cogent ancestry with the books named in Appendix N, and the resulting game of D&D can be easily seen not as a brilliant *creation* but as a brilliant *integration* of the best fantasy conventions from a wide variety of sources. Read the books in Appendix N to feel the mental "click" as you understand why some part of D&D is the way it is: spells, classes, races, combat mechanics, and so on.

Third and finally, that the type of fantastical adventure espoused by D&D—the "spirit of the game" which many modern, nostalgic gamers strive to invoke—is not achieved via specific game rules, but rather by *any rules* and *any style of play* that allows one to *simulate the adventures of classic fantasy heroes*. If your game can accurately accommodate the adventures of doomed Elric, grim Conan, clever Cugel, spontaneous Harold Shea, merry Fafhrd and the Gray Mouser, daring Hawkmoon—if your game can do that, regardless of rules, you have achieved what Gygax and Arneson set out to do.

This author highly recommends returning to these primary sources for inspiration. When writing the *Dungeon Crawl Classics Role Playing Game*, I did not set out to create a retro-clone (in the OSR sense) nor did I intend to create a d20 clone (in the OGL sense). My goal was to create a game that resembled, and enabled, the adventures I read in Appendix N. As a precursor and subsequent companion to the writing of this manuscript, I set out to read the entirety of Appendix N. This is several years' work, and because many Appendix N authors wrote dozens of books, a project that never truly ends, but I did succeed in reading a prodigious supply of classic fantasy literature while authoring this work. I believe the resulting RPG successfully captures the spirit of the original game, using a wholly different rules set. You may question why rules for intelligent swords and planar travel are included in a low-level rules set, but referencing the primary sources reveals the answer.

Below you will find Gygax's original bibliography intact. While concepting and writing this manuscript, I read most of the list: all the books named by title, most if not all of the books from the various specified series (e.g., Burroughs' Mars series), and the generally acknowledged "best" works of authors who are listed with no corresponding title or series (for example, the Silver John series by Manly Wade Wellman).

You will find that the DCC RPG rules easily accommodate any adventure from Appendix N. Having completed a self-directed literary survey of the authors on this list, I highly recommend reading the work of Howard, Lovecraft, Vance, Burroughs, Merritt, and Moorcock. They are extraordinarily inspirational for the adventure author and give direct insight to the origins of fantasy role playing. However, do not limit yourself; start with them, then continue through all of Appendix N. Doing so will strengthen your understanding of the game. Vance is critical to understanding the D&D magic system (you'll read descriptions of classic D&D spells in a work written 20 years before D&D was published!), as are De Camp & Pratt, whose adventures of Harold Shea describe many D&D magic conventions. The original D&D thief class is an amalgam of characters presented by Fritz Leiber, Robert E. Howard, and Jack Vance; the original D&D paladin class comes from Poul Anderson; the D&D alignment system is derived from Poul Anderson and Michael Moorcock; the rules for magic swords and much of the inspiration for planar travel comes from Michael Moorcock, with additional planar travel concepts clearly visible in Roger Zelazny and P.J. Farmer, and at a conceptual level in Edgar Rice Burroughs as well; many monsters and elements of spellcasting are visible in Lovecraft; the concepts of drow and underdark adventures derive from Merritt and St. Clair; and so on.

The most powerful trait of Appendix N, insofar as influencing fantasy adventuring, is what I call "pre-genre storytelling." In the current era, all gamers, and many laymen, have preconceptions of fantasy archetypes: one knows what an elf is like, and what a dwarf is like, and what powers a dragon or vampire should have. Most of the authors in Appendix N, however, were writing before "fantasy" was an acknowledged literary category. The conception of an "elf" as expressed in Tolkien is now "common knowledge," but the elves described by Lord Dunsany and Poul Anderson were completely different creatures. The same is true of dozens of other fantasy conceits. When you read Appendix N, fantasy once again becomes *fantasy*; the concepts escape modern classifications.

In a sense, the *Dungeon Crawl Classics Role Playing Game* is not an attempt to model an experience related to D&D but rather an attempt to model the experience that predated D&D. This game is pre-D&D swords and sorcery. You are

holding the rules that let you experience the same sense of adventure that Gygax and Arneson experienced while they were first developing the game. Where they had to dedicate their energies to creating rules never before devised by man, I have the luxury of drawing on 30 years of game design. And thus I dedicate my energies not to creating rules, but to conveying tone. Hear, then, the tone of Appendix N!

My journey down the road of pre-genre fiction brought me to two other fantasy authors I highly recommended. Clark Ashton Smith was a contemporary of Robert E. Howard and Lovecraft, and an amazing author of horror-shadowed fantasy. His work is inspirational for anyone playing a wizard character, and there are some D&D historians who believe his omission from Appendix N was an accidental oversight on Gygax's part. William Hope Hodgson was one of Lovecraft's inspirations. His work deals primarily with seafaring stories and is sometimes considered supernatural horror rather than fantasy, but it is filled with the kind of adventures that make great D&D games.

Additionally, there are certain films which simply must be viewed to properly understand the history of D&D. The first is *The Raven*—the original 1963 version starring Vincent Price, Peter Lorre, and Boris Karloff. Watch this film

to understand the origins of many D&D spells; the spell duel sequence near the end is clearly an input to the D&D spell system (and certain players in the original Lake Geneva campaigns recall Gygax's fondness for this movie). Another indispensible film for the D&D historian is *Horror of Dracula*, starring Peter Cushing. Part of the Hammer Horror series from the 1950's and 1960's, this film is clearly an inspiration for the cleric's iconic ability to turn un-dead (and the series is known to be a favorite of Arneson's).

One final note; I am a sesquipedalian, and I suspect I am not alone among fans of Gygax's syntax and word choice. Inculcation of Appendix N and ratiocination in regard to vocabulary is concomitant to mellifluous and salubrious logophilia and a prerequisite to possession of a fantasy pandect.

And now, to quote Appendix N:

INSPIRATIONAL READING

Anderson, Poul: *Three Hearts and Three Lions; The High Crusade; The Broken Sword*

Bellairs, John: *The Face in the Frost*

Brackett, Leigh

Brown, Fredric

Burroughs, Edgar Rice: "Pellucidar" series; "Mars" series; "Venus" series

Carter, Lin: "World's End" series

de Camp, L. Sprague: *Lest Darkness Fall; Fallible Fiend; et al*

de Camp & Pratt: "Harold Shea" series; *Carnelian Cube*

Derleth, August, *The King of Elfland's Daughter*

Dunsany, Lord

Farmer, P. J.: "The World of the Tiers" series; *et al*

Fox, Gardner: "Kothar" series; "Kyric" series; *et al*

Howard, Robert E.: "Conan" series

Lanier, Sterling: *Hiero's Journey*

Leiber, Fritz. "Fafhrd & Gray Mouser" series; *et al*

Lovecraft, H. P.

Merritt, A.: *Creep, Shadow, Creep; Moon Pool; Dwellers in the Mirage; et al*

Moorcock, Michael: *Stormbringer; Stealer of Souls;* "Hawkmoon" series (esp. the first three books)

Norton, Andre

Offutt, Andrew J., editor *Swords Against Darkness III*

Pratt, Fletcher: *Blue Star; et al*

Saberhagen, Fred: *Changeling Earth; et al*

St. Clair, Margaret: *The Shadow People; Sign of the Labrys*

Tolkien, J. R. R.: *The Hobbit;* "Ring Trilogy"

Vance, Jack: *The Eyes of the Overworld; The Dying Earth; et al*

Weinbaum, Stanley

Wellman, Manly Wade

Williamson, Jack

Zelazny, Roger: *Jack of Shadows;* "Amber" series; *et al*

APPENDIX O: OSR RESOURCES

 hen Goodman Games published *Dungeon Crawl Classics #1: Idylls of the Rat King* in 2003, it was one of the only products available—whether commercial or amateur—that could be described as "old school." Goodman Games' exploration of the retro-gaming experience now seems prescient of interests to come. As I write this in 2012, there are literally hundreds of old school products available—dozens available on the shelves of commercial retailers and many more online. The OSR, or Old School Renaissance, continues to build momentum. Fueled by nostalgic thirty- and forty-something gamers with discretionary income, prolific blogs, and desktop publishing acumen, the OSR has now produced more supplemental material for the original edition of the game than TSR ever did—by an order of magnitude. This wealth of creativity provides a vast pool of exciting gaming material available for the old-school gamer. Extant among the forums and blogs that comprise the OSR are many variations on the "retro-clone" concept, some of which are inspired, others of which are derivative.

If you find that you enjoyed reading the DCC RPG, you may enjoy reading some of the works offered by the OSR community. The best place to start is to explore the many blogs and forums collected by the community members. Below I will offer an assortment of starting points in your exploration of what the OSR has to offer.

Remember, fundamentally, that all writers need income to sustain themselves, and the greater the income produced by an endeavor, the greater the energies available to continue building momentum for that endeavor. Products such as the one you hold in your hand are made possible by gamers who vote with their dollars. If you want to see the OSR thrive—or prefer that one particular segment become the common voice—support the associated publisher.

To the many and varied OSR publishers, I offer one comment. As Grognardia marks its fourth anniversary in 2012, the OSR has re-published a plethora of variants on the core D&D concepts. The target customer is offered no shortage of retro-clones, adventures centered on goblin raiders, excursions into the underdeep, and genre-based campaign settings. I started work on the volume you hold in your hand because I believe the time has come to break the chains of D&D convention and step back one era further, to the original inspiration of Appendix N, beyond the confines of genre assumptions. DCC RPG offers a free license to third party publishers who wish to publish compatible material. Even if you choose not to take advantage of this license, I ask you to consider moving past the boundaries of "TSR mimicry." The time has come to offer our shared customer something both new *and* old-school.

OSR BLOGS AS STARTING POINTS

(In alphabetical order.)

A Paladin in Citadel: apaladinincitadel.blogspot.com

Akratic Wizardry: akraticwizardry.blogspot.com

B/X Blackrazor: bxblackrazor.blogspot.com

Back to the Dungeon: backtothedungeon.blogspot.com

Bat in the Attic: batintheattic.blogspot.com

Beyond the Black Gate: beyondtheblackgate.blogspot.com

Carjacked Seraphim: carjackedseraphim.blogspot.com

Curmudgeons and Dragons: curmudgeonsdragons. blogspot.com

Cyclopeatron: cyclopeatron.blogspot.com

Delta's D&D Hotspot: deltasdnd.blogspot.com

Dreams of Mythic Fantasy: dreamsofmythicfantasy. blogspot.com

Dungeons and Digressions: dungeonsndigressions. blogspot.com

From the Sorcerer's Skull: sorcerersskull.blogspot.com

Gorgonmilk: gorgonmilk.blogspot.com

Greyhawk Grognard: greyhawkgrognard.blogspot.com

Grognardia: grognardia.blogspot.com

Hack & Slash: hackslashmaster.blogspot.com

Jeff's Gameblog: jrients.blogspot.com

Lamentations of the Flame Princess: lotfp.blogspot.com

Lord of the Green Dragons: lordofthegreendragons. blogspot.com

Maximum Rock and Role Play: maximumrockroleplaying. blogspot.com

Old School Heretic: oldschoolheretic.blogspot.com

Original Edition Fantasy: originaleditionfantasy.blogspot.com

People Them With Monsters: peoplethemwithmonsters. blogspot.com

Planet Algol: planetalgol.blogspot.com

Swords Against the Outer Dark: swordandsanity.blogspot.com

The Mule Abides: muleabides.wordpress.com

The Nine and Thirty Kingdoms: 9and30kingdoms. blogspot.com

The Society of Torch, Pole, and Rope: poleandrope. blogspot.com

Tower of the Archmage: towerofthearchmage.blogspot.com

Troll and Flame: trollandflame.blogspot.com

FORUMS & WEB SITES

Dragonsfoot: www.dragonsfoot.org

Knights and Knaves: www.knights-n-knaves.com

Original D&D Discussion: odd74.proboards.com

The Acaeum: www.acaeum.com

PUBLISHERS, GAMES, & MAGAZINES

Black Blade Publishing: black-blade-publishing.com/

Brave Halfling (Delving Deeper): bravehalfling.com/

Fight On!: www.fightonmagazine.com

Goblinoid Games (Labyrinth Lord): www.goblinoidgames. com/labyrinthlord.html

Mythmere Games (Swords & Wizardry, Knockspell): www. swordsandwizardry.com

EVENTS

Gary Con: www.garycon.com

North Texas RPG Con: ntrpgcon.com

DCC RPG LICENSED PUBLISHERS

Brave Halfling Publishing: www.bravehalfling.com

Chapter 13 press: www.chapter13press.com

Crawl! fanzine: crawlfanzine.com

Travsylvanian Adventures: landofphantoms.blogspot.com

Lands of Legend: landsoflegend.blogspot.com

Purple Sorcerer Games: purplesorcerer.com

Sagaworks Studios: sagaworkstudios.blogspot.com

Thick Skull Adventures: www.thickskulladventures.com

APPENDIX P: POISONS

he greatest peril in fantasy literature is poison: the spider's bite, adder's prick, or scorpion's sting, often rendered more fearful by demonic influence or alchemical extraction. Dangerous poisons should be a realistically fatal danger in your game—a brush with poison should frequently result in permanent debilitation or death.

Here are some poisons that can be introduced into your game by wizards, priests, cultists, and assassins. A single dose of the most mundane poison costs a minimum of 100 gold pieces; the more exotic varieties may fetch 1,000 gp or more per use.

In prior editions of the game, poisons have had various effects: generally damage, sleep, paralysis, death, or ability score loss. The poisons below follow this general model. However, we encourage the judge to expand the notion of "exotic monstrous poison damage" beyond tradition. Leave the players guessing—and afraid! Consider creating your own poisons that reduce Luck, spell checks, armor class, saving throws, languages known, and other aspects of character creation. Poisons of supernatural origin could rightfully have that ability. Imagine a poison from the plane of air that turned a character permanently incorporeal or one from the pits of hell that made a character especially vulnerable to weapons of steel…

Poison	Delivery	Fort Save	Damage on Successful Save	Damage on Failed Save	Recovery
Adder	Wound	DC 22	1d3 Stamina (temporary)	2d4 Stamina (permanent)	Normal healing on successful save
Asp	Wound	DC 20	1d3 Agility (temporary)	1d6 Agility (temporary)	Normal healing
Black lotus	Touch	DC 24	1d3 Intelligence (temporary until healed)	1d6 Intelligence (permanent)	Cannot be healed via normal means; only healed via magic.
Black widow	Wound	DC 14	1 Strength (temporary)	1d4 Strength (permanent)	Normal healing on successful save
Centipede, giant	Wound	DC 13	–	Memory loss (complete amnesia; permanent)	Does not heal
Cobra	Wound	DC 18	–	Blindness (permanent); if blinded, second save or automatic death	Can be healed only via magic
Jellyfish	Touch	DC 16	1d4 hp	1d4 Agility (temporary)	Normal healing
Manticore sting	Wound	DC 16	1 Stamina (temporary)	1d6 Stamina (permanent)	Normal healing on successful save
Medusa venom	Touch	DC 16	1d4 hp	Paralysis (permanent)	Does not heal naturally
Mummy rot	Touch	DC 12	–	1 Stamina per day ongoing (permanent)	Does not heal naturally; can only be healed via magic
Ooze, toxic	Touch	DC 10	Paralysis (1d4 days)	Paralysis (permanent)	Does not heal
Scorpion	Wound	DC 16	–	1d4 Stamina (temporary)	Normal healing
Tarantula	Wound	DC 12	1d4 hp	3d4 hp + 1 Strength	Normal healing
Viper	Wound	DC 16	1d3 Stamina	Death	Normal healing
Wasp, giant	Wound	DC 15	1d6 hp	3d6 hp	Normal healing
(Giant)*		+2	–	+1	–
(Demonic)**		+4	–	+2	Can be healed only via magical means

A giant serpent, spider, or scorpion should have this modifier applied for every 2x multiplier of size. For example, a scorpion that is 4x normal size would have this modifier applied twice; if 8x normal size, this modifier would be applied three times.

**An infernal version of a creature should have this modifier due to its supernatural origin.*

APPENDIX R: RULES COMPLEXITY

he *Dungeon Crawl Classics Role Playing Game* plays like a 1974 game. The rule set deliberately omits many modern concepts in order to speed game play. During playtest, a variety of players suggested varying rules for further defining areas of play. These suggestions were discarded because they increased complexity and had no precedent in the 1974 rules. In other words, if it could be handled ad hoc in 1974, it can be handled ad hoc now.

That said, some judges do wish to expand the game to suit their own style. There are many well-recognized rules categories which have been deliberately omitted herein: miniatures rules, feats, skill points, prestige classes, races distinct from classes, weapon proficiencies, attacks of opportunity, and so on. These spaces are "blank" within the rules so the judge can easily add in those parts he feels are necessary.

Think of it as a map with many undefined places. The DCC RPG rules leave these blank spots deliberately undefined. Now you as the judge should fill in those regions of the map that most benefit your style of play.

APPENDIX S: SOBRIQUETS

hat's in a name? The start of an interesting encounter, that's what. In the DCC RPG, every monster is a uniquely terrifying foe, and as such could be rendered more terrible with a unique name. So, too, is it for NPCs. The author highly recommends the out-of-print title *Book of Names* from Troll Lord Games for inspiration in naming NPCs. Appendix N is also inspirational. For further monikers, consult the following table.

Table of Names

d%	Wizards & Clerics	Warriors & Thieves	Fantastic Creatures	Humanoids
1	Absalom	Akurion	Abathon	Agzan
2	Adompha	Alveric	Ahriman	Arwoor
3	Afgorkon	Amalric	Alagraada	Athbelny
4	Akivasha	Angarth	Anana	Atzul
5	Alcemides	Anuk	Ang'qua'iash	Beloso
6	Anector	Aram	Aphelis	Bokrug
7	Anuradhapura	Argosa	Ariston	Bunda
8	Argaphrax	Athelstane	Astreas	Chand
9	Argelibichus	Camballio	Athle	Chuu
10	Ariadne	Carmac	Atost-rad	Cykranosh
11	Azgelasgus	Cashius	Avalonia	Dejah
12	Baithorion	Cathfytz	Ayodhya	Domnos
13	Bypeld	Cerngoth	Bashan	Eibon
14	Calindonadrius	Cobart	Becar	Emumen
15	Caliph	Constantius	Brytoraugh	Eumar
16	Cardoxicus	Cormoran	Carthoris	Feethos
17	Chongrilar	Cromlek	Chemnis	Galan
18	Dagozai	Cushara	Chiron	Gazal
19	Darunzadar	Cyntrom	Chorondzon	Gebal
20	Dweb	Draupnir	Chryseis	Glosoli
21	Dwerulas	Dugar	Djebel	Gobir
22	Ebanoose	Evadare	Dwalka	Goromé
23	Ebbonly	Faraad	Enion	Grox
24	Eibur	Ganelon	Erohye	Guhic
25	Erasmus	Ghor	Fryx	Gurko
26	Galendil	Gondelor	Ganebon	Gwyn
27	Habruztish	Gug	Gathol	Hoom
28	Hadrathus	Harnam	Gelka	Iblix
29	Hasthar	Hoaraph	Gonlex	Iqqua
30	Hekkador	Istrobian	Gothan	Ischiros
31	Ib	Jadawin	Haade	Jargo
32	Ildawir	Japthon	Haalor	Kadabra
33	Iminix	Jeddak	Hadrubar	Kalu
34	Iomagoth	Kadatheron	Hoje	Kordofo
35	Iquanux	Kalikalides	Horphe	Krug
36	Ishgadona	Kerkadel	Hruengar	Kuruz
37	Izdrel	Khavran	Ilarnek	Liennray
38	Jaspondar	Kishtu	Ishtar	Loford

Table of Names (continued)

d%	Wizards & Clerics	Warriors & Thieves	Fantastic Creatures	Humanoids
39	Khumbanigesh	Kothar	Ispazar	Loischa
40	Leniqua	Krallides	Kajak	Manus
41	Maal	Kulan	Kerim	Mnar
42	Marquanos	Llambichus	Kryth	Naat
43	Matai	Llulch	Kuruz	Nargis
44	Mewick	Loden	Lirazel	Narl
45	Mhu	Maldivius	Lloigor	Narthos
46	Moloch	Matsognir	Lobon	Nehic
47	Nambaloth	Minoc	Mandilip	Niemm
48	Naroob	Mocair	Marentina	Obexah
49	Nichiddor	Morghi	Memphor	Og
50	Nimed	Mors	Mhu	Olgerd
51	Ningorus	Narthos	Mikaded	Ollub
52	Norovus	Nerelon	Mindus	Oth
53	Okar	Noureddin	Modeca	Peshkhauri
54	Olloothy	Oberon	Mornoth	Pnoth
55	Orastes	Oggon	Murcot	Quanga
56	Oryx	Ominor	Nacaal	Rafe
57	Palamabron	Ommum-vog	Namirrha	Rika
58	Pergamoy	Ompallios	Nimer	Rintrak
59	Pharnoc	Orillibus	Niv	Rokol
60	Phenquor	Pallantides	Nouph	Romm
61	Philisia	Pallensus	Omthal	Roska
62	Polarion	Poliarion	Opphus	Rubalsa
63	Ptarth	Prospero	Ouphaloc	Sakumbe
64	Quilian	Publio	Phlesco	Shull
65	Rom	Rannok	Pithaim	Sipril
66	Salome	Rolff	Pommernar	Soinough
67	Sarnath	Sabdon	Puthuum	Sorar
68	Scarabus	Satampra	Quamosmor	Storbon
69	Segovian	Scaviolus	Rakeban	Sybaros
70	Shang	Sigur	Rayat-hin	Taramus
71	Somiator	Simban	Rhul	Taran-ish
72	Sotar	Skafloc	Salensus	Tars
73	Talu	Smelroth	Selestor	Tasarith
74	Thankarol	Snish	Sindri	Teelen
75	Thasaidon	Sotar	Skel'danu	Tewk
76	Theotormon	Tabernay	Slioma	Thaug
77	Thulan	Tamash	Sythaz	Thraa
78	Thulsa	Tarascus	Tarkas	Tinarath
79	Tsanth	Tardos	Tharmas	Tith
80	Tspo	Thekk	Thoris	Tor
81	Tutothmes	Theseus	Threl	Turlogh
82	Uldor	Thremnim	Thuloneah	Uccastrog
83	Urizen	Thulan	Thyllu	Ummaos
84	Vala	Thuvan	Tilutan	Unggo
85	Valbroso	Thyl	Ulassa	Urukush
86	Vallardine	Tiglari	Vandacia	Usk
87	Vathek	Tirouv	Vandy	Vand
88	Veezi	Tonunt	Voormish	Vannax
89	Volphotux	Tortha	Votalp	Vetch
90	Vyldabec	Tredegar	Xicarph	Vladisav
91	Waxenesi	Turmus	Xorex	Vulpanomi
92	Weekapaug	Ujuk	Yandro	Xixthur
93	Xaltotun	Valannus	Yasmina	Yar
94	Xergal	Valerius	Ydheem	Yhoundeh
95	Zapranoth	Vanator	Zdim	Yoros
96	Zelthura	Vixeela	Zenobia	Zang
97	Ziroonderel	Vos	Zermish	Zehbeh
98	Zorathus	Xylac	Zo-kalar	Zeiros
99	Zordanir	Yachpina	Zokkar	Zend
100	Zotulla	Zobol	Zomar	Zhaibar

APPENDIX T: TITLES

illains and allies are more exciting with interesting descriptors. For example, Clark Ashton Smith describes one of his wizards, Atmox, as "master of the doubtful arts" and "vassal of umbrageous powers." The author highly recommends reading Appendix N for inspiration in titling NPCs. To inspire further description, roll on the following table.

Table of Titles

d%	Wizard	Cleric	Warrior	Thief
1	Abjurer	[creature]-binder/-keeper*	Amazon	Apprentice
2	Adept	Abbey	Archer	Arch-rogue
3	Apparitionist	Acolyte	Armigerent	Artisan
4	Archveult	Advocate	Artillerist	Assassin
5	Astrologist	Alienist	Athlete	Balladeer
6	Astrologue	Apostle	Bandit	Bard
7	Augurer	Ascetic	Barbarian	Beggar
8	Baleful	Aspirant	Battler	Bilker
9	Beguiler	Astrologue	Berserker	Body snatcher
10	Bonder	Beatific	Bludgeoner	Boss
11	Capricious	Bishop	Bodyguard	Bounty hunter
12	Chamberlain	Blackcoat	Brave	Bravo
13	Charmer	Blackguard	Brawler	Bully
14	Chronicler	Brother	Brigand	Burglar
15	Clairvoyant	Cabalist	Bruiser	Capo
16	Collector	Caller	Brute	Card shark
17	Conjurer	Cardinal	Bushwhacker	Charlatan
18	Controller	Celibate	Cadet	Cheat
19	Cryomancer	Chaplain	Campaigner	Clockworker
20	Cultist	Cleric	Captain	Con man
21	Curse-giver	Conclavist	Cavalier	Cove
22	Dangerous	Confessor	Champion	Cozener
23	Diabolist	Convert(er)	Charger	Cracksman
24	Diviner	Cultist	Chevalier	Cretin
25	Dreamer	Curate	Chieftain	Crony
26	Elementalist	Deacon	Colossus	Cutpurse
27	Enchanter	Dean	Conqueror	Cutthroat
28	Encylopaedist	Deist	Daring- & roll again	Darksider
29	Ensorceller	Disciple	Defender	Devil
30	Ensqualmer	Druid	Defiler	Dice rattler
31	Epicure	Ecclesiast	Dragoon	Embezzler
32	Evoker	Elder	Duelist	Entrepreneur
33	Factotum	Eternal	Exemplar	Executioner
34	Fortune-teller	Evangelist	Fencer	Expert
35	Fulgurator	Evil eye	Fighter	Explorer
36	Harbinger	Exorcist	First- & roll again	Fence
37	Haruspex	Faithful	Footman	Filcher
38	Herald	Father	Freelancer	Footpad
39	Horologist	First- & roll again	Gallant	Forger
40	Hypnotist	Friar	General	Fortunist
41	Illusionist	Heathen-slayer	Gentleman	Gambler
42	Immolator	Hierophant	Giant	Gammoner
43	Infinitist	Imam	Gladiator	Godfather
44	Insidiator	Initiate	Grand- & roll again	Grand- & roll again
45	Lich	Inquisitor	Great- & roll again	Guildmaster
46	Logician	Judge	Grenadier	Guildsman
47	Mage	Keeper	Guardian	Hedge creeper
48	Magician	Lama	Guerilla	Hit man
49	Magic-user	Medicine man	Headman	Informer
50	Magus	Medium	Horseman	Joungleur
51	Marvelous	Missionary	Huntsman	Journeyman
52	Master	Monk	Impaler	Juggler
53	Mentalist	Mullah	Janissary	Junkman
54	Mesmerizer or mesmerist	Necromancer	Jouster	Killer
55	Mind-reader	Oath-keeper	Justicar	Knave

Table of Titles (continued)

d%	Wizard	Cleric	Warrior	Thief
56	Mnemonist	Occultist	Khan	Liar
57	Mummer	Omen-bringer	Knight	Lorist
58	Mysteriarch	Ovate	Lancer	Lyrist
59	Mystic	Padre	Legionnaire	Made man
60	Necrope	Parson	Lieutenant	Magnate
61	Nigromancer	Patriarch	Lord	Magsman
62	Oath-taker	Petitioner	Man-at-arms	Master- & roll again
63	Palmist	Philosopher	Manslayer	Minstrel
64	Pedant	Pilgrim	Marauder	Moneylender
65	Phantasmist	Pious	Marine	Mugger
66	Preceptor	Pontiff	Mercenary	Murderer
67	Prestidigitator	Pope	Mighty- & roll again	Muscle
68	Prosecutor	Preacher	Myrmidon	Muse
69	Psionic	Priest	Paladin	Pawnbroker
70	Psychic	Primate	Protector	Racaraide
71	Sage	Prognosticator	Pugilist	Raconteur
72	Savant	Prophet	Ranger	Rake
73	Scientist	Proselytizer	Ravager	Rascal
74	Séancer	Psalmist	Reaver	Rhymer
75	Seer	Pupil	Samurai	Robber
76	Shabbat	Quixotic	Scout	Rogue
77	Shibbol(eth)	Rabbi	Sentinel	Rowdy
78	Soothsayer	Rector	Sergeant	Rutterkin
79	Sophist	Reverend	Sharpshooter	Scallywag
80	Sorcerer	Revivalist	Shield-bearer	Scammer
81	Spellbinder	Rakshasa	Skirmisher	Scoundrel
82	Spellslinger	Saint	Soldier	Second story man
83	Spellweaver	Scholar	Squire	Shadow walker
84	Summoner	Seeker	Standard-bearer	Shark
85	Telepath	Sensei	Swashbuckler	Sharper
86	Teratologist	Sermonizer	Swordsman	Shiv
87	Thaumaturgist	Shaman	Tank	Skald
88	Theurgist	Shepherd	Templar	Slaver
89	Thought Master	Shrinist	Titan	Sonneteer
90	Transformer	Soul-saver	Trooper	Spy
91	Transmogrifier	Speaker	Vanquisher	Swindler
92	Trickster	Spirit-raiser	Veteran	Thief
93	Truth-teller	Theist	Vice- & roll again	Thug
94	Tyro	Vicar	Victor	Tomb robber
95	Vigilant	Vowmaker	Viking	Trapsmith
96	Visionist	Wanderer	Vindicator	Treasure hunter
97	Warden	Witch doctor	Warlord	Troubadour
98	Warlock	Witness	Warmonger	Villain
99	Witch	Wonder worker	Wildling	Waghalter
100	Wizard	Zealot	Wrestler	Wordsmith

* Roll for type of creature: (1) demon, (2) devil, (3) dragon, (4) giant, (5) vampire, (6) hydra, (7) medusa, (8) cyclops.

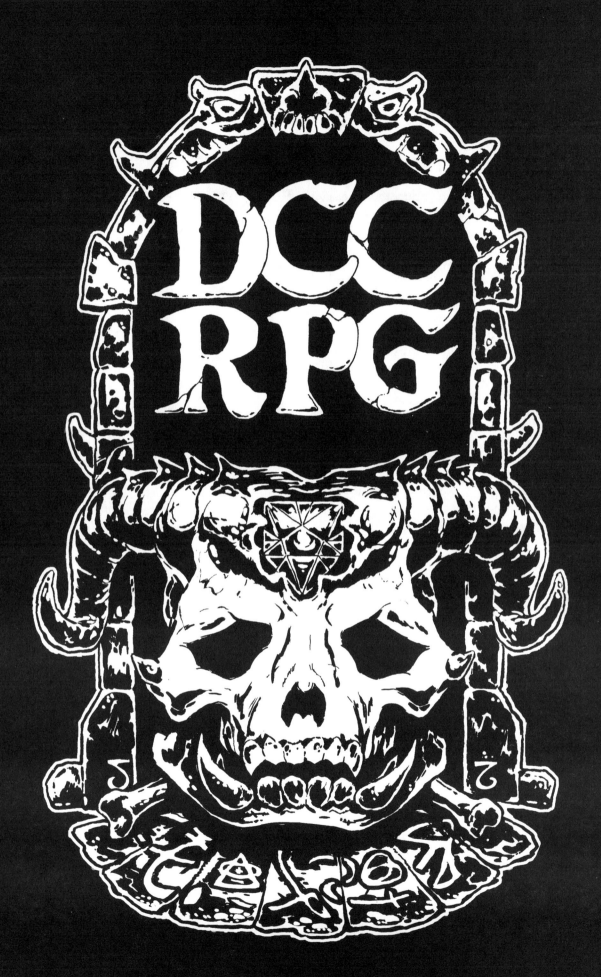

THE PORTAL UNDER THE STARS

A Level 0-1 DCC RPG Adventure
By Joseph Goodman

INTRODUCTION

Seeking wealth and escape from their peasant lives, the characters investigate a supernatural portal that appears only once every half-century when the stars are right. The portal leads to the burial tomb of a war-wizard of eons past. The characters must fight iron men, a demonic snake, the living dead, and a variety of strange statues to recover the treasures left by the war-wizard.

This adventure is designed for 15-20 0-level characters or 8-10 1st-level characters. Remember that players should have 2-3 characters each, so they can continue enjoying the fun of play even if some of their PCs die off. In playtest groups of 15 0-level PCs, 7 or 8 typically survive. The author has playtested this adventure with groups of up to 28 PCs and experienced one complete TPK and several sessions with only a handful of survivors. The adventure focus is on traps and tricks rather than combat, as that ensures the greatest likelihood of low-level survival. Nonetheless, there should be an expectation of the lessons of mortality. The author recommends that the judge tweak the challenge of certain encounters on the fly depending on the size and skill of the adventuring party, particularly area 3 (which has the potential to wipe out the entire party if they cluster around the doors).

BACKGROUND

Eons ago, a primitive war-wizard ruled this land with the aid of barbarian tribes and strange creatures from beyond the stars. When his mortal form was close to expiration, his alien allies instructed him to seal himself away in a protected tomb. Within the tomb the war-wizard could then use astral projection to travel the stars beyond our world. He intended to return later to take possession of his mortal body, which his spirit could do when the stars were properly aligned. However, the war-wizard's extraplanar adventures did not go as planned. Now his body sits perfectly preserved in the tomb built, protected by enchantments and the remains of his barbarian hordes. If these defenses can be bested, the treasures within are ripe for the taking.

ENCOUNTER TABLE

Area	Type	Encounter
1-1	T	Searing light trap
1-2	T	Spear-throwing statues
1-3	T	Flame-launching statue
1-4	C	Ssisssuraaaaggg the immortal demon-snake
1-5	C	Seven piles of living bones
1-6	C	Six crystal statues
1-8	C	78 clay soldiers

PLAYER INTRODUCTION

For long years, you labored in the fields like all the peasants, sweating hot and dirty in the summer, only to shiver under threadbare hides when winter came. This year's harvest ended like all the rest, and autumn's work was hard on Old Man Roberts. When you visited his bedside at the end, he spoke in labored breaths of constellations that hadn't been seen since he was a young lad. The last time the Empty Star had risen in the sky, it was more than fifty winters past, he said. Under the light of that strange star a portal had opened by the old stone mounds. He'd seen jewels in there and fine steel spears and enameled armor, but he'd run when the iron men had attacked. Now, old and dying, he wishes he'd taken the chance on a life of adventure. The Empty Star is once more rising, and a young man with courage could be more than just another peasant – if only he'd take the chance Old Man Robert hadn't.

You're taking that chance. You stand before the monolithic rocks of the old stone mounds, under the dark light of a starry sky. The Empty Star is clear and bright above you. Three of the large stone blocks lean haphazardly together to form an upright rectangular portal about the size of a man. They seem to be placed directly beneath the star's path. As the Empty Star ascends to its brightest point, its light catches in the portal, and a shimmering stone-lined corridor is visible through the stones, but only from one side of the opening. Grasping your pitchfork with white knuckles, you step into the starlit portal which was not there before today, thoughts of jewels and scorching wheat fields foremost in your mind.

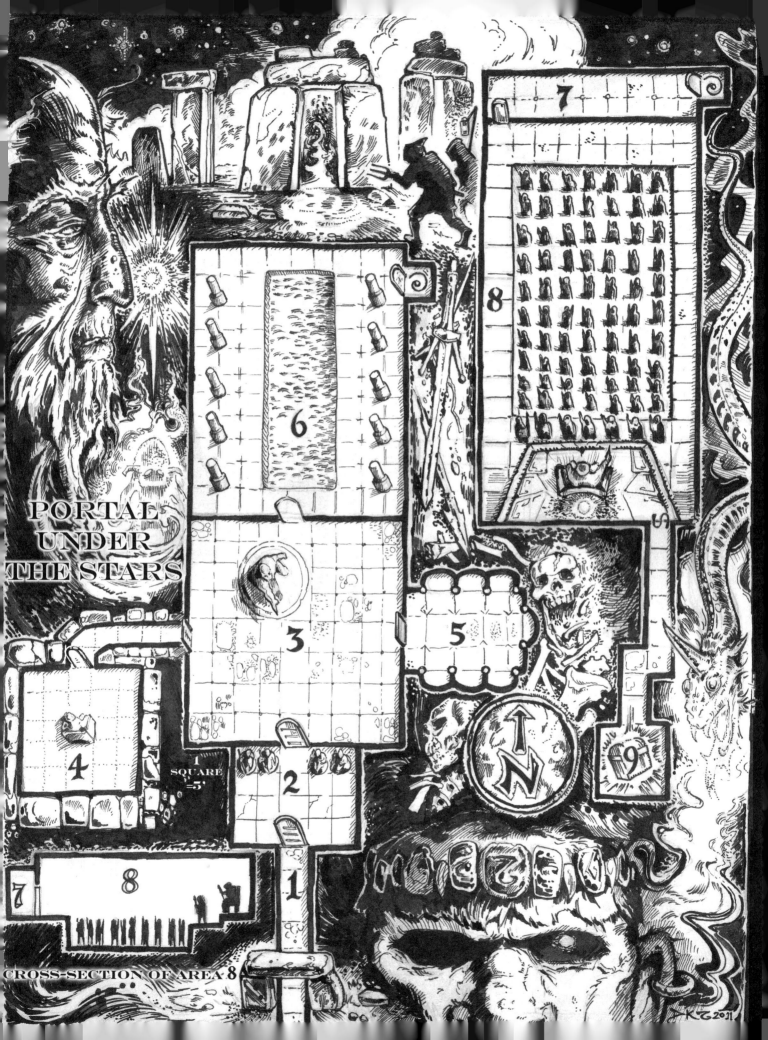

PORTAL
UNDER
THE STARS

1 SQUARE
=5'

CROSS-SECTION OF AREA 8

AREAS OF THE MAP

General Features: Unless otherwise noted, the dungeon is dark and dry. Doors are unlocked unless specified otherwise. Access to the tomb is restricted, so there are no wandering monsters.

Area 1-1 – Portal: *Even though the hallway is visible from only one side of the portal, you tread on solid flagstones. The starlight fades as it reaches into this hallway, which dead-ends ahead at a stout iron-banded door. Jewels or crystals in an odd assortment of star shapes are inscribed on the door.*

The hallway appears only under certain constellations related to the Empty Star. The star shapes on the door approximate the nighttime sky visible through the reverse end of the hallway.

If the characters wait two hours, movement of the nighttime sky makes the view back through the portal reveal the same star pattern as that inscribed on the door. (A character realizes this with a DC 14 Intelligence check.) The door swings open easily for this ten-minute interval.

Door: At any other time, the door will not budge. Treat as locked; DC 15 Strength check to break down; DC 15 Pick Lock check for a thief.

Trap: If the door is forced, a searing light burns from the star-shaped inscription. The character in the lead takes 1d8 damage (DC 10 Reflex save for half). The trap is detected with a DC 20 Search (PC notices arcane arrangement of the star-shaped inscriptions).

Area 1-2 – Guardian Hall: *Across from this room is another stout door. Four iron statues flank the door, two to a side. Each statue depicts a different fighting man in a round iron helmet and thick scaled armor holding a long spear in a throwing position. All the spear-tips are aimed at the door through which you just entered.*

The statues are mechanical creations of the war-wizard. They wait for an opportune moment, then suddenly hurl their spears at the characters. Four spear attacks: +2 to hit (additional +2 if characters stand in doorway bull's-eye), damage 1d8.

The jerky spear-throws are clearly mechanical. The statues remain in the post-throw position and make no further movement. They can be attacked but are made of solid iron and only damage weapons used against them. Their scale mail armor is beautifully enameled with shining black stone. The armor can be removed from the statues and worn or sold for twice the usual price.

The spears can be recovered. The door is unlocked and not trapped.

Area 1-3 – Monument Hall: *This spacious chamber has marbled floors and a door on each wall. At the far end is a towering granite statue of a barbarian, one hand outstretched, index finger pointed toward you. The muscular savage wears animal hides, but his eyes are intelligent and his engraved neckline sports amulets and charms. A grimoire hangs beside a broadsword on the hip of the thirty-foot-tall monument.*

Observant characters (DC 12 Intelligence check) notice many fine scorch marks on the marble floor, as if campfires had been started there.

The granite statue weighs many tons but rotates freely on a well-oiled (but concealed) base. With a deep bass groaning sound, it swivels to track the characters' movements. If the party splits up, it tracks the largest group. The extended hand marks its line of sight.

If any character moves to exit the room (including opening a door or leaving as they arrived), the statue sends forth a scorching burst of flame from its fingertip: +6 to hit, 1d6 damage, 1d6 additional burning damage each round thereafter until a DC 10 Reflex save is made to put out the fire. Once provoked, the statue launches flames continuously, once per round, for up to 5 rounds, at which point its fuel supply is exhausted.

Strong characters who remove the doors from their hinges in areas 1 and 2 can use them as a shield against the statue. This full-body shield increases AC by +4 but reduces movement to half.

The statue can be placated by uttering the name of the war-wizard in whose likeness it is carved. But that name is lost to time. Otherwise, it is so large as to be beyond the ability of the characters to damage.

All doors are unlocked.

Area 1-4 – Scrying Chamber: *A wide stone throne faces you from the center of this square room. The walls are hung with primitive clay tablets, head-high and inscribed with strange symbols. Each tablet is a few feet wide and there are dozens hanging on the four walls. However, your attention is riveted to the enormous snake that has crawled out from behind the throne. It is ringed in crimson bands the color of hellfire and has a demonic horn in the center of its fanged head.*

The immortal demon-snake guards this scrying chamber. It speaks in a sibilant hiss: *"I am Ssisssuraaaaggg, and you intrude on my guardianship."* Then, without parley or hesitation, it attacks.

Ssisssuraaaaggg, the immortal demon-snake: Init +0; Atk bite +6 melee; Dmg 1d8; AC 13; HP 20; MV 20'; Act 1d20; SV Fort +8, Ref +4, Will +4; AL L.

When Ssisssuraaaaggg is killed, its body dissolves into ash, leaving only the demonic horn behind. The horn can be used to commune with a demon, and when meditated upon (DC 12 spell check), confers access to the spell *invoke patron*.

A magical portal hangs on the back of the entry door. If the door is shut, someone seated on the throne looks directly upon the portal, which shows stars unlike any seen before in the night sky. The constellations slowly move across the "sky" shown in the portal. A powerful wizard can use this portal to see far-away places (DC 25 spell check).

Anyone who studies the tablets can make out their story. They tell of an alien race that came from the stars to bring magical implements to a barbarian tribe, who in turn conquered many lands with their new powers. The aliens will return when the stars are right. Many less significant events are foretold by the stars (and tablets) as well: droughts, plagues, the birth and death of kings, and so on.

Area 1-5 – Chieftains' Burial: *This musty room is clearly a burial chamber. Seven shrouded alcoves hold piles of loose bones. Rusty arms and armor adorn the walls beside each alcove and funeral masks are mounted beneath the loose skulls.*

The funeral masks show primitive, almost simian features on stern faces. Examination of the bones shows they are not quite human: the limbs are too thick, the spines too short, and the beetled brows jut out too far.

Each of the seven skeletons was a general in the army of the war-wizard. If the skulls in this room are destroyed, the spirits that animate the warriors in area 8 are released to find peace.

The bones are living dead that have decayed over the eons. They shake and rattle as characters approach; however, they can no longer animate into cohesive skeletons. The skulls clack, clatter, and attempt to bite, but are easily avoided and crushed through normal means.

Seven piles of living bones: Init -2; Atk bite +0 melee; Dmg 1d4-1; AC 8; HP 2; MV 5'; Act 1d20; SV Fort +0, Ref -4, Will +1; AL C.

Most of the weaponry and armor in this room is rusted and worthless, but a hand axe, a battle axe, and a set of chain mail can be recovered. Due to their age and brittleness the two axes are at -1 to attack, and the chain mail offers only +4 armor class for similar reasons.

Area 1-6 – Gazing Pool: *This enormous chamber is filled with a large, rectangular pool of water running the entire length of the room. Diffused light shines upward from the pool, illuminating wide pillars lining the walls. Strangest of all, however, are the man-shaped crystal creatures visible in the shadows. They shuffle about slowly, their strange crystalline bodies sparkling like jewels whenever they catch the light from the pool. There is a door in the far corner of this chamber.*

This room represents the war-wizard's vengeance against his enemies. He transformed his foes into living crystalline statues, then trapped them here. Now possessed of only animal intelligence, they are no longer capable of speech nor do they need sustenance. They have wandered this room for millennia, trapped in the unending hell of their crystal bodies.

There are six crystal statues. Their features are hard to discern because of their translucency, but they are perfect replicas of the eons-old proto-human warriors who were

transformed to create them. They are attracted to light and shuffle toward torches and lanterns. They do not attack, but their approach may seem menacing, and they will defend themselves. If they reach a torch or other light source unmolested, they simply stand next to it and absorb the warmth.

Six crystal statues: Init -2; Atk punch +2 melee; Dmg 1d4; AC 12; HP 8; MV 10'; Act 1d20; SV Fort -2, Ref -2, Will +0; AL N.

The pool is 3' deep. Its bottom is painted pitch black and encrusted with thousands of crystals forming the stars of a nighttime constellation that is unfamiliar. (It is in fact the sky as it will appear twenty thousand years from now, when the war-wizard's strange benefactors will return.)

The light shines through the crystal stars from area 8 below. Each crystal is worth 10 sp and takes 2 minutes to pry out. Prying out crystals causes the water in the pool to drain into area 8. Air bubbles rise, then a current starts, and after 10 crystals are pried out, the draining is obvious. After 50 crystals are removed, the floor buckles. After 100 crystals are removed, it collapses onto area 8, sending any characters within the pool crashing down into to the room below in a sloshing mess (1d6 damage, DC 12 Ref save for half).

Area 1-7 – Strategy Room: *The spiral staircase leads to a long, narrow room with a door in the far wall. There are several ledges holding miniature clay solders and two tables with armies of opposing soldiers are laid out around buildings and hills.*

The war-wizard intended for this room to be a planning station for his afterlife conquests.

Four of the clay soldiers are solid silver. They are the generals, clearly the leaders of the four armies laid out on the two tables. DC 10 Search check; worth 20 gp each.

Area 1-8 – Clay Army: *The door opens upon a breathtaking scene. An enormous, three-tiered chamber spreads before you. An*

oversized throne rests upon a raised dais at the far end of the room. Seated on the throne is a clay warlord that resembles the giant statue you saw earlier. A pulsating light emanates from a crystal globe atop the throne.

Below the dais at floor level seven statues of clay generals stand motionless. Below them, in a huge pit that runs the length of the room stands an army of clay soldiers. There are dozens of soldiers arrayed in marching formation, their clay armor and clay spears equipped for war.

A great stillness pervades the room. It is the stillness of death; the silence of a tomb. Then, suddenly, the stillness is broken as the clay warlord jerkily raises an arm toward his generals. Then, the entire army takes a lurching step forward, shattering the silence with the tramp of doom.

This is the warlord's elite guard, preserved and reanimated for eternity. The characters have no hope of defeating the 70 warriors, 7 generals, and warlord. All share these same stats: Init +0; Atk spear +4 melee; Dmg 1d8; AC 12; HP 9; MV 10'; Act 1d20; SV Fort +2, Ref +0, Will +0; AL N.

However, there are several clever ways to win passage:

- If the clay army is submerged in water by removing crystals to sink the pool in area 6 all creatures in this room take 1d6 damage from falling debris as the ceiling collapses. Additionally, any surviving clay soldiers slowly turn to mud, taking an additional 1 point of damage each round until they dissolve into a puddle.

- The life force of the clay generals is linked to their skeletons in area 5. If the skulls there are destroyed, the clay generals' heads shatter to shards and dust. The characters may arrive to find the generals already destroyed.

- Smart characters may try to assassinate the warlord directly, which quickly ends the threat.

If the warlord and generals are alive, the warriors climb from the pit (1 action) and attack while the generals look on. If the generals are killed, the warriors lack organization and spend a few rounds milling about before moving forward to attack. If the warlord is killed, the entire army loses anima, becoming simply a set of clay statues.

The secret door is found with a DC 14 search.

The crystal globe emits an ongoing light. It is worth 200 gp as a work of art. A wizard who unlocks its secrets (DC 18 spell check plus study time and arcane consultation) understands that he can use it as a scrying ball. Such a wizard can view a location he has seen or has reference to (e.g., can view a creature whose lock of hair he possesses); DC 18 spell check to activate for 1d6 rounds; -2 penalty for each consecutive use in a day. However, once every 1d8 days, an alien countenance appears in the ball to look *back* at the wizard. These are the extraplanar benefactors of the war-wizard, who taught him to use this crystal globe to guide his astral projection, and who occasionally use it to look upon the mortal realm. See also area 9.

Area 1-9 – Treasure Vault: *At the end of the long hallway is a spartanly appointed room containing simple wooden shelves, a camp chair, and a sleeping pallet. The wooden shelves hold a bronze rod, a copper brazier, fine weapons and armor, and a brass-bound tome. In the center of the floor is a large pentacle with a perfect crystal circle at its center. Inside the circle is a stone table on which rests a wrinkled ancient body whose countenance matches the war-wizards. At the head of the table is a concave depression.*

Here are stored the trappings of the war-wizard:

- The bronze rod of rulership is engraved with half of a demon's face. It is worth 150 gp, but read on.

- The copper brazier is worth 10 gp.

- The assortment of weapons includes a longsword, a long bow, 40 arrows with quiver, a mace, a spear, a battle axe, a dagger, and a hand axe.

- There is a suit of scale mail.

- The tome is written in a language so ancient it is indecipherable to modern man. A wizard who studies it may discover (with a DC 14 spell check) a spell of the judge's choosing.

If a character places the crystal ball in the depression on the table, he sees this:

Gazing into the crystal ball, you see an endless field of bright stars on a faint gray background. A ghostly image of the war-wizard drifts in the star-strewn ether, perfectly still. Then a harsh goat-like face fills the full sphere, staring intently at you. "I have waited a long time for someone to take the warlord's place," says the strange goat-man in a deep voice. "His astral voyage was cut short before he could rekindle the spark of his mortal coil. I am still in need of an ally on your world. Fill this copper brazier with wood from a dryad's tree and ignite it with the spark of a living fire. The blaze will reveal the location of the other half of the ruler-ship rod. Find that for me, and you shall be rewarded." Then the globe dims to mere crystal.

They say a dryad has been seen in the forests east of here…

THE INFERNAL CRUCIBLE OF SEZREKAN THE MAD

A level 5 DCC RPG adventure
By Harley Stroh

INTRODUCTION

his adventure is designed for 4 to 8 5th-level characters. If this is your first exposure to DCC RPG, you can roll up 5th-level characters and use this scenario as a contrast to a preceding one to get a sense of low-level versus high-level play.

BACKGROUND

nfamous in the darker cycles of lore and legendry, Sezrekan the Mad was a notorious sage, diabolist, and warlock bent on a quest for immortality. His perilous quest played out over several hundred years, and none can say whether the Old One achieved deification or lost his soul vying with infernal powers.

Sezrekan's pursuit of lost secrets and forbidden lore spanned the face of Áereth. In these far-flung cities and crumbling ruins, the wizard-sage created simple workshops and foundries to aid in his research. Here, amid frothing retorts and forbidden scrolls, the aging warlock plumbed the mysteries of life, death, and time. Every new discovery opened another line of inquiry, leading Sezrekan to abandon the workshop for another city or ruin, never to return.

An untold number of his abandoned workshops remain undiscovered to this day. One such laboratory is hidden in the ancient city of Punjar.

JUDGING NOTES

he *Infernal Crucible of Sezrekan the Mad* presents the adventurers with both a crafty villain and a deadly battle, but the most dangerous challenge is also the most subtle: Escaping Elzemon's trap requires that at least one foe is left alive. Adventurers given to scorched-earth style expeditions will be the instruments of their own demise. If the PCs slay both Elzemon and Sezrekan's Ape, they are left with a gruesome dilemma: Which of their own to leave behind? How the PCs go about making this decision may reveal more about true *character* than the players care to admit.

The adventure is located in sprawling, decadent Punjar. Specifically, the workshop is hidden in the sub-basement of a decaying manor in Smoke – the worst of Old Punjar's wards – where Dim Lane intersects the Shiv. Here, hidden among the crumbling tenements and foul night smokes, Sezrekan was free to pursue his mad experiments without fear of interruption.

Though nominally set in Punjar, the adventure can be easily placed in nearly any location. The PCs can discover the hidden portal in the floor of a musty tomb, in the cellar of their favorite pub or chapel, or even in a forgotten gallery of their own keep.

Elzemon the Forgotten: Unfortunately for those seeking to plunder the wizard's secrets, Sezrekan was notorious amid the infernal hierarchies for summoning demons and devils, and then simply refusing (or forgetting) to release them. One such being, a minor demon named Elzemon, remains imprisoned in this workshop to this day. And in a desperate bid for its own freedom, the demon has transformed the workshop into an elaborate trap.

Elzemon has free reign within the various areas of the laboratory, but cannot escape the complex until the sand in the hourglass (area 1-1) runs out. He begins the adventure in area 1-2 and is quickly drawn to any disturbance.

The demon's downfall is its delight in tormenting mortals. The pot-bellied demon follows the PCs through the chambers, invisible, doing its very best to egg the PCs into wasting precious minutes.

Elzemon the Quasit: Init +4; Atk claw +3 melee (dmg 1d6+2); AC 17; HP 23; MV 35' (fly); Act 2d20; SP Invisible at will; SV Fort +2, Ref +6, Will +5; Immune to Will-effects unless true name is known; AL C.

ENCOUNTER TABLE

Area	Type	Encounter
1-1	P	Puzzle
1-2	C	10 Glyph Worms
1-3	P/C	Sezrekan's Ape
Any	P/C	Elzemon

PLAYER INTRODUCTION

he adventure begins with the discovery – either by assiduous research or by accident – of the entrance to the workshop: a portal set into the floor. Read or paraphrase the following:

Eagerly you scrape away the mud to reveal a circular portal of dull gray metal set into the floor. Set into the center of the portal is a silver bas-relief depicting a two-legged serpent biting its own tail. Above the serpent, cast in gold, is a crown.

The portal is roughly 3 feet in diameter, though attempts

THE INFERNAL CRUCIBLE OF SEZREKAN THE MAD

START

1

2

3

50'

◇ = 5'

DKZ 2011

at precise measurement hint its diameter to be the value of pi. The portal is cast of lead to foil scrying and inter-dimensional travel. Wizards and thieves examining the portal are overcome by a powerful sense that something terrible lurks behind the lead portal.

The portal is three inches deep and can easily be pried free of the floor, revealing a narrow spiral staircase descending into darkness. The value of the raw silver is 15 gp; the value of the gold is 25 gp.

AREAS OF THE MAP

Area 1-1 – The Magic Circle: *A thick coat of dust covers the floor, obscuring what appears to be a magic circle, carved in runes, circumscribing the entire chamber. Stone faces of tormented demons ring the ceiling, and a pit set into the center of the chamber pulses with a hellish crimson light. Beside the pit rests a tall golden hourglass.*

Inspection by cautious wizards reveals that the magic circle prevents the escape of demons. However, just inside the circle of runes is a pentagram, drawn in blood and hidden by dust, that traps any living creature entering the chamber. The pentagram was cast by the demon Elzemon. These two thaumaturgic inscriptions interact in strange, unpredictable ways.

The instant a PC crosses over the runes, read or paraphrase the following:

A thunderous crack echoes through the chamber and electric blue waves of tormented faces cascade through the air, revealing a sinister pentagram scrawled in blood across the floor of the chamber. The hourglass rotates in its base, and the sound of maniacal laughter echoes faintly from below.

No magic shy of a deific patron or infernal power can wrest the PCs from Elzemon's trap. From this moment forward, it is impossible to leave the chamber, save for the pit down.

Sezrekan's golden hourglass stands nearly three feet in height and weighs roughly 30 lbs. A minor relic discarded by the Old One, the hourglass keeps perfectly precise time of any duration, and grants a +2 bonus to spell checks for spells taking one turn or longer to cast. Destroying the hourglass has no effect other than to eliminate the PCs' means of tracking time.

The pit is 50' deep and runs to area 1-2. Given the opportunity, Elzemon flies up from area 1-2, eager for the chance to push a PC into the pit or cut an unattended rope.

Wizard, sages, or lucky thieves pausing to study the interaction between the magic circle and the pentagram can deduce the following principles:

- So long as the thaumaturgic inscriptions remain intact, no creature can be summoned into the crucible.

- At the end of the hour, both the magic circle and the Elzemon's pentagram part for an instant, permitting escape.

- No matter how many exit, at least one living creature must remain inside the circle.

One final principle applies that can only be inferred: The last creature left within the circle is trapped there for all eternity.

Area 1-2 – The Infernal Crucible: *The pit opens into a cluttered octagonal chamber. A sinister, crimson light emanates from web-laden globes that hang from the ceiling, casting a charnel glow over the chamber's contents.*

A large granite table dominates the chamber. It is laden with glass retorts and a series of skulls, ranging in size from a field mouse to that of a tusked giant. An open tome rests on a stand beside the table.

The walls are covered in sheets of hammered copper, stained with vile liquids and scored by acid. The top of each sheet is attached to a chain and counter weights that run to the ceiling and then descending to hang just above the stone table.

There are seven skulls in all: field mouse, monkey, goat, halfling, elf, human, ogre, and the giant. The cranium of each skull is sawn open, and the interior cavity is set with platinum spacers to accommodate a smaller brain.

The tome is open to a dusty page with a simple passage:

a curse upon thieves that dare
to gaze upon the works
of mighty Sezrekan

Beneath the passage is a large glyph inked in red and black. The quickest inspection of the page activates the glyph. It flashes brightly (Ref save, DC 15, or be blinded for 1d3 rounds), and then animates into inky black worms. With horrifying speed, the worms begin to consume every written word within the chamber.

In the first round, the glyph worms consume the tome. In the second and third round, they squiggle behind the copper sheets covering the walls and consume all the tomes and sheaves. On the fourth round, they move on to the PCs, and on the fifth round, the worms consume any spellbooks, maps, tomes, or scrolls in the PCs' possession. The glyphs die in writhing agony on the 8th round.

Glyph Worm (10): Init +2; Atk –; Dmg –; AC 15; HP 1; MV 20'; Act 1d20; SA consume written words; SV Fort -1, Ref +3, Will immune; AL N.

The copper sheets hanging on the walls function as primitive blast shields, protecting the valuables behind them from any explosions that might take place in the main chamber. Pulling on any one of the five hanging chains raises the corresponding metal sheets, revealing five sets of shelves:

The **first set of shelves** is heavy with the weight of time-blackened tomes, stacks of rolled vellum, and sheaves of worn parchment – Sezrekan's discarded research. If collected and studied by a wizard or sage, they yield 1d5 spells (to be determined by the judge or rolled randomly). The shelf

also contains a scroll that holds the true name of Elzemon and details the demon's weakness: striking the demon with lead renders it visible and inflicts 1d4 points of damage per round of contact.

The **second set of shelves** is laden with retorts, strange flasks, and vials stoppered with wax. They once contained elixirs, potions, and concoctions resulting from the Old One's experiments. Time has reduced most of these mixtures to poison. Sages and wizards succeeding on a DC 13 Intelligence check can identify 1d5 vials of strong acids and bases; thieves succeeding on a DC 20 Handle Poison check can identify a similar number of poisons (efficacy to be determined by the judge).

The **third and fourth sets of shelves** are empty.

The **fifth set of shelves** is laden with the raw materials vital to Sezrekan's studies. Four coffers rest on the shelves. Inside the coffers are 10 silver bars (worth 30 gp each), 5 gold bars (worth 100 gp each), 2 platinum bars (worth 500 gp each), and a nondescript pouch containing lead dust shot through with flecks of adamantine (worth 1,000 gp).

Area 1-3 – The Chamber of the Ape: *Water drips in thin rivulets down the walls of this chamber, pooling on the floor. A trio of large clay vessels, each nearly 4' in height, stands against one wall. Beside the strange jars rest a trio of iron rods.*

At the far end of the chamber is heavy iron gate.

The gate is secured with a massive lock that is easily picked (DC 15). Inside the cell is the body of an enormous ape atop wooden planks. Unmoving and unresponsive, the ape is Sezrekan's unfortunate attempt to transplant a human mind into the body of an animal. Branded onto the ape's shaven scalp is the mark of Sezrekan.

The egg-like vessels are primitive batteries. The top of each jar is sealed with clay and pierced by a hole matching the width of the iron rods. If each of the three rods is inserted into a corresponding vessel, the circuit is completed, initiating a rapid series of events:

Arcs of electricity fan into the chamber, striking any PC standing in the pooled water. PCs in the water take 1d4 points of damage per round and must succeed on a DC 17 Fort save to make any actions. The semi-paralysis ends with the destruction of at least one of the vessels (AC 10, hp 10) or by escaping the pool. Other PCs can pull their paralyzed companions from the water, but if they step into the pool, they are also caught by the arcing current.

The current is sufficient to shock Sezrekan's Ape back to life. One round after awakening, it tears the iron gate free of its moorings and casts the twisted wreckage aside. On the third round, it proceeds to do the same with the PCs.

Due to its rage and Sezrekan's mind-altering magics, the ape is immune to the paralysis effect, as well as to any *charm, sleep* or mind-altering effect permitting a Will save.

Finally, if the PCs are loathe to experiment with the rods and vessels, an invisible Elzemon closes the circuit for them, waiting for the opportunity to paralyze the greatest number of PCs.

Sezrekan's Ape: Init +2; Atk fists +5 melee (dmg 1d12); AC 15; HP 65; MV 40'; Act 2d20; SA Rend for additional 1d16 dmg on natural 18 or 19; SV Fort +5, Ref +1, Will Immune; AL C.

INDEX

TABLES

THANKS

Goodman Games extends a hearty "thanks" to the brick-and-mortar retailers who supported DCC RPG through demos, playtests, poster displays, and more! Here is a small list of those who were particularly helpful, and there are many more. We encourage our readers to patronize their friendly local game stores, including those listed below. *This list is organized by state.*

Axis Records and Comics
2743 San Pablo Ave. #5055
Oakland, CA
(510) 851-2011

Game Kastle
1350 Coleman Ave.
Santa Clara, CA
(408) 727-2452
www.gamekastle.com

Game Towne
3954 Harney St
San Diego, CA
(619) 291-1666

Compleat Games & Hobbies
326 N Tejon
Colorado Springs, CO
(719) 473-1116
compleatgamer.com

Emerald City Comics & Collectables
9249 Seminole Boulevard
Seminole, FL
emeraldcitycomics.com
(727) 398-2665

Emerald City Comics & Collectables
2475 McMullen Booth Road, Suite I
Clearwater, FL
(727) 797-0664
emeraldcitycomics.com

FCB Cards, Comics, and Games
9850 Nesbit Ferry Road #21
Alpharetta, GA
(770) 993-6955
freedomcardboard.com

Tyche's Games
1056 S. Lumpkin St
Athens, GA 30605
(706) 354-4500
www.tychesgames.com

Strategy & Games
Silver Lake Mall
Coeur d'Alene, ID
(208) 762-7764
strategyngames.com

Beckmon's Gaming Paradise
1037 Blue Lakes Blvd North
Twin Falls, ID
(208) 733-3901
beckmonsgamingparadise.com

Castle Perilous Games
207 West Main St.
Carbondale, IL
(618) 529-5317
www.castleperilous.com

Fair Game
5150C Main St.
Downers Grove, IL
(630) 963-0640
www.fairgamestore.com

The Game Preserve
100 S. Creasy Lane
Suite 1030
Lafayette, IN
(765) 448-4200

GameQuest
3631 N Clinton St.
Fort Wayne, IN 46805
(260) 482-4983

Amazing Wonders
148 W Tiverton Way Suite 150
Lexington, KY
(859) 272-0750
www.amazingwonders.net

The Rusty Scabbard
820 Lane Allen RD
Lexington, KY
(859) 278-6634
therustyscabbard.com

Dragon's Den
2600 South Rd
Poughkeepsie, NY
(845) 471-1401
gamersgambit.com

Ravenstone Games
1675 Karl Court
Columbus, OH
(614) 844-6463
www.ravenstonegames.net

Ancient Wonders
19060 SW Boones Ferry Rd
Tualatin, OR
(503) 692-0753
www.ancientwonders.net

Guardian Games
303 SE 3rd Ave.
Portland, OR
(503) 238-4000
www.ggportland.com

Rainy Day Games
18105 SW TV HWY
Aloha, OR
(503) 642-4100
www.rainy-day-games.com

That Game Place
230 S. 8th Street
Lemoyne, PA
(717) 761-8988
www.thatgamestore.com

Planet Comics
2704 N Main St
Anderson, SC
(864) 261-3578
www.planetcomics.net

Dicehead Games
200 Paul Huff Pkwy NW #12
Cleveland, TN
(423) 473-7125
www.dicehead.com

The Game Keep
3952 Lebanon Road
Hermitage, TN 37076
(615) 883-4800
thegamekeep.com

Dragon's Lair Comics & Fantasy
6111 Burnet Road
Austin, Texas
(512) 454-2399
dlair.net

Dragon's Lair Comics & Fantasy
7959 Fredericksburg Rd Suite #129
San Antonio, TX
(210) 615-1229
dlair.net

Victory Comics
586 South Washington St
Falls Church, VA
(703) 241-9393
www.victorycomics.com

Central City Comics
113 E. 4th Ave.
(509) 962-4376
Ellensburg, WA 98926

Discordia Games
630 North Callow Avenue
Bremerton, WA
(360) 415-9419
discordiagames.com

Gary's Games and Hobbies
8539 Greenwood Ave. N.
Seattle, WA
(206) 789-8891
garysgamesandhobbies.com

STRATEGIES Games & Hobbies
3878 Main St.
Vancouver B.C.
(604) 872-6911
www.strategiesgames.ca

DCC #67: Sailors on the Starless Sea
A Level 0 Adventure
The legacy of the Chaos Lords and their
corrupted hordes!

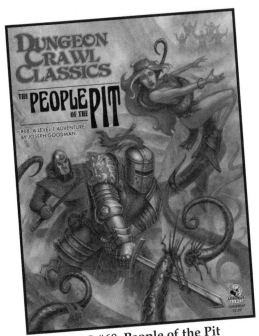

DCC #68: People of the Pit
A Level 1 Adventure
The Great Beast rises from the pit. Is any
man brave enough to end this menace?

DCC #69: The Emerald Enchanter
A Level 2 Adventure
The brooding citadel of the emerald
sorcerer must be breached!

DCC #70: Jewels of the Carnifex
A Level 3 Adventure
Fabled jewels and a forgotten chapel
deep in the slums of Punjar.

r adventures!

DCC #71: The 13th Skull
A Level 4 Adventure
Thirteen generations of devilish secrets
buried and forgotten – until now!

DCC #72: Beyond the Black Gate
A Level 5 Adventure
Journey to an extraplanar ice kingdom
to recover the fabled Horned Crown!

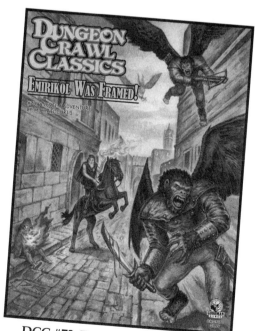

DCC #73: Emirikol Was Framed!
A Level 4 Adventure
Gold and glory for he who penetrates
the walls of Emirikol's Shifting Tower!

DCC #74: Blades Against Death!
A Level 4 Adventure
Test your wits against Death himself in a
bid to save the soul of a friend!

Appendix N
Adventures

COMPATIBLE WITH

New Adventures
New Classes
New Spells
New Gods
New Patrons
New Settings
And Much More!

An adventuring life is a hard life.

One day you are a farmer, a merchant, a scribe, or a woodcutter, the next you are face-to-face and in a life-and-death struggle with unearthly beasts, fiends and horrors.

With every choice you make and every die you toss, your character's story is unfolding right before you.

Appendix N Adventures can help turn that tale into legend!

BRAVE HALFLING PUBLISHING

www.bravehalfling.com

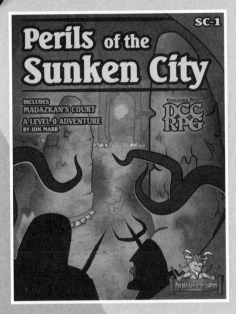

100 years have passed since Mankind revolted and slew the Sorcerer Kings.

Now, the survivors of seven kingdoms begin to rebuild, placing new lives and hopes on the ashes of old. However, even as life continues an ancient and forgotten evil stirs awaiting its moment to strike against mankind.

Join a war-torn land where the struggle for survival continues as new empires arise to impose their will upon the masses. Vicious warlords fight to control territories carved out of fallen Kingdoms. Imposing magicians emerge claiming the legacy of the Sorcerer Kings. High Priests of long forgotten gods and goddesses amass wealth in the name of divine right while Warrior-priests, devoted to a banished god, patrol the lands bringing justice to people abandoned by their rulers.

Tales of the Fallen Empire is a classic Swords and Sorcery setting compatible with the *Dungeon Crawl Classics* Role Playing Game. Within these pages is a detailed post-apocalyptic fantasy setting taking you through an ancient realm that is fighting for its survival and its humanity. Seek your fortune or meet your fate in the burning deserts of the once lush and vibrant land of Vul, or travel to the humid jungles of Xochiquetzal to face the tribes of the Man-Apes and their brutal sacrificial rituals.

Within this campaign setting you will find:

- 6 new classes: Barbarian, Witch, Draki, Wanderer, Man-Ape, & Pirate
- Revised Wizard Class (The Sorcerer)
- New Spells
- New Creatures
- Survival & Scrounging Rules
- A detailed setting inspired by the works of Fritz Lieber, Robert E. Howard, Lynn Carter, H. P. Lovecraft, Michael Moorcock, and Roger Corman

Tighten the straps on your sandals, grab your weapon, and head forth into a land of trouble and turmoil. Adventure awaits those foolhardy to enter the wastelands or for those who fear not the unknown.

WHEN CREATURES PREY ON THE INNOCENT, THE MEEK MUST BECOME THE HUNTERS.

Panic is mounting in the isolated settlement of Sagewood! Frightened villagers speak in hushed tones of "walking frogs the size of men" peering at them from within the woods. And now, a severely wounded local trapper has barely managed to return from Dead Goblin Lake; the fate of his partner known only to the foul creatures that so savagely attacked them.

In a small village without heroes, the townsfolk look desperately towards each other for salvation from this terror.

Those who face the creatures will almost certainly pay with their lives...

Are you brave enough to risk it all?

Attack of the Frawgs is a DCC RPG adventure designed for 8-14 0-level characters but can be easily adapted for 1st-level characters. It can be played standalone or as part of the Princes of Kaimai adventure series published by Thick Skull Adventures.

Writer: Stephen Newton
Interior Art, Layout & Graphic Design: Catherine Harkins
Cover Art: Andrew Harkins

PDF version available at www.rpgnow.com and print versions are available at local game stores.
www.thickskulladventures.com

TIME TO RAISE THE STAKES

TRANSYLVANIAN ADVENTURES

Set aside those "Domains of Despair" for a World of Adventure!

Ancient secrets and epic adversaries lie buried in a land of mists and supersition.

Frightened innkeepers bolt their doors for fear of the stranger at the threshold.

Stoic villagers stand helpless against horrors beyond belief.

It is up to you to turn back the tide of darkness. And it all starts here!

Transylvanian Adventures is a supplement for Goodman Games' *Dungeon Crawl Classics RPG*. New character classes, rules, monsters and a hexmap are all included to capture the feel of adventuring in the land where modern horror began.

No Elves. No Dwarves. No Sparkly Vampires.

TRANSYLVANIAN GRIMOIRE

Eldritch enchantments and ancient mysteries are laid bare in *The Transylvanian Grimoire*.

You'll uncover an entirely new list of spells for the *Dungeon Crawl Classics RPG*, tailored to campaigns of dangerous, yet subtle, magic.

You'll also exhume new patrons and schools of magic like Ritual Magic and Alchemy.

The Transylvanian Grimoire can be used in any existing campaign of DCC to transmogrify it into something heavier on the sword than the sorcery.

No Transylvania Required!

A word of caution, however. *The Transylvanian Grimoire* contains rule modifications that were too terrifying to be considered "essential" rules in *Transylvanian Adventures*.

Invite them to your table, if you dare!

More information at http://landofphantoms.blogspot.com

COMPATIBLE WITH
DCC
RPG

We're with the band.